Change of Season

By Anna Jacobs

THE PENNY LAKE SERIES
Changing Lara • Finding Cassie

THE PEPPERCORN SERIES
Peppercorn Street • Cinnamon Gardens
Saffron Lane • Bay Tree Cottage
Christmas in Peppercorn Street

THE HONEYFIELD SERIES
The Honeyfield Bequest • A Stranger in Honeyfield
Peace Comes to Honeyfield

THE HOPE TRILOGY
A Place of Hope • In Search of Hope
A Time for Hope

THE GREYLADIES SERIES
Heir to Greyladies • Mistress of Greyladies
Legacy of Greyladies

THE WILTSHIRE GIRLS SERIES
Cherry Tree Lane • Elm Tree Road
Yew Tree Gardens

Winds of Change
Moving On
The Cotton Lass and Other Stories
Change of Season

Change of Season

ANNA JACOBS

Allison & Busby Limited
11 Wardour Mews
London W1F 8AN
allisonandbusby.com

First published in 2003.
This paperback edition published by Allison & Busby in 2019.

A CIP catalogue record for this book is available from
the British Library.

10 9 8 7 6 5 4 3 2 1

ISBN 978-0-7490-2511-3

Typeset in 10.5/15.5 pt Sabon LT Pro by
Allison & Busby Ltd

The paper used for this Allison & Busby publication
has been produced from trees that have been legally sourced
from well-managed and credibly certified forests.

Printed and bound by
CPI Group (UK) Ltd, Croydon, CR0 4YY

Chapter One

Louise stuck her head out of the kitchen door and yelled, 'Mum! Dad's on the phone from New York!' then vanished again.

Rosalind Stevenson put down the trowel and walked slowly indoors, rubbing the worst of the dirt off her hands. 'Hello? Paul?'

'There you are at last! Hon, it's good news. I'm coming home to Western Australia on Tuesday.'

As he rattled off the flight time, she scribbled it down automatically, then couldn't help asking, 'How long will you be staying this time, Paul?' He'd been gone nearly six months, dealing with first one crisis then another in the big multinational company for which he worked. And he wasn't the best of correspondents, sending occasional brief emails or making quick phone calls, which usually got interrupted.

He didn't even notice the irony. 'About two weeks. I'm not sure yet which day I fly back. I've got some exciting news and – oh, hell, there's another call on the line. Look, I'll see you on Tuesday. We'll talk then.'

'Paul, wait—' She stood for ages with the receiver buzzing in her ear before she set it carefully down and went back to finish the weeding. The garden was as good a place as any to do some serious thinking.

Tuesday was three days away. She had until then to decide whether to leave her husband of twenty-four years or not. And she was no nearer to knowing what she wanted than she had been a month ago when she had finally admitted to herself that since Paul's big promotion a couple of years ago, their marriage had been virtually non-existent.

The following Tuesday Rosalind stood in Perth Airport and watched Paul wheel his luggage through from customs. For a moment he seemed like a stranger, a tall, attractive man whose middle years sat lightly on him – hair still dark, lean cheeks, hazel eyes and neat nose.

Then he clipped her up in a big hug and as her body remembered how it felt to be loved by him, something inside her softened – just a little.

After kissing her, he held her at arm's length to study her face. 'You look good, hon. I like the jaw-length hair.'

Outside in the fresh air he stopped to stare round. 'I always remember Western Australia like this, clear and sunny. I'll be able to get a good tan before I go back.'

At home he looked round the house as if he'd never seen it before. 'You've got excellent taste in furnishings. I really like the way you've done up the living room.'

She'd consulted him and sent him a photo, so knew he was sweetening her up. But for what?

She didn't say anything, just smiled and went through into the kitchen to get them each a coffee. She heard him stroll round the rest of the ground floor.

'I'm in here. I love these white leather sofas.'

She took the coffee in to him and sat down to pour. 'You said you had some exciting news, Paul. What is it?'

She'd rather get the revelation over with. His ideas of good and hers didn't always coincide. He'd been excited by his promotion to chairman's international rover, troubleshooting for the company anywhere in the world where help was needed, but she'd known immediately what it would mean and had had difficulty hiding her dismay. She'd been right, too. Since then she'd seen less and less of him.

He sipped his coffee, looking at her over the rim of the mug. 'Big changes in the offing, hon. Looks like we'll be able to spend more time together.'

That surprised her. 'You're getting a posting to Australia again?'

'Hell, no! I've moved to the international scene and that's where I intend to stay.'

She watched him put the coffee mug down and study her. It was an effort to keep a calm expression on her face as she waited for the explanation, which she was already sure she wouldn't like.

After a pause during which he sat chewing the corner of his lip, he came out with it. 'I'm going to be based in England for the next six months instead of wandering the world troubleshooting for the chairman – *and* they've arranged for you to live over there with me.' Then he went back to sipping his coffee, keeping a wary eye on her.

She opened her mouth to speak, then closed it again. *Think before you speak, Rosalind,* she reminded herself, a strategy she'd decided on yesterday. She'd always refused to move around with him and a good thing too, or their children would have had no stability in their lives or education.

Until he joined the giant multinational, Marrill Marr, ten years ago, none of Paul's jobs had lasted more than a year or two anyway, some less. Since then the company had dominated his life – and hers too. He'd made several in-house 'career moves' during those years, each to a different part of the world. And now this.

She realised he was looking at her impatiently, waiting for a response. 'But I don't want to go and live in England.'

His voice was low and persuasive. 'Just think about it, hon. The kids have all left home now and—'

'Louise hasn't left yet.'

He rolled his eyes. 'She's about to go to university, isn't she? Which means she's grown up, like Jenny and Tim. Besides, I'm sure your mother would have her for a few months. Lou's seventeen now, past the awkward stage.'

Which showed how much he knew about his children, Rosalind thought mutinously.

'Face it, hon. We're free to live where we please at long last.'

'I live where I please now. Western Australia's a great place – and it's my home.'

He closed his eyes for a moment, sighing as if she'd said something unreasonable. 'Don't you *ever* fancy a change?'

'No, not really. I enjoy my life here.' Which was no

longer true. She'd felt very lonely during the past year or two. Her children had their own friends and interests nowadays and didn't seem to need her, and she was neither fish nor fowl when it came to a social life – married but without a visible husband.

'Look, Ros, I really do need to live a little closer to the action. And you might actually enjoy going back to the country where you were born.'

'I was only two when my parents migrated to Australia. I don't remember anything at all about England. I'd be as much a foreigner there as you are – more.'

'And yet when you write to your sole surviving relative in the UK, you keep promising the old witch you'll go and visit her one day.'

'Well, I will – one day. Just for a holiday. And Aunt Sophie is *not* a witch. She—'

He didn't even try to hide his impatience. 'Quite frankly, you're stuck in a rut here, Ros, and you need to do something about it. You and that little group of friends who all went to school together, not to mention that damned embroidery of yours. In this day and age – embroidery! What a hobby for a modern woman!'

She didn't rise to that old bait. Her embroidery wasn't a hobby but an abiding passion, and she considered raised stumpwork an art form. She was good at it, too, had won several prizes for her embroidered pictures. But for some reason she'd never been able to fathom, Paul hated her doing it.

His next words were etched in acid. 'I don't want to quarrel, but it's time to tell it as it is. You and I *need* some time together, Ros. We're growing apart. Do you want our marriage to go on like this? Or to end? I don't. Think of it as a change of season, a natural part of life. It might even be fun.'

Another silence, then his tone changed. 'Now, how about thinking it over while you make me one of those wonderful gourmet meals. You know I never eat much on the plane.'

That she could do for him, at least.

As she stood up, her attention was caught by her own reflection in the glass tabletop and she stared down in surprise at what it showed. Pastel colours, all of them. Ash-blonde hair, pale pink T-shirt, softly patterned skirt. She didn't look her age, not nearly old enough to have a twenty-two-year-old daughter, but she did look faded and indecisive – and that shocked her.

They walked through to the kitchen together and Paul perched on a stool to chat as she worked, telling her what the chairman had said and how her clever husband had turned a disaster into a profitable deal for the company, thus earning himself a nice fat bonus.

Her thoughts zigzagged all over the place as she put together a salad and nodded occasionally to keep Paul talking. What she kept coming back to – reluctantly, very reluctantly indeed – was that she really ought to give his suggestion serious consideration. The sight of him, the feel of his arms round her had made her feel – well, *married* again.

But the most telling reason of all was: *he* wanted to put things right between them. That mattered very much to her, because it had begun to seem as if he didn't care.

No, she decided as she served the meal, she didn't want their marriage to end – of course she didn't! – but he'd been the one to go away. And oh, she didn't want to live in England, either! She had a suspicion that if she agreed to go, she might not find it easy to come back again.

He was right, damn him, though she wasn't going to admit that yet. Something had to change if they were to stay together.

But why did it always have to be her who made the changes?

The following morning Louise got up late, deliberately waiting till her father went out to the golf club before she left her bedroom. Taking a quick shower, she left her hair to dry naturally. It was dark and wavy like her father's, but she was thinking of having her head shaved to a stubble and perhaps getting a gold stud in her nose. Now that she didn't have to conform to stupid school rules, she could have more fun with her appearance. And she had good enough features to get away with it.

Opening the bedroom door she cocked an ear, but there were no noises from below. Her parents didn't realise how much you could overhear from the upstairs landing of an open plan house like this – which could be very useful sometimes. If her mother did go to live in England, maybe Louise would be able to share a flat with her friend Sandy when she went to uni, instead of living at home. She was definitely not going to live at Gran's. Her grandmother's ideas of what was right and wrong were even more out of date than her mother's.

Going back inside her room, she put on a CD and lay back to enjoy the pure heaven of not having to study or worry about exams.

There was a knock on the door and her mother peered in. 'Darling, you promised to clear up your bedroom today. And will you please turn that music down?' She didn't wait for an answer.

Louise scowled. Why shouldn't she have an untidy room if she wanted to? It was her room, wasn't it? The music throbbed through her, making her feel achy inside her belly. Sexy, she decided. She felt sexy. And she wasn't going to wait much longer to do it, either. Virginity wasn't a treasure nowadays and everyone else in her group had had sex. Of course, she hadn't admitted that *she* hadn't, but she felt left out of the discussions sometimes. Reading about sex in books wasn't the same. She wanted to *know* how it felt to have an orgasm.

Ten minutes later her mother stormed back in, switched off the CD player and yelled, 'Get this pigsty cleared up! I'm putting on some washing in five minutes. If your stuff isn't in the basket by then, you can deal with it yourself.' She waited, hands on hips.

Louise sighed and rolled off the bed. 'I'm supposed to be on holiday.'

'Five minutes.'

When her mother had left, Louise made a quick phone call then stuffed a few necessities into her tote bag, muttering under her breath. She wasn't clearing anything up today. She was going round to Sandy's where there was no one to nag you, in the daytime, at least.

Creeping down the stairs, she held her breath as she crossed the open space near the kitchen. Her mother was sitting there, a mug of coffee cradled in her hands, her back to the world and her shoulders slumped.

What's wrong with her? Louise wondered. *Give me half a chance to go to England and I'm off, outta here, bye bye folks, see ya when I see ya.*

Giggling softly she made her escape, closing the side door quietly behind her. The washing would be done for her when she returned. It always was.

But that evening when she got back, she found her room hadn't been touched. That really threw her. Her mother must be more upset than she'd realised about the trip to England.

She looked round and grimaced before starting to tidy up. She'd get online later. If her father saw the mess in here, he'd hit the roof, and he could be a real bastard if you pushed him too far. She wanted him to think her grown-up enough to be left on her own. Oh, yes.

A few streets away, Liz Foxen was also worrying. She could recognise the signs because she'd seen it all before: Bill looking happy and alert, whistling as he did the gardening, giving long explanations every time he left the house. For a clever man, he was remarkably obtuse about other people. It was right what they said about university lecturers – out of touch with the real world. Too busy playing academic politics. Or screwing one another. Or both.

Who was it this time? Some young tart of a student or a new colleague? There had been one or two changes in the lecturing staff this year.

'I'm fed up with it!' she yelled suddenly, slapping the flat of her hand on the table. This time she wasn't going to take Bill's infidelity lying down, or rather – she paused as an idea slammed into her mind – perhaps she was. 'What's sauce for the goose . . .' she murmured.

Just then the phone rang.

'Oh, Liz!' The voice was hesitant, tearful.

'Hi, Rosalind.' Clutching the telephone receiver in one hand, Liz studied herself in the hall mirror as she listened to her friend. She kept in good trim, didn't she? Worked out at the gym, ate sensibly, dressed smartly. So why did he go after other women?

'Liz, can you come over?'

'Trouble?'

'Mm-hmm.'

Liz sighed. She didn't need someone else's woes on top of her own, but Rosalind had been her best friend since school. 'Put the kettle on, then. But no cake!'

Getting up from the telephone nook, Rosalind made her way to the rear of the house. Her slippered feet made no sound on the tiled floor and she shivered suddenly. It was as if she had no real existence, as if only a ghost had drifted past. A pastel-coloured ghost, at that. Feeling hollow and insubstantial, she filled the kettle and got out the mugs, then went over to touch the vivid green curls of the parsley leaves in her herb pot and stare blindly out of the window.

Before the kettle boiled she heard Liz's car.

The two women embraced and, as usual, Rosalind felt too tall and well-fleshed next to her friend. 'You look great! I love that outfit. It's new, isn't it?'

Liz twirled round, showing off. 'Yes. I was trying it on when you rang. Do you think the skirt needs taking up a fraction?'

Rosalind took a step backwards, studied her friend's outline and shook her head decisively. 'No. Don't touch it. It's perfect as it is. Coffee or tea?'

'Coffee.'

When they went into the living room, Liz kicked off her shoes and tucked her feet up underneath her on the couch. 'What's the matter, then? Tell all.'

'Paul wants us to spend the spring and summer in England and – I don't want to go.'

'Well, you've got plenty of time to think about it. What's the panic today?'

'Northern hemisphere spring, not Australian. I'd have to leave within the month.' Rosalind took a sip of her coffee, then stared down at it bleakly. Little ripples were running to and fro across the surface – just like the apprehension shivering in her belly.

Liz took a sip, made an appreciative murmur and sipped again before she spoke. 'I can't see what the problem is.'

'For a start, it's Louise's first year at university. How can I possibly leave her?'

Liz refrained from saying that lately Rosalind hadn't been getting on with her younger daughter and they'd probably both be happier apart. 'You were there when Tim went to uni. It didn't make much difference, did it? He still bombed out. Where is he now?'

'In America. He's travelling round, working on the sly to pay for it. He emails now and then from an Internet café, and he rang me last month.' She took another slurp of coffee. 'Anyway, a daughter's different. I was there for Jenny and she needed my help.' Though there had been some anxious times, because Jenny wasn't a top student and had found the business course Paul had insisted on really hard going. 'And anyway, I *want* to be there for Louise.'

Liz leant forward. 'You're making excuses, Rosalind Stevenson.'

'Well, the truth is, I don't want to go to England at all. And – and before he came back I was thinking of asking Paul for a divorce.'

Liz choked on a mouthful of coffee. 'You can't mean that! Not *you*!'

'I don't know what I mean, but I have been wondering about our marriage. Only, Paul seems to be – well, making more effort. He says we need time together and he's right.'

All of a sudden Liz was fed up of humouring her friend. 'It's time you thought of him. You've always put the children first before.'

'I haven't.'

'You have, you know!' Her voice softened. 'You might even enjoy staying in England for a few months. You should be thankful Paul wants to spend some quality time together. I'd swap places with you any day, believe me.'

Her voice had such a vicious edge Rosalind realised something was wrong. 'Not – trouble with Bill again?'

Liz nodded, lips tight and bloodless.

'You shouldn't put up with it.'

'I'm not going to this time.'

'You mean – you're going to leave him?'

'Heavens, no! I'm still fond of the old bugger – too fond for my own good. I just got to thinking of giving him a taste of his own medicine for a change. See how he likes that. It's simply a question of finding someone I fancy and diving into the nearest bed.'

'You shouldn't joke about something so important.'

'Who's joking?'

The bitterness in her voice worried Rosalind, but Liz didn't mean what she'd said, of course she didn't.

After her friend had left, Rosalind wandered out into the garden. She sighed as she nipped off a few dead leaves. Perhaps something would turn up to prevent her having to go to England. Paul was always changing his plans and rushing off to deal with an emergency for the chairman.

Oh, please, let something turn up! she prayed.

That evening their elder daughter, Jenny, popped in unexpectedly. 'Hi, Mum! Louise not around?'

'She and Sandy have gone to the movies.'

'Good. I need to talk to you both.' She opened her mouth to speak, then burst into noisy, gulping sobs.

Rosalind hurried across to hug her till she'd calmed down, not saying anything, simply waiting for an explanation.

Jenny finished mopping her eyes. It was her mother she looked at as she said, 'It's Michael. I've left him.'

Paul leant forward. 'Is he the guy I met last time I was home? Well, it's about time you came to your senses. He's a real no-hoper, that one, and I was against you moving in with him, if you remember.'

'What's happened?' Rosalind asked, frowning at him. No need to sound so triumphant when the girl was hurting.

'He's been unfaithful to me and – and he's not even sorry about it!' What's more, when Jenny had confronted him, he'd hit her, though she wasn't going to tell her parents that. She'd known then that the relationship was over. Irrevocably. She wasn't into being thumped. 'The split's been brewing for a while, I guess. Could I stay here? I can't go back. I've got my things in the car.'

Paul gave her one of his icy looks. 'You can't stay for long. The house is going to be closed down. Your mother's coming to live in England with me for a few months.'

Rosalind felt annoyed. She hadn't actually agreed to go yet and he knew it.

'I could look after the place for you,' Jenny volunteered. 'It'd be safer to have someone living here.'

Paul gave a scornful laugh. 'No way. I haven't forgotten the last time you looked after it. That party of yours cost me over a thousand dollars in redecoration, as well as upsetting all the neighbours.'

'But what am I going to *do*? I don't have enough money to pay the bond on a flat of my own.' She began to sob again.

Rosalind put her arm round Jenny's shoulders. 'I'm not turning my daughter away, Paul.'

'I didn't say I wouldn't *help*. And of course she can stay with us till we find her a flat. I'll even pay the bond. But after that, we're closing the house down and we're off on our second honeymoon.'

Jenny smiled at them through her tears. 'That's so sweet. *Second honeymoon*. I'm always glad you two are still together. Nearly everyone else's parents are divorced.'

'No chance of that as long as your mother behaves herself.' Paul grinned across the table.

'And as long as you behave yourself, too, Paul Stevenson,' Rosalind retorted.

'Don't I always?'

Jenny laughed. 'You do when you're at home, Dad. We don't know what you get up to when you're overseas.'

He stiffened. 'I work far too hard to misbehave, believe me, young lady. Even if I were that way inclined, which I'm not.'

They both stared at him in amazement, his tone was so sharp.

'She was only joking,' Rosalind protested.

'Well, it's the kind of joke I can do without, thank you very much.'

After the silence had gone on for a bit too long, Rosalind said, 'How about I get us all a drink, then we can discuss what to do?'

Later, when Jenny had taken up residence in the guest suite, Paul sat down beside his wife on the bed and put his arm round her shoulders. 'Feeling better about the trip now? You *are* coming, aren't you?'

'I suppose so.' She'd made up her mind to give it a try, because she really did want to put their marriage to rights. That was the main reason. She wasn't going to tell him that, of course.

He nibbled her ear. 'What am I going to do with you, woman?' As her breathing deepened, he took her in his arms and kissed her. His hands knew all her body's weaknesses, as hers knew his.

And then, of course, she forgot everything else, for he was a superb lover, always had been. Their reunions were fantastic. She missed the sex greatly when he was away. He must do, too, because he was a passionate man.

Maybe they did need a change – and she loved the idea of a second honeymoon.

Four days later the chairman's personal assistant rang from England. Rosalind handed the phone to Paul feeling faintly anxious. The PA only rang in emergencies. She went to sit in the kitchen because Paul hated people listening in on his business conversations.

After a few minutes a shadow fell across her. She looked up and her heart sank. He was looking excited and alert. She knew that expression of old.

He perched on the edge of the chair next to hers. 'Darling, I'm sorry, but I have to get back to London straight away. They've booked me a seat on the six o'clock plane. *Big* crisis.'

'But you've been home less than a week!'

He shrugged. 'That's how things go in this job, and it's exactly why I want you over there with me.'

'That means I'll have to travel to England alone!'

Breath rasped impatiently in his throat. 'I think you'll be able to find your way to the airport from here, and I'll be there to meet you in London.'

'Promise me you'll meet me. *Promise!*'

'I promise faithfully. Now, come and help me pack, eh? Good thing we found that flat for Jenny, isn't it? And I've been talking to your mother. She's agreed to have Louise.'

'She didn't tell me!'

'I asked her to let me do that.' He held her at arm's length and stared at her with mock sternness. 'So you have no excuse for trying to wriggle out of this trip, my girl.'

'I've said I'll come, haven't I?'

He nodded and let her go. 'I'm rather looking forward to having a wife around. Dinner parties, regular sex, theatres and restaurants. We'll have a great time.'

When she got back from taking Paul to the airport, Rosalind took out her embroidery things and set up the smaller spare bedroom as her workshop again. She always put everything away when he came home to avoid arguments and snide remarks. The routine of arranging her things usually helped her settle down after he'd left – though this time she'd only be here for a couple more weeks herself.

The embroidery worked its usual magic and even when Jenny rang up to complain that the new flat was noisy and Michael was still pestering her to get back together, Rosalind didn't let it worry her. She spoke soothingly and claimed a pan on the stove so that she could end the conversation quickly.

When Paul went away, she always needed a few hours of peace to reorient her life. Everything was so different without him. And this time she had a lot to think about. She'd agreed to spend the spring and summer in England and wouldn't go back on her word.

But next time someone had to compromise about what they were doing with their lives, it wouldn't be her, she was quite determined about that.

INTRODUCTION TO RAISED STUMPWORK

This highly individual type of embroidery flourished in its original form for only a few decades of the seventeenth century ...

Its capacity for conveying life and humour, and the way in which it combines many different embroidery and lace-making techniques makes this work an ideal vehicle for modern embroiderers seeking to achieve similar effects in a contemporary idiom.

(Barbara and Roy Hirst, RAISED EMBROIDERY, Merehurst Limited, London, 1993, p.6 – quotes used with permission)

SIMULATING LIFE

The stitches, techniques, threads, fabrics and other materials used to create a raised embroidery are all carefully selected to express, simulate and describe the subject ...

A sampler of this type might be designed with a particular theme in mind – family, nature, the seasons, a period in history, or a particular event.

(Hirst, p.60)

Chapter Two

The twenty-hour flight to London seemed interminable. Rosalind was too tall to be comfortable in planes and couldn't manage to do more than doze for an hour or two. By the time the plane arrived in London, she was exhausted.

Pushing her luggage trolley, she walked out into the terminal looking for Paul, pleased at the prospect of being with him again. When she couldn't see him anywhere she began to feel apprehensive. He'd phoned last week and promised that nothing, absolutely nothing, would prevent him from meeting her at the airport and helping her settle into the English house. So where was he?

She saw a young woman holding one of those signs with people's names on them and didn't look at it, then something clicked inside her brain and she turned slowly back. It said STEVENSON in ominous black letters.

He'd broken his promise!

'Oh, damn you, Paul!' she whispered. 'Couldn't you even do this for me? Does the company have to come first every single time?'

The woman holding the sign looked across at her and nodded in recognition. She was so trim and well-groomed, she made Rosalind feel huge and even more dishevelled than before.

'Mrs Stevenson? Paul's wife?'

'Yes.'

The woman stuck out one well-manicured hand. 'You look just like the photo on Paul's desk. I'm Gail Johns from personnel. I'm afraid Paul's been called away. He's in New York at the moment, actually.'

'*New York!*' Rosalind could hear her voice wobble, couldn't prevent it.

Gail gave her a reassuring smile. 'You don't have to worry. I've arranged everything for you. Let's have a coffee and I'll explain.' She set off across the concourse.

For a moment Rosalind stood watching her, then sighed and began to push the luggage trolley through the crowds. Around her people were hugging one another, some weeping for joy. Children were running to and fro. Everyone, it seemed, was with family or friends.

Everyone except her. Only pride kept her head up.

And anger.

The refreshments area was seedy and predominantly brown. The tables had been swiped over casually with a cloth and were still smeary.

Gail brought back two coffees and some food for herself. 'Hope you don't mind, but I haven't had any lunch yet.'

She took a huge bite of the sandwich, then got out some papers. 'I have full instructions for you, Mrs Stevenson, all in alphabetical order – so much better than my trying to explain everything now, don't you think? You'd never remember all the details afterwards.'

Her tone was that of an adult dealing with a rather dull child. Rosalind breathed deeply but said nothing. It had been the same when Paul worked in the company's Australian branch. Ambitious young things like this had treated her as if she were in her dotage because she was a mere housewife.

'We've found you a house in Dorset. The chairman's family came from there originally and he always speaks well of it. The house is quite large and there's a nice villagey atmosphere, so you should find it easy to make friends. It's only about two hours' drive from London.'

Aligning the papers carefully on the table, Gail dipped into the briefcase again. 'This is the key to the house – front door key only, the others are waiting for you in Burraford Destan. It's a nice little place and really easy to get to, mostly motorway from here. Paul said you'd be all right with the driving.' She raised one eyebrow questioningly.

'Of course I shall.' Rosalind was absolutely terrified of driving in a strange country, but she'd let herself be hanged, drawn and quartered before she'd admit it to this bright young thing.

Gail picked up the sandwich again, then glanced across the table with it halfway to her mouth. 'Are you sure you're all right, Mrs Stevenson? You look a bit pale.'

'I'm just a bit – um – jet-lagged. It's a long flight.'

'Well, if you're too tired to drive today, we can easily book you into a hotel.'

Rosalind struggled to 'get her head together', as Louise would have said. 'I – what time is it here?'

'One o'clock in the afternoon.'

Rosalind thought furiously as she adjusted her watch. If she booked into a hotel now, she would fall asleep then wake up in the middle of the night. Paul always said it was better to fit into the day–night pattern as soon as you could after you changed time zones, and he ought to know. 'No. I won't bother with a hotel. I've all afternoon to drive down to Dorset, haven't I? So I can just take things easily.' *One step at a time.* Her old motto brought its usual comfort.

Gail devoured the last of the sandwich. 'That's terrific. Though you'd better stop on the way to pick up some groceries. Paul hasn't managed to get down to Dorset yet and there'll be nothing in the fridge.'

'But I thought – Paul told me he'd approved the house himself.'

'Ah. Well, I'm afraid a few things cropped up and he only had time to set the ground rules. But the agency we use for executive relocation is very reliable and I've shown him the photos. Very attractive house, delightful village. I'm sure you'll like living there. Paul really fancies English village life.' She took another gulp of coffee. 'Dorset is a really pretty part of England. I looked it up online. Hills, farms with grey stone walls, very picturesque villages.'

Her description made Rosalind realise that no one from the company had actually checked the house.

'And we have a company flat in London for when Paul

can't get down to Dorset. You can get up to town in two hours by train from nearby Wareham, which is pretty convenient. I've got you a good road map.' She unwrapped a piece of fruitcake. 'Don't know why I'm so hungry today. Must be the cold.'

'Is it very cold outside?'

'Freezing.' Gail licked some cake crumbs from her fingers. 'Everyone's saying how late spring is this year. I mean, almost April and no sign of the sun. Even the trees are late getting their leaves.' She glanced sideways, frowned and offered another glib reassurance. 'I'm sure you'll be all right, Mrs Stevenson.'

Miss Efficiency was still talking to her as if she were a doddery old lady and Rosalind wasn't having that. She straightened up and said crisply, 'Well, if you've finished eating, we may as well go and get the car, eh?'

It was a large, comfortable car and Rosalind had no difficulty driving it, though she felt a bit nervous at first coping with the heavy motorway traffic. Then, half an hour later, the engine coughed and spluttered before picking up. A few minutes later, it began to falter again. 'No! Please, no!' Rosalind begged. But the vehicle lost power and began to kangaroo, jerking forward briefly, then losing momentum.

She signalled to move left, cutting in front of a small truck, which blared its horn at her, then pulling off onto the hard shoulder just as the engine died completely. The car rolled slowly to a halt and she sat frozen in disbelief for a moment before opening the door.

Icy wind howled around her. Traffic fumes assaulted her nose. Dark clouds were massing in the sky. What the hell was the matter? The car had a full tank of petrol, so it couldn't be that. She lifted the bonnet, but could see nothing obviously wrong. The battery connections seemed good, the fan belt wasn't slack and no water hoses seemed to be leaking. Beyond that, she didn't know what to look for.

Cars and trucks continued to drone past her and the wind blew icy dampness down her neck, as well as sneaking chill fingers up her sleeves. She hadn't got a mobile phone yet. Miss Efficiency had expected her to have her own. She could only hope there would be an emergency phone nearby.

Locking the car, she began trudging grimly along the hard shoulder, alternately buffeted by the backdraught from passing trucks and mocked by the wind, which continued to tug at her clothes and suck away what little warmth was left in her body.

The phone got her through to the police, who telephoned the car hire company and then told her someone would be coming with a replacement car, but it'd take a while.

'How long?'

'Sorry, madam. They didn't say. You should remain with your vehicle or it might get towed away. If anyone stops nearby, it'd be safer to lock yourself in.'

She tramped back to wait. Finding half a chocolate bar in her handbag, she devoured it hungrily, then wished she hadn't because it made her thirsty. Time crawled past and the radio programmes were only half-audible because of the traffic noise, so she was left with her own thoughts for company.

'Damn you, Paul Stevenson!' she said aloud at one stage.

* * *

In Australia that same day, Liz looked at her husband and anger rose like bile in her throat, scalding her with its intensity. She'd never felt so furious with Bill before, not even the first time he'd been unfaithful. 'You must think I'm stupid if you expect me to fall for that line.'

'It isn't a line.' He looked at her warily.

She leant her head back and stared up at the ceiling for a moment. 'He does think I'm stupid,' she told it, then looked at him again. 'She's called Marian Hulme and she's just out from England in her first tenured position. She's tall, with dyed blonde hair. And she calls you *William, dear.*'

He went white. 'How did you find out?'

'I can always tell when you're being unfaithful, so I did a bit of snooping, not to mention checking the credit card accounts. You've been wining and dining rather a lot lately. And you shouldn't chat to people in stairwells. I heard everything you said to her yesterday when I was on my way to your office, *William dear.*'

He stared down at the floor.

'This time, I'm *not* going to forgive you. Instead, I'm working on the principle of goose and gander, as in sauce for.'

He jerked upright. 'Liz, surely—'

'Surely what?'

'You don't mean that.'

'I do, actually. I've booked myself a holiday. In Hong Kong. Eighteen lovely days. And while I'm there, I'm going to keep my eyes open for a likely new gander – preferably one a little younger than you and with more hair on his head.' She heard the air whistle into Bill's mouth and felt grim satisfaction at hitting him in his weak spot. Heaven alone knew why it mattered so much to him that he was going bald, but it did.

'Don't do that, Liz. I'll – I'll end it at once, and—'

'Oh, but I shall do it. Go to Hong Kong, anyway. I'll have an affair, too, if I can find someone I fancy. And every time you start screwing around from now on, I'm going to take a lover as well. I'm told I'm quite attractive still – even if *you* don't find me so – and I doubt I'll have too much difficulty getting someone to sleep with me.'

'Liz—'

'I leave in two days for Hong Kong.'

His glance was very level. 'I don't believe you about the lover, but if you want a holiday, well, that's all right with me. I'll make sure everything is well and truly over by the time you return.'

'It'd bloody better be.' She smiled then and delivered her coup de grâce. 'Hope you're feeling in a domesticated mood, because you won't be able to eat in restaurants while I'm away. I'm afraid I've cleaned out our account.'

'*All of it?*'

'Yup!'

'You've got a nasty streak under all that sparkle, Liz. How the hell am I going to manage without money till you get back?'

'I don't actually care.'

She slept in the spare bedroom till she left. And missed cuddling him like hell. But she wasn't going to admit that.

As Rosalind sat waiting for deliverance by an English roadside, in America her son put his last coin into a slot machine and reached for the paper cup of coffee. His hand was shaking. Hell, they had certainly pinned one on last night. What had been in that last pill he'd popped? He blinked and risked a sip of the dirty-looking liquid. Oh, for one of his mother's wonderful coffees! That thought made him snort with laughter.

'What's so funny, man?' Wayne appeared next to him.

'I was just thinking of Mum's coffee. It's the best in the whole world.' Tim took another sip. Well, at least this stuff was warm. 'What are we going to do now? I'm skint. And you're nearly out of money, too.'

'We'll have to earn some more.'

'We don't have a work permit.'

'You don't need a permit for what I've got in mind.'

'I don't think I want to—'

Wayne grabbed him by the front of his jacket. 'I'm getting just a little tired of you and your scruples. If you're not happy here, go back home to your darling mummy. Otherwise, stop moaning and feeling sorry for yourself. We could have earned ourselves some good money working with those guys last night, but oh no, you had to put your foot in it, didn't you?'

'The fat one was a full-on drug dealer and he wanted us to push for him.'

'So what? Everyone's into something nowadays, so why not take advantage of that? You've been doing stuff since you were fourteen, so you're a fine one to talk. Yeah.' He let that sink in, then added, 'Now, either you're with me or you can manage on your own. Make up your bloody mind.' Only then did he let go of his friend's jacket, laughing as hot coffee spilt down it.

Tim shuddered at the thought of walking away from Wayne. America – well, the part they were visiting – scared him silly and he wished desperately he'd never left Australia. Even home was better than this nightmare existence. But he wasn't going to crawl back to his father with his tail between his legs. No way.

'I said I was in, didn't I? And you owe me a coffee now, you stupid bastard. You spilt most of mine and that was my last coin.'

Wayne's face slowly relaxed. 'All right, then. One coffee coming up. Now, here's what we do . . .'

It was nearly three hours before another car drew up beside Rosalind, by which time she was chilled to the marrow and bursting for a pee. She had sunk into a dull lethargy, enduring because there was nothing else she could do.

A man wearing a cap with the hire company logo on it got out and she opened the door to speak to him. A flurry of light rain whispered across them, then trailed away into mere dampness, but judging by the dark clouds more was on the way.

'Mrs Stevenson?'

'Yes.'

'John Trevithin. I've got another car here for you. A tow truck will be along in a few minutes to take me and this naughty girl back.' He slapped the car with an affection Rosalind in no way shared.

'Well, I hope you fix the problem before you hire the car out again. I've been sitting here for *three hours* in the freezing cold!'

'Yes. Sorry. There's a motorway services place just along the road. Go and get yourself a meal and a hot drink. You'll feel a lot better then.' He handed her a voucher. 'Compliments of the company.'

She looked at her watch. Half past four. 'I had intended to get down to Dorset before dark.'

'You'll never make it. Might as well take a break first. Do you good. Not a nice introduction to England, eh, Mrs Stevenson? Never mind. Things can only get better from now on. Enjoy your holiday.'

He didn't look much older than her son, but she felt old today – old, cold and fed up to the bloody teeth. Lips pressed tightly together she started up the car and left him standing there, grinning and waving at her like an idiot. But she did stop at the services to use the ladies', then grab a cup of coffee and a sandwich. Muddy coffee and a pallid sandwich with wilted salad and stringy beef stuck between two layers of anonymous white bread. She left half of it.

It was an effort to push herself up again from the small plastic table. She was exhausted and jet lag was making her whole system scream for sleep. But she didn't want to find a motel, just get this endless travelling over and done with, and take possession of her new home.

It grew dark well before she reached Dorset, but she found a petrol station which sold basic foods and bought enough to last her until the following morning. She grabbed another coffee while she was at it and this time it was proper coffee, freshly brewed. By the time she left, she was feeling slightly more cheerful. Nearly there now.

She turned onto the Wareham–Swanage road, driving through the darkness with a sense of triumph. According to her directions, Burraford Destan was on the right just past Wareham. If she missed the first turn, there was another soon after it. Yes, there was the sign.

She followed the last of the instructions, which she had to admit were excellent, and found Number 10, Sexton Close. She had to stop the car and get out to open the big wrought-iron gates, whose rusty hinges seemed unwilling to move. 'You ought to be here today, Paul Stevenson,' she muttered as she struggled with them. 'For once in your damned high-powered life you ought to be *with* me.'

The gates gave way at last to her desperate shoving and she got into the car, rolling forward slowly round the circular driveway to the front door. She gaped at the house in the beam of the headlights. It really was beautiful, built of some sort of pale grey stone. Even the roof was grey, not covered in tiles but what looked like big slabs of stone.

A steep gable on the right side of the house looked like something from a small-town Disney movie, and all round the edges of the circular drive were daffodils, scores of them, lit up by the powerful headlights of the car. Her spirits began to lift, though she'd have felt better if there had been lights showing in the windows – and would have felt safer, too.

When she got out, she left the engine running and the headlights on. Outside that charmed circle of light everything looked dark and sinister, but she reminded herself of the self-defence course she'd taken. She'd got a commendation for it, too, though she'd never had to use the skills.

Oh, for goodness' sake, she thought, *pull yourself together, Rosalind! You're not some fragile little thing to be easily overpowered.*

The self-defence instructor had said you never turned your back on danger. Well, she'd just like to see him open this door without turning his back on the garden. 'Come on, come on, you stupid thing!' She fumbled with the lock and turned the key just as rain began hissing down again like a grey chiffon cloak between her and the car headlights.

It took a lot of willpower to step forward into the blackness of the hall, even with the car keys poking out between her knuckles as a makeshift weapon. She found a switch and suddenly the place was flooded with light, then something started beeping and she keyed in the security number quickly.

Weak with relief, she leant against the wall, reassured by the feel of something solid behind her as she studied her surroundings.

It was a few seconds before she gathered enough courage to move forward and begin opening doors. On the left a spacious living room led into a small dining room with a very ugly modern table and chairs, all angles and discomfort. On the right was a smaller sitting room and behind it an office. Kitchen and conservatory were at the rear. She left lights on everywhere because it made her feel better, and put the kettle on while she was in the kitchen. Even instant coffee would be wonderful.

Upstairs, according to the brochure on the house, were *'four spacious bedrooms and two bathrooms'* with an *'attic playroom or guest bedroom, plus small shower room'*. Well, she'd investigate those when she'd got her luggage in.

She made two quick dashes to the car and when she switched off the headlights and motor, she felt suddenly terrified that someone might be lurking in the bushes, so raced up the steps and slammed the front door shut behind her. Laughing shakily at herself, she shoved the bolt across.

The kitchen was full of steam because the kettle hadn't switched itself off. There wasn't enough water left in it for a coffee, so she filled the damned thing again. Her teeth were chattering and she had never felt so cold in her whole life. She would not cry! She would not.

But she did. She sipped her coffee with tears trickling down her face and plopping into the cup. Realistically she knew Paul couldn't have refused to do his job, but emotionally she felt he'd let her down.

She shivered. How cold it was! No wonder her parents had emigrated to Australia. Only then did it occur to her. She was an idiot. Miss Efficiency had said there was central heating. She fumbled for the instructions folder, which said: *'Central heating is switched on from the central boiler, located in the mudroom.'* She frowned round. Mudroom? What the hell was one of those?

Suddenly she noticed the door at the back of the casual meals area next to the kitchen. She'd dismissed it as a cupboard, but perhaps this was the mudroom. It was locked. No key in sight nearby. Back to Miss Efficiency's instructions.

KEYS, she read, the only entry under K. Capital letters, neatly positioned on the page. She could just imagine the immaculate Gail typing it on her computer keyboard, red nails flashing. *'The keys are in the top drawer of the bureau in the sitting room to the right of the front door as you go in.'*

Great one! Where else would you keep keys? 'Aha!' Jangling the big bunch in her hand, she went back to the kitchen to try them out. 'No labels on them, of course! Caught you there, Gail Johns! Not good enough. Off with your nails!'

She decided that a mudroom was a utility room, a place for coats and shoes, judging by the hooks and racks. It also contained the controls for the heating system and she left it clucking quietly to itself before trailing wearily upstairs. The quilt in the master bedroom looked fluffy and inviting. Shivering, she crept under it without taking her clothes off. Within seconds she was fast asleep.

Chapter Three

In Australia, Louise waited until her gran was asleep then tiptoed downstairs. Honestly, who went to bed at ten o'clock these days? Some of the nightclubs didn't even open their doors until then. She beamed in the darkness as she slipped quietly along the hallway. She was going clubbing tonight with Sandy, who was now settled in her own flat, the lucky tart.

When the front door clicked softly shut behind her, she raised both fists in a silent victory salute, then got into her mother's car. She'd told Gran she had permission to use it. Well, her mother might have said yes if she'd asked. It made sense, after all. But she hadn't asked, because her mother might also have said no.

She'd look after it because she was a very careful driver, a natural, her instructor said when she'd passed her driving test first time, unlike Tim and Jenny. Mind you, with having to drive on P plates for the first year after passing her test and being underage, she didn't dare drink and drive, but there were other things, less obvious things, that the breathalysers wouldn't pick up – and they could be as much fun as alcohol.

She drove away, turning up the stereo till the bass notes were thumping along her veins. *Yeah! This is going to be a great night out!*

Audrey Worth lay for a moment in the darkness, wondering what had woken her. When she heard the car drive away, music pulsing loudly from it, she leapt out of bed and pulled back the edge of the curtain to see tail lights disappearing down the street and the spare parking bay outside her house empty.

'The young minx! I don't know why Rosalind lent her that car. It was asking for trouble. And trouble is what Louise will get from me when she comes home.'

Only her granddaughter didn't come home – well, not until six in the morning – by which time Audrey was nearly out of her mind with worry and seriously considering calling the police.

And far from listening to the reprimand, Louise shouted back at her, then slammed out of the house again to go to uni without waiting to eat anything or change her clothes.

'I'm not enjoying her company at all,' Audrey told her friend John when he called in later that morning. 'She's very wilful.'

'I've never understood why you agreed to have her in the first place.'

'You don't know my son-in-law. He'd persuade Eskimos to buy ice, that one would. Well, what can't be cured must be endured, I suppose.' But it was going to be a long six months, she could see that. Very long indeed.

In the evening Audrey once more tried to talk to her granddaughter.

Louise glared at her. 'I told you I was out with my friends. What is this, a bloody nunnery?'

Audrey tried to keep her temper. 'Don't swear in my house. We agreed when you came that you'd let me know where you were going and what time you'd be back – and that you wouldn't stay out after midnight.'

'Look, these days nothing starts happening till ten o'clock. Did you really expect me to walk out on my friends at midnight? They'd have laughed themselves silly.'

'Yes, I did expect it. For someone who's supposed to be studying, midnight is quite late enough. Anyway, it's not safe out on your own. Young women disappear, get murdered.'

Louise tried persuasion. 'Honest, Gran, nothing starts till late. And I was perfectly safe. That's why I've got the car. We all went for an early breakfast together afterwards. We always do.' An exaggeration. She'd never been allowed to stay out all night before. However soft her mother was, she had her sticking points.

Audrey's voice was chill and emphatic. 'Both Rosalind and Paul agreed to my conditions and so did you. You can like it or lump it, but you'll be back by midnight from now on, young lady. And if you're in any doubt about that, we'll ring your mother up and ask her opinion. Or your father.'

Louise stamped upstairs. Honestly, you'd think someone who'd left school and started university would be treated like an adult. But no. She had to live with her grandmother instead of sharing a flat with a friend, and she had to be home by midnight. What was this, *Cinderella* revisited?

Only – if she disobeyed and Gran did contact Mum, they'd find out about the car. Or they'd tell her father – and she didn't want *him* coming the heavy. He could be a real bastard sometimes – with everyone except her mother, anyway – though he usually managed to get his own way with her, as well.

Louise went over to stare out of the window, then realised something and swung round to stare at her bedroom. There were no clothes on the floor, only a large dustbin liner in the corner and the bag was half-full. Where had that come from? She went to investigate.

A strong smell of cheesy socks, dirty knickers and sweaty T-shirts hit her nostrils as she opened it and she gasped in fury. Her clean things were in there, all mixed up with the dirty ones. She went back downstairs, dragging the bag with her.

'Gran? What's this?'

'Oh, your washing. I put it all in the bag, dear. I could smell your socks from my room. This is a very small house, you know. I don't intend to wash for you – you keep insisting you're grown-up – so if you don't put your things away, I'll stuff everything into a bag.' She had decided this in the middle of her wakeful night.

'But you put the *clean* things in with dirty, so they'll all smell rotten now.'

'You surely didn't expect me to examine your knickers to see which ones had been worn?'

There was no answering that one. 'What am I going to

wear tomorrow? I particularly wanted to wear this shirt.'

'Up to you, dear. But if you want to do some washing now, the laundry's free and I have some undercover lines. Your things will be dry by morning.'

Glances locked.

Audrey kept a smile on her face only with difficulty.

Louise didn't even attempt to smile. 'I do not need this.'

'Nor do I. In fact, it's inconvenient having you staying here, much as I love you. But I'm sure things will work out once you get used to my ways. You need to remember that this is *my* house.'

The silence was definitely heavy enough to weigh. Cursing under her breath, Louise stormed into the laundry. Before she could sling her clothes into the washing machine, her grandmother was there beside her.

'I can't afford new appliances, so let me show you how to get the best out of this old one.'

Sullenly, Louise listened and obeyed. It certainly was an old machine. She looked round. 'Where's the tumble drier?'

'I don't need one. They're expensive on electricity and besides, things dry on my undercover lines, even in winter.'

Louise let out an aggrieved sigh. *Great! Back to the Dark Ages!*

Later, when she had finished her first assignment from university, she wandered downstairs again. Her gran was watching some dumb documentary on television. The only books on the shelves were romances – Mills & Boon, for heaven's sake, and someone called Georgette Heyer! She picked up one of the romances. 'I didn't know you read this rubbish, Gran.'

'You know enough about romances to pass judgement, do you?'

Louise dropped the book as if it were a hot coal. 'I've never read one in my life!'

'That makes you an excellent judge, then. Anyway, who asked you to read my books – or to comment on them?'

Louise retreated to her room. She was hungry. But she'd put on weight if she ate the things her grandmother cooked. Her stomach growled and she sighed. Maybe she should get some pills to kill her appetite and make her more active. Sandy said they were marvellous. They were a bit expensive, though. She might have to get a part-time job. She switched on her radio and since she and Gran had already had words about noise levels, she turned it down and got into bed. She'd never sleep, going to bed this early. And she'd go mad with boredom in the evenings here.

People who went gallivanting off to England should make better arrangements for their daughters. Sandy complained about her bedsitter being too small, but Louise would swap with her any day.

It wasn't till she was eating breakfast next morning that she realised she'd forgotten to peg out her washing the previous night. She pushed the toast aside with an angry growl and got up to do it. What the hell was she going to wear today?

This was a lousy start to the university year. Absolutely lousy!

The following afternoon the phone rang and Rosalind ran to pick it up. 'Paul?'

'No. It's me. Sophie.'

Disappointment knifed through Rosalind. You'd have thought your husband would at least ring to check that you'd arrived safely, whether he was in New York or not. 'Aunt Sophie! How lovely to hear your voice. How on earth did you find out where I was?'

'Phoned your husband's company. They didn't want to tell me your number at first, but I insisted.'

Rosalind's smile was genuine. 'I was going to ring you this evening.'

'Well, I didn't want to wait. Look, they told me Paul isn't expected back until the weekend, so I want you to come and visit me for a day or two. You haven't got anything else arranged, have you?'

'No. Well, only sorting out the house.'

'Sort it out next week instead. I need to see you now.'

Rosalind chuckled.

'I'd better warn you. I've got cancer. I don't have long to live, so don't be shocked at how thin I am.'

'Oh, Soph, no!' Tears welled in Rosalind's eyes.

'No maudlin nonsense. I'm eighty-three. Got to die of something. Rather have had a quick heart attack, but there you are.' More silence, then, 'Are you coming?'

'Yes, of course!' *Cancer!* Poor Soph! Paul was right – Rosalind couldn't have afforded to wait any longer to come to England. Damn him, why did he always have to be right? And why hadn't *he* phoned?

She went to repack her suitcase and set off within the hour, arriving in Lancashire around three in the afternoon after a trouble-free drive along some delightful country roads, then up some busy motorways.

Southport had such a pretty main street she was tempted to stop for a few minutes and walk round, but resisted that idea and drove on, following Sophie's instructions.

'This can't be it!' she exclaimed as she pulled up. She checked the number again, but it was correct. Somehow, she hadn't expected Sophie to have such an impressive house. Although it was a terraced house, it was far larger than the one she and Paul were renting and was three stories high, with attics above that. But it was an old house and there was no garage, so she had to park in the street.

As she walked along the path the front door was opened by a complete stranger. 'Am I at the right place? I'm looking for my aunt, Sophie Worth.'

'Yes, this is her house. You must be Rosalind. I'm Prue Daking, a sort of nurse-housekeeper. Do come in.' She smiled conspiratorially and lowered her voice. 'Your aunt's been waiting for you impatiently all afternoon.'

At the sitting-room door, Rosalind stopped and tried to keep smiling through her shock. Sophie Worth was skeletal, the faded yellowish skin stretched across her bones like crumpled parchment. She was sitting in a wheelchair and didn't get up, just held out both hands to Rosalind, then pulled her close, cheek to cheek, for a moment.

'I'm so glad you've come, dear.'

'I am, too.'

'Prue, would you get us a tea tray?' Sophie let go of Rosalind's hands and gestured towards the comfortable sofa next to her.

Tears filled Rosalind's eyes. She didn't know what to say.

'You can go away again if you're going to weep all over me.'

'You know I always cry easily, Soph.'

'Well, if I'm not crying, you certainly shouldn't be.' She reached out to pat her great-niece's hand. 'I've had a long life and a good one, too. Never married,' she grinned wickedly, 'but had a few lovers in my time.'

'*Aunt Sophie!*'

'Ha! Shocked you there. Don't know why, though. Did you think we were all sexless in those days?'

Suddenly, Rosalind felt at home. Each time Soph had visited them in Australia, she had felt drawn to her – as she did now. The two of them had corresponded intermittently for years, but Soph had never even hinted at her present health problems.

'What did that husband of yours say when you told him you were coming to see me today?'

'Paul doesn't know.'

'Oh?'

Rosalind shrugged, trying to speak lightly. 'He hasn't been in touch yet. And he didn't meet me at the airport as he promised. If you hadn't told me, I wouldn't even know when he's coming back from America.' In spite of her efforts, her voice wobbled.

'You're too soft with him. I've always said that.'

They both stopped speaking as Prue brought in the tea tray and poured cups for them, her actions quick and efficient, her short dark hair sleek as a seal's coat.

When she'd gone, Sophie continued thoughtfully, 'Paul came to see me – when was it? – two years ago. We didn't get on very well without you to mediate. He stayed for tea, then left for "an urgent business appointment". In Blackpool, he said, but that was just an excuse. He came mainly to value my house and he didn't need much time to do that.'

'Oh, no!'

'Of course he did! Don't stick your head in the sand, girl. He's a businessman. Why else would he visit an old woman he can't abide?'

Rosalind could feel heat creeping across her cheeks.

'Anyway, after he came, I changed my will.'

Rosalind sat up very straight and said stiffly, 'You can leave your money as you like. I don't care about inheriting your property, Soph.'

'Pity, because I've left it all to you.'

'But you said you'd changed your will.'

'I just changed the conditions under which you inherit. My lawyer, Mr Dennison, has all the details.' Sophie gave her niece an urchin's mischievous smile. 'Everything's now left in a trust and your precious husband won't be able to touch a penny of it. You'll get the income, not him, and it must be paid into a bank account that's in your name only. Paul offered to manage my affairs for me, did you know? I told him I could manage them myself, thank you very much.'

'I didn't know any of this.' And the thought of her husband trying to take over Sophie's affairs didn't sit well with her. He not only dealt with their own finances, but wanted to know where every penny went, so that you couldn't even buy him a present without him knowing where you got it from and what it had cost. It was only by saving from her housekeeping money that Rosalind managed to have anything of her own. But whenever she got irritated about this, she reminded herself that he had their welfare at heart.

'Wish I could be there to see his face when the will's read,' Sophie went on. 'He'll be bitterly disappointed not to get his hands on the capital, and you're not to hand the income over to him, either. You're to keep it in your own bank account and spend it yourself. Promise me!'

'Well – if you want me to, I promise. But Paul was probably just trying to help you. He's not quite so – so mercenary.'

Sophie gave her a wry look. 'Of course he's mercenary! If he weren't, he'd not be any good at a job like that. Do you even know how much he earns?'

Rosalind shook her head, unable to meet her great aunt's eyes.

'Well, don't tell him how much money you get from me. That'll even things up. Anyway, that's enough talking about him. I want to tell you exactly what you'll be inheriting.'

'I didn't know you were so rich,' Rosalind faltered when the tale was over. She felt quite shocked at the thought of inheriting so much money. This house was the least of it.

Sophie looked smug. 'I did rather well with my investments, if I say so myself, and a couple of friends left me their money.' Her smile faded. 'It's sad seeing your friends die one by one. I'm the last of my circle left. It's time I went.' She picked up a little brass hand bell and rang it. 'I'm afraid I need a rest now. Can't stay upright for too long these days. Get Prue to show you round the house, then you might like to go out for a walk.'

Prue took Aunt Sophie away to the bedroom they'd made out of the old dining room, then came back a few minutes later to show Rosalind to the large bedroom on the first floor, with its square bay window and big pieces of mahogany furniture. 'Don't keep Miss Worth up too late tonight,' she warned in a low voice.

'How is my aunt? Really, I mean.'

Prue shrugged. 'As you'd expect. The doctors have prescribed something for the pain, but she'll only take it at night, because it makes her so dopey. She's a brave woman and I shall miss her when she dies.'

'So shall I.'

'She likes people to ignore her condition as much as possible.'

'I'll do my best. Um – I think I will go out for a stroll. Sitting in a car all day makes me twitchy.'

On her short walk Rosalind passed a florist's and on impulse went inside. There were so many types of flowers available, even at this season, that in the end she asked for a large mixed bunch.

When Sophie reappeared that evening she looked tired, but had changed her dress and tied her long white hair smoothly back at the nape of her neck with a black velvet ribbon. Rosalind gave her the flowers and her face lit up.

'How lovely! Thank you so much, my dear. I've always loved flowers, but I can't even remember the last time anyone bought me a bunch.' She sighed, her eyes blind with memories. 'It used to be men who bought me flowers, of course. I've had quite a few bunches of red roses in my time. But they're all dead now, the men of my generation. They died so quickly. It's the women who're the survivors. Remember that, Rosalind.'

After a light but delicious meal, Prue went to clear up and the other two sat talking for a while until Sophie rubbed her forehead and sighed. 'Have to go to bed again now. Damned nuisance. Need one of those blasted injections. Call Prue, will you? I'll see you in the morning, my dear. There's some rather fine cognac in the sideboard. I can't drink it now, more's the pity, so don't stint yourself. And watch the television, if you like. It won't disturb me.'

But Rosalind didn't watch television. Instead, she sat staring at the flames of a gas fire that imitated burning logs rather well, while cradling a brandy glass in her hands. Sipping occasionally she let her thoughts wander where they would. The room was crowded with mementoes and ornaments, all Sophie Worth's life set out in careful patterns. But when it came down to it, you went out of the world on your own, as deprived of possessions as you'd come into it.

Perhaps, she thought as she got ready for bed, she'd clung to her own possessions too much.

Perhaps Paul was right about her needing a change.

In the morning Rosalind slept late, for her, because she still hadn't adjusted to the time change. When she got up around nine, she found Sophie waiting for her impatiently downstairs.

'Thought you were never going to surface. I was about to send Prue to wake you. Look – I know you spent yesterday driving, but do you feel like a trip out today?' It was typical of her not to bother with the meaningless small talk she had always despised.

'I'd love it, but ought you to—'

'I hired a car and driver yesterday. Forgot to tell you last night. The injections make me a bit woozy. I want to go to the Lake District one last time. Will you come with me?'

'I'd love to. But there was no need to hire a car. I could have driven you.'

'Oh, no! Much more fun to let someone else do the driving. This way, you'll see more of the scenery and we can talk properly. I've ordered a big car so my stupid wheelchair will fit into the boot.'

The car was a grey Mercedes with a driver in a navy chauffeur's uniform. Sophie giggled and nudged Rosalind as he fussed over them. 'This is doing things in style, eh?'

'Don't you always, Soph?'

The day passed swiftly. They drove north along the motorway to Kendal, then stopped for a while beside Lake Windermere. Rosalind noticed that her aunt was dozing, so sat quietly enjoying the scenery.

'I'd have bought a house up here near the lakes if it wasn't for the holidaymakers cluttering up the place,' Sophie said suddenly.

'You're awake again.'

'Of course I'm awake. Do you think I talk sense in my sleep?' She shifted uncomfortably. 'Need a toilet. One of those bigger ones for disabled folk. Would you mind helping me?'

'Of course not.'

Afterwards Rosalind pushed the wheelchair along the lakeside for a while, worried at how white her aunt's face was. She didn't go far, but found a bench with a lovely view of the water and its fractured reflections of the hills around them. They sat chatting quietly as a light breeze rippled the surface.

'Tell me about your life,' Sophie said abruptly. 'Has it been good for you?'

'Oh, yes. I've made my career out of my husband and family. They're the centre of everything, my whole life and—'

'No!' Her aunt sounded really angry. 'They're *not* your whole life. He's your husband, and important to you, but you're a person in your own right as well. You should have a life of your own and think of *your* needs as well as his. The same with your children. Never forget that.'

Silence sat between them like a chaperone for a few moments, then Sophie sighed. 'Let's go back to the car now. I'm weaker than I thought.'

'Perhaps we should go home?'

'*No!*' Sophie's voice was sharp. She looked at her niece, pleading for understanding. 'This'll probably be my last outing. Let's make the most of it, eh? We'll stop again later and I'll probably have another doze. But that doesn't matter. I'll have seen the hills and lakes again.'

She was very quiet as they drove round by Keswick and stopped near Helvellyn. 'Beautiful, isn't it?' she asked once, then nodded off before Rosalind could answer. She slept most of the way home, too.

Prue took one look at her when they got back and said firmly, 'Bed now, Miss Worth. You're not staying up for dinner tonight, either.'

'Bully!' said Sophie, but went without further protest.

'I shouldn't have let her go out,' Rosalind worried when Prue came back down to join her.

'Well, the doctors would tell you that. But in my opinion she should do whatever she wants. Does it really matter if the outing shortens her life by a few days? She enjoyed it greatly.'

'You're very good to her.'

'Not all my patients are as much fun to be with.' Prue hesitated. 'It's not my place to say it, but you will come and see her again, won't you? She's thoroughly enjoying your company.'

'Oh, yes. I'll come as often as I can. But I'll have to leave tomorrow, I'm afraid, because Paul will be home at the weekend.'

There were tears on Rosalind's cheeks as she drove away from Southport, but she was filled with admiration for Sophie's bravery. Old age was cruel and she didn't know how anyone could face death so cheerfully.

How would *she* face old age? And Paul? It would be worse for him, she was sure. She couldn't imagine him growing old gracefully. He already hated his light sprinkling of silver hairs. But he'd not escape the effects of old age any more than she would. No one did. And growing old was better than dying young, after all. Or one assumed it was.

She clicked her tongue in annoyance at herself for such morbid thoughts and switched on the radio. It didn't do to dwell on things. She had enough on her plate without borrowing trouble from the years ahead.

Some second honeymoon this was! She didn't think she'd ever felt quite so angry at Paul. But she was glad she was here for Sophie, at least.

Chapter Four

It was not until Saturday afternoon that a sleek, dark BMW drew up in Sexton Close and Paul emerged to struggle with the recalcitrant gate. Rosalind had been fidgeting about in the large sitting room with its icy blue décor, because she could see him arrive from there. When she saw the car stop in the street, she debated whether to go out and help with the gates, hesitated then went into the kitchen instead. Let him open the damned gates himself! And let him knock on the door and wait for her to answer it, too.

She heard the protesting screech of the gates being pushed right back, then the sound of tyres on the drive. A car door slammed, footsteps crossed the gravel and someone tried the front door. A muffled curse brought a tight smile to her face, as did the sound of the doorbell being rung, then rung again a few seconds later.

The letter box rattled. 'Ros! Are you there? Ros!'

Only then did she move, walking slowly along the hall towards the front door.

'Darling!' He planted a swift kiss on each cheek. 'Didn't you hear me arrive?'

'No.'

He looked at her, eyes narrowed, assessing the situation. 'In the black books, am I?'

She breathed deeply.

'Oh, give me a proper hug, woman, and stop sulking.' He pulled her into his arms. 'There was nothing I could do about it. The chairman had a crisis on and I had to go to the States. We'd have lost the contract if I hadn't stepped in.'

Something cold shifted uneasily inside her, then perched upon her shoulder, whispering a commentary in her ear. His first remark had been about the latest contract. 'And how are you going on, Rosalind? Are you settling in all right?' she asked sarcastically.

'Hey, don't be like that, hon!'

'You *promised* to be there for me at Heathrow, Paul.'

'But darling, I just explained all that and—'

'There are times when family should come first, family and wife.' She pulled away from him and looked him straight in the eyes. 'Not the chairman, or even the bloody company.'

'Without the company, we wouldn't have all this.' He gestured around them.

She didn't reply to that, didn't say, *But maybe we'd be closer to one another*. She didn't want to start a quarrel. 'Well, now you *are* here, would you like a cup of coffee?'

'Real coffee?'

'Of course.'

'I'd kill for one. You always make the best coffee'

Suddenly she felt ashamed of her churlish greeting. 'Go and bring your things in, then, and I'll make you a cup. The kitchen's straight through the hall.'

'There's nothing much to bring. I've only got this one bag.'

'What? But you took two suitcases of stuff with you from Australia and you keep some things in the company's London flat. I thought you'd be bringing most of it down here now.'

He pulled her into his arms and sighed. His voice came from just above her right ear, low and persuasive. 'A new problem's cropped up. Look, there's no easy way to say this. I'm sorry, hon, but I can only stay till tomorrow.' Another long, sifting sigh. 'Then I'm afraid I have to go to Hong Kong.'

She jerked back against his arms. 'Hong Kong! *Hong – Kong?* But you said you'd be based in England this year. That's why I came here!' She set her hands against his chest and shoved him away. 'Paul, how *could* you?'

He ran one hand through his hair as he pulled away. 'I've only just found out. Yesterday evening, actually. That's why I'm late. Been to a briefing. Pearson in Hong Kong had a heart attack. Yesterday. Died before they could get him to hospital. I have to go and take over for a month or so till they find someone to head the Asian operation permanently. There are some negotiations at a very delicate stage. I'd have flown out this morning if it hadn't been for you. So you see, I *do* put my family first sometimes.'

A chill spread through her body. 'Then I needn't have

come here at all. I'd have been closer to you in Australia. Oh, damn you, Paul, for uprooting me like this!'

She walked into the kitchen and he followed, moving around, peering out of the back window, opening the pantry door, going to investigate the mudroom. He didn't speak, didn't touch her. She knew what he was doing. Allowing her time to come to terms with his news.

Of their own accord her hands attended to the coffee. She was relieved that some part of her was still functioning, because a flock of cockatoos seemed to have settled inside her skull and they were filling it with stupid, meaningless noise, shrieking in derision at her situation, her gullibility. Why in hell's name had she expected things to be different here in England? Why hadn't she held out against him? He could hardly have dragged her here by force, after all.

She plonked the cup down near him, splashing a trail of brown liquid across the white surface. 'So I'll be alone here for a whole month.'

'I'm really sorry about that.'

She filled her own cup and stood cradling it in her hands. 'Some second honeymoon this is.'

'I said I was sorry. Be reasonable, Ros. No one could have guessed that Pearson would have a heart attack.'

'I'm going home to Australia, then.'

'You *can* do that, of course—'

She didn't take in a single word until he finished, 'But I *will* be back in England for the rest of the spring and summer, I promise you. So why don't you reconsider? We can still be together. I have plenty of leave owing, so I'll take a week off when I get back.'

'*A whole week?*'

'Look, it's hard to get even that at this time of the year. And I've just had some time off, though I spent half of it on planes to and from Australia for your sake, so you needn't get snitty with me.'

'It's hard for you to take leave at any time of year. Any year.' He had loads of paid leave owing to him, months and months of it. And he'd fretted around like a lost soul in Australia during the one week he'd spent there. He'd been *bored*! He seemed to have lost the ability to enjoy himself quietly at home like other men, which was one of the reasons she'd been thinking of divorce. She wanted a companion, not a nominal husband.

He put his arms around her again, tugging at her stiff body until it moved to rest against his and nestling his cheek against her hair. 'Don't go back to Australia, Ros. Please. A month will soon pass. I really do want us to spend some time together.' He kissed her cheek. His breath was warm in her ear and his breathing showed he was aroused.

'I'll see.' She pulled away. She didn't feel aroused. Not at all. A month could pass quickly when you had plenty to do, but time could drag when you were stuck in a rented house in a village where you knew no one. Unfortunately, where his work was concerned, Paul was a reinforced concrete wall. No use beating her head against it.

He abandoned the attempt to make love to her, but was subdued for only as long as it took him to drink the coffee, then went to get his briefcase. He saw her dirty look. 'Just some papers I need to look over today, hon.'

'You can't even give me two full days, can you?'

His voice changed, became steely. 'It's the work I do which pays for all this.'

'Then it pays for things I've never wanted. As far as I'm concerned, you're doing all that for yourself.' She went back into the kitchen and started preparing dinner, banging the pots around. Anything to keep her hands busy.

He didn't follow her and presently she heard the sound of papers rustling in the small office. He'd found that room, all right, and taken possession of it without asking her if she minded.

But as they sat and chatted after dinner, she could feel herself softening, because when he set out to charm, no one was better company than Paul. And when they went to bed the touch of his hands, the feel of his body against hers worked their usual magic.

Whatever Liz said, Rosalind couldn't imagine anything better than their loving.

'You're still a damned good lay,' he muttered in her ear afterwards.

'Very romantic!' she teased. 'You're not bad yourself.'

But he was asleep already. She lay awake for ages, listening to his soft, even breaths. If they were going to use the word 'still', she'd apply it to her emotions.

She *still* felt angry with him. Very angry.

She *still* felt uncertain about their marriage, too.

After lunch the next day, Paul looked at his watch. 'I'll have to leave soon, hon.'

She could feel her lips tightening.

'You aren't going back to Australia, are you?'

'I suppose not.' But it was for Sophie's sake, not his, only she wasn't going to tell him about her aunt.

'Good. When I get back, we'll do some entertaining, eh? I owe so many people over here. We've plenty of room for them to stay over. Or the pub in the village has some rather nice en suite rooms, I gather. You could cook some Australian specialities. It'll be fun, make a good impression.'

'I don't see how we can give a decent dinner party here. There's only minimal cutlery and crockery.'

That got his full attention. 'It's supposed to be an executive residence. Everything supplied.'

'It's quite big and the furniture is reasonable, but they've skimped on the kitchen equipment. Six of everything in the crockery line is not enough to entertain with and kitchen gadgets are practically non-existent. There's a hand beater, a plastic grater and a tin opener, and that's about all. I had to buy that coffee plunger myself.'

'Not satisfactory. I'll have a word with Gail and tell her to complain. She's good at that sort of thing.' He grinned. 'It's my bet that in a day or two the agent will get in touch with you and ask your advice about what's missing.'

'What's missing will be you,' she said and couldn't stop her voice coming out choked, but he was carrying his bag and briefcase out to the car and didn't hear her.

'Look, why don't you go up to Lancashire to see that aunt of yours?' he said as he slammed the boot shut. 'Stay a few days.'

She opened her mouth to tell him that she'd already

been to see Sophie, but he was still speaking.

'By the time you've done that and sorted out the house ready for some serious entertaining, I'll be back from Honkers.' He gave her a quick, absent-minded hug. 'Four weeks will pass in a flash. You'll see.'

As she watched him drive away, she knew that wasn't true. Four *days* could seem like an eternity, stuck here on her own, with no family to look after, nothing familiar to comfort you.

In Australia, Jenny Stevenson stood and listened to the scolding from her supervisor with as much grace as she could muster.

'Your heart doesn't seem to be in your work, Jenny,' Mr Bennett said with that solemn expression of his. 'You should remember that you're on probation for six months before we can accept you on our permanent staff – *if* we accept you. It isn't automatic, you know.'

She stared at him in horror. Her father would kill her if she got the sack, and anyway, she needed the money even more now she was renting a flat on her own.

'Is – um, is something troubling you, my dear?'

She stared down at her feet, then realised this was an out. 'I – I've been having trouble with my – my ex-fiancé. We've just split up. I'm sorry. I didn't mean to let my work suffer.' Tears came into her eyes. Michael was still pestering her to get back together again and no way was she going to agree. In fact, he was being more than a pest and had frightened her silly last night banging on her door just before midnight. She'd never go back to him. Never.

The supervisor's voice was more gentle. 'I'm sorry. You should have said something.'

Jenny dabbed at her eyes. 'I'll try to – to do better,' she promised. She really would. However bored she was with office work. However the working days dragged. She didn't dare get the sack without her mother here to help her.

In the middle of the night she woke suddenly. Had she heard something? She lay rigid, listening with all her might.

Before she could get up to look out of the window, there was a crash, which made her squeak in shock and cower in the bed. By the light from the street lamp she saw that someone had thrown a brick through her window.

It must be a drunk! She got up to peer out of the window, but there was no one outside. And although a light had come on in the flat next door, it winked out again as she looked, and she was left staring at the shards of glass sticking out from her window frame.

She cleared up, but couldn't get back to sleep, well not properly, only doze a little, even though being on the second floor meant she didn't have to worry about someone getting in through the window. And she was late for work while she waited for someone to come and fix a new windowpane.

It was only as she was getting into her car that she had a sudden thought. If drunks were around, you usually heard them talking or laughing. She had heard nothing. But – who else could it have been?

'Oh, no!' Her heart plummeted as she admitted what she had been avoiding facing until then. There was only one person who bore her a grudge. Michael. He had rung last night and she had shouted at him on the phone, then slammed it down. She felt a cold shudder run down her spine as she suddenly knew for certain it had been him who had thrown the brick.

'What good does it do?' she whispered. 'I'm not going back to him.'

She kept telling him that. Why wouldn't he believe her and leave her alone?

As she posted a letter to her mother in Australia, Rosalind noticed a craft shop on the corner opposite and was lost.

She'd only intended to buy a bit of canvas on which to do a small sampler, just to pass the time, but she forgot that as she looked round the well-equipped shelves. And the more she looked, the more the determination grew in her to set herself up for her own type of embroidery, raised stumpwork, the thing she loved doing.

Since Paul had left her here, all alone, it was only right that he pay for the new equipment and materials she would need from the housekeeping account. It wasn't going to come out of her own money this time. And she was not only going to do some new pictures, she was going to take over one of the bedrooms and leave her embroidery things lying around all the time. Just let him complain about her 'mess' again! Ever.

She would send for some of her finished pieces, too, and put them on the walls to cheer herself up. She'd get them professionally packed and air freighted out. Rebellion burned through her, hot and reckless, and it felt good, damn good, even if it was only a small domestic protest.

When she got home she spread out her purchases, stroking the hanks of embroidery thread and snipping the new scissors in the air. Her eyes became unfocused as she debated what subject to work on. She had several ideas in mind, but a new one blossomed suddenly. The family. Her family. All of them: Paul, herself, the three children. She'd never done a family portrait before. Of course, she'd have to work out a design and create figures which showed their personalities, but she had photos of her children and husband with her. She'd start sketching a layout after tea as she watched television. Sometimes it took a while to get the right composition.

The icy unhappiness inside her began to thaw, though only a little. She was still missing her family and friends dreadfully. She'd never been away from her daughters before and neither of them was a good correspondent. On that thought, she did a quick calculation of time differences and picked up the phone.

Louise answered it. 'Hey, Mum! How are you?'

They discussed university, then Jenny. 'Yeah, she's got over her split with Michael. Well, he was a real dork, wasn't he? I don't know where she finds them! I wouldn't even fancy him if you blindfolded me. What? No, Gran's out shopping. I'll tell her you called. Of course I'm coping with the studying.' Which was a lie. But no one was going to find that out for a long time.

Phew! she thought as she put the phone down. *Good thing Gran isn't in.* The two of them had had another row this morning. What did it matter if you left a few plates lying around the kitchen? Anyway, what else had Gran to do with her time but clear up?

Louise went to fiddle with the kettle, sighing. The reason she wasn't coping with her studies was that she wasn't finding them at all interesting. *Business studies!* Why had her father insisted on them all doing that sort of degree? Not arts, he'd insisted, because that was an expensive way of joining the dole queue and he was the one paying for all this, thank you very much. And not architecture, either. There were a lot of young architects struggling to make a living.

Well, she didn't really want to do architecture. She'd only said that to stir him up. She hadn't got high enough scores to get into medicine, even if she'd wanted to, but she had toyed with the idea of training as a nurse. First aid had been a non-academic option at school and she'd enjoyed it very much, been good at it, too. She liked looking after people who were injured, and the bloodier the better. Sandy had slashed her wrist by accident one day when they were fooling around in the kitchen and she'd known exactly what to do. The doctor had praised her efforts, too, which was more than her bloody father ever did.

But Dad had the money, so they had to dance to his tune. Life wasn't fair. But at least those tablets Sandy had got her were working. She wasn't at all hungry nowadays – though her Gran hadn't congratulated her on losing the two kilos, just tried to nag her into eating more. Honestly! Her whole family was so far out of touch it wasn't true. If you were fat no one fancied you. It was as simple as that. Thin was in.

The conversation with her younger daughter relieved some of Rosalind's worries, but it wasn't the same as being there and seeing everyone. She rang Liz afterwards, but there no answer. She tried several times over the next day or two, but to no avail. And the answering machine wasn't on, either. She hoped everything was all right. Liz had been in a very brittle mood when she left.

The next time Rosalind rang Perth, she caught her mother in, which was what she really wanted, and they had a nice long chat, though the question of how Louise was doing brought a stiff tone to her mother's voice. Rosalind debated pushing for more information, then decided against it. She had enough problems managing on her own, was hating the loneliness.

At one point she asked if Audrey had seen Liz.

'I met a cousin of hers, who said she'd gone away on holiday.'

'Oh? Where?' Liz had said nothing to her about holidays and they shared their plans with other.

'Singapore or Hong Kong, I think. Or was it both? I can't remember.'

'But the university term has started. How has Bill managed to get away?'

'Liz went on her own, apparently. Her mother said she'd been feeling depressed and needed something to cheer her up.'

'I see.' That sounded ominous to Rosalind. Surely Liz wouldn't be putting her threat into operation? It was bad enough Bill being unfaithful, but two wrongs didn't make a right. 'Strangely enough, Paul's in Hong Kong, too, Mum.' She then had to explain about Pearson dying and it being an emergency, and her mother said all the things she'd been thinking, but of course she couldn't agree with them too strongly because that would be disloyal.

'Wouldn't it be funny if Paul and Liz bumped into one

another?' she said, to divert her mother's attention.

'It'd be a miracle if they did. That place is so crowded you can hardly move around at more than a shuffle, and you can't even see the people across the street clearly for heads bobbing in front of you.'

Rosalind smiled. Her mother had hated her one visit to Hong Kong. Well, she hadn't liked it much herself, either. The people were pleasant, the hotels good and the tour guide had been charming, but Rosalind had found the masses of people everywhere claustrophobic after the wide open spaces of Western Australia.

Liz wasn't enjoying being on holiday alone. The hotel in Hong Kong was big and luxurious, but most of the guests seemed to be passing through as part of tours. She'd tried sitting in the foyer, hoping to strike up a conversation with someone, anyone, but people just walked past her to join their tour groups.

And as for finding a man, forget it, baby! Most of the guests at the hotel were quite elderly. If she was going to the trouble of having an affair, it had to be with someone decent. At this rate it'd probably be no one, but she needn't tell Bill that. She'd invent some gorgeous hunk and describe the encounters in intimate detail. An American tourist, she'd say. Perhaps she should buy a couple of romance novels, see if they gave her any ideas.

But that evening, a miracle occurred. Someone came up to her table in the restaurant and said, 'What the hell are you doing here in Honkers, Liz Foxen?'

She gaped up at him. 'Paul! But you're in England!'

'I was yesterday.' He glanced down. There was only one table setting. Curiouser and curiouser. 'Isn't Bill with you?'

'No, I'm on my own.'

'Want some company?'

'I'd love some.' It was one thing to swan off and leave your erring husband wondering what you were getting up to, but another entirely for a woman to amuse herself on her own at night in a foreign city.

He sat down and beckoned to a waiter.

She watched the man fuss over him. Paul certainly knew how to get good service. Bill always got fobbed off with tables in corners and slow service.

Paul looked up and winked at her as the waiter continued to fuss. 'Want me to order for you?'

'Yes. I don't know what half the things are. I was going to have the bouillabaisse.'

'Wouldn't advise it. Not here. The seafood can be very dodgy because the harbour is so polluted.'

'Whoops! I had prawns last night. Do you think I'll live?'

'Oh, yes.'

His smile was warm and his eyes said he found her attractive. Well, it made a change for someone to feel that way. In fact, it felt wonderful.

The food was excellent. A series of small dishes, each perfectly presented, accompanied by superb wines. Too much wine, perhaps. When the meal was over and Paul suggested a cocktail, she found her head spinning as she tried to follow him to the bar.

'I think you've had enough to drink,' he said with a chuckle, steadying her.

She clung to his arm. Lean and muscular. Bill had let himself go a bit lately, was getting a distinct paunch. 'I never could hold my wine.'

'Come on, then, milady, let Sir Galahad escort you up to your chamber.'

At her door he hesitated, then asked, 'Want to meet for a meal tomorrow evening? I'll be working during the day or I'd offer to show you round.'

'I've booked a coach tour. Going out to see a big Buddhist temple. But I'm free in the evening.'

'Shall we say about eight, then? I'll pick you up here.' He glanced up at her room number.

This was more like it, she thought as she closed the door. Paul Stevenson was a charming bastard when he wanted to be.

It was only then that Liz realised – they hadn't mentioned Rosalind at all, not after the first round of greetings. Not once. How strange! But then, they hadn't mentioned Bill, either. And of course she wouldn't tell Paul what she had threatened to do. That was between her and her husband.

But it'd been great to have someone to talk to! She was really looking forward to the next evening.

WHAT IS RAISED EMBROIDERY?

Although domestic stumpwork/raised embroidery embraces flatwork and a large variety of stitches, the definitive features of this style might be summed up as follows:

• The use of 'needlemade fabrics' in the form of needlelace . . .

• The use of wires and vellum, bound with silk and other threads, to provide texture and decorative relief features.

• The application of a wealth of supplementary ornamentation in a variety of available materials, including embroidered silk fabrics, pearls, beads, semi-precious stones, real hair, feathers, mica, metal threads/strips, braids . . .

• The strong use of figurative subjects within an otherwise natural design.

(Hirst, p.8)

Chapter Five

When Aunt Sophie rang a few days later with an invitation to go to Southport again, Rosalind accepted at once. 'As long as you're not too tired for visitors, Soph.'

'I really enjoyed your last visit, dear.'

This time Southport looked grey and unwelcoming. People were hurrying along the pavements, umbrellas much in evidence, headscarves shrouding women's faces into anonymity. She shivered as she parked outside her aunt's and ran through the pouring rain to knock on the door.

When Prue opened it, her face crumpled and tears filled her eyes. 'I tried to catch you before you left this morning. You're' – she hesitated, then finished – 'too late, I'm afraid.'

'What do you mean?' But she knew, really.

'Your aunt died in her sleep.'

As Prue held the door open, Rosalind walked into the hall and stood there. It was a moment before she could speak. 'I can't believe she's gone. Soph was always so *alive*. And I spoke to her on the phone only last night.'

'I'd grown very fond of her, too. More than I usually do with patients.' Prue wiped her eyes. 'Do you want to see her? The undertakers have attended to things – she wanted to lie in her own home, not in a funeral parlour, and I said I'd stay with her. She looks very peaceful.'

'Oh.' Rosalind swallowed. 'Um, Prue – to be honest I've never seen a dead person before.' Not even her own father. 'Maybe I should just – you know, remember her alive.'

Prue put her arm round Rosalind's shoulders. 'If you want my professional opinion, I think it's better to say goodbye properly. There's nothing to be afraid of, you know.'

'Oh. Well, all right.' Feeling shaky inside and wondering why she wasn't weeping, she who even wept at sad items about complete strangers on the television news, Rosalind followed Prue into her aunt's bedroom, hesitated just inside the door, then walked over to stand by the bed.

To her surprise Sophie dead was still someone she loved. 'She does look peaceful,' she whispered, not knowing why she was speaking in hushed tones.

'Yes. And if it's any comfort to you, I think she was more than ready to go. Though she'd have been sorry not to see you again. Isn't it wonderful that you came to England when you did? That you were able to say goodbye to her properly?'

Rosalind felt a surge of guilt at how reluctant she'd been to leave Australia. Her aunt had been asking her to come and visit for years. 'I'd like to sit with her for a while. On my own, if you don't mind.'

Prue gave her a quick hug. 'Sure. I've put you in the same bedroom as before.'

Rosalind pulled a chair up to the bed and found herself talking to her aunt. 'I'm going to miss you very much, Soph. In fact, I don't know what I'll do without you for the next few weeks.' She blinked her eyes, but no tears came. Why wasn't she weeping?

She sat on for a while, feeling a sense of peace in the quiet, elegant room. Prue was right. It was good to say goodbye properly and knowing how much her aunt had hated her increasing incapacity, she couldn't be sorry that Soph's suffering had ended.

Soon she found herself talking again. 'I'm still annoyed with Paul, you know. He's gone off to Hong Kong. For a whole month. That's why I was counting on coming to see you and—' She broke off. She could hear her aunt's answer to that echoing in her head.

Count on yourself, girl. You're the only person in the whole world you can really rely on. Soph had said that to her so many times before, but it had never meant as much as it did now, when it was merely an unspoken echo.

She sighed and stood up. 'I'll try, Soph.' Then she went off to ring her mother and tell her the sad news.

Her mother seemed a bit uptight, but Rosalind didn't ask if anything was wrong. She had enough on her plate at present coping here. More than enough. If her daughter was misbehaving, she didn't want to know yet.

The funeral was held two days later. Only three neighbours and the solicitor attended, apart from Rosalind and Prue. When the neighbours had left the cemetery, Mr Dennison came up to Rosalind, leaning heavily on his stick. He looked top-heavy with age, like a tree ready to be blown down by the next gale.

'Could you possibly come and see me in my office this afternoon, Mrs Stevenson, about your aunt's will? I only work two days a week now, so if you don't come today, it'll have to be next week, I'm afraid.' He patted his chest. 'Ticker's not doing too well. Got to take things easy.'

'All right. I'll come today.'

He presented her with a business card, then walked slowly away.

The two women strolled back to the car park in a companionable silence.

'Have you made any plans yet?' Rosalind asked as they got into her car.

'No. But if you like – well, your aunt suggested after your last visit that I stay on for a few days to help you go through the house and see what you want to keep. I know where everything is, you see. I've helped her sort out all her things over the past few months. She was very anxious to leave everything in good order.' Prue paused and sighed. 'I shall miss living there. It's a lovely house, a real home. I suppose you'll be selling it?'

'I suppose so, eventually. I'd like you to stay on for a while. I hadn't really thought about dealing with Soph's things.'

As they went inside, Rosalind stared round. She couldn't believe that this gracious old house belonged to her now and still felt more like a visitor than an owner.

At the solicitor's that afternoon, Mr Dennison summarised the arrangements Sophie had made.

Rosalind nodded. 'Yes, she told me all that.'

He looked at her sideways, as if assessing her, then added, 'She was a bit worried about your husband, even so, worried he'd try to take the money off you, or that you'd just give it to him.'

Rosalind flushed. 'She made her wishes quite clear and you can rely on me to respect them. I'll open a separate bank account for the money.' It upset her that Soph had considered her so much under Paul's thumb. It upset her even more that there had been good reason for that belief.

Mr Dennison nodded. 'Right, then. Do we have your address in England? No? Well, could you just jot it down, then? And your phone number? Good. Now – anything else you want to ask me?'

'Um – about Prue's wages? My aunt wanted her to stay on for a few days, to help me clear things out. She knows where everything is, you see.'

'Your aunt provided for that. Just send us a written note when she stops work. Until then, the estate will continue to pay her weekly at the reduced rate agreed upon.'

When Rosalind left the lawyer's office, she decided to go for a walk along the seafront. She needed some fresh air – and some quiet thinking time, too.

She found a series of neat, if uninspired, gardens surrounding artificial sea lakes – well, she presumed they were artificial. They were too regular to be natural, surely? It was a cold day, but sunny, and there were few holidaymakers so early in the season.

At one stage she sat on a bench and held her face up to the sun. More changes, she told it.

It continued to smile down at her. What had she expected? it seemed to be asking. Life was full of change. As if to emphasise that, some clouds passed across it and everything went dull until the clouds moved on and the world brightened up again.

Rosalind sucked in a deep breath, which was shaky with grief not only for Sophie but for herself, for her loneliness and uncertainty, her desperate need to sort her own life out.

What did she really want? To become a company wife and follow Paul around the world – or to put down roots somewhere on her own? She knew what the first choice would entail and as for the second, well, she'd been doing that for years. It was the one thing she'd stood up to Paul about. And it wasn't truly satisfactory being on your own, either.

Sighing, she stood up and began to walk back to the town centre. Since Paul wouldn't be back for a while, she'd make going through Sophie's possessions her first priority.

I'll try to be stronger next time I see him, she vowed as she walked up the garden path. *Even if I do decide to become a company wife, I'll make sure I have my own life too. Things like my embroidery. I must. I can't go on like this, letting him use me as 'a wife'.*

Tim Stevenson edged forward, his eyes darting from side to side. If the cops caught him – if they put him in prison – but the buyer muttered what he wanted, handed over the money and hurried off as soon as he had the small packet. The next sale was just as easy.

When Tim had sold all his packages, he shuddered with relief and walked back to the bar. Handing over the money, he accepting the percentage agreed on – which was quite good pay for an hour's work.

'See,' said Wayne afterwards. 'It was easy. We'll work for a while here, then move on. How about buying me a drink with your profits? And I bought some stuff for tonight. We can share it, if you like.'

'No, thanks. I've got a thumping head. I'm not—' Tim paused for a moment as he realised what his decision meant. But he couldn't be any more unhappy than he had been lately, and it was the only real alternative. He stared at Wayne. 'I'm giving the hard stuff up. It doesn't agree with me.'

Wayne laughed, a sneering sound. 'It's a bit late to stop, isn't it? I mean, you'd need medical help to kick the habit.'

'I've only been using when I could afford it, not every day.'

'You can afford it easily now. Pusher's discount is quite helpful. Quit later, if you must "see the light".' He tittered as if he had made a joke.

'I want to quit now,' Tim insisted. The haggard, sometimes desperate faces of the people who had bought from him underlined what the stuff did to you sooner or later, demonstrating it better than any films and lectures ever could. 'Look, I'm going back to our room now. Don't bring any chicks home tonight, right? I need some sleep.' He didn't even wait for an answer, just turned and walked away.

Over the next week or two, he pushed drugs only to survive and did try to give the stuff up, to Wayne's great amusement. He slipped up a couple of times, but he did cut it down, way down, and that was a start.

His friend, on the other hand, was indulging himself in every new treat that came along and wasn't eating well. Wayne looked thin and feverish, full of energy one minute, sagging around their sleazy little room the next.

Which also kept reinforcing how stupid they were to have got themselves into this mess.

Tim bought a money belt and it never left his body, because with his clearer head he'd realised Wayne had been going through his things when he was out and helping himself. As his belt grew heavier, he found another hiding place for his passport and part of his savings, away from their motel. Risky, but who'd look in a neglected cemetery urn?

When he'd saved enough for the fare, he was going back to Australia and he was never, ever going to leave it again. He didn't tell Wayne or anyone else about his plans. He was just going to take off one day. He'd already sussed out the quickest way to get to the nearest airport. He'd be gone before anyone realised it, flying to another city before booking his flight home. Oh, yes, he had it all figured out.

Sometimes the thought of home and of his mother especially made him want to break down and sob his heart out. He hadn't been fair to her. He'd mocked and scorned her, had encouraged Louise to do the same. His mother didn't deserve that. He desperately wanted to see her and tell her how much he loved her.

Hell! If Wayne saw him crying like this, he'd laugh himself silly. And anyway, becoming sentimental was no way to get out of this mess. Tim knew he had to keep his cool, save his money and run for it when the right moment came.

Louise glared at her grandmother. 'What do you mean: I'm grounded? What do you think I am, a child?'

'Yes, I do. You're only seventeen. That's not grown-up in my book.'

'Well, it is in everyone else's. Anyway, I'm nearly eighteen.' And no longer a virgin. But sex wasn't all it was cracked up to be, not by a long chalk. Or else Todd wasn't very good at it. What a let-down that had been!

'You're not eighteen for three months yet. And why didn't your parents let you have a flat if you're so grown-up? Why did they want you to live here with me while they were away?'

'Because my mother is as stupidly old-fashioned as you are!'

'Well, at least Rosalind is polite, unlike her daughter.'

Louise got up and moved towards the front door. 'Grounded, eh? How are you going to keep me in the house, then?'

Audrey gaped at her. 'Are you going to disobey me?'

'You bet. Just watch!' Louise opened the door, swept a mocking bow and walked out, slamming it hard behind her.

Audrey sank down on the nearest chair, legs trembling. She might be old-fashioned, but she wasn't stupid, and Louise had definitely been taking something recently. Yesterday she'd been all dreamy and stupid-looking when she came home, not expecting her grandmother to be waiting up for her at two o'clock in the morning.

What am I going to do? she wondered. *I wish I'd never taken this on. I'm too old for all these confrontations. But I'm not giving in. This is* my *house and as long as she's here, she'll keep to my standards.*

The trouble was, what other sanctions could she apply? And how to enforce them?

Feeling out of her depth, she went across the street to see John, who was a great comfort to her. He'd told her she was crazy taking Louise in, but he hadn't said 'I told you so!' when he'd been proved right.

Audrey knew if she gave him any encouragement, he'd like to be more than a friend, but she wasn't sure she wanted to live with anyone again. She enjoyed living alone. Her family and friends worried about her, but she had a quiet, happy life – or at least, she had been happy until Louise joined her.

It was nice, though, having John to turn to, to go out with from time to time. Someone who really seemed to care about her problems.

'I'll give Louise a week longer,' she said after talking it over with him. 'If things don't improve, I'll ring my daughter and say it's too much for me.'

'Why not ring the father? He's a damn sight closer to hand.'

'Yes, of course. You're quite right. Anyway, it's about time he took a hand in the everyday problems of raising his children, instead of leaving it all to his wife.'

With Prue's help, Rosalind spent a few days going through the house. She'd expected it to be a chore, but instead found it fascinating. Sophie had been a hoarder and there were mementoes dating back to the 1920s and even earlier, the residue of many lives, other members of the family, people Rosalind had never even heard of before.

Soph had put together a family tree and labelled all the photographs, so that her great-niece would be able to identify them. And oh, Rosalind did love those photographs! Album after album of sepia prints, all neatly labelled as to subjects and year – or approximate year in some cases. 'Aren't they wonderful?' she exclaimed one afternoon.

Prue nodded. 'One or two of them date back to the 1860s. That makes a shiver run down my spine. Miss Worth wrote her memoirs, too.' She went to the bookcase and pulled out a huge bound ledger, the sort they had used in old offices.

Rosalind opened the book at random. Soph's familiar spiky handwriting. It should have made her weep, but it didn't. Why hadn't she been able to weep for her aunt? Why was the grief sitting inside her in a tight bundle? It was so unlike her. 'I shall enjoy reading these.'

'You'd better take them with you, then. You don't want them being carted away with the rest of the stuff.'

'I shan't have anything carted away yet, Prue. I may want – no, I definitely *shall* want to keep some of her things. And I'd like my children to see this place before I close it down. There are some lovely pieces of furniture. I'm going to ship them back to Australia and keep them in the family.'

Before she left, she arranged for Prue to stay on for a few weeks, rent-free, then set off back to Dorset.

She drove slowly. There was so much to think about. What was she going to do about her life? There were still nearly three weeks to go before Paul would return. She had to come to some decisions before then.

Jenny groped through the mists of sleep and picked up the phone. Who could be ringing in the middle of the night? She jerked into full wakefulness at the thought that something might be wrong with her mother in England.

She could hear someone breathing heavily at the other end of the line and yelled, 'Stop this, Michael Lazzoni! You hear me? It won't get you anywhere. I'm not coming back to you and that's that.' She slammed down the phone but within seconds it started ringing again.

She stared at it, her breath coming in gasps, as if she'd been running. What was she going to do about this harassment? She'd asked at the police station, but they said they couldn't really help without proof, and the phone company seemed to think the calls would die down of their own accord. How had Michael got hold of her new number, anyway? She'd only given it to her close friends and had sworn them to the strictest secrecy.

When the ringing began to irritate her, she lifted the phone and let it drop instantly, cutting the connection. But it was ringing again within the minute, so she left it off the hook.

Michael was stalking her – there was no other word for it – waiting outside work and staring at her, following her in his car. She didn't know what to do about it, who to turn to. Let's face it, she was scared out of her mind.

If only her mother was here! Or even her father. She smiled wryly in the darkness. This was actually the sort of thing he'd be the best person to handle. But she couldn't face his scorn. She'd give it a little longer. Surely Michael would grow tired of pestering her?

Soon after Rosalind arrived back in Burraford Destan, the phone rang and Paul snapped, 'Where the *hell* have you been, Ros? I've been calling you for days. I was thinking of getting on to the police to check that you were all right.'

Why hadn't he, then? 'I've been in Southport.'

'But I rang there. Twice. No one answered. I assumed the witch lady was away.'

She felt angry at the way he referred to Sophie and was strangely reluctant to tell him the sad news. 'How's Hong Kong?'

'Great. Busy as ever.'

'Have you run into Liz? She's there on holiday.'

There was a silence, just the sound of the line humming and fizzling.

'Paul? Didn't you hear me?'

'Sorry, bad line. What did you say?'

'I asked if you'd run into Liz.'

'Why should I have done that?'

'She's on holiday there.'

'There are rather a lot of people in Hong Kong, as you know from your own experience. Bloody millions of them, actually! Wouldn't be my favourite place for a permanent posting, I can tell you. Anyway, never mind all that. Tell me how you're getting on with the house? Have you sorted things out with the agents? Some rather important clients will be in town next month. I'd like to give them a country weekend. You'd better explore the district, see if there are any stately homes nearby. Those Americans adore them.'

When she didn't reply immediately, he asked sharply, 'Ros, are you listening?'

'Yes. I'll see what I can do. The agent's authorised me to buy some more equipment.'

'What do you mean, you'll see what you can do? Is there some problem I don't know about?'

She hesitated, but she had to tell him sometime. 'Yes. There is rather. Aunt Sophie died last week.'

Silence, then, 'Did she leave you anything?'

She slammed the phone down.

When it began to ring again, she waited for eight rings before picking it up.

'Ros?'

'Yes.'

'We got cut off. Is something wrong? Why did it take you so long to pick the phone up again?'

'We didn't get cut off, actually. I put the receiver down. I've just lost a relative I loved very much and all you asked about was what she'd left me.'

Silence again, then, 'Hell, don't take things to heart, Ros. You know me. I'm the financial manager of the family.'

'Not this time, you aren't.'

His voice became very soft. 'What – exactly – do you mean by that?'

She smiled as she told him. And afterwards, when he started complaining, saying they'd have to try to overset the will's conditions, she didn't slam the receiver down, but replaced it gently in its holder.

It started to ring but she didn't pick it up. Instead, she poured herself a glass of her aunt's cognac and raised it mockingly. 'Well, Soph, you'd be pleased with me today. The new independent Rosalind's first act of rebellion.' Small but immensely satisfying.

The next day the embroideries her mother had picked up for her and sent by courier arrived from Australia. They felt like old friends. She carried them into the large sitting room and hung them on the wall, stacking the tacky prints they replaced in a corner of the attic bedroom with their cartoon-like blue roses hidden.

Much cheered, she began working on the new embroidery, the family group. Her preliminary sketch was of Paul, taken from a photo she'd brought with her. She'd tried to draw his figure several times, but it hadn't come out as she'd wanted. Now, still angry with him, she tried again. And it was right, so absolutely right.

It would go in the centre of the picture, of course.

She started work on the head first. Muslin face, lightly padded. Dark brown embroidery silk for hair, boyishly tousled. Predator's stance.

At that thought, she stopped stitching. *Predator?* Paul wasn't a predator. He was just – a little aggressive and opportunistic.

He's a predator! Admit it. The voice in her head sounded like Sophie's.

OK, she told it. *You're right, really. He is a predator.*

But there have been times when I've been glad of his strength. And at least he's looked after his family – in his own way. He's not like some men, going off having affairs, behaving irresponsibly.

She continued sewing. Sometimes she had to make two or three heads to get the face right, but not this time. At first try she got Paul right. He was an arrogant figure, arms folded, dominating the foreground, standing on his own. Why hadn't she realised before how dominating he was? Funny how the embroidery seemed to be helping her see things more clearly than usual.

Was she going to continue letting him rule the roost? Her small act of defiance yesterday wasn't going to change much. She shook her head ruefully. She'd never been good at dealing with him in the past, why should she be any better in the future?

No, that wasn't good enough. She looked up and promised Sophie's hovering shade that she'd continue to do what she could to stand up for herself. She'd at least try.

She felt better for that, as well as apprehensive.

HEADS AND FACES

The head is usually the first part of the human figure to be embroidered on the ground fabric or applied to it. The soft-sculpture technique . . . is both versatile and lively . . .

Obtaining a head that is of a correct size for the design is often a question of trial and error . . . Insufficient soft filling will result in a flat, uninteresting face . . .

It is more important to create the desired impression than to copy slavishly from the design source.

(Hirst, pp.42–6)

Chapter Six

During the next few days Rosalind spent a lot of time thinking about her situation and relationships as her clever fingers built up the figure of Paul in her embroidery. This wasn't at all like one of her usual pictures, it was – it was more a search for understanding, she decided during a stormy afternoon, watching the rain march across the hills towards her, then splatter against the windowpanes of the bedroom she used as her workroom.

This wasn't just a pleasurable activity, but a necessity, and it was taking far longer to do than usual because she seemed to be spending a lot of time staring into space, lost in the dark tangles of her own thoughts.

When the figure of her husband was finished, she held the square of material at arm's length and stared at it in amazement. Such a strutting, arrogant creature! And yet – it was Paul!

Was she being cruel to him, creating a caricature? No,

she decided reluctantly, she was being truthful, using her artist's eye.

Paul's experiment had backfired on him. Change of season, he'd called this visit to England. Change of perception, it seemed to be for her – about herself as well as him.

She set the piece aside for a while because working on it was so traumatic. She couldn't face doing herself or her children yet, not if their figures were going to reveal as much as Paul's had.

For the next embroidery she chose a charming thirties scene with children playing in a park, based on one of Soph's old photographs. It was a relief to work on that after the wrenching emotion of doing Paul.

She was no longer sorry she'd come on this trip, because she'd been able to say farewell to Soph.

And the money she'd been left made her feel better about herself, more confident somehow. She'd bought a new computer and a program for designing embroidery pictures – though she was still trying to figure that out. She was on email too, but Liz must still be away and her mother didn't do email.

She'd sent messages to her daughters, giving them her new email address, but they hadn't replied. Had she dropped off the planet or something?

She hadn't contacted Paul, because what she wanted to say to him needed to be done face-to-face. It fretted her that he was so far away, because she wanted, no, *needed* to discuss their future. They hadn't talked enough in the past, not seriously, anyway.

Improved communication could only strengthen their relationship in the long run, surely, even if it was painful. Twenty-four years together must mean they were basically on track as a couple. Paul wasn't like Bill Foxen, after all. He didn't cheat on her.

Liz let Paul swing her round the dance floor and gave herself up to enjoyment. She'd danced with him before, of course she had, but it hadn't felt like this, as if they were alone in the universe. Other faces blurred around them. She looked up and found him smiling down at her.

'Enjoying yourself, Liz?'

'Oh, yes.'

'Me, too.'

As he pulled her closer, Paul couldn't help wondering if Liz had meant what she said to Ros about 'sauce for the goose'. He'd dismissed the idea at the time, but what was Liz doing on her own here in Hong Kong if she hadn't meant it?

He shouldn't think about such things, definitely not. Rule number one: never foul your own nest. But the feel of Liz's small, firm breasts against his chest, the smell of her perfume, the pleasure of her company and intelligent conversation – well, they were all having an inevitable effect. He only hoped it wasn't too noticeable.

It was. Liz smiled as she nestled against him and felt his arousal. She wished the dance would go on for ever. Even if it was only Paul, it was good to feel a man get hard because of her, especially a man as attractive as this one. She'd seen the other women in the restaurant looking at him.

Well, look all you want, ladies! she thought triumphantly. *Tonight, he's mine.*

That made her blink. Whatever was she thinking about? He wasn't hers. He was Ros's. Her best friend's husband, for heaven's sake! What sort of woman was she to fantasise about him, press herself against him like this? She pulled away, only too aware of her own body's reactions. And his.

'I think this is getting too – too—'

He didn't let go of her hand, didn't stop moving in time to the music. 'I'm enjoying myself, Liz. Very much.'

She swallowed hard, then the words crept out of their own accord. 'So am I.'

'Then why stop?' He pulled her closer and started dancing again. She couldn't resist the invitation behind those words, because it was balm to her pain.

Any more than he could resist following up on her unspoken consent. A man's sexual needs were so much more pressing than a woman's. Ros would never have understood that.

One fine but cold day Rosalind decided not to sit around and mope. A really long walk would do her good.

The neighbours, who had invited her in for morning tea one day, had told her about the wonderful scenery you could only see properly on foot, all signposted for walkers, apparently. The lady at Number 7 had even lent her a book of walks, graded from easy to energetic.

Rosalind decided to try something of medium distance to begin with, so flipped through the book. No, a mile wasn't enough. Three miles would be just right. That would tire her out and then she'd maybe get a good night's sleep, for a change.

Lovely, she told herself as she set off. But she'd never been one for solitary walks, or solitary anything, come to that. She was really missing her circle of friends, not just Liz, but the others she'd known for years, the ones she went to the theatre with, or out for cosy little feminine lunches. Her mother, too.

With the sun shining and a moderate wind blowing her along, Rosalind did feel better for a while. The countryside was truly beautiful and there was a blaze of daffodils in gardens and even along the sides of the road sometimes. There were clumps of purple aubrietia, too, forming an attractive contrast with the yellow, and often tumbling out of crevices in the grey stone walls that edged many of the gardens.

She passed picturesque cottages which would look good in an embroidery, even stopping to photograph one or two. But her fingers were so cold with her gloves off that she messed up one shot and had to do it again.

The inhabitants of those cottages probably had more sense than she did and were staying inside, keeping warm. Only idiots went for walks on freezing cold days like this.

She was an idiot. Definitely.

The walkers' trail had been clearly marked so far, but suddenly the path split into three and there was no indication as to which way she should go. She pulled the guidebook out of her shoulder bag, but could get no help from it. Shrugging, she stuffed it back, wrapped her scarf more tightly round her neck and turned left because that looked the most used of the three tracks.

It twisted down a steep slope into a small wood. Leafless trees surrounded her and bare brown branches swept at the grey overcast sky like giant brooms, while the skeletons of last year's leaves were still piled in hollows. When did the new leaves come out here, for heaven's sake? It was April already, allegedly spring, and most trees were still pretty bare.

The sun went in and suddenly everything seemed to take on a sinister feel. Charcoal clouds raced one another across the sky and the landscape lost every vestige of colour. Here in the woods there were only greys and browns and muddy hues – earth and rock and decay. She glanced up anxiously, hoping the rain would hold off until she got back.

One moment she was striding along at a cracking pace, the next she trod on some gravel and felt it roll beneath her feet. She scrabbled desperately to keep her balance, found only other loose stones and cried out as she lost it completely. She felt herself falling awkwardly and called out again. But only the trees heard her.

As she hit the ground, the breath was slammed out of her and she lay half-stunned for a moment. There was no sound to be heard, apart from the howling wind and her own ragged breathing. Her ankle hurt. She moved it cautiously and couldn't help moaning as pain clamped its teeth into her leg. Was the bone broken?

She made an attempt to get up, yelping as she tried to put some weight on that knee and bumped the ankle. And suddenly, it was all too much. She fell back on the ground, with sobs forcing themselves up her throat in painful bursts of harsh noise. She could lie here and die of exposure and no one would know, or even care.

Delayed grief for Sophie hit her in a secondary wave and she lay there weeping helplessly, her head pillowed on her arms, sobbing out her misery on the rocky ground.

On that cold spring day, Jonathon Destan also decided to go for a walk. He'd been meaning to check out the unfenced bit of land above the grove and at least string a token wire barrier across it with a PRIVATE – KEEP OUT notice before the summer influx of tourists. Several walkers had taken a wrong turn the previous year and had then treated the grounds like a public park, leaving litter and other, more disgusting, signs of their passing.

He strolled slowly across the gardens and paused to look back at the house, his gaze softening as it always did. He loved his home. It was as much a part of him as his own body and he didn't intend to let anyone take it away from him. Well, Isabel had no reason to break the family trust – even the courts had recognised that, since everything would go to his elder son in due course – but his ex-wife had certainly taken all his spare money in lieu.

He didn't know how he was going to manage. He'd tried to think of some way to earn money because the days of landed gentry living on their rents were well past. Only – what was he qualified to do except manage this small estate?

He sighed. He wanted to support his two sons and pay for a good education, of course he did, but he also wanted them to have Destan Manor as their inheritance. Not an old ruin no one could afford to maintain, but a beautiful home that had been lived in by the same family for several centuries. A wave of bitterness washed through him. What he had really wanted was to bring up his children here and potter along, keeping the place up to scratch – but Isabel, no doting mother, had taken his sons away from him out of sheer spite and the bloody courts had supported her.

From further up the slope he heard a noise he couldn't place and stopped to listen. It sounded like – oh, hell, it was! – someone was sobbing! He moved forward, peering cautiously through the trees to see a figure huddled on the ground, a woman. Her whole body was shaking with the passion of her weeping.

The last thing he needed just now was to get involved in someone else's troubles, but he couldn't force himself to move on. She sounded so very unhappy. And she was lying in the place the family always called Araminta's Grove, because one of his ancestors had loved that quiet spot above all others.

He'd taken refuge here himself a few times during the quarrel-filled year before he and Isabel split up, finding comfort for both grief and anger. In late spring there were bluebells under the trees and in summer it was a place of filtered green light and whispering leaves.

He studied the woman. She definitely wasn't from the village. He knew all the permanent residents by sight. Another tourist gone astray, no doubt. But it was a strange place to let out her grief. And a strange time of year for walkers.

The sobbing went on and on. *Dammit! I can't leave the poor woman like that*, he thought. He went right up to her without her even noticing him, cleared his throat and asked, 'Can I help you?'

She didn't hear that, either. In the end he had to bend and touch her shoulder, repeating his question.

'Oh!' She jerked upright in shock, then whimpered in pain and clutched at her leg. 'I didn't hear you coming,' she muttered, turning away to brush futilely at her face with her sleeve. But that didn't prevent more fat tears from overloading her eyes and tracking down her wet cheeks.

Oh, hell, how could you leave anyone in such anguish? He knelt beside her, cradling her in his arms. 'Shh! Don't. Whatever it is, we'll sort something out. Shh, now.'

Gradually, the soft comforting sound of his voice penetrated her distress and she began to calm down. As she realised she was sitting weeping against the chest of a total stranger, she gulped a few times and managed to stop sobbing. But when he looked down, Jonathon saw that she was still clutching his rough jacket as if it were a lifeline. Perhaps it was.

Her hair was fair, a sort of ash-blonde, fluffy and longish. Not dyed, as his ex-wife's had been, but quite natural in colour. This close, he could see a few silver hairs among the pale strands and he had a sudden urge to run his fingers through its softness. It smelt of shampoo, just as her skin smelt of fresh soap, not make-up.

Who was she and what was she doing on his land?

As she shivered, he became more aware of the practicalities of the situation. He could feel an increasing dampness in the air and when he looked up, he could see heavy rain clouds piling up. 'It's going to pour down soon. Let's get you to shelter, hmm?'

'I can't walk. I think I've sprained my ankle.'

'Is that why you were crying?'

Her eyes fell. 'Partly.' She drew in a deep breath that still quivered with suppressed sobs. 'And – and you won't be able to carry me. I'm too big.'

'Let's get you standing up anyway, then we'll work out what to do next. The ground's too damp and cold to sit on. Put your weight on your sound foot and try to hold the other in the air. Now, give me your hands.' Holding her gently, he pulled her to her feet.

She tried to muffle a whimper as she bumped her ankle and that again touched something inside him. 'There's my brave girl,' he whispered, holding her upright against him.

'You're very tall,' she muttered.

'Yes. Bane of my life.'

'Mine, too.'

'You're not tall.' He could give her five or six inches, he reckoned. Even his sister was taller than she was, at six feet.

'I'm a hundred and seventy-eight centimetres.' She saw his look of puzzlement. 'About five foot ten. That's a big disadvantage for a woman. My husband says if I ever put on weight I'll look like a carthorse.'

He took an instant dislike to the husband. 'With a face as pretty as yours, you could never look like a horse and you don't appear to be carrying any extra weight to me.'

She blinked at him as if she didn't believe him.

'Now, we need to get you to the house before the heavens anoint us. If I put my arm round you, will you be able to hop?'

They tried it for a few paces, then she sagged against him. 'I – could we rest a minute?'

'Of course. Lean against this tree.' He had a sudden idea. 'Look, we've got an old bath chair in the stables. I could push it up here and get you back to my place in it if you don't mind a bumpy ride. Can you hold on for a minute?'

'Mmm.'

She watched him run down the hillside with long-legged, confident strides. What a bony man he was, taller than Paul and much thinner. He had a nice face, though. Kind. Lovely brown eyes, soft as a doe's, and a long, sharply chiselled nose. It was the sort of face you'd trust instinctively.

How lucky that he'd found her! She felt her face grow hot as she remembered *how* he'd found her, lying sobbing on the ground like a stupid child. Feeling absolutely washed out, she leant her head against the tree trunk. The injured ankle was throbbing, her good leg was aching from supporting her whole weight and she was so cold she couldn't even think straight.

A few minutes later her rescuer reappeared at the bottom of the slope pushing an ancient bath chair made of basketwork which had frayed in places on a frame that was well-rusted. It squeaked in continual protest as he pushed it up the hill, but it didn't fall to pieces.

'*Voilà, madame!*' He flourished a bow. 'Your carriage awaits.'

She couldn't help smiling at his triumphant expression. With his help, she hopped across to her unlikely chariot and collapsed into it, groaning.

His voice was gentle. 'Ankle hurting?'

'Mmm.'

'Hold on, then.'

The going was rough and the jolting hurt, but soon the path levelled out, becoming marginally smoother. Now they were bumping along on crazy paving, which led between unkempt lawns to a house half-hidden by trees. Her rescuer was panting, but laughing exultantly, too, as if this was all a merry adventure, and she found her spirits lifting.

Only when they got closer did Rosalind realise how old the house was, or how large. 'What a lovely building! Do you really live here?'

'Oh, yes. We Destans have been at Burraford since the Middle Ages – though the main part of the present house dates only from the early seventeenth century.'

'You have the same name as the village?'

'It's called after us, actually. My ancestors took over here after the Norman Conquest.' He chuckled and added, 'Somewhat forcibly, I'm afraid. The previous owner had been killed at Hastings. Burrh means a fortified place – near a ford. The river's on the other side of this house. The original keep was much closer to the water.'

'How wonderful to know your family's history so far back!'

'In some ways it is, but there are down sides to it all. These ancient piles cost the earth to keep up, even small places like mine.' And they attracted social climbing women, who then tried to gut them of their valuables – and Isabel would have succeeded, too, if he hadn't come home early by sheer chance, and caught her and her lover stuffing bags full of the smaller pieces of silver into her car.

He pushed the memory of that dreadful encounter away hurriedly. He hadn't realised he had it in him to grow so furiously angry, let alone to punch someone on the chin. 'Houses like these are draughty in winter and stuffy in summer, but—'

She finished for him, 'You love it.'

Her smile was soft and gentle. He felt warmed by it. He'd like to make her smile more often and wipe that sadness from her face. 'Yes. I do. And so far we Destans have managed to keep our home for ourselves, not hand it over to the National Trust.' Though for how much longer, he wasn't sure. He realised she was shivering. 'But I shouldn't stand here talking. You need to get warm. Would you like to come inside? Do you fancy a cup of tea?'

'I'd kill for a hot drink.'

'Then you've arrived at the right place. I rather pride myself on my skill as a tea maker.' He trundled the bath chair to the foot of the front steps and an old dog appeared, tail wagging furiously and nudging his hand for attention. 'Sit, Dusty! Stay!'

He turned to grin at Rosalind. 'This old fellow is a cuddle hound – never has been interested in hunting or guarding things, just likes to coax cuddles out of people. Wait there a mo. I've even got a pair of crutches somewhere from when I broke my leg. They'll be easier than hopping.'

She sat staring up at the house as the first drops of rain landed gently on her cheeks. It was built of what she now knew to be grey Purbeck stone, with the steep stone roof that seemed typical of this part of the world. Three stories high only, with a gabled wing jutting forward at one side and four windows along each floor of the main block. There was an extra tall window in the middle above the entrance, probably to light the stairwell. The gardens needed attention and the front door needed painting, but that didn't destroy the charm and it looked like a home, not a showplace.

He came striding out to join her, brandishing the crutches and beaming. 'Here we are. Just in time.' Easing her out of the chair, he helped her make her slow, painful way up the steps. As he was closing the front door, the rain stopped teasing them and came down with an express-train roar.

'Thank goodness you found me,' Rosalind said shakily. She paused, finding the crutches unexpectedly hard to manage.

He noticed and laid a gentle hand on her arm. 'No need to hurry now we're under cover. I'll adjust them once we've got you sitting down.'

The room he helped her into was so perfectly proportioned that for all her discomfort she couldn't help exclaiming, 'Oh, how beautiful this is! Just look at that plasterwork!' The furniture was old and well-used, big easy pieces you could sink into, and everywhere there were objects to catch your eye: an unusual ornament, a painting, an elegant piece of furniture.

He guided her towards a sofa. 'There. If you sit with your leg up for a while, it should help the swelling. I'll go and make some tea, shall I? I haven't any live-in staff, just a woman who comes in three times a week to clean.'

'Tea would be lovely.'

'Earl Grey all right? No, it's a bit early in the day for that – how about English breakfast?'

'Perfect.' Not the time to tell him you were a coffee addict and all types of tea tasted more or less alike to you.

Rosalind wedged herself into the corner of the high-backed sofa and gave herself up to enjoyment of the room.

Nothing really matched, but everything seemed to cohabit happily. Each piece of furniture her eyes lingered on was a treasure begging further inspection. Old polished wood – dusty in parts – exquisite inlay work, carving, ornate brass handles. She didn't know where to look next. She could spend a whole day in here and still not have studied everything!

Footsteps on the polished boards of the hall, accompanied by the pattering of the dog's paws, heralded her host's return. He set down a wooden tray carefully and picked up a lumpy tea towel. 'I put some ice in this. Thought it might help your ankle.'

'How kind.' She watched him adjust the compress with deft fingers.

'I brought some biscuits, too. Chocolate. I hate plain ones. They look so anaemic.' Deftly he poured her some tea. 'Milk? Sugar?'

'Just a little milk. No sugar.' She balanced the cup in her hand while he fetched a small table.

He turned back to the tray and picked up a plate. 'Biscuit?'

'No, thanks. I have to watch my weight.'

'You're kidding.'

'Thin is fashionable and my husband likes me to – keep up to date.'

She saw him make a moue at that statement – was it because she'd refused the biscuits or because she'd admitted that she watched her weight to please Paul. She realised suddenly that she wouldn't have cared if she'd put on a bit of weight. She spent a lot of time watching others eat delicious food she'd cooked and longed to eat.

The biscuits were still tempting her, set out on an old linen doily with hand-worked edges. He'd gone to some trouble. What harm would one do? 'Well, perhaps just one biscuit. Sweet things are supposed to be good for shock, aren't they?'

His face brightened and he passed the plate, then took one for himself and bit off half of it with great relish, saying indistinctly, 'So, tell me what you were doing in our grove.'

'Trying to find the public footpath so I could get back to Burraford.'

'You're living there?'

'Yes. Temporarily, anyway. We're from Australia.'

'I guessed that from your accent. Who's "we"? You and your husband?'

'Yes. When he's at home. Which isn't often. He works for a multinational company and travels a lot.'

'You must be living in the old Harris house in Sexton Close, then.'

'I don't know about any Harrises, but I do live in Sexton Close. Number 10. How did you know?'

His grin made him look about twelve years old. 'I know everything that goes on in the village. My sister sees to that. She lives just behind the church.' He saw that his visitor wasn't listening and followed her gaze. 'That's Araminta's picture.'

'If it weren't for my ankle, I'd have my nose pressed against the glass.'

'It is rather jolly.' He unwound his long legs and went

to lift the framed embroidery off the wall, setting it down on her lap. 'Here. Take your time.' He took another biscuit and leant back in his armchair, smiling as he realised she'd forgotten him completely.

'This is a very fine example of raised stumpwork,' she said at last. 'About 1670, I'd guess, though there isn't a date on it. The last corner, after her name, is unfinished. What a pity! Did she die? Do you know who this Araminta was?'

'One of our most loved ancestors. She lived all through the Civil War, kept the Roundheads from destroying the place, then died suddenly at the age of fifty-two from a fever. My sister found this in an old chest in the attic, together with Araminta's diary and account books. We had the embroidery framed because we both love it.'

'No wonder. It's a particularly clever use of materials and look how realistic the figures are. And the animals. You could almost stroke that little dog. I've seen photos of pieces like this in books, but this is the first time I've seen one face-to-face.'

'You sound very knowledgeable.'

She shrugged. 'Well, I do a bit of embroidery myself.'

'This sort?'

'Mm-hmm.'

'You've done actual stumpwork pictures?'

She couldn't help smiling at his eager tone. 'Oh, yes. I've got an attic full of them at home in Australia. And I've brought one or two with me – just to make the rented place a bit more homelike.'

'No room left on the walls at home, eh?'

She blushed and fiddled with the edge of the frame.

'Well, not exactly. Such things are not to everyone's taste.'

He looked at her, eyes narrowed. Who had criticised her work and made her so apologetic about it? The damned husband again, probably. 'We have a colour photo of this one, for insurance purposes. Would you like me to have a copy of it made for you?' He watched her face light up. She was lovely when she smiled.

'Oh, would you really? I'd love that. And – and if I could come back with the photo and make notes on the stitches she used. She was a very skilled needlewoman, your Araminta.'

'Of course you can. I'll show you round the rest of the place too, if you like, when your ankle's better. But for the moment, I think we ought to get you to a doctor. That ankle doesn't seem to have gone down at all.' He took the picture from her and brought back the crutches. 'Just let me adjust these.'

She looked down at her leg, the light fading from her face. 'It is rather swollen, isn't it?' It was throbbing. So was her head. How far could she have crawled if he hadn't found her? The thought made her shiver. There was no one to miss her or come looking for her. She could have been stuck overnight and died of exposure out there in the woods.

He helped her up and measured the crutches against her. 'That's better. Now, I think you should see old Doc Barnes. Is there someone you want to call to pick you up?'

Her voice was toneless. 'No, there isn't anyone. My daughters are in Australia and my husband will be in Hong Kong for another few weeks.' And she had no idea where

Tim was, any more than he knew she was in England.

'Then I'll drive you myself, wait till you've seen Doc and take you home afterwards.'

'I couldn't put you to all that trouble. If you'll just call a taxi, I'll get out of your way. Though I'd appreciate it if I could borrow the crutches.'

'It's no trouble. Honestly. I'll pop in to see Harry while I'm in the village.'

'Harry?'

'My sister. Short for Harriet, which she hates. She's a widow – not the merry sort, still grieving. Lung cancer, it was. Went on rather a long time and Phil was a decent chap, didn't deserve to die like that.' He took a deep breath and shook off those memories. 'You stay there and I'll bring the car round the front.'

The doctor examined the ankle, then strapped it up tightly, speaking in curt phrases as if he didn't have time for whole sentences. 'Nothing broken. Bad sprain. Keep off your feet for a few days and you'll be all right.'

Rosalind stared at him in dismay. 'But I can't!'

'Can't what?' He'd already opened the door and gestured to Jonathon, who was sitting outside, to come and help her out.

'Can't stay off my feet. There's only me. What am I going to do?'

Jonathon tried not to say it, but the words were out before he could stop them. 'Harry and I will look after you.'

She turned to him, 'But I can't ask you to – we'd never even met until today—'

He shrugged. 'We're blocking the doorway. Come on. We'll discuss it on the way to Harry's.'

People were staring at them, so she tucked the crutches under her arms and swung painfully and slowly after him. The receptionist wanted her to sign some papers and by the time she got to the car, she felt as if her armpits were on fire.

When he climbed in beside her, she said faintly, 'I think I'd rather go straight home, if you don't mind.'

He looked sideways at her as he started the car. Hell, she was as pale as a ghost. 'All right. I'll phone Harry and ask her to come over to your house for a council of war, if that's all right with you. She'll find a way to help you.'

'You're being so kind, and to a complete stranger.' Rosalind leant her head back against the car seat with a sigh.

Jonathon drove as smoothly as he could, very conscious that she was in pain. There was something about her that touched him. She was so soft and vulnerable, with that swollen trembling mouth and those gentle blue eyes. And anyway, if you couldn't help someone in trouble, you weren't worth much as a human being. Why was she here alone in England when her home was in Australia? And why was that damned husband of hers living in Hong Kong if they'd come to spend the summer here? It didn't make sense.

What was he doing getting involved? That made even less sense. Jonathon smiled ruefully as he parked in front of her house and went to open the gates. Well, if nothing else she'd taken his mind from his own worries and made him feel pleasantly philanthropic. And actually, he liked her. He really did. Such a transparently honest face. There didn't seem to be many people like that around nowadays.

Harry would like her, too, he decided hastily, not letting himself linger on his own reaction to her, though it was the first time since his highly acrimonious divorce that he'd been attracted to a woman in any way at all. Which was probably a good sign. Well, it would have been if the woman in question hadn't been married.

He got her settled on the couch and then said, 'Won't be a jiffy. I'll just phone Harry.' He took out a mobile phone and vanished into the hall.

Chapter Seven

Harriet Larcombe was so intrigued by her brother's call she agreed to join an immediate emergency conference about how they could help this Rosalind Stevenson cope for the next few days. As she put the phone down, she wondered what Jonathon was doing getting involved with a complete stranger? This female must be gorgeous to make him break his vow of abjuring all womankind except his sister.

Only Rosalind wasn't gorgeous, Harry saw instantly. She was a gentle person, the sort others often took advantage of. There was nothing striking about her as there had been about Isabel, who had so ravaged poor Jonathon's life. Nor was this woman trying to attract a man, for she spoke openly of being married.

So it was just Jonathon, who had a chivalrous soul, rescuing a damsel in distress. But perhaps this little adventure would stop him brooding so much on the past and put him into a more positive frame of mind about the future. He hadn't been truly happy since the boys left and she knew he still missed them dreadfully, even two years after the divorce.

'Why don't you move in with me for a few days, Rosalind?' she offered when she saw the two of them looking at her for guidance, as people often did. 'I've got plenty of room.'

Rosalind shook her head, smiling at her visitor, who was a mere six foot tall compared to her brother's six foot three, but equally thin and with the same bony, aristocratic face. 'It's very kind of you, but no. My family will want to contact me and – and my husband prefers to ring me, since he's such a busy person.'

'Why, if he's in Hong Kong and you normally live in Australia, are you here in England on your own, if I may ask?' Harry had been puzzling over this.

'Paul thought he'd be settled in England for the summer on a special project, so he insisted – I mean, he *asked* me to come over here, too.' Rosalind blushed at her slip, but neither of the others seemed to notice. 'Then the man in charge of the Hong Kong office died suddenly, so Paul's had to fill in until they can appoint a replacement.'

'Bit rough on you.' Harry decided they couldn't be short of money if the husband had that sort of job and mentally revised her plans for helping Rosalind to include paid assistance that would benefit another of her protégées. 'We could ask Alice Tuffin to come in each morning for an hour or two until you're functioning again, if you like. Her services are very reasonable and she'll do your shopping for you as well as your housework. I've always found her extremely reliable, if rather outspoken.'

'What a lovely name! It sounds like something out of Beatrix Potter.'

'It's a local surname. She was a Bugg before she married and that's a Dorset name, too.' She shared a conspiratorial smile with her brother and confided, 'The Buggs insist they've been in the area for much longer than the Destans and they may be right. There's a reference to a Thomas Bugg in Araminta's diary.'

'He was put in the stocks several times for drunkenness,' Jonathon added with a grin, 'but we haven't mentioned that to Alice.'

Harry glanced at her watch. 'Look, I have to go soon, but I can pop across here for the next afternoon or two to get your evening meal. The more you rest that ankle, the quicker you'll be walking on it again.'

Rosalind leant back with a sigh of relief. 'I can't believe how kind you're both being to a complete stranger!'

'Oh, it makes us feel nice and virtuous. Christian duty and all that. Now, do you want me to bring anything downstairs for you before I leave?'

'My embroidery, if you wouldn't mind.' She had to explain what she was doing to Harry and Jonathon, who then inspected the embroideries hanging on the wall.

'I say, you *are* good,' Jonathon said instantly. 'As good as Araminta.'

Harry looked at the pieces, head on one side. 'When you've recovered, I'm going to coax you into donating one of these to the fête. We raise funds once a year for the old folks' centre.'

'Oh, I'd be happy to donate one – if you think someone will want to buy it. They're not to everyone's taste.'

She'd said that before, Jonathon thought, frowning. How could she possibly have doubts about such gorgeous work?

They settled Rosalind in the living room with the gas fire bubbling away in the grate and her embroidery to hand.

'I've got a committee meeting at three for the fête,' Harry tossed over her shoulder as she strode out, 'but that'll be over by five at the latest. See you then.'

Jonathon lingered for a moment or two longer.

'You've both been so kind,' Rosalind said.

'Oh, Harry enjoys playing lady of the manor now that I haven't a wife to fill that role.'

'Is such a thing still needed?'

'Well, not really, but she's convinced everyone in the village that things would go to pot without her help, and she does do a lot of good for the village and for charity, so who am I to deny her these little pleasures? Are you *sure* you'll be all right on your own?'

'Yes, of course I will.'

'Right-ho, then. I'll see you tomorrow.'

Rosalind listened to the front door close, then picked up her embroidery. But the weeping and fall had exhausted her. She put her bits and pieces down and let her head fall back on the soft pillow Harry had found for her.

When she awoke the afternoon light was dimming gently outside and Harry had just returned to prepare her evening meal. 'I'll take the sandwiches you didn't eat for my dogs, if you don't mind. You won't want them as well as an evening meal.' She bustled round, making an omelette and salad, clearly not keen to linger, but she did stop to study the pictures on the wall again. 'These are truly lovely. Are you sure you can bear to part with one for our fête?'

'Oh yes. I've got plenty of them at home. I won't give you one of these because they're my favourites, but I'll send for one of the others.'

'Well, we'd be very grateful.' If it didn't fetch too high a price, Harriet might even bid for it herself. She didn't know why those embroideries attracted her, but they did. Each seemed to tell a story, as well as being a work of art.

It occurred to Rosalind as she lay in bed that it had been a good day in a strange sort of way. The burst of weeping had been very cathartic and best of all, she'd made some friends here.

And that embroidery at Destan Hall was glorious, simply glorious. Fancy getting the chance to study a rare old piece like that! She was looking forward to going round the house, too, when she was better. Who knew what other treasures were hidden away there?

Yawning, she snuggled down, feeling better than she had since her arrival in England.

The Hong Kong office was organised so efficiently that it was easy for Paul to keep things on an even keel with minimum input. This looked like being one of the easiest assignments he'd ever had, boring even.

'What have you got planned for tomorrow?' he asked Liz that evening as they ate dinner together. If it was a coach tour, he wasn't going to get involved. He was not the sort to be driven round in a herd of sheep-like tourists and told what to look at.

'I thought I'd wander round the shops, stopping for a coffee or a meal, you know the sort of thing. Why?' She hoped he had a better suggestion because she was finding it hard to fill the days, couldn't afford to buy anything else and was sick to death of coach tours. All day she'd been looking forward to seeing Paul and having someone to talk to.

He smiled at her. 'I'm at a loose end too. We could catch the Star Ferry over to Kowloon and then wander round the place together, if you want.'

'Are you sure you can spare the time? I thought you were here because of an emergency?'

'Well, it turned out that my late colleague had good staff and ran things efficiently. So long as I go into the office each day at some stage, I can easily take time off. It's not part of my brief to interfere with something that's running well. The chairman trusts me absolutely to judge that sort of thing.'

He glanced sideways at her. 'If you *want* some company, that is? You said you had another week here. But perhaps you've made other plans?'

She stared at him across the dinner table. She almost asked why he was suddenly seeking her out, when they'd been disagreeing about everything under the sun for years, but bit back the words. She'd always enjoyed the sparring, now she came to think of it, been exhilarated by it. Perhaps he'd felt the same.

She was glad he hadn't taken her dancing again tonight, though. His lean, muscular body pressed closely against hers had affected her far too much. He really was a splendid specimen of manhood. That hadn't occurred to her before, but it did now – rather too much for her peace of mind.

If she hadn't had such a big row with Bill, made such a point of getting away to think about where their marriage was going, she'd have returned to Australia early and avoided temptation altogether, but she'd shocked Bill rigid and wanted him to stay shocked. Why the hell had she booked such a long holiday in one place, though?

Paul reached out and brushed away a lock of hair that had fallen over her forehead, a small, intimate gesture that made a shiver of awareness run through her. 'You have lovely hair, Liz. Always so dark and glossy. And no grey in sight.'

The shiver did another lap of her body and settled in her belly. For a moment she couldn't breathe.

'Shall we not share a few days?' he asked.

Did she take that at face value, or was he offering her more? She looked sideways at him and he smiled, a lazy, sexy smile. He *was* offering more, definitely. For a long moment she hesitated, tempted, so very tempted, but trying to think of Rosalind. Then she sighed and gave in to the urges that had been humming through her all evening. 'Why not? I'd really welcome the company of a *close* friend.'

He raised her hand and pressed a gentle kiss into the palm, a kiss which seared her skin.

'Why not, indeed?' he echoed, still holding her hand, eyes gleaming. 'We'll keep our encounter to ourselves, though, shall we? We don't want to hurt other people.'

She'd always wondered if Paul was faithful to his wife during those long absences and now she'd found out. *Oh, Rosalind, I'm sorry, but I can't resist this.* After all, what her friend didn't know wouldn't hurt her and Liz could certainly trust Paul to keep quiet, just as she would herself. She would still tell Bill about the affair, of course, but not the name of the man.

Oh, hell, she needed an affair for so many reasons, not

just to get back at Bill, but to reaffirm that she was still an attractive woman. You had to wonder if there was something wrong with you when your husband kept being unfaithful.

She smiled as Paul led the way out of the restaurant.

From then on, neither of them mentioned their spouses.

It took Rosalind a long time to wash and dress the morning after her accident, and she had to sit down on the bed afterwards for a rest. When she could face the ordeal, she eased herself slowly down the stairs on her backside, one tread at a time, then pushed herself upright on the crutches.

The kitchen seemed a million miles away, so she unlocked the front door ready for her new helper before she started the slow trek to the back of the house. After a scrappy breakfast of cereal she went into the sitting room, grunting with relief as she eased herself down on the sofa.

Someone knocked on the front door, opened it and called, 'Hallo-o? Alice Tuffin here. Mrs Larcombe sent me.'

'Do come in!'

A small woman with faded sandy hair, of the body type always labelled wiry, came and stood staring down at Rosalind, head on one side.

'I'm so glad you could come and help out, Mrs Tuffin.'

'Call me Alice.'

'And I'm Rosalind.'

A quick shake of the head at that Aussie egalitarianism. 'How long do you want me for, Mrs Stevenson?'

'A couple of hours a day for as long as it takes my ankle to get better – and Mrs Larcombe said you might do some shopping for me, as well.'

Another nod. 'Wages?'

'Whatever you think right.'

'Same as what Mrs Larcombe pays me. Shall I make you a cup of tea before I start?'

'I prefer coffee. Do you know how to use a plunger?'

'One of them things you press down?' Alice shrugged. 'There's not much to it, is there? How much coffee do you put in?'

'Two measures. Get yourself a cup, too.'

'I might as well try it.'

The coffee wasn't a success with Alice, who grimaced. 'Too strong for me. I'll stick to my tea.' She stared round the sitting room in an assessing sort of way.

By mid-morning, the downstairs rooms were clean and Rosalind knew all about Alice's invalid husband and four strapping sons.

'Eat me out of house and home, they do,' Alice wound up fondly.

When she'd finished attacking the housework as if she had a personal grudge against dirt, she came in with another cup of coffee and lingered to stare at Rosalind's embroidery. 'That's going to be a nice little picture, that is.'

'Oh – er, thank you. It's my hobby. Embroidery, I mean.'

'I like that old-fashioned lady you're doing now better than the picture on the wall there – though that's good, too.'

Rosalind liked it, too. She hadn't even considered working on the family portrait. Doing Paul's figure had left her feeling bewildered about her husband and marriage. It was as if she'd never really looked at him before, as if he was a complete stranger. She wasn't certain who to do next – in fact, was having second thoughts about finishing the picture at all. That wasn't like her. She usually chose a subject and then forgot everything else while she worked on it.

When Alice had left, Rosalind fell asleep again and woke feeling not only refreshed but more cheerful. She phoned Prue, explained about her accident and checked that everything was all right in Southport. Prue had found a daily job, so Rosalind gave permission for her to continue living at the house.

It would be more practical to put the place on the market, but she didn't want to. Not yet, anyway. Her great-grandparents had lived there and she was absolutely determined to show it to her children, to give them a sense of the family's history. The house had passed to her grandfather and then to her uncle.

Her father had been the younger son and had emigrated to Australia in his early twenties, not expecting to inherit anything. When his elder brother had died unmarried and childless, the house had gone to the only girl of the family, Sophie. It made Rosalind feel strange to have the weight of family inheritance on her shoulders and she couldn't help wondering how that sort of thing affected Jonathon, who had so much more to look after for the next generation.

In the late afternoon, there was a knock at the door. Rosalind called out that it was open and Jonathon came in, carrying a basket.

He uncovered it to show a casserole dish. 'My sister's famous boeuf bourguignon. She's had to rush off to Winchester. Her daughter's just miscarried, poor thing. Everyone in the family sends for Harry when something goes wrong.' Even Isabel had done that last year when the boys got a bad dose of flu. Couldn't ask the boys' own father to help, though, could she? She was still trying to keep them apart, hated the fact that they loved not only him, but the house here.

'It smells lovely. Um – I don't suppose you'd care to stay and share it with me? I'd love a bit of company.'

He hesitated, sniffed the casserole with exaggerated relish and nodded. 'All right. There's supposed to be enough for two days, but if I bring round a takeaway tomorrow evening, perhaps that will make up for my eating half of this now?'

'It certainly will.' She fumbled for her crutches. 'Look, come into the kitchen. I have some vegetables and rolls in the freezer and we could do some jacket potatoes in the microwave.'

'You can sit and give orders, but you're not doing anything yourself, milady. I'm not the world's best cook, but I can follow instructions and I have a very stylish way of heating frozen vegetables.'

When the meal was ready, Jonathon slapped his hand against his forehead in mock anguish. 'Oh blast! I am an idiot! I should have brought some wine with me. A red to complement the beef.'

'Don't panic. I have some. It's in the dining room inside the sideboard. We ought to have opened a bottle earlier to let it breathe, but there are a few nice Australian reds there and I don't mind drinking one that hasn't breathed if you don't. Choose any you fancy.'

She hauled herself across to the table. She definitely wasn't going to win a gold medal for crutch-hopping. Her body seemed to get heavier every time she moved. Her foot was still swollen, though not as badly as it had been yesterday, and she didn't think it wise to put any weight on it yet.

As she subsided into a chair, she banged her ankle on the table leg and let out a muffled whimper.

He was there kneeling beside her in an instant. 'Let me help you.' He pushed her and the chair carefully into position, brought a footstool for her from the living room, then carried over the plates of food. 'Start without me while it's hot. I'll just open the wine.'

But she didn't start without him, of course she didn't. She hoped she had better manners than that. In fact, she wasn't all that hungry and although the food was good, she put down her knife and fork when the plate was half-cleared and looked at him apologetically.

He smiled. 'It's all right. You won't get spanked if you don't eat up. Besides, you're not doing much to work up an appetite at the moment, are you?'

'I feel guilty, though. Such lovely food. And such good company, too.' She stared at him. He stared back at her. The silence lasted too long and the very air between them seemed to tingle.

'I'll take your leftovers home for Dusty,' he said at last. 'He much prefers human food.' He studied her with a sympathetic expression. 'It's getting you down a bit, isn't it, being an invalid?'

She nodded.

'And you were weeping when I found you yesterday. Your other troubles won't have gone away overnight. I don't mean to intrude, but if you ever want to talk about it – well, I'm here.'

'Thank you.' But confiding in him would seem disloyal to Paul. She'd intended to confide in Sophie, but had left it too late. So she would just have to work through things herself.

'Come on! We'll have dessert in the living room.'

'I couldn't possibly eat anything else.'

But he brought in a packet of fancy chocolate biscuits, laughing at his own weakness for them, and she found herself taking one and nibbling it while he ate four or five.

As the evening passed she found herself chuckling quite often over his nonsense. Jonathon was uncomplicated and fun. She could feel herself relaxing, laughing, expanding somehow in the warmth of his company, and couldn't remember the last time she'd enjoyed herself so much. She supposed she was quite a simple person, really – or at least, Paul always said she was – and she liked doing quiet, companionable things best of all.

And even when Jonathon had gone, the house seemed full of warmth still, as if the laughter they'd shared was clinging to the walls and wafting round the rooms.

The following afternoon, Jonathon came round to make sure Rosalind liked Chinese food and to let her choose from the takeaway menu. It seemed quite natural for him to stay and make her a cup of coffee.

When the phone rang, he called, 'Shall I get it?'

'Yes, please.' She'd forgotten to bring the portable phone in with her.

'Hallo?'

A voice bristling with indignation said, 'Who's that?'

'Jonathon Destan. And you are . . . ?'

'Paul Stevenson. I was trying to contact my wife.'

'She's here, but she's hurt her ankle. Hold on for a moment and I'll take the phone through to her.' He walked into the living room, rolled his eyes at Rosalind and mouthed, 'Your husband.'

She waited till Jonathon had closed the door behind him before she spoke. 'Paul?'

'Who's that fellow?'

'A friend. He and his sister have been helping me. I've sprained my ankle. If he hadn't found me when I fell, I'd have been in serious trouble, because I couldn't walk and I was miles from anywhere.'

'Did you have it x-rayed?'

'Jonathon took me to a doctor. It's just a sprain.'

'Who exactly is this fellow? One of the locals?'

'The lord of the manor, actually. And his sister lives here in the village.'

'Oh, well, that's all right, then.'

She could feel herself bristling. 'What do you mean – *that's all right*?'

'I just wondered what a man was doing answering your phone.'

'I don't like your tone, Paul. If you don't trust me by now, there's something wrong between us.' She could hear him breathing more deeply, as if restraining anger, so changed the subject. 'Now, what can I do for you?'

'I rang to see how you are, of course.'

'I'm well enough, apart from the ankle.' And apart from feeling depressed. And apart from worrying about Tim, for some reason she couldn't fathom.

'I've been thinking about your aunt's money. That house of hers should be worth a nice little sum. We can sell it and—'

'I told you – everything's in a trust. I get the income from it, but I can't touch the capital without the trustees' approval.'

'Yes, but I'm sure you'll be allowed to sell the house. And anyway, I've been thinking about it all. I know a good lawyer. We'll set him on to see if we can overthrow that trust.'

'I don't want to do that.'

'Look, Ros, you know you don't understand financial matters. Nor did your aunt. She was probably senile towards the end. She seemed completely dotty when I saw her, the things she said. Should be quite easy to prove that. Leave me to—'

Rosalind slammed down the phone on him for the second time in her life and when it rang, she didn't pick it up. Jonathon opened the door and found her glaring at the phone, making no attempt to touch it.

'Get cut off, did you?'

'No. I put the phone down on him. Sometimes my husband can be very infuriating. Will you take it back into the kitchen, please? And – and don't answer if it rings. I shan't speak to him again tonight.'

When Jonathon came back with the coffee he said nothing about the phone that was ringing again and she was grateful for his forbearance. 'Tell me about your children. What are they called?' She could imagine him as a father, teasing, joking, throwing little children up in the air.

'Giles and Rufus. They're old family names. Rufus hates

his, but it's a tradition in our family, so he'll jolly well have to put up with it.'

As he talked, she thought how unfair it was that he had so little access to his sons, but not once did he say anything against his wife.

He smiled as he finished his tale. 'The boys are coming down to Destan for the fête. I'll introduce them to you.'

Jonathon was the easiest person she'd ever met to be with, she decided later as she slid into bed. Unlike Paul. What had got into her husband lately?

What had got into her, too?

Darkness rustled and whispered outside as the wind teased the branches near her window into a lazy ballet. She lay watching the shadows on the curtains and it was a while before she faced the truth and answered her own questions. There was nothing really different about Paul lately, but her perception of him had altered.

And *she* had changed since her arrival in England, was still changing.

She would get the embroidery out in the morning, study it, think about the other figures. It had taught her so much about her husband. Perhaps it would do the same about herself.

She was a little worried about where all these changes were leading. Only – whatever became of her, she couldn't wish them undone. She felt better inside herself than she had done for years. Much better.

EMOTION

Much intricate and ingenious stitchery is used for foliage, flowers, birds, fountains and buildings on seventeenth century raised embroidery, but the whole is brought to life by the small human figures and the stories they represent. Humour, pathos, anger and many other emotions are depicted . . .

   (Hirst, p.38)

Chapter Eight

Paul slammed the buzzing phone down and stood glaring at it, breath rasping in his throat. What the hell had got into Ros? He paced up and down the hotel room, chewing one fingertip and trying to work out how much money the old witch would have left her. He was itching now to get back and sort it all out. What a time to be away!

The phone rang and he picked it up. 'Ros?'

'No, Liz. Watch broken down, has it?'

He glanced at his wrist. 'Oh, hell, I'm supposed to have picked you up ten minutes ago, aren't I? Sorry. I was talking to Ros on the phone. That old aunt of hers has died and left us all her money, but it's the most idiotic will – she's set up a trust fund and no one can touch the capital. And when I suggested contesting the will, Ros hung up on me. I don't know what's got into her lately.'

'She'll be upset. She was very fond of Aunt Sophie.' Liz waited for a response to that, an acknowledgement of

Ros's grief, but clearly her words hadn't even penetrated. Heavens, he might be a good lover, but he was the most selfish man she'd ever met, even worse than she'd thought. How had Rosalind put up with him all these years? She'd rather have Bill any day.

Rather have Bill!

That realisation shocked her rigid. Bill wasn't as good-looking as Paul, wasn't nearly as good in bed and was an unfaithful bastard – but he was infinitely nicer to live with. *Well*, she thought, *one decision made. We soldier on.* 'Sorry, what was that you said?'

'I said Sophie Worth was senile,' he repeated.

'I don't know what you're worrying about. Rosalind still benefits, even if the money has to go through a trust fund. I shall enjoy having a rich friend. Now, why don't you meet me downstairs? I'm famished.'

He went straight down and stood in the lobby waiting for her. When she came out of a lift, he watched her walk across towards him, admiring the vividness of her colouring and the energy of her stride. 'You keep yourself in damn good trim, you know.'

'I work out at the gym.'

'Ros could with toning up a bit,' Paul mused, still looking at Liz. 'Perhaps you could persuade her to go to a gym when we get back?'

'I've enough on my plate keeping my own body in order, thank you very much. And I think Rosalind is just right for her height. The scrawny waif look wouldn't suit her at all. Now – are you intending to eat or not?'

'Of course I am – and after dinner I'll apologise properly

for keeping you waiting.' His voice was husky with innuendo.

'I shall insist on that.'

But she was beginning to wonder if this affair was really worth it, and guilt was beginning to creep in.

She didn't have to psychoanalyse the man, for heaven's sake, just enjoy his rather dishy body and his company. Given the circumstances, he wasn't likely to tell anyone about their affair – which was a good thing, because Paul Stevenson definitely wasn't worth losing her best friend for.

Paul waited three days before ringing his wife again and this time kept the conversation carefully neutral, making no reference to the fact that Ros had put the phone down on him last time. Liz was right. She would have been upset and perhaps he had been just a tad tactless. 'How's the ankle?'

'Getting better now, thank you. The swelling's going down nicely.'

'Good. Good.' She still sounded miffed, probably not liking being on her own in England. 'So what have you done about the house? Is it ready to entertain in yet? We can start thinking about our first house party, if you like. I can phone people up from here and invite them, set it up for my first weekend back, perhaps.'

'The house is all right, but I'd rather not plan anything until after you get back, if you don't mind – after all, I am fairly immobile still, and anyway, you may only be with me for a couple of days.'

'Ouch! I really upset you there, didn't I?'

'You've upset me in a few ways lately, Paul. But I dare say we can talk it through when you come back.' She was absolutely determined to get their relationship on a better footing before they did anything else.

When he put the phone down, Paul grimaced. Talk what through?

Then he smiled. Ros was one of the best hostesses he'd ever met, a good listener who drew people out and made them feel interesting, exactly the sort of wife he needed for the next stage in his career – but he wouldn't tell her about the other changes that were on their way for a while yet.

It'd taken a lot to get her to move away from Western Australia temporarily, and it'd take more to move her permanently, so he'd have to plan his campaign rather carefully.

In the middle of the night the phone rang and Jenny was awake instantly, heart pounding. She didn't answer it, of course. She'd learnt not to do that. When the ringing stopped, she took the receiver off the hook and lay there listening to the dialling tone. On and on. The humming sound nearly drove her mad in the tiny bedroom of this horrid flat, so she unplugged the phone from the wall.

Michael had left a note on her car windscreen at work yesterday asking her to meet him for dinner to talk things over. He said he still cared for her and wanted her back in his life. She hadn't replied to the note, didn't want to speak to him or see him ever again.

Let's face it, the rotten bastard had got her well and truly spooked. She didn't dare go out now at night unless a friend picked her up and came back with her while she searched the flat. Not that that took very long. What was there to search? But it made her look such a wimp and she didn't like that.

When the phone rang the following evening, Jenny looked at the clock. *He* didn't usually ring this early. Taking a deep breath she picked up the phone. 'Yes?'

'Hello, love, how are you?'

'Mum!' Relief flooded through Jenny. 'How are you getting on?'

'I'm fine, though I've sprained my stupid ankle. Have I caught you at a good time for a chat?'

'I've always time to talk to you, Mum. Goodness, I'm missing you.' More than she'd expected to and not just because of this nastiness with Michael, either.

'I'm missing you, too.' They chatted for a few minutes, then Rosalind asked, 'Look, could you do something for me, love? I don't want to ask your gran because I think she's got enough on her plate with Louise.'

Jenny rolled her eyes at the ceiling. Her mother didn't know how right she was. Gran had more than enough on her plate. The last time she'd seen her sister, Louise had boasted about using her mother's car and doing what she wanted with her life, in spite of being forced to live with an old lady who needed a reality implant. The two of them had had a big row about that, but Jenny hadn't been able to make her sister see sense.

'So, what can I do for you, Mum?'

'I need some more of my embroideries sending over to England, and I want them air freighted here, however expensive it is. I know it'll be a bit of trouble, but do you have time to go to the house and get them for me – and fairly quickly? It's only a question of taking them to the same shipper as before. You don't need to do the packing. These are unframed pieces.'

'No problem. Is someone over there interested in them?'

'Well, sort of. There's this fête coming up in the village and I've promised to donate one.' Besides, she missed her pieces. It had surprised her how much she missed them. At home, when Paul was away, she'd sometimes pull down the colour-matched prints that hung on the walls and put her embroideries up instead. 'Do you have a pencil?' She listed the pieces she wanted, knowing exactly where each was stored in the attic.

'That'll be easy. I'll go over tomorrow after work and pick them up – oh no, I don't have a key any more.' Her father had taken her key when she moved out, saying it wasn't good security to leave keys lying around in houses where no-hopers could get hold of them.

Her mother's voice sounded happy and more confident than usual. 'Borrow your gran's key again. And Jenny—'

'Mmm?'

'Get one cut for yourself while you're at it. I don't happen to agree with your father about that.'

'Oh. Well, all right. But don't tell Dad or he'll hit the roof.'

Rosalind chuckled. 'What he doesn't know won't upset him, will it?'

'You don't usually go against his wishes.'

'Well, maybe that's going to change from now on.'

'How are you managing on your own if you've hurt your ankle?'

'Oh, it's only a sprain and it's getting better slowly. I'm

developing a very elegant limp. And I've made some new friends because of the accident.' She was also getting a lot of embroidery done – and seeing Jonathon regularly, so that he felt like a friend of many years' standing by now.

She suspected he was lonely, too. What a lovely man! He'd taken her for a drive yesterday to Weymouth and back and they'd had a delightful afternoon out. She couldn't believe how beautiful and unspoilt the Dorset countryside was. She realised her mind was wandering and pulled her attention back to what her daughter was saying.

'I don't know why you don't put your pictures on the walls at home, Mum. They're so beautiful. When I get somewhere proper to live, I'm going to beg one off you. I love them.'

'You could have had some ages ago!'

'I didn't want to risk them when I was sharing with Michael.'

'I'll let you choose one when I get back.' Rosalind took a deep breath. 'And I agree. I'm definitely going to put some up permanently. I don't know why I haven't insisted before. Your father will just have to lump it.'

When Jenny put the phone down, she shook her head. Dad would find some way to stop her mother putting up the embroideries. He always got his own way. Though how anyone could call her mother's work 'amateur', as he did, she didn't know. The only word that did those pictures justice was 'exquisite'.

On her way home from work the following day, Jenny called at her gran's for the key, and of course had to stay for a cuppa. Louise was nowhere to be seen, thank goodness, and when she asked about her sister, Gran looked unhappy so things mustn't have improved. Jenny had had it with Louise, absolutely had it.

After that, since it was late-night shopping, she stopped to get a key cut for herself and pick up a newspaper. She wanted to look at adverts for flats. She was thinking of moving – and of changing her phone number again. The trouble was, if Michael had found her once, he could keep on finding her.

On sheer impulse she bought herself a scratchie coupon – she never had any luck with them, beyond winning an occasional couple of dollars, but she liked having one in her purse. She always kept it for days, dreaming of what she would do with her winnings and waiting until she felt a lucky moment come upon her. Then she would scratch the coupon and examine the numbers. It was a fun thing to do, a licence to dream.

Her parents' house seemed dark and menacing when she approached it at night on her own. She made absolutely certain no one was around before she got out of her car, glad when the movement sensors switched the outside lights on. Unlocking the front door as quickly as she could, she darted inside and slammed it shut behind her. It was the work of seconds to dial the correct number into the security system, but she still felt nervous.

How her mother had stood it here alone this past year – well, as alone as you got with Louise still living at home, which was pretty much alone – she didn't know.

I've never really liked this house, Jenny decided as she walked up the stairs, switching lights on everywhere. The one where she'd grown up had been much more homelike. This place had too many big, echoing spaces.

She had to steel herself to slide the loft ladder down and go up into the roof storage area, which had only a couple of bare bulbs to light things up. They threw a lot of spooky shadows, but luckily, her mother had everything in pin-neat order and she found the embroideries immediately, sorting out the ones to send, then packing the others up carefully again.

Carrying them down to the kitchen, she hunted in vain for something padded to wrap them in, so went back up for a bath towel. She stopped for a moment to finger the top embroidery and admire the scene on it. Her mother seemed to get the essence of her subjects. Jenny had loved art herself when she was at school, been good at it, too, but of course, her father hadn't let her study it in upper school.

As she was locking the front door carefully behind her, a voice said, 'Hi, Jenny!'

She jerked round in horror. She should have realised that the outside lights being on meant someone was around. *He* was standing there smiling, looking smug.

'Michael!' She tried not to show her fear, but it came slamming into her belly, grappling its way up into her lungs and making her feel short of air. She shot a quick glance around. There was no one in sight on the street – well, people in this district went everywhere by car, didn't they? Would the neighbours even hear her if she yelled for help?

He was barring the way. 'Why didn't you answer my letter, Jen?'

'We'd said all there was to say. Why do you keep phoning me, Michael?'

'I don't remember phoning you.' His smile said he'd enjoyed doing it, just as he was enjoying tormenting her now.

She grew angry. 'I know it was you, Michael. And there's no way I'm getting back together with you. The sooner you accept that, the sooner we can both carry on with our lives.'

His smile slipped and he grabbed her shoulders, pulling her towards him. Although she twisted about and shoved at his chest, she couldn't break his hold. 'Let me go!'

In response, he dug his fingers more deeply into her shoulders.

'You're hurting. Let me *go*!' She kicked his legs and he stopped smiling as he shook her so hard she bit her tongue.

'Why are you doing this?' she whispered when he stopped. 'What do you want?'

'I want to remind you how well we go together.'

She saw his intention in his eyes and froze for a moment. *He was going to rape her!* He pressed himself against her and she could feel his erection pressing into her. He was bigger than she was and much, much stronger. 'Don't, Michael!' she pleaded. 'Please don't do this.'

'That's not what you used to say.' He laughed then. 'Now, we can do it the hard way, or—'

Just then the unlikely happened, the best miracle of her entire life. The woman next door looked over the fence. No warning, just a face suddenly appearing.

'Oh, it's only you, Jenny. I saw the lights and heard voices, and I knew Paul and Rosalind were away, so I—'

Before Michael could say or do anything to stop her, Jenny screamed out, 'Call the police! This man's threatening me.'

The neighbour took one look at Michael's furious face, gaped in horror at the hand upraised to slap Jenny and yelled, 'Stuart! There's an intruder next door! Get the dog! Tommy! Here, boy!' There was the sound of claws clicking on brick paving and human feet thumping as someone ran towards the gate.

Michael shoved Jenny away from him. 'You'll be sorry for this, you bitch! I know where you live and work. It's only postponed.'

He strode out of the garden and Jenny collapsed against the car, sobbing in mingled relief and terror. Angela Coppin came rushing round, followed by her husband and their big Dobermann, woofing and pulling at its lead. There was the sound of tyres squealing and a car driving away.

Angela rushed to put an arm round Jenny, shushing her like a baby. 'You're all right now. He's gone. How lucky I peeped over the fence to check who it was!'

'Very l-lucky,' Jenny managed, but she couldn't stop shaking.

'I'll go and call the police,' Stuart said. 'I couldn't see the number plate on his car, unfortunately.'

'No, don't call them!' Jenny clung to Angela, still shuddering. 'We won't be able to prove anything. He'll say I misunderstood what he wanted, that he was only trying to kiss me. He – he used to be my boyfriend, you see, and he can be a very convincing liar.' As she knew to her cost. How she could have thought herself in love with someone like him, she would never know.

'He's stalking me,' she admitted in a small, shamed voice.

'But you can't just let him get away with it,' Stuart declared.

Angela looked at her husband and shook her head to stop him saying anything else. 'Come into our house for a minute or two, Jenny. You're still shivering.'

'There's my car. Oh, and I've dropped my mother's embroideries.' She bent to pick them up, relieved that they hadn't been trampled on. 'I couldn't bear anything to happen to them.' She clutched the unwieldy bundle to her breast, tears still rolling down her cheeks, wishing desperately that her mother were there. Or even her father.

Stuart held out his hand. 'Let me have your car keys. I'll put the embroideries on the back seat then drive it round to our place. You're in no fit state to get behind the wheel.'

So she found herself sitting in their lounge, explaining what had been happening during the past few weeks and weeping again as she did so. She'd never had much to do with the Coppin family, and knew her father was rather scornful of them because they were into caring for the environment and were members of what he called 'the brown rice brigade', but they were being very kind to her now.

'Haven't you had anyone to talk to?' Angela asked gently as the flood of confidences subsided.

'Not really. It only started after Mum left.'

'Well, if you want my opinion, you need to get away from Perth. Get right away for a while, somewhere he can't find you, then he'll turn elsewhere for his nasty pleasures. I read an article about stalkers.'

'I can't afford to go anywhere. I'm only a trainee manager and the pay's lousy. Besides, I'm not due any holidays yet.' Jenny tried to pull herself together. 'Look, you've been very kind. I won't let him catch me in a vulnerable spot again.

I'd better go home now.' But when she stood up she burst into tears again, afraid to drive off on her own, afraid to go into her flat even, in case he was there, waiting for her.

'We'll drive you back,' Stuart said firmly, seeming to understand her fear without being told. 'You can ride with Angela in our car and I'll drive yours. We'll see you safely inside your flat, too, and check that he's not hanging around.'

'But I can't ask you to – it's right across town.'

'You didn't ask. I've got daughters of my own. I wouldn't like to think of them being so vulnerable.' If he were on better terms with Paul Stevenson, he'd ring him up and tell him what was going on – but you couldn't get close to someone who was never there. Funny sort of marriage that was, with the husband away all the time. Though Rosalind was pleasant enough.

When they had left her, Jenny fastened all the doors and windows in her flat and sat down in front of the TV. But she was too locked in her own thoughts to notice what was on the screen. She felt reasonably safe now because there were people within screaming distance. In fact, there was always someone moving about nearby until the small hours of the morning. The noise had driven her mad at first; tonight she was glad of it.

But if Michael had followed her once and caught her on her own, he could do it again. You couldn't be on your guard every second of the day. You couldn't stop going out, either – and you had to come home each day and worry about whether he was waiting for you.

What the hell was she going to do?

* * *

Jenny met her friend Carla after work the following day and they went for a drink, which led to a visit to a food hall for a quick, cheap meal. Afterwards they went back to her flat together, because she didn't dare go home on her own.

'You know, you really ought to call in the police, Jen,' Carla said as they walked up the concrete stairs. She had been saying that ever since she found out about the attempted rape.

'What can they do? I can't prove what he was *intending* to do, can I?' She hadn't slept properly the previous night and today her supervisor at work had had a word with her about late nights and their effect on work performance. He clearly thought she was partying on. *In your dreams, Mr Bennett!* she thought sourly.

At the flat door, they both stopped dead and Jenny clutched her friend as terror cramped through her. 'I didn't leave the door open. I wouldn't.' She stared at it. 'The lock's broken. He's smashed it.' She hated to put it into words, but it had to be faced. 'He – he may be waiting for me inside.'

'You'd have thought someone would hear the noise.' Carla glanced sideways.

'Yes.' Jenny's arms and legs felt all stiff, as if they'd never move or bend again.

Her friend sucked in a breath, then whispered, 'You peep inside and I'll stay here, ready to scream for help.'

'I don't want to.'

'You *have* to. We can't stand out here all night. Go on! He can't rape two of us and he can't lock you inside, not now he's smashed the door.'

Jenny gulped and forced herself to move. It took a huge

effort to set one foot in front of the other. She was going to be sick. She felt faint. What if he jumped out at her? What if she was so scared she couldn't scream?

Pushing the door fully open so that he couldn't hide behind it, she waited a minute, listening, then exchanged glances with Carla before stepping inside. If Michael did pounce on her, she was sure she'd not be able to run away. Terror had already fused her knees into stiff unyielding lumps.

As she looked round and realised what had happened, a sob wrenched its way out.

From the doorway, Carla yelled, 'What is it? What's wrong?'

'He's wrecked the place.' Jenny looked round the normally neat living area and burst into tears. All the furniture had been thrown about and her brightly coloured cushions had been slashed. In the kitchen area, food was scattered across the floor, margarine trampled into flour and sugar, with drinking chocolate powder scattered artistically across it all in a question mark. Broken eggs were lying in a slimy shell-strewn mess in one corner and some bananas had been ground into pulp at the other side. And there was a strong smell of urine.

Carla called from outside, 'Jenny! *Jenny!* Are you all right?'

'Yes.' But her voice was only a hoarse whisper and it was a moment before she could get it to come out more loudly. 'There's no one in the living area. I'm going into the bedroom. Stand nearer the front door so you can hear me.'

Carla appeared in the opening. 'Hell! The man's a lunatic.' She brandished her mobile phone and jerked her head towards the other door. 'Talk as you go and if you stop talking, I'll start screaming and call the police.'

Jenny went into the room. 'There's no one here, but oh, God! Carla, it's such a mess.' She was weeping helplessly now. 'I'm looking in the wardrobe – nothing here, either – just the bathroom to check now – oh, the bastard! What a mess!' All her make-up had been ground together in the sink and all her perfumes poured down it so that the place was full of a cloying stink. 'He's not here – you can come in.'

Carla walked through the small flat, muttering to herself as she inspected the damage. 'He's sick, that man is, really, really sick. *Oh, my God! Look at that.*'

Jenny turned reluctantly towards the bed. Her best underwear was arranged on top of the covers, as if a body were wearing it. Black lace bra and knickers, the suspender belt she'd bought because *he* said it was sexy. Why the hell hadn't she thrown that away? And there was a condom standing ready by the bedside. But where her heart would have been, just below the black lace bra, a carving knife was sticking up in a pool of red.

'Don't touch anything.' Carla dialled the 000 emergency number on her mobile.

It took an hour for someone to turn up, during which time Jenny jerked in fright at every sound of footsteps in the stairwell, even though Carla had wedged a chair under the front door handle.

The policeman was brisk and factual, examining everything, then calling into the station for someone to come out and investigate more thoroughly. 'It's a sicko,' he said into the phone. 'A real sicko.'

It was three hours before the investigation team had finished with Jenny, by which time she had repeated the sordid details of her affair with Michael and her troubles since they broke up, going over it so many times she felt like a record stuck in a groove.

'Do you have somewhere else to stay tonight?' the woman officer asked as they prepared to leave. 'We'll send someone to make this place secure, but you shouldn't stay here on your own from now on.'

'I – yes, I can go to my gran's – oh, but she hasn't got a spare bed now.' She stood there, feeling utterly dumb, unable to think of an alternative.

'Come round to my place and crash on the floor,' Carla offered. 'Sue won't mind. You can think of something more permanent tomorrow.'

Jenny could only nod. 'I'll pack some things.' She took plastic bags and stuffed every garment she could find that was untouched into them, emptying her drawers and her shelves. She didn't want *him* coming back to finish creating mayhem. And she didn't want to come back here herself, either. Not ever.

It wasn't until the following morning, as they were getting ready for work, that Jenny remembered her mother's embroideries. How lucky she'd forgotten about them and left them in the car boot! As she was fumbling in her bag for her keys, she found the scratchie. Well, she certainly didn't feel lucky at the moment! Still, she got out a coin and scratched off the coating.

As she studied the numbers, she gasped and checked everything again. But she hadn't made a mistake. 'Five thousand dollars!' She raised her voice to yell, 'Carla, I just won five thousand dollars on a scratchie. Oh, I don't believe this!' Then she was weeping again and her friend was comforting her.

'But why are you crying, you idiot? You've won some money. That's good news, for a change.'

'Because this is the answer, don't you see?'

'Call me stupid, but I don't see. Five thousand dollars isn't exactly a fortune.'

'It's enough to get me to England. I'm going to stay with Mum.' Michael wouldn't be able to reach her there or even find out where she was.

'Wow! Good idea.' Carla went back to her breakfast, waving one hand at the phone. 'Be my guest. Phone her now and tell her. And if she's out, you can use my computer and email her.'

Jenny picked up the receiver, then put it down again. 'No. I'm not giving her the chance to speak to Dad. He'll say no for sure and she always does as he tells her. I'm not even going to tell Gran.'

She hugged her arms around her chest. 'I'm really scared, Carla. That policeman was right. Michael's a real sicko. I'm leaving the country. And if that means that bastard's won, well, he's won.'

'What about your job?'

'I'll tell my supervisor what's happened. I think he'll understand. He's been asking me if anything's wrong. And if he doesn't give me leave, I'll quit.' It was better to be alive and unemployed than dead – or raped – or both.

After Carla had left, Jenny rang work and told them what had happened, then phoned the detectives. Before she could say anything about her plans they asked her to go to the police station and answer some more questions.

What they said made her even more determined to leave Perth. Michael had an alibi. Well, of course he did. Two of his sleazy friends had sworn he'd been with them at the hotel drinking, they'd gone there straight after work and stayed until closing time. And a barman remembered seeing him, because he'd complained about a wrong order, but the guy couldn't decide on the exact time for this, as things had been pretty busy around then.

Jenny looked the female detective in the eyes. 'I knew you wouldn't be able to prove anything, but I swear to you it's him.'

'I believe you.'

The male detective looked at her thoughtfully, then nodded. He was inclined to believe her, too. The suspect was a cocky bastard and had smirked the whole time they were interviewing him. He *smelt* bad, as far as Dean was concerned. And the victim was as nice as that guy seemed suspicious. 'We'll keep an eye on him from now on. Your parents' neighbours gave us a clear description, even to the colour and make of his car. We both believe you, Jenny.'

'You do?'

The female detective smiled at her. 'You've got that sort of face, Jenny Stevenson. Honest. So what are you going to do? You'd be best getting away for a while, if you can.'

Jenny managed a near smile. 'I'm going to England to join my mother.'

'Your ex won't know her address?'

'No. It's a rented house. She went there after I broke up with him.'

'Perfect. Leave us your contact details, though.'

It was not until she was sitting on a plane that Jenny remembered the note she'd scribbled to her gran and forgotten to post in her hurry to get away. It was still in her pocket. Oh, well, she'd ring from England. She snuggled down in the seat. She hadn't felt so safe for a long time. Soon she was asleep.

Chapter Nine

The sun was low in the sky and it had been a balmy spring day. Rosalind walked slowly round the gardens of Destan Manor with Jonathon, a short stroll, so as not to overstrain her ankle. Dusty trailed behind them, sniffing at this and that, wagging his tail whenever someone looked his way. Rosalind felt more at peace with the world than she had done for a long time.

She bent to caress a patch of vivid purple aubrietia that tumbled over a low, greystone wall above a clump of bright daffodils, then half-turned to smile at Jonathon. 'These are so beautiful, aren't they? I think I'll do a Dorset garden in spring as one of my next pieces, with an art nouveau kind of lady in the centre, slender and elegant with sweeping skirts that tangle into the flowers till you can't tell which is which.'

'That sounds beautiful.'

'It's good sometimes to escape into fantasy art – though I enjoy capturing reality, too.'

She also enjoyed talking to someone who understood her references. Paul would have asked what she meant, Liz would have told her to do something from the twentieth century, and her children would just have shrugged and said, *Yeah, yeah, very nice* – no, Jenny might have been genuinely interested.

But Jonathon, well, he seemed tuned in to the same cultural things as she was. It was one of the many things which made him such an easy and pleasant companion.

As they reached the end of the alley, he took hold of her hand and swung her to face him. 'I've been trying not to say this, but I can't hold it in any longer. Rosalind, dearest Rosalind, you do realise I've fallen in love with you, don't you?'

She stood and stared at him, mouth open. She had sort of realised it, she admitted to herself, but she hadn't let herself face up to it. She hadn't admitted to her own feelings, either. She was attracted to him, very, though she couldn't understand how this had happened. She hadn't encouraged him to be more than a friend, because she wasn't the sort of person to be unfaithful. Only – she'd seen so little of Paul during the past year or two, and he seemed to have changed . . . and Jonathon was so . . . She didn't let herself finish that thought.

Gnats drifted past them in a cloud, trailing a thin wailing sound that seemed to express exactly how she felt. She couldn't be less than honest with him. 'Oh, Jonathon, why didn't I meet you twenty-five years ago?'

His voice was soft. 'You were on the other side of the world and actually, I took a while to settle down, rebelling against the burden of all this.' He waved a hand towards the house. 'Then Dad died suddenly and it all came to me, so I had no choice. Later I fell in love with Isabel and I think she loved me at first, I really do! Though it's hard to be sure now, after all the acrimony.'

He stared into the distance. 'Only I wouldn't wipe out my sons any more than you'd wipe out your children. We've both reaped the pleasure of children from our marriages, even if other things haven't been – wonderful.'

As she met his solemn gaze, she tried to find the right words to answer him, but failed because her thoughts were in a total tangle.

'But we've met now, Rosalind, and I don't think you're indifferent to me.' He took her other hand and raised it to his lips, gazing into her eyes, trying to gauge her response. He saw only confusion.

Her voice was breathless, soft as everything else about her. 'You must think I'm stupid, but I hadn't realised until now how you felt – or how I felt, either. No,' she corrected, determined to be absolutely honest, 'I had realised, but I just hadn't let myself admit it. I've never even looked at another man before, you see.'

He nodded. 'You seem like the sleeping princess sometimes, slightly out of touch with reality. You're not happy with Paul, though, are you?'

She stared blindly at the masses of colour around them. 'No. I'm not happy with him and I haven't been for a long time.' She closed her eyes for a moment before saying the rest of it and facing things squarely. 'He's good in bed, but not much use as a husband and father. Well, you can't be when you're never there. And where he's heading now isn't where I want to go. I'm not even sure I can pretend any more, let alone follow him further up the corporate ladder.'

Silence whispered around them for a few moments, then she stretched out one hand to touch his cheek briefly. 'I *am* attracted to you, Jonathon, but I've been married a long time and we've both been faithful, so Paul and I do share a bond of loyalty, if nothing else. I can't just walk away from everything. Your marriage is over, you're cut off from your sons and I can tell how that hurts you. If I left Australia, came to live in England, I might cut myself off from my children, too, and I don't think I could bear that.'

And besides, Paul had cared enough about their marriage to arrange this second honeymoon, even if it had gone awry. She'd held on to that thought through her weeks of being angry with him.

She let her hand drop and walked on. Jonathon walked with her, not interrupting, allowing her time to think. Dusk closed in around them, encouraging her to more confidences. 'Paul and I have admitted that we've grown apart and we've agreed to try to – get closer again. I have to give it a chance.'

'And you're not the sort to have an affair.' To him it was part of her charm. 'But would it upset you greatly if I kissed you? Just this once? I've been longing to for days.'

Without waiting for an answer, he drew her into his arms, holding her for a few moments to gaze down into her eyes. Love shone brightly in his face.

When he bent his head to kiss her, she gave in to temptation and with an inarticulate murmur, she put her arms round his neck. She didn't hold back because she wasn't going to do this again and wanted something to remember him by. When they stopped kissing, she rested her head on his shoulder and let him hold her for a long time.

At last he pulled away. 'May I remain your friend, Rosalind? I promise I won't pester or embarrass you about how I feel.'

'You *are* my friend.' She swallowed a hard lump that was sitting in her throat. How quickly she had grown to love this man. *Love him?* Yes, this was love. She couldn't imagine life without him now, couldn't bear the thought of going back to Australia and never seeing him again.

But she didn't voice those thoughts because acting selfishly would mean hurting Paul and her children. She reached out to hold Jonathon's hand, allowing herself that small pleasure, and together they strolled back through the softly shadowed gardens.

By now he knew her real preferences, so made her some coffee and said in a more normal tone, 'I told you, didn't I, that my sons will be visiting me for the fundraising fête?'

She was glad to talk of something else. 'I shall look forward to meeting them.'

He stared down into his cup. 'Isabel doesn't like them staying here – she wants to stop all the family traditions and get Giles to break the trust when he grows up, but the more she keeps them away from Destan, the more the boys seem to love it.' He gave a wry smile. 'There's an extra fascination in the forbidden, don't you think? They come here every year at this time. That's part of our divorce agreement. They think the fête is enormous fun.'

'I'm looking forward to it, too. Perhaps you'd like to bring them round to tea?' Twelve-year-old boys on their best behaviour could be delightful. Or utterly ghastly, if they were in an off mood. She could remember Tim at that age, before he'd withdrawn from any closeness with her.

'I think it'd look better if I gave everyone tea here – you, me, Harry.' He knew Isabel questioned the boys when they got back and would love to find an excuse to keep Giles and Rufus away from him in future.

As they drank their coffee and chatted quietly, Rosalind saw how his glances sometimes betrayed his feelings and wondered if hers did the same. She was very conscious of his body – and of her own. How short a distance his hand was from hers! She kept wanting to kiss him again. Or at least hold his hand.

But she didn't.

And neither did he.

Tim took the money back to the dealer and handed it over.

'Where's the rest?'

'What do you mean?'

'I gave you fifty packets. There's money here for only forty. Where's the rest?'

'I don't have any more.' Tim's mind raced back to his hour on the street. Wayne had come up to chat to him. They'd been laughing and horsing around a bit. Surely his friend hadn't robbed him?

Who else could it be? No one else had touched him, and a serious thief would have taken all the dope.

'Someone must have picked my pocket and—'

'Do you think I came down in the last shower of rain?'
The dealer beckoned and two figures stepped out of the
shadows.

Tim backed away, but the two men dragged him outside.
One of them flung him hard against the wall, then punched
him several times. When the fist slammed into his gut again,
he was violently sick, unable to control himself.

'Hell!' said a voice up above his crouched body. 'This
bastard just puked all over my shoes.'

'Kick him in the balls.'

Tim curled up, trying to protect himself. 'Please, no! I
won't – it was an accident, losing those packets.'

A foot slammed into his back and pain exploded
everywhere. 'Make sure you don't have any more accidents,
man! And don't push for no one else in this town. Got it?'

He screamed, but they ignored that and continued to
beat him till he felt himself losing consciousness. He was
sure by then that they intended to kill him.

He woke early next morning, surprised to find himself
still alive and lying in an alley he didn't recognise. It took
him a while to drag himself painfully to his feet, for every
inch of him seemed to hurt. Although people were passing
the end of the alley, they didn't come to help but hurried
away when they saw him staggering round.

He leant against a wall and began to weep, but it didn't
make any difference. No one came to help him.

After a while, he stopped sobbing and staggered
towards the street. Oh, hell, what was he going to do?
Those bastards had emptied his wallet and money belt. Or
someone else had.

He was only sure about one thing: he had to get out of town fast. He didn't even dare go back to confront Wayne and pick up his clothes.

At first he stumbled blindly along the streets, but he found a ten-dollar note in an inside pocket and a stop at a burger joint for two cups of strong coffee helped him pull himself together. Another stop bought him some aspirin and the pain receded a little. It took him a while to work out what to do, but the only safe place he could think of was the cemetery, so he went there and hid among the tombstones, shivering every time he heard a car drive past.

Come nightfall, he'd retrieve his money and passport and leave town.

He was going back to Australia, even if he had to ring up and grovel to his father for the rest of the ticket money. And once he got there, he was never, ever going to leave it again.

After another disturbed night lying worrying, Audrey went into her granddaughter's room and stared at the smooth, wrinkle-free bedcovers. Seven o'clock in the morning. Bed not slept in again. And no threat seemed to have any effect on Louise's increasingly nocturnal habits.

The girl did clear up after herself now and do her washing more or less regularly. But that was a minor victory. Set it against Louise's blatant refusal to keep reasonable hours or let her grandmother know where she was going – not to mention a certain glassy-eyed look the last couple of times she'd come in late . . . and Audrey knew she was beaten. As for studying, well, she suspected Louise was cutting classes as well, but couldn't prove it.

It's time for someone else to take over now, she decided. *John's right. I've given it a fair go, but I don't intend to make a martyr of myself.*

She waited until about four o'clock, to allow for time differences between the UK and Australia, then picked up the phone and rang Paul's head office. It took a while to persuade them to give her his number in Hong Kong, but she did, because she was absolutely determined. Though he wasn't going to like her telling them there was a problem with his younger daughter, she knew. Well, too bad. There *was* a problem.

When she got through to the hotel in Hong Kong, she felt lucky. Paul answered his room phone at the second ring. 'Yes?'

'It's Audrey here.'

'Ma-in-law! Hey, nice to hear from you. How are things?'

She grimaced as his voice took on that over-jolly, patronising tone he always used with her. How she hated it! 'Not going well, so we'll not waste time on chit-chat. Paul, I can't cope with Louise any longer. You'll have to make other arrangements for her.'

He sighed. 'Have you rung Ros? The children are her business, really.'

'No, I haven't rung her and I'm not going to. You're nearer to Perth by a few thousand miles than she is. I'll expect you to fly down here at the weekend. You can take Louise away then. I've had more than enough of that young woman.'

'Look, put her on the phone and I'll have a very strong word with her. I promise you, I'll make her so afraid she'll—'

'Not good enough, Paul. I'm sixty-seven not twenty-seven. I can't cope and dammit, I won't even try any more. You have until Saturday to fetch her.'

He scowled at the phone. *Stupid old cow!* 'I can't make it on Saturday, I'm afraid, Audrey.'

'Then I'll have to call social services, say she's unmanageable and ask them to take her off my hands. She's not eighteen yet, after all. I think they'll be interested.'

'*You wouldn't!*'

'I would, actually. I don't want the police raiding my house looking for drugs or—'

'*Drugs?*'

'I'm pretty certain she's taking something.'

'I'll be there on Saturday. Don't tell her I'm coming. Let me surprise her.' He'd surprise Liz, too, while he was at it. He'd missed her since she returned to Perth, missed her astringent conversation and sexy body. She'd been very firm about not continuing the relationship, but he was sure he could persuade her to see him while he was there. They'd been good together in the sack. If only Ros were more proactive about sex like Liz was.

As he put down the phone, anger sizzled through him and he thumped the pillow with one clenched fist. Bloody kids! You gave them the best of everything, private schools, expensive holidays, bicycles, and who knew what else – and what did they do to thank you? Went off the rails. Abandoned their studies. Got into drugs. Ran off to America.

Oh, hell, his youngest daughter was doing drugs like her brother. Why? Where had he and Ros gone wrong?

He sat down on the edge of the bed, chewing his lip. Unfortunately Audrey was right to ring him. This wasn't something Ros would be able to cope with. In fact, Ros must have been weaker than he'd thought on the discipline side. First Tim, now Louise. And even Jenny had chosen a no-hoper of a guy when she was let loose on the world, though she'd had the sense to realise that and leave the fellow, at least.

He was going to nip this present mess of Louise's in the bud right away, but first he had to figure out what you did with a seventeen-year-old rebel in Hong Kong?

It wasn't until he was getting ready for bed that an idea struck him. He began to smile. Yes, that should sort it out nicely.

The following day he strode out of Perth Airport and hailed a taxi. At Audrey's he paid off the driver and turned to find his mother-in-law waiting for him at the door. They didn't waste time on greetings.

'Louise is still asleep,' Audrey said in a low voice. 'She didn't get back until about four o'clock this morning.'

Something caught his eye and he didn't follow her inside. 'What the hell is Ros's car doing here?'

'Louise has been using it. She said Rosalind gave her permission.' Audrey's heart sank. *Oh no, not more lies!* And Paul looked so grimly angry today she hardly recognised him.

'Ros definitely didn't do that.' She'd have told him if she had. She'd told him every other goddamn detail of her preparations for England in those boring letters she wrote weekly when he was away. She hardly ever used emails, and hadn't bothered to get online in England, or if she had, she hadn't told him, and she would have done.

He was going to drag her into the twenty-first century, even if she screamed all the way. He pushed those thoughts aside. He had to deal with his daughter first.

'Tell me the details about Louise.' He listened in growing fury, then said in a tight, clipped voice, 'You stay here and I'll go upstairs. This may take a while. You were absolutely right to send for me. You – er, might like to put the radio on. There will definitely be some shouting.'

As he opened the door of Louise's bedroom, he stared round in disgust at the mess. Dirty clothes on the floor, litter everywhere. By the side of the bed was a cotton thing that looked like a shoulder bag made from a flour sack, so he upended it on the desk by the window. A small packet of what looked like herbs fell out. He sniffed it. Pot. Pray that was all she was on. But there were a few pills, too. He didn't know enough about drugs to guess what they were.

He began to search the drawers and all the time his daughter slept peacefully behind him, looking as innocent as the child she had been not long ago. There was also a packet of condoms. Bile rose in his throat. His daughter screwing around. At seventeen! How had she got into all this?

He stood by the bedside, contemplating the child who had always been his favourite, the one who looked most like him. She appeared innocent and pretty still, sprawled on her side with one hand curled beneath her cheek. But she wasn't innocent, she was spoilt, dirty.

What was that? He bent closer and saw the ring in her nose, the streaks of dirty blonde on one side of her hair. She looked so tarty that for a moment disgust rose like vomit in his throat. Then he reached out and shook her – hard.

'Hey! Wh-what? *Dad!*' She jerked upright in the bed. 'What are *you* doing here?'

'Your grandmother phoned. It seems, Louise, that you've been upsetting her, as well as burning the candle at both ends.' He flicked one finger towards the things on the desk.

She gasped and stared at him, her eyes large and frightened, but didn't say anything.

'I thought you had a little more sense, but you didn't waste much time following Tim's example, did you?'

Her voice was sulky. 'Everyone does something nowadays. It's only dope.'

'And the tablets?'

'Amphetamines. To help me keep my weight down.' They gave you the most lovely feeling of energy and optimism, too. Pity they were so expensive. 'They're not hard drugs, Dad.'

'I don't expect *my* children to do *any* drugs. Hard or soft.'

She laughed, a shaky, nervous sound. 'They're no worse than alcohol. The law's stupid. This is the twenty-first century, not the—'

She didn't finish what she was saying because he slapped her across her face, hard, then slapped her again.

After an initial screech, she cowered down on the bed, sobbing noisily.

'I've never hit you before, Louise. Perhaps I should have.' He reached out and held her at arm's length, forcing words past the anger that seemed to have solidified in his throat. 'Now listen, and listen well, young woman.' He gave her another shake for emphasis. 'I learnt my lesson with Tim. I overlooked this and overlooked that – and he carried on mucking around. Heaven knows where he is now – whether he's still alive, even.'

She looked at him in horror.

'Surely that possibility had occurred to you? America can be a dangerous place. He hasn't been in touch for months.' And Paul worried about that, though he hadn't said so to Ros.

Louise stared up at her father and waited for more harsh words – or more slaps. He shook her again, but less violently, then said in a tight, angry voice.

'I'm *not* going down the same path with you, Louise. I trusted Tim to grow out of his silliness and he ran away instead, got in deeper. You have a simple choice ahead of you, really simple. Behave yourself – and I'll be watching closely, so don't think you can pull the wool over *my* eyes as you have your mother's – or get out of my life and family this minute. I shan't give you a second chance, either.'

She could only goggle at him. Get out of the family! He couldn't mean that. But she saw the grim determination in his eyes and realised with a jolt that he did.

He leant forward until his face was almost touching hers. 'Do you believe me? Do you believe that I mean *exactly* what I say, Louise?'

She nodded, gulping.

He moved back and stood there with arms folded. 'Right then, it's entirely your choice. If you don't toe the line from now on, I'll cut you off from the family within the hour – and push you out of your grandmother's front door myself.'

The chairman would have recognised him. The chairman really approved of the way Stevenson cut through the crap when it was necessary. So would one or two cheating managers whose thieving Paul had uncovered, and whom he had sent packing there and then.

But Louise had never seen her father like this and she looked, quite literally, terrified. Good. He wanted her terrified.

'D-dad, don't!'

He looked at his watch. 'I'll give you exactly one minute to decide, Louise. Not one second longer. After all, it's a very simple choice.'

She started sobbing.

'And weeping won't make any difference at all.' Implacable, he waited until she capitulated – as he'd known she would.

Chapter Ten

Rosalind picked up the phone. 'Yes?'

The voice was hesitant. 'Mum? Is that you?'

'Jenny! How nice to speak to you.' Rosalind glanced at the clock. She was meeting Harry in five minutes and they were going to have coffee with the organisers of the auction. Why did people always ring up for a chat when you were in a hurry?

'Mum – oh, Mum, I'm in England, at the bus station in Poole. Can you come and pick me up?'

'*In Poole!* Jenny, what have you *done*?'

There was the sound of sobbing at the other end. 'It's not what you think, Mum. I – please can you pick me up? I'll tell you about it then.'

'Yes, of course. Where did you say you were?' But although she would be glad to see Jenny, Rosalind's heart sank.

She cancelled everything, programmed the satnav and

drove into Poole. Her anger vanished as she hugged her daughter and saw how haunted and jumpy Jenny was looking, not to mention how much weight she had lost. 'What's wrong? Have you been ill?'

'Not exactly. I'll – explain later.'

Jenny picked up her big suitcase and Rosalind took the piece of cabin luggage out of her hand.

'That one's got some of your embroideries in, Mum. I had the rest shipped out – these two may be a bit crumpled, but they're safe, at least.'

Why should things not be safe? What had been going on in Perth? Rosalind looked sideways at her daughter, not attempting to start the car. 'Tell me.'

Jenny's face crumpled. 'It's Michael. He's been – oh, Mum, he's been stalking me. He kept phoning at all hours. I couldn't get a proper night's sleep unless I unplugged the phone. And then he broke into my flat and trashed everything. I've been terrified. If your neighbours hadn't turned up when I was getting those embroideries for you, he'd have raped me.' And every time she thought about that, she wanted to curl up into a ball and scream herself into oblivion.

Rosalind felt horror trickle through her as she took Jenny in her arms, shushing her and patting her back as she had done when her daughter was a child. Now, Jenny was five foot nine and a woman grown, but she needed holding just as much as the child had.

When the tears had subsided and Jenny had blown her nose several times, they looked at one another.

'You aren't – angry with me, Mum?'

'Only with Michael. But how did you get the money for your fare, love?' If it was from her mother, it'd have to be paid back at once. Rosalind knew Audrey had very little to spare.

Jenny gave a hiccupy laugh as she explained about her timely win. 'I took the money and ran, Mum. Fled for my life. I was terrified. I thought – no, I *knew* he was going to kill me if I stayed in Perth.'

'*Kill you?*'

Jenny nodded. 'The policeman said he was a sicko.' She explained about the underwear laid out on the bed, the knife and mock blood.

Horror kept Rosalind silent for a moment. 'You did the right thing, then. But Jenny, if you'd rung and explained what was happening, I'd have sent you the money for your fare earlier.'

'I thought of that, but Dad didn't want any of us to come here with you. He'd have persuaded you not to help me – or arranged something else. Only you see,' her voice quavered, 'I needed *you*. Do you mind very much?' She reached across to take her mother's hand.

'I don't mind at all, not now I understand.' Rosalind squeezed the fingers that were quivering against hers. 'And your father doesn't dictate everything I do.'

Her voice was so quiet and sure Jenny stared at her in surprise. 'He usually tells you – well, he tells us all what to do.'

Rosalind stared down blindly at the steering wheel. 'I've let him do that in the past, to my shame. But he won't be giving me quite so many orders from now on – or at least, if he does, I won't be obeying them.'

'You sound different.'

'Yes. I think I am. We can talk about that later, though. We're both shivering, so let me get you home. The countryside round here is gorgeous. There's nothing like pretty scenery for soothing the savage breast.'

When they got to Burraford, Rosalind settled Jenny in front of the fire with a big mug of coffee and tried to ring Paul, breaking her normal rule of not disturbing him when he was working on a project. But although it would be the middle of the night in Hong Kong, he wasn't in his room, and the hotel receptionist said he was away for the weekend. Which seemed very strange. He didn't usually take holidays when he was working on a project. 'I'd like to leave a message, then. And tell him it's extremely urgent . . .'

That evening Jonathon decided to ring Rosalind simply because he wanted to talk to her. Another few days and his sons would be here, and after that her husband would be back. Oh, hell, he didn't want this interlude to end, this brief idyll when they'd forged a friendship and fallen in love.

'Hello?'

He smiled at the way her voice always sounded as breathy and uncertain as a young girl's. 'It's me, Rosalind. Do you fancy going to the pub for a drink?'

'I can't, I'm afraid. My daughter's just arrived from Australia. Jenny, the eldest. She's been having trouble with an ex-boyfriend.' She lowered her voice, 'He's been stalking her and she's very upset.'

'Anything I can do to help?'

'Not really.'

'I shall miss you.' He didn't have to spell it out that her daughter's arrival meant their closeness had ended sooner than they'd both expected.

'Yes. I shall, too.' She didn't dare talk more openly to him. She had done nothing to be ashamed of – *nothing but fall in love*, that truthful little voice said inside her head – but even their public friendship would have to be lower-key now. And perhaps that was a good thing. Though it didn't feel like a good thing.

When he had put the phone down, Jonathon poured himself a whisky, then went to pace up and down the long gallery upstairs as he did sometimes when he was upset. The creaking floorboards suited his mood today, as did the frayed hangings and worn carpets.

At first he was angry that the daughter had come, then he got annoyed with himself because stalking was a very serious matter and any mother worth her salt would naturally drop everything to look after that daughter in those circumstances. But the thought of not being with Rosalind hurt even more than he had anticipated.

'Oh, sod them all,' he told the last bit of amber liquid in his glass, 'I've never had any luck with women.'

Well, at least the boys were coming down the following weekend. That was something to look forward to. And he'd get Harry to invite him, Rosalind and the daughter round for coffee. He had to see his lovely, gentle darling sometimes, to make sure she was all right, at least. He poured the rest of the whisky down in a gulp and went to refill his glass.

Not even his divorce had made him feel this bad emotionally, because by then all affection between himself and Isabel had been gone and he'd only been left with anger at her rapaciousness – and relief at being rid of her.

The house creaked and shifted around him and the ghosts of his ancestors rustled past, as they always seemed to do when he was alone in this room. Thin, spindly people like him and Harry, with sad narrow faces. He never quite knew whether he was imagining them or whether they really did gather round him, but they felt real enough. And certainly, when this mood came upon him, Dusty grew uneasy, whining and twitching at the shadows. But dogs were like that. They could sense your mood – and perhaps see your family ghosts. He looked down at the furry face and wagging tail. Dogs didn't pretend. They gave their love wholeheartedly and unconditionally. As he'd like to give his.

For once, he drew no comfort from the sense of solid continuity to Gilles D'Estaing, who had carved out his own territory in the conquered foreign land of England, or to the many ancestors who had allowed their name to be twisted into a more English sound. He raised the glass, drinking a silent toast to Araminta Destang, his favourite ancestor, who had saved the estate from destruction during the Civil War. 'Paul Destan!' he toasted next. The poor fellow had lost an arm at Waterloo, but had gone on to sire four sons. And had made the final name change.

Jonathon went to look for some more whisky, opened his reserve bottle and drank to Rosalind's health, trying to ignore the tears trickling down his face. Who said men didn't cry? He'd cried when the court awarded custody of his sons to Isabel. And he was crying now.

How was Rosalind feeling? Was she missing him? Would she weep into her pillow tonight?

In Australia Paul Stevenson paced up and down the hall of his own house. Louise was in bed after a very unpleasant day, having cried herself to a complete standstill as he and Audrey went through her room with a fine toothcomb, exposing the evidence of her peccadilloes, which were not as bad, thank goodness, as he had feared. Though he hadn't said that to her. No, he had acted as if she were ripe for the gallows and he the hangman, while she wept and sobbed and promised him whatever he demanded.

'Take out that bloody nose ring for a start!' he'd roared, and when she'd done so, he'd tossed it into the rubbish bin.

And while he ranted on at Louise, Audrey had sat and watched, tight-lipped. He hoped she was upset behind that stoical mask. She should be. She'd failed lamentably and she knew it, the silly old bat. But at least she hadn't wept on him as his daughter had.

God, how he hated snivelling women! And although Louise had promised faithfully not to misbehave any more, he wasn't going to leave her in Australia. You couldn't trust seventeen-year-olds to live on their own. You needed to watch them all the time.

His two youngest had taught him that, by God they had, and he didn't intend to fail with Louise as he had with Tim. She was going to grow tougher and she was going to do well in life. He hated other people boasting about how successful their grown-up children were, hated being unable to match tales with them. Hated most of all the thought that *his* children had grown into fools and wastrels.

For the first time he wondered if Ros had been right and it had been unwise to take her away at precisely this time in Louise's development. Then he shrugged. It was essential to his career that his wife loosen her ties to Perth. That had to come first. Perhaps he should have let Louise come to England with them, then? On reflection, he supposed so – and would have done if he'd known all the facts. But he hadn't really wanted a teenage daughter hanging around. He still didn't.

Hell, he was horny tonight. Solving a crisis always had that effect on him. And Liz was only a few hundred yards away. He listened. Not a sound. Louise had been so exhausted she'd barely made it up the stairs before tumbling into bed. Maybe he could arrange something? He could sneak out to Liz's place if Bill was at one of his meetings – or he could meet her in the garage here so they could screw themselves silly on the old couch. Worth trying. He always thought better when he wasn't in lust.

He went into his home office and picked up the phone.

Louise, who'd been lying in bed pretending to be asleep and worrying about what her father intended to do with her, heard the sound of the phone and sat up. Who was Dad phoning at this time of night? If he was planning to dump her on someone else, she wanted to know about it.

She crept into her parents' bedroom and picked up the receiver carefully. She'd listened in a few times from here. The phone system was in excellent order because her father had brought the company back several times to fix things like echoes on the line or clicks from other extensions. As long as you didn't make a noise and put down the receiver *after* the other person, no one knew you were listening in.

Her father's voice. 'Liz?'

Louise frowned. What was her father phoning *her* up for? Liz was her mother's friend and he didn't get on all that well with her.

'Paul?'

'Who else?'

'I thought we'd agreed not to get in touch.'

'I'm here in Perth.'

A hiss of indrawn breath.

'Any chance of seeing you?'

'No.'

'Liz, baby, we're good together. You know we are.'

Louise listened, stunned. Her father's voice had gone all warm and smarmy, the way it did when he was charming someone. But this was *Liz* he was talking to, her mother's friend, and from what he'd said . . .

'Surely we can seize an odd moment or two to satisfy our mutual needs? You said Bill was a second-rater in bed. You said you were never satisfied with him. I think you were quite satisfied with my performance, though.' He chuckled softly.

Louise wrinkled her nostrils in disgust. How gross, to screw her mother's best friend! And *he* called what she'd done bad!

'I thought I made it plain that I don't want to continue the affair. The last thing I want to do is hurt Rosalind. I must have gone crazy in Hong Kong, but I'm not crazy any more. It's over. Finito.' Her voice softened for a moment. 'It was great, it really was, but it's finished. Enjoy your life.' She put the phone down without waiting for an answer.

From below, Louise heard the sound of a phone slamming down, set the handpiece gently in its cradle and hurried into her bedroom, lying with her back to the door so that her face was hidden. Who'd ever have thought it? Liz and her father! *Oh, wow! Wait till Tim hears about this.*

She sighed, remembering that he wasn't here any more. She did miss her brother. The two of them had always been close. They were both into *Living* – with a capital L. Jenny was a wimp and Mum a doormat. A nice doormat, but she still let everyone tread on her. Though actually Dad was a lot kinder to her than to anyone else, so he must have some feelings for her – if not enough to stay faithful.

When she heard footsteps in the stairwell, Louise closed her eyes and started breathing slowly and evenly. He came in to check, of course. He'd said he would and he always did as he'd threatened. He'd told her that if she so much as put her nose outside the house without his permission, she wouldn't get back inside again. A shiver ran down her spine. He meant it, too. Indignation followed the shiver. Who was he to preach at her when he'd been cheating on her mother? Probably for years.

Tim had hinted at that sort of thing before, said he'd seen Dad out with a young chick once in Sydney, but she hadn't believed him. She did now. Oh, she wished her brother were here to talk to! He was the only one who understood her.

And she wished she knew what her father was going to do with her. The thought of him tossing her out, so that she had to get a dead-end job and manage on her own, definitely did not appeal. Why should she anyway, when her father was rich? Well, comfortable. So OK, she'd have to toe the line for a bit and that didn't really appeal, either.

Those oldies forgot what it was like to be young and full of energy. Well, she was full of energy when she took those pills, but how the hell was she going to manage without them now? She'd lost a lot of weight and she looked good. She'd kill herself if she got fat again. Nobody loved you when you were fat.

A tear trickled down her cheek, followed by another. If only Mum was here. Dad was never as bad when Mum was around.

The following morning Paul woke Louise at six, dragging her from the bed, having had an idea about how he could start the new regime. 'Come on! I'm going running and so are you. I want you where I can keep an eye on you.'

'*Running!* But I – Dad, stop! Hey, I don't do things like that.'

His smile made her shiver. 'You don't think I'm going to leave you alone in the house, do you, Louise? You must think I'm a fool.'

'But I haven't had any breakfast!' She hadn't eaten anything at all yesterday and she was hollow inside.

'You don't get breakfast until afterwards. One exercises on an empty stomach. Hurry up, or I'll drag you outside in your pyjamas. You'll need shorts and a T-shirt – and wear some joggers that aren't simply a fashion statement.'

His expression was so grim she hurried, slumping down breathlessly in her seat as he drove them down to Cottesloe beach. He'd put her mother's car away and brought out his own. Normally she loved riding in its luxury. It was used so rarely, it was like new. While he'd been away, she'd even toyed with the idea of borrowing it and taking it for a spin, but hadn't quite dared.

She shivered. A light rain had begun to fall and it was chilly. Well, it was autumn now, after all. 'Can't I just stay in the car and watch?'

'Certainly not. I thought young women liked to keep themselves fit and trim. You're always worrying about putting on weight. Maybe this is the answer. Those pills certainly aren't.'

'I've kept my weight down without any of this exercise crap.'

His gaze was as chill and assessing as a meat inspector looking at a carcase. 'You're thin, yes, but grossly unfit.' He gave her upper arm a squeeze and pulled a face at its lack of muscle tone, then slapped her thigh. 'Flabby! To look good, flesh needs to be firm.' He got out of the car. 'Come on! I'm going to run up and down the beach where I can keep an eye on you and if I see you stop moving, you're in deep trouble. You can do a hundred yards running and a hundred yards walking until I tell you to stop. That's how beginners start training.'

Anger burned in her, but she kept her mouth closed and did as ordered. She'd watched Tim blurt out defiance and get nowhere with it. Her bastard of a father always had all the answers. At first she did run, thinking she might as well get some benefit from this, but soon her feet felt like lead, an iron band settled round her chest and she could only stagger along. But every time she looked along the beach she could see him staring at her, so she didn't stop moving.

When he came jogging over to see why she'd slowed down, he looked fit and energetic for all he was nearly fifty, and she could see a couple of young women giving him the eye. She was panting and puffing, was soaked to the skin, felt like death warmed up, and no doubt looked it, too. She hated him – *hated* him!

'You're in worse condition than I thought. All right, I'll make it a short session today. It's nearly breakfast time. We'll go home and shower, then we'll find a café. There's nothing to eat at home. It's very different without your mother's efficient organisation, but it's no use stocking up!'

Louise brightened. This was more like it. She loved having breakfast in a café.

But when they got there, he ordered for her – fresh fruit salad and a low-fat muffin – not even asking what she wanted.

'Couldn't we have croissants?' she begged, trying to make her voice as girlie-soft as she could.

'Full of grease and calories. You are about to get fit, young lady, really fit.'

He didn't even look up from his newspaper as he spoke.

Louise sat there, fuming inside but not daring to interrupt him. She was so hungry she ate the bloody muffin and picked up the crumbs from her plate with a dampened fingertip.

When he'd read the paper from cover to cover, he leant back and studied her. She hated it when he did that. You could never outstare him.

'I've decided to take you to Hong Kong with me, then on to England. Since I can't trust you on your own here, I'll find a cramming school for you in England.'

Her initial surge of joy turned into leaden horror. 'A school! But I've left school.'

'You obviously left it too soon, before you were mature enough.'

'But I'm not going to be in England long enough to do any proper studying.'

'And did you do any proper studying here? Your exam results were pretty pitiful. I had to pull a few strings to get you on that course, you know.'

She slumped down in her chair glaring at him. 'But I've started the course here now.'

'Don't worry. I'll arrange a deferral. Or find you somewhere else to study. You do need some qualifications, I agree.'

They drove home in silence, then she went up to sit in her bedroom while he made phone call after phone call. At first she stood behind her bedroom door and listened to his voice floating up the stairs. Hell, he certainly ordered people around! After a while, she grew tired of business talk, put on some music and turned it up loud, trying to lose herself in the beat.

She nearly jumped out of her skin when he erupted into the bedroom and switched the CD player off. 'No music. Get a book and come downstairs where I can keep an eye on you.'

'What do you think I'm going to do, climb out of my window?'

He slapped her face, leaving her speechless with shock . . . and fear.

'I don't think you've quite realised, Louise, how angry I am. Or how little latitude you have. Now, find yourself a book – no, not a rubbishy spy novel, something worth reading – and come downstairs. We'll be leaving Perth tomorrow. You can spend this afternoon packing. We'll pick up the rest of your stuff from your grandmother's later on.'

'I've never been to Hong Kong,' she ventured after sitting for a while staring at the travel book he'd provided, a dull thing on ancient temples in Indonesia. Her mother had used something from it for an embroidery. It had looked good, too. 'What is there to see? What shall I pack?'

'This won't be a tourist visit. We'll be going on from there within a few days to England, so pack for the English spring. A bit like our winter.'

She huffed one shoulder and pretended to read. Stupid pictures of Asians in silly costumes. Who cared about such things?

Paul turned back to his own book, but his mind was on other things. He'd have to find her a minder for the next few days while he tied up the loose ends at the Hong Kong branch. Still, that should be quite easy in a place where labour was cheap. He smiled grimly. She was in for a few shocks, one way or another, his darling little daughter was. All his family were.

He was about to take charge properly. Should have

done it years ago, should have *insisted* on Ros moving to New York or London. Well, better late than never.

Rosalind examined the embroideries Jenny had brought and pressed them carefully. They hadn't suffered any damage, thank goodness. She invited Harry round to choose one – and couldn't resist inviting Jonathon, too, feeling guilty but looking forward so much to seeing him and spending a little time in his company.

Jenny hardly left her side all day. 'I'm sorry to hover – I'm a bit nervous still. It hasn't got through to my emotions yet that I'm safe. Do you mind?'

'Not at all. I'll try to ring your father again.'

When she didn't get Paul, she tried her mother and what Audrey had to tell her made her feel quite sick with shock.

Jenny, who had been watching, waiting to have a quick word with Gran, came up and put an arm round her mother as she put down the phone and stared around blankly. 'What's the matter? Mum! Talk to me, please, Mum!'

Rosalind let Jenny help her to a chair because her legs had turned to rubber. 'Did *you* know Louise was misbehaving?'

'I knew she wasn't studying much. And that she'd got in with a strange crowd.'

'You should have told me.'

'It's a bit hard for one sister to tell tales on another. I did talk to her, try to make her see sense, but you know what Louise is like.'

'She's been using my car, as well. Told your grandmother I'd given her permission.'

Jenny nodded unhappily.

'And,' Rosalind had to take a deep breath even to get the dreadful admission out, 'your grandmother says she's been on drugs. *Drugs!* At seventeen!' And sex, too – her mother had found condoms in Louise's drawers. 'I *told* your father she was too young to leave on her own.'

'Too immature, you mean. She's like Tim, greedy for life. Take, take, take.' Jenny was still worried about her mother's pallor. 'You can't babysit her for ever, Mum. She has to go out and face the world sometime, even if she mucks things up. It's the only way she'll learn. Shall I make you a coffee?'

Rosalind stared at her blindly, without answering. When the doorbell rang, she didn't even seem to hear it, just continued to stare into space and pleat the material of her skirt.

Jenny went to open it and found herself facing two strangers, both very tall and bony, obviously related. 'You must be Jonathon and Harry Destan.'

'Yes, we are. And you're Jenny.' The woman smiled at her. 'You look so like your mother.'

'Yes, I suppose I do. Look, come in. I'm afraid Mother's just had a bit of a shock.'

'What's wrong?' Harry nudged her brother as she spoke because he looked as if he was about to rush off to find Rosalind. Luckily Jenny was gazing towards the kitchen not at her visitors.

'Not – news about your brother?' Harry enquired. They both knew how worried Rosalind was about her son.

'No. Mum phoned Gran and found out that my younger sister has gone off the rails a bit and my father's had to fly down to sort things out.' Jenny led the way into the family area near the kitchen. Her mother was still sitting there, but when she saw the visitors she stood up and tried to remember her duties as hostess.

'Harry, Jonathon. Do come and sit down. I'll – um, get you some coffee and—' She stopped and shook her head saying hoarsely, 'I'm sorry. It's not a good time just now. Could you come back tomorrow?'

Only when they'd gone did it occur to Rosalind that if Paul was in Perth he'd probably be at home. Even before the front door had closed on her visitors, she was picking up the phone. 'Paul! Oh, thank goodness I've caught you. How's Louise?'

'Subdued. Look, I'll tell you all about it when I get back. It's not the sort of thing to discuss on the phone.'

She had to know. 'Mum said drugs – and sex.'

'Yes to both.'

'Oh, Paul.'

'I'm dealing with it, Ros, all right?' His voice was impatient. 'Louise and I are flying out to Hong Kong together tomorrow. I'll keep her with me there and bring her back to England next week.'

'Yes. Yes, of course.'

'There's another call on the line, Ros—'

She grew angry at his patronising tone. 'Let them wait.' She took a deep breath. 'I'm afraid I have some other news. Jenny's here in Dorset with me.'

'*Jenny!* What the hell is *she* doing there? Has she lost her job? My God, what have I ever done to deserve such stupid, useless children?'

Rosalind thumped the kitchen surface and shouted down the phone, 'For once, just shut up and listen, Paul. Jenny's ex-boyfriend has been stalking her. She's been in danger and terrified. He tried to rape her, then he broke into her flat and trashed it.'

Silence, then, 'Did she call in the police?'

'Yes, of course. They haven't been able to prove anything, so they said it was better she get away for a while. He must be deranged judging by what he did. *They* reckon he is, anyway.'

'That's all I need! How did she get the money to fly to England? Did you send it her or did Audrey lend it her?'

'Neither. She won it on a scratchie.'

'She *what*? She should have stayed there and faced him out.'

'Are you mad?' She explained the exact state of Jenny's bed and the carving knife.

'Then he's definitely crazy. I told you he was a no-hoper. And you say the police can do nothing?'

'Nothing. Michael has set up an alibi. She says he's cunning.'

'He was never clever enough to impress me. Well, it looks like we'll all be playing Happy Families in England for a while, Ros. *You* should enjoy that, at least. So much for a second honeymoon.'

She ignored the gratuitous sarcasm. And she would not, she knew, enjoy having Louise around. Or even Jenny at the moment, when she was discovering so much about herself. She'd just settled into a quiet happy routine and – oh, face it, she was missing Jonathon's company already. 'Do you, um, want to speak to Jenny?'

'Yes, of course I do. I'll get the details and see if there's anything I can do to help the police.' He had a few contacts. Or no, maybe he'd pay someone to watch that sick bastard full time. He wasn't having anyone thinking they could get away with stalking his daughter.

She passed the phone to Jenny, who was standing nearby looking apprehensive.

'I'm not going back!' Jenny hissed as she took the phone.

'Of course not.'

'Hello, Dad – yes, well, I—' She rolled her eyes at her mother.

Rosalind patted her daughter's shoulder in encouragement, then wandered out into the back garden. The grass was damp and looked very green. The next-door garden was full of trees, some with fat buds on them, nearly ready to burst into leaf, but there were only two trees here, cropped to within an inch of their lives, standing stiffly on guard at each rear corner of a square of manicured lawn which had a foot-wide flower bed all round the fence edge. Daffodils alternated with aubrietia with ruthless geometric precision, courtesy of a fortnightly gardener, who didn't like 'meddling' by tenants. She really missed having her own garden.

When she went back inside, Jenny was sitting in a corner, looking upset. 'How was I to have known Michael would turn out like this? Honestly, Dad is the most unreasonable man I've ever met! It's never *his* fault if things go wrong, and he doesn't have any sympathy for anyone else's troubles. You'd think I'd encouraged Michael to stalk me just to annoy Dad.'

She jerked to her feet. 'I think I'll go for a walk into the village.' She was desperate for some fresh air and she'd be quite safe here. She had to keep reminding herself of that, reminding herself to get on with her life. 'Do you want anything from the shops?'

'Yes, I do, actually . . .'

When her daughter had left, Rosalind went up to her workroom and took out the embroidery of the family. She picked up the sketch pad and began to rough out her own figure, with a few glances in the mirror. Vulnerable, submissive, too soft for her own good. She was beginning to see that now. Could she show it all in her embroidery? She didn't know, but she was certainly going to try.

When she'd cut out the paper figure, she studied herself in the mirror. Her face was more determined than the one in the sketch – but that was now. This picture was going to show how she and her family had been for all those years. If she embroidered it, she'd understand it all better. She didn't know why, but she would. Placing the paper figure next to Paul on the embroidery, she studied the effect. Heavens, that was so *like* him, the best figure she had ever done. She was startled every time she looked at it.

After a minute, she frowned and moved her own figure, settling it eventually at the far left side of the embroidery. Yes. That was where she belonged. Not next to him. Not together. They hadn't really been together for quite a while. She could see that now, as well. And she'd do herself in pastel colours, to contrast with the bold dark colours of Paul. She looked down at herself. Why did she always choose such faded colours?

She'd been far too accommodating with him. Jenny was right. *He* wasn't at all reasonable.

After another thoughtful pause, Rosalind sighed. Neither were her children, not even Jenny. Had she been a bad mother, brought them up wrongly? She'd loved them all, done her very best for them, but – she had to admit it, though it hurt like hell – her love and care hadn't been enough. Tim and Louise had both gone off the tracks, and Jenny – she gasped in horror as she realised it – Jenny had followed in her own footsteps, going out with a dominating man.

Well, everything was going to change. For both herself and Jenny. She'd think of her own needs as well as theirs from now on, and never, ever again would she fall in with others' wishes if they felt wrong for her.

A sad smile curved her lips for a moment – *Change of season*, Paul had said about this trip. She'd not been able to get that phrase out of her thoughts. Change of every bloody thing, it seemed to her.

He wasn't going to like some of the changes, but that didn't make any difference. They had happened now, were still happening and evolving. No one could turn the clock back.

She didn't even want to try.

Chapter Eleven

Rosalind decided she needed to do something to cheer Jenny up and take her mind off her worries. 'Want to come and look at my inheritance from Aunt Sophie?'

'But I thought it was at the other end of the country?'

'It's a small country, love. Southport is six or seven hours away by car – you can do part of the driving if you like. After all, you'll want to see a bit of England while you're here, surely?'

Jenny's face brightened. 'I'd love to see it.'

'I'll give Prue a ring, then let Harry know we're going away for a few days. We'll get back for the fête, though.' She was picking up the phone even as she spoke. 'Prue, just to let you know – my daughter Jenny and I are coming up to Southport for a few days. We'll be there sometime tomorrow afternoon. My elder daughter, yes. It's a long story. Tell you when I see you.'

And a minute later, 'Harry – Jenny and I are heading

north for a few days. You couldn't come round and choose an embroidery now, could you? It need only take a few minutes. Yes, I'm definitely feeling better, but we're both a bit down in the dumps, so I thought a trip would cheer us up.'

As she put down the phone, Rosalind saw her daughter's amazed expression and grinned. 'I'm learning to act more decisively – well, trying to.'

Jenny hugged her. 'About time, too, Mum. You go for it!' But would her mother remain decisive once her father arrived? Jenny doubted it. She knew from her own experience how hard it was to stand up to him.

At the other side of the village, Harry put down the phone and nodded in satisfaction. That'd get Rosalind out of poor Jonathon's hair for a while. He was moping around like a sick puppy worrying about her. Poor old thing. Still, the boys would be coming to Burraford soon and that'd take his mind off Rosalind.

She grabbed her raincoat and drove over to Sexton Close, humming tunelessly under her breath. She didn't really like this part of the village. Full of newcomers. And the houses were the sort which tried to look bigger than they were. Places for yuppies, she always thought. Still, the occupants would come to her fête and spend their money with carefully calculated generosity. They always did. Liked to show themselves as part of the village. Ha! You had to be born here to be really part of it. Though some did fit in after a while. Rosalind was that sort – well, she would be if she were free to stay – which she wasn't. Damned pity, that.

When Rosalind spread out the two embroideries, Harry beamed in delight. 'They're absolutely gorgeous,' she said at last, touching one of the figures gently. 'How can you bear to part with them?'

Rosalind shrugged. 'I have plenty more. They only sit in the attic at home. And besides, it's in a good cause. But you'll need to have whichever one you choose framed. I'll pay for that, of course, part of my contribution. Sarah at the craft shop will get it framed for you. I hope it can be done before the fête.' She gestured towards the paintings on the wall. 'Something like that for a frame – you can take it with you, if you like, to show her.'

Harry nodded, but her attention was still on the embroideries, which had surprised her with their beauty. She had wondered if the two on the walls were the best of the crop, but these others seemed just as good to her untrained eye, and showed how skilful her new friend was. Her friend George Didburin was going to be very interested in them indeed, she was sure. She picked one up to examine the details more closely, fingering the figures and backgrounds. 'I don't know how you have the patience to do this, but they're fine efforts, damned fine.'

In the end she chose a picture in sepia tones of some slum children of Edwardian times, who had a little dog leaping about beside them. Bare feet, ragged clothes, with that hollow look that long-term poverty gives sometimes, and yet still full of mischief. 'How did you get the dog to look so alive and frisky?' she marvelled.

'Not easily. That's the third dog figure I made. The other two were rather wooden-looking. But this one seemed OK.'

Rosalind sneaked a surreptitious glance at her watch. 'Is this the piece you want, then?'

'If you don't mind.'

'Take it.' She had expected to feel upset at losing it, but she didn't. Jenny's troubles were serious, worth getting upset about. These embroideries were simply a hobby, well a bit more than that, but she was the only one who truly cared about them. It'd be nice to know one had found a good home with someone who loved it enough to bid money for it. If anyone did bid. She saw Harry looking at her in concern and dragged her attention firmly back to the present.

'Yes, we will be back in time for the fête. I wouldn't miss it for anything.'

Harry nodded. 'It is pretty popular.' In fact, her fête was getting a solid reputation, because she focused on quality, not silly bouncy castles and such rubbish. Old-fashioned country games like skittles, which she'd played in her youth. The tourists loved them. And the local kids loved to run them, which convinced the outsider kids that they weren't – what was that word young Jim Tuffin had used the other day? She'd forgotten it again. She was out of touch with this modern slang.

'Jonathon opens up his home on fête day, too,' she told Rosalind, 'donating the entrance money to our charity, plus there are a few houses in the village with rather nice gardens which are also open. We run horse charabanc trips from the fête to Destan House. Take one lot of people over, dump them and fetch the previous lot back. No hanging around or wasted journeys. The trick is to offer the grokkles lots of things to do, so that they don't have a chance to be bored.'

'Grokkles?' Jenny queried.

Harry grinned. 'Tourists.'

'I love the word. And the fête sounds good,' Jenny said. 'If I can help out in any way, just ask.'

Harry looked at her, decided she meant it, then looked at her watch. 'Look, I'm sorry to take the picture and run, but I have a few million things to do. And thank you, Jenny. I'll definitely take you up on that offer. Be prepared to work hard on the day.'

When Harry had left, Rosalind smiled at her daughter. 'Let's set off now and stop somewhere overnight on the way up. The Wye Valley is supposed to be lovely – we could find somewhere to stay in Shrewsbury. Brother Cadfael country.'

Jenny beamed at her. 'Wonderful. I'd love to see Shrewsbury.' She and her mother were both Brother Cadfael fans – and even Louise didn't scorn those books, though she usually read novels with more modern themes than a medieval monk who was also a detective.

What was her younger sister doing now? Jenny didn't envy her spending time with their father when he had one of his snits on.

Paul listened to the phone ringing out again. 'Where the hell is she?' He opened his office door and the secretary assigned to him looked up enquiringly. 'Keep trying this number, will you?' He rattled it off. 'I need to speak to my wife.'

There was no reply by the time he was ready to go back to the hotel. Nor had Louise and her minder returned. He paced up and down his office, fretting. What the hell had got into his family? Why were they doing this to him?

When the minder eventually brought Louise back, the woman was obviously annoyed and his daughter was wearing her sulky look – though that tarty blonde patch had been redyed to match Louise's dark hair, thank goodness.

'What happened?' he demanded, cutting through the polite phrases.

'Your daughter wished to go elsewhere. We had a small – disagreement.'

Louise let out a long, aggrieved sigh. 'I only wanted to go on the harbour cruise.'

'Your father wished you to do otherwise,' the woman said quietly, but her face had a steely look to it, which was why she'd been hired.

Paul suppressed a quick memory of Liz, laughing beside him on one of the cruises, then lying under him in bed. He was having a lot of trouble getting Liz out of his mind. She was some woman. That wimpy Bill didn't deserve her. 'You're not here to go touristing,' he told his daughter curtly.

'But it's such a waste if I don't see *anything*!'

He turned to the minder, whose official title was personal trainer. Bloody expensive, but sharp enough to read the agenda behind the overt reasons for hiring her. 'Did she do her exercise after you'd been to the hairdresser's?'

'Yes, sir. We kept active.'

He grinned. He intended to make sure Louise was so tired every night that she slept soundly and thus didn't give him any trouble. Last night she'd nearly fallen asleep over dinner.

As if to reinforce his satisfaction, Louise yawned and

sagged against the wall. The minder gave her a poke. 'Good posture, Miss Stevenson. We've already discussed its importance.'

Louise's scowl deepened, but she straightened up.

Back at the hotel Paul gave his daughter ten minutes to get ready for dinner and smiled at the look of panic on her face. He got through his own ablutions with his usual speed and tried the phone again. Nothing. And the answering service wasn't even on, though he'd told Ros to fix one up. But that was Ros all over. Dreamy and impractical. Heaven knew what she'd have done without him.

The thought of someone else managing her money was still worrying him. The sooner he got back to her and sorted that out the better.

The lawyer he'd consulted hadn't been too optimistic about overturning a trust when the money from it went straight to Ros. But Paul wanted to know what she was *doing* with all that income. When she'd told him how much it would be approximately, he'd felt sick. She was probably wasting it.

She'd always spent far too much on books and embroidery equipment. As if he didn't know what she got up to while she was away. He'd seen those pictures of hers stacked up in the attic. How many hours had she wasted on that old-fashioned rubbish? He intended to clear them out when they got back, give them to some charity. If any charity wanted them.

And when they moved to the States, embroidery would definitely not be on the agenda. He'd get her to join a health club, get her body into shape. Firm. Like Liz's.

He pressed the redial button and the phone rang again, on and on. Dammit, where was she?

The day of the fête dawned cool but fine. They'd got back the previous day after a golden interlude in Southport and Rosalind was feeling in need of exercise. She peeped into her daughter's room, but Jenny was still asleep, curled up into a tight ball like a child, with her long fair hair spread out on the pillow. She was looking so much better now, thank goodness, though she was still a bit jumpy after dark.

From the look of the early morning sun, it was going to be fine for the fête. Good. Rosalind grabbed an apple and set off, intending to pick up a newspaper. There were people bustling about the village already and an air of expectancy everywhere.

When she got back, Jenny was sitting frowning over a cup of tea.

'Something wrong, love?'

'Dad rang. Woke me up.'

'Oh?'

'He was in a foul mood. Why does he have to be so – *jarring*? You and I were away for four days and we didn't have a single cross word. Anyway, he says you're to ring him the minute you come in.'

'Oh, does he!'

Jenny looked at her in surprise. 'Aren't you going to?'

'No. Why spoil a lovely day?' Paul never rang unless he wanted her to do something, and what she intended to do today was go to the fête.

'He'll be furious.'

Rosalind shrugged.

After breakfast Jenny came down in jeans and a shirt, with a sweater tied round her waist.

Goodness, she looks so like me, Rosalind thought and felt awed, remembering the tiny baby whom she'd adored on sight. She blinked as fingers snapped in front of her face and saw her daughter laughing at her.

'Wake up, Mum! I've asked you twice what time you want to leave.'

'Oh, whenever you like.'

As they walked into the village together, Jenny asked, 'Can we go and see Jonathon's house?'

Rosalind looked at the cars turning off the main road to park in the field and the people strolling up and down, pointing to the 'quaint' houses and the 'cute' things in the shops. 'Not with hordes of other people there. I'll get him to show us round another day, just you and me. It's a lovely house and full of beautiful old objects.'

Jenny glanced sideways. 'He's been a good friend to you, hasn't he?' She felt like a voyeur at the expression on her mother's face, the tight, controlled sadness quickly replaced by that bland look her mother used as a barrier against her father when he was in one of his fusses. But why did her mother need a barrier now? Surely she hadn't fallen for this Jonathon? No, that was unthinkable. Not Mum.

'Harry and Jonathon have both been good friends to me,' Rosalind said carefully. 'Though he was the one who found me when I fell and twisted my ankle, of course.'

'You'd have been in trouble if he hadn't.'

'Oh, I dare say I'd have managed to crawl for help.'

She took a deep breath and summoned up a smile from somewhere. 'Well, let's get into it. At least we live close enough to come home if we're bored.'

But they weren't bored because Harry pounced on them as soon as they walked through the gates of the schoolyard. 'Going to treat you like locals, I'm afraid. I need someone to help out in the tea tent. Would you mind, Rosalind? And Jenny, would you help out at the skittles? I've got my nephews setting them up for people, but I need an adult to collect the money. Meg Loder's let me down again – not that it's her fault – her youngest is always catching something.'

Still talking at the top of her voice, she led Jenny through the groups of people. 'These are my nephews – Giles and Rufus.'

Jenny smiled at the two boys, both at that thin pre-puberty stage of bony limbs and jerky movements. They were very like their aunt and father. 'You'll have to explain to me what's going on. I don't know anything whatsoever about skittles.'

They stared at her solemnly, then nodded as if she'd passed some unseen test. 'All right,' one said. 'It's not hard, really.'

'I'll be off, then.' Harry left her in charge of a small table and cash box with a float of change.

The two boys hovered next to her. 'You're Australian, aren't you?' one of them asked.

Jenny grinned. 'Too right. G'day, mate.'

'I say, do people really say that?'

'Sometimes.'

And from then on, whenever there were no customers they plied her with questions about Australia, which Giles was 'doing' for a geography project and which the other boy seemed equally fascinated by.

Just before lunch, two young men appeared in front of Jenny.

'Phil Ross,' said one. 'Here to relieve you.'

The other bobbed his head. 'Ned Didburin. Mrs Larcombe sent me to guide you to food. She's got refreshments set out for the helpers in that old green tent at the rear.'

'Oh, good! I'm starving.'

He began to stroll along beside her. 'Is that an Aussie accent?'

'Mmm.'

'Thought I recognised the twang.' He looked at her sideways. Pretty. And gentle-looking, as if she had no malice in her. He liked the look of her. 'Um – you wouldn't like to come for tea with me later when the auction's over?'

Jenny stiffened. 'No, thank you.'

He gave an exaggerated sigh. 'Something I said or do I just not appeal?'

She looked at him warily. He had a kind, open sort of face. She didn't want to upset him. 'Just – something someone else did. I – haven't quite recovered.' To her horror, her voice trembled.

He looked aghast. 'I say – sorry to have roused the sleeping tiger.'

'N-not your fault. You couldn't be expected to know.' She hurried off before he could say anything else, but she was trembling still and couldn't face a crowd of people, so wandered down the main 'street' of activities. But there were people everywhere, people she didn't know, who made her feel nervous as they pushed against her, so she turned back and made her way reluctantly towards the green tent.

Ned Didburin watched her go, upset by the fear he'd seen on her face.

Later, it seemed as if fate was smiling down on him for once, for he ran into her again, this time looking even more distressed as two young guys – from London by the sound of their accents – had her cornered between two displays and were trying out their wit on her.

'Sorry lads, the lady's with me!' he called out, striding forward and hoping they wouldn't cause trouble. He wasn't the macho sort and never had been. For a moment it was touch and go, then one of them shrugged and moved off.

The other hovered, frowning in puzzlement at Jenny's distress. 'Only 'avin' a bit of fun, you know, gel. Didn't mean to upset you.'

She turned her back on them, not wanting anyone to see the tears of relief that had started flowing the minute Ned came to her rescue.

'They really didn't mean any harm,' he said softly from behind her.

She looked down at the handkerchief he had pushed into her hand and shook it out, swallowing hard as she mopped her wet face. But the tears continued to trickle down her face. 'S-sorry.'

'It must have been bad, whatever it was that upset you,' he said gently. She was still gulping and trying so desperately not to sob that his heart went out to her. 'Look, no one can see you with me standing here, so if it helps to cry it out, go ahead and water away.'

She was caught between a sob and a hiccup of laughter. 'You must think I'm a fool.'

'No. I don't, actually. The ones I think are fools are the people who keep their emotions under wraps and get all het up inside. Terrible for the old health. I was brought up that way, but I've found my way out of it now.' Thanks to an ex-girlfriend, to whom he would be eternally grateful.

She found the sound of his crisp English voice vaguely comforting. The tears had stopped now, so she mopped her eyes and blew her nose, then looked down at the handkerchief in dismay. 'Oh, I'm sorry. You must tell me where you live and I'll wash it before I give it back to you.'

'All right.' He fumbled in his pocket and produced a business card, delighted to have an excuse to see her again.

Edward Didburin, Didburin Fine Arts, Dorchester

She held out one hand. 'I'm Jenny Stevenson.'

'My friends call me Ned.' He clasped her hand, trying to think of an innocuous question. 'And what are you doing in Dorset, Miss Jenny Stevenson from down under?'

She gave him a half-smile. 'I'm taking a bit of time off to – recover. I'm a management trainee, graduated last year.'

'And do you enjoy managing things?'

'Not really.' She shrugged. 'It was Dad's idea of a good career for me.'

'You're staying round here, then?'

'Mmm. Dad's rented a house in the village. Mum's been here a while, but I only arrived a week ago. It's a lovely part of the world, Dorset. I'm really looking forward to exploring. Mum and I've just spent a few days in Southport – at a relative's house.'

He wanted to stay and talk to her. She was so soft and fair and feminine-looking. Apart from that golden tone to her skin, she wasn't at all what he'd imagined an Australian girl would be like. But a quick glance at his watch made him exclaim, 'Oh, hell! Got to go to the auction. I'm here on duty for my father, I'm afraid. Got to bid on one or two pieces. Unless – you wouldn't care to come with me, would you? It's jolly interesting.'

She looked at him doubtfully. He was only a little taller than she was, with thinning brown hair which would probably leave him bald by the time he was forty. He had kind blue eyes, not gleaming black ones, and for some reason she felt safe with him. 'That would be nice. I want to go to the auction anyway because Mum's got an embroidered picture in it. I want to be there to give her support. She's worried no one will buy it.'

'Not the slum children thing?'

'Yes.'

'But that's a *gorgeous* piece. It's the main thing I've been sent to bid on, actually.' Another glance at his watch. 'Come on, then. Let's go and see what happens to it.'

When he caught hold of her hand so they didn't get separated, she didn't draw away, but let him race her off to the auction tent, where they both arrived breathless and laughing, collapsing into two empty seats at the end of a row just as the bidding began.

* * *

Rosalind sat down at the back of the auction tent and tried to look as if she were studying the catalogue. Not that she was here to bid for anything. But she had to see what sort of person bought her picture and what price it fetched.

Harry mounted the dais, ready to get things rolling. She gave a nod of satisfaction at the turnout, then smiled at the plump, bald man who had come to sit beside her, saying something that made him smile, too. After Harry had introduced him, he tapped a hammer to quieten people down and the auction started.

It was an hour before Rosalind's embroidery came up for sale, and she was delighted to hear the woman behind her whisper, 'Wish I could afford that one. It's gorgeous, isn't it? Bound to go for tons of money.'

'Mmm. Must be an heirloom piece. Don't know how anyone can bear to part with it.'

'Doesn't say so in the catalogue. Says it's a modern piece in the Jacobean style of raised stumpwork.'

'Let's start the bidding at a hundred pounds,' the auctioneer called.

Rosalind gasped aloud. *Start* at a hundred! Did he expect it to go higher, then?

But no one bid, so the amount went down to seventy pounds, then fifty. She could feel her face going red. Perhaps Paul was right. Perhaps people didn't like that sort of old-fashioned stuff nowadays.

Then someone raised a hand and the auctioneer pointed a finger towards him. 'Thirty pounds I'm bid. I'll take it in tens from now on.'

Only a few seconds later, he pointed again, 'Forty, lady in the blue coat.'

From then on the bidding climbed steadily and Rosalind sat there in a state of shock.

'A hundred pounds.'

'Hundred and seventy . . . three hundred . . . five . . .'

'Six hundred and fifty. Any advance on six hundred and fifty?' The auctioneer looked round, gavel raised. 'No more bids? Right then, going once, going twice, sold to the gentleman in the fawn jacket. Now the next item is . . .'

Rosalind got up and stumbled out of the tent, avoiding people, slipping between the big auction tent and the smaller grey tent next to it, desperate for a moment to herself. *Six hundred and fifty pounds!* And several people had wanted to buy her picture! Joy filled her and pride, too. If someone had paid all that for her embroidery, it wasn't worthless. Or amateur.

'You all right?'

She looked up with a smile. 'Jonathon. Yes, I'm fine. Just a big overwhelmed. Did you see how much my picture fetched?'

'I did indeed. Congratulations.'

Without knowing quite how she got there, she found herself in his arms, hugging him, letting him hug her. When he bent his head, she kissed him back because it seemed the natural thing to do.

Jenny, who had followed her mother outside to congratulate her, stopped in shock at the sight of the entwined figures then tiptoed away. That was no kiss of friendship, that was the kiss of a man and woman who really fancied one another – or loved one another. Her mother's expression had been radiant as she turned to greet Jonathon and he'd been beaming down at her.

Oh, heavens, she hoped Dad never found out. He'd go off his face.

She walked to and fro at the other side of the tent, waiting for Ned to finish paying for the picture and thinking about what she'd seen. She didn't blame her mother for being tempted by a nice man like Jonathon Destan – her father had treated her like an idiot for years. Only . . . she did hope this wouldn't break up her parents' marriage.

Another thought occurred to her, a much happier one. Her father would be furious when he found out how much the embroidery had fetched and how many people had bid for it. If her mother didn't tell him, she would. Maybe from now on, he'd stop criticising her mother's hobby and realise how good her work was.

The other thing, the attraction to Jonathon Destan, was just a passing fancy, surely? Perhaps her mother had needed that to stiffen her spine. Good for the old morale to know someone fancied you.

Which brought Jenny's thoughts back to Ned. She really liked him. He wasn't good-looking, but he was kind and fun. Not at all like Michael – or her father. She not only felt safe with him but he made her chuckle with his wry remarks.

Turning, she saw him coming towards her and smiled. When he held out his hand, she put hers into it without hesitation.

Chapter Twelve

Rosalind spent the morning unable to settle to anything as she waited for Paul and Louise to arrive. When she saw his car turning into the drive, she was conscious of a strong desire to flee. She didn't want to see him. Or Louise. She sighed and remained in the bedroom.

A couple of minutes later, a voice called, 'Mum! Dad and Louise are here!'

'I'll be down in a minute, Jenny. Can you open the front door?' She'd deliberately left it locked like last time, so that he wouldn't be able to take her by surprise.

It wasn't until she heard voices in the hall that Rosalind went downstairs. Paul was so busy ordering Louise to fetch the rest of the luggage in, he wasn't even looking round for his wife.

Louise tossed a huff in her mother's direction, then slouched off.

'I'll come and help you.' Jenny pushed her sister out of the door.

Paul gave Rosalind a quick hug. 'Well, woman, I'm back now for a while.'

'Good.' But it didn't feel good. It felt as if a trap had closed round her. 'Come and have a coffee.'

Louise came back in, hesitated, then at a nudge from Jenny put the luggage down and went over to hug her mother properly. 'Fancy us all being here in England together.'

'Not quite all. Tim's not here.'

Louise's eyes filled with tears. 'I miss him.'

'Well, you've got Jenny and me, so you won't exactly be lonely.' To her surprise, Rosalind saw Louise shoot an uncertain glance at her father.

'We'll see about that.'

The air was suddenly full of tension.

'Louise has let us all down,' Paul said, giving his daughter one of his icy looks, 'behaved badly to her grandmother, *stolen* your car and used it, and worst of all, got into drugs.'

For heaven's sake, Rosalind thought, *why is he making such a drama of it? He's already told me this on the phone.*

'I haven't decided yet what to do about her, or whether I can even trust her to behave if I leave her here with you.'

Louise looked so unhappy Rosalind went straight across to put her arm round her, feeling the initial stiffness give way to a convulsive hug. 'Well, until you have decided, I shall be able to enjoy the company of both my daughters.' While he, no doubt, would be going away within a day or so, even if he did intend to use this as his base from now on.

Oh, Lord, she was doing more talking inside her head than she was with her mouth. She had to stop this.

As they sat and drank coffee, Rosalind realised she and her daughters were all watching Paul and guarding what they said. He was the only one who seemed at ease as he told them about Hong Kong and the project there. 'The chairman doesn't hang around when a new man needs selecting.'

Later, he went upstairs to change. When his wife didn't follow, he called down impatiently, 'Rosalind? Aren't you going to come and unpack for me?'

She didn't really want to be alone with him. Aware of her daughters' eyes on her, she gathered her strength together for the first minor confrontation. 'I'm busy down here at the moment. If you stick your dirty clothes in the linen basket, I'll put a wash on later.'

There was silence from upstairs, no sound of movement, even.

Louise stood up. 'I – I'd better unpack, too.' She saw her mother and sister's surprise. 'He can get grouchy if you – if—' She burst into tears.

Rosalind, who had never seen Louise so cowed, went to put her arms round her again. 'Well, before you do go up, let me say again how lovely it is to see you, even if I don't approve of what you've done.'

Louise stared at her for a moment, eyes wet with tears. 'I'm glad to see you, too,' she said in a gruff voice, then glanced upstairs. 'I'd better go and unpack, though.'

When she'd gone Jenny looked at her mother and whispered, 'What's he been doing to make her so meek?'

'I don't know.' And she definitely didn't like it. Louise had misbehaved, and badly, but it seemed wrong to knock all the spirit out of her. She'd always been such a lively child.

Paul came clumping down the stairs and went to dump some things in 'his' office. 'Not a bad house, really, is it?' he asked from the kitchen doorway.

Rosalind, who'd been talking quietly to Jenny, broke off and nodded. He turned away again.

'He always expects us to jump to attention, doesn't he?' Jenny asked softly.

'He does, rather.' Rosalind heard him go into the living room and her heart started pounding in her chest. She had left her embroideries up on the wall for the first time ever.

'Ros? Could you come here a moment?'

'Don't let him take them down,' Jenny whispered.

'I won't.' She took a deep breath and walked into the living room. 'Something wrong?'

'Why have you brought those?' he demanded, pointing to the embroideries. 'You know I hate the damned things.'

'Since you weren't here, I decided to please myself. I happen to like having them around.'

He had already unhooked one. She took it from his hand and put it back on the wall. 'Leave it, Paul.'

'There were already pictures up, a matching pair, which went well with the décor of this room, so there was no need for this. How did you get them out here so quickly? What did that cost, eh?'

'I don't see why you're making such a fuss about this if they're so unimportant.'

Their eyes met, held, then a look of scorn came over his face. 'What do you think people will say if we have those old-fashioned things displayed on the wall? I thought you had a bit more sense than that, Ros, I really did. What you do in your own time is one thing, but what you show the world is quite another ball game.'

'Apparently I haven't any sense at all, because I love to have my pictures hanging where I can see them and I don't care what other people think. I'm the one who lives here, after all.'

'Well, they're coming down when people visit. They're too amateurish.'

Jenny appeared in the doorway. 'They're not amateurish at all, Dad. They're beautiful.'

He turned to glare at her. 'You can keep out of this, young lady.'

'I don't see why. I like looking at them, too, and those prints were trashy. Besides, I don't think Mum will tell you, but one of her embroideries fetched six hundred and fifty pounds at a charity auction two days ago. There was intense bidding from several people, but a fine art dealer bought it – to sell in his gallery.'

'You're making this up.'

'Why on earth should I?' Jenny went to put her arm round her mother's shoulders, feeling the tension there, angry that he'd been so unkind within minutes of arriving. 'I'm very proud of Mum. And everyone here has *admired* her embroideries. People did at home, too. There's only you who doesn't like them, actually.'

The silence was heavy with menace. 'Well, I definitely don't. And I have to live here, too.'

Rosalind intervened. 'How long are you staying this time, then, Paul? One day? Two? I think you can put up with them for that long.'

'I'm leaving tomorrow.' He saw the scorn on her face and snapped, 'I have to report in, don't I? I've brought our younger daughter down for you to keep an eye on, so I did *put family first*, contrary to what you accused me of last time. But now I have to go up to London to make a full report to the chairman about Hong Kong.'

Rosalind's voice was without inflection. 'Yes. Of course.'

'But I'll be spending the weekends down here from now on, so I should have some say in what I have to look at.'

Did he never give up? she thought wearily, wondering if this was worth it. There was a knock on the front door before she could answer him.

'I'll get it.' Jenny was worried about the anger on her father's face. Why was he being so brutal about her mother's embroideries? 'Oh, Mrs Larcombe! How lovely to see you! Won't you come in? Mum and Dad are in the living room. You haven't met Dad yet, have you?'

Harry marched forward with her usual aura of energy and purpose to plonk two kisses in the air above her friend's cheeks. 'Rosalind! How are you today?'

After the introductions, they sat down to chat while Jenny went to make some coffee.

'Nice girl, that,' Harry said. 'Big help on the skittles.' She turned to Paul. 'You must be very proud of your wife.'

'Must I? Why?'

'Why, because of those.' Harry waved one hand towards the wall. 'Damned fine work. A much smaller one fetched six hundred and fifty pounds at the fête.'

His smile had quite vanished. 'Amazing. But some folk will buy anything to support a charity.'

Harry stared at him incredulously, then turned to Rosalind as if he hadn't spoken. 'I popped round because George Didburin wants to come and see you about your work. He's interested in representing you. All right if I give him your phone number and address? You do have other pieces for sale, don't you?'

Happiness surged through Rosalind. 'Yes. And I'd love to talk to him.'

'You don't need to huckster your work around,' Paul snapped. 'You'll have enough on with—'

Harry was not to be deflected. She held up one hand. 'Just a minute!' she said, before turning to Rosalind again. 'Did you mean it about repairing Araminta's embroidery for us?'

'Of course I did.'

'Who's Araminta?' demanded Paul. 'And why can't she repair her own embroidery? My wife's not a damned sewing woman!'

Harry guffawed. 'Araminta's one of my ancestors, seventeenth century, and your wife offered to repair an embroidery she did then. It's rather valuable.' She'd taken an instant dislike to this man, who reminded her of her stockbroker – good at his job, she'd guess, but would tread on anyone to get a profit.

It was with relief that Rosalind showed Harry to the door ten minutes later, because Harry gave as good as she got, was impervious to subtle insults and was quite prepared to be downright rude to Paul.

On the doorstep Harry leant close to Rosalind and whispered, 'Don't let that husband of yours put you down!'

Then she winked and raised her voice. 'George wants to make your embroideries the centrepiece of his next needlework exhibition. So don't give away any of them from now on – except one to me for next year's fête, of course.'

Rosalind stood by the door watching her friend stride down the drive, then took a deep breath, squared her shoulders and went back inside the house.

I don't even want to see Paul, she thought. Guilt shot through her at the memory of Jonathon kissing her, congratulating her, being glad for her. She stopped moving for a moment till it faded. *He* didn't bark orders at her and disparage her embroideries.

Paul appeared in the doorway of the sitting room. 'Ros? For heaven's sake, are you going to stand out there all day?'

She sighed and went in to continue the battle.

By afternoon Rosalind was near screaming point. Paul was in his office, fiddling with something on his laptop. 'I – um, think I'll go out for a walk,' she told her daughters. 'Anyone else want to come?'

Louise shook her head. 'Dad'll want me to go jogging soon. That's enough exercise for one day.'

'You – jogging?'

'Yes. It's his idea of rehabilitation.' Louise started fiddling with the handle of her mug. 'And I have lost some flabbiness, even in the short time since we started. He hired this personal trainer for me while we were in Hong Kong. I thought she was just – you know, a minder for the naughty girl. But she really was a personal trainer and she taught me all sorts of things. So I might keep the exercising up. See how I go.'

'You look all right to me, love. You've definitely lost weight, however you did it.'

'Oh, Mum, I'm just thin. I don't have any tone. And,' she blushed, 'I lost the weight because I wasn't eating. I was – you know, taking these amphetamine pills. They were wonderful. You didn't feel at all hungry and you were simply bursting with energy – but I wasn't *seriously* into drugs, whatever Dad says! I was just – you know, trying things out. Pot isn't a hard drug. Everyone smokes it. It ought to be legalised. It's no worse than alcohol.'

'So they say. I'm not so sure. They wouldn't ban it for nothing.' Sadness gripped Rosalind suddenly. 'Tim used to smoke it, too, didn't he? Then he went on to worse things.'

'I suppose so.' There was silence, then Louise looked over her shoulder and asked in a low voice, 'You haven't heard from him, have you? I mean, I know he wouldn't contact Dad, but I hoped he might have at least written you a card. Just to let you know he's OK and all that.'

'I haven't heard a thing since that last postcard, which you saw.'

'Are you worried about him?'

'Very. I worry about you all. But Tim – well, he could be dead and I,' her voice broke, 'I wouldn't even know it.'

Louise was near tears. 'He isn't! He can't be!'

There was silence, then Rosalind said, 'I must get out while I can.' She went to find Jenny, who was reading a book in the conservatory. 'Do you want to come for a walk, love?'

'Not just now, thanks. Ned said he might ring.' Jenny didn't want to get heavy with anyone, but it'd be nice to have a date or two.

'I'll go on my own, then.'

Paul came in. 'Go where?'

'Out for a walk. And to pick up a couple of things at the shops.'

'It's going to rain. Take the car.'

She was always surprised at how little he used his own feet. Oh, he trained in the gym. And jogged. Religiously. But he rarely walked anywhere for the pleasure of it. She didn't take the car but picked up her umbrella instead. And when the rain got heavy she went to sit in the little café in the village.

Jonathon came in and saw her gazing sightlessly through the rain-streaked window. It seemed like the answer to a prayer to him. He'd been wondering how to contact her.

She saw him and her sad expression lightened as she gestured to the seat next to her.

Beaming, he hurried across. 'On your own?'

'Yes. I'm the only real walker in the family. When it started to rain, I took shelter here.'

'Mind if I join you for a cuppa?'

'I'd love it.' She realised her voice had been too warm and looked down at the table, saying more temperately, 'Please do.'

When his pot of tea and chocolate cupcakes had arrived they sat in silence, then he said, 'I miss you dreadfully, Rosalind.' He didn't look at her, just stirred his tea round and round.

She couldn't be less than honest with him. 'I miss you, too.'

Another silence. 'Harry says you're going to repair Araminta's picture for us.'

'Yes. I'd really like to do that. Perhaps you could bring it round to the house sometime?'

'Or you could come and get it?'

'You must be sick of people invading your house. Harry said the horse charabanc was full every trip on the day of the fête.'

'I enjoy having people round, actually. It can get very lonely with the boys away. And I left showing folk round to Mrs Durden-Jones, who runs the local historical society. She knows nearly as much about the place as we Destans do, but she puts it across better and handles the groups better, too.' He leant forward and said conspiratorially, 'I'm a failure at handling crowds, actually. I'm too soft with them.'

She sighed. 'I've been too soft with everyone, I think.'

'How's it going? Now your husband's home, I mean. How's it really going?'

A shrug was the only answer and seeing the distress on her face he started talking about the fête instead, telling her how pleased Harry was about the takings, which looked like creating a record.

As they were parting Rosalind said, 'I miss you so much, Jonathon dear.' Then, as if terrified by what she had said, she turned and rushed off.

He wished he had the right to follow her.

Chapter Thirteen

Paul answered the front door. 'Yes?'

'George Didburin.' The man on the doorstep was plump and bald, but held himself with casual confidence. He was dressed immaculately and spoke with a drawling, educated accent, very English. He proffered a business card and waved one hand towards his companion. 'My son and partner, Ned. We're looking for Rosalind Stevenson. She's expecting us.'

Paul took the card and examined it cursorily, not at all impressed by the accent or appearance of his visitor. 'Ros! It's that art fellow for you.' He was annoyed at all this fuss over his wife's hobby, felt betrayed by it. Who'd ever have thought people would get excited about bloody embroideries?

Still, if there was money to be made from them, he'd better make sure no one cheated her. She hadn't the faintest idea how to push for the best bargain. He held the door wider. 'I suppose you'd better come in.'

George stepped into the hall, taking in far more than

was immediately apparent. Good-looking chap, Stevenson, but the smile didn't reach his eyes. He wondered what the wife was like. He hadn't had a chance to meet her after the fête. Ned said she was pleasant but with no sparkle.

Well, sparkle or not, George hoped she had some more pieces like the one of those children. Very touching scene, that. Brilliant needlework, too, with some unusual uses of materials. But it was the artistic style that made it valuable, the eye for a composition. He hoped the other pieces were of the same quality. It had been a while since he'd discovered a new talent.

Rosalind hurried down the stairs, wishing the art dealer had come after Paul had left. She advanced across the hall, with her right hand outstretched. 'Mr Didburin? I'm *so* pleased to meet you.'

Why doesn't she tell him how humbly grateful she is for his interest while she's at it? Paul thought, watching her closely. Honestly, she was such a fool. Look at her body language. Even a blind man could read it. She was putting all the cards into her opponent's hand before the game even began.

George presented Rosalind with a business card – you had to be careful nowadays when dealing with a husband and wife, treat them equally and all that, and anyway he was here to see *her*, not that cold fish beside her. He clasped her hand in both of his, holding on to it for a minute as he studied her. Well, at least her smile reached her eyes but what the hell was she nervous of? People didn't usually find him intimidating. Then he saw her glance flicker uncertainly towards her husband and back again. Ah.

'Shall we go and sit down, Ros?' Paul prompted, his voice impatient.

'Oh, yes. Yes, of course. Do come this way, Mr Didburin.'
She led the way into the sitting room and indicated a chair.

George didn't even see her gesture because he'd noticed
the pictures on the wall. 'Do you mind?' He didn't wait for
an answer but walked across to examine them. 'Aaah!' He
wasn't aware he'd made an approving noise, wasn't aware
of anything except the pieces. They were exquisite. Oh, yes!
Abso-bloody-lutely exquisite.

Excitement filled him, rushing along his veins and bringing
a slight flush to his fair complexion. There was nothing to beat
the thrill of discovering a new talent, nothing. And such an
unusual talent, too. Her pictures weren't just pretty, they had
guts. That was the only way he could phrase that indefinable
something that meant an artist had captured some essence
of life, some wonderful essence that would bring people of
discernment flocking to buy their work.

'What do you think?' Paul asked as the silence dragged
on and the guest made no attempt to take a seat.

George continued to ignore him. He stabbed a finger
towards an Elizabethan lady in full costume with a miniature
ruff, wondering how Mrs Stevenson had managed to do
that so accurately on such a small scale. 'This one is pretty
and will sell, but this other,' he stabbed a finger at an old
lady sitting on a park bench, looking suspiciously at the
world as she watched some children play, 'is masterly. You
should stay away from the pretty scenes and capture Life –
with a capital L. It'll sell better.'

Rosalind flushed. 'Oh, well, I—'

'Could you tell us a bit about yourself, Mr Didburin?' Paul
cut in smoothly. 'We're happy that you like the embroideries,

of course, but what are your credentials for handling my wife's work? Or for passing judgement on them?'

Rosalind stared at him in horror.

There was the sound of a phone ringing, footsteps, then Louise called, 'Dad! It's for you. The chairman.'

Paul froze in instant response to that magic word, murmured something which might have been an excuse and left swiftly, pausing to hiss at his wife, 'Leave any negotiations about prices to me.'

Embarrassment reddened her cheeks. He had sounded like a schoolmaster ordering a pupil around – and a scornful schoolmaster dealing with a stupid pupil, at that.

'I'm afraid I prefer to deal directly with the artist,' George said mildly to Rosalind, feeling sorry for the poor downtrodden woman. 'I like to develop a *personal* relationship with my clients. No intermediaries.'

She felt overwhelmed with embarrassment at Paul's all-too-obvious assumption that she couldn't handle things herself. 'I'll explain that to my husband, because I'd prefer to deal directly with you, as well. If you're going to buy more of my work, that is.'

'I hope I am. Do you have much completed?'

'About fifty pieces. But most of them are back in Australia.'

He nodded, smiling gently, exhilaration still coursing through him. *Fifty!* Oh, yes! He had definitely made a find. 'If they're as good as this lot, I won't guarantee to make you rich, but I will guarantee you recognition of your talent. And a fairly steady income.'

'Oh.' She went pink with pleasure. 'Are you sure I'm – well, good enough?'

He looked at her incredulously. She really meant it. She was that uncertain of herself. 'Yes, very sure. I'm a bit of an expert on embroideries, actually. And these are first-rate.' It was about time for a revival of interest in this particular form of needlework.

'Dad's the top expert in Britain on raised stumpwork pieces, actually,' Ned put in. 'In Europe, even.'

George smiled deprecatingly at Rosalind. 'Bit of a passion of mine, embroidery. And in my judgement, Mrs Stevenson, you have considerable talent.' He paused, unable to think of a tactful phrase. 'Do you really want your husband to negotiate prices in advance for you?'

'I'm not sure what you mean by that.'

'Well, let me try to explain how I usually work before you decide. Prices are a delicate point until I've got you established as an artist. I'd much rather take a few of your embroideries – about twenty or so would give me enough for a good display – pay you a retainer and then arrange an exhibition. In the meantime I'll show your pieces round and gauge reactions, though I'm pretty sure your stuff will take.' He patted his chest. 'I get a feeling here when I discover a new talent. I've got it now. Strongly.'

Delight flooded through her. 'You make me feel very happy, Mr Didburin, with your expert appreciation. And I'd definitely like you to handle my work. I couldn't work with someone I didn't – well, trust and respect. The embroideries mean too much to me.'

'Call me George. And,' he remembered what her husband had called her, 'you're – Ros, is it?'

'No. Only my husband calls me that. I prefer my full name, actually – Rosalind.'

'Rosalind it is, then. Can you get the other embroideries sent over from Australia?'

'Yes.' She hesitated. 'But there are a few I don't want to sell. They mean too much to me.'

'Would you consider showing them anyway? We could put a sold sticker on them. If they're good, they'll help draw people in.'

'I – yes, why not?'

'How soon can you have them here?'

'Oh. Well, I can phone my mother. She'll go round to the house and take them to the shipper. They'd be here within the week, I should think, air freight. They're not framed or anything, though.'

He sighed in delight. 'Great! I'd prefer my own framer to deal with them anyway. She's one of the best in the country at preparing and framing embroideries! Give me a call when they arrive, then bring them over and have lunch with me in Dorchester. I'll show you round my little gallery.' His eyes twinkled and he lowered his voice. 'On your own, perhaps?'

'Yes, definitely.' Paul was probably packing already. The chairman never rang just to say hello.

George got up and went to examine the pictures again, the framed ones on the wall, then the unframed ones on the dining-room table, the ones Jenny had brought. He was still standing near the latter when his host came back.

Paul consulted his watch. Was that fellow going to spend all day gaping at these bits of cloth? He needed to set off for London and would do so as soon as these two had left. That fellow was damned rude. Hadn't even turned round to acknowledge his host's return. He waited a moment, then prompted, 'Well, what do you think?'

'I like them very much.'

'How much are they worth?'

Rosalind interrupted. 'It's too soon to tell that, Paul. I'm sending for some of the others from Australia before we settle anything with Mr Didburin.' She was ashamed of how nervous she felt, how hard it was to stand up to Paul.

'There will be no discount for quantity,' Paul said severely.

George stared at him, absolutely gobsmacked, then said in a chill tone, 'It's not a question of *quantity* with works of art as wonderful as these, Mr Stevenson. When the others arrive, we'll put on a display in my gallery, invite a few selected buyers from the trade and a few of the top collectors, and that'll help us gauge the market.'

Paul snorted in disgust. 'I prefer to talk prices *before* I begin a contract.'

George had had enough of this. He walked across and looked his host firmly in the eye. 'But I shan't be signing a contract with *you*, Mr Stevenson. I'll be dealing with your wife. She's the one with the talent.'

At the sight of Stevenson's outraged expression, Ned hastily converted a choke of laughter into a cough, hiding his face in his handkerchief and clearing his throat loudly before he dared take it away.

'Nonetheless, I am the one with business understanding in this family and if I'm not satisfied with the terms, we'll take them elsewhere.'

Shame stiffened Rosalind's backbone. 'Paul, I'm quite happy with what Mr Didburin wishes to do. How can he decide anything when he's only seen a few of my pieces?'

The look he gave her was icy, then he glanced at his watch again and clicked his tongue in exasperation. 'I have to leave right away. The chairman wants a full briefing, then we have a shut-up, lock-up planning session for a few days. Very well, then, Didburin, we'll leave it at that for the moment. Nothing agreed to. Nothing to bind either of us. We'll send for some more stock. Negotiate when that arrives.'

George closed his eyes in pain at that word. *Stock!* What a philistine this man was!

'I'll see Mr Didburin out while you start packing.' Rosalind led the way hastily towards the front door. The men exchanged curt nods of farewell, then Paul ran up the stairs two at a time whistling under his breath, a busy, tuneless sound that meant he was already mentally far away.

As they walked into the hall Ned wondered how best to ask to see Jenny. Hearing footsteps, he glanced sideways and there she was. 'Jenny, hi!' he called, forgetting the others in his pleasure at meeting her again.

She had been deep in thought but smiled at the sight of him. 'Ned! How nice to see you!' He'd told her he might phone and she'd been hoping he would, because she was desperate to get out of the house and spend time with someone of her own age who was pleasant and uncomplicated. You could cut the atmosphere here with a knife since her father's arrival.

Ned moved towards her, taking her hand, holding it in both his own. 'I was going to phone you, then Father said he was coming over, so I tagged along. Your mother's other embroideries are absolutely wonderful.'

Jenny beamed at him. 'I hope you told Dad that.'

'Yes.' He hesitated then whispered, 'I don't think he believed us, though. He started talking about "no discounts for quantity" and "not signing a contract" – that sort of thing.'

She began to look anxious, which was not what he'd intended.

'But your mother stood up to him,' Ned added hastily.

Her eyes were wide with what was surely disbelief. 'She did?'

'Well—' He sighed. He didn't want to lie to her. Not now, not ever. 'Sort of. She slid sideways, so to speak, and managed to postpone a decision – on his part, not on hers or ours. We would definitely like to develop your mother as an artist and I think she'd like us to represent her.'

'Dad won't admit to himself how good she is.'

'Well, luckily he got summoned to the phone and we were able to set the ground rules while he was out. My father has a top reputation in the trade. He'll deal fairly with your mother, I promise you.'

She betrayed the same nervous embarrassment as her mother had. 'Oh, I'm sure he will. It's just – well, Dad might interfere.'

He saw his father and Mrs Stevenson watching them from the front door and got to the point. 'Look, my father's going to have lunch with Mrs Larcombe after this. He's got a bit of a soft spot for her, values stuff for her every year for the fête, then has a post-mortem on prices afterwards. I wondered if you'd take pity on me and come out for a pub lunch or something while they're nattering.'

'Oh. Well, I don't know.'

'Just to the pub and back,' he urged gently. 'You'll be quite safe with me there.'

'You – understand? It's not you, it's—' Her voice trailed away and tears filled her soft blue eyes.

'I can guess. A little.' He laid one hand on his chest and put on a mock-solemn expression. 'I promise you I'm trustworthy and reliable, Ms Stevenson. In fact, I can get references to that effect. In triplicate. Or centiplicate – if there is such a thing. I'll take a lie detector test, too, if that helps.'

She gave a gurgle of laughter. 'Now you're being silly. All right. I'd love to come and have lunch with you. You go ahead and I'll meet you there.' She didn't want her father interfering.

'See you in half an hour, then, at the Destan Arms. Turn right when you come in from the car park.'

'Lovely.'

She watched him stride along the drive. He seemed so nice and uncomplicated. Surely she wasn't making a misjudgement this time?

'What was all that about?'

Jenny jumped in shock and turned to see her mother smiling at her. She'd been miles away. 'I'm going to have lunch with Ned at the pub.'

'Good. He's a nice boy. I like him.'

'Boy? He's not a boy. He's—' She broke off, realising how little she knew about him.

'His father is a close friend of Harry's, so I'm sure you'll be safe with him.'

Jenny leant her head against her mother's shoulder for a moment, in wordless acknowledgement of her understanding. Then she pulled away. 'I've got to go and get ready. Come and help me choose something to wear.'

'All right. But we'd better be quick. I have to do your father's packing.'

The thought of Paul leaving filled Rosalind with relief. She'd never expected it to be so difficult to get on with him. He seemed much worse than usual. Had he changed so much in such a short time?

Or had she?

As she waved him off a short time later, worry and guilt sat heavily on her. But she didn't intend to let him negotiate with George. Definitely not. She smiled faintly. And she hadn't done too badly at standing up for herself – for a beginner. She would improve with practice. She was determined to.

And Paul would adjust too, learn that she wasn't to be ordered around.

Surely he would?

Tim tried to phone his parents from a public phone in a large city, and the answerphone gave his grandmother's number, so he phoned her instead. He was amazed when she told him his parents and sisters were in England, but delighted. It was so much closer and he could afford the air fare without having to beg help from his father.

When he got off the plane at Heathrow, he fretted his way through customs and then tried to vanish into the crowd as quickly as possible, because officials made him nervous. Not that he was carrying anything illegal. He wasn't that stupid.

He had no luggage to collect, since he'd lost everything he'd taken to America except the passport and money he'd hidden in the cemetery. His hand luggage contained a change of underclothing, a couple of new T-shirts and basic toiletries.

He found his way to the coach station and bought a ticket to the nearest stop, then waited for the coach to leave, leaning against a wall, his head aching and that ever-present need for a fix gnawing at his belly.

I'm on the last stretch now, he told himself. *I can hold out. Once I'm with Mum things will start to improve.* He needed quite desperately to see her. And even if the old man was around, seeing him wouldn't be a problem for long. It never was, because he rarely stayed for more than a day or two.

Rosalind dialled her mother's number, delighted to hear Audrey's voice. 'Mum?'

'Darling! I was just going to call you. How are you?'

'I'm well. Mum, I've got such good news! An art dealer has bought one of my embroideries for over six hundred pounds. And it was quite a small one, too.'

'Goodness!'

'And – and he wants to see the rest of my work. He says he can sell them for me. He really likes them.'

'Oh, Rosalind, I'm so happy for you! You have a real talent there and it deserves recognition.'

Rosalind beamed at the phone. 'Could you go and get the rest of the finished embroideries from the attic for me and have them shipped out as soon as possible? You've got my credit card number. Use that to pay for them.'

'Yes, of course I can. I'll get John to help me.' She took a quick decision. 'Rosalind – I have some other news for you.'

'Oh?'

'Tim phoned. From America.'

'Tim did! *Tim!* Oh, Mum, is he all right? I've been so *worried* about him, absolutely frantic.' Tears welled in her eyes. Paul refused point-blank to discuss their son, got angry if she so much as mentioned his name, but not mentioning Tim didn't stop her worrying about him.

Audrey took a deep breath. 'I'm pretty sure he's in trouble.'

That didn't surprise Rosalind. She'd felt for a while that something was wrong. She wondered sometimes if she was fooling herself when she got these premonitions, or if all mothers felt like that at times. 'I wish I could see him.'

'You can. He's on his way to join you in England.' She waited for an exclamation of pleasure, but there was nothing, no sound at all. Had they been cut off? 'Rosalind? Are you still there?'

'Yes, Mum. I just – I can't help it. I – oh!' She turned blindly to Louise, thrust the phone at her, then collapsed on the telephone seat, sobbing loudly. She'd been out of her mind with worry, but now she knew he was all right, it had all come bursting out. He was alive, her Tim was alive – and coming to join them in Burraford. Oh, it was the best news she'd had for a long time! The very best.

Louise held a short, excited conversation with her grandmother, then put the phone down and hovered beside her mother, who was still sobbing loudly. In the end, she couldn't bear to see such pain, put one arm round the heaving shoulders and gave her mother a hug.

After a while, she coaxed her into the living room. 'I'll get you a cup of coffee, shall I?'

'Please.'

'Tim will be all right now.'

'Yes. I hope so. But it's been so long. What has he been *doing*?'

When Louise set a mug down beside her mother, she, too, had suspiciously bright eyes. 'I've missed him,' she confessed, 'and I've been worried about him, too.'

Then they both wept, putting their arms round one another and sobbing for ages. It didn't occur to Rosalind until much later how close she'd felt to Louise at that moment. Or how much comfort her daughter had been to her, as if she were another adult, a friend.

She was deeply relieved Paul hadn't been there to mock her foolishness – and that she would have Tim to herself for a while before her husband came back.

In the Destan Arms, Jenny and Ned chatted carefully, both feeling rather self-conscious. Neither paid much attention to the food, but each paid a lot of surreptitious attention to the other.

'Would you like to come out with me one night?' he asked. 'For a meal or to the pictures – or they have some good shows at the theatre in Bournemouth sometimes? It's not all that far to drive.'

'I—' The thought of going into Bournemouth at night with someone who was still a virtual stranger made her feel nervous, much as she liked Ned. 'We could go out for a meal perhaps. Here? It's a nice pub. Just – chat, get to know one another.'

'Whatever you like, Jenny. Just as long as I can see you. How about tonight? In fact, let's just stay here in this corner for the rest of the day.'

That made her chuckle and feel warm inside. 'Are you sure about coming here? You'll have to drive over from Dorchester again.'

'It'll be more than worth it to see you.'

She let him take her home, but didn't invite him in.

And the news that was waiting for her inside made her feel even happier. Tim was safe! The three women opened a bottle of wine and drank to his health, not even waiting till the evening meal.

'We'll drink to your embroidery, too,' Jenny said, raising her glass. 'Here's to my famous mother.'

'To your embroidery, Mum!' Louise echoed. She took only a small sip and put her hand across the top when Jenny tried to refill her glass. 'Wine's not good for the figure or for my fitness level.' To her surprise, she was now enjoying the jogging.

'We're not going back to that dieting stuff again, are we?' Rosalind asked with mock severity. 'I don't want a daughter who looks like a stick insect topped by a skull, thank you very much.'

The entente cordiale faded a little. Louise scowled at her mother. 'What I want is—'

Rosalind stood up, her mood of euphoria evaporating suddenly and exhaustion setting in. She needed to be on her own now. 'I don't really care what you *want*, Louise. Other people have needs, even mothers, and it's about time you noticed them. You don't live in a vacuum, you know. You're part of a family.'

Louise's voice was aggressive. 'Well, I don't think—'

'Your father's left a long list of instructions about what you're to do with yourself for the rest of the week. I've put it on your dressing table. I agree with him absolutely about the need to watch you carefully. I've been too soft with you in the past. I don't feel quite as soft any more. You should understand that. *Everyone* should understand that.'

She saw them both staring at her in amazement, mouths gaping in shock. 'I'm going up to my room now. I need a bit of peace and quiet. I don't want disturbing unless it's an emergency.'

The sisters exchanged glances as she walked out of the room.

'He's pretty rude to her sometimes,' Jenny whispered, 'but she's learning how to fight back at last.'

'He's pretty rude to everyone. But that's not my fault. And anyway, she should have stood up to him years ago.'

'Oh, yes? Like you stood up to him when he found out about your cavorting?'

'You just mind your own bloody business, Jenny Stevenson!'

Although the row was very loud indeed, their mother didn't come down to stop the quarrelling, as she usually did.

And when the shouting had petered out and they'd both – separately – got themselves a cup of coffee, Louise looked upwards and asked, 'Do you think she's all right?'

'I don't know.' Jenny remembered her mother kissing Jonathon Destan at the fête. They'd looked so right together, so tender. Suddenly she felt tired. Her mother wasn't the only one who needed a bit of peace. 'I think I'll go up and get ready for Ned. He'll be here soon.'

Louise was left with the television. And her own thoughts. Anger was still simmering inside her, but she didn't dare poke her nose outside the house. Her father's scribbled instructions had been very specific about that.

Here she was in England, but not where there was anything going on. No, she had to be stuck in the middle of nowhere being treated like a child. It wasn't fair.

Then she brightened. But Tim was coming. Things would brighten up when he arrived. They always did. He'd work out a way to get round these stupid restrictions, though she might keep up with the running, persuade him to join in, even. Her body was getting firmer, developing quite a good shape, actually. She didn't like to admit that her father was right about that, but he was, the bastard. She picked up the half-empty bottle of wine, pushed the cork in and put it in the fridge.

In her room, Rosalind shut her ears to the noise from below. To help her resist the urge to go down and tell them both off – which had never done any good in the past and wasn't likely to do any good now – she went and got out her embroidery.

She sat for a moment or two staring at the pretty art nouveau scene, not really seeing anything, still trying to control the confusion inside her head. When she felt calmer, she put that piece away and took out the family portrait.

Concentrate on Life with a capital L, George Didburin had said. Well, this family portrait was no pretty scene. Her own figure with its wishy-washy pastels upset her – but it was true to life – or at least, true to what she had been for so long. Paul's figure continued to disturb her.

She would never exhibit or sell this piece. It was for her and her alone, and it was going to reflect her whole life, which was turning out to be a failure in so many ways. When she saw it all more clearly, surely she'd know what to do about it.

Jenny, she thought. *I'll make a start on her figure today.* She got out her family photos and the sketching materials, but ruined several drafts. The happy smiling girl in the photo wasn't the Jenny of today or the younger Jenny of her memories. She closed her eyes, trying to visualise the figure she needed and suddenly realised how nervous her elder daughter often was. In fact, Jenny had always been slightly nervous of life.

Rosalind took out a fresh piece of paper and this time the sketch grew beneath her fingers like a thing alive in its own right. When she put her pencil down, she stared at it, knowing it was good, really good. Or it could be. But would she be able to translate the drawing into an embroidered figure? Well, she could only try. Carefully she cut the sketch out.

Now, where to put Jenny? As if of its own volition, the figure settled at the back of the scene, standing by itself. Only it was the wrong size to go there, so she took another piece of paper to sketch it smaller. Yes. That was right. Poor Jenny. As alone as her mother.

No, Rosalind frowned, Jenny hadn't been quite alone. There had been the dog. Zip had been more Jenny's than anyone's, spending a lot of time cuddled up to her. She'd taken him for walks, fed him and looked after him very responsibly, even when she was quite small. And when Zip had died at the age of thirteen – why did dogs live for such a short time when they could be such a comfort to people? – there had been a cat because Paul had refused to have another dog. Sasha, the cat had been called. A nice creature, again devoted to Jenny.

Then Sasha had been killed by a car and Jenny had begged and pleaded for another dog. Paul had refused point-blank, even though it would hardly have affected him.

Guilt shot through Rosalind. *I should have let Jenny have her dog*, she thought, *I really should. I was wrong. Paul wasn't around half the time, even then. If we'd got a dog while he was away and presented him with a fait accompli, he'd not have been able to do anything about it.*

Or would he? You never knew with Paul. He could be ruthless at times, not against her of course, but against other people. She frowned. No, she was fooling herself. He was ruthless with her, too – though he meant it for her own good. At least, she'd always believed he did. Now she was no longer sure of that.

Under her fingers – such clever fingers tonight – Zip took shape, almost as big as Jenny because that was how he came out, and then the cat, slightly smaller than the other two, but certainly not cat size. They'd been such a comfort to Jenny, those animals. It was right to show them larger than life. And all three of them were looking away from Paul. Funny, that.

But Rosalind had come to believe lately that her needle didn't lie, so she didn't attempt to change the figures.

She knew it would upset Jenny if she saw this portrait – well, it hurt Rosalind to do it – but she continued working. She heard Jenny call farewell and go out with Ned. She heard the television blaring from downstairs. When Louise came up to bed, calling out goodnight, she answered, but didn't go out to see her.

Later Jenny came home, humming as she ran upstairs. She

hesitated outside her mother's workroom, but went to bed without coming in. Which suited Rosalind at the moment.

The house fell silent. She didn't go downstairs, because she wasn't hungry. For some reason she was consumed by impatience to get the figure done. At one point she got herself a drink of water from the bathroom, but continued sewing until her eyes grew too tired to focus. And by that time, the essence of Jenny had been captured.

Only then did she go to bed, feeling drained and sad. Her last stray threads of conscious thought were of her son. She hoped Tim would turn up soon. Even if it did add to the discord in the house. He'd never been easy to deal with but she had to see for herself that he was all right. Not until then would she be able to do his picture.

And if necessary she'd find a way to keep Paul off their son's back. She must learn to stand up for her children, as well as herself.

A researcher can be confused, as well as charmed, by the profusion of pictorial and decorative detail on stumpwork embroideries, and also by the strange absence of scale. Flowers, insects, animals and trees jostle for position in scrapbook fashion and mix indiscriminately with fountains and fish, country mansions and castles, and costumed figures, as well as lions and leopards, all in an improbable English countryside, where the sun and moon shine at one and the same time.

(Hirst, p.10)

Chapter Fourteen

The phone rang as Rosalind was passing through the hall. 'Yes?'

'Mum?'

The voice was so wobbly it took her a minute to realise who it was. '*Tim?* Is that really you, darling? Where are you?' Tears started pouring down her cheeks, tears of such relief and joy that it was hard to focus on what he was saying.

Louise came pounding in from the kitchen at the sound of her brother's name, trying to put her ear close to the phone and listen in. Jenny hung over the banister.

'I'm in Poole, Mum. At the coach station,' Tim said.

'Wait there. I'll come and get you.'

'How long will it take you to get here?'

'An hour, perhaps less.'

'There's nowhere comfy to wait, nothing to do. Look, there's a shopping mall across the road. I'll go in there and get a cup of coffee. I'll meet you in an hour near the mall entrance, the one that's opposite the coach station. And Mum – it's great to hear your voice.'

'It's great to hear yours, love.'

Louise grabbed the phone, but he'd already put it down. She glared at her mother. 'You *knew* I wanted to speak to him!'

'There isn't time for chatting. We have to leave at once.'

'Well, you might have bloody well let me say hello, at least.'

'If you don't apologise for speaking to me like that, I'll not even take you with me to Poole. Do you really think you can be polite to your father and rude to me?'

Louise's mouth fell open in shock. She had never seen such an expression of determination on her mother's face.

'Well? I'm still waiting for an apology.'

'I'm sorry. I didn't think. I didn't mean to upset you, Mum.'

'Well, you did upset me. I've lost count of the times you've upset me by your rudeness in the past year or two, and I simply won't take it any longer. Do you understand that?' Her voice was still quiet, but steely in tone.

'Yes, Mum.'

'Now go and get ready.' Rosalind raised her voice, 'Jenny? Are you coming with us to meet Tim?'

'Wouldn't miss it.' As Jenny walked back into her bedroom to grab her coat and bag, she couldn't help grinning and making a triumphant fist in the air. Wow! Her mother was really getting tough.

She paused. No. Not tough. Mum could never be tough in that sense and had spoken as quietly as she always did. But she was starting to stand up for herself – not waiting till she was goaded, like before, and then bursting out with a hysterical-sounding protest. This time she'd spoken straight away, as soon as the put-down started, and had stayed in control of herself. About time, too.

As she came downstairs, Jenny suddenly remembered her date. 'Oh, can you just wait a minute, Mum? I want to cancel my date with Ned. I'm not going out with him on my little brother's first night back.'

Tim put the phone down, then went into the shopping centre, where he bought a cup of coffee and sat watching the crowds.

When an hour had passed, he went to the entrance and found his mother and sisters waiting, looking anxious and scanning the crowds. He hurried across to them, tried to hug them all at once and then said in a shaky voice, 'Get me out of here.'

'Where's your luggage?' Rosalind asked.

'Lost.'

It seemed a long walk to the car. Tim sank into the back seat and huddled down. 'I'm exhausted!' He was holding tears back only with great difficulty. It was so wonderful to see them. So bloody wonderful.

'So where have you been in America?' Louise asked. She was sitting next to him in the back of the car, worrying about how ill Tim looked.

He shrugged. 'Here and there.'

'But where exactly?'

'We wound up in New York.' Which was a lie.

'You and Wayne?'

'Yeah. But we split up.'

Silence.

'It's lovely to see you, Tim,' Jenny ventured from the front seat.

He nodded, but didn't say anything.

'I'm delighted to have all the family together again,' Rosalind said softly.

Tim jerked forward in his seat. '*All* the family? Dad's not down here, is he? Oh, God, I can't face *him* yet!'

Rosalind frowned, wondering why she'd said 'all' when Paul wasn't going to be with them for a few days.

Louise laid a hand on her brother's arm. 'It's all right. Dad isn't here just now. The chairman called and he rushed off to London again like a tame little piggy-wig. He won't be back for a few days because he's going to some sort of live-in planning meeting.'

Tim buried his face in his hands, relief making him shake. 'Thank goodness! Oh, thank bloody goodness!'

In the front, Jenny and her mother exchanged astonished glances. In the back, Louise sat and worried some more.

By the time they reached the village, Tim had calmed down again.

'This is it,' Louise said, waving one hand scornfully. 'Burraford Destan. Dad's English country dream. Centre of the bloody universe it isn't.'

'It looks wonderful to me. Peaceful and full of real people.'

She stared at him. What had happened to make Tim welcome the idea of living in a dead-end hole like this? She would get it out of him later. He always told her things.

* * *

In Australia, Liz stared at the doctor in horror. 'No! I don't believe it. We had tests, lots of tests. I can't have children. We tried for years. It must be something else, gastric flu maybe.'

The doctor sighed. She hated to see women react like this to the news that they were pregnant. 'According to your records, the tests showed you weren't highly fertile because you don't release many eggs, but you could definitely conceive. Your husband was in a similar position – under-fertile – which made it very difficult for you both.'

'But we've never taken any precautions, not since those tests. And I've never got pregnant.' She'd boasted about that to Paul, who had produced some test results giving him a clean bill of health and had then boasted in return that he chose his partners very, very carefully and she had no need to worry about catching anything, if she wanted to really enjoy sex without those bloody condoms.

The doctor cleared her throat to bring her patient's attention back. 'There's no mistake. You are definitely pregnant.'

Liz buried her face in her hands. She hadn't let Bill near her since she got back. And although it was only a short time and she'd only missed one period, she was feeling wretched, nauseous all day. She'd gone to the doctor for help, worried that she'd picked up a virus in Hong Kong. She hadn't even asked what the tests were for.

'It isn't my husband's child,' she said in a voice still muffled by her hands. 'I'll have to get rid of it.' Her voice rose hysterically. 'I'll have to!'

'Ah.' The doctor steepled her hands. 'Well, if you really

want to do that, we can discuss it later, but it's too soon to make a decision.'

Liz raised her head and glared at her. 'What do you mean, too soon? What else can I do? And surely the sooner we do something, the better?'

'You could tell your husband and ask him to accept the child. After all he wanted children, too, or he wouldn't have gone for the tests.'

'That was a long time ago. And he wanted his own children, not another man's.' Bill had flatly refused to consider adopting, becoming aggro at the mere idea. Telling him about this child would mean her accepting his screwing around, as well as him accepting her little affair and its consequences. She'd never get an edge over him after this. *If* he accepted the child. *If* she decided to have it. *If* they managed to stay together. Oh, hell! What a bloody mess! She groaned aloud.

The doctor shook her head and gave Mrs Foxen a moment or two more to pull herself together. Patients never ceased to amaze her by the complexities of their emotional and sexual lives. 'Well, it's still too soon to think of an abortion. You tried for years to have a child and at your age this may be your final and only chance. My advice is to go away and think it all over very carefully. Take a few days. We don't need to rush into anything.'

Liz stared at her. It was good advice – for other people. She could see that. But *she* could never have this child. Still, you had to go through the formalities, the rigmarole and procedures the medical profession had set up. If the doctor wanted her to wait, there was nothing she could do about it.

Just as she was about to agree, however, a thought struck her. 'I don't think I can hide it from my husband for much longer. The sickness is so violent in the morning he's bound to guess.'

'I can give you something which may help. But it probably won't stop the sickness completely.'

Liz accepted the prescription and walked out to sit in her car and try to come to terms with it all. She was going to get rid of it, of course she was. Oh, hell! What a stinking, rotten mess!

She'd been a fool, an utter fool.

When they got back to Sexton Close, Tim gulped down a coffee, smiled faintly at the empty mug and looked at his mother. 'I used to dream about your coffee, Mum. It's still the best in the world.'

Rosalind gave him a quick hug as she passed. 'Well, now you can drink it till it comes out of your ears.'

'Yes. I can.' He tried to smile. Didn't succeed.

'Have something to eat.'

'I'm not really hungry, Mum.'

'Just a snack, then. To please me.'

'OK.' He picked at some food, then pushed the plate away. 'What I'd really like is a bath. I must smell awful. I've been in these clothes for days.'

'What happened to your own stuff?' Louise asked.

'Stolen.'

Rosalind hadn't commented, but he did smell pretty high. 'I'll find you something of your father's to wear.'

'I have a tracksuit that's unisex,' Louise volunteered.

'Thanks.' He trailed up the stairs without even looking at her.

'Shall I clear your stuff out of the spare bedroom?' Louise asked her mother, trying to be helpful.

'Why?'

'Well, why do you think?' She sighed. Honestly, her mum could be so vague. 'Tim's back. He'll need somewhere to sleep.'

Rosalind fixed her with a cool gaze. 'There *is* another bedroom free. The attic. If you don't think it's suitable for your brother, you can move up there yourself. I have my room all set up as I like it, so I see no need to change things.'

Louise opened her mouth, caught her mother's eye and shut it again. 'I'll go and make the bed up in the attic for Tim, then, shall I?'

When she had gone clumping up the stairs, Rosalind looked at Jenny and for a moment her courage faltered. 'He looks so ill,' she whispered. 'He's nothing but skin and bone.'

Jenny had seen people looking like that before, at university. 'I think – it's only a possibility, mind – but he might be seriously addicted to hard drugs. Or just coming off them.'

Rosalind closed her eyes and took a few slow breaths. 'Yes. That had occurred to me, too. But he's not going to take drugs in my house.' She began to fiddle with things in the kitchen, trying to find something to keep her busy. 'How about a roast chicken for tea?'

'Fine.'

'I'll defrost one.'

She sat and listened to the microwave pinging and whirring as it defrosted the chicken, listened, too, to the sounds from upstairs. The bath lasted a long time, then slow footsteps climbed up to the attic.

A short time later Louise came into the kitchen. 'He's fallen asleep.' She looked a bit miffed. 'He had a shower, lay down on the bed, grunted at me and fell asleep.'

'Perhaps that's what he needs most.'

'I wanted to *talk* to him, ask him about America.'

Jenny made a choky little noise to show her disgust. 'You always think about what you want. Try thinking about what other people need for a change.'

'Has Mum been talking to you?'

'What about?'

'What you just said.'

Jenny looked at her in puzzlement.

'Oh, forget it!' Louise stamped out of the room.

They took it in turns to go up and check, but Tim slept all through the rest of the afternoon and the evening, too. Feeling emotionally drained, Rosalind had a nap as well, something rare for her, waking with her son's name on her lips.

The girls stayed up till ten o'clock, then went off to bed, yawning. Rosalind hesitated in her bedroom doorway, then shook her head and went to work on her embroidery. She couldn't sleep yet.

She sat quietly with the door open, listening to the sounds of her daughters getting ready for bed, tossing and turning about, then falling asleep.

At about one o'clock she went to bed herself, but lay there

wakeful, worrying about her son. In the end, she gave way to temptation and tiptoed up the attic stairs in her bare feet.

Louise had left a lamp on at the side of the bed. Tim was lying sprawled across it in the way he always had done, even as a very small child.

As she watched, he opened his eyes, jerked upright and stared round him in what looked like sheer terror. Not until he saw her by the door did he sink back on the pillows again. 'I thought it was all a dream and I was back there again.'

She went to sit by the side of the bed. 'Do you want to tell me about it?'

He reached out for her hand and they sat holding one another for a few minutes. She saw tears on his cheeks, then he sniffed and looked at her.

'Yes. I do want to tell you about it – some of it, anyway. But – do you really want to know, Mum? It isn't nice. I'm not proud of what I've done.'

'You're still my son.'

He smiled through his tears. 'And you're still the best mother in the world. I wanted you dreadfully when – when things went bad.' Then he began to tell her.

She sat very quietly, holding his hand, not interrupting, not even allowing herself to exclaim in shock.

When he'd finished, she gathered him in her arms and held him for a long time, rocking him slightly. Only after he pulled away did she move again.

'I've stopped taking the drugs, Mum.'

'Do you need help with that? I have plenty of money now. I can get you into a clinic—'

'*No!*' He took a deep breath and tried to smile, but failed completely. 'I don't want to be shut up anywhere. Can you understand that? Even the plane – and the bus – made me feel bad. What I want to do is spend as much time as I can in the fresh air, in quiet places. Like beaches. Or woods.'

'Well, there are plenty of places like that round here.'

He didn't seem to have heard her and the confidences were still pouring out of him like pus from a boil. 'When it gets bad, Mum, when I'm hanging out for the drugs, I go out and walk till I'm exhausted. It helps. If I can live here quietly for a while and get my head together, I think I'll come through it.'

'Well, no one will stop you going for walks. I did it myself when I was first here because I missed home so much. But I warn you, I shall try to feed you up.'

He shrugged. 'I don't feel hungry these days.'

'But you'll eat a little – to please me?'

'Are you sure you're not a Jewish momma?' he teased with a brief return of his old self.

'In the sense of feeding you up, I'm as Jewish a momma as they come, so beware.' She watched his smile fade. 'Look, I'll go and get you a tray. I won't bring a lot of food, but you must eat something.'

When she got back, he was staring blankly into space. She set the tray in front of him and sat down. 'I'll feel better if I see you eat something.'

So he forced down two of the delicate sandwiches, and drank half the glass of milk. Then he looked at her pleadingly. 'If I eat any more, I'll chuck up.'

She took the tray. 'Do you want to get up or stay here?'

He sounded surprised. 'I think I can sleep again. I'll have a pee, then come back.'

'It's not the most comfortable bed on earth.'

'It feels pretty wonderful to me.'

'Then I'll leave you in peace.'

Before she went to bed, she wrote a note to Louise and propped it at the foot of the attic stairs, warning her to let Tim sleep, then she went to bed. She thought she'd never get to sleep, but her exhausted body had a different view of that and she didn't wake until ten o'clock.

She found all three of her children gathered in the living room looking sad. She decided to think and act positively. 'When I've had something to eat, would anyone like a ride to the nearest beach?'

'Sounds great,' said Tim. 'I'd like to sit quietly and look at the water.'

'All right,' said Louise. 'I can do my running there, I suppose. I'm getting quite fit, Tim. You could join me when you've picked up a bit.'

'Yeah, sure.'

'I think I'll stay here,' Jenny said. 'I'm not much into beaches.' And she was finding being with Tim a strain. He looked so miserable it hurt her to see him, because every time he came into a room, she was instinctively expecting the old Tim, the one who bounced round the house, talked rebelliously and couldn't even sit quietly to drink a cup of coffee.

'If your father rings,' Rosalind said quietly to Jenny as they left, 'don't tell him about Tim yet.'

'No.' She could understand that.

But Paul didn't ring.

And they were all glad of that.

In fact, Rosalind was so dreading Paul's return that she was even thinking of taking Tim up to Southport before he came back and staying there with him. Tim seemed to need to be with her. He didn't say much, but often sat nearby watching her. He particularly liked watching her embroider and he was the only one to whom she showed the family picture she was working on.

He stared at it for a long time. 'You're really good, Mum. I didn't realise how good. You've got that sod down to a T.'

'And myself,' she said with a wry smile. 'All pale and wishy-washy.'

He studied her for a minute then shook his head. 'That was the old you. You've changed. You're still quiet – but you're more – more colourful.'

She treasured that compliment.

Chapter Fifteen

A few days later Jenny went quietly upstairs, listened to see whether Tim was awake and heard the sound of low voices. Her younger brother and sister sounded as if they were having another heart-to-heart, so she went outside and wandered round the back garden, restless, worried about her mother, not knowing what to do with herself.

As usual she felt to be the odd one out, though Tim was a lot kinder to her than he had been in the past. It was just that he and she had never been close and now she wanted to bridge the huge gap yawning between them, only couldn't think how to start.

She also wanted to talk to someone about her feelings for Ned, only Louise and Tim seemed to have monopolised her mother's attention.

Was she ready for another relationship? She didn't know, only felt she didn't want to lose him.

On an impulse, she picked up the phone. 'Ned?'

'Jenny? Hi there, gorgeous one!'

She didn't waste time on chit-chat. 'Ned, are you doing anything for lunch?'

'Not if there's any chance of seeing you.'

'I thought I'd catch a bus into Dorchester, have a look round the shops – and whatever else there is to see. But I don't want to – to—' Her voice tailed away.

'It's a wonderful idea. Come and meet me for lunch, then go off and do your own thing for the rest of the afternoon. If you can hang around till five-thirty, I'll drive you home after work and take you out for tea in Burraford. Might as well make a day of it.'

'You're too kind to me, Ned.'

'I enjoy your company, Jenny. You know that.'

When he put the phone down, Ned was beaming.

'Good news?' his father asked.

'Yes. Jenny's coming over to Dorchester to have lunch with me. You don't mind, do you? It's not likely to be a busy day.'

'I don't mind at all.'

He wanted to talk about her, mention her name. 'She's great company, Jenny is.'

His father looked at him over the top of his half-glasses. Not like Ned to chat about his girlfriends. What he saw on his son's face made him sound a warning. 'She's very like her mother. Too soft for her own good.'

Ned stared in surprise. 'Don't you like her?'

It wasn't a question of liking or not liking. He wanted a stronger sort of woman for his son, because Ned was soft, too – the sort of gentle person who kept getting hurt. There had been one or two young women in the past whom George could have cheerfully strangled.

He saw that his son was still looking at him, waiting for an answer. 'I'm not sure whether I like Jenny or not. I've hardly exchanged two words with her. But you seem taken by her.'

'I am. Very.'

'Well, that's what matters then, isn't it? But don't rush into things, eh? And don't forget the appointment in Weymouth this afternoon.'

'No. Of course not. But that isn't till three.'

He turned away, smiling to himself. *Don't rush into things!* He'd been gone from the moment he first set eyes on Jenny Stevenson at the fête – and he rather thought she'd fallen for him quite quickly, too. You just knew, somehow.

Jenny turned up at the gallery around twelve and found Ned hovering near the door. She was surprised when he kissed her hard on the mouth by way of a greeting, but instinctively wound her arms round his neck and reciprocated with interest.

When the kiss was over, they both suddenly realised how public their situation was and pulled apart, each a little pink.

'Like that, is it?' she teased softly.

'Yes, it is like that. Very much like that.' He offered her his arm. 'I thought I'd show you round the gallery, then we'd go to the pub round the corner. It's my favourite watering hole.'

'Do you always eat out in pubs?'

'Most of the time. I don't booze at lunchtime, of course, but I still like the feel of a pub – and when you go to the same place regularly you get to know people. Besides, Karen at the Nag's Head does the best sandwiches in town. Huge. Full of goodies. Just wait till you see them. Now, come and have a look round.'

The gallery was larger than she'd expected, crammed with interesting and beautiful things. Half of them were antiques, half were works of art. Some embroideries were displayed in one corner. They were pretty, but not as telling as her mother's, somehow.

At the rear, two larger rooms were each devoted to a show by one artist. Jenny wrinkled her nose at the dark landscapes in the first room, at least, she thought they were landscapes.

'Don't you like them?'

'Not really. They make me feel uncomfortable.'

'They're supposed to. Landscapes of nightmare, the artist calls them. I'm always surprised at how well his stuff sells.'

'People read a lot of horror novels nowadays. These follow the same trend, don't they?'

He looked at her with surprise as well as respect. 'Good girl. Absolutely right.'

She flushed. 'I used to like art at school.'

'Then why did you take business studies at university?'

'Dad.'

'Ah.'

By the time lunch was over Ned had come to the conclusion that something was wrong. He took Jenny's hand. 'Want to talk about it, whatever it is?'

She smiled, then the smile faded and she looked at him wistfully. 'I do, rather. Do you have to go back to work now?'

'I have to drive over to Weymouth to see some stuff

we've been offered. You could come with me, if you don't mind sitting in the car while I'm wheeling and dealing.' He grinned. 'It's an old lady actually, with a cupboard full of rather nice ornaments. Shouldn't take more than half an hour to value them.'

'I'd really like to come with you.' He made her feel hopeful, loved. She blushed at the last thought and was glad he didn't ask her to explain the blush.

It was a quiet drive. Ned didn't make conversation just for the sake of it and Jenny was lost in her own thoughts. But both were glad to be together.

He dropped her reluctantly on the seafront at Weymouth while he went off to see old Mrs Trouter. Jenny watched him drive away, then turned to study the town. She fell instantly in love with the huge stretch of windswept promenade and after a cursory inspection of the famous statue of George III, which Ned had dutifully pointed out to her, she set off for a brisk walk.

A few people were sitting huddled in shelters, for it was a cool day, showery and with more rain to come, judging by the clouds piling up. The place was almost deserted and even the sand looked as if the rain had washed it down. She welcomed the wind, cold as it was, feeling cleansed by it, liberated briefly from her worries. Throwing back her head, she sucked in the salty air. If there hadn't been people around, she'd have run along the sand, skipping and dancing like a child.

When she looked at her watch she realised she was late so ran all the way back, arriving at the statue breathless and pink.

'You look gorgeous.' Ned pulled her towards him for another kiss, his eyes full of promises.

She smiled and nestled against him for a moment. It was right between them, it really was – only she needed to tell him about Michael now.

On the drive back to Burraford, he turned the car down a small side road and stopped on the verge. 'Look!' In the distance, on a mound of land nestled at the bottom of the rolling folds of the Purbeck Hills, was Corfe Castle.

They got out and she stared, entranced. 'Oh, wow! This has got to be one of the most picturesque places in all England. It's like something out of a movie. Is it real?'

He was pleased with her reaction. 'So real I'll take you round it one day.' There were many things he'd like to share with her. He hoped she liked Dorset, for he could never think of living anywhere else.

A shower had just passed and the sun had come out, together with a rainbow, but there were more clouds looming. Silence settled between them and he saw the anxious look reappear on her face. 'Tell me what's worrying you,' he said quietly. He put his arms round her, so that she was leaning back against him, not facing him.

She looked at the rainbow and its colours began to blur and run together. Only then did she realise she was weeping – silently, helplessly, the pent-up anguish of the past few weeks overflowing at the sight of all that beauty.

'Tell me,' he said again, holding her close, hurting for her. 'What did that bastard do to you?'

'He – he . . .' And suddenly the words poured out of her in harsh spurts of shame and pain and guilt.

'Why did he pick on me? What did I do wrong? I've never understood what I did *wrong*,' she wailed when the story was told. By this time, her face was muffled in his chest.

He held her against him, dropping kisses on her hair. '*You* didn't do anything wrong. The policeman was right. That bastard was sick. You were just in the wrong place at the wrong time.'

'It doesn't – put you off me?'

'Never.' When there were no more confidences and she hadn't mopped her eyes for a few minutes, he suggested they go for a stroll to stretch their legs. After a short time, they came back and leant against the car, watching another rainbow. 'That one's ours,' he said softly.

As she turned a glowing look on him, he admitted to himself that he loved her. Deeply. The sort of love which led to a lifetime together. But he wasn't sure she was ready for that so he didn't speak of his feelings.

Rain hissed down suddenly and they laughed as they both dived into the car for shelter, then sat there for a while longer, hand in hand, looking out through the miniature rivers on the windscreen at the rainswept landscape and the romantic ruined castle below them.

She leant across to kiss his cheek. 'Thank you for listening and understanding. You're a lovely man.'

He eyed her speculatively. 'Then you like me enough to keep going out with me, me and no one else?'

'Yes, definitely.'

'That's smashing!'

He gaped, for she was quite convulsed with laughter. 'What's the matter?'

'That word. "Smashing". It sounds so corny. I didn't think you Poms still used it.'

'Well, we do. And it *is* smashing that you're going to continue seeing me. In fact, it calls for a celebration,' he allowed a pregnant pause, 'and I have just the thing.'

'Champagne?' she joked. 'Caviar? Red roses?'

'No, this.' He produced a bar of chocolate from his pocket, wrapper torn and crumpled, with pieces missing from one end. 'Want some?'

She chuckled, feeling light and happy again. 'Definitely. I didn't know you were a chocoholic.'

'Unfortunately, yes.' He patted his waist – not fat, but not thin either.

'Well, I'll let you into a secret.' She leant closer. 'I adore – chocolate.'

She linked her arm in his and leant her head against his shoulder, letting him feed her piece by piece, letting the damp wind blow through the open car window now the shower had passed, so that her hair fluttered around her face.

She had the strangest conviction that her troubles with Michael were blowing away, too, in that soft, damp wind.

Then the heavens opened again and they had to close the car windows quickly.

She was flushed and pretty, so he kissed her again. He was, he decided, going to marry her one day if she would have him. Definitely. But he'd better not say anything about that yet. He suspected she needed a little more time to recover.

It took only two days for Tim and Louise to start bickering. She wanted to be with him – he wanted to be alone. Or he wanted to be with his mother.

When Louise started to complain to him about being cut off from the world in a dead-end dump like Burraford, he turned on her, terrified the rot had set in with her, too – for he felt himself to be rotten now, terminally sick like a fungus-ridden tree. He would lie there in his narrow bed, half-awake, imagining he could feel pieces crumbling away: a fingernail here, a toe there, hair, ears – there were lots of bits you could lose and still keep stumbling along in a semblance of life.

So when Louise complained about this lovely, peaceful place, he glared at her and it was a moment or two before he could force any words through the haze of anger. 'You don't know what you're talking about, you stupid – *you child*!'

Her anger was as swift to rise as his. 'I do know, too. And I'm not a child any more. You're not the only one to have done drugs, you know. And I've had sex, too. Lots of times.'

'Well, I'm not doing drugs now and look how hard it is for me to kick the habit. What have you been on?'

Sulkily, she told him.

He sighed with relief. 'You've not got really hooked, then? Not on the hard stuff?'

'On the allowance Dad gives me?'

He sighed in relief and grasped her arms, so that she had to look him in the face. 'Look, Lou, I've seen what happens to drug users – and I've seen the sort of lowlifes who make money out of the suckers. I'm not going to be a sucker again and if I ever see you doing drugs I'll tell Dad right away.'

She jerked away. 'Well! Thanks for nothing, Big Brother!'

He looked at her, sad and solemn. 'There's nothing clever, either, about giving sex away for kicks. They sell it on the street every day. That sort of sex is a cheap commodity.' His voice softened. 'You should wait till there's some love going with it. That's what makes it really special, worthwhile.' He'd been fond of a girl once, though she'd got fed up of him. And who could blame her?

Louise snorted. 'Ha! Who believes in love and romance these days? You don't think Mum and Dad are in love, do you? I want to *live*, not stifle to death in a cosy little house!' She stormed off.

He went to find his mother and sit quietly, watching her work in the kitchen, so efficient, so clean, so *warm*. 'If you're worrying that I'll be a bad influence on Lou, Mum, I thought you might like to know that I'm trying to talk a bit of sense into her.' He tried to please her by eating one of her newly baked scones, but couldn't finish it, so slipped half of it surreptitiously into his pocket to be flushed away later.

'Thanks, Tim love. I am worried about Louise, I must admit. She's been very foolish, but your father's too harsh with her. Perhaps some of what *you* say may get through to her.'

He studied his coffee gloomily, thinking how little it had meant to him when people tried to talk sense into him, how eager he had been to follow Wayne to America – eager enough to steal the money. His mother didn't know about that and he hoped she would never find out, either. 'I don't think anything helps really, except a dose of capital L-I-F-E. Why didn't Dad let Lou go into nursing? That's what she really wanted. It'd have suited her, too.

She's always,' he managed a faint smile as he remembered, 'been good at mopping up blood and gore – usually mine.'

'Paul wouldn't even countenance it. And in those days I had no money of my own, so I couldn't help her.'

'But you do have money now . . .' He let the words trail away suggestively.

She nodded. 'Yes. But I'll only help her if it's what she really wants and she'll promise to give it a fair go. No good will come from pushing her down another blind alley.'

'Yeah, that's for sure.' He looked sideways at her. She'd changed. Was more sure of herself now, though still quiet. He liked that quietness, needed it.

Only – how would she be when his father came home? How did a gentle person cope with a bully like him? Tim was thinking seriously of asking his mother for a loan and getting the hell out of this place before his father got back. Very seriously. Only he couldn't seem to get round to planning it yet. All he wanted to do was to rest. And be with his mother. It was hard enough managing without the drugs. He couldn't manage without her yet.

Next time Tim and Louise had a spat he yelled, 'The sort of life you hanker after, little sister, leads to young kids dying in back alleys from an OD. Drive-by shootings. Crims with guns. Hunger and dirt and old people with hopeless faces waiting to die.'

'I don't believe you. I won't. There's *got* to be more to life than this!' she waved one hand scornfully.

'Of course there is, but not if you're greedy and in a hurry to grab things. Like I was. I didn't make it to the nice parts of America, where the normal people live and exciting, fun things happen.' Thanks to Wayne.

But would staying here bring trouble to his family? That still worried Tim a lot in the endless hours of fidget-filled darkness, tangled sheets and equally tangled thoughts. No, of course it wouldn't. Those crims didn't know where he was now. The thing to concentrate on was kicking the habit. It was harder than he'd expected. Much harder.

'Are you listening to me?'

'Sorry, Lou. What were you saying?'

'I don't want to get into that sort of sleaze, Tim, of course I don't. But there must be *something* more interesting than business studies. I'll go mad if I have to go back to that, right round the bloody twist.'

'Why don't you try nursing? Talk to Mum about it.'

'Ha! What good would that do? She always does as Dad tells her.'

'Mum has money of her own now. If she thought you really meant it, she'd help you. She said so.'

Louise frowned at him. 'I'll think about it. I can't see her standing up to Dad about something like that, though.'

'I think she would – now.'

When Jonathon rang early one morning Rosalind spoke to him briefly. She couldn't help smiling. Just to speak to him was – wonderful.

'How's it going?' he asked. 'Enjoying having your son back?'

'Just a minute.' She went to close her bedroom door. 'It's not going all that well. Tim's – damaged. That's the only word for it, Jonathon. Damaged. Badly. And I don't know if I can put the pieces together again.'

'Let me know if I can help. In any way.'

'I'd be hammering on your door, don't worry. But there's nothing anyone can do that isn't being done. They say time is the best healer, but I don't know about cases like this. I just – well, I hope they're right.'

Tears welled in her eyes so she said goodbye in a voice that came out choked and put the phone down before she started crying in earnest. Jonathon would understand her abruptness. He always understood things. She wished – oh, she wished desperately he could be here to help her through all this. She felt so alone.

She thought of her husband and grimaced. These mammoth planning sessions for the company went on for ages sometimes. Paul hadn't rung, so he didn't even know Tim was back. Not that he'd have come home for that. She wasn't sure he'd be much help in the future, either. His way had never been right for Tim. That was why she hadn't called him out of his planning session.

And although it was good that Paul had got Louise interested in exercise, he was still insisting on her doing the same sort of university course. That wouldn't work, she was sure. Louise was a doer, not a thinker. Why could Paul not see that?

Not long afterwards Audrey rang, sounding querulous. 'For days I've been expecting someone to call about Tim. I presume he arrived safely?'

'Oh, Mum, I should have rung you. I'm so sorry. I'm sorry for *all* the trouble we've caused you lately.'

'It's not your fault, love. But I'm too old for all these fusses now. I said so to John only yesterday.'

'Not too old to have a boyfriend in tow,' Rosalind teased.

Audrey's voice softened. 'No. I thought I was, but I've changed my mind. Do you like John?'

'Yes. Very much. And if he makes you happy, I'll like him even more.'

'Good.'

'Well, I must go now. Lovely to speak to you.'

Audrey's voice was suddenly urgent. 'Don't let those children run rings round you, Rosalind. Stand up to them as well as to Paul. *You* have needs, too.'

'I am standing up for myself,' Rosalind assured her mother. 'Well, starting to.'

'Good. Don't expect to change completely in a few weeks. Bye!'

That night Tim let himself quietly out of the house shortly after midnight. The girls were sound asleep, but Rosalind heard him leave and wondered about stopping him, then shook her head. No. He'd said walking helped him cope with the withdrawal symptoms. And this wasn't an inner city, after all. He should be safe enough in the quiet Dorset countryside.

She knew she wouldn't get back to sleep till she heard him return, so she got up and went to her embroidery, her usual refuge and comfort.

Jenny's figure was finished, so this time Rosalind drew Tim – drew him as the thin, anguished creature he now was, not the lively young lad he had once seemed. He'd been unhappy for a while now, and she'd been unable to find a way through the tangles of family relationships to help him.

Perhaps no one could have done that. She didn't know.

She only needed to do one sketch. As she stared at it, she knew it was right, terrifyingly so. As instantly right as Paul's figure had been.

When she heard Tim come in again two hours later, she made no attempt to conceal the fact that she was up.

He came into the back bedroom, bringing a cold damp smell with him, but looking more at peace with himself. 'Can I see what you've done today?'

She leant backwards and gestured to the partly finished piece. 'I'm still working on the family portrait. It's not going to be a pretty one. I'm trying to see us as we are.'

He was silent for a moment or two, studying it, then nodded. 'It's good. Really good. That's Jenny to the life. Christ, Dad's so arrogant! But you're not like that figure any more.' He touched the pastel-coloured Rosalind, standing sideways, looking at her family with a faintly anxious air. 'You used to be, but not now.'

'Mmm. I know.' She hesitated, then confided, 'Actually, I'm thinking of putting another me back to back with that one, a more brightly coloured figure, sort of like a Siamese twin, looking out at the world.'

'Worm turning?' he asked softly, not looking at her.

'Yes.'

'Good. About time.'

He went back to studying the embroidery. 'It's a good one of Zip, too. Funny how he was always Jenny's dog, isn't it? What about me? Have you done a sketch of me yet?'

She pulled the piece of paper out from underneath the pad and passed it to him.

He was quiet as he studied it, then nodded and handed it back. 'That's me, all right. You've got a real flair for this sort of thing. You're good enough to do portrait sketches. I dare say you'll become very famous with your embroideries, then I'll go round boring everyone about my clever mother.'

She smiled, but her thoughts were still on her sketch of him. 'You look a bit young here, that's all.'

'Don't change it, not if you want the truth. I feel young sometimes, young and stupid. And yet old, too.' Tears were running down his cheeks. 'Oh, hell, why am I crying? What a wimp!'

She'd found a book about drugs and getting over them on a shopping trip into Poole, had gone there deliberately to see if she could find something to show her how to help him. 'You have to expect mood swings and a very emotional state while you're detoxifying. It's part of the process.'

He grinned through his tears. 'Found a book on it, have you?'

'Yes.'

'You and your books.' He looked down at his wet, cold feet. 'Well, this one's right, I can tell you. Only, I don't know how I'm going to cope with it all for much longer. It's – it's like something gnawing away at me, this need. I'm even snapping at Louise and all the poor thing wants is to be with me.'

'Thanks for trying to talk sense into her.'

'I'm not sure I got anywhere – well, not very far, anyway.'

He looked at his mother, naked anguish in his eyes. 'You don't deserve kids like us, you know.'

'You're my son, Tim. I love you whatever you do.'

He came over to her and put his arms round her, laid his cheek against hers and said in a choked voice, 'I love you, too.' They stood silently for a while, then he yawned and pulled away. 'I think I'll manage to sleep now. See ya, Ma.'

'Don't call me that,' she said automatically and saw him smiling at her. But she couldn't seem to smile back. Tonight everything felt too charged, too sad.

Paul was called out of a meeting for an urgent phone call. It wouldn't look good, this. But it'd have looked worse to refuse to take the call.

The receptionist directed him to a phone booth in the foyer. 'Hello?'

'It's me, Paul.'

'Liz?' Her voice had been husky, anxious. 'Is there a problem?' Don't let it be his mother-in-law! That'd send Ros scurrying home to Australia and he'd never get her away again.

'I'm pregnant.'

The world seemed to lurch around him. 'You *can't* be!'

'I am. I was a bit surprised myself.'

'You *are* going to get rid of it?' Silence. 'Liz?'

'I'm thinking about that.'

'What do you mean, thinking? Haven't you seen a damned doctor?'

'Yes.'

'And—?'

'She wants me to think it over for a few days, then she'll help me if I still want an abortion.'

'I thought you were sterile.'

Her voice wobbled. 'So did I.'

'Well, I don't see a need for us to upset Ros over this.'

Suddenly Liz wished she hadn't rung, didn't want to speak to him any more. What had she expected from Paul Stevenson, for heaven's sake? Support? Warmth? She should know by now what he was like. 'I just thought you ought to be aware of it,' she said wearily. 'I'll deal with it.'

'If you need any money . . .'

There was a sudden buzzing. The bitch had put the phone down on him. He stood there, anger roiling through him. Suddenly he thumped the wall with his clenched fist. He didn't need all this hassle! He had a living to make, a career to get on with. Had the whole world gone mad lately?

Liz didn't find the doctor's anti-nausea remedy much use. Oh, it gave her time to get to the bathroom before she threw up, but it didn't do much else. So when Bill came out of the spare bedroom where he was still sleeping, opened the bathroom door and stood there watching, she knew the game was up.

Another wave of sickness hit her and she had to concentrate on hitting the toilet bowl. When she'd finished, she washed her face and went out into the bedroom to face him.

He was sitting at the dressing table, arms folded. 'That's not an upset stomach. You're pregnant.' His voice was flat and definite, making a statement, not asking a question.

'Yes.'

'Hong Kong?'

She nodded and slipped under the bedcovers, shivering with the after-effects of the vomiting.

'Cup of tea any use?'

She looked at him and saw he meant it. Tears flooded her eyes. She hadn't expected kindness from him, given the circumstances.

When he came back, she accepted the mug of tea gratefully, sipping it and holding its wonderful warmth between her hands while she waited to see if it would stay down. After a minute, she tried another sip, saw him watching and explained, 'Sometimes there's a double whammy with the sickness. I have to be cautious.'

He held out the plate of biscuits. 'Want one of these? I read somewhere that a dry biscuit helps.'

She shook her head, tears scalding down her cheeks. 'Stop being so damned kind!'

'Well, I'm not going to beat you up, you fool, but we do have to talk.'

'Yes. If it's any consolation, I went to see the doctor, told her I wanted to get rid of it. I don't expect to land you with – with someone else's offspring.'

'Bit drastic that, isn't it?'

'Yes. But I couldn't see any other choice. And she s-said – she said to think it over – and I thought what a load of crap, why doesn't she just sign the bit of paper? Get rid of it quick before anyone finds out. But last night I dreamt of it – a little boy – and he smiled at me – and I knew I couldn't do it, couldn't kill him.'

The dream child had looked too much like Ros's son, Tim, as a child. But if she did have it, how was she going to manage when Bill left her, because she hadn't had to earn a living for over twenty years?

He looked solemn, stern, not at all like the easy-going man she normally lived with. 'Don't do anything yet. I'll need to think about it, too.' At the door he turned. 'Do you know who the father is, by the way, or did you just screw anyone?'

She threw the mug at him then, scattering hot tea all over the quilt. 'Of course I know who he is! I only screwed one person, dammit! Unlike you!'

He didn't duck but the mug fell short, smashing against a chair leg and breaking into dripping pieces of fractured clay. When the door closed behind him, Liz couldn't take her eyes off that mug. Was her life going to break into pieces, too?

She wished she hadn't phoned Paul. What was the point of telling him about the baby? Did he really think she'd go shouting her mouth off to Rosalind, her best friend?

More tears flooded her eyes and she mopped at them with the edge of the sheet. She felt ashamed of what she'd done, desperately ashamed. Burying her head under the covers, she wept again.

But Bill didn't come back to comfort her.

Chapter Sixteen

Tim felt really bad that day. He spent most of it in his room, sweating and resisting the urge to scream, to smash things, to take out his body's agony on anything and everything. And he succeeded in keeping control. A small victory. Well, each day was a small victory at the moment, wasn't it? What was it his mum always said? One step at a time.

But what terrified him was: they said you never lost the desire, never, whatever you did. That the need for a fix always haunted you. And he didn't think he could take a lifetime of this.

There was a tap on the attic door. Louise poked her head round it. 'Want a cup of coffee?'

'Yeah. Thanks.'

She came back with two mugs and a plate with a piece of cake on it. 'Mum said you might like to eat something.'

He looked at it with loathing. 'And then again, I might not.'

'Shall I dispose of it for you down the toilet? We can pretend you've eaten it?'

Somehow that idea was loathsome to him. He had even felt guilty about flushing away the piece of scone the other day. 'No. I'm not going to lie to Mum.'

'Everyone else does.'

'What do you mean by that?'

She shrugged. 'Shan't tell you.'

He lay back, rolling his eyes at the ceiling. 'I'm not in the mood for childish games. If you can't talk sense, go away and play at getting fit.'

'What do you mean "play"? I *am* getting fit.'

'Well, go and get fitter, then.'

Rosalind, crossing the landing with some clean towels, heard the sound of them quarrelling and let out a growl of exasperation. Sometimes Louise did more harm than good, with Tim in this fragile state. She went across to the attic stairs, the small noise her slippered feet made on the bare wooden treads masked by the raised voices above her.

Just as she got to the attic door, she heard Louise yell, 'Well, Dad does lie to her all the time. He's having an affair with Liz at the moment. Mum's best friend. And he's probably had lots of affairs before that. He's even more of a nightmare than we thought.'

Rosalind stood in frozen horror on the stairs. *Liz and Paul!* It couldn't be true! It just – it wasn't possible. She didn't move away, though, couldn't. She had to know the truth. Louise wouldn't say something like that without a reason.

Tim's voice was low and scornful, amazingly like his father's. 'I don't believe you. Even *he* wouldn't – not with Mum's best friend. I've seen him with young chicks a couple of times, not with older women. And how did you find out about it, anyway? You must have made a mistake.'

'I overheard him phoning her when he came to get me in Australia, talking about being together in Hong Kong, asking her to meet him for a screw.'

Rosalind believed it suddenly. She put one hand across her mouth to hold the shock and pain inside. There was the sound of someone moving inside the attic, then Louise yelping in shock.

Tim's voice came out in jerks, as if he were shaking his sister. 'If you ever – say one word – about this to Mum – I'll kill you myself.'

'I haven't. I wouldn't.'

'You'd bloody better not.'

There was silence now from inside the room. Rosalind looked round blankly, realised where she was, dumped the pile of towels on the landing and tiptoed down the stairs. She had to get out of the house, couldn't face anyone yet, could hardly face her own thoughts even. She went quickly into her bedroom, snatched up her handbag and rushed downstairs, passing Jenny on the way.

'Are you all right, Mum? You look—'

She pushed past her daughter, not daring to let her feelings out.

Jenny stared after as the front door slammed and there was the sound of a car engine. It faded away into the distance and the house became silent. Too silent.

Why couldn't they all be happy, like other families? she wondered as she went into her own bedroom.

Eyes half-blinded by tears, Rosalind drove out of the village more by instinct than by good judgement. Then suddenly she could go no further, so she pulled the car up at the tree-shadowed end of a lay-by, switched off the engine and sat there, back to the world, bowed over the steering wheel. The tears she'd been holding in overflowed, rolling down her cheeks.

So many pieces had suddenly fallen into place, like tumblers clicking inside a lock, which then let the door swing back to reveal the hidden things behind it. Nasty things, growing like poisonous fungi in the dark.

Paul *had* been unfaithful! She knew it with an utter certainty as she sat alone in the car. But why with Liz? *Liz, of all people!* Any woman was bad, but her best friend . . . She couldn't help sobbing, a harsh, strangled noise that surprised her.

It had happened in Hong Kong, of course. They'd both been there at the same time. Liz had sent only one postcard and hadn't replied to Rosalind's letters since.

She suddenly remembered a silence on the phone once when she'd mentioned Liz to Paul. And how her friend – who was now not her friend, who could never be her friend again – had declared before she left that she was going to get her own back on Bill. Sauce for the goose, she'd said.

'But why use *my* husband to pay him back?' Rosalind whispered. 'Oh, Liz, how could you do that to me? *How could you?*'

Was Liz just a one-off aberration? For a moment

Rosalind tried to cling to that hope, then shook her head slowly and sadly. No. A man like him couldn't cope without regular sex. And even he wouldn't be unfaithful for the first time with Liz. When he was home he was always so lusty, wanting to make love every day. Twice a day sometimes. He loved sex. So did she. It had been hard for her to get used to the periods of enforced celibacy.

Why had she believed he could do it – would even try?

She let out her agony in a raw, moaning sound. Oh, what a credulous fool she'd been! All those years she'd made their marriage and their family the centre of her life. Even when Paul began to go away for long periods, she'd tried to adjust, to be a supportive partner, to be a good mother. Dammit, she'd tried so *hard*.

Rain spattered against the car windscreen, then worked itself up into a frenzy, pounding on the metal roof. She welcomed the cacophony because it shut her in, gave her a sense of utter privacy. Even when the tears had dried on her cheeks, she sat on, with cars droning past behind her back and rain pattering down more gently now. She didn't know what to do. Her whole life had just fallen apart.

No, said Sophie's voice inside her head, *not your whole life. He's your husband, but you're a person in your own right. You have a life of your own, needs of your own. Never forget that.*

'He might not be my whole life,' Rosalind told the hovering shade of her aunt, 'but he's a damn big part of it, Soph, whether he was there in person or not.'

Traffic thundered past, wind blew so strongly that the car rocked with the force of it. The main thing Rosalind had to decide was – should she forgive him? No, even that wasn't the full pattern of her truth. She admitted it to herself at last. The main thing was did she really *want* to stay with him now?

She didn't think so. Not when she'd experienced the warmth and companionship of another sort of man.

Which made her mentally unfaithful. That thought startled her, then eased the pain a little.

Only – how could she break up her family?

The following day Jenny met Ned for lunch. As she ran towards him, he held out his arms and gathered her close, swinging her round.

'Oh, hell!' he said suddenly, stopping and looking down at her, 'I can't hold it in any longer, Jen. I love you. I want to marry you.'

She stared up at him, her mouth open in shock, then gradually a smile crept across her face.

'Trust me to blurt it out,' he said. 'I meant to propose all romantically, only the sight of you coming towards me was too much. I couldn't wait a second longer.' He raised one of her hands to his lips to kiss it, then did the same to the other. 'Oh, Jen, you will say yes, won't you?'

She flung her arms round his neck. 'Of course I will. I can't imagine what you see in me, but yes, Ned, I love you, too. And yes, I will marry you.'

A woman bumped into them and muttered something about 'cluttering up the pavement'. Ned came down from his rosy cloud for long enough to guide Jenny into the pub and sit down in the corner with her.

'I don't know what to say,' he admitted. 'Except that

I don't think I've ever been as happy in all my life.'

'Me, too.'

They ordered sandwiches, which neither of them finished, and drinks, which they left almost untouched on the table. They said very little, but smiled and held hands, telling each other the things lovers have always said, yet which always seem new and wonderful to each couple.

As the lunchtime rush ebbed, Ned realised what time it was and grimaced. 'Should have been back at the gallery an hour ago.' He pulled her to her feet. 'Come on! Let's go and tell Dad our news.'

'Now?'

'Yes. And later we'll go over to see your mother.'

As they walked into the gallery together, Jenny suddenly felt shy. Ned's father peered out of a door at the back, waved one hand in greeting and waited for them to join him.

'What time do you call this?' he demanded in mock anger.

Ned beamed at him. 'I completely forgot the time. I've been proposing, you see, and Jenny has just agreed to marry me.'

George gaped at his son. 'Goodness me! Well, you *have* taken me by surprise.' He gave Jenny a bear hug, muttering 'Great! Great!' in her ear as he patted her back. 'I'm delighted about this and my wife will be, too.' Then he held her at arm's length. 'Welcome to the family, Jenny, my dear. I hope you two will make each other very happy.'

He went on to give Ned an even more crushing hug, pounding him on the shoulders repeatedly. 'About time, you young scamp, about bloody time. Your mother's been fretting for a year or two.' He winked at Jenny. 'Wants grandchildren before she's too old to enjoy them.'

She blushed. And wondered if many other fathers hugged their children so naturally. She would make sure Ned hugged theirs. She couldn't remember her father ever hugging any of them.

Ned detached himself, grinned and put his arm round her again. 'A bit premature, to think of grandchildren, don't you feel, Dad?'

'OK. We'll wait a bit for that.' George gestured to the phone. 'Do you want to tell your mother or shall I?'

'I will.' Ned took the phone and pressed the automatic dial key. 'Mum?' He pulled a face. 'No, I'm fine. Look, Mum, will you *listen*?' He took a deep breath. 'Jenny and I have just got engaged.'

There was a shriek at the other end of the phone. George rolled his eyes at Jenny and grinned as a gabble of words had Ned nodding and murmuring.

At one stage he passed the phone to Jenny so that she could 'meet' his mother.

Afterwards, he said, 'We need to buy an engagement ring, Dad. All right if I take the rest of the day off?'

'Be my guest. It's not every day my only son gets engaged. Do you want to look at our antique stock of jewellery first? Or are you going to buy a new ring?'

Ned looked at Jenny questioningly.

'I think I'd like a new one, if you don't mind.' She wanted everything to be fresh and new in this relationship.

'I don't mind at all. We'll go and hunt round the shops.' He was already guiding her towards the door as he turned to his father. 'Oh, and Mum wants us all to do lunch tomorrow, to celebrate. Will you book a table?'

'Fine.'

When his son had left the gallery, George picked up the phone again. 'Stella? No, he's just gone. We can talk now.'

'How did he look?'

'Absolutely besotted.'

'What's she like?'

'Gentle. Pretty. Looks as besotted as he is. They're clinging to one another like a pair of damned leeches.' He chuckled. 'Ah, young love! Yes, one o'clock tomorrow, usual place. Don't overdress. She's not a fashion plate. And don't overpower her with your enthusiasm for grandchildren. She blushes easily.'

When he put the phone down he leant back and smiled round him. 'If she makes him happy, she'll do,' he told his favourite statuette, a bronze art nouveau lady with flowing skirts and hair. Pulling out a large handkerchief, he blew his nose vigorously.

Jenny arrived home at teatime looking windswept but happy. Ned came into the house with her and they both went upstairs to see Rosalind, who was in her workroom.

She turned to greet them, hoping the make-up had hidden the redness of her eyes. Then, as she saw the linked hands, the beaming faces, she guessed what had happened and tried to respond joyfully to their news. It had been so long since she'd seen that happy look on her daughter's face, she didn't want to spoil things now by confiding her own troubles.

She led the way downstairs, calling to Tim and Louise to join them and opening a bottle of wine for a toast.

After they'd chatted for a while, Tim excused himself.

He had been very quiet, but had smiled at Ned and taken a few sips of wine.

Rosalind watched him go, trying to hide her anxiety. Seen next to Ned, he seemed blurred, no more than a shadow in their midst. And surely he was getting thinner?

Louise looked at her mother and pushed herself to her feet. 'I'll go and – see if he's all right.' She turned to her sister and gave her another hug, 'I'm really glad for you two.'

Rosalind tried to sound hearty and happy. 'We'll need to tell your father. I'm sure he'll be delighted.'

'Yes, I suppose so.' Jenny looked at Ned, then back to her mother. 'We can wait till Dad's finished this conference thing, though, can't we?'

'Yes.' Which meant Rosalind would have to wait for her own confrontation with Paul until after that. And she didn't know whether to be glad or sorry. Relieved mostly. She had a lot of thinking to do. Finding out about his unfaithfulness had thrown her emotions into turmoil and she wasn't sure what she wanted any more.

'Would you mind if I went out to the pub with Ned for dinner, Mum?'

'No one will mind at all, love. Go and enjoy yourselves.'

Ned came to hover in the doorway of the kitchen while Jenny was changing. 'Any sign of the other embroideries arriving?'

'What? Oh. Oh, yes. They arrived a few days ago. I forgot to tell you.' She led the way into the dining room. She hadn't even opened the box. 'Why don't you take it with you tonight, Ned? You and your father can have a look through them, see what you think.'

'Don't you want to open them yourself? Check they're all right?'

She made a huge effort to concentrate on business. 'No. I've – um, got something on my mind just now. Don't sell any till I've told you which ones I want to keep, though.'

Ned looked sideways at her. Under the make-up her eyes were reddened. It was probably something to do with Jenny's brother. He had a lot to answer for, Tim Stevenson did. But he looked as if he was paying for it. He looked awful. Like an AIDS sufferer, all hollow-faced and big-eyed, his body a series of sharp angles.

'I know your father will look after them.' Rosalind pushed the box towards him with her toe.

'He definitely will. I'll pick them up when I bring Jenny back. I don't want to leave something so precious in the boot in a pub car park. I'm really looking forward to seeing them.'

He glanced over his shoulder to check they were still alone and his face became solemn. 'Um – Jenny told me about – about that fellow Michael she used to be with – and what happened in Perth. I just wanted you to know that she'll be quite safe with me.'

Ned's tender concern for her daughter was another spear stabbing into Rosalind's guts, but the years of putting on a public face at Paul's functions stood her in good stead. 'I know she will.'

She waved them goodbye, then pleaded a headache, leaving Tim and Louise to get their own tea. They'd obviously made up their quarrel, but both were subdued.

About ten o'clock she heard Jenny come back and help Ned carry the box of embroideries out to the car. Afterwards there was a long silence from the hall, filled with faint rustlings and murmurs, then the front door closed behind Ned, and Jenny then went straight to bed.

About eleven o'clock, Louise went to bed, too.

Tim stayed downstairs watching TV, then went up to the attic about midnight.

About two o'clock, he woke Rosalind as he crept out. To her surprise he took her car. She usually kept the keys in her handbag in her room, but now she remembered that she'd left them on the hallstand tonight, she'd been so upset. Was he insured to drive the car? She didn't know. The company had leased it for her.

She couldn't get back to sleep, but lay and worried about him. Well, she always worried when he went out at night, but somehow, tonight, she felt more worried than usual. As if – oh, she didn't know what she thought. She didn't know anything any more.

But why had he taken the car? He usually went walking.

Eventually she dozed a little, then woke up and saw grey smudges against the cloud-filled darkness of the sky. Nearly dawn. She rose and went up to Tim's room, thinking he might have come in while she was asleep.

He wasn't there.

She peered out of the window. Neither was her car.

After frowning at the untidy attic, she searched all the drawers, sighing in relief when she realised his clothes were still there and there was no sign of a farewell note. She'd been desperately worried that he might take his own life, he seemed so lacking in hope sometimes. There were no clues to his absence, none at all. The bed had been lain on, but not slept in. The radio was still muttering quietly to itself. Irritated by its faint rasping noise, she went and snapped it off, then went back to her own room.

Where was he?

In the shower, she thought she heard the car and ran into the bedroom dripping wet, only to see the man next door turning into his drive. Disappointed she trailed back to the shower, which was still hissing away.

When she was dressed, she went downstairs to make some coffee, but couldn't galvanise herself into doing anything useful after that, so sat on alone in the quiet kitchen, hoping to hear the sound of Tim's key in the front door.

But he didn't come back. And the sky was fully light now.

She threw away the cold coffee that half-filled her mug and made some more. He'd never stayed out so long before.

Something must have happened to him!

She felt a quick lurch of terror in her belly. He might be lying somewhere in pain, suffering from withdrawal symptoms like those described in her book, or he might have been driving carelessly and had a car accident. 'Please let him be safe,' she whispered. 'Just let him be safe. Never mind the car, it's Tim who matters.'

Time trickled past and the second mug of coffee grew cold. She considered making more, but couldn't focus on such mundane things.

Where the hell was her son?

Chapter Seventeen

Liz was standing in the kitchen waiting for the kettle to boil when the phone rang. She picked it up listlessly. The early morning nausea wasn't as bad today but she still felt pretty ghastly. It was a wonder that women ever had more than one baby, she decided, a triumph of instinct over common sense. 'Yes?'

'Hi there. How are things? Can you talk?'

She glanced quickly round, but Bill was still upstairs. 'What do *you* want?'

'Just to find out how you are. Have you – er – dealt with that little problem?'

'Not yet.'

'Need any money?'

'No.' She hesitated, then malice made her add, 'I'm thinking of keeping it, actually.'

His voice grew hard and angry. 'I'll deny everything.'

She felt perverse, not wanting to make it easy for him.

'But will people believe you? Ros, for instance? Plenty of hotel staff saw us together – that barman who made the beautiful cocktails. I can easily prove we were together if I have to – and then there's DNA testing.'

His voice sounded incredulous. 'You're going to *tell* Ros? And you call yourself her *friend*?'

'I'm a better friend to her than you are a husband, you rotten sod. I've betrayed her once. How many times have you betrayed her?'

A sound made her glance round and she saw Bill standing behind her, his face like stone.

He walked forward and took the phone from her hand, shouted 'Go to hell, Stevenson!', then slammed the receiver into its cradle. After breathing in and out deeply several times, he finally raised his eyes to look at Liz. 'I'm disgusted by what you did. Utterly, totally disgusted.'

'You're a fine one to talk.' But her protest sounded weak and unconvincing, even to herself.

He stared at her for a moment, then shrugged. 'I've broken my marriage vows, yes – several times. But I've never betrayed my best friend and, strange as this may seem, I've never stopped loving you. What's more, I've dealt fairly with the other women. They all knew the score, knew I wasn't about to break up my marriage.' His voice grew thick with revulsion. 'How could you do it to her, Liz? *Rosalind Stevenson*, of all people? The gentlest, kindest person I know. How could you even think of it?'

She was sobbing now, her whole body shaking with the violence of her feelings. 'I don't know. I don't *know*, dammit! I think I went mad for a time. I was furious with you and so bloody bored up there in Hong Kong. I was even thinking of coming home, that's how bored I was, only I wasn't going to give you the satisfaction. Then Paul arrived and turned on the charm – and that bastard can be very charming when he wants, believe me. And I fell into his arms like a ripe cherry. Only *you* ripened me, you know you did.'

She looked up for long enough to hurl at him, 'Don't you think I'm sorry? Even without this,' she gestured towards her belly. 'Don't you think I feel like the lowest kind of – of worm, doing that to my best friend?' The minute the plane took off coming home from Hong Kong the guilt had started to nag at her, and she'd been amazed that she had even thought of having an affair with Rosalind's husband.

When her husband didn't speak, she asked, 'You aren't – going to tell her, Bill?'

'Me? Of course I'm not. What do you think I am?'

She covered her face with her shaking hands. 'Sorry. I know you won't. I don't know why I said that.'

'Will *he* tell her?'

'He's managed to keep all the others from her,' she said in a dull voice.

'*All* the others?'

'Yes. It appears he's made quite a hobby of it, says he enjoys the variety.'

'He was just making use of you, then.'

'Yes.' After a moment she stood up, wanting to escape, unable to stand his calm scrutiny and the scorn in his eyes, but she stumbled and would have fallen headlong had he not jerked forward to catch her. Then she started sobbing loudly, clutching at him, calling his name. 'Bill,

Bill, Bill!' On and on. She couldn't stop herself.

Bill sighed and closed his eyes, keeping hold of her, patting her shoulder occasionally. She was right. He had to take some share of the blame, he knew that, but could he take another man's child along with it? She was still weeping helplessly against him, the whole of her small body shaking, her eyes drowned in tears. The only other time he'd ever seen her weep like that was when they'd told her she wasn't likely to have children.

'Shh, calm down, Liz. This isn't good for you or the baby. We'll work something out – together.'

She looked up, hope dawning in her eyes. 'Bill?' she said again, uncertainly this time.

'Don't – push things.' His decision was made, really, but he didn't want to say it out loud yet.

She stared at him, not daring to voice her hope in case she broke the fragile gossamer threads that were starting to draw them together. After a moment, she laid her head against his shoulder with a weary sigh and they stood there in silence.

Finally he muttered, 'Oh, hell, I don't want us to split up, Liz.'

'Neither do I.' She huddled against him, praying for a miracle.

'And I definitely don't want to kill a baby.'

Another silence. Much longer this time. She hardly dared breathe as it dragged on.

Then, 'You'd better be a bloody good mother, though.'

The old Liz revived enough to ask, 'Will you be a good father?'

He nodded, holding her at arm's length and looking very solemn. 'I like kids. I always have. I was wrong about not adopting. But you're not to tell anyone it's not mine. Ever. That's my only condition.'

'I won't. Oh, Bill, I promise I won't.'

Then she was weeping again, tears of joy this time, and they were kissing one another as they hadn't kissed for years, hungrily, needily. Excitement flared between them and they started tearing at one another's clothes as they sank down together onto the soft vinyl of the kitchen floor.

Flesh against flesh, stripped of all barriers, they started to grow together again.

Tim drove through the darkness and when it started to rain, he didn't switch on the windscreen wipers, laughing as he nearly ran off the road. Maybe that was one way to end it? But something made him switch the wipers on and slow down just a little.

He came to Poole, eventually. Everything looked quiet, but when he got down to the docks area, there were signs of life, lights here and there, the odd person walking or stumbling along.

He stopped the car and got out, waiting till a man came along and asking bluntly, 'Where's the action?'

'Piss off.'

The words were slurred and Tim could smell the beer on the other's breath. He stepped back and watched the man stumble away. Patient now, because the end of his agony was in sight, he waited for someone else.

This man tried to avoid him, but when Tim repeated his question, 'Where's the action?', the fellow stopped and stared at him suspiciously.

'You want to score?'

'Yes.'

After a careful scrutiny of both him and the surrounding area, the man nodded. 'You're in luck. I've got some. Cost you, though.'

Tim fumbled in his pocket. His mother had had quite a stash of money in her handbag, thank goodness.

When he got the stuff, he had to ask, 'I've lost my equipment.'

The fellow laughed. 'Cost you some more.'

Tim paid, then walked away, twitching now for a hit. The only question was where. He didn't want anyone interrupting him.

He remembered the pub in the village. It was further than he really wanted to go, but still, it'd be deserted at this hour of the night and the car park was hidden from the road.

He got into the car and drove off again, this time switching the windscreen wipers on immediately and even humming along to the radio. Not long to wait. Just a hit now and then so that he could think straight, get his life in order. If you controlled the habit, it wasn't so bad. It was when you let the need control you that it was dangerous, and he'd proved he could live without it most of the time.

Rosalind felt as if she'd been sitting in the kitchen for a very long time when Louise got up and joined her.

'Ooh, Mum, you gave me a shock, sitting there so still!' She was dressed for her run and had already begun the warming-up exercises. She finished and realised her mother hadn't moved. 'You all right?'

'Tim hasn't come back. He went out last night, took my car. He left about two o'clock and – he hasn't returned.'

'He might have stopped somewhere for breakfast.'

'Where? This isn't a large city, with cafés open all hours. This is a small village, with one olde worlde tea room that doesn't open till ten.'

'Perhaps he stopped off at a garage for a coffee or something.'

'I can't see that, somehow. He's been avoiding other people ever since he got here.'

'I'll go and check his room.'

Louise ran upstairs, there was silence, then the sound of her coming down again slowly. 'His loose change is lying on top of the chest of drawers, just as it was last night when we were talking. I kept staring at it, seeing the patterns of the coins while we talked. It hasn't been moved. So he can't have stopped anywhere for breakfast.'

Fear dug its claws right into Rosalind's guts. 'What if something's happened to him?' She gave a shamefaced laugh. 'I expect I'm just getting worked up over nothing. He probably stopped the car somewhere and fell asleep. He'll be back soon.' Surely he would?

Jenny, who had been woken by Louise's footsteps pounding up and down the attic stairs, came into the kitchen in her dressing gown. 'What's wrong?'

'Tim went out last night and took Mum's car. He hasn't come back.'

'Oh.'

'I should have taken him straight back to Australia,' Rosalind worried. 'Gone with him and made him seek proper treatment. I *will* when he gets back. In fact, we'll all go home.

I'm fed up of living here, with your Dad popping in for an odd day. And now, well, he'll only rub Tim up the wrong way, he always does. I'll book our fares as soon as Tim gets back.'

Jenny and Louise exchanged worried glances.

The words *if he gets back* might have been written in fire around the walls.

'I don't want to go home to Australia. Not now,' Jenny said. 'Ned and I have only just got engaged and – well, I'm not going back.'

Rosalind went across to hug her. 'I've plenty of money. You can rent a flat in Dorchester or somewhere. I just – think Tim is in danger if he doesn't kick his habit. I have to *do* something. Help him. I trust our doctor at home. He's known us for years. He'll help me save Tim.'

Louise didn't go out for her run. Half an hour later she looked at the clock again. Nine o'clock. 'Oh, Mum, where *is* he?'

Another hour passed, long, tedious minutes dragging by between short bursts of awkward conversation.

'Should I ring the police, do you think?' Rosalind asked suddenly.

It was Louise who spoke. 'It wouldn't hurt. They could tell you if there'd been any accidents, couldn't they.'

So Rosalind found the number and dialled the nearest police station. To her surprise, they took her seriously. 'Has there been an accident?' she repeated.

'No, ma'am. What sort of car did you say it was?'

She told them, impatient now to get off the phone in case Tim was trying to ring home. The car had probably broken down, that was all.

'And the number of the car is?' the voice pressed.

'Thank you. And your address? If we hear anything we'll get back to you.'

She put down the phone and turned to smile shamefacedly at her daughters. 'He's probably just broken down. If he didn't take any money, he'll not be able to ring us.' She picked up her handbag from beside the phone. It felt too light. She peered inside. 'Anyone seen my purse?'

There was dead silence.

She looked from Louise to Jenny and back again. 'He wouldn't have. He wouldn't.'

They searched the house carefully, but there was no sign of her purse.

'I probably left it in the car,' she said uncertainly.

Louise shook her head. 'You're very careful with your purse, Mum. Ever since it got stolen that time.'

Tears filled her eyes. It seemed all too obvious Tim had taken it.

Louise put one arm round her mother, guiding her into the kitchen. 'I'll make us all some fresh coffee, shall I?'

At midday, still with no sign of Tim and no word from the police, Rosalind could stand it no longer. 'I'm going to ring your father. Ask his advice about what to do.' At that moment she'd completely forgotten about Paul's affair with Liz, forgotten everything except her anxiety for her missing son.

'Yeah,' Louise nodded, 'I'll say that for him – Dad usually knows what to do in a crisis.'

The secretary was insistent that she couldn't possibly disturb Mr Stevenson, whereupon Rosalind stopped being polite and yelled, 'This is a matter of life and death, and if you don't fetch my husband now, I'll have to send the police to do it.'

There was a gasp from the other end, then, 'I'll see what I can do. I'll call you back.'

When the phone rang a few minutes later Rosalind snatched it up. It was Paul and he was furious. 'What the hell do you mean by ringing me here, Ros? You know I'm working.' Twice now this had happened. What would the chairman think?

'It's Tim. He turned up a few days ago. He'd got himself into trouble in the States. Drugs.'

'*What?*'

'He was trying to kick the habit, and I *know* he hasn't taken anything since he's been with me. Only,' she had to gulp back the fear before she could put it in words, 'now he's taken my car and – and disappeared. My purse is gone too. Should I call in the police and tell them?'

'What do you mean "disappeared"?' Paul questioned her with the skill he usually brought to his work, drawing more details out of her. What he discovered made him splutter with rage. 'The stupid young bastard! What did he think he was playing at? And why didn't you let me know before?'

'If you can only mouth off at me, I'll put the phone down,' said the new Rosalind. 'For the last time, should I or should I not call in the police and tell them everything? I think – I feel sure he's in trouble. Serious trouble.'

'Not yet. I'll come straight home. It'll take me about two hours. Don't do anything at all until I get there. Not a single thing. Is that clear?'

'Yes.'

* * *

When a car turned into the drive a couple of hours later they thought it was Paul and all three of them went rushing to the front door. But it was a policeman. He had a woman with him, not in uniform, but she looked like some sort of official, too.

Rosalind took one look at their solemn faces and guessed what they were going to say. So when blackness rose around her, she let herself slip into it gratefully.

From a long way away she heard Louise's voice. 'She's coming round. Don't stand too close. Let her recover before you say anything.'

A mutter of voices.

Rosalind didn't want to open her eyes, but knew she had to. Had to face it. Had to.

She was surprised to find herself lying on a sofa in the living room. How had she got here? Louise was kneeling beside her, there was a wet cloth on her forehead and Jenny was standing behind the couch, gripping it with white-knuckled hands. Rosalind felt their anxiety and their support even before she looked across to the two strangers sitting stiffly on the other sofa.

'He's dead, isn't he? Tim's dead.'

They nodded.

'Sorry,' said the woman.

'How?'

'Overdose. He was sitting in your car behind the pub. You'd contacted the police earlier about it, if you remember, asking if there'd been any accidents.'

Rosalind tried to take it all in. It was the sort of thing you heard about on the television news. She always felt sorry for the families. And why wasn't she crying? Shouldn't she be crying? Only there were no tears, just a huge block of ice forming slowly inside her, layer upon chill layer.

After a while, she found she had to know one thing above all others. 'Did he – feel any pain?'

The man shook his head. 'Shouldn't think so. I don't think he'd even have realised what was happening. And it must have been very fast. The – er – needle was still in him.'

'Probably the heroin was too pure,' the woman said, 'and he gave himself an overdose by mistake.'

Rosalind couldn't speak or move, still trying to come to terms with the idea that her son was dead. They didn't try to pester her with any more questions, thank goodness.

At last, she forced herself to sit up properly but couldn't think what to do or say next.

Jenny slipped round to sit on the sofa beside her. Louise came and perched on the sofa arm at her other side.

Rosalind reached out to touch them, needing to make contact. Jenny was weeping. Louise looked frozen, stricken.

Another car drew up outside and someone pushed open the front door. 'Ros! Where are you, Ros?'

'That's my husband,' she told the police officers quietly, relief surging through her. For once Paul had put his family first. She found that comforting. If anything could be comforting on a day like this.

'We're in here!' Jenny called, her voice breaking on the words.

He stopped in the doorway and glared at Ros. 'I told you not to call in the police till I got here! Do you never bloody think before you act?'

It was Louise who got up and stood toe to toe with him. 'Don't you talk to Mum like that! *We* didn't call the police in. They came to tell us that Tim's body had been found in the car.' Her voice wobbled for a minute, then she forced herself to continue. 'He's *dead*! So don't start throwing your weight around because we don't need any aggro from you today!' Then she collapsed against her mother, sobbing wildly.

Rosalind put her arms round Louise and watched her husband. He looked stunned. She was glad he was here, but she didn't want to go to him, just wanted him to take charge. She continued to hold Louise and patted Jenny's hand from time to time with her other hand.

'Tim's – dead?' Paul's voice was the merest scrape of sound.

Rosalind nodded.

Paul couldn't move for a moment. Tim dead. His son. His only son. And the last time he'd seen him, they'd argued, shouted – said dreadful things to one another. He shuddered and tried not to think of that.

The policeman seemed to materialise at his side. 'Come and sit down, sir. You've had a bit of a shock.'

Paul shook the hand off his arm and found his own way to a chair. 'Tell me the details. I need to know.'

So once again they described what had happened.

He tried to focus on the police officer as he listened, but his eyes kept sliding back to Ros, sitting with a daughter on either side of her, weeping, being comforted. Why was no one trying to comfort him?

The woman cleared her throat. 'I'm sorry to do this to you,

sir, but someone will have to come and identify the body.'

Paul stared at her in horror. 'But you've just told us he's dead, so you must know already who he is. What good would it do for us to go and see him?' And with a shock, he realised that for the first time in a lot of years he couldn't do what was expected of him. He just – he simply couldn't. 'You shouldn't even ask it of us, dammit.'

Rosalind surprised them all by standing up. 'I'll go and identify the body, officer. I *want* to see my son.' She had to, in order to accept that he was dead. Her boy. Her baby. Her agonised young man of the embroidery.

Louise stood up. 'I want to see him, too. I need to – to say goodbye.'

Jenny shook her head in response to their questioning glances. 'I'm sorry. I c-can't face it.'

'We'll take you in the police car, Mrs Stevenson,' the woman said quietly. 'And bring you back afterwards. We'll get your own car back to you as soon as possible.'

'I'll get the leasing company to change it,' Paul said at once. 'You won't want to drive that one again.'

Rosalind looked across at him. He sat down, shook his head blindly and put it in his hands without saying a word. He didn't attempt to speak to her, let alone comfort her. And she found she had nothing to offer him, either.

She looked at her younger daughter and put an arm round Louise's shoulders, feeling Louise's arm round her waist. Together they walked out of the house with the police officers.

When they'd gone, Jenny scowled across at her father. 'You couldn't even help her do that, could you?'

He glared at her. 'You didn't go with them, either.'

'I'm not her husband. You are.'

She went to phone Ned.

Paul sat there and tried not to weep. He hadn't wept since he was a small boy and it'd do no good now, no good at all. He kept seeing images of Tim, hearing faint echoes of their many quarrels – and wishing he'd seen him alive once more and made up the quarrel.

In the end he went and poured himself a large whisky. It was the only comfort he could think of.

By the time Rosalind got into the police car, the news was all over the village, because one of the Tuffins had found the body.

Feeling upset about the dreadful news, Harry drove over to see Jonathon. Better if she told him about it so that he didn't give himself away. She came straight to the point. 'Have you heard?'

He was working in the big formal dining room, sanding the floorboards in preparation for a new coat of stain. 'Heard what?'

'Heard about Rosalind's son?'

'Tim? No. What's he done now?'

'He hasn't done anything. He's dead. Drug overdose.'

Jonathon stood up, turning white and leaning one hand against the nearest wall. 'Dead?' he whispered. 'That poor lad's dead?'

'Yes. Alice Tuffin told me. Her eldest son found the body in the car park behind the pub. This morning. Just sitting in the car, she said. She thought I'd want to go and see Rosalind.

But – well, I thought I'd better come and tell you first.'

'Oh, hell and damnation! Hasn't she enough to bear with that selfish brute of a husband? Does she have to bear this, too?'

'Tim was twenty, that's all. Twenty.' Harry looked at her brother. 'Got any gin?'

'Yes.' He escorted her through to the small sitting room he used in winter to conserve fuel. 'Sit down. I'll get us both a drink.'

They sipped at gin and brandy respectively, sitting in silence. Once he got up to put some more wood on the fire. Once she opened her mouth as if to speak, then closed it again. Nothing you said made any difference at a time like this. She'd found that when her husband died, had often wished her kind friends would just go away and leave her to grieve in peace. But today she sat on in case Jonathon needed her.

'What hurts,' he said at last, 'apart from the tragedy of a young life lost, is that I have no right to go and comfort her. And I can't see that damned husband of hers being much use at a time like this. Can you?'

'He'll probably deal with the practical details very efficiently – which will spare her that trouble, at least,' Harry said. 'There are a lot of details to sort out when someone dies. I'll call in on them tomorrow, if you like, then let you know how things are going.'

He shook his head. 'I'll call myself.' He had to make sure Rosalind was all right.

'We'll go together, then. It'll look better, don't you think?'

He raised his eyes to stare at her. 'You know, don't you? How I feel about her, I mean?'

'Oh, yes. Sticks out a mile. Well, to me it does. Pity she's married. I like her, too. Bit soft for her own good, but nice. Heart's in the right place.'

But for once Harry was wrong. Paul Stevenson wasn't dealing with anything efficiently. While he sat and waited for his wife to return, he drank a whisky quickly, then poured another one, drowning his grief in gulps of amber comfort.

By the time the car turned into the drive, he was sitting in an owlish stupor and Jenny was fiddling around in the kitchen, trying to keep herself occupied while she waited for Ned to arrive. She went into the hall, expecting her mother and Louise to be in floods of tears, but they weren't. They were very still and white. For the first time ever she saw a faint resemblance between them, something about the expressions on their faces.

She took their coats, hesitated, then whispered, 'Dad's drunk. In the sitting room.'

Rosalind looked in to see Paul slumped down in an armchair, snoring, a glass with an inch of whisky in it tilting dangerously in his hand. And was glad. She didn't want to face him yet. Not about anything.

'What shall we do?' Jenny whispered.

'Nothing. Leave him to sleep it off.' She switched the living-room light off again, turned back into the hall, hesitated, then gave in to temptation. 'I'm going out. I'll take your Dad's car.'

'To see Jonathon?' Jenny asked.

Rosalind looked at her, startled.

Jenny blushed and said in a very low voice, 'I saw you kissing him at the fête.'

'How long ago that seems now.' It was important to set the record straight. 'We're not sleeping together, you know.'

'You don't need to tell me that. You wouldn't.'

But she'd wanted to, Rosalind thought. Heavens, she'd wanted much more than Jonathon's kisses. Did that make her as guilty as Paul? Did it matter? Did anything matter now?

At the door she turned. 'If your father asks, would you mind saying you think I've gone to see Harry? If he wants his car, ring Harry and explain.'

Jenny rushed forward to give her mother a hug, then watched her walk stiffly out of the house. Strange. She'd expected her mother to crumble, not her father. She went to sit with Louise in the kitchen and pick at a sandwich. 'Ned's coming over tonight.'

'Good. I'm glad you've got him.'

'What about you?'

Louise looked at her blindly. 'I'd actually prefer to be on my own.'

She heard Ned arrive and go upstairs with Jenny, but sat on alone with her thoughts and memories. Tim had looked so peaceful in the morgue it had surprised her, almost as if he'd been ready to die. 'Have you done anything to – um, make him look better?' she'd asked the assistant as they all stood there in that chilly room, gleaming with stainless steel and smelling of antiseptic – and of something else she didn't like to think about.

'No. We haven't touched his face at all. That's how he looked when he was found.'

At that moment Louise had been certain he was glad to be out of it and she even wondered if he'd done it on purpose, though she'd never say that to her mother, of course. He'd said a few times that he felt used up, exhausted. When she'd tried to talk about the future, he'd said he couldn't see one for himself.

But *she* had to carry on, and her future didn't look very rosy, either. She had to face her pain at losing her brother and also sort out her own life. Probably that'd mean rows with her father.

She wandered into the sitting room and stared down at him, taking the glass from his hand. He didn't move and she didn't try to rouse him.

You've let her down, she thought. *Mum needed you to be strong and you let her down. You should have gone with her today, then comforted her when she got back. I'm not going to be like you when I grow up.*

Tim was right. She still had a long way to go before she could consider herself mature. But she was sure of one thing: she was never, ever going to let anyone down again.

And then it all overwhelmed her in a great black wave of sorrow. She had to run up to her bedroom and bury her face in her pillow so that her father wouldn't be woken by her sobbing, so that her sister wouldn't come in.

Chapter Eighteen

When someone hammered at the big front door of the manor and kept on hammering, calling his name, Jonathon ran along the hall and flung the door open. He drew Rosalind into his arms. 'Oh, my love! My darling girl, come in!'

He took her into the small parlour and sat down beside her, his arm round her shoulders. This wasn't a time for large rooms and echoing spaces, but for the cosiness of the womb.

As her grief eased a little, he poured them both a brandy, then they sat together quietly on the couch. When she looked at him, he said gently, 'No need to talk unless you wish to, my love.'

So she didn't try to speak at first, not until she had drawn enough solace from his presence. She simply sat there pressed against him, feeling his arm light yet strong round her back and clasping her hands round the brandy goblet as she soaked up the peace of Destan Manor. Nobody could bring Tim back, but friends could share your grief, acknowledge that you had borne and loved a son, and that his passing was momentous enough for them to stop their own busy lives for a moment or two.

She sipped the brandy from time to time and focused on small things to distract herself from the pain – the warmth of the liquid in her mouth and throat, the visual comfort of a wood fire flickering in the grate, the interesting textures in the worn fabric on the arm of the sofa. When at last she'd pulled enough of herself together, she started to tell him what had happened over the past few days – quietly, not weeping, because tears wouldn't help. What did help was the warmth of this man's body next to hers and his unspoken offer of anything he could give her. It helped so much.

When she'd finished the tale, they sat on in the quietness of the night, the dog lying nearby, sighing from time to time as if in sympathy. Once Jonathon got up to refill their glasses, later he dozed against her, his head on her shoulder, his fine, thinning hair tickling her cheek. The occasional grey strand filled her with compassion for the way the years marked them all. You couldn't go through life unscathed.

She didn't wake him because his presence was all she needed. She was deeply grateful he'd made no attempt to fill the night with meaningless chatter, but she couldn't, she simply couldn't sleep. Not yet. This wakeful night was, in some strange way, her special tribute to her son.

Later still, Jonathon raised his head, blinked at her like a thin, nervous owl and said, 'Sorry. Didn't mean to fall asleep on you.'

She smiled and stretched out one hand to brush the soft

hair from his eyes. 'What are you sorry for? You were there for me. That's all I needed.'

He caught that hand and raised it to his lips. 'Always.' But he didn't labour the point. After a few minutes, he yawned. 'It's nearly morning. Do you want a coffee? I've got your favourite brand.'

'I'd love one. And a piece of toast, perhaps?' The thought that he'd bought the plunger and coffee specially for her, since he much preferred tea, made her feel loved. Of such details, she thought dreamily, were lives made. And relationships.

So they walked through the creaking, shifting old house to the kitchen and made coffee and toast, sitting at a scrubbed wooden table just as the first fingers of brightness were tearing the mourning veils from the sky and signalling the end of her darkest night.

Not until it was fully light did she leave. 'Thank you,' she told him, kissing his cheek and then fleetingly, impersonally, his lips. 'I can think better now. I have to go back and – and deal with it all.'

He could not help asking, 'Are you – do you think you'll stay with him?'

'I don't know. I can't decide that now.'

'No. Of course not. But – I do love you, Rosalind. And I want to be with you. Remember that, won't you?'

A fragile smile flickered briefly on her face. 'I will. And I love you, too, Jonathon. Very much.'

When Paul woke up, he couldn't think where he was for a moment. He winced at the stiffness of his body and groaned when he moved his head incautiously. A hangover started to thump behind his forehead, circling his skull with a leaden band and drumming a message of pain whenever he moved. He swallowed and grimaced at the sour taste in his mouth. Hell, what had made him tie one on?

Then he remembered.

Tim was dead.

He stood there, thumping his thighs with his clenched fists, until he had his damned emotions under control, then stumbled up the stairs to the master bedroom, stopping at the door in shock as he found it empty, the bed not even slept in. 'Ros?' He peered into the en suite but she wasn't there. He went pounding back downstairs into the kitchen, the dining room, the conservatory. Not a sign of her.

But there was a youngish man, a complete stranger, sleeping on the floor in the office. He mumbled in his sleep when the door opened, but didn't wake up.

Who the hell was he? Paul wondered as he closed the door quietly. The stranger looked familiar, but he couldn't quite place him, and he definitely didn't feel up to accosting the fellow and asking what he was doing there. Not till he'd had a strong coffee and put some food into his rumbling stomach. He never thought well when he was hungry. Now he came to think of it, he hadn't had any dinner last night. No wonder the drink had gone to his head.

Back upstairs. One room was full of her embroidery. Bloody stuff! He picked up the frame and as he saw what she was doing, he froze and stared down at it. He had never thought her good before, but this – it was clever, there was no denying that. She'd caught him perfectly, shown him as he liked to think of himself, confident, in control of himself.

She'd caught herself, too, with those damned pale colours – he was going to take her to a fashion consultant before they went to the States, smarten her up. His eyes slid over the image of Jenny and that bloody dog of hers, then he saw the sketch of Tim. A wave of anguish took him by surprise. Was that what Tim had become? That thin, haunted creature? He couldn't bear to look at it, even.

He tossed the frame down on the table, but it wasn't enough. The sketch of Tim was still there, still looking up at him accusingly. With a growl of anger, he knocked everything on the table flying, then kicked the frame with its stretch of canvas out of the way. It went spinning across the room and he was glad to hear the wood crack.

Where the hell was Rosalind? *Tim's room!* he thought suddenly. *She'll be up there, mooning around.* But there was no one in the attic. Tim's things were lying scattered around as if he'd just stepped out and that made Paul gulp and back out. He could feel tears filling his eyes again. Hell, you'd think he could control himself better than this!

He went and opened the front door and saw that his car was missing, which made him feel angry. He concentrated on the anger, which was better than the other emotion. What if she had an accident? Did no one in his family care about the liability of driving a car that wasn't insured for them? And where had she gone anyway?

He went back upstairs. Perhaps the girls would know.

'Jenny!' He shook his elder daughter awake.

She lay staring at him in surprise for a moment, then

remembered Tim, sobbed and covered her swollen eyes with her arm.

He shook her again. If he let her cry, she'd start him off, and he wasn't, he definitely was not, going to parade his emotions like some sodding half-man of a poofter. 'Where's your mother gone? I can't find her anywhere. And she's taken my car.'

Jenny had no trouble lying to him this time, she who normally blushed and stuttered if she even tried to fudge the truth slightly. 'She'll have gone to Harry's, I expect. They're good friends.'

'Harry?'

'Harriet Destan.'

Ah, he remembered now. Sister of the lord of the manor. 'Well, she has no *right* to go out and leave us. No right at all. Fine way of showing her grief that is!'

'It's better than getting drunk and *snoring*!'

'I do not snore.'

'You were rotten drunk when Mum came back from identifying Tim yesterday afternoon and you were definitely snoring. Loudly.' Like a hog, a disgusting hog.

'Well, that's neither here nor there. Get up and make me some breakfast.'

She couldn't believe what she was hearing. 'Go and make your own damn breakfast. I'm not Mum, waiting on you hand and foot.'

'Get up, I said!' He hauled her out of bed.

After an involuntary squeal of surprise, she resisted him, shouting and yelling.

Then Ned was there, pushing past her father to stand between the two of them. 'Leave her alone, you bully!'

'Who the hell are you? And what are you doing in my house anyway?'

Jenny clutched Ned's hand. 'He's here at my invitation. This is Ned Didburin. We're engaged.'

'Well, well. I only had a drink to blur my grief, but you brought someone round here to screw your troubles away.'

Whereupon Ned, peaceful, unaggressive Ned, punched him on the jaw.

And Paul, unprepared for anyone so wimpy-looking to stand up to him, rocketed backwards, crashed into the door frame and overbalanced, to fall sprawling on the landing floor. He lay for a moment, grunting, shaking his head.

Louise, woken by the noise, stepped over him and arranged herself by her sister's side. 'What's caused this?'

'He wanted Mum. When he couldn't find her, he ordered me to get up and make his breakfast. I didn't happen to feel like waiting on him.' Tears began to trickle out of Jenny's eyes. 'I wanted to stay here and pull myself together. So he tried to force me to get up. Then,' she gulped audibly, 'Ned came up to see what was happening and Dad accused me of screwing him to – to block out what happened to Tim.'

'What a nasty sod he is!'

Ned was still standing dumbfounded, gaping down at his fist, then goggling at Paul, who was pulling himself to his feet with an ugly expression on his face.

Louise went to stand between them. 'Get out of here, Dad. Jenny wants to get dressed.'

'Oh? And is lover boy going to stay here and help her, then?'

Louise raised her chin and took a step forward, nudging her sister aside and facing not only her father, but the years of fearing him. Staring him in the eyes, she said, 'What Ned and Jenny do is none of your business.'

Then she took her father by surprise by shoving him back out onto the landing before he realised what she was doing. 'Leave them alone, Dad. If you need waiting on, I'll come and make your breakfast for you.'

Rosalind walked in just then and looked up as the door to Jenny's room opened and Ned peered over the banisters.

'Good morning, Ned. I'm glad you came over to be with Jenny.' Rosalind ran lightly up the stairs and went to kiss Jenny, then Louise, who gave her a watery smile.

Still with her arm round Louise, Rosalind turned to stare at her husband who was glaring at her.

'I'll just have a quick shower and change my clothes, Paul, then I'll come and make your breakfast. We'll leave Jenny and Louise to get up at their own pace.'

He grunted something which might have been agreement and followed her into the master bedroom.

She got out some clean clothes, the darkest garments she could find, though she owned nothing black. *Pastels*, she thought, looking along the neat row of hangars, *they're nearly all pastels*. She had a sudden longing for jewel tones, for shiny fabrics and rich patterns, for clothes with more *life* to them.

Paul flung himself into the small armchair in the bay window and watched her sourly. 'Where the hell have you been?'

'With friends.'

She walked into the bathroom and locked the door on him, needing a few quiet moments to pull herself together.

Paul sat down on the edge of the bed and closed his eyes, rubbing his aching forehead, not sure what to do next.

At a nod from the inspector, Constable Thelma Simpton knocked on the front door. They waited, but no one came.

'Knock again!' he ordered.

Paul went to peer out of the window, muttering, 'Oh, sod it. Can't the bloody police leave us alone for a minute?'

In the bathroom the water cut off abruptly. Wrapping a towel around herself, Rosalind went into the bedroom and joined Paul at the window. When he didn't move, she pushed it further open and looked down at the police officers. 'Yes? Can I help you?'

The inspector cleared his throat. 'Police here. Sorry to intrude on your grief again, Mrs Stevenson, but could we come in and speak to you?' He gestured around him. 'This place is a bit public for a discussion.'

'The door's not locked. I'll be down as soon as I'm dressed.' Rosalind threw on her clothes at top speed and turned in surprise to Paul, who had flopped into the chair again and was sitting with his head in his hands. 'Aren't you coming down?'

'In a minute. And for Christ's sake, put some coffee on.'

As she went downstairs, she saw the two police officers waiting in the hall.

The inspector nodded. 'Sorry to intrude.'

'You have your job to do. Come through here.' She

led the way into the sitting room. 'Sorry everything is in such a mess. We haven't had time to clear up yet this morning.'

He brightened. 'Does that mean no one's touched your son's room?'

'I don't think they have.'

Behind them Louise said, 'No one's been in Tim's room except me, and I only stood in the doorway for a minute to see if he'd taken any money with him. Oh, and I think Dad went in when he was looking for Mum this morning.' She went to link an arm in her mother's.

Rosalind clasped her daughter's hand as it lay on her arm. Who would have expected Louise to be so steady and dependable in a crisis?

Paul came clattering down the stairs to join them, his tight business expression back on his face, the front of his hair damp. But he was still wearing the same crumpled clothes and his face looked ravaged. That touched Rosalind's heart a little. She couldn't have borne it if he'd been unmoved by Tim's death.

'Would you mind if we checked your son's room, Mrs Stevenson? We need to find out if he's been storing drugs here.'

Paul breathed in deeply. 'Come upstairs. I'll want to be there while you search Tim's room.'

'I'll come with you, too,' Rosalind added quietly. 'I know more about my son's possessions than my husband does. He didn't see Tim this time.' Alive or dead. And would presumably never see him again. None of them would. She felt the grief solidify in her chest as if ice was still building up. She couldn't weep out her grief until it melted.

'Very helpful of you, madam. We're much obliged. If there's anything my officers can do to help, don't hesitate to ask.'

There wasn't, of course, but you said things like that to offer them comfort, make them feel you were on the ball – well, you said it to the nice ones, anyway.

He sighed as he walked downstairs again. There had been nothing in the room to show that the boy was a junkie, but judging from the condition of his arms, he'd been well into the stuff, though not recently.

Maybe it was time to take that early retirement he'd been offered after all. He'd seen too many grieving, bewildered families, people he'd wanted to help and couldn't, because the accountants had got into everything and the talk nowadays was all of bottom lines and staying within budgets, instead of service to the public.

When the inspector had left, Rosalind went into the kitchen and picked up the phone. Paul followed her and put his hand across the dialling pad. 'Who are you calling?'

'My mother.'

'Surely that can wait till after breakfast?'

'I don't want any breakfast. And I can't face cooking.' She pushed his hand aside and began to dial. 'If you're hungry, get something.'

'I don't know where anything is in this house.'

'Try opening a few cupboard doors and looking. They're not locked. Ah, Mum.' Her voice was quite steady. 'I have some very sad news, I'm afraid . . .'

He watched her in disbelief as she told her mother

about Tim, not weeping, speaking calmly, doing her best to console the older woman, whose sobbing was quite audible from where he stood.

He looked at her in puzzlement. Ever since it happened, he'd been expecting Ros to collapse, give way to her grief, but she hadn't done. He didn't understand how she could be so strong about this when she was so weak about everything else.

As for Tim – Paul stood still and fought yet again to contain his grief – as for Tim, well, that was over and done with. He didn't have a son any more. You just had to get on with things. But he'd make sure his daughters didn't go off the rails, by hell he would! And as for that chinless wimp Jenny said she was engaged to, they'd see about that. She was useless at picking men, absolutely useless.

After the phone call, Ros went up to do her hair and calm herself in the en suite with the door locked. By the time she came down again, Paul had made himself some toast and instant coffee, and was crunching an apple. The sound was obscene.

'The bathroom's free,' she told him and felt nothing but relief as he grunted an acknowledgement, took the plate of toast and went upstairs, not running as usual, but walking slowly and heavily.

The phone rang. 'I'll get it,' she called. 'Yes?'

'Harry here. I'm so very sorry to hear about Tim. Anything I can do to help, Rosalind?'

'I'm not sure. I'll get back to you if I need you.' She heard someone else breathing and realised that Paul was listening in, spying on her. Anger filled her for a moment.

'You won't hesitate to call on us?'

'No, of course not. You and Jonathon have been good friends to me.'

'I told Alice Tuffin you'd ring if you wanted her. She'd be happy to help, too. She says to tell you no charge.'

'Thanks.'

'Jonathon sends his love. I'm with him now. You sure you're managing all right?'

'Yes. Thank him for me. Bye now.'

Upstairs, Paul frowned. Her voice had grown warm as she spoke to those damned friends of hers. But if this woman had to ring and ask how she was, Ros mustn't have gone to see her last night. Where had she been, then? He pulled his clothes off, leaving them scattered across the floor, and took a very long shower, emerging in better control of himself, thank goodness.

Downstairs Rosalind brewed some more coffee, taking a cup upstairs to Jenny.

'Where is he?'

'Showering.'

Jenny looked towards the master bedroom. 'We'll come down now. Can I get Ned something to eat?'

'Of course you can.' Rosalind nodded to him. 'I'm so glad Jenny's got you, Ned.' She felt warmed by the sight of their love. The lump of ice inside her cracked just a little at the way they were holding hands.

Louise's bedroom door opened. 'All right if I go for a jog?' She lowered her voice. 'Don't want to face Dad yet.'

'Do whatever you want.'

Louise hesitated, then came across to give her a hug. 'I love you, Mum.'

Rosalind's composure slipped for a minute and the ice cracked still further. 'I love you, too.' Her voice came out husky and she had to blink away the tears.

'Tim said I'd been a fool and he was right. I won't let you down again, Mum. Or him.'

'Good.' Rosalind flicked away a tear, but it was followed by another. Funny what set you off. 'You go for your run, love.'

'Sure you'll be all right?'

'Yes.' She still had Paul to face about the other thing. But she wasn't going to have a confrontation about his infidelity with her son lying unburied.

She was nearly sure now that she was going to leave him. But not till all this – this main trouble was over.

It was a big decision to make. She couldn't rush it, had to be very sure of what she was doing.

Chapter Nineteen

Paul stared at Rosalind incredulously when she explained that Jenny and Ned had gone out for a while, and Louise had gone jogging.

'At a time like this? Her brother dies and all Jenny is concerned about is being with lover boy. And who said they could get engaged? No one asked me.'

Rosalind was getting tired of him yelling. She kept trying to tell herself that it was just his way of dealing with this tragedy, but it was a way that took no account of others' needs. 'She hasn't been sleeping with him. He's been here offering her comfort and support.'

A nasty grin curved Paul's mouth. 'Don't you believe it, Ros. I know all about that sort of comfort. He was in her bedroom, helping her to dress, for heaven's sake. How you can be so incredibly naïve at your age, I can't understand.'

At least she wasn't cruel to someone grieving.

She nearly told him what she knew about him, but

managed to turn away, taking several deep breaths. Not now. She'd promised herself not to do or say anything about their marriage until after the funeral. 'I'm going out to the shops. We need something for tea.' It'd be a relief to get away from him.

'Why bother? We'll go out somewhere for a meal tonight.'

'You can go out, if you want. I shan't. There's only the local pub to go to, anyway.' Rosalind didn't want to face a sea of sympathetic faces.

'Well, all right, but be quick. I'll stay here in case the police want anything else.'

As if she needed his permission to go shopping!

In the convenience store the staff and other customers left her alone, except for bobs of the head and sympathetic murmurs as they passed her. They didn't seem to expect a response, for which she was grateful. She slung food into the trolley as quickly as she could and when she was waved to the head of the small queue, she nodded her thanks, but didn't speak or make eye contact with anyone.

Back at the house, she put the groceries away and stayed in the kitchen wondering what to do with herself.

Paul came into the kitchen. 'Fancy making us a cup of coffee?'

'No.' If she did that, he'd expect her to join him, and then she might blurt something out, like, *Was Liz a better screw than me?* She went upstairs to her embroidery.

When she saw what had happened there, however, she stopped dead, then rage boiled up in her, absolutely boiled. Paul had taken out his feelings on her things. 'Oh, you bastard!' she muttered under her breath. 'You nasty, rotten bastard!'

She went first to pick up the broken frame from the floor

in the corner, checking every inch of the family embroidery carefully and breathing a sigh of relief when she found it intact. Had he even noticed the picture? Surely he'd have said something if he had, because his figure was very prominent in it, very recognisable and not at all flattering. No, he must just have hit out in blind fury.

She was picking up her skeins of thread when he poked his head in the doorway. She turned to look at him and said loudly, 'If you ever touch my embroidery things again, I'll make interesting patterns on your business suits with my scissors.'

He scowled at her, the apology he had intended to make dying in his throat. 'I might have known you'd come here. You're sick, do you know that? Stuck in a bloody time warp, spending your life on an outmoded pastime that no one respects nowadays.' He slammed the door behind him.

Rosalind sat on the floor looking at her sketch of Tim, which had drifted under the worktable. *I'll do you justice, love*, she thought. *I really will. If I have to redo your figure a hundred times.*

But she didn't have to. She mended the embroidery frame with insulation tape, then worked on her son's head. As it took shape, it turned into Tim, giving her his half-smile, looking rebellious, yet lost and afraid in a hostile world. A few tears fell and the ice that was weighing down her chest cracked a bit more.

She needed to finish the family embroidery, even though she knew she would never be able to hang it on the wall. It was too full of pain. All their pain.

But she needed to *know*.

* * *

That afternoon she rang up the police station. 'I was wondering how soon we can bury our son?'

'Have to be a post-mortem, even though we know what he died of. Sorry about that, madam. Say three days, four at most. The undertakers will know what to do if you tell them what's happened. Munham's in Wareham is well thought of.'

'Thank you.'

Paul came out of the living room. 'What did they say?'

'Three or four days. There'll have to be a post-mortem.' She started up the stairs.

'Is that all you're going to do? Sit and bloody embroider? Your son lies dead and you fiddle with embroidery silks?'

She paused only long enough to say, 'It's better than quarrelling, don't you think? If you want something to do with yourself, go and book the funeral.' She didn't care about the details. They were irrelevant. However they did it, it would be her son they were burying.

She had to stand very still for a moment on that thought. She had known of agony like this, but only intellectually. The reality was far worse, a bleak cliff of pain that she had to scale an inch at a time. She realised Paul was speaking.

'Yes. I'll go and do that. Where should I go, do you think?'

'Munham's. In Wareham. They're used to these cases, apparently. You can probably find their address online.'

She heard him go into his office. She let some of the tension sift slowly out in a long breath, but her relief was short-lived. A few minutes later she became aware of him standing in the doorway. She covered the embroidery instinctively.

'I'm not going to touch your precious toys. I've seen what you're doing there. A pitiful attempt at a family portrait.'

'Did you want something?'

He scowled. 'I think you should come with me. I don't know anything about arranging funerals. You've just done one for that old witch.'

'*Don't*,' her voice was so sharp it surprised her as well as him, 'call Aunt Sophie that.'

In her bedroom, eavesdropping as usual, Louise grinned. *Good one, Mum.* She made a sign of triumph with an upraised fist.

'Don't be so bloody touchy! It's only a nickname.'

'Well, it's one I don't care for. I was extremely fond of my aunt.' Rosalind sighed, but put down the sewing and shepherded him out of the room. 'Very well. We'll do this together.' She knocked on Louise's door. 'We're going to sort out the funeral. Do you want to come with us, love?'

Louise recognised the look of pleading in her mother's eyes and steeled herself. 'Yes. I'd like to be part of it, Mum.' And found to her surprise that it was the truth.

'Thanks.' Rosalind squeezed her daughter's hand.

Watching them, Paul thought how successful his methods had been with this child, at least. Louise had fallen into line, just as he'd known she would. It took discipline, something Ros wasn't good at. These housewifely types never were, but they made the best sort of wife for a man like him.

'You drive,' he said outside, waving a hand at Rosalind. 'You know the district. I'll just program the address into the satnav.'

She couldn't remember the last time he'd asked her to drive him. And he was very quiet on the journey – amazingly quiet, for him – sitting staring out of the window with a grim look on his face.

Louise was just as quiet in the back.

When they got home, Rosalind fidgeted round the house then decided to go for a walk. She had to get out of this brooding atmosphere for a while if she was to continue coping. As she came downstairs, dressed in her outdoor things, Paul peered out of his office, where he'd been making phone calls and sending faxes intermittently, as well as doing a lot of staring into space. 'Where are you going?'

'For a walk.'

'Where?'

'Just out.' She tried to pass him, but he grabbed her arm.

'I need to know where you'll be, in case the police want you.'

She had promised herself no confrontations till after Tim was buried, but suddenly she'd had enough. She tore her arm out of his and shrieked, 'I'm going out and I don't *know* where. I just need a bit of peace, so damned well leave me alone.'

She went out before he could say anything, and judging by the way he was gaping, her outburst had startled him. *Well, that's just the beginning, Paul Stevenson.*

In Western Australia Audrey decided to ring round her daughter's friends and let them know what had happened. 'Liz? Audrey Worth here. Yes, I'm fine. Liz – I have some bad news.'

Liz braced herself to hear that Paul and Ros had split up.

'Tim's dead.' Audrey took a deep breath. 'Overdose.'

Liz collapsed onto the nearest chair, speechless, shocked. 'Are you still there?'

'Yes. I just – I don't know what to say.'

Audrey's voice was thick with tears. 'I thought you might like to ring Rosalind. You two have always been so close. Do you have her UK number? Oh, well, here it is, then.'

'Thank you.' She wasn't sure what to say, just knew she had to offer her sympathy. Liz put the phone down and sat there, feeling numb. Then she looked at the clock. No, not a good time to ring.

When Bill came in, she was sitting in the kitchen with an empty mug in front of her. She didn't even look up.

'Something wrong?' He was getting quite used to the idea now, was looking forward to being a father. He would *make* himself the child's father, and let anyone try to say different. He'd been wondering about moving away from Perth, too. It'd been hinted lately that he needed to broaden his experience, work overseas for a while. If he found somewhere to go for a year or two, it'd get Liz out of the Stevensons' way, and keep the baby out of that bastard's hands, too.

Liz shook her head and managed a faint smile. 'No. No, it's not that. It's – oh, Bill, Tim Stevenson's dead, an overdose.' Her eyes filled with tears again. 'What must Rosalind be feeling?'

He came to stand beside her, his hand on her shoulder. 'You'll have to ring her.'

'I can't. Bill, I just can't face her.'

'You have to.'

So a little later, when it would be morning in England, she picked up the phone. 'Ros? Liz here. I just heard. I—'

'Go to hell, you cheating bitch!' Rosalind slammed the phone down.

Liz sank to the floor in the hall, burying her face in her hands. Rosalind knew. How long had she known? Had he told her? Surely even *he* wouldn't do that?

Bill peered out of the living room, saw her and rushed over. 'What's wrong?'

'Rosalind knows.'

'Oh, hell!'

Liz burst into tears and wept till she was so exhausted and wrung out that Bill was seriously thinking of calling out the doctor to sedate her.

When she stopped sobbing, he brought her a cup of camomile tea and sat beside her while she drank it, steadying her shaking hand round it at first, but not saying anything. What was there to say? The harm had been done. Nothing they could do would make things right again, not between Rosalind and Liz, anyway.

Hearing the phone, Paul came into the hall. 'Who was that?'

Rosalind stared at him blankly for a moment. 'What? Oh, wrong number.'

'But you told them to go to hell.'

'Nuisance call, then. What is this? The Inquisition?' She drifted up the stairs into her own room, not to embroider, no, just to sit and stroke the face she had made for Tim's figure. And to wish this dreadful waiting time would end. Not until her son had had a proper funeral would she feel like facing the rest of her life.

A little later she went out in the car. Paul heard her go

but didn't ask where she was going this time. He stood in the hall watching her drive away through the glass of the front door, feeling abandoned. They'd all gone out, Jenny with that fellow – God, she could certainly pick 'em, what a weak-looking prat! – Louise for a run – 'Keeping fit, Dad,' she had said brightly as she left – and now Ros. Didn't they realise he had feelings, too?

There was a knock on the door and he went to open it. A woman was there with a big arrangement of flowers in her hands.

'Special delivery,' she said in a hushed, sympathetic voice.

He took them off her and she drove away. It was a while before he realised he was still standing there, with the door wide open, clutching the damned things.

He set the flowers down on the hall table. What good did flowers do? But when he looked at the label, he felt a bit better. From the chairman himself. He studied them again. They must have cost a packet.

But the flowers didn't solve the problem of what he was going to do with himself for the rest of the day. He tried ringing work to catch up with a few things, see how the workshop had ended, but everyone insisted they could manage, speaking to him in gentle tones, as if he were ill.

He'd rather have worked. Much rather. It'd have stopped him thinking so much, stopped him regretting so much, too. He cut that thought short. He wasn't going to allow himself to get maudlin again. He'd follow Louise's example and go for a run.

It didn't help as much as he'd expected.

* * *

Rosalind drove for a long time, eyes blind with memories. Then she realised where she was and turned right. 'Why not?' she asked the wind as it buffeted the car. The cold spring was being featured on the news every night now – one of the coldest Mays on record. That suited her, somehow. It was much better than soft, sunny days, which would have seemed to mock her grief.

Jonathon opened the door, glanced round and saw that she was alone, so simply opened his arms.

She walked into them, resting her head against his chest with a weary sigh. 'Can we go into one of your lovely rooms and just sit? The one with Araminta's embroidery, perhaps?'

'Of course.'

They walked along the hall arm in arm and she let him fuss her into an armchair near the unlit fire.

He struck a match and soon flames were crackling in the hearth. 'Want a cup of coffee?'

'Mmm.'

When he got back, she was sitting there, staring into the fire with her hand on Dusty's head, stroking him absent-mindedly.

She looked up. 'I'm not very good company, I'm afraid.'

'I don't need entertaining. Would you like me to leave you alone here?'

She considered this, head on one side, then nodded. 'I would, actually. I love this room. I need to be alone and quiet. Paul's so – loud and demanding.'

'Want me to take the dog with me?'

She looked down and seemed surprised to see her hand lying on the soft fur. 'No. Leave him.'

'Come and join me when you feel like a bit of

company. I'm varnishing the gallery floor upstairs.'

The peace and silence enfolded her like a lover's arms. Like Jonathon's arms. Only she couldn't make him her lover. Well, not physically, anyway. And perhaps not in any way. During the long hours of the night she'd woken several times and begun to worry about it, to wonder if she could leave Paul now.

She had to face the fact that she'd lost some of her certainty about what she was going to do after the funeral. There was no doubt Paul was upset in his own way. She'd never seen him behaving so irrationally. He'd even looked at her pleadingly a couple of times. Could she just abandon him after all those years together? She didn't know.

Only – she didn't think she could continue as his wife, either. The thought of him touching her sexually after playing around with Liz made her feel like vomiting.

Dusty nudged her with his head, asking for more caresses and she obliged, finding the action soothing on herself as well as gratifying to the animal.

Oh, hell, she thought after a while, she didn't know anything any more. She had just been starting to get her act together, just been finding herself. And now she was lost again.

Chapter Twenty

It was a long, dreary week, whose only brightness for Rosalind was seeing Jenny and Ned's love for one another. Paul mocked the engagement when his daughter wasn't around, though he was more or less civil when Jenny brought her fiancé home.

Ned was never anything but stiffly polite to Paul, refusing to be provoked again and hiding behind that peculiarly glassy politeness at which the English were experts.

Rosalind took herself and her daughters into Bournemouth one day to buy some black clothes for the funeral. Afterwards they had lunch together then strolled along the promenade and cliffs, which were magnificent. They didn't say much, just enjoyed walking slowly along the miles of walkways that overlooked the water.

None of them mentioned a reluctance to return to Burraford. They didn't need to.

Paul was in a foul mood again when they got back.

'Didn't think to ask if I wanted to come, did you?' he snapped as soon as Rosalind walked through the door.

Her voice was cool and disinterested. 'No. I wanted to go with the girls.'

'I'll just put my things away, Mum,' Jenny murmured, hating the way he was glowering at them, then hesitating, feeling guilty for leaving her mother to face him. He was getting nastier by the day. She didn't know how her mother coped, she really didn't.

'Will you take my parcels upstairs, Louise?' Rosalind nudged her younger daughter. The girls might as well stay out of the firing line. She went to sit in the living room and he followed.

Coming in here with him is an act of bravery, she thought, and smiled briefly at herself.

'Have a big spend-up, did you?' He threw himself on a chair opposite her.

'We spent what was needed.'

'How did you pay for it?'

She was puzzled. 'By credit card, of course.'

'That's right, spend my money. I'd have thought you could start using your own now for clothes and things. You've certainly got plenty.'

'We've only just got probate. I haven't sorted out Aunt Sophie's money yet.'

'And you still don't intend to follow my suggestion of contesting the terms of the will?'

'Of course not. Aunt Sophie had a right to leave it how she wanted. And besides, I like having my own money.' She ignored his snort and got up, going to nip a couple of dead leaves off the plant in the window that was struggling to cope with the nearby central heating radiator. If he carried on like this, she'd walk out. She'd done that several times this week. Had sought refuge with Jonathon on two of those occasions, brief encounters that had nonetheless strengthened her backbone.

'Did you think to get me a black tie?' Paul threw at her.

She didn't turn round. 'No.' She had spent the day trying not even to think about him.

'Well, thanks for nothing.'

'If that's the sort of mood you're in, I'll go upstairs and unpack my new clothes.'

'That's right, run away. You're good at running away from trouble, always have been.'

She didn't turn to refute that, just walked out. Upstairs she sighed and sat on the bed with her head in her hands, making no attempt to open any of the parcels.

After a minute or two Jenny came in. 'Dad's in a foul mood today. Even worse than yesterday. I think I'll go over to Dorchester this evening, if you don't mind. I can catch the five o'clock bus.'

'Yes.'

'Don't let him upset you, Mum.'

'No.'

Louise peered round the bedroom door, saw no sign of her father and joined them. 'It was good to get out of the house,' she said wistfully. 'Just us three.'

'Yes.' Rosalind gave each of them a quick hug. 'I'm glad I've got you two here. You're such a comfort.'

Of course Jenny dissolved immediately in tears, but Louise nodded and said 'Good' in a gruff voice.

'Could – would one of you fetch me up a cup of hot chocolate? I think I'd like to lie down for a while. I'm not sleeping well.' She kept waking up and jerking away from any contact with Paul's body. If he had tried to touch her in that way – but he hadn't – which was not like him. She was too tired to puzzle that out now, though.

'I'll get it.' Louise left.

Jenny leant against her mother. 'I hate the thought of the funeral,' she said. 'I don't know how I'll cope.'

Rosalind patted her hand. 'We'll face it together, love. And you'll have Ned for extra support.'

She was dreading tomorrow just as much as her daughters were, not only because of saying a final farewell to Tim, but because she'd decided to confront Paul afterwards. He was already speaking of getting back to work in London. Well, he wasn't leaving here without them having a serious talk about their future. Definitely not. If she had to, she'd lie down in front of his car to prevent him.

'Um, Jenny – after the funeral I'd like to talk to your father on my own. Do you think you and Ned could take Louise out somewhere? Give us a couple of hours to iron a few things out?'

'Yes, of course.' She began to fiddle with her skirt. 'Is something wrong?'

Rosalind hesitated, then said, 'Yes.'

'Are you going to leave him?'

'Would it matter to you if I did?' she glanced quickly sideways, wincing internally as she saw the anxiety on her daughter's face.

Jenny nodded. 'It would, rather. I know he's – difficult. But you're my parents and I've always been so glad you've stayed together. For better, for worse. Isn't that how the service goes? And this is the worst our family has ever had, isn't it?'

Guilt speared through Rosalind.

Louise came back with a steaming mug. 'There.'

'Thanks. I think I'll have a rest now.'

The sisters went into Jenny's room to whisper together as she got ready to go out and meet Ned.

'She wants to talk to *him* tomorrow after the funeral,' Jenny worried. 'On her own. She asked me and Ned to take you out somewhere for a couple of hours afterwards.'

'I hope she's going to tell him she's leaving him,' Louise said fiercely. 'And if she does, I'm going with her.'

Jenny began smoothing a corner of the bedspread. 'But why should she leave him after all these years? I mean – Tim's death isn't a reason to leave someone, is it?'

Louise chewed her bottom lip, then decided to put her sister in the know.

Jenny listened in horror to the tale of her father's infidelity with Liz and others. 'Oh, no!' she kept saying in a hoarse whisper. 'Oh, no! Not Mum's best friend. How could he?'

The door opened without so much as a by-your-leave and Paul stuck his head round it. 'Louise, I – oh, hell! What's she upset about now?'

'Tim.' Louise jerked her head towards the door, hoping he'd take the hint.

He scowled but left.

'He just walks in without knocking,' Louise fumed. 'What if I'd been standing here naked, eh? He'd probably have enjoyed the sight of another female body, knowing him.'

When Jenny left, Louise accompanied her to the bus stop, calling, 'I'm going for a walk, Dad,' as they passed the living room, just to be safe from recriminations when she returned.

But he didn't answer. He was pouring himself a glass of whisky.

'He's drinking a lot,' Louise said.

'Guilty conscience.'

Louise snorted. 'He doesn't know the meaning of the word. Oh, I do hope she's going to leave him. I do, I do.'

'Well, I don't.'

Louise stared at her. 'You still don't? Even knowing about Liz?'

'No.'

'Are you into sado-masochism or what? Get real, Jenny! And let Mum get a life.'

Left to herself, Rosalind lay down and tried to rest, but her thoughts were in turmoil. She didn't want to hurt Jenny, who couldn't understand the sense of betrayal you felt when you realised you'd been living in a fool's paradise for nearly twenty-five years. Or the utter humiliation of finding that your husband had been unfaithful with your so-called best friend!

She knew Jonathon wanted her to leave Paul and she'd been secretly hoping he'd ask her to go and live with him. She felt so right with him, as if they'd known one another for ever. And she fancied him, too, loved his long, lean body and his gentle hands. Since she'd started that embroidery, she hadn't really fancied Paul. And after finding out about him and Liz, she wondered if she ever would again.

But splitting up was such an irrevocable step to take. Jonathon wouldn't pressure her to leave Paul. She knew that. It would have to be her own choice for it to be right with him. And it would be, if – when she made the break.

But there were other things to consider as well. Did she want to leave Australia and spend the rest of her life in a foreign country, for a start? What about her mum? Then there were Jonathon's sons to think about. They'd seemed like nice lads at the fête, polite, well-brought-up, but with a certain liveliness. They'd got on well with Jenny, too. But how would they deal with a stepmother? And did she want to bring up stepsons? She hadn't made a brilliant success of bringing up Tim. At the thought of him she sucked in a long breath that was barbed with anguish too deep for tears, and it was a while before she could continue thinking things through.

She kept coming back to the same old question. Leaving Paul. Could she do it? Should she do it? He'd admitted their marriage was a bit shaky and had brought her here because he wanted to patch it up. She had to suppose the interlude with Liz meant nothing to him. There must have been others over the years. Were they all meaningless?

But his infidelity wasn't meaningless to her.

Oh, hell, what was she going to say to him tomorrow?

In the end she stopped trying to rest and went to her embroidery, starting on Louise, trying two or three sketches until she got the figure right. Tomboy looks, like Paul physically. Hands in the pockets of her jeans, short dark hair, chin thrown back as she scowled at the world. Yes, that was right.

She heard the front door slam and Paul's car drive away. He came back a short time later, presumably having found a black tie, but she didn't go down to him. And even when she heard him come upstairs and stop outside the closed door, she didn't call out to him as she once would have.

He went away without saying anything and she let a sigh of relief sift slowly out as she bent her head over her work again.

She didn't go to bed until long after he was asleep.

The smell of whisky made her wrinkle her nose with disgust.

The following day they were all very self-conscious over breakfast. The funeral was to be held at ten o'clock, but no one mentioned it. No one ate much, except Paul, who ploughed through his usual cooked breakfast.

The smell of bacon sickened Rosalind and in the end she just had a piece of toast with a scrape of jam. Even that was too much for her to finish.

'I'll go and change,' she said when she'd finished her coffee.

'I'll clear up,' said Jenny.

'I'll help,' Louise volunteered.

'I wonder how long this sisterly closeness and co-operation is going to last?' Paul sneered.

He wandered off into the small office, to sit there and scowl at the fax machine, drumming his fingers on the desk, staring into space, but seeing only his son's face, shouting defiance at him. That scene kept replaying in his mind.

Again he fought for self-control, breathing deeply and clenching his fists.

Bloody hard, this. The worst. The pits. Bloody children! Were they worth it? He didn't know. He didn't know anything today.

Rosalind was relieved when the big black funeral limousine turned up. As it swallowed them up, it muted the colours of the landscape with its tinted windows. The black upholstery heightened the sense of gloom.

In front of them, driving with agonising slowness, the hearse carried Tim's body. Alone. Covered by flowers whose colours ran and bled together as tears welled in Rosalind's eyes. She didn't look at Paul, didn't even want to turn to him for comfort, and he made no attempt to touch her. But she saw that opposite them, the girls were holding one another's hands. She was glad of that.

Jonathon and Harry were parked at the end of the street and their car joined the funeral cortège.

'Who invited *them*?' snapped Paul, peering over his shoulder.

'I did,' said Rosalind struggling to keep her voice quiet and even. 'They're good friends of mine.'

Behind them drove Ned, who'd also lingered outside rather than go into the house and face his future father-in-law's nasty remarks. Paul had refused point-blank to let Ned ride with the family, so Rosalind had suggested he come in his own car. That way he'd be able to take the girls out for an hour or two afterwards while she spoke to Paul.

The cemetery was small and Paul's voice seemed twice as loud as usual as he grumbled about the time it took the men to get the coffin out of the hearse.

'What do we do now?' he asked Rosalind in an undertone, scowling round. 'I hate this sort of mumbo-jumbo.'

'We follow the coffin into the chapel.' As they began to inch forward at a slow pace, she found Louise on her left side, holding her arm, but Paul made no attempt to touch her or to keep pace with anyone.

'The chairman offered to send someone to represent the company,' he said, too loudly, as they walked along, 'but I told him it wasn't worth it. They didn't know Tim, after all. But it was a nice gesture, don't you think?'

Rosalind didn't attempt to answer. She was watching her son's coffin, saying a mental farewell to his body, hoping his soul was now at peace.

It was Louise who surprised herself and everyone else by bursting into tears and sobbing so loudly that the last part of the ceremony came to a halt for a moment.

Rosalind sat with her arm round Louise's shaking shoulders, relieved when the service was over and the coffin had vanished behind the curtains. What it contained wasn't really Tim any more. Her son was inside her now – in her heart, in her memories – there for ever.

From a short distance away Jonathon watched Rosalind whisper to the girl and hug her. He watched Paul lean over to say something in a low, angry voice and saw Louise wince. He wished – oh, how he wished he were able to share Rosalind's burdens on this terrible day.

Why do we do all this? he wondered, as he had wondered at his own parents' funerals. *Why the hell do we put ourselves through the agony of a public performance at a time when we're still trying to come to terms with our grief in private?*

He saw tears trickle down Harry's face. Funerals reminded her too much of her own husband, but she'd made the effort to come today. He fumbled for her hand. She gripped his tightly and whispered, 'Damned shame!'

After the coffin had gone the small group of mourners gathered at the front of the chapel.

'So sorry,' said Harry. 'So very sorry, Rosalind.'

'Ros,' corrected Paul.

'Rosalind,' the owner of the name said firmly. 'You know I prefer my full name.'

'I've called you Ros all our married life,' he said, affronted that she would correct him in front of strangers.

'And I've preferred Rosalind all our married life, too.'

Jonathon had to content himself with holding her hand in his for a moment, meeting her eyes and hoping she would feel his love. As he stepped back, he murmured, 'If we can help in any way . . . ?'

'Very kind of you,' said Paul, seeing Ros neglecting her social duties, 'but we're going back to Australia soon.'

Every member of his family gaped at him.

'You never said anything about that before!' Louise blurted out.

'Why should I? It's my company who's paying for this jaunt of yours. I've decided it's a waste of time and money, so we're going back.'

It was at that precise moment that Rosalind felt anger begin to take over from the sorrow. 'This isn't the place to discuss it,' she said in a chill voice, turned on her heel and walked over to the waiting limousine.

Paul started to apologise for her, but found himself

looking at two tall, thin backs as Harry and Jonathon Destan also moved away.

'We're going with Ned. We'll find our own way home, Father,' Jenny called.

He shrugged and followed his wife to the limousine.

'Let's go to the pub, eh?' Ned was in the know about leaving Jenny's parents alone – and the reason for it. He put an arm round Louise's shoulder as well as Jenny's as they walked to the car. His future sister-in-law gave him a watery smile of gratitude.

'I wish I could be there to look after Mum,' Louise said. 'Dad's in a rotten mood. Foul. I hate him.' That wasn't an exaggeration. She did hate him.

'She can look after herself,' Jenny said. 'She's grown very strong, Mum has.'

They both looked at her in surprise.

'We've all relied on her for years,' Jenny explained. 'I've been thinking about it. And I suddenly realised that she's always been the strong one where the family is concerned, though she doesn't brandish her strength at you or try to bully you like Dad does. I wish—' Her voice faded for a moment.

'What do you wish?' Louise prompted.

'I wish I hadn't told her yesterday that they should stick together. You're right, Louise. She should leave him.' Tears came into her eyes. 'Did you see how Jonathon Destan looked at her? How she looked at him?'

They nodded.

'That's how couples should be. Dad's done nothing but shout at her since Tim died. What help is that?'

Louise could only shake her head.

As the silence lengthened into awkwardness, Ned said, 'Let's decide what we want to do.'

They looked at him in puzzlement.

'If your family is going back to Australia, Jenny, you and I have to decide about our own future.'

'Heavens, yes!' Louise looked at them. 'Do you want me to leave you two on your own? I could go for a walk.' Though she didn't really want to. She needed company just now, needed it badly.

'No. You're part of my family, now, as well.' Ned gave her a hug to prove it. 'And you feel like family, too. But your bloody father doesn't.' And never would, he was sure.

As the funeral limousine pulled away from the house and left them alone there, Paul stared at Rosalind. 'Why did the kids go out?'

'I asked them to give us some space. We have to talk.'

'Oh? That makes a change. You usually go and hide in your little playroom to avoid talking to me.'

She ignored his gibe and walked into the living room, feeling clammy and apprehensive. But as she remembered how insensitive he'd been at the funeral, the anger began to rise again and she encouraged it. She would need its fire to carry her through this.

'I want to talk about your infidelity,' she began, as she had planned.

That made him sit very still. 'How the hell did you find out?'

'What does that matter?'

He shrugged. 'Always like to understand the game, that's all.'

'*Game?* It's not a game! It's us, our whole life together!'

'Calling it a game is just a way of looking at things, for heaven's sake.'

'You want to understand so that you can *play* it better next time, I suppose?'

He shrugged.

She waited for an apology for the infidelity, but it didn't come. He sat there with an assessing look on his face, watching her.

As the silence dragged on, Rosalind suddenly couldn't stand it any more. She didn't want to play games. The words exploded out of her mouth. 'You're not even going to offer me an apology, are you?'

'What for? I'm only human. We've had long spells away from one another. What happened was partly your fault for not moving around with me, so why should I be the one to apologise? *You* haven't apologised to me for your stick-in-the-mud attitude and that's what drove me to it.'

She ignored his accusation. 'You're not sorry at all, are you?'

'I'm sorry you found out. Sorry you're hurt.' He really was. It surprised him how much. He didn't want to hurt her. 'And to find out now of all times – well, I deeply regret that, Ros.'

'And that's all?'

'This is the twenty-first century. We're both grown-ups. No one believes in fairy stories and happy ever afters nowadays.'

Hell, he could do without this. Didn't she know he was upset, too? At least she had seen Tim. He hadn't. They hadn't even bothered to tell him his son was back.

Seeing how bright with tears her eyes were, he tried to explain, to soften the blow. 'The other women – well, they didn't make any difference to the way I felt about you, I promise you, Ros. It was just – opportunism. A man's physical needs are so much more pressing than a woman's. You know that.'

He was doing it again, Rosalind realised, twisting the argument his way, putting the blame onto someone else. 'Well, whether the women mattered to you or not, I'm leaving you.' She had the satisfaction of seeing his jaw drop.

'You're bloody not!'

'You can't stop me.'

'I can talk sense into you, though. We've lost one member of the family. This is not the time to break up the rest of us. For the girls' sake, if not for ours. Give yourself a few days, at least. Think things through. You'll see I'm right. And – and I do apologise for hurting you.'

'*Speak the speech, I pray you, as I pronounced it to you, trippingly on the tongue,*' she said scathingly. It was from *Hamlet*. Another tragedy. Very apt. The rest of the words she had once learnt by heart for homework came back to her suddenly and she hurled them at him, '*If you mouth it as many of your players do, I had as lief the town crier spoke my lines.*'

'What the hell are you talking about?'

'I'm quoting the Bard. He was talking about actors and you were just acting out an apology.' She sucked in oxygen and tossed at him, 'How *could* you do it with Liz? Of all people, *Liz*!'

He stared at her in shock. She even knew about Liz. Oh, hell! After a minute of searching for words to put the best spin on things, he could only think of, '*She* did it with me, too – was eager for it. To get back at Bill, she said.'

'And you couldn't resist seizing a freebie – even if it was with my best friend.' Rosalind's voice wobbled as she fought for control.

He shrugged. 'I suppose you're going to break up a lifelong friendship now just for a few screws?'

'No. For the betrayal.'

'Betrayal!' He threw back his head and roared with laughter. 'Oh my God, join the twenty-first century, will you, Ros?'

'*Rosalind!*' she screamed at him. 'I'm called Rosalind and that's how I think of myself and always have done. *Rosalind!*'

'Bit late to tell me that, now.' He went across to the decanter and poured himself a large whisky. 'Want one?'

'No, I don't. But you go ahead and get drunk again. Your only son is dead, your marriage is over and you turn to the bottle. Very helpful, that.'

He could feel himself getting really angry. He'd been very forbearing, but it took two to work out a reconciliation. Suddenly he wanted to wound her. 'Anyway, Tim might not be *my* only son. She's pregnant. Liz is, I mean.'

'*What?*'

'Yeah.' He patted his crotch. 'Everything's still working all right. Shook me when she told me, though.'

'Pregnant?' The word was a hiss of sound. '*Liz – is – pregnant?*'

'Yeah.' He raised his glass in an unvoiced toast. 'So I might still have a son.'

She could bear it no longer. He wasn't sorry for what he'd done, not in the least sorry, only sorry that she'd found out. And for all her good intentions, she'd not handled it as firmly as she had hoped. That upset her, too. She turned and ran from him, not pausing to grab a coat, just snatching her handbag and throwing open the front door.

He set down his glass and followed her, but she had the car door open and the motor running before he could do anything. By the time he started down the porch steps, hands outstretched to tell her to stop, the car was moving. He leapt in front of it.

And she kept moving, not caring whether she knocked him over or not. He had to jump sideways to avoid her.

'Damn you, you stupid bitch!' he yelled after her from where he lay sprawled among the dying daffodils.

Their season was over now.

'Jonathon!' She hammered on the door of Destan Manor. 'Jonathon, where are you? Jonathon, I need you.'

No one came to answer and she slid to the floor, sobbing and weeping loudly like a hurt child. The ice inside her was breaking up now in great chunks and pain was running like meltwater through her whole body. Harsh noises kept erupting from her throat and she couldn't stop them.

When Jonathon found her, he pulled her to her feet and supported her as she stumbled into the house. Then he held her while all the ice melted and she cried out her sorrow for her son and her marriage.

He understood what she was going through. He'd been there himself. And he knew better than to let her make any irremediable decisions in this frame of mind. If she came to him, she had to come for all the right reasons. Not because her insensitive husband had trampled all over her again.

Chapter Twenty-One

'I'm not going back to Australia yet,' Jenny decided as they sat in the pub. She looked at Ned. 'You want me to stay here, don't you?'

'Of course I do. You can come and live with my family.'

'I don't think I'd better. I—'

He took hold of her hand, kissed it, then kissed her cheek for good measure. 'You've seen how happy all this is making my mother. She's been itching for me to get married. Besides, we've tons of room at home. You must definitely come and stay with us while you and I look for a house of our own. We'll get married as soon as we can. None of this fancy wedding fuss. It's you I want.'

Louise excused herself and went to the ladies'.

Jenny didn't notice her sister's departure, but sat smiling at the thought of having her own home, her own life. With him. Then it occurred to her that she'd be completely dependent on Ned and that thought didn't please her quite so much. 'There'll be formalities to go through. I'm an Australian citizen. And I'd like to find myself a job, though *not* as a trainee manager.'

'Fine, we'll go through the formalities together. No one will turn a gorgeous girl like you down. And if you want a job, I'll help you hunt for one.' He raised his glass and drank a silent toast to her. 'Though you could come and work in the gallery, if you wanted. It's hard to get part-time staff. Mum comes in sometimes when we're busy. You might enjoy it.'

She frowned. 'Is this a pretend job, or a real one?'

'It's as real as you care to make it, love. Up to you.'

Her face brightened. 'Then I accept. I always used to like art at school and I'd love to learn about antiques.'

Louise came back and sat down, smiling at them both. 'It makes me feel there's hope in the world, seeing you two looking all smoochy.' Her smile faded and she stared down into her lemon, lime and bitters. 'I'm underage, though, and *he* still has power over me.'

'Only for a few weeks then you'll be eighteen,' Jenny said consolingly. 'At that age you're technically an adult – I think.'

'Yeah, but what do you live on, whether they call you an adult or not?'

'Mum has some money now.'

'I suppose so. Do you think she'd mind supporting me for a bit till I find my feet?'

'I think she'd love to.'

Louise began to look thoughtful. 'I'll still need to train for something. Perhaps nursing.' She blinked her eyes furiously. 'Tim suggested that and I think he was right.'

She'd thought about it several times since his death and the idea pleased her greatly. It meant he would be with her in a sense, would have given her a permanent legacy. Then reality bit and she shook her head. 'Dad will find some way to stop me, you know he will. If Mum makes him mad enough, he'll do anything he can to hurt her – through me, if he has to.' She shivered. 'He frightens me when I'm on my own with him, you know. He thumped me around quite a bit when he came to get me in Perth.'

Jenny gasped. 'No!'

'Mind,' Louise allowed, 'I probably needed it. But he didn't need to enjoy it, which he definitely did. And I was terrified. Absolutely terrified,' she repeated, remembering that day with a shiver.

'He's always made me nervous. Tim used to say—' Jenny broke off for a moment, then continued unsteadily, 'that I should stand up to him. But I'm not like you two. I'm soft. Too soft. More like Mum, really.'

Ned frowned. 'I don't like your father, I must admit, but is he really so bad?'

Jenny nodded. 'Well, he does like to be the big boss man and make everyone's decisions for them, though to give the devil his due, he's always supported us in style. But he's had Mum under his thumb for years.' She paused, then added, 'Well, except for her embroidery, though she puts that away when he's home.'

Ned shook his head. 'He was very scornful about it when he was talking to my father, but she's a brilliant artist! How can he not see that?'

'That's probably the reason he hates it,' Louise said

gloomily. 'He doesn't like anyone else to shine too brightly when he's around. You should see him perform at a party. Mr Wonderful in person.'

They stayed on in the pub until nearly three o'clock, then Louise sighed. 'I think we'd better get back, don't you? She might – you know, need us.'

'You drop us outside,' Jenny told Ned. 'No need to stir things up further by you and Dad having a confrontation.'

'Are you sure?'

'Yes. Very sure.' She linked her arm in Louise's. 'Besides, there are two of us, not one.'

'Three. Don't forget Mum.'

But their mother wasn't at home and their father was on the phone as usual, talking about—The two sisters looked at one another apprehensively. He was ending the lease on this house.

'Didn't she tell Dad?' Jenny whispered.

'I don't know.'

Paul came out of his little office. 'Come into the living room. I want a word with you two.' He waited until they sat down together on one of the sofas, then said, 'We're all going back to Australia as soon as I can book seats on a plane. Go and get me your return ticket, Jenny, and I'll rebook you with us – I presume you did have a return ticket?'

She took a deep breath. 'I'm going to stay on in England with Ned's family. We're going to get married quite soon.'

'You can get married later.' His smile became frosty at the edges. 'Your mother needs you at the moment. She's rather upset by all this. So go and get the ticket, there's a good girl.'

'I'm sorry, but I'm not going back with you.'

He glowered at her. 'Don't make me have to come and find the ticket.'

Her mouth fell open. 'But—'

'I mean it, Jenny. What this family needs now is pulling together and I intend to do just that.' He set his hands on his hips and stared at her challengingly. 'Well, are you going to get that ticket or am I?'

'I'll – it's in my room.' She stumbled upstairs wondering how to buy time, feeling as if she were living in a nightmare. Whatever had happened between her parents had made her father go all aggro. Had her mother given in to him again? Surely not? And where was she?

Jenny took out the plane ticket, looked at it and shook her head. She'd paid for it. It was hers and he had no right to take it off her. She tiptoed out on the landing to see what was happening downstairs. He was shouting at Louise now, ranting on about people who went off for a drink in the pub at a time when the family should stick together.

'And with a stranger, too!' he roared.

'Ned's not a stranger. He's going to marry my sister.'

'Not if I have any say in the matter. I don't want a wimp like him for a son-in-law.'

Upstairs Jenny's hand flew up to her mouth. She knew her father and Ned had hardly had the most promising of introductions – but she hadn't thought even *he* would try to stop them getting married. If she went back to Australia, she'd be stuck there without the money to return. Well, she'd have the rest of her winnings, but why should she have to buy another ticket with it when she was here already?

No, she wasn't going. She was staying here and marrying Ned. Letting out a long, slow breath, she murmured, 'Sorry, Mum.'

She stuffed the plane ticket into her handbag, together with all her remaining money. Then she shoved some underwear into a plastic carrier bag. After a hasty glance round to see if there was anything else she could grab quickly, she crept out onto the landing, ducking back with a gasp as her father came into the hall.

He yelled over his shoulder, 'And you, young lady, are going back to your studies next semester. *Business studies*. The only sort of qualification that gets people jobs nowadays. You can do better for yourself than nursing, by hell you can!' He strode off towards the kitchen, not even glancing upstairs, and there came the sound of running water and the kettle being switched on.

As cups rattled and cupboard doors slammed, Jenny tiptoed down the stairs. Passing the open door of the living room, she saw Louise sitting disconsolately on the sofa and paused, her heart going out to her sister. When Louise looked up, Jenny raised one hand in farewell and blew her a kiss.

Louise made shooing motions with one hand.

Jenny managed to get the front door open without her father hearing and didn't even try to close it behind her. Once outside she took off at a run, haring down the street as if pursued by all the demons from hell.

When she saw the Dorchester bus chugging round the corner towards her, it seemed as if fate was on her side. Hope springing up anew at this miracle, she sprinted to the pole with its little BUS STOP sign at the top and its faded timetable under a pane of cracked glass, signalling to it to stop.

With a grin the driver pulled up. 'Nearly missed it there, young lady, didn't you? If I hadn't been running late, you'd have had to wait another hour.'

Joy filled Jenny. 'Yes. What a bit of luck! A single to Dorchester, please.' She slid into the seat and sat smiling out at the world. She wasn't going back to Australia yet. Not even for her mother's sake. And since she was almost twenty-three, there was no legal way her father could make her.

If Ned's family didn't want her, she'd simply find somewhere else to stay and get a job. She had just cast her vote with her feet. *Stuff you, Dad*, she thought. *Go and find someone else to bully.*

There was nothing she could do to help her mother except take herself out of the equation. Now her mother only had Louise to worry about.

When Rosalind's tears dried up, she poured out all the details of the encounter with her husband to Jonathon, then lay back on the couch, numb with tiredness and reaction.

'You needed to cry it out,' he said. 'You really did.'

'Yes.' The lump of ice inside her was gone now, but she was left with a sea of churning panic in its place. 'I'm going to leave him, Jonathon.'

'Are you sure about that?'

She nodded. 'Very sure.' She waited a minute and when he didn't say anything, she asked, 'Can I come here to you?'

When he didn't immediately reply, she looked sideways. 'Jonathon?'

'I want you to leave him, of course I do. And I want us to try living together. But I'm not sure—' He began to chew one corner of his lip.

'Not sure of what?'

'Of whether you really do want to make a life with me. Or whether you just want to leave him.'

'*Jonathon!*'

'And I don't think you're completely sure yet, either, which is more to the point. One doesn't break up a long marriage like yours in a fit of anger. If you want my opinion, you need to go back to Australia and make certain you really can leave everything – home, country, friends.' His eyes were shadowed. 'I've made one very serious mistake, Rosalind, and I'm not about to make another. Even to help you.'

'I thought,' her breath caught on a sob, 'you loved me.'

'I do, very much indeed, but I'm too old and wary to toss everything aside because of it. That's not enough for me or for anyone. You, of all people, should know that. You loved Paul once. Greatly, if I'm any judge.'

More tears filled her eyes, trickling from the lake of meltwater within her. 'Yes.'

'So I'm not going to rush into anything – not even with you, my dearest Rosalind. When things have calmed down, when you've found your feet again, we could try living together. I'd really like to get to know you better in – more normal circumstances,' he gave her a wry smile, 'and for you to get to know me, warts and all. I actually believe we stand a good chance of building a successful, and I hope long-term relationship – but not now, not while you're so upset with him. I won't be held responsible in future for breaking up your marriage, not by you or by anyone else.'

After a short silence, he gave her a hug, then put her resolutely away from him. 'Come to the kitchen. I'll get you a cup of coffee and a biscuit.'

She went with him, feeling shattered. She'd failed with Paul. Was she failing with Jonathon already?

Was he failing her?

Or was he right?

Did she need more time to come to terms with the failure of her marriage? She didn't know. She didn't feel as if she was very wise at all. The whole world, herself included, was a puzzle to her lately, incomprehensible as a high-walled maze that she'd strayed into by sheer chance on a moonless night.

'Thanks.' She sipped the coffee, avoiding his eyes.

He sat jiggling a teabag in his own cup, then fussing over the milk and sugar.

When the caffeine had started to kick into her system she stood up. 'I'd better get back, then.'

He stood up too and tried to take her in his arms.

'Don't.' She pushed at him. *'Don't!'*

He stood looking down at her, an anxious question in his eyes.

And suddenly she knew she wouldn't be certain of anything until she got back to her own home and possessions, the home which had been the centre of her world for so long.

'You're right,' she said, turning to walk out of the house. At the front door she stood on tiptoe to kiss his cheek. 'I do need to go home before I commit to anything else. How wise you are! And there's Louise to sort out, as well. I can't abandon her to Paul's tender mercies.' She looked at him searchingly. 'I'll write. And phone. If you want me to.'

'I do.' He didn't have her Australian address and still he let her go, watching her drive away, aching to call her back. But he couldn't do that. Didn't dare. He wanted Rosalind whole in heart and mind – or not at all.

He wanted to spend the rest of his life with her, to see her grow and expand, to make her happy, to be happy himself.

Was that too much to ask?

He wouldn't settle for anything less.

At home Rosalind found the mail on the floor in the hall. She picked it up and began to open her own letters, not wanting to see Paul yet. She could hear him upstairs. It sounded as if he was packing his things, whistling cheerfully.

He knew she was back, but he didn't come down to see her. He expected her to go to him.

There was a letter from her mother, written just after Tim died, which made Rosalind weep a little, and there was a letter from the solicitor in Southport to say they'd got probate. The money to which she was currently entitled would have been transferred into her account by the time she received this. The sum he mentioned was so large it made her gasp. She stuffed that letter hurriedly into her pocket.

She and Paul had enough problems to sort out without him trying to get hold of her money. Or trying to fool her into believing he was a reformed character, because of the money.

Besides, this was her ticket to freedom – if she decided to leave him.

'I have to go up to London first thing tomorrow,' Paul said as she entered the bedroom.

He didn't even turn his head to look at her, she thought resentfully.

'I've booked us three on a plane to Australia leaving Heathrow Saturday teatime. I wanted to book Jenny, too, but she ran out of the house and took her return ticket with her. Went off to join that twit, I suppose. So bugger her. She can fend for herself from now on.'

Rosalind felt a spurt of relief trickle through her. Jenny was safe, then. But there was still Louise to worry about. 'I think that's the right thing for Jenny,' she said carefully. 'Ned will look after her.'

'I don't agree. I think she should bloody well put family first at a time like this.'

She didn't state the obvious, that this was the first time he'd put family first in all their years together – if he was putting it first, if this wasn't part of some devious scheme or other. No, surely not! Even Paul wouldn't be scheming at a time like this. She contented herself with, 'Ned *is* her family, now.'

'Well, she needn't come to me to pay for a fancy wedding if she won't do the right thing by you.'

'She's doing exactly the right thing by me – marrying

the man she loves.' And if Paul didn't pay for the wedding, Rosalind would. Not a huge, extravagant one, which she thought a waste, but a nice wedding. And she'd certainly come back to attend it.

Oh, it felt so good to have Sophie's money behind her. 'I'll leave you to pack your things, then.'

He looked at the jumble in his suitcase. 'Could you just sort this out for me . . . ?'

'No, I couldn't. I'm exhausted.' And besides, she didn't want to touch his things. Or him.

What did that say?

'Thanks for nothing.' His lips curved in a particularly nasty sneer. 'Wept all over your dear friends, have you?'

There was no point in denying the obvious. 'Yes.'

'Feel better for it?'

'Not really.' She turned partly away from him.

He paused halfway towards her, arms outstretched, then let his arms drop. 'I see. I'm still in the doghouse, eh?'

'Very much so.'

'Ros, I'm not going to beg you to stay with me, but I'll reiterate – what I've done doesn't make any difference to our marriage. It never has.'

She looked at him as if he were a stranger. He felt like a stranger. 'So you say. And my name's Rosalind. It always has been. And fidelity happens to be something I value very highly indeed. You've had that from me.'

He let out a long, aggrieved sigh and turned back to his case, cramming things in with a bit more care.

'I'll be back on Friday evening to pick you and Louise up and I'll drive us to Heathrow on Saturday morning. We'll get the hire firm to pick up your car up from here.' He hesitated. 'You *are* coming back with me, aren't you?'

'Yes, I'm definitely coming back to Australia. I could perfectly well drive the car up to London myself, though. Save you a journey.'

'No need. I'll come and get you.' He zipped up the suitcase. 'Oh, and if Jenny comes to her senses, phone me through her flight details, will you? I can still change her ticket.' Scorn filled his eyes. 'That girl is too soft by far. We should have done something to toughen her up.'

'Why?'

'Because life, as you have recently found out, my dear sheltered wife, is never simple and one needs to be able to cope with it. I'd have thought the episode with Michael would have taught Jenny something, but no, she's walked straight into another relationship. I'm not a wicked ogre, as you all seem to think. I'm actually trying to look after my family, though a fat lot of thanks I get for it.'

He waited for her to say something and when she didn't, his voice became slower, with a patronising edge to it. 'Jenny's new relationship has been formed on the rebound. It won't last. And I don't like that Ned. He's as soft as she is. He'll not make a good husband for her. She needs someone stronger, someone who can look after her. As I've looked after you. That's why I wanted to get her back to Australia.'

She couldn't bear to listen to him making these ridiculous statements any longer, as if he had looked after her, when he'd spent so much time away from home and gone with other women. She walked out and went downstairs.

He came to the bedroom door and yelled after her, 'You stupid bitch, come back! Stop walking out on me! We have to *talk*!'

She carried on, ending up outside in the garden, breathing in the fresh air in big gulps and blinking her eyes furiously. She wasn't going to cry any more. She was not.

He came out to see her, radiating anger, grabbed hold of her arm and shook her.

She let out a mew of surprise, because he'd never laid hands on her before.

'Pull yourself together, Ros. We have *got* to talk.'

He let go of her arm, but she could still feel the painful spot where his fingers had dug in. As she stared at him, something inside her balked at speaking, so she kept her mouth firmly shut.

The words spurted out of him as if they'd been forced through a very narrow space. 'I definitely *don't* want us to split up. I never have wanted us to split up.'

She tried to turn away, frightened by his anger, but he grabbed her arm again. '*Listen*, will you! You made a big thing about me listening to you, now it's your turn to listen to me, dammit.'

So she stood there numbly, waiting for him to speak.

'I'm coming back on Friday evening and if you're not here, I'll scour England for you. I mean that, Ros. We're going back to Australia together, you, Louise and I. I want us to remain a family. I *really* want that.'

She couldn't think what to say.

'After the funeral I wanted us to make up, get closer, not –

not—' He paused to gulp back the emotion that welled in him.

She stared in shock at the tears in his eyes.

'But no, you have to choose this moment to make a stand, *Rosalind*. See. I do remember what you want to be called. Well, I'm upset about Tim, too, and I've had it with this place.' He scowled round at the house as he fished out a handkerchief and blew his nose.

'We're not only going back to Australia, but we're going to sort things out between us. I want that. I really do.'

She nodded again, not having the energy to do anything else at the moment. Those were definitely tears in his eyes. She hadn't expected that, and it made her uncertain of what she wanted as nothing else could have done.

'Good,' he said in a softer voice. 'And tonight you and I are going out for a meal together. I've booked a table at a place I saw in Wareham.'

'I don't want to—'

'Can't you even spare me a little time? Just you and me. No children.' he asked. 'Can't we even *try* spending time together? After all those years of being married?'

She opened her mouth to refuse, then closed it again and shrugged. 'All right.'

The restaurant in Wareham was small and discreetly lit. Waiters fussed over them. A candle flickered on the table, next to a white rose in a slender bud vase. Rosalind stirred the food round on her plate and tried to look as if she was eating.

After the main course, however, Paul looked at her. 'This isn't working, is it?'

'No.'

'Want to leave now?' He pushed aside his plate, of which he'd eaten perhaps half.

She sighed in relief. 'Please.' It was such a parody of a romantic evening. And they had both been really struggling to find neutral subjects to talk about.

On the way home he stopped the car in the car park of Corfe Castle. As the engine died, he leant his head on his hands for a moment, then looked sideways at her. 'I don't want us to break up, Ros – I really don't.' His voice broke.

She was shocked to see tears glinting on his cheeks again. 'Paul—' she said hesitantly, not sure what to do or say.

And suddenly, he was weeping, harsh sounds that filled the car. She hadn't thought he *could* weep.

'I didn't even see him!' he sobbed. 'I never even saw Tim again! He was my son, too, you know!'

She took him in her arms and shushed him as if he was one of her children, and when he turned and clutched her, she let him, patting his back, murmuring meaningless words of comfort. It took a long time for the tears to stop.

'Oh, hell!' he said shakily at last. 'You must think me a real wimp.'

'No. I'm glad you cried for him.'

'Ros,' he gulped audibly, 'I can't lose you as well. You – you won't really leave me, will you? Please don't!'

'I can't promise anything yet. We'll have to – to see if we can grow together again.' And she'd have to see if she could forget Jonathon.

'But you'll give it a chance.'

'I'll try, yes.'

He rubbed at his eyes, gave a shamefaced laugh and asked, 'Got a handkerchief?'

She fumbled in her handbag and passed him the little packet of tissues she always carried. 'Here, use these.' She could hear how raw his breathing was and see an occasional tear tracking down his face.

She moved back a little and stared out of the window.

'Want to leave now?' he asked eventually.

When she nodded and looked at him, he reminded her for a moment of a much younger Paul, the man she had fallen in love with and married. But only for a moment. Perhaps it was a trick of the moonlight. But if it wasn't . . .

When they got in Paul went straight upstairs and Rosalind followed him slowly. She could hear Louise moving around her bedroom, the CD player making a faint rhythmic sound. Louise didn't call out and Rosalind didn't go in to see her.

But she had to force herself to follow Paul into the bedroom. She hesitated in the doorway. What she needed now was time to think. Away from him. Time to assess her own feelings. She felt as if the universe had heaved beneath her feet tonight.

Paul looked at her with a frown. 'What are you doing?'

'Getting my night things.'

'Aren't you going to sleep with me?'

'No. Not yet.'

He closed his eyes for a moment, his lips a tight, thin line.

When he didn't try to persuade her, she nearly weakened, then shook her head in annoyance at herself. He hadn't been pretending to cry, he really had been racked with anguish for their son's death and she thought he truly wanted to stay married to her.

But did she truly want to stay married to him? A marriage was for two people, not one. She still wasn't sure she could trust him. Would he really try to change?

Could he?

In the morning, Paul was subdued, eating a rapid breakfast and leaving by six-thirty. 'I'll ring you tonight, Ros – *Rosalind*, to check that everything is all right.'

He leant forward as if about to kiss her cheek, but she pulled back, so he muttered something and turned on his heel.

Only when she'd heard his car drive away did she start to think clearly again. She went back into the kitchen, breathed in the delightful peace without his abrasive presence and put the kettle on.

She couldn't get the thought of his tears out of her mind, though.

A voice from behind her said hesitantly, 'Mum? Has Dad gone?'

'Yes. Come and have a cup of coffee with me, Louise. We need to talk.'

'Are you going to leave him?'

'I don't know. I shan't know till I get home.' Maybe not even then. She was torn every which way at the moment.

'Mum, don't let him persuade you. You deserve your own life now.'

'I won't let him persuade me,' Rosalind promised. 'But you don't lightly toss away twenty-five years of marriage.'

* * *

Jenny stared round the comfortable bedroom with its single bed. Mrs Didburin – Stella – had been kind to her, and so had Ned. She smiled involuntarily as she looked at the bar of chocolate by the side of the bed. He'd pressed it on her 'for comfort' last night. Dear Ned. What a lovely teddy bear of a man he was! But she felt very guilty for leaving her mother alone to face her father.

'Jenny!'

'Yes?' She poked her head out of the bedroom door and Stella's voice floated upstairs. 'Phone call for you. You can take it in the hall.'

'Who is it?' If it was her father, she wasn't going to speak to him, whether that was cowardly or not.

'Your mother.'

'Thanks. I'll be right down.' Jenny rushed downstairs. 'Hello? Mum, are you all right?'

'Yes, of course. Are *you* all right, love? Your father didn't hurt you yesterday, did he?'

'No. Never mind me. I've got Ned. How are *you* – really?'

'I'm – oh, you know – coping.'

'I'm sorry to leave you in the lurch like that, Mum. I just couldn't take any more. He was going to take my ticket from me *by force*.'

'Leaving was probably the best thing for you to do, darling. I'm phoning to say your father's gone back to London. You and Ned had better come and collect the rest of your things today. I have to pack and close up the house. We're flying out on Saturday.'

'You're going back to him? After all he's done.'

Disappointment flooded through Jenny's body, tasting bitter in her mouth.

'I'm going back to Australia. To my home. As to the other, I don't know.' She repeated the formula she had used for Louise. Bland words, masking a turmoil of contradictions that were tearing her apart. 'It's not an easy thing to do, you know, break up a marriage after all this time.'

She would telephone Jonathon later today and confirm that she was leaving on Saturday, give him her email address, so that he could write to her.

Jenny put the phone down and burst into tears on Ned's broad chest. 'She's going back to Australia with him! He'll smother her – he'll never let me see her again.'

The plane took off on time. Rosalind leant back and sighed in mingled relief and tiredness. There had been so many things to sort out. Embroideries to discuss with George Didburin. Food remnants to go to Alice Tuffin. Other bits and pieces to Harry, to be disposed of as she saw fit.

By far the hardest of all had been sorting out Tim's few possessions. She and Louise had done that together, weeping over how little he had to show for his life.

And all the time Louise had kept begging her not to go back.

'I have to,' she'd said each time. 'I have to go back to my home and begin sorting my life out from there.' Because that was where it had all started. Because her home had always been so important to her.

She'd spoken to Jonathon on the phone, not daring to see him again till she was sure of herself. He'd showed his usual understanding of her needs and in the end she'd had to say goodbye because she couldn't speak through her tears.

'Penny for them.' Beside her Paul smiled and patted her hand, but she couldn't return his smile and she pulled her hand away. She looked sideways at him, this man with whom she had spent all her adult life. Did she know him? Did anyone really know another person?

'You all right, Ros?' He saw her expression. 'Oh, very well, *Rosalind*, then. It'll take me a while to get used to it. Rosalind.' He sat with his head on one side and repeated it again, like a child learning a poem. 'Sounds quite good, actually. Dignified. I shall enjoy introducing you to people as *my wife, Rosalind Stevenson*.'

Trust him to make small concessions gracefully once he felt sure he'd won the major battle. She felt naked without her daughter there. You shouldn't need an intermediary with your own husband. But she did. 'I wish you'd let Louise fly business class with us.'

'Whatever for? She's young enough to cope with those narrow seats and mass troughing conditions. Waste of money to pay more than double the fare for her.' He turned to smile at the hostess, who was offering him a glass of champagne. 'Thank you. Ros, do you want one?'

She shook her head. She needed to keep a clear head. Was he drinking more heavily because of Tim? Or had it been going on for a while and she'd not noticed before?

After the first meal, he sat back, replete and mellow, sipping a glass of cognac now. 'What did you do with your embroidery things? I haven't seen any extra suitcases. Didn't you bring them back with you?'

'Just a couple of pieces I've been working on.' The family portrait was almost finished now, but she still had to complete her own figure. For that, she had to understand what she had become and where she was going.

His face brightened. 'I know you've done quite well with it, but I still think embroidery was a stupid occupation for the twentieth century. There are machines to do that sort of thing now. You just program them and they do it for you.'

A black mark for that, Paul, she thought. *You can't even give me my own creative space, can you?* She changed the subject. 'So – what are your plans for the coming year? Where is the chairman sending you next?'

'I've got a month's compassionate leave to see you settled in at home first. What with Tim and all. And talking of home, I have a small piece of news for you. I got a phone call from Australia yesterday.'

'Oh?'

'That fellow who attacked Jenny. Michael Whatsit.'

'What about him?'

'I put a private detective on to him, a good one. Rod followed him, caught him attacking another woman, knocked the bastard out and called the police. So it's quite likely dear Michael will serve a prison sentence. I've informed the police that my daughter will be happy to make a statement to help the prosecution, but I suppose they can get that from England.' He smiled at Rosalind, waiting to be praised.

'I'm glad he's where he can't harm anyone else. That must have cost you a lot of money.'

He shrugged. 'No lowlife scum hurts *my* daughter and gets away with it.'

She nodded and let him take her response how he wanted. From the smugness of his expression, he had decided her reaction meant approval. Actually, she was trying not to ask whether he saw Jenny as a person in her own right, or only as *his* daughter.

Whether he saw his wife as a person in her own right or only as *his* wife. The sort of question she should have asked years ago.

But in the end she decided it'd do no good to ask. He wouldn't even understand the point she was making. She doubted he would ever understand such subtleties.

They took a taxi home from the airport, sitting in silence except when Paul commented on the beauty of the Perth foreshore. No one answered him. Louise was glowering out of the window. Rosalind was looking inwards, surprised how much a stranger she felt here now.

Perth in late May was cool. Almost winter. Another change of season, she thought ruefully, but one she had always liked far more than the hot summers. If only she could be sure what the right thing was to do.

Stay or go?

Forgive and forget?

Or remember and reject?

Twenty-five years of marriage was a long time. Jonathon was right. She did need to make her decision more carefully, not in the heat of the moment.

If Paul would let her. His cheerfulness on the flight back had come as something of a shock. Did he think things were settled now? Surely not?

At the house her mother was waiting, warned by Paul to expect them.

Rosalind surprised them all, herself included, by bursting into tears and throwing herself into her mother's arms. Then she noticed the man standing behind her mother. 'John. I didn't see you. Sorry to ignore you. I'm a bit – emotional.'

'You have every reason to be. I can wait in the car if you'd rather be alone with your mother.'

'No, no. Of course not!'

They all went inside. Rosalind excused herself to go up to the bathroom. She needed a moment before she could face them.

When she went down to the sitting room she viewed it with fresh eyes. It was like an ice cavern. Pale cool colours, chill marble floor, stark glass and brass. What a change from the small rooms in English houses, the busy wallpapers, the fussy ornaments! Even the big rooms in Jonathon's house were fussy compared to this one.

Her smile faltered for a moment as she thought of him, of Destan Manor and the village, of Jenny left behind with Ned, Jenny weeping as Ned drove her away the other night after she'd packed her things. Of Jenny trying not to accept the cheque her mother had given her, but in the end agreeing. Rosalind knew Sophie would have approved of that use of her money. 'You need some independence,' she'd told her daughter firmly. 'Even from Ned.'

As everyone sat down for a cup of coffee, Audrey and John looked at one another self-consciously. 'We have some news for you,' she said, reaching for his hand.

'Audrey has done me the honour of agreeing to become my wife,' he said in the fussy, precise way he always spoke.

But his expression was young and happy as he exchanged smiles with Audrey and that delighted Rosalind. 'Oh, I'm so glad for you both!' She went across and gave them both big hugs.

Paul's congratulations were more temperate and he tried not to show the jubilation he felt. Another stumbling block to going to America removed for him, just like that. Couldn't be better. The cards were certainly falling in his favour. Even that damned burst of weeping had had good results. He still felt hot with shame as he thought of that.

And now they were home, they'd have none of that other nonsense. Separate bedrooms, indeed! He'd seen where she'd dumped her suitcase. What did she think he was? A celibate monk? He was nearly bursting for a screw and he'd get one out of her tonight. A bit of romance never failed with her and she was easy to arouse, always had been.

There was a ring at the door and when he went to answer it, a florist's van was parked outside.

'Delivery for Stevenson,' the woman said.

He carried the red roses back into the sitting room, smiling. It'd have been better timing if the flowers had arrived after Audrey and that moon-faced old fogy had left, but never mind. You played the cards you were dealt.

'For you,' he said to his wife, flourishing a bow as he presented them to her.

She stared. 'What?'

He felt a fool in that silly position and straightened up. 'Aren't you going to take them?'

She did so, setting them on the low table immediately, where the dark red of the roses was echoed in reflection as an even darker dried-blood colour. It made her shiver. 'To Ros, with love from Paul,' she read aloud and gazed at him blankly. 'Oh.'

'Now that's a nice touch,' Audrey said, leaning forward to examine the flowers. 'Beautiful, aren't they? Pity they don't have a perfume, though. I always think flowers should have a perfume.'

Louise didn't join in the chorus of admiration. Surely her mother wasn't going to fall for that old red roses trick? She was getting very worried about what was going on. Her father was looking smug, not chastened, and her mother had become very distant and vague again, like she'd been before they went to England.

She'd seen where her mother dumped her things when they arrived here, though. In one of the spare bedrooms. And seen her father's scowl as he watched her. So maybe there was still hope?

But these roses worried her. He was clearly trying to get back into her mother's bed again. Oh, hell, he was up to every trick in the book, that randy bastard was. And if her mother didn't leave him, Louise would be forced to stay with him, too, though not for long.

She would be eighteen soon and she wasn't going back to business studies whatever he said. Nursing, she'd decided. Helping people who were sick, who really needed you – as she'd tried to help Tim, but hadn't been able to. She'd make up for that, though, by helping others. She really would. She'd make Tim proud of her and she'd do something for which she was suited. Best of all she'd be proud of herself.

'Well, we'd better go and leave you three to settle in,' Audrey said, putting down her empty coffee cup. 'I'm sorry Jenny isn't here, but Ned certainly sounds a nice young man.'

'He's thirty,' Paul cut in, 'running to fat and already going bald. Not exactly young. And he's a typical public school wallah. No chin and no fire in his belly.'

'I like him,' Rosalind said, frowning at Paul, 'and I'm sure you will, too, when you meet him, Mum.'

'Are they coming over for a visit, then?' Audrey asked eagerly.

'No. But if you two are getting married, I'd like to offer you a trip to England as a wedding present. You could go there for a honeymoon. Check Ned out for yourself. Go up to Southport for a few days, perhaps. I haven't closed Sophie's house. Prue is going to caretake it for me. I think she's met a guy in Southport. I hope it works out for her.'

Louise nearly wet herself trying not to laugh at her father's outraged expression. He'd hate her mother spending that much money on a present, even if it wasn't his money. And he clearly didn't know about the house in Southport still being open.

Louise escorted her grandmother out to the car, but stopped outside the front door. 'I just want to say how sorry I am for how badly I behaved when I was staying with you, Gran. I was out of line and – well, I'm sorry. Tim told me I'd been a fool, but I had to,' her voice wobbled for a moment at the thought of her brother and the talks they'd had, 'had to realise that for myself.'

Audrey reached out to hug her. 'I'm really glad to have my granddaughter back.' She looked back towards the house. 'Are they all right? Paul and Rosalind, I mean? They seem a bit – strained.'

'I hope they're not all right. He's been rotten to her.' Louise looked over her shoulder to check that he wasn't nearby, and added, 'He's been unfaithful, actually. And she's very upset about it.'

Audrey's mouth dropped open in shock.

'Don't say I told you. I just thought that if you knew – if she needed help – you'd not say the wrong thing. You see – it was with Liz.'

There was a moment's silence, then Audrey whispered, '*Liz?*'

'Mmm. Him and Liz. And now she's having a baby – Dad's baby. It's so sordid.'

John cleared his throat. 'I'm glad you've told us, young lady. You can be sure it'll go no further. Your poor mother!' He shook his head. 'And having to face it at a time like this, too.' Then he coaxed a tearful Audrey into the car.

When they'd left, the thought that her mother wasn't completely under his thumb yet, that she'd had the courage to offer her own mother a big wedding gift, took Louise upstairs more cheerfully to unpack her things. It felt good to be back in her own room. But it felt awful to pass Tim's door. Not that he'd been there for ages, but still – knowing he'd never come back hurt so much.

In the kitchen, Rosalind set about washing the dishes.

Paul came in with the box of roses. 'You haven't put them in water yet.'

She turned to him and her voice was like ice. 'Did you really think that cheap trick would win me over again?'

'It wasn't a cheap trick.'

'Oh, yes, it was! Believe me, the only way you'll get me into your bed at the moment will be by force!'

He threw the roses at her, muttering something which sounded like 'Stupid bitch!' and slammed out of the house.

Chapter Twenty-Two

The next morning, Rosalind went to the shops, partly to avoid Paul and partly because they needed some fresh fruit and vegetables. She was walking down an aisle in her favourite supermarket when she felt a hand on her arm. She looked up, saw Liz – and froze.

'Rosalind, could we talk?'

'No. There aren't any words which can possibly heal the way you've hurt me, Liz.'

Her ex-friend paused, tears starting to trickle down her cheeks. '*Please!*'

'No. I wish you well, I really do. And I hope the child brings you joy. Is Bill going to accept it?'

Liz nodded, her eyes welling with tears.

'Good. I'll say goodbye, then.'

There was uncertainty in Liz's face now. 'You seem – different.'

'Well, a lot has happened to me lately, hasn't it? My

whole life has changed.' And was still changing.

'I'm sorry about Tim.'

'Yes.' Determinedly, she pushed Liz's trolley aside. 'Goodbye.' And walked away, her back straight. She could never forgive Liz for what she'd done. Not in a million years. And the encounter had made her realise that she couldn't forgive Paul, either. Just – could – not.

She cut short the shopping trip, feeling uncomfortable among the cheerful crowds.

When she got home, she saw a strange car outside the house with a sticker on its side saying DOOLIFFE & JONES – REAL ESTATE. She frowned as she drove into the garage. What was that doing here? Real estate salesmen didn't usually call in person unless invited. Usually they pushed leaflets through your letter box. Dozens of leaflets every year. Such a waste.

When she went inside, Paul was sitting talking to a woman. She was blonde and ultra-smart, and there were papers – forms, they looked like – spread out all over the table.

She hated that table, Rosalind decided suddenly, hated its nasty, chilly surface that took all the warmth out of people whose reflections were trapped in it.

Paul stood up. 'Ros! I didn't expect you back so soon.'

She looked from one to the other. 'Obviously.'

He turned to the woman. 'Please excuse me a minute.' Then he put his arm round Rosalind's shoulders and led her through into the kitchen. 'I was just getting a couple of valuations. I wouldn't have done anything without consulting you. But you need to think ahead when you're selling houses and—'

'You should have spoken to me first. I haven't decided anything yet.'

'I'll – um – ask her to leave.'

'Do that.'

When he'd left, she buried her face in her hands. He was walking on eggshells, tiptoeing around her, but it wasn't working. It wouldn't work, either, whatever he did. The decision she'd been pushing to the back of her mind because it terrified her surfaced suddenly, complete with answer.

They'd both changed too much. It was too late to mend their marriage.

Worst of all, she didn't want to mend their marriage. A vision of Jonathon floated in front of her and she smiled involuntarily. She wanted to be with him, needed a gentler man than Paul at this season of her life. It all seemed so much clearer now she was home. No, not home. This wasn't her home any longer and never would be again.

But back in Australia she knew where she stood, somehow.

When Paul came into the kitchen, he was rubbing his hands together, looking bright and cheerful. 'You're right, Ros – *Rosalind*. It's too soon to put the house on the market. We'll look into all that together, once we've settled in.'

As far as she was concerned, his cheerful confidence was the last straw.

He didn't speak, just sat down and smiled. Confidently. He was humouring her. He'd soon be playing games with her, as soon as he felt it was safe to move on.

'Was I intended to find out yet about selling the house, Paul?'

'I wasn't selling it, just getting it valued. I told you.'

He came and put an arm round her, planting a kiss on her cheek. Impatiently she shook him off.

He looked at her through narrowed eyes. 'Something else wrong?'

'Many things. You know that.'

'Oh, for heaven's sake, Ros, don't make such a meal of it. We've agreed to work things out, but we won't be able to do that if you keep taking a huff at the slightest thing. I can't change completely overnight.'

He moved towards the coffee plunger. 'There's something else we need to discuss. I didn't want to bother you yet – wanted to give you more time to get over things.'

'How kind!'

'But maybe we should lay all the cards on the table. No, you go and sit down. I'll deal with this. It's nice to be among our own possessions again, isn't it?'

'How would you know? You've spent very little time here. I'm amazed you could even find your way home from the airport.'

He clapped one hand to his chest, as if wounded. 'Sharp, Ros, bit too sharp, don't you think?'

'Rosalind.' She had decided to correct him every time he shortened her name. It might be petty, but it satisfied something inside her.

He rolled his eyes at the ceiling and said nothing.

When he came over to the table with a steaming mug, she shoved the bags of shopping piled there aside, her mind on her problems. One fell onto the floor and glass tinkled as something had broken.

'Steady on!'

She shrugged and took the cup, holding it in her hands as she waited for him to explain the 'something else'. And when he didn't, she didn't speak, either. She used his own tactic and waited him out this time. Enjoyed doing it, too.

In the end he sighed and said, 'The thing is, I've been offered a promotion.'

'So? What difference will that make to the house? Why do we need to sell it? You surely don't want somewhere bigger?'

'We need to sell it because the new job is in the old US of A. We'll need to live there, all of us. We'll probably have to take out American citizenship eventually. The chairman doesn't think there'll be much problem about that, not if the company sponsors me. It's good news, isn't it? I'm on the chairman's senior team now. Can't get much higher than that.'

'Have you accepted the promotion already, then?'

'Of course I have. On the spot. You don't turn down an offer like that.'

'Without asking me.' She said it as a statement, not a question. He hadn't asked her when he became the chairman's international rover, either.

'I was going to tell you after—'

'*Tell* me – not *ask* my opinion, let alone listen to my views.' She stared at him, feeling in control, for once.

He frowned. 'You wouldn't understand my career needs, hon. You'll have to trust me for that. And anyway, I thought you'd be glad to make a fresh start. On all counts.'

'In the USA.' She looked round slowly, making him wait, then said quietly, 'The answer is no.' She didn't need to shout any more. The last of her emotional shackles had just fallen off.

'Ros, you can't—'

'Rosalind.'

'Stop doing that, dammit. I'll get used to it. No need to pick me up on it every time.' He picked up his mug of coffee.

'I saw Liz at the shops.' She saw the mug jerk away from his lips and coffee splash onto his hand. 'The baby doesn't show yet, but she has a softer look on her face. She wanted to talk. I refused.'

'Bit harsh of you. After all, none of us is perfect.'

'No. And I'm not setting myself up as perfect. Far from it. I'm just not able to consider her a friend any more.'

'Your choice. But think about this: Jenny's left the nest for good, your mother's getting married again, your best friend is lost to you. It seems to me a most appropriate time to make a move. Another change of season, eh? A big one, this time.'

She smiled at him, feeling sadness at this finale to a relationship that had started with so much hope. The biggest and most important of all the recent changes were inside her, and he hadn't really noticed them. She'd gained a tiny bit of wisdom, she hoped – and some courage, too. 'It *is* time for us to move on, Paul. You're right about that.'

He gave his snarling tiger's smile of triumph. 'So you'll come to the USA with me, make a fresh start?'

Upstairs on the landing Louise clenched her fists, fighting not to burst into tears.

Rosalind let the silence drag on for a minute or two, till the smile on his face faded a little and puzzlement crept in. 'No, Paul. I won't be coming to the USA. I'm definitely leaving you. I'm going back to England to live in my aunt's house for a while and think about my options.'

Suddenly his expression was ugly. 'Oh, now that you have the money, you've suddenly got *options*, have you? I suppose you stayed with me before because I was the best *option* at the time – with the most money to offer you.'

She shrank away from him, he looked so vicious. Then she got angry with herself for reacting like that and sat up straighter, staring right back at him across the kitchen table. 'Actually, my favourite option has nothing to do with money. I met a man while I was over there, you see, Paul. A very kind man. We get on really well and—'

Upstairs Louise was weeping helplessly, relief turning her into a jelly. *Oh, thank you*, she kept murmuring. *Thank you, thank you, God, or fate, or whatever you are up there. She's going to escape.*

And so am I.

Paul's mouth dropped open, then he made a quick recovery, thumping the table with the edge of his clenched fist. 'So you've been unfaithful to me, you bitch! And there you were going on at me, treating me like a pariah.'

'No, I haven't been unfaithful. Not physically, anyway, which is the only thing you'd understand. I wouldn't do that while we were still married.'

'Who is it? Do I know him?' He snapped his fingers suddenly. 'Not that thin streak of nothing. That blue-blooded waffly creature with the bossy sister?'

'Yes.' A smile suddenly overtook Rosalind at this description of Harry and she felt warm inside, absolutely right about what she was doing. 'Yes. It's Jonathon.'

Paul thumped the table again and one of the coffee cups fell off it, shattering, scattering brown liquid on the grey and white tiled floor. Neither of them bothered to pick it up.

When the silence continued, Paul swiped at one of the carrier bags of food that was still sitting on the table, knocking that down on top of the coffee. 'Rich is he, your precious Jonathon? Richer than me? As well as better connected? You're more cunning than I'd realised, Ros. Made very sure of your options, didn't you, before you decided to leave me?'

She tried to explain, knowing it would be useless, but at least she tried. 'Jonathon's quite poor actually. That house of his is a sort of trust. No one can dispose of it, just guard it for future generations.' She would be proud to help with that if he'd let her, though she wanted to spend time in Australia, too, didn't think she could abandon her country entirely.

'So he's after your money, then.'

She smiled, very certain of that. 'No, he isn't.'

'He is, you know.'

'Is that the only attraction I can offer him? I think not. Anyway I'm not going to live with him at first. I'm going back to live in Aunt Sophie's house.' She waved one hand around her. 'To make things easy, I'll agree to sell this place as soon as you like and split our possessions down the middle. I've never really liked the house. It's a cold and heartless. *You* chose it, not me.'

He folded his arms. 'Our younger daughter is staying with me, then.'

'No, I'm not.' Louise came into the room, trying to look calm, but actually feeling a bit shivery inside. He was looking so black, like a thunderstorm about to crash down on them. She'd crept downstairs in case her mother needed help, but she wasn't having them decide about her future without her being involved.

Rosalind stood up and Paul followed suit, moving to stand between her and her daughter.

Louise ducked away from him and darted across to join her mother.

'I doubt you'll get custody – even if you're foolish enough to try,' Rosalind said thoughtfully. 'I believe children get a say in such things these days as long as they're old enough to understand what's happening, which Louise clearly is. And anyway, she'll be eighteen in another month or so. You couldn't even get the case to court before her birthday.'

'I want to come with you,' Louise said. 'You will let me, won't you, Mum?'

Paul made an inarticulate noise and grabbed her. 'You're staying with me from now on.'

When she struggled against him, kicking him in the shins, he slapped her face.

Rosalind moved to stand between them. 'Stop this, Paul.'

When he raised his hand a second time, she reacted automatically, moving quickly, as her instructor had once taught her, and taking him by surprise. She kneed Paul hard in the groin before jabbing the side of her hand into his neck. Then she watched with intense satisfaction as he folded up with a quiet 'Oof!' and rolled about on the floor, agony written all over him, unable to breathe properly.

'I went to self-defence classes one year, Paul. Don't you remember? I was worried because you were away so much and I got nervous going out at night on my own. I've always wondered if I'd have the guts to use the techniques. Now I know.'

'Ros—' His voice was still half-choked and he was rocking about, his hands splayed protectively around his genitals.

'My name is Rosalind,' she said firmly, 'and I think we've said everything there is to say. If you'll move out of this house, I'll get it ready to sell. I can make a big difference to the price if I have things looking really nice – or if you won't move out, we can lose a lot of money. That's up to you.'

He glared at her as he tried to straighten up and couldn't.

She put an arm round her daughter's shoulders. 'Come on, love, let's go and tell my mother our news. Later today, when your father has moved out, we'll come back and start getting the place ready to sell.' She looked back at Paul, who had dragged himself to a chair, but was still clutching his crotch and looking shocked as well as winded.

'I'm sorry it's ended like this. But there's no hope of my staying with you, whether Jonathon and I work something out or not. You see, you don't seem to have learnt anything from what's been happening. Didn't you see how alone you were in my family portrait? No one was standing near you, not even your wife.'

'What the hell has that embroidery to do with this?'

'Everything. It mirrors life, our life.'

But he didn't understand that. She'd take the family

portrait with her when she went to her mother's, though, just for safety. What a good thing most of her embroideries were still in England.

'I'll fight you – for everything,' he rasped. 'I've earned – the money that paid – for all this.'

'But I raised your children and played my part in the marriage. I believe the courts always take that into account.' She had seen a few of her friends' marriages break up over the years and knew the ropes. Had never expected to walk down the same path herself, but now found the prospect inviting. Very.

'You didn't do a very good job with the children!' he snarled. 'Tim was a total failure. I blame *you* for that.'

Pain shafted through her again, as it did every time she thought of her son. 'I blame myself, too, and I always shall, but I think I've time to make a difference with Louise.' She looked at her daughter, who was smiling proudly at her, not even looking at her father. 'I don't want to force you into anything, though, Lou.' She used the pet name Tim had sometimes called his sister by.

'I want to come with you, Mum. I need you.'

'I'm glad. Will you nip up and fetch my suitcase? And yours. Just in case your father doesn't move out.'

Louise ran off.

Paul found the breath suddenly to yell, 'Well, who wants an old-fashioned lump like you for a wife. I'll find myself a new one who's twice as smart – in every way!'

'I hope you do. And she'll ditch you as soon as you lose your edge. You'll deserve each other.' Then she turned her back and began walking out.

After Rosalind pulled the front door closed behind her, however, she clutched her daughter's arm and took a deep, shuddering breath. 'Get me to the car, Lou. I feel sick.'

'Hold on to me, Mum. Don't let him see that you're chucking a wobbly.'

They walked out together, arms linked, each carrying a suitcase.

'You'll have to drive. I'm shaking.' Rosalind slid into the front passenger seat. She sat up very straight until they'd turned the corner, then slumped down and began to weep noisily.

When Louise stopped the car and tried to cuddle her, she held on to her daughter for a few moments, then blinked away the tears. 'Changes as big as this hurt like hell,' she said huskily. 'But it's done now – well, the decision is taken, anyway.'

'You – won't change your mind? About leaving him, I mean?'

'Oh, no. That is quite definite, whatever else happens. Only I had to come here to – to close things off. How do you think you'll like living in England?'

Louise started up the engine again. 'I don't know. But it'll be better than living with him. I still want to train as a nurse. I dare say I can do it there just as well as here.'

'I think you'll make a good nurse. I'll help you all I can.'

'Thanks, Mum. But until I can start training, I'll be getting a job. I'm going to stand on my own feet from now on.'

'I'm glad. It's what I want for you – and for myself.'

As they drove away, Rosalind not only felt closer to her daughter but at peace beneath the sadness. If it didn't work out with Jonathon, she'd still be better off without Paul. And she had her embroidery. George Didburin was very enthusiastic about her future as an artist. She meant to work very hard, really make something of herself. It was about time.

She sat up straighter. She'd begin another piece soon. A woman – on her own, head up, wind blowing. Herself. But not in pastel colours. That was what was wrong with the family portrait. Her own figure. She was such a faded creature in it. She would do another half-figure of herself in brighter colours and place the two Rosalinds back to back, as she'd once told Tim, almost like Siamese twins.

Then, and only then, when she'd seen herself as she had become, would she be finished with the past and ready to step forward into the future. Whatever that might be.

LIFELIKE EFFECTS

Almost without exception, extant work reveals remarkable inventiveness and dexterity, displayed in a myriad of small embroidered slips and constructed artefacts, and an even greater ingenuity in their assembly into a finished piece of work.

(Hirst, p.8)

ASSEMBLING THE EMBROIDERY

[Like life] A raised embroidery is built up in a series of layers . . . Succeeding layers must follow in the correct order of precedence. In reality, the process is a continuous one . . .

(Hirst, p.74)

ANNA JACOBS is the author of over eighty novels and is addicted to storytelling. She grew up in Lancashire, emigrated to Australia in the 1970s and writes stories set in both countries. She loves to return to England regularly to visit her family and soak up the history. She has two grown-up daughters and a grandson, and lives with her husband in a spacious home near the Swan Valley, the earliest wine-growing area in Western Australia. Her house is crammed with thousands of books.

annajacobs.com

A Short History of
Sociological Thought

Second Edition

Alan Swingewood

Lecturer in Sociology, London School of Economics

MACMILLAN

First published 1984 by
THE MACMILLAN PRESS LTD
Houndmills, Basingstoke, Hampshire RG21 2XS
and London
Companies and representatives
throughout the world

ISBN 0–333–55860–X hardcover
ISBN 0–333–55861–8 paperback

A catalogue record for this book is available
from the British Library.

Printed in Hong Kong

First edition reprinted 1988, 1989
Second edition 1991
Reprinted 1992, 1993

A Short History of Sociological Thought

Also by Alan Swingewood

The Sociology of Literature (co-author)
Marx and Modern Social Theory
The Novel and Revolution
The Myth of Mass Culture
Sociological Poetics and Aesthetic Theory

Contents

Contents

Contents

HISTORY OF SOCIOLOGICAL THOUGHT

Origins

Eighteenth-century social thought (Vico, Montesquieu,
Smith, Ferguson, Rousseau)

The development of nineteenth-century sociological
positivism (Comte), sociological evolutionism (Spencer) and
Marxism (Marx and Engels)

↓

Classical Sociology

Weber, Simmel, Pareto
(the tradition of *verstehen*
sociology and critique of
positivism and evolutionism)

Durkheim's critique of the
positivist tradition

The development of Marxism after Marx involving a critique of materialism
and evolutionism: Labriola, Gramsci, Sorel, Lukács

↓

Modern Sociology

Phenomenological Sociology (Schutz)
Freud, Mead, Mannheim

↓

Functionalism
Systems Theory and Action Theory
(Parsons)
Structuralism

↙

Structuration Theory
Critical Theory (Habermas)

Introduction

This book is neither a history of sociology nor of sociological theory but a selective history of sociological thought from its origins in eighteenth-century philosophy, history and political economy. By sociological thought is meant an awareness of society as a distinctive object of study, as a system or structure objectively determined by laws and processes. Eighteenth-century social thought was sociological in this sense although it failed to develop an adequate sociological concept of the social, too often assimilating it to political and economic elements. In effect eighteenth-century social thought posed many of the critical issues of sociology without resolving them sociologically. In contrast, early nineteenth-century sociological thought (specifically Comte, Spencer, Marx) sought to define the social both in terms of society as a complex structural whole and in its relation with specific institutions, notably the division of labour, social classes, religion, family and scientific/professional associations. Society was industrial society and the broad themes of the early sociologists were those of social conflict, alienation, community, social cohesion and the possibilities of evolution and development. The task of social science was to identify the forces promoting historical change. Early sociological thought was concerned with the separation of an autonomous social sphere (or 'civil society') from centralised state institutions (or 'political society'). It is this notion of 'finalisation', that history has a meaning apart from the actions of everyday life, which differentiates early sociological thought from later, classical sociology and the various schools of 'sociologised' Marxism.

Early sociological thought was broadly optimistic: the

1

certainties of the natural sciences could be applied to the social sciences unproblematically. Classical sociology emerges as a reaction to this form of positivist scientistic thought. The broad themes of classical sociology were pessimistic: industrialisation produces social structures which alienate the individual from the community, transform cultural objects into commodities, rationalise human life into bureaucratic systems of domination and effectively strip the individual of autonomy. Classical sociology becomes centred not on large-scale changes but on the human subject: 'voluntarism' and action replace the historical determinism of nineteenth-century systems theory. It is this distinction which sets the agenda for the later development of modern sociology.

Modern sociological thought begins with the breakdown of the classical, voluntarist model. The dominant paradigm becomes functionalism, its pre-eminence bound up with the emergence of American sociology in the years following the Second World War. Classical sociology had been almost entirely European: the rise of European Fascism, Communism and the Second World War shifted the focus of sociological thought across the Atlantic. And it was not until the 1960s that new schools of sociology – phenomenology, action theory, structuralism, Marxist humanism – which drew much of their inspiration from classical sociology, emerged.

In this book I have attempted to describe these developments. In particular, there is extended discussion of Marxism both as a distinctive theory of society and for its influence on classical and modern sociology. It has become fashionable to argue that Marxism is a sociology. I suggest that Marxist thought is certainly sociological and as such has been absorbed into sociology itself and, increasingly, that Marxism assimilates sociological concepts and thought in order to offer adequate accounts of modern industrial society and historical development. Many of the crucial differences between sociology and Marxism resolve themselves around the relation of centralised state structure to decentred social structures. By defining its object of study as civil society sociology developed theories which emphasised the differentiated and potentially autonomous nature of modern industrial society. In contrast, Marxist thought articulated a theory of the social formation

2

built around a deterministic relation of economic 'base' to socio-cultural 'superstructure'. It is this decentred, sociological concept of the social which links together the various schools of sociological thought. This does not imply a single sociology. Since the rise of classical sociology there have been many different sociologies but they share a common object of study and their focus is broadly similar.

Part I examines the historical rise of sociological thought and its development into positivism, evolutionism and Marxism. Part II describes the complex reaction to positivist social science and Marxism by classical sociologists such as Weber, Durkheim, Sombart and Simmel. Because Marx's thought played such an important role in the formation of classical sociology I have discussed his theory of class and power in Part II contrasting it with Weber's work on social stratification. This is not an argument that sociology developed through a 'debate with Marx's ghost'. Indeed, classical sociology 'debated' with Kant as much as Marx. Kant's epistemology and moral philosophy played as vital a role in the development of classical sociology as Hegelian dialectics in the development of Marxism. Part III explores the development of modern sociology, first in the form of sociological functionalism, and then in its attempts to rediscover the insights of classical sociology. It is the depth of this renewal which suggests a convergence of sociological thought in the midst of apparent fragmentation and diversity.

The development of sociological thought is the result of collaborative, communicative and dialogic interaction involving individuals, social groups and communities. Of all areas of the history of sociology this is perhaps the most complex and neglected although there have been valuable contributions by Coser, 1971; Jay, 1973; Clarke, 1973; Schwendinger, 1974 and Therborn, 1976. Certain themes – race and gender, for example – are not discussed, largely because they have not been in the forefront of sociological thought. This book is, as I have said, a selective history. At the end I have listed a number of works by chapter which refer the reader to further general discussion as well as more specialised studies. A history of sociological thought – from Vico to Bakhtin – can easily become a 'shopping list' of great names: I have tried to avoid this by concentrating

3

in some detail on major themes of sociological relevance as well as significant thinkers.

November 1983   ALAN SWINGEWOOD

Note to the Second Edition

For this second edition I have substantially revised the accounts of critical theory and structuralism. I have also made a number of minor changes to the chapters on Marx, Weber, Durkheim and Marxism after Marx. In this way I hope to have strengthened the basic argument of the book and made it more useful for students studying sociology and related subjects.

August 1990   ALAN SWINGEWOOD

PART I
FOUNDATIONS

1
Origins of Sociology

There was no sociology before the advent of the nineteenth century, if by sociology is meant a systematic corpus of knowledge, specific methodology and conceptual framework which clearly differentiate it as a distinctive discipline, with its own object of study, from the related studies of economics, history, philosophy and law. The term sociology was coined by Auguste Comte in the early nineteenth century although the study of society as an historical and empirical object had begun much earlier, especially in eighteenth-century France and Scotland, where a commitment to historical and scientific modes of thought and inquiry shifted the prevailing discourse of political and moral philosophy away from traditional concerns with the universal and the transhistorical to a grasp of the specificity of the social. This is not to suggest that eighteenth-century social theory constituted a sociology, rather it remained a peculiarly invigorating mixture of political philosophy, history, political economy *and* sociology.

The work of Montesquieu, Ferguson and Millar exemplified a sociology in the making. In discussing the development of sociology it is crucial to distinguish between those writers who discussed broad sociological themes within a non-sociological discourse (Aristotle, Plato, Hobbes, Locke) and those genuine precursors who defined both a method of inquiry and a concept of society as a distinctive object of study, a dynamic structure of institutions and processes analytically separate from political society.

Human nature and social order

Two pre-sociological theories – those of classical Greek thought and the Social Contract – are sometimes regarded by historians of sociology as laying down the foundation for a science of human society. Both Plato (427–347 B.C.) and Aristotle (384–322 B.C.) defined society in holistic terms as an organism in which the constituent parts were necessarily related to the whole. Plato particularly emphasised the unity of the social organism, the parts defined in terms of their subordination to the whole. In contrast, Aristotle conceived society as a differentiated structure in which separate elements, while contributing to the whole, remained independent of it. Thus Plato analysed society as a unified system, structured around the division of labour and social inequality. Social health, or social order, was the product of 'wise legislation' in which the interests of the whole exerted priority over those of the individual parts. Plato's ideal state has thus been described as a form of communism in that the separate elements, such as private property and the family, functioned in relation to the higher unity of the whole.

Aristotle's concept of society was equally anti-atomistic: as a complex, differentiated structure the social whole consisted of groups not individuals. For Aristotle, the origin of society lay in human nature; humanity was by nature social and political and thus destined to live with others in communities. Social structure consisted of social groups based on function and social wealth (food-producers, warriors, tradesmen; the rich, the poor, the middle class). Aristotle's *Politics* is full of sociological insights into the nature of human society and contains one of the first systematic attempts to analyse and classify social phenomena, such as government, into ideal types (tyranny, oligarchy, democracy). Yet Aristotle's social thought remains within the framework of traditional political philosophy. As with Plato, there is no clear distinction between the state and society. And for Aristotle social institutions are derived from basic human instincts such as sexual desire which predispose individuals to form groups and associations which then function to further develop essential human nature. Society was thus the expression of an inherent sociability with

8

social relationships the culmination of this instinct. Aristotle's formulations blocked the possibility of defining society in terms of objective laws and historical processes.

Aristotle's static world view was not challenged until the sixteenth century. Medieval social organisation did not generate a philosophy oriented to problems of social change and secular political obligation. Social contract theory developed as an alternative world view rejecting notions of Divine Law and religious conceptions of sovereignty. Social contract theory sought the origins of society in a structure of contractual obligations and reciprocal social relationships. Human nature was still an important component of the theory but Aristotle's essentialist sociability was replaced, in the work of Thomas Hobbes (1588–1679), by an asocial, egoistic and individualistic humanity. In the pre-social state of nature, Hobbes argued, there was an absence of social bonds and a condition of permanent warfare. A peaceful and unified civil society was made possible only through the renunciation of certain individual rights: a contractual obligation linked the individual with a sovereign state that guaranteed order and harmony under the rubric of positive law.

Social contract theory prepared the way for the secular social theory of the eighteenth century even though it remained tied to asocial notions of human nature. Society was conceived as partly the product of human and not divine action. Not all social contract writers were as pessimistic as Hobbes: John Locke (1632–1704) argued that the state of nature was rather a state of peace, good will and reciprocal relationships, the development of social conflict and diverging interests the result of the growth of private property and thus of social inequality. Both Hobbes and Locke grasped the secular historical nature of human society but assimilated this notion of the social to an underlying concept of a pre-social, transhistorical human nature: egoism for Hobbes, sympathy for Locke. In the eighteenth century Jean-Jacques Rousseau (1712–78) further developed Locke's dichotomy of a sociable humanity existing in a state of nature and the corrupt, egoistic humanity of modern civil society; humanity as the product of nature versus humanity as the product of society and culture.

In the writings of Aristotle, Plato, Hobbes, Locke and

Rousseau there are numerous sociological themes relating to problems of social differentiation, inequality, social conflict and social cohesion, the development of the division of labour and private property – but this does not make these theorists sociologists. Locke is more sociological than Aristotle in his analysis of property and social differentiation; Rousseau is more sociological than Locke in his awareness that society creates more complex needs and therefore a more complex humanity than that found in the state of nature. Pre-eighteenth century philosophy, however, was largely dominated by a weak, not strong concept of the social: society was not defined as an objective structure of secular institutions and processes, but the product of asocial forces and the voluntary acquiescence of pre-social individuals in the formation of modern states and political obligation. The emphasis on human nature as the basis of human society and social order led to the view of the social as the expression of an immanent transhistorical process. There was no conception of society as a complex structure of different levels – the economic, political, cultural – dependent for their functioning on specific, objective laws. In this sense the true precursors of sociology are Giambattista Vico and Baron de Montesquieu.

Vico: science and history

The New Science of Giambattista Vico (1668–1774), first published in 1725, is one of the most remarkable works of early eighteenth-century social thought; a vast comparative analysis of the history of human culture which discusses the rise of property, religion, and the development of language, art and literature. The third edition of 1744 preceded Montesquieu's *Spirit of the Laws* by four years and together they stand as the first major attempts to theorise society as an organic whole and relate its varying cultures, values and institutions to a specific stage of historical development.

Vico's *New Science* sought to make history intelligible by defining it as a process characterised by three distinct stages of development – the age of the Gods, the age of the Heroes and finally the age of Men – and thus invested with immanent

10

meaning. The theory itself is perhaps less significant than Vico's attempt to apply scientific concepts to the study of human history. His starting point was the affirmation of humanism – the creative, active role of the human subject. 'In the night of thick darkness', he wrote, which envelops the remote past 'there shines the eternal and never failing light of a truth beyond all question: that the world of civil society has certainly been made by men' (Vico, 1948, Section 331). Vico thus rejected the fixed concept of human nature which had characterised the social thought of Aristotle, Hobbes and Locke: the general argument of the *New Science* was that human society was historical, social institutions and human relationships defined as the product of action. For Vico, society and human nature were dynamic categories: he accepted that human nature rested on certain principles to be unfolded and revealed in the historical development of institutions such as the family. Vico's dynamic sense of history contrasts sharply with the anti-historical rationalism of social contract theory which, assuming society as the expression of an unchanging human nature, postulated a static notion of the social which failed to account for the richness and variety of traditions and customs and the ways in which elements of the past survived actively into the present.

Vico's concept of history as an active, creative process made by humanity, clearly differentiates his social thought from the mechanistic materialism of Hobbes and Locke with their emphasis on the determining influence of the environment on human action. Vico was also opposed to the scientific rationalism associated with the natural sciences: the *New Science* rejects many of the assumptions of Newton, Galileo and the philosophy of Descartes. Cartesian rationalism, a potent influence on philosophy and science at this time, assumed that the only certain knowledge was derived from principles and concepts drawn from mathematics and physics. Descartes advanced what he called the 'geometrical method' as the basis for understanding both the natural and the social worlds. True knowledge, therefore, was essentially deductive, the application of rules that were universal and timeless. But mathematics itself, Vico argued, was man-made and the knowledge derived from mathematical propositions was true knowledge only

11

because humanity itself had created it. Here Vico states one of his revolutionary new principles, that humanity can know only that which itself has created: the true (*verum*) and the made (*factum*) are convertible. It was not, therefore, a question of passively recording, classifying and observing an external reality in the manner of the physical sciences, for 'the world of human society has certainly been made by men, and its principles are therefore to be found within the modifications of our own human mind'. Vico's distinction between 'inner' and 'outer' knowledge derived from his humanist, anti-mechanical and anti-determinist standpoint: factual knowledge of the external world was clearly inadequate as the basis for human science since it eliminated the active core of human culture, diminishing the making in favour of the made.

For Vico, then, the subject matter of the natural sciences differed from that of the human sciences. Social theory must be based on the human subject as an active agent, on human experiences and mental states. But for all its revolutionary implications, perhaps because of this, the *New Science* found little response among the major philosophers and political theorists of the eighteenth-century Enlightenment. It was not until the nineteenth century that Vico's work was given its true recognition. His concept of society as an organic whole was clearly opposed to the atomistic individualism of French philosophical materialism. Yet Vico's work was typical of one important strand of eighteenth-century thought which culminated in the holistic theories of society and culture advanced by Hegel, and later, during the nineteenth century, by Comte and Marx. Vico's humanist historicism is important here for the argument, central to both Hegel and Marx, that human action has meaning only in terms of the whole. History is conceived as a process which succeeds in binding together the often contradictory and chaotic actions of individuals in such a way that they form a coherent whole. At the end of the *New Science* Vico restated his 'first incontestable principle' but added that

this world without doubt has issued from a mind often diverse, at times quite contrary, and always superior to the particular ends that men had proposed to themselves . . . Men mean to gratify their

12

bestial lust and abandon their offspring, and they inaugurate the chastity of marriage from which the families arise. The fathers mean to exercise without restraint their paternal power over their clients, and they subject them to the civil powers from which the cities arise (Vico, 1948, Section 1108).

This notion of the unintended effects of social action is developed by Vico as part of his general theory of historical change. As we shall see it was to exercise a great influence on eighteenth-century social theory.

Montesquieu

Eighteenth-century philosophy remained unreceptive to Vico's humanist historicism. When Montesquieu visited Venice the *New Science* was recommended but there is no evidence that he either read or acquired the work. It was Montesquieu, not Vico, who influenced the sociological writings of the Scottish School of Ferguson, Smith and Millar. Like many other eighteenth-century intellectuals, Montesquieu (1689–1755) was not a specialist but a man of letters trained in classics and philosophy. His work combined the study of history, political science, criticism, political theory and sociology, but he has been described as the first, and greatest sociologist of the Enlightenment. In the 'Preface' to *The Spirit of the Laws* (1748) he emphasised his scientific intent: 'I have not drawn my principles from my prejudices but from the nature of things.' Such was his reputation that in 1767 a despairing Adam Ferguson noted that 'when I recollect what . . . Montesquieu has written, I am at a loss to tell why I should treat of human affairs'.

Montesquieu, employing a richer and more detailed mode of historical analysis, more extensive and systematic than anything found in previous social theory, was able to define society as a structural whole and, more significantly, attempt to locate the specific causes of different social phenomena. The laws of

13

society, although the embodiment of human reason, must nevertheless suit the physical context and its social institutions. Legal codes and customs are discussed from the perspective of their relationship with social structure; the role of the legislator is one of balancing the requirements of an 'ideal' constitution with the situation or 'milieu'. It was this aspect of Montesquieu's thought that Emile Durkheim regarded as significant for the development of sociology: to accept the view that legislators alone framed constitutions and social customs was tantamount to denying 'any determinate order in human societies, for if it were true laws, customs and institutions would depend not on the constant nature of the state, but on the accident that brought forth one lawmaker rather than another' (Durkheim, 1965, pp. 11–12).

Montesquieu's point of departure is clearly indicated in the 'Preface' to the *Spirit of the Laws*:

I have first of all considered mankind, and the results of my thoughts has been, that midst such an infinite diversity of laws and manners, they were not solely conducted by the caprice of fancy.

And in the first book he writes:

They who assert that a blind fatality produced the various effects we behold in this world talk very absurdly; for can anything be more unreasonable than to pretend that a blind fatality could be productive of intelligent beings? (Montesquieu, 1949, Book 1, Section 1).

Montesquieu is arguing that although society presents itself as a chaotic and diverse phenomenon, there exists beneath the surface a definite structure comprising regularities of behaviour, institutions and laws. Social institutions and processes are thus the product of definite material conditions which can be discovered by empirical and historical analysis. Regular relationships exist between these objective forces. In his study of the Roman Empire (1734) Montesquieu wrote:

It is not chance that rules the world. Ask the Romans who had a continuous sequence of successes when they were guided by a certain plan, and an uninterrupted sequence of reverses when they followed another. There are general causes, moral and physical, which act in every monarchy, elevating it, maintaining it . . . All accidents are controlled by these causes (Montesquieu, 1965, p. 165).

All social phenomena are interconnected, 'every particular law is connected with another law'. Montesquieu's concept of society is thus couched in holistic, not atomistic, terms; societies are self-contained, integrated wholes.

Montesquieu's main concern was forms of government. But his types of government are effectively types of society. Law must accord with social context, but Montesquieu attempts to define context more precisely as a structure consisting of soil and climate, occupations, religious institutions, 'commerce, manners and customs'. His analysis of law is far from narrowly political, for as laws express the 'spirit' or inner essence of society as a whole, the distinction between the political and the social is purely formal. Thus although adhering to Aristotle's classification of government – republics which include aristocracy and democracy, monarchy and despotism – Montesquieu concentrates his analysis on the distribution and exercise of power within them and the principles or 'spirit' binding them together – virtue, honour and fear.

Montesquieu emphasises that his classification is of ideal rather than real types: the fact that a republican government exemplifies virtue (through the frugality and equality within its city states) does not imply that all republics express virtue only that they 'ought'. Montesquieu's forms are effectively ideal types, logical constructs, abstracted from the rich and varied historical details of reality to facilitate analysis, a methodological standpoint which clearly differentiates his thought from the classic Aristotelian political tradition. Aristotle's governments were essences – timeless, universal abstractions based on a limited historical experience. Montesquieu's awareness of the relation of the social to the political effectively yielded a classification of governments and societies.

But in making this break from political philosophy Montesquieu failed to develop a theory of social change; he did not analyse the ways in which one type of society passed into a different form. His typology was broadly synchronic, concerned with describing the typical elements of different formations as they unite in a coherent unity; Montesquieu's sociological 'formalism' is thus insensitive to the problems of genesis and change. The important question of transition is never raised and in this sense Montesquieu was not historical enough, his formal classification, although of great significance for sociological method, blocking the development of a dynamic concept of civil society. The writers of the Scottish Enlightenment, while indebted to Montesquieu's typology and formal historical sense, were more concretely aware of social change and the transition from one type of society to another. Thus they attempted to identify those elements within society which led to social change.

Montesquieu's synchronic approach led him to define society as a system in which the various elements had meaning only in terms of the whole. The basic elements comprising this system were climate and geography: other writers had advocated physical factors as the basis of social analysis but Montesquieu was the first to analyse their contribution to the structure of society as a whole. Montesquieu's concept of environment, or milieu, implied the concept of a system in which the political 'superstructure' and culture express the spirit of the whole. Of course, Montesquieu overstates his case: suicide, slavery, marriage are all mechanically and causally related to specific climatic conditions and peculiarities of geography. But there can be no doubting the scientific spirit behind these arguments. Also Montesquieu did not suggest a totally monistic view: there are moral, as well as physical causes, and in Book XIX of *The Spirit of the Laws* he argued that

> Mankind are influenced by various causes: by the climate . . . religion . . . laws . . . maxims of government . . . morals and customs; whence is formed the general spirit of nations. In proportion as, in every country, any one of these causes acts with more force, the others in the same degree are weakened. Nature and climate rule almost alone among the savages; customs govern the Chinese.

The structure of any society thus hinges on the workings, not of one single factor but of many factors; society is the product of an equilibrium between a multiplicity of elements. Social development gradually weakens the influence of purely physical elements and strengthens the moral. The role of the legislator is to discover a balance between physical and moral forces, the latter by their nature more amenable to human manipulation. The milieu is thus the framework in which physical and moral factors operate, a structure of multi-causality which allows Montesquieu to adopt a voluntaristic position, the legislator mediating between the emerging influence of the moral and the weakening influence of the physical. Nevertheless, the broad implications of Montesquieu's concept of society is that the individual is merely the instrument of historical change, a passive element within a system conceived as the ceaseless interaction of moral and physical forces that climaxes in the spirit of the nation. Virtue, honour and fear function to create social unity and maintain social order.

The sociological core of Montesquieu's thought is undoubtedly the attempt to discover an underlying pattern of relationships between the different elements of society; beneath the apparent diversity and chaos of empirical reality exists a structure and system which, once clarified, illuminates the cause of diverse phenomena and thus generates meaning. His comment on the feudal system is apposite:

> The feudal laws form a very beautiful prospect. A venerable old oak raises its lofty head to the skies; the eye sees from afar its spreading leaves; upon drawing nearer it perceives the trunk but does not discern the root; the ground must be dug up to discover it (Montesquieu, 1949, Book XXX, Section 1).

It was this task which fell to Adam Ferguson and John Millar.

The Scottish Enlightenment

As I have suggested earlier, the atomistic individualism of the French Enlightenment prevented the further development of Montesquieu's sociological conceptions, especially the notion of society as an integrated, systemic whole. Thus Diderot's

17

project, the *Encyclopedia* contains no entry for society; Voltaire, like Diderot, remained firmly within the individualistic rationalism and philosophical scepticism of post-1750 French thought. Rousseau is one exception, for as I have noted earlier, in the discussion of social contract theory, sociological themes saturate his works. In *The Social Contract* (1762) and the *Discourse on the Origins of Social Inequality* (1755) Rousseau analysed the rise of property and its relation with the division of labour, inequality and social conflict. And like Montesquieu, he grasped both the distinctiveness of the social and society as an organic whole in which individual interests were assimilated into a common, general will. Society was not a collection of atomised individuals. But unlike Montesquieu, Rousseau was concerned with origins: for him society was the result of a contract, an act of association which generated a moral and collective order greater than the individual wills comprising it. Society was thus the product of both the principles of nature (the original state of nature and natural man) and those of reason. There is here a sharp distinction between the concept of society in Montesquieu and Rousseau. For Montesquieu, society was a system built around objective structures or elements; for Rousseau, society was an organism based on individual wills collectively organised into a quasi-mystical general will.

In the development of sociology Montesquieu was the more potent force. During the second half of the eighteenth century a group of intellectuals working in Glasgow and Edinburgh advanced the scientific study of human society in directions opposed to social contract theory. Such were the achievements of David Hume (1711–76), Adam Smith (1723–90), Adam Ferguson (1723–1816), John Millar (1735–1801) as well as the historian William Robertson (1721–93) that Edinburgh became known as the Athens of the North, compared only with Paris as the major centre of learning during the latter half of the eighteenth century. For this group of intellectuals society as a distinctive object of study could not be assimilated to a contractual relation between individual and government, but defined empirically, as a distinctive structure with a natural or 'theoretical history'.

While there has been much comment on the intellectual

18

achievements of the Scottish Enlightenment, there has been a tendency to concentrate on its contributions to philosophy and economics and to underemphasise the sociology. Smith, Ferguson and Millar raised critical sociological issues and problems analysing the social role of property, forms of government, the development of the division of labour, the alienation of industrial work and the development of language: these were not mere themes within their work but constituted a core of sociological thought and theorising within the broad framework of economics, philosophy and history.

Of these intellectuals the least sociologial was David Hume but his influence on Smith and Ferguson was crucial. Hume was an empiricist: experience, fact, utility constituted the backbone of his epistemology and social philosophy. He rejected the social contract theory of society arguing that to locate the origins of political society in the voluntary acquiescence of individuals was to ignore the real historical world of human experience and facts. Social contract theory was effectively dismissed for its lack of sociology. Society could not be deduced from universal principles of human nature, for although characterised by uniformity it is moulded by the social context especially education, custom and habit. Hume emphasised the role of social factors which affect human character. One of the most important is sympathy which is defined socially in that 'the mutual dependence of man is so great in all societies that scarce any human action is entirely complete in itself, or is performed without some reference to the actions of others, which are requisite to make it answer fully the intention of the agent'. Writing of justice Hume remarked that it is established by common consent 'and where every single act is performed in expectation that others are to perform the like'. Sympathy is social because 'the propensity to company and society is strong in all rational creatures'. In a similar way he argued that custom and habit were not irrational forces but elements essential for the proper workings of society. Hume failed to develop a conception of society as a structure, and in general his model remained atomistic and his method deductive. Thus although human association was the product of human nature, Hume's concern lay with the forms of sociability which human nature takes within society. He continually defined human action as social because it is oriented towards the actions of others: 'Reduce a person to solitude and he loses all enjoyment except either of the sensual or speculative kind; and that because the movements of his heart are not forwarded by correspondent movements in his fellow creatures.' A non-social man, like the state of nature, is a mere 'philosophical fiction'.

Hume's essays are full of proto-sociological themes. Authority, he notes, is always a 'mixture of force and consent' made generally acceptable by its practical utility. He argues for the close relation of property and power, advocating a functional balance between them. But the existence of sociological themes does not make a philosopher into a sociologist; nor do they necessarily cohere into a theory of society as an independent object of study. Unlike Hume, Ferguson, Smith and Millar defined the basic unit of analysis as groups – Ferguson's 'troops and companies' – which thus constituted a definite patterned structure. Hume followed Aristotle in defining society as coeval with the human family, a social group which unites and preserves sexual union until 'a new tie takes place in their common concern with their offspring'. From sexual desire Hume deduced the universality of the human family and therefore society. Ferguson, while agreeing with Hume on the importance of sexual desire in the process of family formation, and noting the existence of human instincts, was more concerned with the institution of the family and its contribution to socialisation and forging the necessary bond between parent and child. This distinction, however, between Hume's deductive approach and Ferguson's inductive, empirical standpoint is by no means clear-cut, but the tendency towards a sociological analysis of the institutional and structural basis of society is markedly present in Ferguson, Smith and Millar. Ferguson's *Essay on the History of Civil Society* (1767) marks a distinct advance on Hume's more speculative essays of the 1740s.

Problems of method

As I have suggested, there was no sociology that can be separated from economics, philosophy and history until the nineteenth century. A distinctive sociological framework, or perspective, did not exist in eighteenth-century thought, but rather a core of sociological concepts and an empirical methodology subsisting within economic, political and historical perspectives. In the writings of Adam Smith three distinct, although related levels of analysis can be identified: the economic, the philosophical and the sociological. In *The Wealth of Nations* the emphasis falls equally on the economic and social consequences of the division of labour. What is significant about the contribution of the Scottish Enlightenment to sociology is the clear awareness that society constituted a process, the product of specific economic, social and historical forces that could be identified and analysed through the methods of empirical science. Society was a category of historical investigation, the result of objective, material causes.

The Scots rejected both the theory of the 'divine origins' of society and the theory of the great legislator. Theoretical, or 'conjectural history', as the approach was termed – misleadingly since the intention was a science of history and society, positive not conjectural knowledge and therefore theoretical in the best sense – was superficially similar to Montesquieu's broad comparative perspective. But the Scots were concerned above everything else with the problem of social change and the causes which lead to the transition from one type of society to another. As Millar wrote:

In searching for the causes of . . . systems of law and government . . . we must undoubtedly resort . . . to the differences of situation . . . the fertility or barrenness of the soil, the nature of its productions, the species of labour requisite for procuring subsistence, in the number of individuals collected together in one community, their proficiency in the arts . . . The variety that frequently occurs in these and such other particulars must have a prodigious influence upon the great body of the people; as, by giving a peculiar direction to their inclinations and pursuits, it must be productive of corresponding habits, dispositions and ways of thinking (Millar, in Lehmann, 1960).

Social diversity is thus explicable in terms of an underlying structure consisting largely of economic factors. Millar's comparative approach, however, sought to analyse diversity and uniformity in terms of the change from 'rude' to 'polished' society. Similarly, Ferguson related forms of government to property, social stratification, division of labour and social conflict. Ferguson's standpoint was civil not political society. Thus the Scots' typology of societies: savage, barbaric and polished (Ferguson), hunting, pastoral, agricultural and commercial (Millar, Smith), constituted forms based on the dominant mode of production in each. And having defined societies in these terms the Scottish writers analysed their dominant institutions and mechanisms leading to social change. One institution which occupied much of their thought was social stratification.

The emergence of class

Neither Hume nor Montesquieu discussed social stratification in any depth. Montesquieu's concerns lay with societies as organic wholes and not with possible sources of conflict and differentiation. Montesquieu lacked a theory of transition, his synchronic model of society eliminating the sources of energy and thus of structural change.

For Adam Smith, the development of a commercial society produced a social structure divided into three clear classes, landowners, capitalists and labourers, 'the three great and constituent orders of every civilised society'. Like Ferguson and Millar, Smith did not employ the concept of social class, but there can be no doubt that in his work, and that of Millar particularly, a theory of class as a sociological category is articulated. The relation between Smith's three social 'orders' and the economic elements is unambiguous: the three groups derive their revenue from rent, from stock, and from wages. Property forms the basis of social differentiation, 'the natural source of influence and authority' closely bound up with social change and pervading 'every corner of society'. Millar argued, indeed, that social development necessarily engendered social inequality ceaselessly introducing 'corresponding gradation and subordination of ranks'. An economic interpretation of history is suggested:

The distribution of property among any people is the principal circumstance that contributed to reduce them under civil government, and to determine the form of their political constitution. The poor are naturally dependent on the rich, from whom they derive subsistence; and, according to the accidental differences of wealth possessed by individuals, a subordination of ranks is gradually introduced and different degrees of power are assumed without opposition, by particular persons (Millar, in Lehmann, 1960).

In pre-industrial society, Millar argued, social stratification was based largely on function: in fishing and hunting communities, for example, outstanding personal accomplishments, such as courage, strength and military skill, constituted the basis of authority. But distinctions hinging on function are unstable and 'cannot be productive of any lasting influence and authority'. But with the growth of agriculture and settled mode of subsistence property became increasingly accumulated in private hands and thus a permanent differentiation of ranks emerged: authority became stabilised and institutionalised.

For Millar, commercial society produces damaging effects through the division of labour. Both Millar and Ferguson, aware of the relation of social stratification to the division of labour, treated work specialisation sociologically. Their analysis represented a sharp break from previous discussion, for although Montesquieu and Hume had noted its economic significance they minimised the division of labour's social effects and failed to grasp its broad, structural significance. Thus Ferguson pointed out that the division of labour was a social as well as an economic institution separating those whose function commanded skill from those for whom work required neither thought nor the exercise of 'ingenuity'. Work thus becomes more efficient 'under a total suppression of sentiment and reason' and where 'ignorance is the mother of industry as well as of superstition'. In a famous passage Ferguson wrote:

Manufactures . . . prosper most where the mind is least consulted, and where the workshop may, without any great effort of imagination be considered as an engine, the parts of which are men (Ferguson, 1966, pp. 182–3).

23

As mechanical labour is divided so too are other activities: 'In the progress of society, philosophy or speculation becomes, like every other employment, the principal or sole trade and occupation of a particular class of citizens . . . subdivided into a great number of different branches.' Division of labour is a total process; Ferguson has outlined, indeed, the basis of sociology as a distinct and separate field of study. The norms of efficiency and dexterity apply equally to philosophy and industry, 'more work is done . . . and the quantity of science is considerably increased by it'. Specialisation, Ferguson suggests, leads to a loss of the whole. Manufacturing occupations, unlike the occupation of philosopher, stultify the human intellect; the more minute the task, the fewer the ideas; the more that men work the less time they have for thought and study. Social development is indeed double-edged. As Millar wrote:

> As their employments require constant attention to an object which can afford no variety of occupations to their minds, they are apt to acquire an habitual vacancy of thought, unenlivened by any prospects, but such as are derived from the future wages of their labour or from the grateful returns of bodily respose and sleep (Millar, in Lehmann, 1960).

One of the unintended effects of industrial development, the consequence of a 'polished' society, is that humanity increasingly resembles machines, stripped of its mental powers and 'converted to a mere instrument of labour'.

The dialectics of social change

The concepts of class and industrial society are implicit in the Scottish analysis although remaining untheorised in comparison with later nineteenth-century sociology. Ferguson and Millar identified industrial change as a source of progress in human culture but which, inevitably, brought with it dehumanisation and alienation. Social development was contradictory. It is the analysis of the transition from one stage of social development to another which lies at the heart of the Scottish contribution to sociological thought.

Social development occurred both through economic forces as well as the combined efforts of groups and generations. Social change was grasped as a collective not individual phenomenon involving physical situation, economic and political organisation and the division of labour. Property was the key factor. Such a rigorously deterministic concept of social development circumscribes the activity of the human agent, and while Millar introduced accidental causes and personalities into his historical schema, the basic tendency is mechanistic. Yet Ferguson continually emphasised the active nature of the human agent, the natural disposition to 'remove inconveniences' and improve the situation. Man, he wrote, was 'not made for repose . . . every amiable and respectable quality is an active power . . . and all the lustre which he casts around him, to captivate or engage the attention of his fellow-creatures . . . shines only while his motion continues'. In opposition to the utilitarian concept of humanity as pleasure seeking, Ferguson noted that 'the most animating occasions of human life, are calls to danger and hardship, not invitations to safety and ease', while Robertson argued that 'no small part of that fertility which we ascribe to the hand of nature, is the work of man'.

Vico's 'voluntarism' thus finds an echo in these formulations, but the dualism implied in the concept of an active agent and determining environment was never adequately solved. The important point is the way in which social change was conceived, as a process with both an objective structure – especially the mode of production – and active subject. Change is dialectical in that it emerges as the largely unintended result of human action. 'Every step and every movement of the multitude', Ferguson wrote, 'are made with equal blindness to the future; and nations stumble on establishments, which are indeed the result of human action, but not the execution of human design' (Ferguson, 1966, p. 210, 45). Vico's 'incontestable truth' takes on a sociological meaning in Ferguson's analysis; while in Smith's *The Wealth of Nations* private and egoistic interests are converted into the collective social good by an 'invisible hand' which advances 'the interest of society' without intending or knowing it. Smith's conception is similar to Vico's in that the historical process rectifies and corrects human selfishness and failings: there is, in other words, a logic to history which escapes its active agents. Smith's theory of unanticipated effects of human action is implicitly historicist; Ferguson's, by contrast, is empirical and anti-historicist. Thus discussing the development of commercial society, Smith described initially the structural forces which led to the decline of feudal society and property and the necessary evolution of trade and manufacture. The key to understanding this transition, Smith argued, was the actions of two contending social groups, the rich barons whose concern with social status and ornament led to their gradual impoverishment and the more secular, and efficient, merchant class whose manufactured goods brought the ruin of the great landowners. The rising merchant class replaced the landed groups, buying their agricultural holdings and making them efficient and profitable. Smith's assumption here was that wealth from agriculture was more durable than that derived from commerce, but his more significant point is that social change was unconsciously effected by social groups pursuing their own interests and without the slightest regard for the public good:

> To gratify the most childish vanity was the sole motive of the great proprietors. The merchants and artificers, much less ridiculous, acted merely from a view to their own interests, and in pursuit of their own pedlar principle of turning a penny wherever a penny was to be got. Neither of them had knowledge or foresight of that great revolution which the folly of the one, and the industry of the other, was gradually bringing about (Smith, 1970).

Smith's 'hidden hand' – an historicist and religious notion ultimately – succeeds in regulating the centrifugal tendencies of civil society, the complex structure of property ownership, division of labour and social classes, into a harmony of interests and equilibrium. Smith's conception is basically optimistic: the bad effects of the division of labour can be mitigated by education and religion and the collective workings of market forces.

Ferguson, in contrast, developed no link between the social actions of individuals, as members of social groups, and the wider, collective historical process. Indeed, for Ferguson the individual, as with the state of nature, was merely a fiction. Man is a member of a community, 'part of a whole', his actions social because they are collective. There is nothing of Smith's individualism in Ferguson's concept of the unanticipated effects of social action, or the facile optimism that separated historical meaning from the human subjects which themselves constituted history. Of course there was harmony but also conflict within society, a conflict not to be assimilated to an underlying historical process. Without conflict there was no society, no structure, no process. Without the 'rivalship of nations and the practice of war', Ferguson wrote, 'civil society itself could scarcely have found an object or a form'. Conflict functions to strengthen social bonds and the sense of community. The state itself was founded in war becoming institutionalised in those 'polished' societies characterised by 'collisions of private interest'. It is precisely in these formulations that Ferguson, of all the eighteenth-century writers, approaches a modern sociological standpoint.

The atomistic individualism of the post-Montesquieu French Enlightenment blocked the development of a genuinely sociological concept of society. For Ferguson, society was conceived as a definite structure in which the relation of part to whole constituted the 'principal object' of social science. Like Montesquieu, the writers of the Scottish Enlightenment emphasised the structural nature of social phenomena rejecting the view of society as the product of a haphazard and accidental process. In their notion of the unintended consequences of social action Ferguson and Smith went beyond the static limitations of Montesquieu's synchronic, systemic definition of society to embrace a concept of society as both structure and process. It is this complex relation between human agent and structure which lies at the heart of the Scottish contribution to social theory and not, as some historians of sociology have argued, their emphasis on the social aspects of humanity and their analysis of the social effects of specific material forces. Many of the insights developed in the work of Ferguson, Millar and Smith would be lost in the subsequent emergence of nineteenth-century sociology. But Vico, Montesquieu and Ferguson had laid the foundations and posed the essential problems of a science of human society, culture and historical change, of the relationship between human action, objective social structures and historical evolution. The concept of society as an organised system developing through definite laws and stages had been established. The real history of sociology begins at this point with the work of Saint-Simon, Comte and the positivist tradition.

2
Industrialisation and the Rise of Sociological Positivism

The social thought of Vico, Montesquieu and Ferguson is characterised by a profound belief in humanist values, the application of science to the study of human culture and history and to humanity's control over the environment. The eighteenth-century Enlightenment had produced what David Hume termed the moral sciences – psychology, political economy and a nascent sociology – all of which argued a common theme, that social development brought with it increasing sociability: industry, knowledge and humanity, Hume wrote in his essay, 'On Refinement in the Arts', were linked together by 'an indissoluble chain'. The emergence of these separate, but related sciences was in part the product of the development of a new reading public which, while remaining relatively insignificant in relation to the widespread illiteracy of the great mass of the population, was nevertheless a real and an important element in the secularisation of culture and the emancipation of the writer from patronage. In Diderot's novel, *Rameau's Nephew* (1779), the first ambition of the artist is stated as securing 'the means of life without servitude' an attitude widely shared by contemporary composers, philosophers and economists. A prosperous, liberal middle-class reading public encouraged the growth of literary institutions, clubs and societies; publishing, as a trade, further encouraged the growth of a secular humanism. Man, wrote Diderot, is and will always be at the centre of things for his presence makes existence meaningful. Ferguson expressed this humanist core of Enlightenment thought in his rejection of all biological or organicist metaphors: the proper study of humanity is man 'and we can learn nothing of his nature from the analogy of other animals' (Ferguson, 1966, p. 6).

The relation of the Enlightenment to the development of sociology, however, goes beyond the mere assertion of humanism: the Enlightenment involved the philosophical emphasis on reason, freedom and individualism and emphasised the concepts of society and social development as objective, collective forces. Three broad streams of thought can be identified as contributing to nineteenth and early twentieth-century sociology: first, the humanist historicism of Vico with its emphasis on the creative and active human subject and rejection of any simple application of natural science methods to cultural analysis; secondly, the mechanistic social theory of Montesquieu, Millar and, to a lesser extent, Ferguson, concerned with objective facts and the relevance of natural science to the study of society; and finally, the *philosophes*, Voltaire, Diderot and Rousseau, whose critical rationalism was dedicated to a scientific understanding of the social world, a rationalism that would free the individual from superstitious beliefs and intellectual error. Both the Scottish and the French Enlightenment were built around the principles of modern science, the rejection of metaphysics, the separation of facts from values, and a belief in the possibility of objectivity. Science was positive based on facts not conjecture: the origins of nineteenth-century positivism can thus be traced to the work of Montesquieu and Ferguson, a positivism which was critical and, given the historical context, revolutionary.

Empiricism and positivism

Positivism formed an integral part of the Enlightenment tradition: science and facts opposed metaphysics and speculation; faith and revelation were no longer acceptable as sources of knowledge. Positivism in this extremely general sense must, however, be distinguished from empiricism although both are closely connected historically and theoretically. Sociological positivism dates from the early nineteenth century in the work of Auguste Comte (1798–1857) whose attack on metaphysics was as sharply drawn as that of Hume who had described all forms of metaphysical philosophy as containing no 'reasoning concerning matters of fact and existence' but pages of mere 'sophistry and illusion'. Hume's philosophy was essentially empiricist committed to the concepts of experience and objective facts a standpoint common to sociological positivism.

Eighteenth-century empiricist philosophy, deriving from the work of Bacon, Locke and Descartes, developed an epistemology which located the foundation of human knowledge in experience and the basis of science in experiment, induction and observation. Empiricism assumed the existence of an external world made known through the senses; only that knowledge which could be tested against experience was genuinely scientific. Knowledge was thus defined as a social product, useful and functional, secular and innovating. The transformation of the raw data of experience into knowledge, however, was not a simple mechanical process; it was the function of the human mind to process the data through immanent categories such as judgement, measurement and comparison. Thus although Descartes had argued for the importance of sensory experience in the formation of knowledge, he advanced the view that knowledge equally developed from principles derived from mathematics and logic. Empiricism was in effect an inconsistent doctrine, a materialist epistemology which declared that there existed, independent of experience, laws of mind and laws of thought. It is this dualism between the active and passive properties of cognition which positivism developed by strengthening the mechanical, passive aspects of the subject's relation to experience. As empiricism sought the laws of mind, so positivism established the external laws of historical change and defined society as an external datum, a structure of facts known and verified through observation and experiment.

Positivism, therefore, developed a concept of society while empiricism a theory of concepts. Both empiricism and positivism tended to minimise the active element in human consciousness: some Enlightenment philosophers, for example, sought to eradicate the emphasis which Locke and Descartes had accorded to the innate activities of the human mind thus defining the human subject as the product of an external environment. At the heart of Enlightenment philosophy lay a contradiction: on the one hand, the concepts of human perfectability and progress, the triumph of reason over ignorance and superstition, the belief in the role of ideas in the education of humanity; on the other, the theory that ideas themselves were largely the necessary results of the external situation and of experience. Thus the human subject was conceived in passive terms: both subject and ideas constituted epiphenomenal forces, their existence dependent on the operations of other, different elements. This is not to suggest that every Enlightenment philosopher accepted this mechanical form of materialism: others argued that knowledge flowed from deductions based on *a priori* categories and that human reason, once liberated from mystical and religious thought, would be free to develop objective knowledge.

The *philosophes* in particular developed an extreme form of philosophical dualism arguing that on the one hand material conditions determined forms of human consciousness and modes of action, and yet, on the other, advancing the voluntaristic view that through notions of freedom and reason humanity would be educated out of ignorance and servitude to traditional ideologies. The rationalist optimism of Enlightenment philosophy was thus built around the free individual who, guided by the precepts of science, could reconstruct society through the principles of human reason. In effect, reason was higher than empirical reality.

The French Revolution and sociology

As we have seen, positivism originated in the materialist philosophy of the Enlightenment. As a philosophical and sociological movement positivism embraced a number of different meanings which included a belief in science as the foundation of all knowledge (scientism as it has been called), the employment of statistical analysis in social theory, the search for causal explanations of social phenomena and the fundamental laws of historical change or of human nature. But eighteenth-century Enlightenment positivism was essentially critical and revolutionary, its fundamental tenets of philosophical individualism and human reason largely directed against the irrational powers of the Absolutist state, organised religion and residual social institutions. Institutions, it was argued, should accord with the principles of reason. Knowledge is acquired only through experience and empirical inquiry: reality cannot be comprehended through God.

The transformation of this critical positivism into nineteenth-century sociological positivism occurred in post-revolutionary France. From its beginnings it opposed the individualistic atomism of Enlightenment philosophy. It needs emphasising that with the exception of Montesquieu and Ferguson eighteenth-century social thought had failed to develop a theory of society as a system and objective structure. A theory of society as a totality is fundamental to sociology as an independent empirical science; the relation of parts to whole constitutes the methodological axiom guiding research into the social role and functions of institutions such as religion and the family. It was precisely this concept which could not develop within a rationalist atomistic framework. Enlightenment philosophy had effectively minimised the significance of institutions which the *philosophes* had labelled irrational. In particular the problem of continuity within change could not be posed adequately given the prevailing emphasis on human perfecta-bility and progress. So-called irrational institutions, such as religion, formed in the historical past, could not be conceptualised in their active relation with the present: lacking a concept of society as a whole, rationalist thought defined religious ideas as peripheral and residual exercising no significant and *positive* role in the maintenance of society.

The French Revolution had the effect of challenging these rationalist assumptions. Enlightenment philosophy was judged deficient in its analysis of those traditional institutions which effectively create the social bonds necessary for a functioning society. Edmund Burke (1729–97), Louis de Bonald (1754–1840) and Joseph de Maistre (1754–1821) were three influential critics of philosophical rationalism who rejected the individualistic concept of society developed by the Enlightenment philosophers, identifying its 'negative' and

33

'critical' principles with the collapse of traditional modes of authority and the organic nature of social bonds.

Society was defined as an organic whole in which 'irrational' and traditional elements played an active, constitutive role. Religion and the family were integral parts of the whole. The Enlightenment slogan of the natural rights of man and the rational principles enshrined in the social contract theory were rejected in favour of a concept of society which emphasised hierarchy, duty and the collective good. As Bonald expressed it: 'The schools of modern philosophy . . . have produced the philosophy of modern man, the philosophy of I . . . I want to produce the philosophy of social man, the philosophy of we.' As an organism, society was defined in terms of its inner 'spirit' or 'soul', an essence fundamentally religious in nature. Bonald and Maistre thus developed a concept of expressive whole, the various parts manifesting the inner essence and spirit. All elements of the organic whole were integrally linked as expressions of an irreducible essence.

Linked with this organic notion of totality was the rejection of empirical science as the means of analysing social forms. For Maistre and Bonald society was apprehended through intuition, not reason or science. This belief in intuition and feeling is linked with attempts to discover a new source of political authority in the post-revolutionary world that followed the collapse of the old regime. Revolution and industrialism were creating a new kind of society, one in which the old traditional values no longer held sway. The result was a concept of society which emphasised the creative role of the family, corporations and a hierarchical structure of authority similar to the rigid estate system of feudalism. It was through these institutions that the individual participated in the social whole, the 'I' transformed into a 'We'. The post-revolutionary critique of emerging industrial society was thus couched in terms of pre-industrial organic values: modern society was conceived as a calculating, individualistic system built around pragmatic, material values and interests with authority vested in formal rules and written contracts. Such a society could eventuate only in the collapse of social bonds and render problematic the organic relation of the individual to the collective.

For Maistre and Bonald society did not consist in an

aggregate of individuals: society was the expression of a whole culture, a collective concept which decisively influenced the sociological positivism of Auguste Comte. Equally important was the emphasis on the positive role of traditional institutions and the problem of authority in the post-revolutionary world of the early nineteenth century. Burke, Bonald and Maistre mourned the passing of the traditional legitimacy of the old society and in their work posed the question of new modes of political obligation. It was in this spirit that Saint-Simon wrote of the eighteenth century as critical and negative, while the nineteenth would be positive in laying the foundation for social reorganisation. Only positivism, wrote Comte, provided the necessary basis for the new society pointing the way forward from 'the critical condition in which most civilised nations are now living'. Ideas were of paramount importance either governing the world or throwing it into chaos:

> The great political and moral crisis that societies are now undergoing is shown by the rigid analysis to arise out of intellectual anarchy . . . whenever the necessary agreement on first principles can be obtained, appropriate institutions will issue from them, without shock or resistance; for the causes of disorder will have been arrested by the mere fact of the agreement. It is in this direction that most must look who desire a natural and regular . . . state of society (Andreski, 1978, pp. 37–8).

Comte's preoccupation with social order and progress developed within a sociological framework that owed much to the work of Bonald and Maistre notably their emphasis on the nature of the social bond. But in the development of sociological positivism the irrational and negative view of science advocated by these philosophers was rejected: the moral crisis of the post-revolutionary age could be resolved only through the application of positive science and the principles of industrial organisation derived from the empirical study of social development. The work of Henri Saint-Simon was decisive in this process.

The concept of industrial society: Saint-Simon

Saint-Simon (1760–1825) introduced the term industrial society into European social theory. He defined the process of industrialism as essentially pacific in contrast to the militaristic spirit of feudal society. Saint-Simon was particularly concerned with the transition from feudal type societies, structured around consumption, to industrial societies centred around production. Saint-Simon's status in the history of sociology has always been ambivalent: on the one hand his concept of industrial society emphasised the centrality of social classes, the importance of property and the structural significance of the division of labour in the process of class formation. His collectivist notion of society was broadly socialist and materialist; but on the other hand, Saint-Simon's analysis of technology and the role of science and intellectual élites – mostly composed of scientists and industrialists – combined with his theory of moral crisis suggests a conservative standpoint close to the sociological positivism of Comte. In a very general sense Saint-Simon can be claimed as an influence on both nineteenth-century sociology and the development of socialism and Marxism. What is not in doubt, however, is that Saint-Simon's work represents a theorisation of the emerging separation of state and civil society, the development of a public sphere consisting of economic, political and cultural institutions independent of centralised, bureaucratic administration. More emphatically than Adam Smith, Saint-Simon defined the state administration as parasitic and hostile to the needs of production and the newly emerging social classes engendered by the process of industrialism. By its nature, he wrote, mankind was destined to live in society, first under governmental or military regimes and then, with the triumph of the positive sciences and industry, under an administrative and industrial regime. The administrative institutions of industrial society would no longer be centralised in the state but rather in the institutions of civil society.

Saint-Simon's basic argument is of the necessary relation between property and power. Political constitutions should express the state of society itself; they must be structured firmly in social reality. In his *Industrial System* (1821) Saint-Simon argued that society could, and should be organised on scientific, positive principles with the economic and political systems working in harmony with each other. The study of politics was transformed from the conjectural to the positive, from metaphysics to physics. For Saint-Simon, science was positive, and therefore, through its principles of prediction and verification, formed the basis of practice. Like Adam Smith, Saint-Simon's model of society was based on astronomy: 'The astronomers only accepted those facts which were verified by observation; they chose the system which linked them best, and since that time, they have never led science astray' (Ionescu, 1976, pp. 76–8).

Saint-Simon coined the terms 'social physiology' and 'social physics' and, following Maistre and Bonald, defined society as an organic unity. The positive stage of development was dominated by the centrality of science and the growth of systematic social knowledge especially in relation to the laws which regulated the social whole. Saint-Simon's model of society was thus holistic: he defined a 'healthy' society as one in which the various parts subsisted in a state of functional harmony with the whole. Social health was closely identified with production and the role of the productive social classes. Industrial society, in contrast to all previous forms of social organisation, was not based on a centralised power structure but rather built around the institutions of civil society. Saint-Simon did not argue for the abolition of political institutions only that decision-making must increasingly devolve on the institutions associated with science and technology. Politics does not express the 'good will' but an equilibrium subsisting between economic and political structures. Saint-Simon described industrial society in terms of collaboration and consensus: under the old system force constituted the means of social cohesion, but industrial society creates partners not subjects and associated modes of co-operation involving labourers and the wealthiest property owners. The principles of free production generate moral solidarity. Saint-Simon contrasted the authority structure of feudal society, in which corporations symbolised coercion, with the unequal, hierarchical nature of industrial society arguing that industrial institutions were, by their nature, both functional and spontaneous.

Society would become a vast workshop organised around the production of goods, and authority transformed from authority over individuals to authority over things.

Saint-Simon's social theory was thus a theory of the rising bourgeoisie and he emphasised the class struggle between the industrial classes and the old feudal classes. 'The entire history of civilised mankind', he wrote, 'is inevitably divided between these two great systems of society.' The French Revolution had not completely destroyed ecclesiastical and feudal power but merely 'diminished confidence in their basic principles' as the basis of social order. Only industry which embraces all forms of useful work, theoretical and practical, intellectual and manual, can produce the values that will hold modern society together. Industry has ushered in 'a new era' signalling the end of government by force in favour of consultation and consensus. In effect, what Saint-Simon calls 'administrative action' comes to replace feudal–military action so that administrative power finally dominates military force:

> In the end soldiers and jurists must take orders from those most capable of administration; for an enlightened society only needs to be administered . . . The guiding principles of social force should be supplied by the men who are most able to administer; now, as the most important industrialists are those who have given proof of the greatest administrative ability, since it is their competence in this sphere that they owe what importance they have acquired, in short, it is they who should necessarily be given the direction of social interests (Ionescu, 1976, p. 188).

But the nineteenth century was still dominated by the 'critical' spirit of the Enlightenment and was failing to adopt the organisational character organic to it. A disjunction existed between the institutions of industrialism, especially administrative action, and the broader culture. Saint-Simon's writings during the 1820s point to a major issue which had largely eluded the eighteenth-century philosophers and social theorists of progress: in the past, civil society and the state were bound together with social regulation flowing from traditional institutions and the structure of traditional values. But with the separation of the state from civil society the problem of social regulation was posed in an acute form. Traditional modes of authority, and their associated values, had collapsed in the face of a triumphant critical philosophy with its beliefs in the rights of the individual over that of the collectivity. Traditional authority could no longer legitimise political forms: a moral vacuum therefore arose within modern society. Saint-Simon rejected the view of the political economists that the market worked to harmonise different and often conflicting interests into a social and therefore moral unity. Social cohesion would not flow from the free play of purely economic forces. Industrial society required a strong moral centre which he described in his last work, *The New Christianity* (1825), as a secular religion opposed to the egoism of philosophical individualism and functioning through a priesthood of artists, scientists and industrial leaders whose interests were identical with those of the masses.

Social regulation is thus described as a process directed from above by an élite of intellectuals. Although Saint-Simon's image of industrial society was one of co-operative enterprise, he defined industrial society as a system organised around the principles of functional hierarchy, rational discipline and selective leadership. Saint-Simon, however, was not advocating a new form of centralised authority; authority is returned to civil society and vested, not in control over individuals but within the institutions of planning, co-operation and production. Industrial society was not a communist Utopia but a hierarchical structure which had produced a new governing class of scientists and industrialists. Scientists were associated with the spiritual realm, industrialists with the temporal: together they would create the leadership and the values necessary for a functioning modern society.

There is, here, an authoritarian strand to Saint-Simon's thought, a distrust of democracy and representative institutions, a lack of confidence in the masses, or the people, to create for themselves a culture of self-government. His distinction between productive and non-productive, or 'idle' classes is polemical rather than scientific. Saint-Simon failed to develop a sociological theory of class: his main concern was always with those who produced and those who consumed, industrial proprietors, investors and bankers were productive, the military, nobility, lawyers and those living off profits were the idlers. Those producing 'useful' things were the only valuable members of society and for this reason politics was defined as the science of production and the new society, emerging from the ruins of post-revolutionary Europe, industrial, technocratic and undemocratic.

Comte and positive science

Saint-Simon did not develop a distinctive sociology. Auguste Comte (1798–1857) who, at one time, acted as Saint-Simon's secretary publishing his early works under Saint-Simon's name, founded the first comprehensive system of sociology, one that was strongly influenced by the work of Saint-Simon and his belief in science and technology (elements found in eighteenth-century philosophers of history and champions of progress such as Turgot, 1727–81 and Condorcet, 1743–94), and 'that immortal school' of Bonald and Maistre with their concept of society as an organic, harmonious whole composed, like medieval society, of different and static social orders. Comte attempted to reconcile the anti-atomistic theories of Bonald and Maistre with the rationalist concept of progress and notion of the perfectability of man. Like Saint-Simon, Comte's work was produced at a critical period of French history, the period following the revolution in which the old regime had disintegrated and a new industrial regime was in the process of formation. Comte's sociological positivism was forged at the same time as Balzac was describing in fictional form the irresistible rise of the industrialists and the bankers within a French culture still permeated by the old aristocratic values.

Comte never held a full-time academic position. Sociology was not yet institutionalised; Frederic Le Play, who wrote a massive study of the European family during the 1850s and the leading French sociologist before Durkheim attained an academic position but only as a Professor of Mining. Comte remained a marginal figure in French intellectual culture, ridiculed in academic circles, suffering from periodic bouts of madness and suffering the indignity of being listed as deceased in a contemporary bibliography. J.S. Mill, who corresponded with Comte, argued that his influence in the development of social science was greater than his actual achievements and that while not creating sociology as a science Comte's work nevertheless made it possible. Thus although Comte's interpreters note his strong conservative bias and deprecate the influence on his sociology of Maistre and Bonald as well as 'the illustrious Gall' (1758–1828), as he described the founder of phrenology, his place within the history of sociology is guaranteed by his attempts to explain the origin and growth of industrial society and his analysis of the social effects of the division of labour, increasing wealth and development of individualism and his rejection of metaphysics in favour of positive empirical methods in the study of social facts. Yet these elements had already been widely discussed by eighteenth-century writers such as Ferguson, Millar and Montesquieu: the Scots especially had provided a detailed empirical account of the emergence of industrial society, social class, social conflict, the division of labour and the mechanics of social change. Since Comte knew the work of Adam Smith and Ferguson, as well as minor writers such as Lord Kames, it is obviously important to grasp the ways in which his own approach differs from theirs and assess the extent to which Comte's sociological positivism assimilated and developed this proto-sociology.

Comte's attitude to the Enlightenment was, of course, negative: although he accepted the theory of progress, especially Condorcet's notion of social evolution developing through the workings of specific natural laws, he rejected the critical positivism of eighteenth-century philosophic rationalism abhoring its 'negative' attacks on the values of traditional authority and morality, on religious institutions and the family. In particular he rejected the Enlightenment view that preindustrial society, especially the Middle Ages, constituted the dark age of civilisation. For Comte, Condorcet's one-sided devaluing of the past, in his *Sketch for a Historical Picture of the Progress of the Human Mind* (1794), was rounded out by the positive approach of Maistre and Bonald:

Right views upon the subject were impossible . . . until full justice had been rendered to the Middle Ages, which form at once the

41

point of union and separation between ancient and modern history. Now it was quite impossible to do this as long as the excitement of the first years of the revolution lasted. In this respect the philosophical reaction organised at the beginning of the century by the great de Maistre was of material assistance in preparing the true theory of progress. His school was of brief duration, and it was no doubt animated by a retrograde spirit; but it will always be ranked among the necessary antecedents of the positive system (Comte, 1875–6, Vol. 1, p. 50).

Comte's *Cours de Philosophie Positive* (1830–42) is essentially an attack on the 'negative' philosophy developed by eighteenth-century individualistic philosophy. He agreed with Saint-Simon that the eighteenth-century had only destroyed rather than provided the foundations for a 'new edifice'. This new structure was to be directed exclusively in the interests of social order and social consensus. The 'essential aim of practical politics', he wrote, was 'to avoid the violent revolutions which spring from obstacles opposed to the progress of civilisation'.

From the beginning, the *Course* set itself the task of social reorganisation: writing from within a society which appeared close to anarchy it seemed obvious to Comte that 'true science' was nothing less than 'the establishment of intellectual order, which is the basis of every other order'. Comte's positivism, a science of stability and social reconstruction can thus be seen on one level as a response to the negative and critical traditions of Enlightenment philosophy by seeking to unite the notions of order and progress. The task of social physics would be wholly positive:

> Under the rule of the positive spirit . . . all the difficult and delicate questions which now keep up a perpetual irritation in the bosom of society, and can never be settled while mere political solutions are proposed, will be scientifically estimated, to the great furtherance of social peace . . . the positive spirit tends to consolidate order, by the rational development of a wise resignation to incurable political evils. A true resignation . . . can proceed from a deep sense of the connection of all kinds of natural phenomena with invariable natural laws. If there are political evils which . . . cannot be remedied by science, science at least proves to us that they are

incurable, so as to calm our restlessness under pain by the conviction that it is by natural laws that they are rendered insurmountable (Comte, 1896, Vol. 2, pp. 185–7).

On this definition, therefore, sociology prescribes a wholly passive and fatalistic orientation to the social world and contrasts sharply with Vico's injunction that the social world was the work of humanity. The active relation of human labour and thought to the development and transformation of social forms is effectively assimilated to a theory of objective, determining facts. The polemical thrust of Comte's positivism is thus clear: but what of his concept of science?

Sociology was defined in its relations with other sciences and Comte's stated aim was the synthesis of all available knowledge, a task facilitated by the law of three stages and hierarchical classification of the sciences. Both these conceptions had been stated by previous writers notably Turgot, Condorcet and Saint-Simon: in their beginnings all the sciences, wrote Saint-Simon, are conjectural but end by being positive, developing from the simple to the complex. Comte systematised these arguments tracing the evolution of the sciences in great detail. All human thought, he argued, has passed through three separate stages, the theological, the metaphysical and the positive. In the theological state the human mind seeks for origins and final causes analysing all phenomena as the result of supernatural forces; feelings and imagination predominate and Comte divided the theological state into three separate periods of fetishism (nature defined in terms of man's feelings), polytheism (a multitude of gods and spirits) and finally, monotheism (the existence of one God and the gradual awakening of human reason with its constraint on the imagination). For Comte, each stage and sub-stage of evolution necessarily develops out of the preceding one: the final sub-stage of monotheism prepares the way for the metaphysical stage in which human thought is dominated by abstract concepts, by essences and ideal forms. In the final stage of evolution thought abandons essences and seeks laws which link different facts together through the methods of observation and experiment; absolute notions of causes are abandoned and the emphasis shifts to the study of facts and their invariable relations of succession and resemblance. Each science develops in exactly the same way passing through these separate stages, but they do so at different rates: knowledge reaches the positive stage in proportion to the generality, simplicity and independence of other disciplines. As the most general and simple of the natural sciences astronomy develops first, followed by physics, chemistry, biology and sociology. Each science develops only on the basis of its predecessors within a hierarchical framework dominated by the law of increasing complexity and decreasing generality.

Sociology is particularly dependent on its immediate predecessor in the hierarchy, biology. The science of biology is basically holistic in character beginning not from isolated elements, as in chemistry and physics, but from organic wholes. The distinctive subject matter of sociology is society as a whole, society defined a social system. Sociology is thus the investigation of the action and reaction of the various parts of the social system. Individual elements must be analysed in their relation to the whole, in their mutual relation and combination. As with biological organisms, society forms a complex unity irreducible to its component parts: society cannot be decomposed into individuals any more than 'a geometric surface can be decomposed into lines, or a line into a point'. Knowledge of the parts can flow only from knowledge of the whole, not vice versa.

Society was defined, therefore, as a collective organism characterised by a harmony between its individual parts and whole. The analogy between biology and sociology is constantly reiterated:

. . . in biology, we may decompose structure anatomically into *elements*, *tissues* and *organs*. We have the same things in the social organism . . . forms of social power correspond to the *tissue* . . . the *element* . . . is supplied by the family, which is more completely the germ of society than the cell or fibre of the body . . . *organs* can only be *cities* the root of the word being the nucleus of the term civilization (Comte, 1875–6, Vol. 2, pp. 223–6).

Although Comte warns against pushing the analogy too far – cities are organic wholes themselves or aspire to be so – his

44

theory of social order derives almost entirely from biology especially his concepts of harmony, equilibrium and social pathology. Pathological situations develop within the social organism, for example, when the natural laws governing the principles of harmony or succession are disturbed by elements analogous to diseases in the bodily organism. Social evolution proceeds in accordance with biological laws and the general intent of Comte's positivism is to subordinate the study of society to biological concepts. The absence of a spontaneous harmony between the parts and the whole of the social system indicates the existence of social pathology. Harmony is consensus; conflict is equated with pathology. While Ferguson had rejected the biological analogy, Comte assimilated biological terms and models to his sociology arguing that the distinction between anatomy and physiology enabled sociology to differentiate structure from function, dynamics from statics, social order from social progress. All living beings exist under dynamic and static relations: statics investigates the laws of action and reaction of the different parts of the social system which 'normally' produce an equilibrium between parts and whole, a functional interrelationship of social institutions. Comte's notion of statics is concerned with clarifying the interconnection between social facts functional for a social system such as the division of labour, the family, religion and government and is clearly synchronic in nature. Dynamics is the empirical study of these interconnections as they change in different types of society and Comte describes this aspect of sociology as the historical method.

Comte describes the historical method as specific to sociology. It is clearly important to grasp what Comte meant by this term since it suggests a movement from analogical representations of societies to empirical analysis of social processes. 'If the historical comparisons of the different periods of civilization are to have any scientific character', he wrote, 'they must be referred to general social evolution' (Comte, 1896, Vol. 2, pp. 252–7). The comparative method belongs to statics, the historical method to dynamics. He defined the comparative method as

The comparison of different co-existing states of human society on

45

the various parts of the world's surface – those states being completely independent of each other (Comte, 1896, Vol. 2, p. 250).

The historical method links these states of society with evolution through the dynamic laws of social development which effectively relate to the growing solidarity and unity of society structured in the co-operative functions of the division of labour and the universal principles enshrined in religion and language. Social evolution, in other words, works through the existence of certain invariable laws which synthesise order and progress. It is in this sense that Comte repudiates empiricism. Sociology is not a science which accumulates mere desultory facts but seeks to interpret and connect them with each other through theory: facts are not strictly speaking based on observation but are constructed by the guiding hand of theory. Real knowledge can never be based on observed facts alone but on laws which connect all social phenomena through resemblance and succession. No real observation is possible, wrote Comte, 'except in as far as it is first directed, and finally interpreted, by some theory'. Observation and laws are 'indispensably connected' (Comte, 1896, Vol. 2, p. 243).

Comte's awareness that facts and theory are mutually connected suggests that sociology is an interpretative science, a formulation which goes beyond the critical positivism of the Enlightenment. Comte was the first theoretical sociologist who was thoroughly sceptical that observed facts will, as it were, speak for themselves. But the theory which Comte developed was essentially a speculative theory of historical change, a philosophy of history. The result was a conception of the historical method extremely abstract and non-historical: specific historical events, and the specifically historical character of institutions, fell outside the framework of sociological positivism. States of development are abstractly conceived, the sequences are conceptual and ideal, neither empirical nor chronological. One result of Comte's abstract formulations of the historical method and the distinction between static and dynamics was to separate the study of concrete events, or facts, from the study of social change as an historical category.

Positivism and determinism

All social phenomena are subject to invariable laws and once these have been scientifically established humanity must, from necessity, submit to their dictation. Science makes possible social control and Comte defined 'true liberty' as the 'rational submission' of the individual to the laws of nature. Positivist sociology effectively abolishes 'the absolute liberty of the revolutionary school . . . and, by establishing social principles, will meet the need at once of order and progress'. From science comes 'prevision' and from 'prevision comes action', for 'to see in order to foresee is the business of science'. Eighteenth-century philosophy had laid the foundations of social science through the law of human progress, while the French Revolution had generated the need for order.

What Comte's 'wise resignation' means in practice is a submission to the facts of inequality within the emerging industrial society. The law of progress, as Comte described it, clearly affected social groups differently. Thus in his discussion of the role of the working class Comte described their 'inevitable lot' as existing on the 'precarious fruits' of labour and to suffer constant deprivation. Positivist sociology, while recognising this as a 'great social problem', would seek to ameliorate the workers' condition, but not at the cost of 'destroying its classification and disturbing the general economy' (Comte, 1896, Vol. 3, pp. 36–7). In his early writings of the 1820s Comte agreed with Saint-Simon's argument that the aftermath of the French Revolution had created a spiritual vacuum and absence of 'any moral discipline whatsoever'. The result was a state of 'anomie', a state of normlessness, of deregulation. Saint-Simon's solution was an ethic of universal love – a new Christianity – which in Comte's work became the Religion of Humanity interposing itself as a remedial agency between the working class and the governing classes. In this way the economic and political 'imperfections' of modern society, the products of 'intellectual and moral disorder' and the prevailing states of consciousness, were solved. What particularly concerned Comte was the maldistribution of wealth since it provided 'a most dangerous theme to both agitators and dreamers'. Only by convincing humanity of the superiority of

47

moral over political solutions would these 'quacks and dream-ers' relinquish their 'dangerous vocation'. The solution to inequality and class differences and interests was the organic society in which the positive concept of 'duties' replaced the negative concept of 'rights'. A moral education would inculcate an awareness of the individual's rightful social status: the subordination of the working class to their employers would be seen as resting wholly on their less 'extensive actions' and responsibilities. And once established this gradation would be acceptable because of its clear principles and awareness that the working class are 'privileged in that freedom from care . . . which would be a serious fault in the higher classes, but which is natural to them'. Following Saint-Simon, Comte conceived industrial society as a system dominated by the moral influence of a 'Speculative' stratum of scientists and philosophers, in which capital is 'useful to society at large' thus rendering the distribution of property unimportant to 'popular interests' (Comte, 1896, Vol. 3, pp. 313–35).

Like the socialists of his day, therefore, Comte accepted the structural significance of the industrial working class but differed from their analysis by his stress on the inevitable laws of social evolution which point to their integration into an unequal society. There was no question of class organisation and practice: the individual might 'modify' the course of social development and assert a freedom of action over 'blind fatality', but ultimately the natural laws of society are higher in their practical efficacy than human action. Social evolution, which for Comte was the progressive development of the human mind as it finds its expression in the three stages, is thus a process without a subject, a universal history of humanity which claims the importance of knowledge for the ends of social reorganisation, but subordinates the individual to the inevit-able 'realities' of social life: the needs of order and progress.

Sociology, political economy and the division of labour

Comte defined the social as the only universal point of view, the only perspective which grasps all scientific conceptions as a whole. The relation of the social to the political is described as one of 'spontaneous harmony'. Comte separates the social both from the political and the economic arguing that in modern society social cohesion – social authority – flows essentially from moral and intellectual, not political or economic, forces. Government fulfils its obligations not by exercising force but through moral and intellectual leadership. Comte was particularly critical of previous social theorists who had minimised the crucial, constituting role played by these 'spiritual' elements. Only morality provides an adequate regulation of economic activity, only morality can sustain social harmony. For Comte, the 'essential vice' of political economy was its tendency to define social order in natural terms as the expression of market forces and thus free of regulation by artificial (positivist) institutions.

Yet although Comte disagreed with the *laissez-faire* principles of classical political economy, he accepted its pessimistic and largely negative conclusions on the social consequences of an advanced division of labour. Specialisation of work, while an essential element of an advanced society, tends to 'restrict human understanding' and promote ignorance and squalor among the working classes. Comte cited the example of pin manufacture: workers engaged in this tedious and routine labour cannot develop their faculties to the full with the result, 'a miserable indifference about the general course of human affairs' and a fundamental 'dispersion' of ideas, sentiments and interests. Comte drew a radically different conclusion from the political economists, arguing that the division of work necessarily entails moral regulation by external institutions.

Comte's solution to the problem of the division of labour was the institution of 'wise government' with its principles fundamentally religious and universal thus consecrating and regulating command and obedience. Civil society itself is judged incapable of generating from within its own spontaneously developed institutions the values necessary for social cohesion. Comte's distrust of democratic institutions is explicit; society is to be regulated from above. Humanity must learn to accept inequality and the natural laws of social subordination. Fortunately the masses recognise the intellectual superiority of their rulers and thus experience the sheer 'sweetness' of consigning 'burdensome' responsibilities to 'wise and trustworthy guidance'. The division of labour creates the intellectual and moral skills on which all systems of government and stratification rest: 'Thus do individual dispositions show themselves to be in harmony with the course of social relations as a whole, in teaching us that political subordination is as inevitable . . . as it is indispensable' (Comte, 1896, Vol. 3, pp. 294–8).

Comte's sociological positivism strips the division of labour of its *negative* effects and transforms it into an agency of social harmony although regulated by an élite of positivist intellectuals. Conflict relations engendered by the division of labour as constituting a source of social change was simply unthinkable. By emphasising the essentially religious nature of social bonds Comte advocated moral solutions that were conformist and ideological. Comte's positivism celebrates industrial society in its early capitalist form as the end of history: humanity must accept its place within the natural order of things and adapt to the necessary equilibrium between parts and wholes.

The anti-democratic nature of Comte's sociological positivism was a theme taken up later in the nineteenth century by Durkheim, while the analysis of the division of labour in the process of social development and the relation of civil society to economic production and political forms formed part of Marx's contribution to social science. Comte failed to develop the notion of society as an empirical and historical totality, conceiving it in organismic terms as a system dominated by external natural laws that reduced the efficacy of human action. The separation of dynamics from statics was artificial and theoretically misleading and in the discussion of the division of labour the dynamic aspect virtually disappeared in favour of static moralising.

Nevertheless, Comte had laid the foundations of a sociological positivism which was to remain the dominant paradigm during the course of the nineteenth century. But the positivism which developed after Comte increasingly abandoned his speculative philosophy of history and his theory of social evolution as the evolution of consciousness and mind through definite stages of social development.

Evolutionism and sociological positivism: Mill and Spencer

Comte's positivism conceived the concept of the social as a distinct sphere clearly separated from economics, politics and history; society was an autonomous object of scientific study, conceptualised as a system evolving in the direction of industrialisation. The development of sociological positivism after Comte took two forms: first, the widely accepted view that the methods of the social sciences were no different from those of the natural sciences involving the establishing of laws, the employment of experiment and observation and the elimination of the subjective element in social analysis – society was defined in terms of an organism evolving through the workings of specific natural laws. And secondly, the increasing awareness of empirical method and the value of statistics in the framing of hypotheses and modes of validation. Both forms of sociological positivism emphasised the necessity of eliminating philosophical concepts such as free will, intention and individual motives from social science and establishing sociology as an objective science. Two of the most important sociologists working within this broad positivist framework were J.S. Mill and Herbert Spencer, although both were critical of Comte's philosophy of history and, in the case of Spencer, sought to distance his sociological theories from positivism.

Mill's most significant contribution to sociology was his *System of Logic* (1843). Mill (1807–73) claimed that he was laying down the foundations of a science of society, a science based on 'general laws', experiment and observation. Unlike Comte and Spencer, he never developed an all-encompassing system of sociology, one embracing society, history and nature. Nevertheless, he accepted Comte's basic sociological principles, the theory of stages, the distinction between dynamics and statics, the historical method of analysis, and the concept of consensus. Comte's main conclusions, he wrote, were in all essentials 'irrefragable'. He agreed also with Comte's scientism arguing that there was no fundamental difference between the methods of the natural and the social sciences: science depended on its ability to predict, and comparing the social sciences with the physical sciences of meteorology, tidology

51

(the science of tides) and astronomy, Mill concluded that while these sciences established the underlying laws governing the weather, the tides and planetary movements, with the exception of astronomy they failed to generate precise modes of prediction. Prediction necessitated knowledge of all the antecedent elements within a particular context and only in the case of astronomy was this possible. Mill thus concluded that social science was quite capable of achieving a comparable degree of prediction and thus of scientific status.

The context examined by the social sciences consisted of human beings: unlike Comte, Mill believed in the importance of psychology and to this end he advanced the claims of ethology as the science of the laws of human nature. Psychology was not part of Comte's hierarchy of the sciences; he believed that Gall's 'cerebral physiology' explained the source of thought and mind in terms of its physical location in the brain. But Mill argued that all social phenomena were structured in the laws governing the drives and motives of human nature. Describing his approach as the 'inverted-deductive' method, Mill argued that social science consisted of the empirical laws of sociology, demonstrated in statistical studies and surveys, the laws of psychology, derived less from empirical studies than philosophical reflection, and finally, linking the sociology and the psychology, the laws of ethology, the fundamental laws governing human nature:

> The laws of the phenomena of society are, and can be, nothing but the laws of actions and passions of human beings united together in the social state . . . obedient to the laws of individual human nature. Men are not, when brought together, converted into another kind of substance with different properties as hydrogen and oxygen are different from water (Mill, 1976).

Human nature is thus fixed: the socio-historical context constantly changes so that the task of positivist social science lay in explaining empirical observations and sociological laws by deductions from the universal law of human nature. In effect Mill proposed a reduction of the specifically social to the psychological:

All phenomena of society are phenomena of human nature generated by the action of outward circumstances upon masses of human beings (Mill, 1976).

If human thought and action are dependent on fixed laws then clearly all social phenomena must conform to similar fixed laws. From this standpoint it is not surprising that Mill failed to develop either a systemic concept of society or an adequate sociological theory of social structure, social institutions and social change.

Mill's positivistic nominalism was ultimately less significant for the development of sociology than the positivist organicism of Herbert Spencer (1820–1903), who combined, within a broad evolutionary model of social development, a notion of society as system and as aggregate of individuals. Spencer's main focus was on the evolutionary growth of social structures and institutions and not mental states. Comte, he wrote, accounts for 'the progress of human conceptions . . . ideas' and seeks to interpret 'our knowledge of nature'; in contrast, 'my aim' is to account for 'the progress of the external world . . . of things' and to interpret 'the genesis of the phenomena which constitute nature'. Comte is subjective not objective. Nevertheless, as Comte sought to unify all knowledge in his hierarchy of the sciences, so Spencer aimed to unify all knowledge in his concept of evolution. The evolution of humanity was Spencer's theme in which society constituted a special instance of a universal law. 'There can be no complete acceptance of sociology as a science, so long as the belief in a social order not conforming to natural law, survives' (Spencer, 1961, Ch. XVI).

During the latter half of the nineteenth century Spencer's writings were enormously popular among the burgeoning middle-class reading public. His work attempted to synthesise a radical individualism based on *laissez-faire* political economy with a collectivist organicism derived from the natural sciences especially biology and physics. Spencer, in effect, offered a theory of progress built around the prestige of the natural sciences and the individualistic and competitive nature of nineteenth-century capitalism. Spencer had already formulated the basic constituents of his theory of evolution when

Darwin (1809–92) published his *Origin of Species* in 1859. Although he acknowledged the significance of Darwin's concept of 'natural selection' for the evolutionary process, Spencer tended to accept Lamarck's theory of the inheritance of acquired characteristics. He thus remained an evolutionary optimist arguing that through the transmission of both mental and physical innate elements humanity must necessarily develop to higher and higher levels of intellectual perfection.

Spencer's model of society was organismic. Societies were like living bodies which evolve out of a state of undifferentiated unity to highly complex, differentiated structures in which the individual parts, while becoming more autonomous and specialised, nevertheless come increasingly to depend on each other. This interdependence of parts implies integration for 'unlike parts' are 'so related as to make one another possible' and come to form an aggregate 'constituted on the same general principle as is an individual organism'. In simple societies the lack of differentiation means that the same individuals are both hunter and warriors. Society thus develops through progressive changes in the *structure* and *functions* of its basic institutions; social evolution does not depend on individual intentions and motives. Thus from a state of homogeneity human society *naturally* develops to a state of complex heterogeneity, a process which Spencer saw as characteristic of the inorganic world of matter, where evolution begins, the organic world of nature, and finally the living organisms in society, the last stage of evolution.

Spencer identified three laws of evolution: the law of 'the persistence of force' or the conservation of energy, from which is derived the law of the indestructability of matter and the law of the continuity of motion. The notion of the persistence of force forms the basis of Spencer's deductive system: the universe is characterised by a continual redistribution of matter and motion in terms of the processes of evolution and dissolution. Spencer noted four secondary propositions to these three laws: that laws are uniform in their workings; that force is transformed never lost; that everything moves along the line of least resistance or the greatest attraction; and finally, the principle of the rhythm, or alteration, of motion. All these laws and propositions are governed by the law of universal evolution which states that with the integration of matter, motion is dissipated and as matter becomes differentiated motion is absorbed: 'Evolution is an integration of matter and a concomitant dissipation of motion during which the matter passes from a relatively indefinite, incoherent homogeneity to a relatively coherent heterogeneity and during which the retained motion undergoes a parallel transformation.'

The evolution of society is defined by Spencer as the gradual socialisation of humanity, a process occurring independently of human practice. The actual origin of human society is located as the result of population pressure which compelled individuals to enter the social state and thus develop both social organisation and social feelings. But having identified the genesis of society Spencer analysed social formations in terms of the biological analogy. As with Comte the historical dimension of society disappears; the organismic analogy has the effect of emphasising synchronic rather than diachronic analysis.

Spencer's ahistorical and anti-humanist perspective is especially brought out in his frequent defence of the concept of the social organism which he sometimes defined as a useful analogy and at other times as a reality. Thus in *The Principles of Sociology* he writes that it is the character of both living and social bodies 'that while they increase in size they increase in structure', that as they acquire greater mass their parts multiply and differentiate. And in his article, 'The Social Organism' (1860), he defined society as a 'thing' which grows, evolving from small 'aggregations' so simple 'in structure as to be considered structureless' in which there is 'scarcely any mutual dependence of parts', to complex, differentiated structures in which the separate parts acquire mutual and functional dependence: society is a structure characterised by co-operation between parts and whole. Should anything 'disturb' this consensus, Spencer adds, the equilibrium of the whole system is endangered (i.e. if government artificially interferes with the workings of economic and social life). Although noting the differences between the biological organism and society – the parts are more dispersed and independent from the centre of society, individual members may die but the whole persists, in the biological organism the elements exist for the good of the

55

whole while in the social organism the whole exists for the good of its members – Spencer tended to equate the two:

> While comparison makes definite the obvious contrasts between organisms . . . and the social organism, it shows that even these contrasts are not so decided as was to be expected . . . Societies slowly augment in mass; they progress in complexity of structure; at the same time their parts become more mutually dependent . . . The *principles* of organisation are the same, and the differences are simply differences of application (Spencer, 1969a, p. 206).

Spencer distinguished 'militant' from 'industrial' societies in terms of this holistic approach. Militant societies were defined as lacking complex structural differentiation, dominated by a centralised state, rigid hierarchies of status and a tendency towards conformism; industrial societies, developing through the general law of evolution, were more complex and structurally differentiated and characterised by a multiplicity of beliefs, independent institutions, decentralisation and a tendency to individualisation. The organismic analogy, however, prevented Spencer from grasping the contradictions and conflicts of interest which industrial society actually engendered: unlike Ferguson, who rejected the organismic analogy, he failed to integrate the dialectical elements of social change into the holistic model, that evolution creates both differentiation of structure and differentiation of interest, that parts become independent through collective social organisation and the development of a common awareness by the members of different specialised organisations, and that their interests differ from the interests of others. Spencer had no conception of interest as a collective phenomenon, as class interest, group interest, etc. Rather, interests were conceived strictly in terms of Smithian individualism, that although society consisted of different, atomistic interests they nevertheless harmonised into a unity through the operation of a 'hidden hand' which synthesised private interests with the common good. Individuals seek private ends but because such actions take place within a complex society built on the interdependence of institutions, the human agent unconsciously and unintentionally serves the higher needs of society as a whole. In this way

Spencer attempted to reconcile his sociological individualism with his collective concept of the social organism.

One consequence of this argument was a rejection of social regulation as conceived by Comte and the forms of state intervention which Spencer saw increasingly dominating industrial society. For Spencer, society was regulated adequately if individuals were allowed to pursue their own interests free of collectivist intervention. Hence his hostility to state education, state medicine, the provision of free public libraries: institutions which 'artificially' preserve its 'feeblest members' lower the moral and intellectual standards of society as a whole. Spencer remained rigorously individualistic in his conception of human society. In *The Principles of Sociology* (1873), discussing the controversy between nominalists and realists, he argued that society was essentially 'a collective name for a number of individuals' and that there 'is no way of coming at a true theory of society but by inquiring into the nature of its component individuals' (Spencer, 1961, Ch. VI). In one important sense, therefore, Spencer's positivistic organicism and sociological individualism failed to develop much beyond Mill's psychological reductionism: on the one hand, society constituted the sum of individual actions and sociological analysis must focus on the biological and psychological characteristics of individuals; on the other hand, society was a system, a complex, highly differentiated structure consisting of phenomena that had evolved at the superorganic level. Spencer's sociology could not resolve this dualism, the conflict between a biological and evolutionary determinism and a profound belief in individual human action as the source of unity and social harmony. As Peel has observed, 'Spencer had no real sense of either the historical actor, or the sociologist, intervening or participating in the flow of events'. The pattern of evolution could not be changed by 'any "extra-evolutionary" action' (Peel, 1971, p. 164).

Spencer's sociological system, his concept of evolution as a cosmic process, his sociological individualism and organicist holism had no deep, lasting effects: some of his ideas crossed the Atlantic and found a congenial reception within early American sociology, but European sociology, in the general reaction against positivism at the close of the nineteenth-century, debated with Spencer's theories (especially Simmel and Durkheim), only to salvage such basic sociological concepts as structure, function, system, equilibrium, institution. Nevertheless, the anti-historical bias of Spencer's sociology influenced the later synchronically oriented sociologists and deflected attention away from those structural elements in societies which, through conflict and differential interests, promote social change. Spencer's organicist positivism, however, did succeed in grasping society as a structure, a system, and he was one of the first social theorists to identify industrialism with a new, decentred mode of social organisation. In this respect he differed sharply from the centralising notion of society developed by Comte. Indeed, Spencer's lasting contribution to sociological theory may well be his notion that an advanced society – industrial society – built around increasing differentiation of structure and differentiation of function and reciprocal relations between different institutions as well as between parts and whole, necessarily lacks a single, dominant centre. Comparing the social and the biological organism he noted that 'while in the individual organism there is but one centre of consciousness . . . there are, in the social organism, as many centres as there are individuals' (Spencer, 1969, p. 282). Spencer expressed the concept of decentred structure in atomistic terms but it is, nevertheless, an important insight. The implicit focus of Spencer's sociology is on civil society and its separation from the state. Of course, his synchronic, individualistic approach prevented a profound theorisation of the historical, systemic and contradictory nature of modern industrial society, that as industrialism expands the framework and frees the institutions of civil society it simultaneously generates centralising trends within the state itself. Spencer's concept of industrialism and social differentiation could be said to be deficient in one important respect: that it failed to grasp the historical specificity of industrialism as class structured, as a capitalist process.

3
Marxism: A Positive Science of Capitalist Development

Comte's theory of historical change had emphasised the concept of determinate laws, that history necessarily moved through a succession of stages culminating in the scientific epoch of positivism. For Comte, as with Montesquieu, Smith and Ferguson social change was not a random process dependent on purely subjective and accidental elements, but the result of an underlying structure of forces – material and moral – that generated both direction and meaning. As was argued in the previous chapter, many of Comte's fundamental ideas were derived from Saint-Simon, but in Comte's reworking of Saint-Simon's theories the concepts of industrialism, production, class formation and class conflict were stripped of their contradictory and negative aspects and integrated into an organismic, consensual model of society. But Saint-Simon's writings contain both positivistic and socialist elements. The development of socialism as both an intellectual current and socio-political movement owed much to the influence of Saint-Simon's followers. The Saint-Simonian school, in particular the writings of Enfantin and Bazard, argued that production must be socially organised, run by the producers themselves (not the parasitic 'idlers' and 'unproductive classes'), and society develop from rule by government and military organisation to administrative and industrial rule. During the 1830s this notion of the socialisation of production, and therefore of private property, became the corner-stone of

59

socialist theory: employed for the first time by the Saint-Simonian, Pierre Leroux in 1832, socialism demanded the abolition of private property rights, the elimination of poverty, the assertion of equality and the organisation of production through the agency of the state.

Positivist sociology and socialist theory thus share a common source even though both socialism and sociology, as theories of social and political organisation, existed before they were named. But it was only during the crucial period between 1789 and 1830, in response to rapid political and economic changes, that the intellectual and institutional basis of sociology and socialism were laid as expressions of a developing opposition to the dominant ideas of political liberalism, individualism and the market economy.

Nineteenth-century socialism and sociology emerged after the intellectual consolidation of classical political economy largely in response to the doctrine of the immanent rationality of individual interests: sociologists and socialists both agreed that the private pursuit of interests must eventuate in the collapse of social and moral solidarity; the anarchy of the market place could not lead to social cohesion and stability. Comte's solution was authoritarian moral leadership; the Saint-Simonians demanded a socialised system of production. But socialist ideas made little impact on the nascent labour movement that had developed rapidly after the ending of the French revolutionary wars. In England working-class leaders worked closely with the bourgeoisie, advocating liberal rather than socialist ideas in opposition to the political domination of the aristocracy. The success of the 1832 Reform Act had the effect of separating the working-class movement from the bourgeoisie and instituting a distinct socialist alternative – Owenism and the Chartists in England, the Saint-Simonian school and Fourier in France. Both Robert Owen and Charles Fourier insisted on the necessity for co-operation not competition as the means of social organisation advocating the development of communities in which the worker would enjoy 'the fruits of his labour' to the full.

The early socialists tended to offer a moralising and Utopian critique of industrial capitalism, that as labour constituted the only source of value everyone, apart from the 'unproductive' workers, should work together and produce a society based on mutuality rather than private gain. The capitalist was effectively depriving the worker of that which was his own, an action clearly immoral and socially divisive. The solution was thus social transformation through moral criticism and action, a standpoint which led Engels to characterise Owen, Fourier and others as 'Utopian' not scientific socialists. In the sense that pre-Marxist socialism lacked both a theory of social change and a grasp of society in terms of the relations between economic organisation and the social and political system then it was utopian, basing the necessity for socialism on changes in human nature. And, of course, it was precisely the scientific grasp of social change that Engels admired in the work of Saint-Simon, especially the concept of historical laws, the necessary historical conflict between social classes – feudal and bourgeoisie, idlers and producers – and the central argument that changes within the political system depended, not on moral actions, but on economic institutions. Equally significant for the development of Marxist socialism was the assimilation of the Saint-Simonian doctrine that socialised production was possible only through the organisation of a centralised state. The emphasis on the ethical component of socialism, which plays such an important role in the work of Owen and Fourier, disappears in the socialism of Marx and Engels: the moral element is entirely dependent on the structure of the economy and polity.

The development of Marxism is thus organically bound up with a burgeoning labour movement – especially in England and France – the rapid growth of industry and the new social relations of capitalist production. Equally important was the critique of this new social order by 'dissident' intellectuals influenced by classical political economy, especially the labour theory of value, and the revolutionary trends associated with democratic republicanism. During the course of the 1840s and 1850s Marxism emerged as the first sociological theory which identified scientific analysis with the interests of a specific social class, the industrial proletariat; a theory of historical change grounded in the struggle between social classes and the priority of economic factors in the shaping of social and political structures. In effect the scientific study of historical development disclosed the necessity of socialism as the resolution of internal conflicts generated by capitalist production: Utopian socialism had disclosed no law-governed process in history, no historical necessity, and thus had ended with moral appeals in which socialism was defined as an ideal state realisable through education and co-operation.

The development of Marxism

Marx's first writings (1841–5) were largely philosophical, concerned with the problem of human alienation and freedom. It was only with *The German Ideology* (1846) that Marx 'settled his account' with his 'philosophic conscience' and developed the first outlines of what later would be called 'the materialist conception of history'. Co-written with Engels, *The German Ideology* advanced a sociological concept of society as a definite structure built around antagonistic social classes, division of labour and forms of private property. Ideas themselves are rooted in specific material contexts and have no independent existence apart from the social formation. Specific modes of production characterise historical development: society develops through different stages from slave and feudal, to capitalist. In the works which followed *The German Ideology – The Poverty of Philosophy* (1847), *The Communist Manifesto* (1848), *Wage Labour and Capital* (1849) – these themes were further developed within Marx's general historical theory, that social change occurs through conflict and struggle and more precisely through the contradictions existing between the productive forces of any society and its social relations. There is thus a pattern, a meaning to historical development located within the necessity for modes of production to develop towards higher social formations: socialism is thus given a scientific basis in necessary social change.

During the 1850s Marx produced a number of historical studies dealing with the problems of socialism and the working-class movement in Europe, especially France. But his most important work was the massive study of the economic foundations of modern capitalism, the *Grundrisse der Kritik politischen Okonomie* (*Outline of a Critique of Political Economy*), which remained unpublished during his lifetime becoming widely known only after its publication in East Germany in 1953. The importance of the *Grundrisse* in the development of Marxism lies in the continuity which it establishes between Marx's early writings on the alienation of labour and the concept of the active human subject, and the later, supposedly more scientific work, in which capitalism is defined as a social system governed by specific laws of motion and development. Nevertheless, while Marx employs the concept of alienation in the analysis of economic forms there are significant differences between the *Grundrisse* and the earlier works: the term labour-power replaces the concept of labour (labour power had been noted in *The Communist Manifesto* but only in a general sense); production is emphasised at the expense of exchange and the basis laid for the theory of surplus value, capital accumulation and economic crisis. These are the themes which dominate *Capital* (1867) of which only the first volume was published in Marx's lifetime. Yet the theory of alienation and dehumanisation are central issues in these later largely economic analyses and Marx remained faithful to the essential principles of Hegelian dialectics and humanism to the end of his life: capitalism was conceived as a system of production structured in contradictions, a social system which transformed human values into external things. In analysing Marx's sociology therefore, it is important to begin with Marx's own starting point.

Alienation of labour

In the *Economic and Philosophic Manuscripts* (1843–4) Marx defined labour as 'man's self-confirming essence', the activity which political economy had succeeded in transforming into an object, an external thing. For classical political economy the worker was 'an abstract activity and a belly . . . increasingly dependent upon all the fluctuations in market price, in the employment of capital, and in the caprices of the rich'. Human activity is thus defined in terms of the non-human.

But the concept of alienation was not part of political economy's conceptual structure or language and it was from

Hegel's dialectical philosophy that Marx derived the theory of alienation. In Hegel's *Phenomenology of Spirit* human culture was assimilated to the concept of 'Absolute Spirit' which progressively unfolds throughout history in a series of dialectical contradictions, eventuating in the expansion of human consciousness and increased self-knowledge; the ultimate stage is the assimilation of 'Spirit' to the 'ethical world'. History was thus defined as enclosing an immanent meaning in that it embodied a ceaseless activity and drive towards unlimited, total consciousness. 'Spirit' was, of course, humanity and the specific historical situations which constitute historical development are analysed by Hegel as 'moments' which, in their material form, embody the dialectical development of 'Absolute Spirit' from an unreflective unity to an organic and conscious unity with culture (the Renaissance, the Enlightenment, the French Revolution). But as 'spirit' unfolds dialectically it is confronted by each specific moment as part of itself, something its own activity has created; it thus experiences this activity as external and alien. 'Spirit' seeks to recover these alienated moments thus creating the movement which drives it towards total unity and thus a non-alienated consciousness.

Marx inverts Hegel's idealist account arguing that such speculative history ignores real individuals and real conditions; through his grasp of political economy Marx defined labour as the basis of human culture. Culture is no longer the expression of a supra-historical force but the product of human activity through labour. Alienation becomes a process in which humanity is progressively turned into a stranger in a world created by labour. This materialist inversion of Hegel was made possible by arguing that religion was merely humanity's essential nature refracted through ideas: religion, Ludwig Feuerbach (1804–72) wrote, 'is nothing other than the essence of man . . . the God of man is nothing other than the divinised essence of man'.

In the *Economic and Philosophic Manuscripts* Marx redefines religion and philosophy as constituting more than the embodiment of humanity's essence, the product of specific economic forces. Marx analyses alienation in terms of the division of labour arguing that it succeeds in creating vast accumulations of wealth at one pole of society, an increase in the value of things achieved only at the cost of a progressive devaluing of human life itself. Human labour becomes an object: 'This fact implies that the object produced by labour, its product, now stands opposed to it as an alien being, as a *power independent* of the producer. The product of labour is labour which has been embodied in an object and turned into a physical thing; this product is an objectification of labour'. Marx distinguishes objectification from alienation arguing, against Hegel, whose philosophy embraced both as synonymous terms, that objectification is a process through which humanity externalises itself in nature and society, producing tools for example, and thus necessarily entering into social relationships; alienation, however, occurs only when humanity, having externalised itself, encounters its own activity, its essence, operating as an external, alien and oppressive power. For Marx, objectification was unavoidable and as such not identical with alienation. By assimilating objectification to alienation, Hegel had concluded that humanity (the 'Absolute Spirit') must remain forever trapped in alienation as its essential and ultimately tragic condition. But by locating alienation with economic and material elements Marx defined it as an historical not universal state.

Marx identified four main characteristics of alienation: man's alienation from nature, from himself, from his 'species being' (a term taken from Feuerbach) and from others. Capitalism alienates humanity from its own activity, from the product of its labour ('alienation of things') thus turning labour's product into an alien object. The more the individual works the more he is dominated by the world of objects that labour has created: 'The worker puts his life into the object, and his life then belongs no longer to himself but to the object. The greater his activity . . . the less he possesses. What is embodied in the product of his labour is no longer his own. The greater this product is . . . the more he is diminished.' Man's 'self-confirming essence', his labour, turns increasingly against him under capitalist industry, becoming a 'forced activity', a denial of his being, serving to stunt his faculties, induce misery, exhaustion and mental despair. Work is wholly instrumental; a form of activity which is specifically human, becomes an oppressive necessity, an alien, external activity in which the individual feels free only outside work in leisure or with his family. Man feels free as an individual and is thus alienated as a species being, for unlike the animals man, through his activity, produces not simply for himself but for the whole of nature. He has, too, an awareness of this activity and continually repro- duces himself in both consciousness and in real life. But alienated labour turns the product of labour from an activity of the species into an activity of the individual dominated by purely biological needs. Capitalism effectively defines the worker as possessing a saleable object, labour, which is thus purchased by 'another' so that his activity is no longer his own.

Marx's early writings thus propound two basic themes: first, that while humanity creates the social world through its own activity, the world is experienced as alien and hostile; and secondly, that both idealist philosophy and classical political economy, the theories which first disclosed this trend towards alienation, depict human relationships not as relations between persons but rather as relations between things. This process of reification is especially marked in political economy.

> It is self-evident that political economy treats the proletarian . . . [as] a *worker*. It can, therefore, propound the thesis that he, like a horse, must receive just as much as will enable him to work. Political economy does not deal with him in his free time, as a human being . . . but . . . conceives the worker only as a draught animal, as a beast whose needs are strictly limited to bodily needs (Marx, 1963, p. 132).

As the most alienated social class in capitalist society the proletariat exist on the basis of private property, itself the source of alienated labour. It is for this reason that Marx identifies the working class as a universal class 'for all human servitude is involved in the relation of the worker to production and all types of servitude are only modifications or conse- quences of this relation'. It thus follows that the whole of society is alienated, from capitalists whose life is dominated externally by the demands of profit, to writers and artists who sell their creative talents to the highest bidder. A total revolution is thus called for and the spearhead is the modern industrial pro- letariat, a class which constitutes the 'effective dissolution' of capitalism, for its demand that private property be abolished is only 'a *principle for society* what society has already made a principle *for the proletariat* and what the latter already involuntarily embodies as the negative result of society'. The dehumanised relation of capital to labour saturates the entire social structure; 'an inhuman power' rules everything.

Political economy could probe no further into the structure of alienated labour and explain the contradiction generated by an alienated social world and increasing material affluence. Political economy ended by celebrating bourgeois society and bourgeois thought as the close of history and as universal activity. The contradictions, the negative elements generated by this process, were simply eliminated: 'Political economy conceals the alienation in the nature of labour in so far as it does not examine the direct relationship between the worker ('work') and production.' Alienation is thus a denial of creative human potentiality, the dehumanisation of the subject and an obstacle to the building of a truly human community.

In Marx's early writings alienation is conceived both in socio-historical and philosophically abstract terms as, for example, the 'fragmentation' of labour and the 'fragmentation' of the human essence. It is important to note that Marx develops a concept of the *whole man* whose human stature is diminished by the external power of capital; man thus needs to be returned to a non-alienated state, reunited with nature, other men and society. As late as 1846, in *The German Ideology*, Marx could describe Communism in terms of these Utopian elements arguing that the division of labour would not function merely to allocate individuals to specific occupational roles but allow them 'to hunt in the morning, fish in the afternoon, rear cattle in the evening, criticise after dinner . . . without ever becoming a hunter, fisherman, shepherd or critic'. (Marx and Engels, 1964, Part 1.) Nevertheless, there is, within this particular text and those which followed, a shift of emphasis and the argument that the concept of alienation in the *Grundrisse* and *Capital* is identical with that of the *Economic and Philosophic Manuscripts* suggests the untenable view that, while Marx's theory of society and social change underwent extensive revision and development in the post-1845 works, the theory of alienation remained at the conceptual and empirical level of the earlier texts. By the 1850s Marx's economic theory, together with his

67

political outlook, had changed considerably. Thus from a purely logical standpoint those concepts retained in the later writings clearly imply radically different meanings from their earlier usage. The present appeal of the *Economic and Philosophic Manuscripts* undoubtedly lies in their depiction of humanity as the ultimate arbiter of the social world and man as an active subject duplicating himself and his powers through his actions. Yet the picture which emerges from these writings does not suggest the voluntaristic theory which has often been claimed for them, for if alienation dominates the social world to the extent of wholly debilitating humanity's creative and natural powers, transforming the individual from an active subject into a passive object, then how is it possible for change to occur. *How is praxis possible?* Marx's concept of alienation suggests the impossibility of radical human action, for consciously planned change. It is this contradiction between the notions of *active* subject and *total* alienation which leads Marx to posit Communism as an ethical ideal which humanity ought to strive for, and the proletariat as the universal class which negates capitalist alienation. Marx's humanist concept of alienation, although based on the keenly felt empirical structure of classical political economy, is ultimately deterministic, philosophical and speculative lacking the sociological and economic framework of the later *Grundrisse* and *Capital*.

Between writing the *Economic and Philosophic Manuscripts* and *Capital* Marx decisively rejected Feuerbach's humanist philosophy as the starting point for social theory. His main criticism related to Feuerbach's essentialist concept of man: humanity constitutes the totality of social relations and thus research must investigate not man in general but man in society and society as a system structured around laws of change and development. But Marx did not abandon humanism. In *Capital* the concept of alienation is sparingly employed but the related notions of the 'fetishism of commodities' and reification are frequently discussed and form an important part of Marx's analysis of capitalist economic structure. In the *Grundrisse*, for example, the emphasis shifts to production; labour is defined as labour-power, a unique commodity found only within the capitalist mode of production. In the early writings Marx had followed Smith and Ricardo in defining labour as 'abstract general and social labour', an approach which succeeded in mystifying the precise relation between the creation of value (expressed in money, for example) and human activity (expressed in labour). Labour-power constitutes a commodity; labour in general does not. The creation of wealth is possible only through the exploitation of labour power, the transformation of labour from an affirmation to a denial of human values. Thus in *Capital* Marx argues that commodity production entails the separation of two specific kinds of value, exchange and use value, values which either command a price or satisfy a human and social need. All commodities embody both values but it is only capitalism as a system of commodity production which aims at the expansion of exchange value.

Human activity increasingly becomes subordinated to the external compulsions of exchange value. Money becomes the objective bond of society, the real community in a system dominated by exchange values. When in the first volume of *Capital* Marx refers to 'commodity fetishism' he describes a process in which human subjects no longer control the objects of labour as their own. The worker exists only to satisfy the demands of the economic system; material wealth does not exist to satisfy the needs of the worker's development. The social process of production effectively negates the need for community, co-operation becomes alienated and replaced by compulsion. Human relations become 'atomised' assuming a material character independent of human control and conscious activity. This process is especially expressed by the fact that products take the form of commodities (Marx, 1958, Vol. 1, Ch. XXVI).

In a society dominated by exchange value, the real social foundations of the unequal relation of capital to labour is hidden. In a famous passage Marx writes of the commodity as 'a mysterious thing' which disguises the social character of labour presenting the relations between the producers and the totality of their labour 'as a social relation, existing not between themselves, but between the products of their labour'. Social relations within capitalism are wholly inverted, 'every element, even the simplest, the commodity for example . . . causes relations between people to appear as attributes of things'. The social world of modern capitalism is a perverted world, the products of labour generating an apparent independence, in which objects begin 'to rule the producers instead of being ruled by them', while those engaged in production 'live in a bewitched world', their own relationships appearing to them 'as properties of things, as properties of the material elements of production'. Humanity becomes dominated by a world of things, by processes its own activity has created but which, through the workings of the capitalist economic system, turn against them, as objective independent processes (Marx, 1958, pp. 72–3). In the *Grundrisse* Marx writes that 'social wealth confronts labour in more powerful portions as an alien and dominant power . . . a monstrous objective power which, created through social labour belongs not to the worker, but . . . to capital'. The emphasis, Marx notes, is 'not on the state of being *objectified*, but . . . of being *alienated*, dispossessed, sold' (Marx, 1973, pp. 831–2). And, in almost identical language, he writes in *Capital*:

We have seen that the growing accumulation of capital implies its growing concentration. Thus grows the power of capital, the alienation of the conditions of social production personified in the capitalist from the real producers. Capital . . . as a social power . . . no longer stands in any possible relation to that which the labour of a single individual can create. It becomes an alienated, independent social power, which stands opposed to society as an object, and as an object that is the capitalist's source of power (Marx, 1962, p. 259).

The extraction of surplus-value, the control over labour-power invested in the individual capitalist and capital, results in the development of a social world which progressively devalues human values and exalts the world of objects and things. In the *Economic and Philosophic Manuscripts* Marx had analysed this tendency: 'The worker becomes an ever cheaper commodity the more goods he creates. The devaluation of the human world increases in direct relation with the increase in value of the world of things.' The relation between the early and later writings is thus clearly stated; in a world dominated by commodity production and exploitation the worker's labour-power is quantified, measured as precisely as possible, treated entirely as an external thing. The analysis of capitalism as a system in the *Grundrisse* and *Capital* is based on similar concepts employed by Marx in his humanist critique of capitalism of the early writings. But in both the early and later writings reification is depicted as a process which so penetrates human and social relations that individuals comprehend the products of their labour as autonomous, objective forces unconnected with human activity.

This process of reification manifests itself most sharply in consciousness: those who comprehend the social world through reified categories emphasise the externality and inexorable *natural* determinism of a world apparently governed by blind laws beyond the control of human beings, a world in which things constitute the only active elements. In pre-industrial society, where use value was not dominated by exchange value, social relations were clear and unequivocal based on personal-ised ties and obligations, unequal relationships grounded in custom and tradition. The social structure of capitalism, however, is built around impersonal relationships based on the dominion of exchange value. In societies where exchange value has replaced direct use value a formal equality masks class relations; the world of capitalist commodity production appears as a world of equals bound by freely negotiated contracts. The exchange between capital and labour bears the illusion of a free exchange of equivalents (labour for wages) and it is at this point that the mystification of social relations occurs: the worker acts as if labour-power is not exploited, that in return for 'a fair day's work' there will be just reward. Capitalist inequality is thus defined as natural and therefore essential for the adequate functioning of society. The worker fails to understand that he has become part of capital itself and is but a special mode of its existence:

> Hence the productive power developed by the labourer when working in co-operation is the productive power of capital. This power is developed gratuitously, whenever the workmen are placed under given conditions, and it is capital that places them under such conditions. Because this power cost capital nothing, and because, on the other hand, the labourer himself does not develop it before his labour belongs to capital, it appears as a power with

which capital is endowed by Nature – a productive power that is immanent in capital (Marx, 1958, p. 333).

Marx's theory of alienation has thus become more empirical, historically specific and sociologically grounded in economic structures. In his early writings Marx had written of the 'inhuman power' dominating social life, frustrating humanity's essential powers and transforming him/her into an object. In *Capital* the concept of alienated subject is retained but within a theoretical framework which defines capitalism as an objective system and alienation in terms of the inner and contradictory movement of capitalist production, an alienation embodied in the transformation of labour power into a commodity. One result of this trend is the increasing importance of ideology for the development and maintenance of capitalist society.

The concept of ideology

Although the term ideology originated at the end of the eighteenth century in the work of the French philosopher Destutt de Tracy, Marxism is often credited with defining its relation to determine social, political and economic conditions and elucidating the process whereby the material 'base' of society (its economic infrastructure) necessarily generates a 'superstructure' (specific forms of thought). Society is explained not through ideas but rather ideas through society: ideas have no history other than as elements of society and history. In *The German Ideology* Marx and Engels postulated a strict, causal and mechanical relation between thought and the social world defining ideas as expressions of class interests. This theory of ideology therefore assumes a relation of correspondence between social structure and thought systems; ideas are merely the passive reflections of an external economic order. Knowledge is epiphenomenal, the product of objective social interests and thus incapable of exercising an active role in society and social change.

The concept of ideology as distorted thought, as a false consciousness which mystifies real relations in defence of class interests, is developed in great detail in *The German Ideology*.

Ideological thought conceives reality 'upside down', an inversion of the objectively real, as with religion which defines human life as an extension of God in opposition to the materialist doctrine of religion as a social product. In this first formulation ideology is equivalent to consciousness, the transposition of 'interests' into mere 'reflexes and echoes' of the 'life process':

The phantoms formed in the human brain are . . . sublimates of. . . material life-processes, which is empirically verifiable and bound to material premises. Morality, religion, metaphysics, all the rest of ideology and their corresponding forms of consciousness, thus no longer retain their semblance of independence. They have no history, no development; but men, developing their material production and their material intercourse, alter, along with this real existence, their thinking and the products of their thinking. Life is not determined by consciousness but consciousness by life (Marx and Engels, 1964, pp. 37–8).

This thesis of a strict causal relation of economic base and ideological superstructure reappears in Marx's 1859 text, *A Contribution to a Critique of Political Economy*, in which it is argued that the forces of production 'constitute the economic structure of society, the real foundation on which arises a legal and political superstructure and to which correspond definite forms of social consciousness. The mode of production of material life conditions the general process of social, political and intellectual life' (Marx, 1971, pp. 20–1). In many of Engels's discussions of ideology it is this deterministic concept which predominates:

Ideology is a process accomplished by the so-called thinker consciously indeed, but with a false consciousness. The real motives impelling him remain unknown to him, otherwise it would not be an ideological process at all (Marx and Engels, 1962, Vol. 2, p. 497).

On this basis all thought must qualify as ideology including Marxism itself. Engels's argument suggests a thoroughgoing relativism, a position not sustained consistently in his work for he clearly believed in the non-ideological advances made in nineteenth-century natural science. Engels insists that although ideology enjoys no independent existence apart from society, no separate history as an autonomous reality, there is, nevertheless, a degree of partial autonomy and although an inversion of the real world, and thus 'false', ideology is not wholly an epiphenomenal and passive reproduction of the socio-economic structure. Engels thus emphasises the *reciprocal* not mechanical nexus of ideas and society:

> The economic situation is the basis, but the various elements of the superstructure, political forms of the class struggle . . . juristic, philosophical theories, religious view . . . also exercise their influence upon the course of the historical struggles and in many cases preponderate their form (Marx and Engels, 1962, Vol. 2, pp. 488–9).

Mutual interaction between all elements exists but in the final resort 'the economic movement . . . asserts itself as necessary'.

Engels's formulation is full of ambiguity. To argue that the economic factor is one among many influences, yet the ultimate arbiter of ideology and all forms of knowledge, does not in itself suggest any criteria for judging truth from error or the means of validating one social theory over another. For example, are some social interests less likely to produce ideological distortion than others; and if this is so how is the economic factor ultimately decisive? In effect, Engels reverts to pre-Marxist concepts of multiple causation and context-bound explanations which fail to specify the exact relation of ideas to society, the structure of determinations and thus of autonomy. Writing of philosophy, for example, he argues:

> . . . through the operation of economic influences (which again generally act only under political etc. disguises) upon the existing philosophic material handed down by predecessors. Here economy creates nothing new, but it determines the way in which the thought material found in existence is altered and further developed, and that too for the most part indirectly, for it is the political, legal and moral reflexes which exercise the greatest influence upon philosophy (Marx and Engels, 1962, Vol. 2, pp. 495–6).

Engels's standpoint is that of eighteenth-century materialism, Montesquieu and Ferguson, mutual interaction of different elements within a given situation; the notion of partial autonomy in this context is merely another way of saying that complex situations are characterised by complex modes of interaction.

A second, more dialectical theory of ideology, one grounded in the category of mediation is, however, implicit in Engels's distinction between what he calls the 'higher' and the 'lower' ideologies ('pure' thought as opposed to concrete, economic thought). The closer that thought approaches abstract ideology the more it will be determined 'by accidental elements in its evolution . . . its curve will trace a zig-zag'. The interconnections 'between concepts and their material conditions of existence becomes more and more complicated, more and more obscured by intermediate links' (Marx and Engels, 1962, Vol. 2, p. 397). This is crudely expressed but it does suggest that the history of ideas is a dialectical and not a mechanically evolutionary process. In the *Grundrisse* Marx had posed the question of the relationship between economy and culture, art and social structure arguing that 'certain periods of the highest development of art stand in no direct connection with the general development of society, nor with the material basis and the skeleton structure of its organisation' (Marx, 1971, pp. 215–17). Ancient Greek art surpassed its economically undeveloped economic system while the developments in eighteenth-century French and German philosophy cannot be assimilated easily to the pre-industrial, semi-feudal structure of French and German society.

Marx's most important contribution to the theory of ideology, however, is his extensive critique of eighteenth and nineteenth-century political economy. Here Marx clearly distinguished science from ideology and the complex relation of class interests with thought. In the 'Afterword' to the second edition of *Capital* (1873) he argues that classical political economy (Smith and Ricardo) 'belongs to the period in which the class struggle was as yet undeveloped', a period characterised by rapid advances in economic science. But with the sharpening of class conflict at the beginning of the nineteenth-century and the eventual conquest of political power by the

French and English bourgeoisie 'the class struggle, practically as well as theoretically, took on a more and more outspoken and threatening form. It sounded the knell of scientific bourgeois economy . . . In place of disinterested inquiries there were hired prize-fighters; in place of genuine scientific research the bad conscience and the evil intent of apologetic'. From the moment when the bourgeoisie assumed the mantle of a dominant class then the class struggle between bourgeoisie and aristocracy became a conflict between bourgeoisie allied with the aristocracy against the burgeoning industrial proletariat (Marx, 1958, p. 15). Political economy now becomes entwined with the claims of ideological legitimation. In the *Theories of Surplus Value* Marx established two crucial elements of ideology:

1. All social thought adopts necessarily a position towards it object of study which is directly related to the practical interests and activity of its leading intellectuals: thus Smith and Ricardo expressed the interests of 'a revolutionary bourgeoisie' in conflict with the landowners.
2. Ideological knowledge will subvert scientific knowledge if the standpoint is that of an economically declining social group, what Marx describes as 'transition classes', such as the aristocracy and landowners.

Thus in his analysis of Smith and Ricardo, Marx frequently describes their work as 'honest inquiry' emphasising their commitment to a rigorous and objective scientific approach. Smith, in his discussion of labour, adopts the standpoint of capitalist production and approaches 'the very heart of the matter, hit(s) the nail on the head' by distinguishing unproductive from productive labour (unproductive exchanging for revenue such as wages and profits, productive producing capital). Smith's distinction was never made from the standpoint of the worker, rather from that of the capitalist. In contrast, Ricardo describes the necessary conflict engendered by the economically unequal relation between capitalist and worker and Marx comments that Ricardo 'wants production for the sake of production' irrespective of its social effects, 'a ruthlessness . . . not only scientifically honest but also . . . a scientific necessity from his point of view'. Ricardo's political economy thus expresses the historic triumph of the industrial bourgeoisie over society as a whole and in this sense his work is, in Marx's terms, genuinely scientific although, as with Smith, penetrated by ideological elements:

> Ricardo's conception is . . . in the interests of the industrial bourgeoisie, only because, and in so far as, their interests coincide with that of production or the productive development of human labour (Marx, 1964–72, Vol. 3, pp. 118–19).

Marx distinguishes, then, between ideological and scientific knowledge: 'The rough cynical character of classical economy' – its honesty – is in effect 'a critique of existing conditions', and he cites Smith's description of the clergy as 'unproductive labourers . . . maintained by a part of the annual produce of the industry of other people' bracketing them with 'lawyers, physicians and men of letters'. Marx writes:

> This is the language of the still revolutionary bourgeoisie which has not yet subjected to itself the whole of society, the State etc. All these illustrious and time-honoured occupations . . . are from an economic standpoint on the same level as the swarm of their own lackeys and jesters maintained by the bourgeoisie and by idle wealth (Marx, 1964–72, vol. 1, pp. 290–2).

As an intellectual expression of a 'rising class' classical political economy penetrated more deeply into the social and economic order than previous economic theory, its concepts organically bound up with its practice as an historically 'progressive' class whose worldly activity, in business and industry, linked it, not with past societies, but with the capitalist and industrial future. The work of Smith and Ricardo thus reflects the practice of a social class which had yet to establish its hegemony within the burgeoning capitalist order. Ricardo's economic theories justify capitalist development and the historic claims of the bourgeois class but this in itself does not make them ideological. Both Ricardo and Smith produced work which did not mystify the social world and conceal contradictions but rather illuminated the very nature of capitalist economic and social relations. Ricardo's contemporary, Malthus, in contrast produced economic analysis which justified the 'rents, sinecures, squandering, heartlessness' of the landed aristocracy, admiring and praising those groups within the state which Smith had criticised as unproductive labourers. To legitimise a 'transition' class clearly leads to ideology:

> But when a man seeks to accommodate science to a viewpoint which is derived not from science itself (however erroneous it may be) but from outside, external interests, then I call him 'base'. . . . It is not a base action when Ricardo puts the proletariat on the same level as machinery or beasts of burden because (from his point of view) their being purely machinery or beasts of burden is conducive to 'production'. *This is stoic, objective, scientific* (Marx, 1964–72, Vol. 2, pp. 114–19).

From these texts it is possible to define more precisely Marx's concept of ideology. The relation of knowledge to society is conceived dialectically, characterised by contradictions, uneven in its development; knowledge is not a direct reproduction of class and economic interests. These formulations are clearly anchored in Marx's dictum that social existence, the 'ensemble of social relations', determines consciousness through the 'sensuous activity' of the human subject. Yet it might be argued that all Marx has demonstrated is that between 1760 and 1830 the English bourgeoisie 'needed' a specific mode of knowledge consonant with its historic role, and that political economy emerged as an historically necessary intellectual response to the burgeoning capitalist economic order. In other words, a functional not dialectical relation subsists between forms of knowledge and forms of society. But the fact that specific forms of knowledge are associated with specific material interests does not imply that the degree of determination automatically classifies all the knowledge-products as ideological. Marx makes the important distinction between the 'ideological component parts of the ruling class' and 'the free spiritual production of this particular social formation', arguing against a mechanical reduction of ideas to economic interests: economic structure develops unevenly and does not constitute a homogeneous unified whole which presents a coherent set of interests. Marx's arguments point to a concept of knowledge as objective and scientific, a reality independent of economic and social forces although necessarily linked to these elements for its social existence.

In contrast, ideology is epiphenomenal tied directly to economic and class interests, its function one of concealing contradictions, mystifying social relations and fetishising the world of appearances. Ideological knowledge, as distinct from scientific knowledge, begins from the alienated nature of human relations and is incapable of grasping the socio-historical foundation of alienation and its influence of social relations. Marx's theory of ideology is thus inseparable from the concept of alienation developed in his early writings: ideology cannot develop an adequate methodological stand-point to the study of society as an historical and sociological reality. Classical political economy combined both ideological analysis and objective scientific study of capitalism and thus produced from within its theoretical framework an empirical methodology which stressed the objective nature of economic facts and processes, while failing to comprehend the contradictions its own analysis yielded.

This complex relation of science to ideology, methodology to ideology is brought out with great clarity in Marx's analysis of the famous 'trinity' formula of 'vulgar' economics which asserted that production flowed from three factors of capital, land and labour, each constituting a separate source of value. In this formulation, writes Marx, the mystification and reification of social relations is accomplished by separating the historically specific forms of social production from the labour process, parts isolated from the whole, 'the enchanted, perverted, topsy-turvey world in which Monsieur le Capital and Madame de Terre do their ghost-walking as social charac-ters and at the same time directly as mere things'. But as with many such formulations of classical political economy, the 'trinity formula' contains elements of truth: the producers *are* separated from the means of production, the revenue forms the income of three great classes of capitalism. 'These are relations or forms of distribution for they express the relations under which the newly produced total value is distributed among the owners of the various productive agencies'. The trinity formula, however, is more ideological than scientific based as it is on an acceptance of the surface pattern of economic relations rather than the 'inner, basic but hidden essential structure, and the conception corresponding to it'. If appearance and reality always coincided, Marx notes, all science would be superfluous: the task of social science lies precisely in discovering and analysing the underlying forms, the structures of society that lead to the 'law of appearances'. Thus the critical importance in Marx's thought of *method* (Marx, 1958, pp. 500, 877, 205).

Marx's method: base and superstructure

Marx's early writings, produced within a culture dominated by the idealist philosophy of Hegel, although employing Hegelian categories such as alienation, had rejected the metaphysical abstractions and methodology of the larger philosophy. But by 1858 Marx's view of Hegel had changed and he now described Hegel's *Logic* as rendering in an accessible form 'what is rational in the method which Hegel discovered but at the same time enveloped in mysticism'. This is the distinction Engels made later between Hegel's *method* and his *system*, the necessity to extract 'the rational kernel within the mystical shell' and develop a materialist dialectic. To achieve this Marx adopted the category of totality, not as a speculative, philosophical principle, but as a methodological instrument which grasps the relations of the simple to the complex, the part to the whole.

Thus Marx begins *Capital* with the simple form of value, the exchange of one commodity for another, arguing that the commodity contains the basic contradictions of capitalism. But the commodity is also a *part* which must be related to a *whole*, a totality, capitalism as an economic, political and social system. Marx's method, therefore, opposed the atomistic approach of methodological individualism (e.g. Utilitarianism, Rationalism) as well as those philosophies which defined the concept of whole as the simple sum of its parts: for Marx, totality is structured in the interconnectedness of phenomena, facts are not isolated and external datums but internally related elements existing in a necessary relation to the whole although enjoying independence from it. 'The relations of production of every society', Marx wrote, 'form a whole' and can be understood and analysed only in this sense.

In analysing society as a totality Marx distinguished between its 'real' foundations in the mode of production (the economic base including technological and human resources) and the superstructure, the cultural, ideological and political practices and institutions. Relations of production (the ways in which production is socially organised through the division of labour, authority, law) correspond with the economic structure. Marx's model assumes an homologous relation between forces and relations of production, with the latter serving the interests of production as a whole, the primacy of economic forces subordinating the superstructure to epiphenomenal status. Hence the young Marx's statement that 'the handmill gives you society with the feudal lord; the steam-mill, society with the industrial capitalist' (Marx, 1961, p. 109). But in his mature writings Marx frequently departs from such rigid, functionalist models, emphasising that in the production and reproduction of social life the superstructural elements play a crucial role. Thus in *Capital* he notes that 'Protestantism, by changing almost all the traditional holidays into work days, plays an important part in the genesis of capital' (Marx, 1957, p. 276). The so-called 'ideal' features of society contribute to social reproduction as material forces.

In any account of the base and superstructure model it is important to distinguish objective and subjective conditions of production. Much of the confusion which has surrounded Marx's sociology is linked to a misunderstanding of his methodology which actively seeks to unify the subjective and objective nature of social reality and social analysis. In the 'Preface' to *Capital* he writes that 'in the analysis of economic forms neither microscopes nor chemical reagents are of use. The force of abstraction must replace both', and in the *Grundrisse* he argues that while the correct scientific approach superficially begins from 'real and concrete elements', actual preconditions such as population or the world market, such a procedure is wrong for the apparently concrete is in reality abstract:

Population is an abstraction if, for instance, one disregards the classes of which it is composed. These classes in turn remain empty terms if one does not know the factors on which they depend e.g. wage, labour, capital and so on. These presuppose exchange, division of labour, prices, etc. For example, capital is nothing without wages, labour, . . . value, money, price, etc. If one were to take population as the point of departure, it would be a very vague notion of a complex whole and through closer definition one would arrive analytically at increasingly simple concepts; from imaginary concrete terms one would move to more and more tenuous abstractions until one reached the most simple definitions. From here it would be necessary to make the journey again in the opposite direction until one arrived once more at the concept of population which is this time not a vague notion of a whole, but a totality comprising many determinations and relations (Marx, 1971, pp. 205–6).

Scientific method in the study of society is therefore the opposite of factual observation which always begins from the concrete and works towards the abstract; scientific inquiry does not adopt the standpoint of the raw material itself but seeks the 'inner structure' of the object by beginning from the general categories. Thus classical political economy was correct to start with population but wrong to define it as a concrete fact rather than as an abstract whole, which necessarily approximates to an ideal, general form emptied of complex and chaotic empirical material. To advance 'from the abstract to the concrete is simply the way in which thinking assimilates the concrete and reproduces it as a concrete mental category'. Thus the study of capitalism as a system must begin, not from particular capitals, competition and other elements which constitute its historic reality, but from 'capital as such', 'capital in general'. 'The introduction of many capitals must not interfere with the investigation here. The relation of the many is better explained after we have studied what they have in common, the quality of being capital . . . Capital in general as distinct from particular capitals does indeed appear (1) only as an abstraction; not an arbitrary abstraction, but one which grasps the specific differences which distinguish capital from other forms of wealth . . . (2) however, capital in general, as distinct from particular real capitals, is itself a real existence' (Marx, 1973, pp. 517, 449).

Capitalism is thus studied as an abstraction, a pure form, leaving out all the complex, historically specific complicating features, the 'appearance' as opposed to its 'inner essence or structure'. Marx's holistic methodology therefore assumes an ideal capitalism, one which is never actually present in reality, a model which is employed throughout his analysis of social change, class formation and social structure. The analysis of production, for example, is usually thought of in terms of specific persons or historical periods, but all stages of production share common features: '*Production in general* is an abstraction, but a sensible abstraction in so far as it actually emphasises and defines the common aspects and thus avoids repetition.' Marx argues that some features are found in 'the most modern as well as the most ancient epochs', but the 'so-called *general conditions* of all and every production . . . are nothing but the abstract conceptions which do not define any of the actual historical stages of production' (Marx, 1971, pp. 189–93). The relation between production, distribution, exchange and consumption can be established only by isolating the inner nature of production, the determinations common to all its forms and grasping the ways in which the historically specific elements depart from the general since in this lies the secret of their development.

Marx's method is thus to begin from a pre-given whole, such as population, production, the state, etc., and to abstract further the elements comprising the whole; then, through a process of successive approximations, relate these elements organically to the whole itself. When he writes that 'the subject, society, must always be envisaged . . . as the pre-condition of comprehension', Marx implies that no category, by itself, can constitute an adequate starting point for scientific social analysis. Both explanation and comprehension, the historical and genetic determinations of an object, together with a grasp of its inner structure and relations with the whole – the diachronic and synchronic – are unified within Marx's dialectical methodological framework. Thus, in the first two volumes of *Capital*, Marx abstracts and simplifies capitalist society to one basic relation, of capital to labour, its inner structure, arguing that if this constitutes the dominant relation then it becomes possible to determine the existence of laws, trends and the possibility of prediction. It is for this reason that any account of Marx's sociology of class, conflict and social change must relate to his discussion of methodology.

Class formation and class consciousness

In the *Philosophy of History* Hegel had argued that scientific understanding presupposed the ability of science to distinguish the essential from the inessential. For Marx, the 'leading thread' of his socio-historical-economic studies during the 1850s, led him to identify and isolate the mode of production as the basic determinant of social structure, class formation, class conflict and ideology. Marx's earlier writings had not accorded production a central role in the analysis of class formation and, in general, a simplified two-class model is postulated which derives its force, not from the concept of surplus value, but from a speculative, philosophical view of social development. In *The Communist Manifesto* the logic of capitalist economic development is described in terms of a sharp polarisation of class forces: 'Our epoch, the epoch of the bourgeoisie, possesses . . . this distinctive feature; it has simplified the class antagonism. Society as a whole is splitting up into two great hostile camps, into two great classes directly facing each other: Bourgeoisie and Proletariat' (Marx and Engels, 1962, Vol. 1, pp. 34–5).

In his polemical writings Marx frequently advanced this oversimplified model of capitalist stratification; in his more scientific and historical studies, however, this simplistic, dichotomic structure is repudiated. In his *The Eighteenth Brumaire of Louis Bonaparte* (1852), for example, Marx distinguished between the financial, industrial and petty-bourgeoisie, proletariat, landlords and free farmers, while in other studies of France and Germany he noted the existence of bourgeoisie, farmers, peasants, agricultural workers, lumpen-proletariat (the 'dangerous classes') and feudal lords. Marx describes some of these categories as 'transition classes' their existence contradicted by the necessary historical development of capitalism, a standpoint which comes close to asserting that only bourgeoisie and proletariat constitute the essential structure of capitalist social formations. But, in general, Marx never articulated a simple two-class model as an *historical* fact emphasising rather the *complexity* of class formation and structure within capitalism.

Marx's second theory of class develops the concept of plurality of structure in which the category of middle class is especially important. The middle classes are defined as variegated groups comprising small producers, petty-bourgeoisie (employers of small fractions of labour), those engaged in the 'circulation of commodities' (marketing, buying, selling), the middle men (wholesalers, shopkeepers, speculators), those who 'command in the name of capital' (managers, etc.) and their assistants, supervisors, book-keepers, clerks, and finally 'ideological classes' embracing lawyers, journalists, clergy, state officials such as the military and police. In his historical studies the simplified model of the earlier philosophical writings disappears and Marx argues that the basic tendency of capitalism is not necessarily towards class polarisation but towards augmenting the middle classes especially those performing important 'social functions' such as professional groups, since they exercise significant roles in the maintenance of bourgeois society. As capitalism develops its productive forces, this class increases in size and influence and Marx suggests that 'the constantly growing number of the middle classes which, situated between the workers on the one side and the capitalists and landlords on the other side, [living] mainly and directly on revenue . . . press like a heavy burden on the labouring class, enlargening the social security and power of the upper ten thousand' (Marx, 1964–72, Vol. 2, p. 573).

These statements clearly contradict the view that Marx's theory of class is dichotomic for he accepts Thomas Malthus's statement, in his work on political economy (1836), that the growth of the middle classes and a constant decrease in the working proletariat is in effect 'the course of bourgeois society'. But to understand these statements it is essential to relate them to Marx's methodology. The analysis of capitalism was based initially on a 'pure' model purged of all complicating historical factors such as foreign trade, monopoly, colonialism, trade unions, the role of the state, a model dominated by the capital–labour relation. In the course of analysis, throughout the three volumes of *Capital* more and more empirically specific and complicating features are reintroduced so that the model increasingly approximates to a complex, rich, concrete historically specific capitalism.

In *Capital* Marx was mainly concerned with English capitalism as the most highly developed form in the nineteenth century and his comments on class are particularly significant. He identifies three broad social classes, the owners of labour-power, capital and land, their sources consisting of revenue, wages, profit and ground rent, arguing that they constitute the 'three big classes of modern society based on the capitalist mode of production'. In England, Marx adds, although the economic structure is highly developed, 'the stratification of classes does not appear in its pure form. *Middle and intermediate strata* even here obliterate lines of demarcation'. The tendency of capitalism in its pure form is to concentrate property in fewer hands, force the middle classes downwards into the proletariat and transform all labour into wage labour. But in reality capitalist development produces a complex structure of classes and class relations. Class is never a single homogeneous unity but rather a cluster of groups, or fractions, sharing a similar work function, values, aspirations and interests. This complex structure leads to frequent conflicts within the class itself, between the differentiated interests, as in the case of revenue derived from ground rent which is common both to landowners, mine-owners as well as property owners. Thus the dominant class is never a simple homogeneous whole but consists of fractions representing different economic and political interests, such as industrial and financial bourgeoisie, officials of the state apparatus and the leading 'ideological classes' within civil society, the law, politics, journalism. Similarly, the working class is differentiated through the various branches of industry, different skills and pay, and the weight of traditions. But Marx was insistent that a class is a class only when it is conscious of its interests and organised for pursuing those interests through its own institutions. This is the meaning of his remarks on the French peasantry:

Their mode of production isolates them from one another instead of bringing them into mutual intercourse . . . In so far as millions of families live under economic conditions of existence that separate their mode of life, their interests and their culture from those of other classes and place them in opposition to them, *they constitute a class*. In so far as there is only a local connection between the small-holding peasants, and the identity of their interests *begets no community, and no political organisation*, they do not constitute a class (Marx and Engels, 1962, Vol. 1, p. 334).

The working class is thus only a class when organised for class action: 'There is one element of success the workers possess: its great numbers. But numbers will weigh in the balance only when united by organisation and guided by knowledge.' But in many ways the actual historical evolution of nineteenth-century capitalism suggested that revolutionary class consciousness would be sapped by 'complicating' elements such as Engels noted with the reformist policies pursued by trade unions. Marx's abstract, pure model of capitalism excluded any possibility of social mobility which would clearly function as a stabilising process in a context of class inequality. In volume three of *Capital*, as the analysis of capitalism approximates more closely to historical reality, Marx noted the possibility that numbers of propertyless individuals, by their own efforts and through their ability, accede to the capitalist class: 'Although this circumstance continually brings an unwelcome number of new soldiers of fortune into the field and into competition with the already existing capitalists, it also reinforces the supremacy of capital itself, expands its base and enables it to recruit ever new forces for itself out of the substratum of society . . . the more a ruling class is able to assimilate the foremost minds of the ruled class, the more stable and dangerous becomes its rule' (Marx, 1958, p. 587).

How then is change possible? The simple class conflict model postulated an inherent conflict of interests between bourgeoisie and proletariat leading inevitably to a heightening of class consciousness and the possibility of revolutionary practice. But if the course of capitalist development negates the development of a polarised class structure does this suggest that revolutionary consciousness is impossible, or at least extremely unlikely? To answer these questions it is necessary to examine Marx's theory of class in terms of his larger analysis of capitalism as a system dominated by objective laws of development.

Laws of development: the problem of historical determinism

Marx defined capitalist society as a system, a structured whole dominated by the mode of production and the contradictions generated between privately owned economic forces and collective, social relations of production. This law, which attributes social development to internal contradictions within the 'base' 'superstructure' model, is expressed in terms of the dichotomic structure of class forces in *The Communist Manifesto*, and capitalist society is characterised as splitting into two 'hostile camps' with irreconcilable interests. In *Capital* Marx discusses class at the end of the third volume and only then in fragmentary, unfinished form. His comments here will appear strange if his methodology is misunderstood, for, as I have argued, Marx is seeking the 'essential structure', the 'secret' of capitalist development, in the first two volumes of *Capital*. Marx's two-class model, 'the working class, disposing only of its labour-power, and the capitalist class, which has a monopoly of the social means of production', assumes that the 'laws of capitalist production operate in their pure form' and therefore:

1. With the labour–capital relation as the dominant element which structures the development and form of the capitalist social formation the analysis of change eliminates any active influence of the 'superstructure'.
2. The capital–labour relation is reduced to its simplest form, capitalists and workers defined as standard types 'the personifications of economic categories, embodiments of particular class relations and class interests'. The capitalist is thus portrayed as 'fanatically bent on making value expand itself' and 'ruthlessly' forcing

humanity to produce for the sake of production and the development of the productive powers of society.

The first volume of *Capital* operates at a high level of abstraction, the analysis of 'capital in general' with its assumption of society consisting solely of capitalists and workers; volume two deepens the analysis as Marx discusses the accumulation of capital, its reproduction and circulation, while in volume three 'capital in general' becomes 'many capitals', their relationships and thus capitalism as an historical–empirical reality. The abstractions underlying the first volume – commodities exchanging according to the cost of production in standard man-hours, the absence of monopoly, the appropriation of the entire economic surplus by the capitalist class (the state taking nothing), the two-class model, etc. – produce laws which must not be taken as concrete predictions about the future since they may be 'modified' by 'other circumstances' that comprise the specifically historical.

Marx's model of capitalism is a complex totality in which the 'superstructural' elements exercise an increasing role in modifying the generalisations of the first volume. This is particularly the case with Marx's concept of capitalist crisis which has frequently been interpreted as the historically inevitable consequence of economic laws working with 'iron necessity' towards intensified class conflict and social breakdown. It is true that in *Capital*, volume one, there are many passages which support this historicist interpretation, but when the concept of crisis is integrated within the context of totality a radically different view emerges:

> From time to time the conflict of antagonistic tendencies finds vent in crises . . . momentary and forcible solutions of the existing contradictions . . . violent eruptions which for a time restore the disturbed equilibrium. The contradiction . . . consists in that the capitalist mode of production involves a tendency towards the absolute development of the productive forces regardless of the value and the surplus-value it contains, and regardless of the social conditions under which capitalist production takes place; while on the other hand, its aim is to preserve the value of the existing capital

and promote its self-expansion to the highest limit (Marx, 1958, pp. 243–4).

The law of the falling rate of profit can thus co-exist with the expansion of total profit and clearly Marx does not postulate a simple breakdown theory. Indeed, his emphasis on the active role of ideology and consciousness point emphatically towards practice if a transition from capitalism to socialism is to be possible. Marx emphasises that social change is not a mechanical process which casts humanity as passive onlooker; humanity is not simply a medium through which external historical laws operate.

Yet this was Engels's interpretation in his definition of historical materialism as historical explanation which seeks the 'ultimate cause' of the economic development of society in changes within the modes of production and exchange, division of labour and differentiation of society into antagonistic social classes. Engels defined Marxism as economic determinism, the ineluctable workings of the infrastructure of society, and the abolition of the creative human subject. This is clearly an inadequate interpretation in terms both of Marx's methodological standpoint in *Capital* and his insistence on the active role of the superstructure, and thus of ideas, on the course of social change. Social development is not inevitably mapped out by the workings of economic laws since historical laws exist only through individuals, through collective human action. Of course, socio-historical laws can be analysed as objective results of extra-human forces; but this process of mystification and reification is foreign to Marx's thought. The role of the active human subject in social development constitutes the most important element in the continuity that characterises the early and the later writings of Marx. Marx's concept of diachronic historical laws is not positivist for while the positivist trend in nineteenth-century natural science exerted a powerful influence on socialist thought it was Engels, not Marx, whose formulations approximated to scientism.

In *Anti-Duhring* (1877), for example, Engels argued that 'modern materialism is essentially dialectical, and no longer needs any philosophy standing above the other sciences. As soon as each individual science is bound to make clear its position in the great totality of things, a special science dealing with this totality is superfluous. That which survives independently of all earlier philosophy is the science of thought and its laws – formal logic and dialectics. Everything else is subsumed in the positive science of nature and history'. Engels thus dismisses philosophy in favour of a 'positive knowledge of the world', a 'positive science' which effectively eliminates the active role of the subject as is evidenced in his conceptions of base and superstructure and economic determination in the last instance. Other Marxists have followed Engels's positivist interpretation of Marxism restricting it to a method and mode of investigation, a heuristic device which facilitates analysis of the relations between discrete social and historical elements.

But Marx's theory of social change cannot be assimilated to this positivist reading: the active and creative role of the subject remains at the centre of the theories of class formation, conflict and consciousness. Unlike Comte, Marx did not summarily reject philosophy and when, in the writings of the early 1840s, he discussed the necessary abolition of philosophy he implied not its total repudiation but a transition to a self-conscious practice which would realise its immanent values socially and thus free it from abstract, speculative and alienated forms. In his eighth thesis on Feuerbach he postulated the dialectical union of human cognition and practical activity, a theoretical position he maintained throughout his life's work:

> Social life is essentially practical. All mysteries which mislead theory into mysticism find their rational solution in human practice and in the comprehension of this practice (Marx and Engels, 1964, pp. 645–7).

Practice negates passive contemplation as the basic structure of philosophical and thus worldly understanding; the significance of Marx's activist epistemology for his sociology cannot be exaggerated. Unlike Comte's sociological positivism, Marx depicts humanity as the active producer of the social world which transforms the external world as it transforms itself, not as isolated individuals, or individual wills, but as members of social groups and classes.

Nevertheless, Marx's sociological analysis of capitalism tends to conflict with his liberterian epistemology. He describes the underlying tendency of capitalism *as a system* to transform active individuals into passive objects, and produce a social world experienced and understood as an external, constraining datum eliminating all sense of creative autonomy. For the mature Marx humanity was conceived precisely in its relations with this social world, and although he argues that the course of social development hinges on the objective application of science and technology to production, it is humanity which ultimately changes the world. In the *Grundrisse* he writes:

> Nature builds no machines, no locomotives, railways . . . These are the products of human industry; natural material transformed into organs of the human will over nature, or of human participation in nature. They are organs of the human brain, created by human hand; the power of knowledge objectified (Marx, 1973, p. 706).

In the same humanist spirit he describes the development of west European agriculture:

> Not only do the objective conditions change in the act of reproduction, e.g. the village becomes a town, the wilderness a cleared field, etc. but the producers change too in that they bring out new qualities in themselves, develop themselves in production, transform themselves, develop new powers and ideas, new modes of intercourse, new needs and new language (Marx, 1973, p. 494).

It is impossible to understand the relation of Marx's 'iron laws' of capitalism – the concept of capitalism as a system existing independently of the individuals who comprise it – to his emphasis on the creative, individual subject – a collective subject organised in groups – unless these contradictory formulations are analysed in terms of his theory of civil society. Marx describes capitalism as effectively liberating civil society from the domination of the state and fostering the creation of a separate and independent spheres in which the new industrial classes, the bourgeoisie and the proletariat, develop their own distinctive institutions, political organisations and modes of activity. Capitalism as a mode of production made possible an enlargement of human practice and the reality of an active subject. Although initially 'the development of the capacity of the human species takes place at the cost of the majority of human individuals and even classes, at the end it breaks through this contradiction and coincides with the development of the individual; the higher development of individuality is thus only achieved by an historical process' (Marx, 1964–72, pp. 117–18).

The fundamental contradiction in Marx's social theory lies between the centralising trends of capitalist economic forces his work outlined, and the real expansion of human freedom and autonomy engendered by these same processes which find their expression in the form of social and cultural institutions. Capitalism, as a highly centralised system of economic production, comes into conflict with its potentially democratic culture. Marx's sociology of capitalism is structured around this contradiction: as with Comte, Marx defines society as a system in which objective laws operate independently of, and frequently against, the will of individuals; yet, as Marx emphasised, capitalism makes possible human practice, control and planning, the active intervention of the human subject in historical development. Marx's concept of laws, of course, differs sharply from Comte's: laws are man-made and not natural and thus open to drastic change through human intervention. But there is a limit to effective human intervention: capitalism *as a whole* eludes conscious control and Marx, following Smith, Ferguson and Hegel suggests again and again that social development emerges from the unintended effects of economic forces and human action. Marx's sociological model, therefore, is one which incorporates human action and practice into a systemic structure of collectivist and historically necessary forces.

This is the contradiction which lies at the heart of Marx's dialectical social theory illuminating the problems of the democratic strands in the theory of civil society – that change evolves through the collective, democratic actions of ordinary individuals seeking to develop their own social, political and cultural institutions – and the strongly collectivist elements of the capitalist social and economic order which suggest the eclipse of individuality and representative institutions. Marx failed to resolve the contradictions in his thought between the historicist notion of economic necessity and his humanist sociology.

PART II
CLASSICAL SOCIOLOGY

4
Critique of Positivism: I Durkheim

Durkheim and the development of sociology

Emile Durkheim (1858–1917) has the distinction of being the first professional, academic French sociologist to be appointed to a Chair in Sociology (Paris, 1913). For Durkheim, sociology was a vocation. Almost single-handed he forced the academic community to accept sociology as a rigorous and scientific discipline. In his teaching and in his research Durkheim laid down the standards whereby sociology was to be judged. In 1895 he published the first major methodology study of sociology in which he observed that none of the nineteenth-century sociologists – Comte, Mill, Spencer – 'hardly went beyond generalities concerning the nature of societies, the relationships between the social and the biological realms' and were largely 'content . . . to make a cursory inquiry into the most general resources that sociological research has at its command' (Durkheim, 1982, p. 48.) Durkheim set himself the task of defining the object of sociology and the methods appropriate to it. His contributions to the study of industrial-isation, suicide, religion, morality and the methodology of social science aroused enormous controversy, but their influence on the development of sociology as well as other areas of social science, especially anthropology, have been far-reaching.

Durkheim began his career in sociology at a time when the French educational system was being expanded and modern-ised. This was the period which followed the national humiliation of defeat in the Franco-Prussian war (1870–1) and the German annexation of Alsace-Lorraine. The intense nationalism of the third French Republic formed the ideological context for the secular reforms carried out by the state throughout the higher educational system. Durkheim's sociology has been described as contributing to the formation of a new civic ethic, a modern republican ideology which rejected both traditional French Catholicism and a deeply entrenched social conservatism. Thus the educational reforms of the 1880s and 1890s were mainly designed to free the French university system from the grip of traditional ideological influences especially those associated with residual, pre-bourgeois social groups.

In 1887 Durkheim took up a teaching appointment at the University of Bordeaux, which was the first French university to provide organised courses in the field of the social sciences especially sociology. The teaching of social science had a practical basis in supporting the modernising ideals of educational reform. Durkheim's first courses, for example, were specifically addressed to teachers and covered an impressive range of topics from ethics, social change, suicide, the family and education to socialism and the history of sociology itself. Durkheim was particularly concerned to clarify the scientific status of sociology and clearly differentiate it from socialism. In late nineteenth-century France sociology was often regarded as synonymous with socialism and therefore hostile to bourgeois culture and values, to religion and the family and peaceful social change.

In the years between 1887 and 1902, when he became Professor of Education at the Sorbonne, Durkheim produced a series of studies which defined the nature of a scientific sociology. *The Division of Labour* (1893), *The Rules of Sociological Method* (1895), *Suicide* (1897) together with *The Elementary Forms of the Religious Life* (1912) are works in which Durkheim set out his conception of sociology as 'the science of institutions, their genesis and their functioning' (Durkheim, 1982, p. 45) in opposition to the eclectic, individualistic and often crudely journalistic approaches of other contemporary social scientists. In particular Durkheim sought to distinguish sociology, as the science which studies the objective reality of 'social facts', from psychology which he defined as the study of individual consciousness. Sociological explanation dealt with collective, not individual forces. The concept of social fact became one of Durkheim's 'fundamental principles' referring to all objects of knowledge which have to be built up, not through mental activity, but from observation and experiment. Social phenomena were external things reflecting a reality very different from the reality conceived by an individual. In the genesis of a social fact, Durkheim argued, individuals exercise a role but 'in order for a social fact to exist several individuals . . . must have interacted together' (Durkheim, 1982, p. 45).

Durkheim's definition of the field of sociology – the study of external social facts – does not necessarily imply a thorough-going positivism. Social facts were not simple objects, or things, existing independently of human consciousness and action and therefore objectively 'visible' to the observer. A social fact was a collective entity – family, religion, professional organisation – characterised by an underlying order, or structure, hidden from ordinary perception. Durkheim's sociology was an attempt to establish the pattern which lay behind all observable phenomena. Thus Spencer's 'individualism' contrasts sharply with Durkheim's 'methodological collectivism'. Social facts were thus defined by Durkheim as structures which, through their manifest forms, constrain and regulate human actions. External to the individual, social facts are 'invested with coercive power' which enable them to 'impose' their influence on individuals even against their will: 'We can no more choose the design of our houses than the cut of our clothes – at least, the one is as much obligatory as the other' (Durkheim, 1982, p. 58). Thus language is a social fact in Durkheim's sense, a system of rules which determine the nature of individual utterances although the speaker will have no knowledge of the rules that govern ordinary speech performance.

Social facts thus become internalised and rule individuals 'from within' becoming 'an integral part' of the self. In this way society enters the individual as a moral force. Sociology was therefore not the study of external facts but rather the ways in which social facts are saturated with moral elements. In *The Division of Labour* Durkheim described morality as the 'least indispensable, the strictly necessary, the daily bread without which societies cannot exist'. Sociology was concerned essentially with social cohesion and social order, the ways whereby individuals are integrated into a functioning social whole.

Thus although committed to the ideals of objective, empirical science Durkheim's work, especially in *The Division of Labour*, falls firmly within the Grand Theory Tradition of nineteenth-century social thought. His theory of the development of society from a 'mechanical' to an 'organic' type is similar to the philosophy of history which underpins the sociology of Comte and Spencer. Beginning from philosophy Durkheim was frequently brought back to its central issues in his later work; he remained extremely sensitive to the relation of sociology to philosophy, his many discussions and analyses of concepts such as anomie, social change and the division of labour are saturated with philosophical implications. The concept of social crisis, for example, is defined largely in moral terms and clearly indebted to Saint-Simon and Comte, a point emphasised in the 'Preface' to the first edition of *The Division of Labour*. It was not a question of extracting ethics from science, he argued, but rather of establishing 'the science of ethics', treating the facts of moral life according to the methods of the positive sciences. Although the study of reality does not necessarily imply any reforming commitment 'we should judge our researches to have no worth at all if they were to have only a speculative interest'. Social science must study the 'state of moral health' in relation to changes in the environment. The result, Durkehim argued, is not intellectual indifference but 'extreme prudence'; social science governs practice in that science provides 'the rules of action for the future', and by establishing the laws of society distinguishes the 'normal' and 'healthy' forms of social organisation from the 'pathological' and 'abnormal' (Lukes, 1973, pp. 87–8).

In many important respects, therefore, Durkheim remained a faithful disciple of Comte's positivism. He rejected Comte's theory of the unity of the sciences and the law of three stages as metaphysical speculation, but accepted Comte's notion of consensus and the sociologism and scientism that underpinned the fatalistic concept of the human subject. Durkheim defined society as the sum total of social facts, objective, thing-like elements, moulds 'into which we are forced to cast our actions' which resist all attempts to change and modify them by individual volition. Humanity is thus determined by things which stand outside itself for 'even when we succeed in triumphing, the opposition we have encountered suffices to alert us that we are faced with something independent of ourselves' (Durkheim, 1982, p. 70). But in what sense do social facts control human actions? As we have seen, Durkheim argued that the individual experiences objective reality subjectively acting in conformity to its constraining nature. But this formulation assumes a passive relation of subject to object, a position which Durkheim does not sustain in all his sociological studies notably *Suicide*, where he comes close to accepting that action which follows the constraining influence of social facts does so because the individual, the subject, has interpreted the external facts in specific ways. Nevertheless, there is a strong, mechanical element in Durkheim's sociology as, for example, when he argues that 'states of consciousness can and ought to be considered from without and not from the point of view of the consciousness experiencing it', a standpoint reiterated in his brief discussion of Marxist methodology:

> We consider as fruitful this idea that social life must be explained, not by the conception of it held by those who participate in it, but by the profound causes which escape consciousness; and we also think that these causes must be sought chiefly in the way in which the associated individuals are grouped. We even think that it is on this condition, and on this condition alone, that history can become a science and sociology in consequence exist (Lukes, 1973, p. 231).

Durkheim's sympathy towards mechanical materialism was clearly related to his attempt to rid sociology of the atomism inherent in other contemporary social theorists such as Tarde, but the result was a conception of society less the product of collective human labour than as a constraining abstraction. Durkheim's epistemology has the effect of splitting society into two separate structures, 'social milieu as the determining factor of social evolution' enabling the sociologist to establish causal relations, and the subjective state defined as a passive process of socialisation.

In Durkheim's writings the concept of milieu plays a crucial role. The term itself characterised virtually all forms of nineteenth-century positivism (Taine, for example) but was never adequately theorised. Durkheim's usage derived also from the natural scientist, Claude Bernard, who employed milieu as the key to analysing the internal system of living organisms, the blood system, its various fluids, their functional relations in the maintenance of a constant body temperature and thus equilibrium. It is not surprising that Durkheim's sociology enjoins the methodological principle of externality with the concept of society as an inherently equilibrating organism.

But Durkheim did not hold to a rigidly mechanical conception of society. For Durkheim society was a moral reality. Thus he was especially critical of Spencer's contractual notion of social relations in which the moral element played no part: 'The division of labour does not present individuals to one another', he wrote in opposition to Spencer's exchange theory of the division of work, 'but social functions'. Social solidarity could never flow from an atomistic concept of individuals freely pursuing their own private interests: social reality could not be defined in terms of individuals who exchange goods and services and thus contribute to social cohesion.

Durkheim firmly rejected utilitarian atomism as an adequate perspective for social science. Society was a moral fact and science must recognise this. Thus he was equally opposed to the influential work produced by the German sociologist Ferdinand Tönnies (1855–1936), *Gemeinschaft und Gesellschaft* (1887) (translated as *Community and Association*), which advanced the view that modern industrial capitalism, a society increasingly dominated by purely economic forces, was losing the authentic naturalism of earlier, pre-industrial social formations. Tönnies's depiction of modern society was one in which the cash nexus penetrated all spheres of social life determining the basic forms of social relationships. For Durkheim, Tonnies's concept of society, which largely derived from the writings of Marx and the German socialist, Lassalle, represented everything in their darkest colours, a simple dichotomy being established between the assumed spontaneous social solidarity of pre-industrial village life and the atomised, egoistic individualism of modern urban culture (Tönnies, 1973, pp. 245–7). Tönnies's analysis suggested that social cohesion and social regulation were possible only through the intervention of an external institution, namely the state.

Durkheim's early sociological writings, while defining society externally, posed the problem of social cohesion in terms which suggest that as social solidarity is moral it can never flow from above, that is, be imposed on civil society itself. Durkheim agreed with Tönnies in rejecting Spencer's notion of an immanent harmony of individual interests that by themselves promote a spontaneous cohesion, but they disagreed on the role which centralised authority must play in a modern industrial society. In this sense Durkheim's sociology was opposed both to Comte's authoritarian Positivist Church as the means of promoting social solidarity, as well as Marxist socialism with its central tenet of a centralised state functioning as the prime agency for social reorganisation and development of human communities.

It is this latter emphasis which has led some critics to argue that Durkheim's sociology was merely an attempt to combat 'the positions of the class conscious socialist movement' which had developed during the latter half of the nineteenth century (Therborn, 1976, p. 269). During the 1890s many of Marx's important writings appeared in Franch translation and a distinctive Marxist intellectual and political culture emerged. French university students formed reading groups explicitly to study *Capital*, while many of the leading academic journals discussed Marxist ideas, reviewed books on Marxism and posed the whole question of the scientific status of Marxist theory. Durkheim criticised Marxism for the class bias of its theory noting, in 1899, that the 'malaise' within modern society was not something centred on a particular class 'but is general throughout the whole of society', affecting both employers and employees although taking different forms in each case, 'an anxious and painful restlessness in the case of the capitalist, discontent and irritation in that of the worker'. State socialism was not the solution, for the crisis of modern society was not one of conflicting material interests but essentially a matter of 'remaking the moral constitution of society' (Lukes, 1973, p. 323).

Durkheim rejected, therefore, the political assumptions and theory of revolutionary socialism insisting that class conflict derived less from any basic structure within capitalism than from the necessary transition from traditional to industrial society, involving the disintegration of one set of values without their replacement by other cogent values: property ownership was secondary to this problem as was the forms of class tension. Both Marx's theoretical and revolutionary socialist conceptions, although widely discussed in French intellectual circles especially through the work of Georges Sorel (1847–1922) who at one time sought to synthesise the work of Marx and Durkheim, exerted little influence on the development of Durkheim's sociology. Nevertheless, Durkheim was acquainted with Marx's writings and followed the debate between Marxists and other social scientists with great interest although inclining to the view that the value of *Capital* lay in its 'suggestive philosophical perspectives' rather than its 'scientific' conclusions. Durkheim's understanding of Marxism, however, relied almost entirely on secondary sources and these tended to be mechanistic and positivist. The Marxist and socialist movement which developed both in France and in Germany during the latter part of the nineteenth century has been described as intellectually shallow, simplifying and vulgarising Marx's theories into a crude economic determinism. Contemporary Marxism in fact made no lasting contribution to the development of sociology being largely defined as a mistaken, although useful doctrine against which the genuinely scientific claims of sociology could be tested.

Durkheim's main thrust against Marxism was its emphasis on centralised authority as the only viable foundation of social order and therefore the assimilation of the social and the political to the economic. By 1902, in the second edition of *The Division of Labour*, Durkheim was advocating occupational associations centred within civil society as the most effective means of regulating the anomic state of modern industry, arguing that with 'the establishment of an occupational ethic and law in the different economic occupations, the corporations, instead of remaining a confused aggregate, without unity, would have to become again a defined, organised group ... a public institution'. It was only through such collective institutions that the individualistic and particular interests of modern society might be subordinated harmoniously to the general interest: 'A group is not only a moral authority which dominates the life of its members; it is also a source of life *sui generis*. From it comes a warmth which animates its members, making them intensely human, destroying their egotisms.' The relation of state and corporations, state and individuals is 'intercalated', mediated by 'a whole series of secondary groups' close to the individual and thus able to integrate him/her into 'the general torrent of social life'. It is the 'density' of these occupational groups that enables them to exercise a regulative moral role and fill the void, for without such a system of organs 'the normal functioning of the common life is found wanting' (Durkheim, 1964, pp. 26–9).

Durkheim's concept of modern society, then, separated the state from civil society, identifying the sources of social solidarity within the civil institutions. The implication of Durkheim's formulations is that without a living, vibrant and independent civic culture society as a whole must disintegrate into anarchy and anomie. There is, therefore, a contradiction between the views expressed in *The Division of Labour* that the individual is basically passive, the product of society (the standpoint of nineteenth-century positivist sociology) demanding an external mode of social regulation, and Durkheim's later views which emphasise the concept of society as constructed through the mediations of autonomous institutions which, by their very nature, are organically bound up with the individuals they effectively regulate. This subtle shift of emphasis in Durkheim's sociology is related to the whole problematic of positivism.

Durkheim's method: social facts and society

Durkheim's sociology was initially conceived within the evolutionary theoretical framework of Comte and Spencer. Society constituted an organic whole in which the various elements functioned to maintain equilibrium. Durkheim rejected Spencer's version of methodological individualism and its utilitarian postulates, as well as the prevailing atomism of contemporary French social scientists such as Gabriel Tarde. Sociological explanation, he argued, must be independent of psychology and subjective consciousness. Writing in the 'Preface' of the second volume of *L'Année Sociologique* he advocated techniques of social investigation that would establish types of laws and the interconnectedness of facts:

> The principle underlying this method is . . . that religion, juridicial, moral and economic facts must all be treated in conformance with their nature as social facts. Whether describing or explaining them, one must relate them to a particular social milieu, to a definite type of society (Wolff, 1964, p. 348).

Wholes cannot be analysed sociologically in terms of individuals: the unit of analysis is 'milieu', the collective forces and facts which thus constitute the object of social science. For Durkheim, the social was irreducible, a *sui generis*, and thus the psychological element was irrelevant. Durkheim's social realism was clearly opposed to those social scientists who adopted a voluntaristic, subjective and psychological standpoint. In his debate with Durkheim, Tarde wrote: 'I am a nominalist. There can only be individual actions and interactions. The rest is nothing but a metaphysical entity, and mysticism' (Lukes, 1973, p. 313). In *Suicide* Durkheim explicitly took issue with Tarde's sociological atomism arguing that social facts were objective datums, things which exist independently of individuals, of individual psychology and human interactions: social facts can never be reduced to another order. In 'affirming the specificity of social facts' he was following the Comtist sociological tradition: 'No further progress could be made until it was established that the laws of society are no different from those governing the rest of nature and that the method by which they are discovered is identical with that of the other sciences. This was Auguste Comte's contribution.' The social constitutes the true object of sociology and must be rigorously distinguished from other levels of human existence: the social is 'a reality *sui generis* in society, which exists by itself and by virtue of specific and necessary causes, and which, consequently, confound themselves with man's own nature' (Lukes, 1973, p. 68).

To distinguish sociology from the other social sciences Durkheim argued that sociology had its own specific object, 'a reality which is not in the domain of the other sciences', the domain of social facts. In defining the specificity of the social Durkheim identified three groups of social facts: 1) those related to the morphological structure such as the volume and density of population, territorial organisation, technology (buildings, machines); 2) social institutions, such as family, religion, political and economic institutions, involving beliefs and practices (the normative sphere); and finally, currents of opinion, collective representations, involving moral concepts, religious dogmas, political and legal rules. Social facts are external structures realised socially through individuals while remaining independent of them. Social institutions, for example, socialise both existing and future generations by inculcating and maintaining traditions and practices.

For Durkheim, the morphological level represented the most basic, constraining structure of any society, severely limiting the possibility of human choice. But as society evolves historically the expansion of institutions enables the individual to achieve varying degrees of autonomy. Collective representations further underline Durkheim's concept of social facts as modes of interaction between individual and society. To treat social facts as things, therefore, does not imply that they are things. Similiarly society is no mere aggregate of social facts but rather an organism which combines, chemically not mechanically its various elements into a higher, dynamic reality than that of simple, individual experience. Historical and objective, society is structured in 'emergent principles', a *sui generic* reality transcending the individual spatially and temporally.

The analysis of social facts demanded a sociological method both comparative and historical:

> For instance, by comparing the curve which expresses a suicide trend over a sufficiently extended period of time with the variations which the same phenomenon exhibits according to provinces, classes, rural or urban environments . . . we can succeed in establishing real laws without enlarging the scope of our research beyond a single country . . . When, on the other hand, we are dealing with an institution, a legal or moral rule . . . which is the same and functions in the same manner over an entire

country, and which only changes over time, we cannot limit ourselves to a study of a single people (Durkheim, 1982, pp 155–6).

What Durkheim called 'the supreme instrument for sociological research', the method of concomitant variations, established the principle that if two or more social facts varied together a causal relation was involved. Thus the causes of the division of labour are certain variations in the social milieu such as increasing moral density (heightened social interaction between individuals) and growing population density. For Durkheim the same effect always corresponded to the same cause. Thus 'if suicide depends on more than one cause it is because in reality there are several kinds of suicide'. Whether comparing social facts within a single society or tracing their development over time the method of concomitant variation derived causal relations internally not externally, demonstrating that 'they are joined by some inner bond'. Durkheim stressed that the sociologist should study general not isolated variations and having proved 'that in a certain number of cases two phenomena vary with each other, we may be certain that we are confronted with a law' (Durkheim, 1982, p. 151).

In these formulations Durkheim adheres to a positivistic model of sociological method, the search for causal relations and laws which exclude, as part of this process, the active involvement of human agency. At the heart of Durkheim's method is the assumption that what happens must happen: there is never any sense that some other course of action might have occurred, no possibility of alternative paths. Thus although describing social facts as modes of interaction and differentiating his method from 'materialism' through its 'application of the spiritual principle' to the study of social life, Durkheim failed to develop an open-ended voluntarism. The emphasis lay rather in the ways human action contributed to maintaining a given society.

Nevertheless, Durkheim's positivism is not that of Comte. From *Suicide* onwards he grapples with the problem of autonomy and agency, the role of ideals and morality in social life. In his account of social solidarity, for example, the key

element is the autonomy of moral action. Durkheim's sociology is permeated by rationalist principles that lead away
from his dogmatic positivism. In *The Division of Labour*, for
example, he argues that 'a mechanistic conception of society
does not preclude ideals', for demonstrating that 'things
happen in accordance with laws, it does not follow that we
have nothing to do'. Durkheim never satisfactorily solved this
dualism of the autonomy of the moral act and the determinism
of social facts and his later sociological work revolves around
this problem of human action and a constraining milieu.
Comte had remained insensitive to the human dimension of
social evolution, Vico's injunction that the social world was
the work of man; Durkheim's positivism grapples precisely
with this problem.

Both Comte and Durkheim argued that the social system
necessitated social regulation and as early as 1886 Durkheim
wrote that society must be bound together by strong social
bonds that were moral in nature. The point here is that
although society is an organism it does not spontaneously
produce equilibrium. Its normal, healthy state is one of
harmony between its various elements, but Durkheim emphasised that in the absence of a strong moral centre society must
inevitably collapse into anarchy and destruction. Sociological
positivism defines society as a system, a structure of social facts
in which unity develops only through moral action. It is in this
sense, therefore, that Durkheim's sociology is rationalistic in
that social cohesion is less the product of the workings of social
milieu than the moral dimensions of social facts themselves.
Pessimistic about humanity's possible sociability, with its
insatiable appetites and egoism, Durkheim argued that there
was nothing 'within an individual which constrains . . .
appetites'; they can be constrained effectively only by external
forces. If these are absent from the system then the result is
general 'morbidity'

What is needed if social order is to reign is that the mass of men be
content with their lot. But what is needed for them to be content, is
not that they have more or less but they be convinced they have no
right to more. And for this, it is absolutely essential that there be an

authority whose superiority they acknowledge and which tells them what is right (Durkheim, 1958, p. 200).

Social solidarity is not spontaneously produced by the internal workings of the social system. Durkheim's solution was a sociology which sought to integrate the subjective factor within his general positivist methodology. In the latter part of *Suicide* Durkheim argued that social life was made up of 'collective representations', collective symbols through which society becomes 'conscious of itself'. Society can be constituted only by the creation of ideals which 'are simply the ideas' through which society sees itself. A mechanistic, purely external concept of society he now argued, tended to eliminate its 'soul which is the composition of collective ideals' (Durkheim, 1952, pp. 312–16). Social facts are objective entities, Durkheim emphasised, but they also contain a significant subjective element which, combining within the individual's consciousness, forms representations of the social world. Collective life – social life – is thus reflected in these representations which effectively 'become autonomous realities independent of individuals' (Durkheim, 1953, pp. 23–6). Durkheim emphasised that collective representations differ from individual representations: for example, the conception of religion is more than individual feelings, rather a system which unifies states of mind, 'a characteristic way of thinking of collective existence'. In his essay on 'Pragmatism and Sociology' (1913) Durkheim noted democracy and the class struggle as further examples of collective representations, authority which imposes itself on the different members of the social group. Collective representations thus constitute the source of all human action for humanity is never motivated entirely by purely physical needs and desires but rather by residues from the past, 'habits', 'prejudices' all of which exercise an active role in social life.

Durkheim's positivism is thus shorn of its empiricist trappings: social facts were not mere external things; social reality is saturated with moral elements. In his essay, 'The Determination of Moral Facts' (1906), he identified morality with the universality of religious belief, arguing that social life itself can never 'shed all the characteristics it holds in common with religion' (Durkheim, 1953, p. 48). Morality and religion are inextricably interwoven: there has always been 'morality in religion, and elements of the religious in morality'. It thus seemed to follow that moral life, and thus social life, possesses a 'sacred character' which inspires respect, awe and obedience. 'In the beginning, all is religious', wrote Durkheim, in opposition to the Marxist thesis that social and cultural life constituted mere derivatives of economic forces, with social change the automatic product of material conditions. Social life is more than this, a moral structure consisting of universal precepts built around religious values and ideas.

Durkheim's concept of the social realm is one which diminishes the productive role of social life in the genesis of culture and ideology: as an 'organism' society is theorised ahistorically and abstractly. Hence his distinction between the 'normal' and the 'abnormal', social health from social disease. A social fact is normal if found in a society 'at the correct phase of its development' either as an effect or as an adaptation of the species to the specific conditions. Thus crime, statistically omnipresent in modern society, is normal since it functions to maintain solidarity by reinforcing collective attitudes to morality and law. The normal are those forces promoting social health, social integration with the collectivity, while the pathological reflect the breakdown of social solidarity. Durkheim's concept of sociology as a science of morals, his concern with social regulation and the possibility of community is central to his studies of the division of labour and suicide.

Division of labour, social cohesion and conflict

The Division of Labour develops a theory of historical evolution in which societies pass from a state of mechanical to organic solidarity, a process necessarily determined by the structure of the division of labour. In the 'Preface' to the first edition Durkheim noted that the origins of the division of labour were bound up with the relation of the individual to social solidarity:

111

'Why does the individual, while becoming more autonomous, depend more upon society? How can he be at once more individual and more solidarity? Certainly these two movements, contradictory as they appear, develop in parallel fashion . . . what resolves this apparent antinomy is a transformation of social solidarity due to the steadily growing development of the division of labour'. The relation of the division of labour to social solidarity is conceived in moral terms, for although fulfilling specific material needs, its existence is bound up with relations of friendship and community: Dukheim writes that the 'true' function of the division of labour is 'to create in two or more persons a feeling of solidarity'. Mechanical forms of social solidarity are defined as essentially pre-industrial; social organisation is highly undifferentiated, characterised by similarity of functions, resemblances and a common consciousness. Its morphological structure is segmental consisting of different organs co-ordinated and subordinated to a central authority, a low level of interdependence and weak social bonds, a low volume of population and material and moral density. Collective sentiments and beliefs predominate and the individual consciousness is scarcely identifiable; the social and religious are unified so that religious ideas saturate the whole society. Law is repressive, expiatory and diffuse, functioning not through specialised institutions but the whole society: 'In primitive societies . . . law is wholly penal, it is the assembly of the people which renders justice' (Durkheim, 1964, pp. 37–8, 56, 76). The essence of Durkheim's concept of mechanical solidarity is well summed up in a passage employing the collective pronoun to good effect: 'When *we* desire the repression of crime, it is not *we* that *we* desire to avenge personally, but to avenge something sacred which *we* feel more or less confusedly outside and above *us*' (Durkheim, 1964, p. 100).

Mechanical solidarity is defined as a structure of resemblances linking the individual directly and harmoniously with society so much so that individual action is always spontaneous, unreflective and collective. In contrast, the basis of organic solidarity is the division of labour and social differentiation; the social structure is characterised by a high level of interdependence, industrial development and a high volume of population and moral and material density. Solidarity through social likeness is replaced by solidarity through difference and a strengthening of social bonds. The individual is no longer wholly enveloped by the collective conscience but develops greater individuality and personality. In this situation it is necessary that 'the collective leave open a part of the individual conscience in order that special functions may be established there, functions which it cannot regulate. The more this region is extended, the stronger is the cohesion which results from this solidarity . . . each one depends as much more strictly on society as labour is more divided; and, on the other, the activity of each is as much more personal as it is more specialised'.

Initiative and individuality create a society 'capable of collective movement', one in which 'each of its elements has more freedom of movement'. Durkheim compares this form of solidarity with that of the 'higher animals' in which each organ 'has its special physiognomy, its autonomy . . . the unity of the organism is as great as the individuation of the parts is more marked' (Durkheim, 1964, p. 131). Thus the term organic solidarity refers to a system of differentiated and specialised functions unified by the relations between its various parts; the individual depends on society through a dependence on the parts which comprise it. Law is restitutive and co-operative; social norms create the legal rules which permeate civil law, commercial law, administrative and constitutional law, all of which operate through specialised organs such as administrative tribunals and an autonomous magistracy. While repressive law 'corresponds to the heart, the centre of the common conscience', restitutive law is less central and more diffuse (Durkheim, 1964, p. 112).

Durkheim's main focus in *The Division of Labour* was on the social problems engendered by the transition from one social order to another, and the problematic nature of the social bonds which united individuals with each other and with society as a whole. He praised Comte for recognising that the division of labour was more than an economic institution but was sociological and moral in its necessary relation with social solidarity, even though its practical workings had the effect of creating social disintegration and moral deregulation. Durk-

113

heim was particularly critical of Herbert Spencer's individualistic concept of the division of labour and his argument that if left to itself the mechanism of specialisation would lead to the unity of the whole. Durkheim rejected Spencer's contractual theory of society since its atomistic individualism failed to grasp that every contractual relationship involved both third parties and antecedent social norms which regulated the relationship. For Durkheim, the advance of science and industry, in the absence of universalising moral norms, must eventuate in anomie, a moral vacuum. The evolution of societies from mechanical to organic forms of solidarity would not result in the harmonious social differentiation envisaged by Spencer, but rather 'extreme moral disorder' and 'egoism' if the process remained unregulated by a consensus of moral beliefs.

Durkheim argued, against Comte, that this 'moral vacuum' was not the result of the inherent nature of the division of labour but rather the absence of a moral consensus regulating the division of labour: normally the division of work produces social solidarity, social reciprocity and shared moral values which then regulate the various branches of industry and social life generally. It is only through what Durkheim called its 'abnormal forms' with its dispersion of interests that organic solidarity is undermined. Durkheim's concept of the abnormal refers essentially to modern industry, capitalist forms of the division of labour exemplified in economic crisis and class conflict. Durkheim identified social inequality as the major source of the abnormal form arguing that 'external inequality' has the effect of threatening organic solidarity by no longer enabling natural ability to correspond with social status. For Durkheim, a normal mode of production was one in which the work of each employee of an organisation was functionally co-ordinated and unity achieved. The point here is Durkheim's assumption that given 'normal' circumstances organic solidarity is self-regulating; but if abnormal forms predominate social order is clearly threatened.

There is, however, more than structural instability within the system: although agreeing with Saint-Simon that the social crisis was essentially moral in nature, Durkheim accepted Comte's one-sided view of human nature, that humanity is basically in need of control because of 'insatiable appetites'. In

The Division of Labour and *Suicide* Durkheim couched his theory of anomie, 'normlessness', in Hobbesian terms although with one crucial difference. In the course of the eighteenth and nineteenth centuries the function of egoism in social theory changes from its polemical standpoint in Hobbes, as a criticism of residual feudal elements and ideology in favour of capitalist enterprise and values, to a moral–evaluative and negative standpoint in Comte and Durkheim. The glorification of capitalist values embodied in the concept of egoism demanded a one-sided characterisation of human nature which, in the writings of late eighteenth-century thinkers, became increasingly problematical. Adam Smith, for example, conceived egoism and altruism as two distinct components of human nature which he treated separately, egoism in *The Wealth of Nations*, altruism or sympathy in the *Theory of Moral Sentiments* (1759), a division which prompted the so-called 'Adam Smith problem' in academic scholarship based on the failure to integrate these polarities into a unified whole.

But egoism as a conservative and universal precept develops only at the end of the eighteenth and beginning of the nineteenth century in the work of Burke and Comte in which it is identified as the source of the disintegration of social bonds. Durkheim's description of modern society in terms of a 'malady of infinite aspirations', 'a thirst [for] novelties, unfamiliar pleasures, nameless sensations' and an absence of 'a healthy discipline' is moral–evaluative and not scientific, a philosophical and conservative analysis which identifies egoism with conflict and normlessness. The problem of reconciling a biological concept of human nature with a sociological concept of regulation persists throughout Durkheim's work and is particularly acute in his studies of class conflict and suicide.

In *The Division of Labour* the anomic and normless condition of modern society is linked with trade and industry, a sphere of life in which deregulation is most pronounced. Yet to describe nineteenth-century industry as 'normless' seems hardly credible: the evidence adduced by Durkheim, that an anomic division of labour was responsible for class conflict and industrial crises replacing organic solidarity, can easily be interpreted as evidence of working-class solidarity and cohesion mediated through specific working-class institutions (trade unions) expressing opposition to capitalist regimentation and inequality. A strike of nineteenth-century industrial workers constituted a 'healthy' and normal rather than 'morbid' and 'abnormal' form of social activity. That Durkheim interprets industrialisation in these terms is somewhat surprising since the basic thrust of his argument of an increasing organic solidarity in modern society suggests that co-operation and mutuality are precisely the characteristic effects of the 'true' functioning of the division of labour. Indeed, he argues that the values of individualism ('the culture of the individual'), generated by the French Revolution and Enlightenment philosophy, constitute part of the movement towards organic solidarity: the progressive emancipation of the individual from a centralised authority and culture implied a strengthening, not a weakening, of the social bonds. Thus individualism progresses in proportion to the diversification of labour and is not necessarily to be identified as egoism since the breakdown of the social bond flows only from one form of individualism. The nineteenth-century labour movement clearly represented individualism in the form of wage-labour, labour which was free and dependent on market forces; it was necessarily combined with collectivism and mutuality and the strengthening of social bonds within the working-class communities.

Anomie

What, then, does Durkheim mean by anomie? Anomie is identified with the goals sought by the individual and their possible realisation; these goals, desires, are partly biological, partly social. In general Durkheim analysed nineteenth-century industrial society as one in which norms regulating the 'getting' were either weakly institutionalised or absent. It is this absence of norms which Durkheim analysed as anomie, a situation occurring when 'society is disturbed by some painful crisis or by . . . abrupt transitions . . . In the case of economic disasters, indeed, something like a declassification occurs which suddenly casts certain individuals into a lower state than their previous one'. For Durkheim, anomie is clearly centred in the economic structure: in the sphere of trade and industry social life is in 'a chronic state' since economic development has severed industrial relations 'from all regulation', from the discipline exerted by religion, and occupational associations. Appetites have thus been freed 'and from top to bottom of the ladder, greed is aroused', aspirations are no longer effectively contained, no one recognises 'the limits proper to them'. With the growth of industrialisation desires multiply and 'at the very moment when traditional rules have lost their authority, the richer prize offered these appetites stimulates them and makes them more exigent and impatient of control. The state of deregulation or anomie is thus further heightened by passions being less disciplined, precisely when they need more discipline' (Durkheim, 1952, pp. 252–4).

For individual passions can be checked only by an authority which everyone 'respects' and to which they yield spontaneously. Only society itself possesses the power 'to stipulate law and set the point beyond which the passions must not go . . . It alone can estimate the reward to be prospectively offered to every class of functionary, in the name of common interest'. In the 'moral consciousness' of society the limits are vaguely fixed and generally accepted: the worker usually knows his position and 'realises the extreme limit set by his ambitions and aspires to nothing beyond. At least if he *respects regulations* and is docile to collective authority, that is has a *wholesome social constitution* . . . Thus an end and a goal are set to the passions'. Not that these goals are rigidly defined for some improvement is always possible but the point remains 'to make men contented with their lot while stimulating them modestly to improve it' (Durkheim, 1952, pp. 249–58).

Durkheim's discussion of anomie, organic solidarity and individualism suggest a theory of compliance with the existing society in terms of its basic institutional structure. At the same time he was critical of the failure of industrial society to achieve a 'normal' division of labour which might adequately regulate human passions and establish a 'normal' relation between natural and social inequality. Durkheim's idealised concept of the division of labour has the effect of eliminating all relations of conflict from analysis and assimilating contradictions to an underlying unity. To conceptualise social development in terms of ahistorical abstractions – mechanical and organic solidarity – is to empty sociology of historical specificity and define society less as an empirical whole but as the expression of an inner essence – the 'normal' state from which modern industrial societies deviate in terms of their lack of regulation. Thus Durkheim's sociology of industrial society oscillates between two distinct poles: on the one hand it outlined theoretically the development of complex, multi-layered social structures in which the collective forces enabled individuals to become increasingly autonomous; and on the other it failed to grasp that this process of structural differentiation is effectively a democratisation of culture, an expansion of civil society and its institutions which enabled individuals, collectively organised into unions, political parties and professional associations, to articulate specific interests which bring them into conflict with other groups, classes and the state itself. Structural differentiation in effect allows for greater participation, democratisation and activity within the institutions of civil society: anomie is thus an expression of the increasing autonomy of the human subject struggling against social forces which seek to control and repudiate his/her interests.

Durkheim had no adequate theory of the subject. He conceived evolution from one type of society to another largely as the product of impersonal natural laws; equally, he failed to understand that structural differentiation itself flows from human action, the pressures exerted continuously from 'below' the major, 'official' institutions of society, from within the culture of the broad masses. But like Comte, Saint-Simon, Marx and his contemporaries, Pareto, Michels, Weber and Mosca, Durkheim mistrusted popular democracy and feared the consequences of that process of democratisation which industrialism and the division of labour had set in motion, and which his own analysis had disclosed.

Suicide and social solidarity

Durkheim never analysed social stratification in ways which would have filled out or modified his general social theory. Instead the concept of anomie is illustrated, statistically, through his study of suicide. He intended this analysis not simply as a closely argued monograph on a specific sociological problem but as a general contribution to the analysis of the culture of industrial society.

Suicide, one of the most private and personal acts, was studied by Durkheim because although superficially a phenomenon more suited to psychological, not sociological explanation, the act itself clearly related to the problem of social cohesion and the social bonds holding society together. There was, too, the practical issue of a falling birth rate and the possibility that the family might decline in significance. 'A high suicide rate', Durkheim wrote in 1888, could - indicate a regression of 'domestic solidarity' in which the 'cold wind of egoism freezes ... hearts and weakens ... spirits' (Lukes, 1973, p. 195). Suicide had been widely studied in France, Belgium and Germany, first as a moral and then as a social problem with correlations established between the suicide rate and numerous social factors which included rapid social change, economic depression, socio-economic status, and urbanism. But the originality of Durkheim's discussion, as Anthony Giddens has pointed out, was to develop a systematic and coherent sociological theory of differential suicide rates within a sociological framework that assimilated the existing empirical findings (Giddens, 1977, p. 324). The language which Durkheim employed in his study reflects this sociological concern: the causes of suicide are linked to the state of society, currents of opinion, excessive individualism, and pessimistic currents within the culture – an emphasis on notions such as 'forces' and 'currents' which tend to disguise his concern with the socio-psychological conditions for social health. This aggressive sociological language, Steven Lukes has suggested 'was altogether less suited to what he wished to say than the language of "social bonds", attaching individuals to social goals and regulating their desires' (Lukes, 1973, p. 216).

Durkheim identified four types of suicide – egoistic, anomic, altruistic and fatalistic (this latter type is not discussed in any detail and is noted simply as resulting from 'an excess of regulations'). The types are closely bound up with Durkheim's theory of morality and social solidarity, that the degree of cohesion present in a society will generate a tendency to certain

119

forms of suicide. Suicide is social and collective; suicide proneness exists only in relation to specific social conditions. Thus the suicide current is defined externally, a social fact related to certain types of social structure. Egoistic and anomic suicide, for example, are mainly found in modern industrial societies, in social structures characterised by an absence of strong regulative norms and lack of integration. It is the currents which determine the suicide rate and in this sense Durkheim's sociological explanation was not designed to account for individual suicides. This has led many critics to point out that both the rate of suicide and the specific individual act must flow from the same cause and therefore Durkheim's account is, and must be, both an explanation of the collective as well as individual acts of suicide. Yet he insisted that the causes of suicide must be determined 'without concerning ourselves with the forms they can assume in particular individuals'. It is psychology which studies the question, *who* commits suicide; sociology studies the broad social concomitants, the social currents that determine suicide as a collective force. Durkheim was surely right to argue that to explain suicide as a social phenomena, as a unified structure with permanent and variable features, analysis could not begin from the individual suicide since such a procedure would never account for the specific statistical distribution of suicide as a whole. The individual only exists as an individual within the framework of a social whole: 'We start from the exterior because it alone is immediately given, but only to reach the interior' (Durkheim, 1952, p. 315). But while establishing suicide as an external structure, *Suicide* is, in effect, a complex and subtle study of the relation between individuals and the social whole and the mediations involved in this process, of the institutions which function to integrate individuals by attaching them to certain social ends and values, thus moderating their biological desires and appetites through social and moral regulation.

In *Suicide* Durkheim established a number of correlations between the suicide rate and specific socio-cultural elements and values. Catholic countries enjoy a lower suicide rate than Protestant countries although both religions condemn the act itself. The suicide rate decreases during wartime and in periods of political turmoil (an example of what Durkheim termed, 'acute anomie'). Married women have a lower suicide rate than single women of the same age although married women without children are more likely to kill themselves than unmarried women (an example of 'chronic anomie'). A higher 'co-efficient of preservation' characterises married women with children than childless marriages. Thus the suicide rate varies inversely with the degree of religious, political and family density. Durkheim concluded that the suicide rate was closely connected with the presence of society within individuals: anomic forms of suicide result from the failure of social norms to restrain individual passions.

He argued, then, that 'suicide varies inversely with the degree of integration of the social groups to which the individual forms a part', and that Protestants have a much higher suicide rate than Catholics for the following reasons:

1. Catholic communities possess the stronger traditions and shared beliefs conducive to an integrated 'state of society' and 'a collective life' which restrains the suicidal tendencies endemic in industrial society.
2. The causes of suicide lie in the weakening of the power of 'collective representations' through the collapse of 'traditional beliefs' and cohesive communities in the face of industrial development and social fragmentation.

Durkheim established a positive statistical relationship between the suicide rate and educational and religious institutions. The influence of education is particularly important because the more educated a social group the more it is prone to question tradition and authority. Durkheim also provided an explanation of differential suicide rates in terms of the consciousness of those committing suicide, that is, by reference to 'collective representations'.

Superficially his argument is simple: the state of society produces either strong or weak suicidal currents and the extent to which a particular individual is affected depends entirely on the nature of the social bonds and degree of his/her integration in the social group. Discussing egoistic suicide, for example, Durkheim cited evidence showing that education and suicide were closely connected in that the more educated Protestants kill themselves more frequently than the less educated Catholics. Education fosters a spirit of free inquiry and develops a critical attitude towards traditional authorities. But Jews, who are more educated than Catholics, have a markedly lower suicide rate. Now this could mean that those Jews with a higher education kill themselves more frequently than those with a poor education. Durkheim, however, did not differentiate the different layers within a social group. By so doing he might have preserved the correlation between education and the suicide rate: but this would have meant cutting across his main argument that it is the lack of integration within a religious group which constitutes the fundamental cause of suicide, and more particularly, the break with tradition engendered by education and individualism.

Durkheim argued that 'free inquiry' – 'the relentless spirit of criticism' – is especially marked among Protestants but this in itself is not the cause of suicide. The need for 'free inquiry', he suggested, has a cause of its own – 'the overthrow of traditional beliefs', the questioning and criticism of established authority:

> . . . for ideas shared by an entire society draw from this consensus an authority which makes them sacrosanct and raises them above dispute (Durkheim, 1952, Ch. 2).

High suicide rates flow from a weak social morality. And morality, for Durkheim, was closely bound up with religion. With this in mind his account of the low suicide rate among English Protestants is particularly illuminating for the statistics clearly threatened the whole thrust of Durkheim's analysis of suicide. As with the example of Jewish suicide statistics, Protestant English statistics are simply assimilated to another explanatory structure and interpreted as buttressing, not invalidating, Durkheim's argument. For the statistics are not what they seem: in England there exist laws sanctioning 'religious requirements', the power of Sunday observance and the prohibition of religious representation on the stage, respect for tradition is 'general and powerful' so much so that 'religious society . . . is much more strongly constituted and to this extent resembles the Catholic Church' (Durkheim, 1952, p. 161).

122

Durkheim offers no evidence for this assertion, but the significance of his remarks lies in the shift of emphasis from the concept of the suicide rate as a social fact, a *sui generis*, correlated closely with specific forms of social structure to a view of society that depends for its validity on the interpretation by the subject. For to argue that in England society is cohesive and regulated, that social bonds are strong notwithstanding the pervasive influence of Protestant ideology, is to postulate that this is how individuals actually perceive the social structure.

Similar problems confronted Durkheim in his analysis of Jewish suicide statistics, for having claimed an external link between the decline of traditional authority and education (the Protestants in France) he was forced to analyse these as an exception. Religious minorities, Durkheim suggested, suffering from continuous persecution, use knowledge 'not . . . to replace [their] collective prejudices by reflective thought, but merely to be better armed for the struggle'. In other words, education has a different meaning for Jews than it has for Protestants, and therefore Durkheim concluded that a high degree of education does not necessarily imply a weakening of traditional authority among the Jews. In effect, Durkheim has imported meanings into his sociological analysis to explain away statistics which cannot be adequately analysed in terms of external social facts and social forces.

The construction of meaning on the part of the acting subject is as significant for the analysis of suicide as the external determinations. Durkheim claimed, on the one hand, that suicide was a collective phenomenon characterised by a definite external structure and laws; and, on the other hand, he stressed the internal nature of such facts thus implying some notion of meaning. As was argued above, Durkheim never solved satisfactorily the dualism of internal consciousness and meaning and external socio-moral determinations. Thus in *Suicide* he failed to discuss attempted suicide which is far more common than successful suicide: attempted suicide, as a 'cry for help' constitutes a communicative act involving the construction of meaning on the part of the actor and its assumed effects on those for whom the act is intended. But Durkheim was less concerned with the subject as creator of meaning than the reactions of subjects to collective social forces; *Suicide* was a paradigmatic study of the dislocations within modern society, the implications for the human community of the collapse of social bonds. There is a strong ideological thrust to Durkheim's theory of suicide exemplified in his uncritical acceptance of official statistics, his reliance on coroners reports and their commonsense definition of suicide. The collection of suicide statistics is itself highly problematical: many social groups, for religious and social reasons, tend to under-report suicide. The statistics on which Durkheim relied were inherently biased by official definitions and method of classification, but nevertheless unproblematically integrated into his general theory.

Functionalism, holism and political theory

Although Durkheim rejected Comte's philosophy of history he accepted his attempted synthesis of science and reform. Comte's sociological positivism was based on the natural laws of social evolution governing human society and the strict application of natural science to the study of social institutions. Durkheim defined society as a social fact but also as a moral reality. As a moral structure society dominated the individual, its various parts functioning in relation, not to the individual, but to the whole. Durkheim's debt to Comte is thus clear: the holistic concept of society suggests that the basic tendency of its institutions – its parts – is the promotion of social 'health', social solidarity, stability, equilibrium. As with Comte, Durkheim defined the normal state of society as one of social harmony in which social forces work to produce conformity to the dominant norms.

By defining society as an organic whole Durkheim analysed social processes and institutions in terms of their relevant functions for the needs of the system. To explain a social phenomenon, he argued in *The Rules of Sociological Method* (Ch. 5), it is necessary to separate the 'efficient cause' which produces it from the 'functions it fulfils'. Thus in *The Elementary Forms of the Religious Life* Durkheim analysed religion in terms of its functions for strengthening social bonds and integrating the individual into society. Religious beliefs express the collective nature of society through representations, while religious rites organise and regulate its functioning. Religion expresses universal values, a role which is indispensable for the adequate functioning of all human societies. Similarly, the division of labour normally contributes to the promotion of social solidarity while both the 'forced' (specialisation being no longer based on the natural talents of individuals) and the anomic forms are abnormal in that they fail to contribute to the development of social co-operation and cohesion. Durkheim's central argument, in his studies of the division of labour, suicide and religion, was the necessity for a moral order that adequately regulated social institutions thus facilitating the promotion of social solidarity. Functions are thus explicated in terms of the 'needs' of the social system.

One result of Durkheim's holistic functionalism was a somewhat paradoxical argument of the social function of 'deviant' behaviour such as crime and suicide. Crime, for example, was 'normal' in those societies not dominated by a *conscience collective*, in which individualism has developed a sense of moral responsibility, and where some individuals will diverge from the collective norms; only in this way was moral change itself possible. Durkheim was opposed to the assimilation of the individual into the collectivity, advocating the development of personal autonomy and individual differences as the only viable basis of genuine individualism. The relation of the individual to the collectivity preoccupied his later writings as he sought to define the mediating institutions between the individual and the state. A social function cannot exist without moral discipline: economic functions, for example, are only a means to an end which is the harmonious community. Durkheim thus advocated occupational groups, or corporations, which would morally regulate economic activity and provide the basis of genuine social solidarity. In the 'Preface' to the second edition of *The Division of Labour* he described these secondary institutions as professional groupings consisting of lawyers, judges, soldiers and priests; the various industries would be governed by an elected administrative council exercising broadly similar functions to those of the old guilds such as labour relations, regulation of wages, conditions of work, promotion, etc. These groupings would also exercise a more general function, that of developing and encouraging intellectual and moral solidarity.

These proposals formed part of Durkheim's general theory that organic solidarity gradually dissolves coercive power in society so that a co-operative social order emerges regulated not by state institutions but increasingly by professional associations and their ethic of service to the community. In his *Professional Ethics and Civic Morals* (1957) he argued that these institutions were essential if the state was not to oppress the individual. The state must be subordinated to civil society although the institutions are closely related to it; state intervention is not abandoned but Durkheim's essential point was that the state could never constitute the source of moral unity for a modern complex society. It was for these reasons that he rejected Tönnies's form of state socialism, for while the intermediary institutions were largely autonomous they nevertheless were supervised by the state.

Durkheim's arguments are important because they focus on one of the central problems of sociology, that of maximising individual freedom and personal autonomy with the increasing collectivist trends of modern industrial society. A democratic society was one in which the source of moral obligation flowed out of the institutions of civil society, the source of social solidarity was immanent and not something imposed externally from above. Nevertheless, Durkheim remained within the positivist paradigm in that the mediating institutions were never defined in ways which maximised human activity and reflected popular democratic forms: Durkheim's professional associations are close to a bureaucratic structure whose function is the maintenance of social harmony; they are not institutions through which popular dissent and the conflict of interests can find expression, but the means of assimilating such elements to an underlying concern with social order. Their function is quasi-religious in the sense of expressing a system of collective beliefs and practices which command obedience, the symbols and sentiments which transform society into a community in which individual differences, while significant, are merged ultimately into a higher unity.

For Durkheim social cohesion remained the highest principle to such an extent that his notion of mediating institutions is itself collectivist, its bureaucratic implications clearly detracting from its democratic potential. There is a sense in which Durkheim's reifed concept of society finds its expression in a reifed notion of mediation. Durkheim's holistic functionalism defines society in static terms, minimising the historical basis of institutions as the products of human action in favour of institutions as things which regulate human action. Society was an organism and thus Durkheim writes of the 'pathological state' of modern society, its 'morbidity', 'pessimism' and 'abnormal', 'anomic' division of labour: the social organism has 'reached a degree of abnormal intensity'. Thus anarchists, mystics and socialist revolutionaries share a profound hatred of the present and 'disgust for the existing order' developing only 'a single craving to destroy and escape from reality'. Life is often harsh, Durkheim writes, 'treacherous or empty' and the task of sociology is to identify the means of establishing a collective authority which will regulate the degree of 'collective sadness' in society and prevent it from reaching 'morbid' heights' (Durkheim, 1952, pp. 360ff). Yet, as one of Durkheim's students, Maurice Halbwachs observed, if high suicide rates are found in all advanced societies in what sense can they be categorised as 'morbid?': 'Are all European societies unhealthy? Can a single society remain in a pathological state for three-quarters of a century?' (Lukes, 1973, p. 225).

Critique of Positivism:
II Social Action

Understanding and the social sciences: Dilthey

The dominant methodological orientation of nineteenth-century sociology was positivism: society was defined in holistic, organicist terms as a system determined by the existence of specific laws which worked to promote change and cohesion through different stages of evolution. It was assumed that a fundamental continuity subsisted between the realms of nature and society. The methods appropriate to the study of the natural sciences were thus appropriate to the study of human society and culture.

In Germany the emergence of sociology as a distinctive discipline owed much to this positivist tradition, but in striving to define its own specific methodology and concept of society many of the central assumptions of positivist orthodoxy were abandoned. The major influences on the development of German sociology were philosophers – Wilhelm Dilthey (1833–1911), Heinrich Rickert (1863–1936) and Wilhelm Windelband (1848–1915) – concerned with epistemological issues and problems of methodology in the social and cultural sciences. Towards the end of the nineteenth century positivism had become an increasingly significant current of thought within German intellectual culture. For these philosophers, the Comtist notion of sociology as the queen of the sciences represented a serious threat to the study of human action and human culture. It was argued that positivism foundered first because human society constituted a realm of unique, not recurrent, law-like processes in which human autonomy and freedom were decisive elements; and secondly, because society itself did not exist in any meaningful sense apart from the individuals who comprised it together with their unique human actions. Thus the methods of the natural sciences were considered inappropriate for social and cultural study. Effectively, therefore, the possibility of sociology as a science was rendered extremely problematic.

One of the fundamental assumptions in this critique of positivism was that the socio-historical realm could be understood only because it had been created by humanity. 'Mind can only understand what it has created', wrote Dilthey. 'Nature, the subject-matter of the physical sciences, embraces the reality which has arisen independently of the activity of mind. Everything on which man has actively impressed his stamp forms the subject-matter of the human studies' (Dilthey, 1976, p. 192). Dilthey made an important distinction between explanation and understanding: to explain an event, or an institution, assumed an external, mechanical relation between the human subject and the world of reality; explanation was conceived in terms of mechanical causation which effectively eliminated the subjective aspects of human life from the analysis. But human culture consisted also of the category of understanding, the interpretation of reality by human subjects which saturates everyday life and without which society would be impossible. Because positivism treated human subjects externally, as objective datums, it failed to integrate this element of understanding into its methodological framework.

For Dilthey, understanding and interpreting constituted the true methods of the human sciences: 'All functions are united through them. They contain all the truths of the human studies. At every stage the understanding reveals a world.' The understanding of others develops through experience 'and on our understanding of it, and on the continuous interplay of experience and understanding'. The task of the cultural sciences, Dilthey argued, was to systematise this simple form of understanding, which exists at the everyday level, into a coherent, conceptual tool that embraces the higher, complex forms of understanding.

Dilthey's distinction between the simple and complex forms of understanding is not easy to grasp: he seems to suggest that as everyday life is shaped by momentary interests everyday understanding is so determined, while complex understanding seeks to link human activity with definite goals within a broad, historical and human context. Elementary understanding, he argues, contains 'no return to the life-complex as a whole'. The simple form of understanding is that through which the individual grasps the meaning of the actions of others, a pragmatic form of understanding that differs from hermeneutical or historical understanding which seeks to interpret the meaning of culture as a whole. Understanding in this latter sense reveals a whole, not simply the isolated individual act. For Dilthey, understanding relates to the historical context seeking to link together circumstances, ends and means with the 'life-structure'. The emphasis is therefore on both explanation *and* understanding, although explanation is not defined in positivist terms. To explain is to incorporate those subjective elements in human action which orientates the individual to ends and means.

Methodologically, understanding is not simply the re-experiencing of the actions of others, the re-enactment of an individual experience. Understanding is always connected with the concept of cultural whole:

> Life consists of parts, of experiences which are inwardly related to each other. Every particular experience refers to a self of which it is part . . . structurally interrelated to other parts: interconnectedness is, therefore, a category originating from life (Dilthey, 1976, p. 211).

The historical world, out of which understanding develops, is thus defined both in terms of its constituent parts, individual experiences and interactions that constitute the source of values and purposes, and as a 'comprehensive, structural whole'. Dilthey's holism is methodological in that a totality, or a cultural artefact, can be understood only through its individual elements and their relations with the whole itself; a complete understanding of each element necessarily presupposes an understanding of the whole. Meaning, therefore, is determined by the relations of parts to whole for every experience is significantly connected with a whole as words in a sentence. Individual events in the external world have a relation to something they signify.

From these arguments it is fairly clear that Dilthey's concept of understanding is historicist: the meaning of any human act flows from the task of inserting it into an objective world of culture and in so doing elucidating its inner structure. Dilthey opposed the reduction of understanding to psychological categories and the reliving of the experience of others. Hermeneutic understanding seeks to produce *historical knowledge* – not psychologial knowledge – of the part to whole. Understanding is, therefore, not a form of empathic penetration and reconstruction of individual action and consciousness, but an interpretation of cultural forms that have been created and experienced by individuals. In this sense humanity only becomes the subject-matter of the cultural sciences 'when we experience human states, give expressions to them and understand these expressions'. The natural sciences had defined humanity as a physical fact apprehended through the senses; the cultural sciences – the moral sciences, *Geisteswissenschaften* – mould their subject-matter by seeking to penetrate the subjectivity of humanity (Dilthey, 1976, p. 175). Dilthey includes history, economics, politics, literature, music, aesthetics in the category of the cultural sciences, but not, significantly, sociology. The study of contemporary society is subsumed under history: sociology is identified with the naturalistic positivism of Comte and Spencer, the reduction of historical reality and culture to mechanistic laws and materialist concepts which excluded the category of understanding. It must be emphasised that Dilthey was not opposed to empirical method and his critique of positivism was directed against its assimilation of complex human experience to deterministic external processes. It is impossible, he argued, to integrate the category of meaning into a methodology that emphasised the externality of the social and cultural world. Human actions and experiences were not external datums but idiosyncratically subjective and formed part of a humanly created historical whole.

Dilthey's separation of the natural from the cultural sciences was a distinction between what Windelband called the *nomo-*

thetic sciences, concerned with establishing general laws, and general phenomena, and the *idiographic* sciences which were concerned with unique and unrepeatable events. Rickert further developed this distinction by equating the scientific with the *nomothetic* methodology and the cultural with the *idiographic* methodology. The essential difference between the sciences was defined not so much in terms of subject-matter or content, but rather in terms of their distinctive method: as an individualising method, the cultural sciences were concerned with the analysis of reality in terms of values not laws. Rickert emphasised that the cultural sciences explored questions of meaning in relation to the concept of culture as something produced through human action and thereby saturated with human values. The methodology of the cultural sciences was individualising and related to values (what Rickert termed, 'value-relevance'). In contrast, the natural sciences investigated objects separated from values. The cultural sciences should, however, avoid value-judgements seeking merely to relate objects to values. It was this concept of value relevance – or value-relatedness – which played an important role in the development of Weber's interpretative sociology. Rickert did not imply the necessity to make *a priori* judgements on the value of cultural elements or actions, only that cultural forms can be analysed in terms of the values of the culture of which they form part.

In general Rickert was concerned with method. To interpret socio-cultural phenomena in terms of value and meaning did not mean abandoning causal analysis:

> History, too, with its individualising method and its orientation to values, has to investigate the causal relations subsisting among the unique and individual events with which it is concerned. These causal relations do not coincide with the universal *laws* of nature, no matter how far general concepts may be required as constructive *elements* of historical concepts in order to represent *individual causal relations*. The only thing that matters is that the methodological principle governing the selection of what is *essential* in history involves reference to values even in the inquiry into *cause* (Rickert, 1962, p. 93).

Rickert's opposition to universal laws of nature, and the teleology this implied, was shared by Dilthey. But Rickert differed sharply from Dilthey over the question of causality within the historical and social realm. Yet if understanding is to be linked with explanation, as Dilthey seems to suggest, then it clearly demands the kind of causal analysis that was to be proposed in the sociology of Weber.

Formal sociology: Simmel and sociation

Rickert had argued that the object of study in the cultural sciences must be constructed by the researcher through methodology; he rigorously opposed the 'naive realism' of historians by postulating a concept of reality as formless and chaotic unless ordered through theoretical categories. One result of this standpoint was to empty the concept of society of all substance other than unique individuals who comprised it. Society was no objective datum governed by laws of development, no whole exercising ontological priority over its parts. Society was defined in nominalist terms and in the sociology which emerged out of the methodological debate over the status of the cultural sciences the categories of understanding and the human subject lay at its centre.

Although important differences distinguish the sociology of Ferdinand Tönnies (1855–1936) and Georg Simmel (1858–1918), they shared a common humanist notion of sociology defining its subject-matter as forms of social interaction between active human subjects and arguing that the structure of such action always involves complex cultural meanings. It was not, therefore, a question of individuals as such, but of the ways in which individuals act socially: thus Simmel rejected the positivist argument that society constituted an objective system dominating its members; Simmel defined society as an intricate web of multiple interactions and relations between individuals which embody the principle of sociation. Society consisted of individuals connected by interaction; institutions such as the family, religion, economic organisations and bureaucracy constituted the forms taken by the social content of such interaction. The object of sociology was thus sociation.

Tönnies equally rejected the organismic holistic concept of society and sought to differentiate sociology from other disciplines especially biology and psychology. The sociological perspective, he argued, was concerned primarily with the facts of 'reciprocal affirmation', of social relations as mutual relationships in which each individual 'makes and asserts a claim to a certain – regular or occasional, more or less permanent – conduct of the other person or persons'. Tönnies argued that all apparent non-rational thought and action implied a meaning 'reducible to human volition'. The social, he concluded, flows from human action, from the intentions of human subjects to relate to one another. Social reality, therefore, exists only in the sense of being perceived, experienced, known and willed by individuals (Tönnies, 1971, p. 89).

Both Tönnies and Simmel attempted, on the basis of this humanist standpoint, to develop a 'pure' sociology in which concepts such as Tönnies' *Gemeinschaft* and *Gesellschaft* provided the necessary order to the variety and complexity of empirical reality. Tönnies' concepts clearly do not refer to existing societies; they do not describe objective facts, but constitute abstractions from 'real situations', from the facts of social interaction. All societies are characterised by elements from both *Gemeinschaft* and *Gesellschaft* but as concepts they are purely formal, ideal types essential for the sociological analysis of historical reality. This is one of the fundamental themes of Simmel's sociology through which he opposed the positivist assumption of laws of social development and thus concepts which reflected this necessary process.

Simmel's work covered an enormous range of topics and issues, including problems of methodology in the social sciences: *Problems of the Philosophy of History* (1892) which influenced Weber's work on methodology, 'The Problem of Sociology' (1894), 'How is society possible?' (1908) 'The Field of Sociology' (1917); contributions to cultural theory – *The Philosophy of Money* (1910), *Philosophical Culture* (1911); and essays and studies in philosophy, music, literature, fashion and general problems of aesthetics.

His first important sociological work, *On Social Differentiation*

(1890), was written under the influence of Spencer and positivism, although the central argument that society progresses from a state of undifferentiated group existence to a condition in which human autonomy and individualism are possible, because of differentiated social structures, remained a significant element in the later anti-positivist and anti-evolutionary sociology. Yet even in Simmel's early writings the influence of Dilthey was marked. Dilthey had defined society in terms of interactions and the individual as an element in the various systems of interaction. Simmel criticised Dilthey, however, for dismissing the claims of sociology on this basis, that society was merely individuals interacting with each other. Simmel sought to define this principle of interaction sociologically by conceptualising society in terms of forms. In the *Problems of the Philosophy of History* he defended the notion of man as the cognitive subject whose actions produce the historical world. Historical knowledge is possible, not as a simple reflection of an external reality, but as a form of human experience. The world itself becomes an object of knowledge through the analysis of forms (Simmel, 1977, pp. 16–18, 60–1). What Simmel meant by form was a category, or number of categories, through which the world of experience becomes transmuted into a taxonomy, a conceptual scheme with both epistemologcal and ontological status. Law, sexuality, society are thus forms in this sense. Forms provide coherence to the world of diverse and incoherent objects: Simmel suggests that the concept of form is immanent and can never be deduced from the context or from the artefact (Simmel, 1980, p. 6).

Thus for Simmel the problem of social reality was solved by recourse to Kantian philosophy. Kant had argued that knowledge was possible only through the immanent categories of the mind and not by reference to experience and context. Similarly, Simmel argued that social reality becomes meaningful only through the organising principles associated with specific, universal forms. It followed that science did not develop out of content, which was merely random, objective facts pertaining to experience; rather, science always implied interpretation and ordering according to concepts which remain *a priori* for the different sciences. In the elaboration of science, concepts have priority. There are no objective laws, no totality. Simmel rejects the hypostatised notion of society found in Comte and Spencer in favour of an active, ceaseless interaction of many elements that constitute a complex structure. Simmel was opposed to those modes of sociology which reifed society, defining it as a reality external to the individual and existing as if it had a life of its own separate from human action. The concept of form enabled Simmel to analyse institutions and social processes objectively while retaining the notion of the active human subject. Sociation did not imply isolated individuals who lack development and therefore interaction. Without forms there is no society; forms inhere in reality itself although reality in its empirical immediacy is structureless. It is only through what Simmel calls the 'great forms' that the complex reality of human society is rendered intelligible.

There is, therefore, a structure, or order, which expresses itself in sociation. Form is rigorously separated from content. Simmel writes:

> I designate as the *content*, as the *material*, as it were, of sociation. In themselves, these materials with which life is filled, the motivations by which it is propelled, are not social. Strictly speaking, neither hunger nor love, neither work nor religiosity . . . are social. They are factors in sociation only when they transform the mere aggregation of isolated individuals into specific forms . . . subsumed under the general concept of interaction. Sociation is the form . . . in which individuals grow together into units that satisfy their interests (Simmel, 1950, p. 41).

It is these reciprocal forms of sociation which constitute the object of sociology, not individual actions or isolated elements which Simmel identifies as the content or material of sociation. Through the forms of sociation individuals develop into a unity; love, purposes and inclinations become transposed from individual properties into the social through their realisation in forms. Forms of sociation include hierarchies, corporations, marriage, friendship; forms do not produce society, forms *are* society. If all interaction ceased then society itself would no longer exist. Simmel's distinction between form and content enables him to argue that although the content of institutions and actions may vary, the forms remain. Thus the form of sociation among a band of robbers may be the same as that characterising an industrial enterprise; economic interests may be realised in forms of competition as well as co-operation. Power becomes a sociological form through a structure of interaction which links the dominator and the dominated: absolute power, for example, always involves an interaction, an exchange between the action of the superordinate and the subordinate.

Perhaps the best known of Simmel's forms is the dyad which he defines as a relation of two individuals involved in immediate reciprocity. The dyadic form can comprise different contents such as teacher/student, doctor/patient, husband/wife, etc., but its essential character hinges on the dependence of the whole on each individual: the withdrawal of one destroys both the relation and the whole itself. But should another individual join the group creating a triad a qualitative change occurs in which there is no longer immediate reciprocity but mediation. The dyad is not experienced as a supra-individual element, a collectivity; in contrast the triad is experienced as a social structure standing outside and independent of the individual.

In these formulations Simmel opposed the reductionism of psychology which failed to grasp the sociological fact that a change in the forms of sociation, a change in numbers, necessarily engendered the development of new properties which cannot be derived from studying the individuals alone. Similarly, in his discussion of secrecy, which he describes as 'one of man's greatest achievements', Simmel analysed it as a form which enhances, not diminishes, human life in that it produces an intimate, private world alongside the public world, a world in which the exclusion of outsiders leads to a heightened sense of moral solidarity on the part of those who share the secret. But as secrecy is surrounded by the permanent possibility of detection it therefore generates tension between the individual's capacity to keep the secret or a weakness to reveal it: 'Out of the counterplay of these two interests, in concealing and revealing, spring nuances and fates of human interaction that permeate it in its entirety ... every human relation is characterised, among other things, by the amount of secrecy that is in and around it' (Simmel, 1950, pp. 118–20, 330–4).

The task of sociology, as Simmel formulated it, was thus to identify the 'pure forms' of sociation and engage both with the uniqueness of historical phenomena and the underlying uniformities. Society is the product of human activity in the sense that society is sociation, and sociation itself exists at the level of ordinary everyday life as forms which bind individuals together. Forms have no separate reality apart from content in the same way as the individual has no separate reality from society. Individuals create society and forms; and simultaneously exist externally to both. The individual's relation with society is dualistic, both within and outside it, 'both social link and being for himself, both product of society and life from an autonomous centre' (Simmel, 1956, pp. 22–3). Without sociation the human subject could hardly exist; but the forms of sociation restrict his autonomy. Simmel's concept of society is one built around the dualisms of human existence: sociation entails conflict and harmony, attraction and repulsion, hate and love, independence and dependence. Clearly this is a different sociological standpoint from the nominalism of Tarde: society is not conceived in atomistic terms but is structured through forms that realise both the individuality and regularity of human action.

Nevertheless, Simmel emphasised that human existence is real only in individuals and that to confine sociology to the study of 'large social formations resembles the older science of anatomy with its limitation to the major, definitely circumscribed organs such as heart, liver, lungs, and stomach, and with its neglect of the innumerable . . . tissues'. The study of major social formations constitutes the traditional subject-matter of social science, and by accepting this approach 'the real life of society as we encounter it in our experience' would play no role in sociological analysis (Simmel, 1965, pp. 312–32). The object of sociology is interactions 'among the atoms of society', and in his essay, 'The Problem of Sociology', Simmel rejected the notion that sociology was defined by its contents. Sociology was neither a dumping pot for the other human sciences, history, psychology, jurisprudence, nor a summation of other disciplines. Sociology was defined as a distinctive method, an instrument of investigation: 'In so far as sociology is based on the facts that man must be understood as a social being and that society is the medium of the historical process, it contains no subject matter not already treated in one of the existing sciences.' The study of form clearly distinguishes sociology from the other sciences: thus sociation constitutes a form stripped of all psychological, biological and historical elements and although these latter disciplines are useful in the description of facts they always 'remain outside the purpose of sociological investigation'. As forms are not reducible to, or defined by, their content so sociology is conceived in terms of the categories of its analysis and perspective. Sociology abstracts from the complexity of social life that which is 'purely society', that is, sociation. The sociological approach is therefore its mode of abstraction, the means whereby the essential features of concrete phenomena are extracted from reality and exaggerated so that the underlying configurations and relations, which are not actually realised in reality itself, are clarified. In this way it becomes possible to compare social phenomena that have radically different contents but share a similarity of form (Simmel, 1965, pp. 312–32).

The purpose of these 'ideal types' is to facilitate the analysis of meaning. In his discussions of forms such as the dyad, secrecy and fashion, Simmel's main concern is always with the meanings of the actions that comprise the structure, understanding the modes of sociation from the standpoint of both the subject and the whole. Social interaction is always more than the sum of the actions, involving both the form or structure as well as the relations within the form itself. Society is not analysed from a holistic standpoint but from the perspective of social interaction conceived as a network of hidden relationships.

Simmel's sociological approach has been characterised as a form of sociological impressionism, the network of interrelationships constituting a labyrinth rather than system, his sociology dismissed for its failure to develop a constructive view of society as a whole. But the significance of Simmel's sociology lies precisely in the fact that it opposed the anti-humanist, scientistic approaches of positivism and vulgar Marxism and sought to recover the concept of society as the product of socially mediated human action. Thus forms explain the resilience of human society, its toughness, elasticity, colourfulness, 'so striking and yet so mysterious', the interactions that constitute sociation producing the social bonds which 'makes for the wonderful indissolubility of society, the fluctuations of its life, which constantly attains, loses and shifts the equilibrium of its elements' (Simmel, 1965, p. 328). The point is, of course, that Simmel *was* concerned with society as a whole, with large-scale social formations, but not as external structures stripped of their human determinations. Simmel's sociology rejected all modes of reifying social institutions and processes for while forms are external to individuals they only *appear* as autonomous entities. 'The deepest problems of modern life', he wrote, 'derive from the claim of the individual to preserve the autonomy and individuality of his existence in the face of overwhelming social forces, of historical heritage, of external culture, and of the technique of life' (1950, p. 409).

Simmel had developed a sociological perspective which exerted a great influence on subsequent German sociology especially that of Max Weber. Although Durkheim's *The Rules of Sociological Method* was translated into German and published in 1904, it had little impact and it was Simmel's notions of understanding, social action and methodology which triumphed. Durkheim's *positive* sociology contrasts sharply with Simmel's *ambiguous* sociology. In a review of Simmel's work written in 1900 Durkheim had drawn attention to what he considered an entirely arbitrary distinction between form and content: but Simmel constantly emphasised the impossibility of rigorously distinguishing form and content. It is 'impossible to avoid ambiguity', he wrote, 'the treatment of a particular problem will appear to belong now in one category, now in another'. Ambiguity even extended to methodology and Simmel argued that there existed no clear technique for the application of his fundamental sociological concept of sociation (Simmel, 1965, p. 324). It was the implication here of the arbitrary nature of sociological method, as well as the ambiguity over form and content, which clearly differentiated Simmels's humanist sociology of modernity from the nineteenth-century positivist tradition and it was these themes which were further developed in Weber's sociology.

Understanding and the problem of method: Weber

The sociology of Max Weber (1864–1920) sought to synthesise the positivist emphasis on causal analysis with the hermeneutic concept of understanding. Although Weber shared with Simmel a concern with integrating the human subject into the cultural sciences within a social action framework, he differed from Simmel in his emphasis on macrosociological studies of institutions and processes conceived from a broad historical perspective. Both were concerned with the fate of the individual within modern culture, but whereas Simmel focused his analysis on the atoms of society Weber dealt with such holistic categories as the Protestant ethic, pre-industrial social structures, bureaucracy and the nation state. The range of Weber's empirical and historical studies is truly encyclopaedic covering economic history, political economy, the comparative study of religions, and the methodology of the social sciences.

Originally trained in jurisprudence and the history of law, Weber's first studies examined the structure of East German agriculture and the recruitment of Polish workers; in 1896–7 he published studies of the decline of the ancient world and the stock exchange. At the outset of his intellectual career Weber was not a sociologist and rarely used the term in his first writings. At university he lectured on law and political economy and at the age of thirty-one became Professor of Political Economy at Freiburg before moving to Heidelberg in 1896. Weber thus came to sociology from economics and history; his early sociological writings reflect a concern with the methodological and epistemological issues raised by the positivist intrusions into German historical scholarship during the latter part of the nineteenth-century. German social science had been strongly influenced both by the evolutionary theory of society conceived by Comte and Spencer, as well as the burgeoning Marxist intellectual culture that emerged in the 1890s. Under the leadership of Karl Kautsky and Eduard Bernstein, the German Social Democrats became the single most important Marxist political party in Europe commanding widespread support from the German working class. The rise and institutionalisation of German sociology effectively co-incided with the development of a political mass movement committed to Marxism and an intellectual culture which attempted to systematise Marxist materialism into a coherent science of society. Weber's sociology developed both as a response to evolutionary positivism on the one hand and to dogmatic Marxism on the other.

Weber defined Marxism as a form of economic determinism, a theory postulating a strict functional relation between modes of thought and economic interests: ideas, whether they were religious or political, were merely epiphenomena lacking any vestige of autonomy. For Weber, Marxism defined knowledge as ideology, as the reflection in consciousness of class and economic interests: concepts were scientific in so far as they reproduced this objective reality while pointing the way forward to the historical inevitability of socialism and communism. Society was thus a system dominated entirely by its mode of production and laws of development. Human subjects exercised no constituting role but were the passive objects of an historically evolving whole.

Weber's opposition to the concept of objective determining laws was based on the argument that such laws – whether Marxist or positivist – eliminated the active and conscious elements of a culture transforming all ideas to the status of automatic reflexes of external, material forces. Like Simmel, Weber adopted a nominalist standpoint arguing that holistic and collectivist concepts such as the state, corporation, and bureaucracy could be analysed only as the results and modes of organisation embodied in human action. Bureaucracies do not act. The burden of his early methodological essays is to demonstrate that the fundamental task of social science lies in analysing society as a structure of meaning-endowing actions centred on the human subject.

In his essay, 'Objectivity in Social Science' (1904), Weber outlined his approach in terms of understanding 'the characteristic uniqueness of the reality in which we move', a reality which consists in 'an infinite multiplicity of successively and co-existing emerging and disappearing events, both "within" and "outside" ourselves'. The study of so-called objective laws, or the relations between the various external elements that constitute a social system, does not, by itself, generate meaning. Weber insisted that the category of meaning is produced only through social action when the acting subject attaches a subjective meaning to behaviour. For Weber, history possessed no immanent meaning as historicists had suggested: history is simply the human context in which individuals and groups struggle to define and achieve certain values and goals. Weber followed Nietzsche's stoic refusal to accept the existence of universal values: there is no meaning apart from the concrete actions of human subjects (Weber, 1949, p. 72).

Weber defined society in terms of sociation, 'social relationships' which 'denote the behaviour of a plurality of actors in so far as, in its meaningful content, the action of each takes account of that of others and is oriented in these terms'. Social action is oriented towards human subjects not things, the acting individual saturating the social context with meanings. This concept of social action assumes intentional behaviour involving motives and feelings; sociology as a cultural science is thus concerned with meaningful action rather than with purely reactive or mechanical behaviour. Sociology is defined as a science 'which attempts the interpretative understanding of social action in order . . . to arrive at a causal explanation of its course and effects' (Weber, 1964, p. 118). Explanation is interpretative in the sense of seeking to understand the meanings of the actor through empathy, and causal in the sense of seeking to relate the action to means and ends. Weber did not define sociology as a subjective, intuitive mode of investigation: because human action is subjective it does not follow that it is unpredictable. Social action hinges on the subject selecting means to realise specific ends and it is this rational component which separates human action from natural processes. Action which is social is thus governed by norms relating to the means–ends continuum and it is this patterned aspect of social action that Weber identifies as the element enabling the sociologist to undertake causal analysis (Weber, 1964, p. 88).

Objective knowledge, then, is possible within the cultural sciences; the fact that the object of study is cultural values does not imply a subjectivist sociology. Weber distinguishes evaluation (*wertung*) from value-relatedness or value-relevance (*wertbeziehung*) to emphasise the point that social phenomena have significance only through their relation with a specific value system which will clearly influence the ways in which the scientist selects the object of study but not the analysis of it. Ethical neutrality forms an essential element of a valid social science, and Weber stresses that the social scientist must never impose his own values on the mode of investigation and interpretation of empirical material. Cultural science cannot evaluate ends only render explicit those ideas which underpin the ends themselves. 'It is self-evident that one of the most important tasks of every science of cultural life is to arrive at a rational understanding of these "ideas" for which men either really or allegedly struggle' (Weber, 1949, pp. 53–4). The task of social science is not to pass judgments but to isolate the structure of values within a given social context and demonstrate the relevance of these values for an objective understanding of social action. Interpretative understanding (*verstehen*) and causal explanation are essential modes of analysis for the attainment of scientific, objective knowledge. The subjective meaning of social action is grasped through empathy and reliving, but unlike Dilthey, Weber's interpretative understanding becomes scientific through its integration into objective, causal explanation. Thus Weber criticises Simmel for his failure to distinguish between subjectively intended and objectively 'valid' meanings which are often treated 'as belonging together' (Weber, 1964, p. 88).

Culture is the realm of values but 'empirical reality only becomes "culture" to us because and in so far as we relate it to value ideas'. Culture in this sense includes those elements which are significant because of their value relevance and it is impossible to discover 'what is meaningful to us by means of a "presuppositionless" investigation of empirical data'. Weber's argument is that not everything within culture is worth investigating for 'only a small portion of existing concrete reality is coloured by our value-conditioned interest and it alone is significant to us' (Weber, 1949, p. 76). The positivist separation of facts and values is here clearly articulated, the choice between values regarded as a matter of faith not of science. But to accept the existence of certain values which predispose the researcher to the selection of the essential from the non-essential segments of reality and on this basis develop a methodology is to ignore the problem of ideology. Weber's standpoint is agnostic positivism, the acceptance of differing and possibly antagonistic cultural values (although this aspect is never adequately discussed). Thus he argues that in order to make sense out of the flux which is reality, a concept must be 'highly selective' and valid only 'within the scope of its own postulates'. Weber writes:

> Life with its irrational reality and its store of possible meanings is inexhaustible. The *concrete* form in which value relevance occurs remains perceptually in flux, ever subject to change in the dimly seen future of human culture. The light which emanates from these highest evaluative ideas always falls on an ever changing finite segment of the vast chaotic stream of events, which flows away through time (Weber, 1949, p. 111).

Totality has been eliminated from social theory; there is no whole, no 'essence' to history and society, but a constantly fluctuating culture of meaning-endowing social actions; social relationships are conceived in inter-subjective terms as embodying purposive activity. Social structure is therefore the product of action and social collectivities such as bureaucracy, corporations, and states treated as results of subjectively understandable action. Weber thus rejects the methodology 'which proceeds from the whole to the parts' arguing that this can accomplish only a preliminary analysis of reality: as there is no external, objective social world determined in its structure by laws of development so there is no correspondence between scientific, sociological concepts and an objectively 'real' datum.

Sociological concepts are pure types which do not reflect reality but, through the processes of abstraction and selection governed by value-relevance and significance, embody the essential elements of different phenomena. Weber's ideal types are in effect Simmel's pure forms, analytical constructs enabling the researcher to make comparisons with many different phenomena which, although characterised by different content or material, belong to the same form. These forms are constituted through action. As there are no objective laws governing society so action must be defined in terms of 'probability' rather than 'necessity' and the structure of sociological concepts built around this probabilistic perspective.

Ideal types and social action

Weber's sociology sought to combine explanation with understanding; social action was both subjective and objective; but subjective understanding was the specific characteristic of sociological knowledge. Weber did not advocate intuitive understanding, for human relationships enjoy regular and consistent patterns so that causality can be defined but only in terms of probability. Probability refers to the chances that in specific contexts human subjects will orient their behaviour to certain norms so that a given observable event will be followed, or accompanied, by another event. Social action is always probable rather than certain because the unique nature of social relationships generates the possibility of deviation from the expected course of action. The ideal type is the means of analysing the probability that actors will follow one course of action rather than another.

Ideal types are concerned with the subjective elements in social life, those unique and unrepeatable elements of culture disregarded by positivist social theory. Ideal types involve selection,

> . . . the one-sided accentuation of one or more points of view and by the synthesis of a great many diffuse, discrete, more-or-less present and occasionally absent concrete individual phenomena which are arranged according to those one-sidedly emphasised viewpoints into a unified analytical construct (Weber, 1949, p. 90).

The ideal type is no description of reality but a mental construction which incorporates the essential, not the average, properties of a particular phenomenon. The term ideal type implies no moral standpoint; it is a methodological concept which facilitates the understanding and explanation of social phenomena. It neither corresponds with an external objective reality nor constitutes 'essence' in the manner of an Hegelian 'spirit'. Ideal types are pure forms; some of its features will therefore be absent from its concrete forms. For Weber, ideal types were tools of analysis, their value purely heuristic, a mode of 'revealing concrete cultural phenomena in their interdependence, their causal conditions and their significance' (Weber, 1949, p. 92).

146

Weber's method is thus to construct unreal relations in order to analyse real historical relations; reality is known through concepts and abstractions. He identified three distinct ideal types: historical formations such as modern capitalism and the Protestant ethic characterised by their specificity; abstract ideal types such as bureaucracy and feudalism which characterise different historical and cultural periods; and finally, types of action. The level of abstraction varies with each of these ideal types although Weber argues, as we have seen above, that social formations and large-scale institutions always designate categories of human interaction and that the role of sociology is to reduce these concepts to understandable action, to the actions of participating individuals. He identifies four types of social action:

1. Rational action (*wertrational*) oriented to the attainment of an absolute value which may be aesthetic, religious, ethical; the goal is pursued for its own sake and not because of the possibility of success.
2. Rational goal-oriented action (*zweckrational*) in which goal and means are rationally chosen.
3. Affectual action determined by the emotional effects on the actor.
4. Traditional action which is guided by custom and habit.

These four types of social action are defined in terms of their distance from the borderline of meaningfully oriented action: thus *wertrational* and *zweckrational* action both involve some measure of conscious choice in ends and means while affectual and traditional action approaches the borderline of purely reactive behaviour. Weber was especially concerned with rational action, rationality being defined exclusively in terms of the means not the ends, the latter being outside the province of science.

For Weber, action governed by rational norms is always more predictable in its possible effects than so-called irrational action. The more a value is absolute so the action corresponding to its achievement becomes irrational for 'the more unconditionally the actor devotes himself to this value for its

own sake, to pure sentiment or beauty ... the less is he
influenced by considerations of the consequences of his
actions'. The norm of rationality against which all social action
is measured is the ends–means relationship, the goals defined
by the acting subject as well as the choice of means necessary to
attain them. Rational action is social action in so far as the
subject must take account of others in his course of action.
Rationality and irrationality – irrationality being deviations
from the rational norm – are structured, therefore, in the
concrete, existing situation, the world as it is, the world of
human experience. Weber, here, approaches a positivistic
standpoint. The ideal type, which does not exhaust all the
possibilities of a particular phenomenon is the conceptually
pure form to which actual action closely approximates, the
classification being useful only in terms of its results (Weber,
1964, pp. 117–18).

Weber is arguing, then, that sociology seeks to formulate
type concepts and generalisable uniformities: human behaviour, whether external or internal, displays relations and
regularities which are understandable in terms of the cultural
significance attached to them by the acting subject. Sociology is
both interpretative understanding of the complex structures of
meaning of typical social actions *and* causal explanation based
on the probability that one event will be followed by another.
Ideal types must therefore be constructed both in terms of their
'adequacy on the level of meaning' and causal adequacy.

The sociologist must interpret the meaning of social action as
rigorously as those explanations which are offered in the
natural sciences. Weber's distinction between the methods of
the natural and the social sciences does not imply that the social
sciences are less scientific, less objective and do not offer
grounds for verifying hypotheses. Objective knowledge and
certainty constitute the aims of sociology even though the
nature of reality as defined by Weber makes it virtually
impossible to achieve these ends. In analysing social action it is
not necessary to invoke any mode of intuitive understanding or
seek to grasp the whole of a person's experience: one does not
have to be Caesar in order to understand Caesar. Weber's
concept of understanding differentiates behaviour from action,

the former lacking subjective meaning being simply habit or reactive behaviour, and he postulates two distinct modes of understanding: direct, observational understanding and explanatory or motivational understanding. By direct understanding Weber means explanation in terms of observable, objective properties within a given context and which are immediately understandable, such as the action of someone chopping wood, or the writing down of the formula $2 \times 2 = 4$; explanatory understanding, in contrast, involves knowledge of motives, the subjective meanings attributed to the action by the actor.

This distinction is not particularly helpful however. To take the example of the woodcutter: the action involved in cutting wood contains a referential meaning in that the act always assumes an end to which the product of the act – wood – is to be used, for making toys, for building, for fire; this meaning is built into every act of chopping wood even in those cases where the individual is merely engaged in physical exercise. Both direct and explanatory understanding imply a context of meaning and it is virtually impossible to differentiate them in Weber's terms. Weber's ambivalent attitude to positivism is evident here: the context of meaning and its norms are given datums. The ends of human action, too, are defined as falling outside the domain of science. But in criticising positivism Weber argues that before explaining why an individual followed a specific course of action it is essential to understand the meaning of the action itself. Sociological analysis must be adequate both in terms of meaning and causality. Ideal type categories of action, therefore, are constructions in which actors are related both to other actors, or subjects, and to the historical context; ideal type analysis is interpretative-causal linking meanings to ends.

For Weber, sociological positivism and Marxism lacked the categories of meaning and motivational understanding other than as derivations from external laws and inevitable historical development; the human subject was determined by the workings of laws to the extent that historical events automatically occurred irrespective of the subjective intentions of the actors. In contrast, Weber emphasised that meaning is inter-subjective and not, as with Marx, systemic, the social whole conferring historical meaning on individual actions. But one such whole, capitalism, is defined by Weber as a structure of social actions and seeking an explanation of its specific and unique historical development involves the sociologist in asking the question: what motivated individuals to save and invest rather than to spend and consume.

Religion and social action: capitalism and the Protestant ethic

Weber's first major sociological study was *The Protestant Ethic and the Spirit of Capitalism* (first published in article form, 1904–5) in which he raised the problem of the sociological analysis of a unique social formation, modern European capitalism and sought to explain its historical development through the method of the ideal type. By 1904 Weber was turning increasingly away from historical studies towards sociology, although he continued to employ the concept of culture rather than the concept of society in his writings. The influence of Rickert is clearly evident in Weber's concept of cultural significance which linked the uniqueness of the historical phenomenon with its interpretation in terms of specific cultural values. Ideal types bring out the cultural significance of that particular segment of reality defined as significant; and they function, too, as heuristic tools investigating questions of cultural values. Weber emphasised particularly the historical dimension of social phenomena arguing that cultural significance can be judged only on this basis. The study of the relation of Protestant theology and capitalism is both a study in historical sociology and a methodological exercise in systematic sociology through the application of typical constructs to complex empirical material.

For Weber, capitalism was the product of a unique historical phenomenon, ascetic Protestantism, and its cultural significance was bound up in these 'ideal' origins and resulting motivational structure which effectively predisposed certain individuals to a particular orientation to work and rational social action. The relation of religion to economic activity had been widely discussed by many scholars before Weber, although it was not until the turn of the century that detailed statistical analysis which linked religious affiliation with occupation became available. A negative correlation was established, for example, between Catholicism and successful business activity. Weber was particularly concerned to demonstrate that ideal elements, such as religious ideas, were not mechanically linked to the economic structure but actively shaped the ways in which individuals carried out their ordinary day-to-day activities.

Weber's study was initially intended as a preliminary analysis, although subsequent criticism has often assumed it as a final statement. During the years following the publication of the articles, Weber replied to his many German critics and in particular began work on a vast comparative study of world religions. In 1920 he published a new introduction to the Protestant ethic study and shortly after his death further important material was published in his *General Economic History*. In these writings Weber rejected the commonly held view that his study merely reversed the Marxist argument of the priority of economic forces in social change making religious ideas the causal factor in social development. In the 1920 introduction he emphasised that his analysis was treating 'only one side of the causal chain', while in the early articles he pointed out that he was not substituting for the 'one-sided' materialist approach of Marxism 'an equally one-sided spiritualistic causal interpretation of history and culture' (Weber, 1930, p. 183). His comparative studies of world religions sought to analyse the plurality of factors which influenced the course of economic development and explored in greater detail the broad cultural implications of religious ideas on the formation of capitalism as a system. Only if Marxism is defined as a one factor theory of social change can Weber's study be regarded as its opposite and its refutation.

The question Weber posed in his preliminary analysis of Protestantism, and in his later studies of Chinese, Indian and Palestinian religions, was why did capitalism, defined as a highly rationalised system, develop only in Western Europe. In India, Palestine and China the material infrastructure of capitalism also existed – markets, division of labour, money economy, trade routes – yet only in Western Europe did ıpitalism fully emerge out of such conditions. Weber notes, for xample, that Indian geometry, natural sciences, medicine, political and historical thought, while all highly developed, lacked systematic concepts and methodology. In China science remained unorganised; there was no 'rational, systematic and specialised pursuit of science'. The existence of specific material conditions is insufficient to form a basis for capitalist development and in particular capitalist economic action 'which rests on the expectation of profit by the utilisation of opportunities for exchange, that is on [formally] peaceful chances of profit'. One of the most important points Weber makes is that if capitalism is defined loosely as a mode of money-making then it is characteristic of all civilised societies, China, India and Mediterranean antiquity:

> The impulse to acquisition, pursuit of gain, of money, of the greatest possible amount of money, has in itself nothing to do with capitalism. This impulse exists and has existed among waiters, physicians, coachmen, artists, prostitutes . . . gamblers and beggars . . . it has been common to all sorts and conditions of men at all times . . . whatever the objective possibility of it is or has been given . . . Unlimited greed for gain is not in the least identical with capitalism, and still less its spirit (Weber, 1930, p. 17).

By capitalism Weber meant a system characterised by a rational organisation of formally free labour, the separation of business from the household, the development of rational book-keeping and rational systems of law and administration. Weber was careful to distinguish his concept of capitalism from contemporary sociologists such as Simmel and Sombart: Simmel, in his *Philosophy of Money*, assimilated capitalism to the concept of 'money economy', while Sombart, in his *Modern Capitalism*, identified capitalism with economic 'adventurers' (entrepreneurs seeking to maximise their profits through courage and excessive risk taking) and high consumption particularly in luxury goods. Neither consumption nor the money economy was unique to the West: but a world view which abjures consumption and luxury demanding of those who accept its tenets that they work and invest, not to expiate sin as with Catholicism, but for the promise of salvation, is unique to

Western Europe. The unique, economic structure of Western capitalism is thus homologous with the unique Protestant theology, especially Calvinism, which developed during the sixteenth and seventeenth centuries. Weber adds that by the eighteenth century capitalism had become effectively independent of its religious foundations.

For Weber, then, sociological explanation of the capitalist social formation, while recognising the importance of purely economic factors, identifies the modes of rationalism which are unique to it with forms of social conduct and action. The fundamental issue between Marxism and Weber's sociology lies ultimately in Weber's rejection of the Marxist philosophy of history, the view that capitalism necessarily develops through the workings of objective, economic laws determined by material forces which effectively render the subjective component – human action – irrelevant. This interpretation of Marxism assimilates meaning to historicism: human actions have meaning only in terms of the developing whole and the ultimate end of the historical process, the reconciliation of contradictions in Communist society. For Weber, Marxism lacked a concept of motivation: change occurs through the workings of external, impersonal forces in which human action is reduced to the status of total passivity. But change is always change through the actions of human agents: human subjects are motivated to act in specific ways, to accept or reject the prevailing system of ideas, to reject luxury and immediate consumption, to postpone their worldly gratification and avoid 'all spontaneous enjoyment of life' in favour of a rigorous asceticism. It is the motivational structure of action which constitutes the spirit of capitalism, a spirit not found in India or China, but bound up with Protestant ideology.

The term, spirit, suggests some notion of essence outside history and society, a metaphysical concept rather than sociological category. Although there is ambiguity in Weber's formulation the weight of his argument nevertheless suggests that spirit is the active element of a world view which, in its everyday forms, structures human action. In his 1905 essay he defines spirit as 'a complex of elements associated in historical reality which we unite into a conceptual whole from the standpoint of their cultural significance'. The spirit of capitalism is thus a methodological concept, an abstraction 'put together out of the individual parts which are taken from historical reality . . . a conceptual formulation . . . that is the best from the point of view which interests us'. As such the spirit of capitalism is expressed in a rationalising attitude to life, in such maxims of conduct as be prudent, diligent, punctilious in repayment of debts and loans, avoid idleness since time is money, be frugal in consumption and so on. The spirit of capitalism is a social ethic, a structure of attitudes and behaviour closely identified with ascetic Protestantism and its associated religious sects such as the Puritans and the Calvinists (Weber, 1930, pp. 47–53).

Although Puritanism, Pietism, Methodism and the Anabaptist sects exemplified the capitalist spirit, Weber particularly emphasised the significance of Calvinism. For Weber, Calvinism constituted a form of inner worldly asceticism built around the notion of worldly vocation or calling. It was Luther, however, who originally emphasised that the fulfilment of worldly duties 'is under all circumstances the only way to live acceptably to God . . . it alone is the will of God, and hence every legitimate calling has exactly the same worth in the sight of God'. But Luther's attitude to capitalism, argued Weber, was broadly traditional identifying 'absolute obedience to God's will with absolute acceptance of things as they were'. The individual was encouraged to remain in the station and calling which God had determined and 'restrain his worldly activity within the limits imposed by his established station in life'. Thus Lutheranism could never establish any new connection between worldly activity and religious principles (Weber, 1930, pp. 81–5).

Of all the Protestant sects it was the Calvinists who successfully combined the notion of calling with values appropriate to capitalist development. Calvinism advocated the concept of predestination which superficially suggests a fatalistic rather than positive approach to the world on the part of the believer. Weber's argument is that it was precisely because the Calvinists had to prove their election through good works that their religious beliefs acted as a dynamic and not passive element in social change: the Calvinist, he writes, 'creates his own salvation, or, as would be more correct, the conviction of it'. Hard work and the moral pursuit of a calling, while not constituting infallible evidence of salvation, nevertheless functions to assuage the fear of damnation. The Calvinists effectively required some sign, some criteria 'by which membership of the *electi* could be known'. It was not a question of accumulating good works, as with Catholicism 'but rather (of) systematic self-control' in relation to material pleasures and 'the constructive use of time'. Idleness, gambling, excessive sleep are proof only of imperfect grace. The faithful must attend not simply to their ordinary spiritual obligations, such as prayer, but strive hard in their worldly callings. Weber stresses that there was nothing especially original in the maxims of Protestantism: many religions had condemned idleness and hedonism but the Calvinists went much further in demanding adherence to their maxims of everyday conduct, not as proof of salvation, but as evidence that one may not be among the damned. Religious grace 'could not be guaranteed by any magical sacraments, by relief in the confession' but the individual must methodically supervise 'his own state of grace in his own conduct, and thus to penetrate it with asceticism . . . a rational planning of the whole of one's life in accordance with God's will . . . something which could be required of everyone who would be certain of salvation' (Weber, 1930, p. 153).

Weber concludes by arguing that only as long as the psychological sanctions which develop from the notion of predestination and the concept of proof remain efficacious 'does such an ethic gain an independent influence on the conduct of life and thus on the economic order'. It is not, therefore, Weber's argument that the ideas of specific theologians exercised a decisive role in the genesis of capitalism, but of the influence 'of those psychological sanctions which, originating in religious belief . . . gave a direction to practical conduct and held the individual to it' (Weber, 1930, p. 197). Religious leaders did not set out consciously to produce an ethic for capitalism; the unintended consequences of social action effectively led to that situation. The human subject, non-consciously but actively, transforms humanity, ideas and society.

Weber has, therefore, linked action with the social system and social development, although his stated methodological approach rejects collective concepts in favour of methodological individualism. The 'elective affinity' between the norms of ascetic Protestantism and the psychological–motivational structure of capitalist values eliminates any notion of a deterministic relation of economic 'base' and cultural 'super-structure'. It must be emphasised that Weber is not arguing that the existence of ascetic Protestant values automatically led to capitalist development – the most frequent criticism of Weber's thesis is to identify different countries, and different areas within a country, where Protestant asceticism existed but capitalism failed to develop, such as Calvin's own homeland of Switzerland and seventeenth-century Scotland – rather that the social ethic constitutes one of many elements which, through a process of mutual interaction, leads to social change.

This is not to suggest that there are no problems with Weber's formulation of a necessary link between religious ideas and economic forms. The evidence which he selects to defend his thesis is largely derived from writers who lived after Calvin such as Richard Baxter (1615–91), John Wesley (1703–91) and particularly, Benjamin Franklin (1706–90) and his analysis assumes a direct relation between the ideas expressed in their literary works and social action. He offers no independent evidence that prominent Protestant businessmen subscribed significantly to ascetic Protestant ideas, or that Protestant business communities adhered to the theological maxims regulating everyday conduct. What is more striking is Weber's failure to elucidate the precise ways in which businessmen interpreted Protestant maxims, to grasp the meanings of theological concepts for the subject. Meanings are in effect *imputed* to the subject on the basis of an interpretation of texts by the sociologist. As many critics have pointed out, Weber offers no other evidence in support of his thesis. Finally it has been suggested that Weber's exemplary figure of Franklin, far from embodying ascetic norms of conduct, enjoyed a private life dominated by hedonistic principles, engaging in extra-marital affairs, cultivating a taste for good food and wine, theatre and sports. Franklin was a far more complex figure than the single-minded Puritan portrayed by Weber (Kolko, 1960).

In a similar way, critics have emphasised that many Protestant businessmen were involved in 'traditional' economic activity such as war-profiteering, colonial expeditions, land and currency speculation. But no evidence is advanced which relates to such individuals and groups. Weber's thesis is at its weakest here: the evidence offered in support of his thesis is largely derived from the social teaching of the Protestant sects (itself culled from Ernst Troeltsch's work on the Christian Churches and their social values) and never from the actors themselves (Marshall, 1982, pp. 116–19).

Weber's basic argument is, however, clearly against reductionist, mono-causal explanation. There is scope within Weber's general approach to account for the ways in which capitalism itself affects Protestant values:

> For those to whom no causal explanation is adequate without an economic (or materialistic as it is still unfortunately called) interpretation, it may be remarked that I consider the influence of economic development on the fate of religious ideas to be very important . . . religious ideas themselves simply cannot be deduced from economic circumstances. They are in themselves . . . the most powerful plastic elements of national character, and contain a law of development and a compelling force entirely their own (Weber, 1930, pp. 277–8).

In rejecting one-factor theories of social development Weber approaches an agnostic, pluralistic perspective: the causal chain, he argues, can run from the technical to the economic, at other times from the political to the religious. It is impossible to bring this process of pluralistic causation to a single resting-point. Yet as he shows in the study of the Protestant ethic, there exists immanent properties within certain religious ideologies which successfully effect a transformation of the culture: thus although rejecting evolutionary theory, Weber seems to adopt a similar standpoint with his argument on rationalisation. The rationalising process is immanent within the Protestant religion, and as the major characteristic of Western culture rationalisation constitutes a law of development. Yet Weber's study of religion stresses the active role of the subject: social development is not inevitable, the fate of humanity has not been decided in advance. Weber's sociology thus moves ambiguously between the poles of certitude and agnosticism, between the subject as active agent and society as external determining process.

The logic of rationality: Simmel and Weber

The sociology of culture, as it developed in the work of Weber, Tönnies, Simmel and Sombart identified culture as a unique realm of values which expressed an immanent historical process. As we have seen with Weber's study of Protestantism, culture exercised an active role in social action and the development of social formations: it could not be reduced to a reflection of economic forces. Comparing the specific and unique development of Western rationalised capitalism with the failure of capitalism to emerge as a system in India, China and the Near East, Weber argued that it was the absence of a cultural orientation to the world, a motivational structure built around rational values, which accounted for the difference. Why did not all societies follow the Western path to modernity? For Weber the answer lay in the specific culture of the West, in the systematic application and discipline of impersonal rules and regulations to the conduct of social life. The whole of Western architecture, mathematics, science and music, he suggested, could be identified as products and as active elements of a rationalising culture. In his unfinished study of music – *The Social and Rational Foundations of Music*, written in 1912 but not published until 1921 as an appendix to *Economy and Society* – Weber attempted to show how Western music, once it became an autonomous art-form based on tonality, polyphony and the study of counterpoint, and modern musical notation which facilitated structural composition leaving little scope for improvisation, became highly rationalised: sonatas, symphonies, operas, together with instruments such as the organ, piano and violin were unknown in non-Western cultures. Thus although polyphonic music was known in other cultures the absence of rational harmony was the decisive element (Weber, 1958b).

Weber's theme of the rationalisation of culture informs much of Simmel's work notably his *Philosophy of Money* (1900) which, in many ways, constitutes a pioneering study of the cultural foundations and crisis of the modern capitalist economic system. Unlike Weber, Simmel was not concerned with investigating the historical genesis of large-scale social formations; Simmel's concept of sociation predisposed him to the study of the small-scale, the molecular processes involved in such significant social relationships as the dyad and secret society. His range of interests was far greater than any other contemporary sociologist: he wrote extensively on aesthetic problems, on art and literature (essays and reviews of Rembrandt, Dante, Michelangelo, Stefan George, Rodin, Goethe), architecture, the structure of the human face, the cultural significance of fashion, the relation of thought to urban life (in his 1903 essay 'The Metropolis and Mental life'). But his major contribution to the sociology of culture was *The Philosophy of Money*, a work which influenced the later studies of reification and culture carried out by Lukács and the Frankfurt School.

On one level *The Philosophy of Money* is an abstract, non-historical, non-genetic, 'phenomenological' analysis of the social and cultural significance of money in modern industrial society. Simmel knew Marx's work and clearly regarded his own contribution as supplementing *Capital*, constructing 'a new story beneath historical materialism such that the explanatory value of the incorporation of economic life into the causes of intellectual culture is preserved, while these economic forms themselves are recognised as the result of more profound valuations and currents of psychological, even metaphysical preconditions' (Simmel, 1978, p. 56). Clearly, cultural analysis required the methods of the cultural sciences. Simmel regarded culture as irreducible to the economic structure, a 'form' in which purposive social action finds expression. Simmel's sociology assumes the world as a structureless mass unless organised into forms, for while experience constitutes the content of the form, ultimately the world is apprehended through what Simmel calls the 'great forms'. Forms shape the raw, unmediated reality into a coherent order. The world is thus a totality of forms – art, science, religion – which bring together diversity and unity: without forms there would be only 'an indifferent simultaneous juxtapostion of contents'.

The Philosophy of Money examines the ways in which the money economy transforms cultural forms into external objects and breaks up the unity of individual and society. For Simmel, culture is a specifically human and meaning-endowing activity of the subject, for 'by cultivating objects, that is, by increasing their value beyond the performance of their natural constitution, we cultivate ourselves . . . In refining objects, man creates them in his own image'. Culture, as 'the supra-natural growth of the energies of things, is . . . the embodiment of the identical growth of *our* energies'. What Simmel terms the 'tragedy of modern culture' is the simultaneous development of science, technology and art, the availability of knowledge, and the decline of individual culture. 'Every day and from all sides', he writes, 'the wealth of objective culture increases, but the individual mind can enrich the forms and contents of its own development only by distancing itself still further from that culture . . .' The result is the domination of objective culture over subjective culture (Simmel, 1978, pp. 446–8).

Thus culture, the realm of human purposes and meanings, becomes externalised. In his essay on urbanism he noted the 'frightful disproportion' between the immense culture embodied in material things and the subject's understanding and knowledge of this process. Like Ferguson and Smith, Simmel identified the division of labour as the factor responsible for reducing the individual to a 'negligible quantity' able to cope less and less with the growth of objective culture, becoming a 'mere cog in an enormous organisation of things and powers which tear from his hands all progress, spirituality, and value in order to transform them from their subjective form into the form of purely objective life' (Simmel, 1950, p. 422). Thus, although the culture of modern society enables the individual to participate in more groups and circles than the culture of pre-industrial society – the individual is no longer immersed wholly in kinship groups or guilds to the detriment of individuality – this shift from cultural homogeneity to cultural differentiation is wrought at great cost. Simmel develops a dialectical concept of social development structured around the notion of sociation as dualistic, the simultaneous embodiment of harmony and conflict, attraction and repulsion, love and hatred.

On one level, therefore, Simmel advanced the view that social development leads to a decentred culture in which there is no dominant structure which wholly absorbs the individual: modern culture is essentially characterised by multiple participation in a complex of social circles which, for Simmel constituted the most important criterion of human development. But as modern society becomes institutionally decentred, culture becomes increasingly rationalised and money, with its 'colourless and indifference' the common denominator of all values: the modern mind is calculating, quantitative values replace qualitative values, the world is fixed by mathematical formulas, dehumanised by 'stable and impersonal' time schedules; punctuality, calculability and exactness pervade all spheres of culture. The tension between objective culture and subjective culture becomes increasingly marked with the development of the division of labour and a money economy. In *The Philosophy of Money* Simmel depicts this fragmentation and alienation as the result of a specific historical process which transforms cultural objects, created by human subjects for human subjects, into autonomous *things* which have the appearance of 'autonomous mobility'. Modern man, he writes, 'is so surrounded by nothing but impersonal objects that he becomes more and more conditioned into accepting the idea of anti-individualistic social order (i.e. socialist ideas) . . . cultural objects increasingly evolve into an interconnected enclosed world that has increasingly fewer points at which the subjective soul can interpose its will and feelings'. The real tragedy of culture is thus the tendency to turn the creative subject into an object, to reify the products of human culture and effectively eliminate purposive human action (Simmel, 1978, pp. 296–7, 448–61).

For Simmel cultural development necessarily entails both the objectification of social relationships brought about by the money economy (social relationships in modern urban society are mediated by pecuniary considerations which have the effect of creating a functional distance between different individuals), and the increasing separation of individuals from the products of their labour (the relation of the subject with the object is mediated through money, and thus commodity values, leading to an increasing mental distancing from the objects themselves). Simmel's concept of 'distance' is important for his general theory of culture for it is only by standing back from the cultural objects that the human subject can grasp reality at all. A money economy, especially advanced capitalist forms, develops this sense of distance (for example, credit transactions which effectively reduce the personal and therefore the psychological immediacy of monetary exchange). Thus cultural development is structured around irreconcilable contradictions: the source of Simmel's cultural pessimism lay in his awareness that the realisation of human potential depends in part on the expansion of objective culture, that the growth of subjective culture with its rich inner life flows from the reification of culture itself.

Simmel's analysis of the cultural effects of economic rationality, of the increasing penetration of the money economy into social life, are echoed in Weber's account of modernity. Although noting Simmel's 'brilliant analysis' of the spirit of capitalism, Weber went much further than Simmel in grounding his analysis of rationality in comparative historical sociology. Whereas Simmel's analysis focused on the ways individuals experience the fragmentary and fleeting moments of everyday life within an increasingly rationalised culture, Weber conceived rationality as a broad, collective process existing within historical time and space.

What did Weber mean by rationality? Although he invested the term with ambiguous, multiple meanings, the core meaning seems to refer to the application of precise modes of calculation and available means in the pursuit of specific goals and ends. A comprehensively rationalised reality is grounded in rational and methodical action free of all magical influences. Weber identified Judaism as the religious source of Occidental rationality: its fundamental concepts of a rational ethic and world open to rational action were further consolidated in the inner-worldly asceticism of Protestantism. With its emphasis on discipline, depersonalisation and calculation, Protestantism rationalised religious belief itself: salvation became linked to an impersonal God, the unintended effects being growing secularisation and worldly 'disenchantment'. Rationality comes to pervade all aspects of social life, business, science, politics and law. In this way the process of rationality undermines the coherent and unified world views of the pre-modern world generating multiple, secular beliefs and values which saturate modern pluralist culture. The world process loses its 'magical significance', merely existing, signifying nothing. Modern culture is characterised by competing 'value spheres' – the political, economic, intellectual/ scientific and aesthetic/erotic (the personal sphere) – each with its own inner logic, structure and autonomy. Further, the rationalisation process makes possible 'a de-centred world', one lacking a dominant world view or ideology, a social order which enables individuals to produce meanings free of dogmatic religious constraints.

Weber's discussion of rationality contrasts sharply with Simmel's narrowly pessimistic perspective. For inherent in Weber's theory of rationality is the Enlightenment belief that the values of science combined with those of social justice and equality will lead to human emancipation. Weber terms this 'substantive rationality', the structuring of social life in action linked with 'ultimate values', ideals, goals, ends. But the rationalisation process is double-edged: substantive rationality becomes increasingly subordinated to the practical dictates of 'formal rationality', the domination of means over ends, the application of quantitative calculation to the purposes of life. Political parties, educational and cultural institutions, the administration of government, all become dominated by a rationally calculating specialisation. Such developments presage the triumph of the machine over human autonomy. This 'iron cage' of modernity is always possible, the total domination of bureaucratic ideals over the ideals of life (Gerth and Mills, 1948, pp 280–93).

Thus although the scope for human action is circumscribed by formal rationality, the ideals of substantive rationality, of autonomy and freedom, do not disappear: there exists permanent tension between the two forms of rationality, between social action guided by 'world images' created through ideas, and social action oriented to fragmented, dehumanised bureaucratic ideals.

Social action and social system: Pareto

Weber and Simmel rediscovered the active human subject through their critique of the holistic, systemic approaches of positivism and determinism of sociological evolutionism. As we have seen, both thinkers were concerned with the sociology of everyday activity, with sociation and the meaning–structures of culture. Although Simmel's sociology can be criticised for its tendency to adopt an excessively abstract and atomistic concept of social structure, Weber was more rigorously histori- cal in his approach to the relation of subject to society. Weber's theory of social action is not, strictly speaking, separable from a theory of social system. In his study of Protestantism the role of the subject is conceived in terms of its relation with capitalism as an economic system, an objective structure both historical and sociological. The social action and social system perspec- tives co-exist within Weber's sociology in a state of fruitful tension. Sociological positivism had conceptualised the social system, often in organicist terms, as an external constraining datum built around an inherent need for order and equilib- rium: social action theory, more optimistic through its concept of human agency, strove to integrate the meaning–endowing role of the subject with the larger, external socio-cultural whole. The sociology of Weber and Simmel is therefore opposed to the holistic determinism which was later developed by American Functionalists who absorbed the notion of system at the expense of action.

Although the concept of system is implicit in much of the empirical and historical work of the founding fathers of modern sociology – Tönnies, Simmel, Durkheim, Weber – it was the Italian sociologist, Vilfredo Pareto (1848–1923) who, in the course of criticising nineteenth-century positivism, evolution- ism, Social Darwinism and especially Marxism, defined society explicitly as a social system. Pareto's sociology constitutes a complex mixture of voluntarism and determinism, a rejection of the humanist tradition in social theory (especially Vico) in favour of a pessimistic and fatalistic notion of a fixed human nature, while simultaneously advancing the concept of society as the product of *non-logical* social action.

A controversial figure in the history of sociology (Mussolini offered him a seat in the Italian Senate which he refused), Pareto began his intellectual career in engineering, mathema- tics and the natural sciences, gravitating towards economics and sociology later in life. His early work reflected the influences of positivism and Social Darwinism elements of which can be found in his later writings. Like Durkheim he was concerned with *facts* not metaphysical theories or speculative doctrines which mixed fact with values. *Les Systemes Socialistes* (1902) is a sustained and hostile critique of Marxism which praised Marx's sociological theory of class and class conflict, while rejecting his claim to have established a scientific socialism and scientific theory of society as a whole. In 1916 Pareto published his monumental study, *A Treatise on General Sociology*, which, in striking contrast to the contemporary sociology of Durkheim and Weber, is less concerned with the specific historical development of industrial society than with the history of human society and culture from the earliest times. For Pareto, history was to be ransacked to provide examples and proofs for broad, general theorems. Throughout the *Treatise* Pareto exhibits a cavalier disdain for the 'rules of sociological method', with arbitrary illustration, wrenched from its historical context, employed as the basis of verification. The *Treatise* is characterised by a poverty of empirical research, absence of specific socio-historical data carefully collected and systematically ordered, combined with a withering contempt for previous sociology. Pareto rejected nineteenth-century theories of progress, condemned Enlightenment philosophical rationalism, debunked humanitarian philosophy and modern mass democracy. Political theories such as Marxism and Liberalism were of interest only because they were popular and therefore required psychological explanation. Pareto's hostility towards humanism and collectivist democracy flowed from his belief that historical development was the work of 'active minorities' invested with attributes enabling them to dominate the passive masses.

Pareto's sociology is built around two fundamental principles: first, the concept of science as logico-experimental employing the method of induction and based on experience and observation. The purpose of sociology, he wrote, was 'to discover theories that picture facts of experience and observation' (Pareto, 1963, p. 1511). Thus although one of the first social scientists to discuss the sociological phenomenon of social mobility, Pareto presented, as evidence for his arguments on the rise and fall of social groups and societies, largely anecdotal evidence drawn from speculative observations (the *Treatise* examines, among other things, the decline of Rome, the development of the Reformation, thirteenth-century Venice and nineteenth-century Germany, the 1789 French Revolution and the English suffragette movement). In this respect Pareto is closer to Comte than to either Weber or Durkheim.

It should be noted that although critical of positivism, Pareto differed from Weber in accepting natural science as a basis of sociology: the emphasis on an objective world of experience as the basic datum of sociological study eliminated the problem of interpretation and meaning from sociological analysis. The social sciences, in Pareto's view, have not yet achieved the precision of the logico-experimental method of the natural sciences. Pareto's second principle is the concept of society as a system: he emphasised continually the necessity to analyse human society as whole not, however, in terms of objective social structures and institutions, but rather as the synthesis of a plurality of non-logical action: there is nothing in the *Treatise* that approaches the empirical–historical analysis of cultural institutions and their relation with economic structures which characterises Weber's sociology; nor is Pareto interested in identifying the specific processes of change which occur between different elements of the social whole. Perhaps Pareto's most extraordinary achievement is to define society as a system in abstract, ahistorical and ultimately non-sociological terms. For Pareto, society is a unity, never perfectly integrated 'because the requirement of uniformity is very strong in some individuals, moderately strong in others, very feeble in still others, and almost entirely absent in a few'. Society, in other words, is the product of psychological forces, the result of the workings out of human nature (Pareto, 1963, p. 1727).

Pareto defined sociology as the study of non-logical action, a category he believed had been largely neglected by sociologists. Non-logical action refers to the realm of values, beliefs, sentiments. In his analysis of the social system Pareto was especially concerned with these elements, or parts, which determine the nature of society. Individuals or actors were the molecules of the system, their actions influenced by non-human forces within the environment, but more significantly by the immanent properties of the system itself, by interest, knowledge, 'residues' and 'derivations'. Pareto's *Treatise* is largely concerned with the latter two categories. The social system achieves a state of equilibrium according to the distribution of residues and derivations within the population as a whole.

What does Pareto mean by these terms? Residues, he argues, 'correspond to certain instincts in human beings' although they must not be confused with them: residues are manifestations of sentiments and instincts which work to maintain society; derivations, much more variable, approximate to subjective explanation of events, the rationalisations employed by individuals to explain their conduct and beliefs. Pareto defined six classes of residues: the instinct for combinations; group persistences or persistences of aggregates; the manifestation of sentiments through external acts such as religious ecstasies; residues of sociality such as social ranking, self-sacrifice, asceticism; the residue of personal integrity that produces action which seeks to restore lost integrity; and finally, a sixth class, the sex residue. The six classes are further subdivided into other elements but the essential point is that Pareto's classification is both arbitrary and intellectually sterile. For example, no explanation is offered for the choice of six groups as opposed to twelve or more. Nor does Pareto attempt to validate his concepts through detailed empirical and factual analysis: discussing Class IV residues, for example, he observes:

> Sentiments of ranking on the part of inferiors as well as superiors are observable in animals. They are very widespread in human societies . . . no human society at all complex could survive without them. Relationships of superiority and inferiority are changed in forms, but none the less kept, in societies that ostensibly proclaim equality for all individuals. A sort of temporary feudalism is the rule in such societies, with a progressive descent in rankings from the politicians at the top to the politicians at the bottom. Anyone doubting this need only try to obtain something, in Italy and France . . . without the support of the local 'boss' . . . the 'powers that be' in art, science and public service (Pareto, 1963, p. 686).

Pareto's *Treatise* is full of such commonplaces: propositions stating the distribution of residues within a particular society, or social class, are illustrated from journalistic, literary and classical sources. Although residues are observable they are never analysed historically: Pareto assumes that residues are fixed and that historical change is one of endless repetition. Rejecting evolutionary theory Pareto advocated a theory of historical cycles pessimistically concluding that while historical and social forms change the inner forces remain the same. These latter are the residues. The distribution of Class I residues of combination and Class II residues of the persistence of aggregates within a population effectively determines the nature of the social equilibrium. For Pareto, class circulation depends on the proportion of Class I and Class II residues within the élite especially its 'governing class' (those involved in some branch of government).

History is thus 'the graveyard of aristocracies' since all élites necessarily decay, not only in numbers, but also in 'quality in the sense that they lose their vigour' by the decline 'in the proportions of the residues which enabled them to win their power and hold it'. Elites become incompetent through the concentration of inherited wealth and power, processes which prevent the free circulation of ability. The governing class is restored through the rise from below of 'superior elements' within the lower classes 'possessing residues suitable for exercising the functions of government and willing enough to use force'. Pareto describes this process as historically inevitable and natural:

> In virtue of class-circulation, the governing élite is always in a state of slow and continuous transformation. It flows on like a river, never being today what it was yesterday. From time to time sudden and violent disturbances occur. There is a flood – the river overflows its banks. Afterwards, the new governing élite again resume its slow transformation. The flood has subsided, the river is again flowing normally (Pareto, 1963, pp. 1430–1).

Revolutions thus restore society to its former equilibrium and prevent its total disintegration. The role of conflict and force is crucial in those situations in which class mobility has slowed down or ceased altogether. Normally the distribution of residues work to produce a dynamic equilibrium. Pareto's conception of system and change is thus superficially similar to Marx's notion that social stability is augmented to the degree that the dominant class assimilates the best brains from the lower classes. 'It is far more difficult to overthrow a governing class when it successfully assimilates most of the individuals in the subject class who show those same talents, are adept in those same arts, and might therefore become the leaders of (the subject class)', for 'left without leadership, without talent, disorganised the subject class is almost always powerless to set up any lasting régime' (Pareto, 1963, pp. 1516–17). Domination is thus defined in terms of the ability of the ruling class judiciously to employ a mixture of force and fraud, a Machiavellian conception which ignores the subjective, consensual component that is so important for Weber.

In general, the most enduring ruling class would combine Class I and Class II residues. Pareto distinguishes two classes of individuals, the lions and the foxes whose actions dominate the political sphere. Lions, as the term suggests, are prepared to employ force in pursuit of their interests and are strong in Class II residues, of loyalty to family and group, solidarity and patriotism; foxes are less direct in their methods, employ innovation and scheming, attaining their ends through cleverness and the manipulation and control of economic and political institutions. Foxes are more likely to maintain power through ideology and propaganda, by combining and recombining different ideas. Class II residues, however, are clearly more important and Pareto emphasises that they 'constitute the foundations of society and stimulate the belligerent spirit that preserves it'. Thus the preponderance of Class II residues will support the pretensions of the lower classes who will inevitably replace the governing class of foxes in which Class I residues have grown stronger while Class II have grown weaker. In this situation the ruling class becomes less and less capable of resorting to force and an unstable equilibrium results. Modern mass democracy is identified by Pareto as a form of society in which the governing class is 'overrich in Class I residues' but 'woefully lacking in Class II'. The result is widespread corruption, 'spineless humanitarianism', degeneration of character and the creation of 'an opening for those who have both the will and the power to use violence in shaking off the yoke of the ruling class' (Pareto, 1963, pp. 1824, 1556, 1797).

Class circulation is thus the master key for understanding the history of civilisation. The residues and derivations, because they embody action, provide the 'energy' which produces change within the social system. Society is thus determined by the ways in which the various elements act on each other; and society as a system, as a whole, acts on the elements themselves. Social structures are never randomly produced but flow from the immanent, structured properties of the system. Thus change is not external but emerges from within the elements that constitute the social system. Whereas positivism conceived society as the product of external relations between different elements acting mechanically on each other, Pareto grasped the immanent active properties of the constituent elements of the social system. Nevertheless, Pareto's sociology is ultimately a dead-end. For although the residues are unevenly distributed throughout a population, their universal and static qualities obfuscates rather than clarifies the complex structures of modern industrial societies. Typical of Pareto's method is his attempt to explain the economic development of Germany and France during the late nineteenth century as the result of the weakness or the intensity of Class I and Class II residues: whole peoples, whole social classes, are analysed in terms of the abstract category of residues, the inner, structural complexity of social classes and social groups, which Simmel's sociology brings out so vividly, reduced to essentialist socio-psychological forces. Pareto's social theory is less a sociological explanation of human society and its historically specific modes of development, than an all-embracing speculative philosophy of history. The richness and diversity of human culture are assimilated to a psychological theory of the human subject, in which action is stripped of its social and communicative properties and yoked to a pessimistic and deterministic notion of the social system.

6
The Sociology of Class and Domination

The foundations of sociological theory were laid down in the work of Durkheim, Weber and Simmel. For these sociologists the object of study was industrial society and particularly the problems of social cohesion, legitimacy and democracy. They were concerned with the conflicts and tensions generated within civil society by bureaucratisation, rationalisation, alienation and rapid social change in the transition from preindustrial to large-scale industrial, urban communities and cultures. Social development was analysed in implicit dialectical terms: increasing social complexity, autonomous individuality and richness of culture on the one hand, collectivism, conformity and sterile, calculative culture on the other. Society was theorised both synchronically and diachronically; society was a structure loosely integrated around values and human action. Weber, Simmel, and to a lesser extent, Durkheim, in examining society as a structure and as a process involving active human subjects, were led to explore the objective, institutional, basis of authority and domination in its bearing on human action.

Although the concept of domination and its relation with economic and social institutions had been analysed by Saint-Simon and Alexis de Tocqueville (1805–59) from the standpoint of the political after-effects of the French revolution, it was Marx who provided the first systematic theorisation and sociological account of domination in capitalist industrial society. Comte and Spencer contributed few insights into the sociological study of social conflict, class structure and the

171

distribution of power: organicist evolutionism, with its concern for social order, consensus and equilibrium deflected attention away from the role of force, conflict and ideology in social life (other than as the struggle for existence), assuming social order to be unproblematical (the result of individual interests synthesised into a universal good by the operation of the hidden hand of the market economy) or imposed autocratically from above (Comte's Positivist Church). The shift of emphasis from the concept of social differentiation to the concept of the division of labour in Marx, Durkheim, Weber and Simmel focused attention on the cleavages of interest within industrial society and the conflicts engendered by class division.

Marx's theory of domination

Marx was not the first writer to emphasise the class nature of industrial society or the conflicts generated between dominant and subordinate classes. 'What I did that was new', he wrote, 'was to prove, (1) that the existence of classes is only bound up with particular historical phases in the development of production, (2) that the class struggle necessarily leads to the dictatorship of the proletariat, (3) that this dictatorship itself only constitutes the transition to the abolition of all classes and to a classless society' (Marx and Engels, n.d. p. 86). In this formulation (itself made during private correspondence and therefore never intended for publication) Marx advanced a dogmatic notion of the centralising role of the state in the transition to socialism. And in *The Communist Manifesto* Marx and Engels described the modern state as a 'committee for managing the common affairs of the whole bourgeoisie', defining political power as 'the organised power of one class for oppressing another'. The implication in this formulation is that power flows from the ownership of economic resources and is simply a reflection of class interests. Class domination is thus the product of class antagonisms based on economic inequality, and while Marx emphasises that economic inequality and exploitation were characteristic of all modes of production beyond simple tribal communism, it was only capitalism which transformed all social relations into economic relations. In pre-capitalist society the social relations of serf and landowner, for example, functioned through a personal as well as an economic nexus: the class domination of the landowner was based on feudal ties of bondage and vassallage, personal elements which capitalism destroys, 'the motley feudal ties that bound man to his "natural superiors" ', leaving only naked self-interest as the bond between individuals. It is in this sense that Marx wrote of class relations under capitalism becoming 'simplified' and 'universalised' with the result that power was increasingly concentrated in the major economic and political institutions.

Marx distinguished between three modes of domination: economic, social and political. Economic and social domination refers to the ways in which *capital* determines the functioning of institutions generally, while political domination refers to the ways in which the state creates and maintains the legal framework for bourgeois rule. Although Marx never used the term 'ideological domination', it is implicit in his analysis of ideology, referring essentially to the need for legitimation within capitalism with the rise of democratic institutions.

In *Capital* Marx depicted capitalist society as a system in which capital acts as an independent force, the capitalist class directly appropriating the whole surplus labour and surplus product in ways which augment the 'domination of capital over labour'. Like Saint-Simon, Marx argued that political institutions expressed basic economic interests; a relation of strict functional correspondence characterised economic and political institutions. Thus in *The Communist Manifesto* a simple, reciprocal base-superstructure model of political power is advanced in which the state – 'political society' – is conceptualised as an ideological institution which supports and defends the rights of private property. The state is a class state. But, in his later, historical writings, especially those analysing contemporary British and French history, Marx developed a more complex model of power, distinguishing between the different fractions within a dominant class and suggesting that the state apparatus was often controlled, not by the bourgeoisie, but by what he called 'a governing class'.

Thus in his analysis of the British political system Marx argued that although the Tory party remained the party of the nobility, it nevertheless carried out the policies of the bourgeoisie: 'The whole aristocracy is convinced of the need to govern in the interests of the bourgeoisie; but at the same time it is determined not to allow the latter to take charge of the matter itself' (Marx and Engels, 1962, pp. 351–8). The dominant class consists of its ruling and non-ruling fractions: the ruling class – the governing class – exercises power through the state on behalf of an economically dominant class such as the nineteenth-century English bourgeoisie. In a similar way Engels describes the German Junkers as the governing class of a Germany which was industrialising and transforming itself into a modern bourgeois society: the conflict of interests between the rising bourgeoisie and the emerging proletariat were overcome by raising the state apparatus over the whole society.

In the *Grundrisse* Marx noted that this internal complexity of class existed at the economic level also: as profit consisted of two separate forms of revenue, the existence of financial and industrial capitalists 'express nothing other than this fact' (Marx, 1973). The dominant class is therefore never a homogeneous whole but a structure of different and potentially conflicting interests. There is no simple mechanical relation, therefore, between class power and economic dominance: power is mediated through political institutions which, developing at a different tempo from the economic forces succeed in exercising an autonomy in respect of class interests.

The state and class domination

From certain of Marx's writings the theory of domination appears as unproblematic: power is the reflection within political society of economic structure. But in analysing the theory of domination as it developed within Marx's work, it becomes clearly essential to distinguish Marx's polemical writings from his historical and scientific works; and further, to distinguish Marx's works from those of Engels.

In general, Engels held to a crude, reductionist theory of domination and his popular summaries of Marxism such as the *Anti-Duhring* and *Socialism: Scientific and Utopian*, together with his historical studies such as *The Origin of the Family, Private Property and the State* tend to restate the position outlined in *The Communist Manifesto*. It should also be emphasised that Marx's concept of the state outlined in his early writings (1841–5) differs from the standpoint of *The Communist Manifesto*: in the former the state is identified with the realm of alienation, founded on the contradiction between public and private life, general and particular interests. In 1844 Marx argued that the unsocial nature of life in civil society, the egoism engendered by the forces of private property, trade and industry constituted the 'natural foundations' of the modern state. The state is not simply the form of organisation that the bourgeois class necessarily adopts to guarantee its property and interests, but an institution which develops out of the alienated social relations of civil society.

Marx's most important works on the state, however, are the historical studies: *The Eighteenth Brumaire of Louis Bonaparte* (1852), *The Class Struggles in France* (1850) and his analyses of the Paris Commune (1871–2). He originally intended to complete his study of capitalism with a final volume devoted to the state but died before finishing the economic analysis. In this sense, therefore, there exists no theory of the state in Marx's work or any analysis of the state system comparable to Marx's economic analysis. Perhaps for this reason it is a relatively simple task to find a number of different concepts of the state ranging from the notion of state as class power to the state as autonomous institution. Bearing in mind, therefore, that Marx failed to develop a coherent theory of capitalist domination the theory of the state can best be approached by focusing on two related, although contradictory themes: that human emancipation depends on civil society being independent of state domination; and the argument that the abolition of capitalism necessarily involves centralised authority.

In Marx's early writings the state is separated from civil society: the state expresses the condition of civil society and is indeed described as its 'official expression'. In his essay, 'On the Jewish Question', Marx accepts Hegel's concept of civil society describing its creation as 'the achievement of the modern world' but he criticised Hegel for defining the state as the institution, together with bureaucracy, which produces

175

social cohesion. Although Hegel's notion of civil society had been largely derived from the writings of the eighteenth-century historians and political economists, he was particularly critical of Adam Smith's depiction of civil society as a harmonious sphere in which conflicting individual interests were synthesised into a unity by the workings of a 'hidden hand'. Hegel defined civil society rather differently as comprising institutions which, by themselves, were incapable of producing social order and unity. Some of these ideas passed into Marx's theory of the state and civil society; Marx's early writings depict the working class as wholly alienated, outside society, their integration possible only through a total revolution and, by implication, the workings of a beneficial state. In *Capital* Marx drew a different picture: the industrial working classes succeed in developing their own characteristic institutions which mediate the relation of class and state, institutions centred in civil society and democratically organised. Marx's analysis of the social relations of capitalism thus suggest the possibility that the working class, through its democratic institutions, can lay the basis for socialist transformation.

It is this latter theme that indicates an anarchist element in Marx's thought and his writings on the Paris Commune are particularly eloquent in defending this standpoint. Nevertheless, the influential Marxist theory of the state, the bourgeois state as embodiment of class power which can be changed only by the centralised socialist state – Marxist–Leninism that is – derives more from Engel's writings than from Marx. Engels declared unequivocally that in 'the last instance' the economic is decisive, a reductionist argument which leads him to characterise the state as the embodiment, in a highly concentrated form, of 'the economic needs of the class controlling production', its historical development the automatic product of economic forces. The modern state, he argued, is the organisation which 'bourgeois society takes on in order to support the external conditions of the capitalist mode of production against encroachments of workers as well as individual capitalists'. For Engels, the state was simply 'a capitalist machine, the State of the capitalists, the ideal personification of the total national capital' (Marx and Engels, 1962, Vol. 2, pp. 148–9). In the 'last instance' the state reflects the economic needs of the class which controls production, an external, coercive apparatus for maintaining class domination.

Engels's formulation suggests that in capitalist society the state is fully and consciously controlled by the economically dominant class. The political structure, therefore, enjoys no autonomy but is simply an ephiphenomenal form of the economic order. Similar arguments inform Marx's own writings, especially *The German Ideology*, which describes the historical evolution of the modern state in terms of the division of labour and mode of production, the separate spheres of administration (law, army, police, civil service) which emerge from the increasingly specialist division of work creating a sense of national unity, an 'illusory community' which seeks to conceal the facts of class struggle and conflicting material interests: 'The state is the form in which the individuals of a ruling class assert their common interests . . . [it] acts as an intermediary in the formation of all communal institutions and gives them political form' (Marx and Engels, 1964).

By the end of the 1840s Marx had yet to work out his theory of social change, surplus value and exploitation: the analysis of capitalism turned on a polarised model of conflict between two classes. This dichotomic model of class structure and social formation underwent profound change in his work of the 1850s and 1860s. One of the most significant historical developments which occurred during the course of the nineteenth century, especially in the advanced capitalist countries, was the increasing centralised nature of capitalism as a system. Marx integrated these developments into his theoretical model of capitalism. He argued that although previous revolutions, such as the French Revolution, had embraced the ideals of freedom and democracy against authoritarian power, the actual results were always 'a perfecting' of the state. The centralised state machine had originally been forged during the period of Absolute Monarchy 'as a weapon of nascent modern society in its struggle of emancipation from feudalism', and although the French Revolution had sought to create national unity necessary for the growth of bourgeois society, this development could be effected only by enlarging the powers of the institution which the ideals of 1789, liberalism and freedom, opposed (Marx and Engels, 1971, p. 149). In the years between the publication of

The Communist Manifesto and the analysis of the failure of the Paris Commune Marx gradually abandoned the reductionist standpoint adopted in the *Manifesto*, with its implication that in socialist revolution the working class would simply take over the existing state machine and use it for the task of reconstruction. In the 'Preface' to the 1872 German edition of the *Manifesto* two crucial changes are apparent:

1. The rapid development of the labour movement resulting from the growth of capitalism had created the potential for democratic change from within civil society itself, through the institutions of the working class.
2. Because of the increasing centralisation of capitalism as an economic system, the state itself becomes more centralised so that the task of socialist transformation is not the reform of the state but its abolition: 'The working class cannot simply lay hold of a ready-made State machinery (as different factions had done in their ascendence to power) and wield it for its own purposes' (Marx and Engels, 1971, p. 270).

Marx's hostility to the state now becomes total: in his writings on the Paris Commune he describes the centralised state machine of modern society as enmeshing 'living civil society like a boa constrictor', functioning as 'a parasitic excrescence on civil society', 'unproductive and mischievous', an 'incubus' which must be 'smashed' (Marx and Engels, 1971, pp. 149–70, 202–3). Whereas in *The Communist Manifesto* and the *Address to the Communist League* (1850) Marx had argued that socialism would necessarily produce further centralisation now he advocated a decentralising transition to socialism.

These political themes are closely bound up with Marx's theoretical analyses of the state as a separate sphere from civil society, partially autonomous from the dominant class yet necessarily linked with it. The bourgeoisie must develop a centralised state structure to facilitate capitalist progress (the state being responsible for communications, education, taxation, foreign trade and law) but because 'the real life' of the bourgeoisie lay in the sphere of civil, rather than political society, the state is always more than a mere agent of this class. This aspect of Marx's theory of domination is especially brought out in his analysis of Bonapartism: in 1851 Louis Bonaparte abolished the Parliamentary institutions of the French bourgeoisie, arrested deputies, deporting socialists and republicans, and outlawed free speech and a free press, all in order to safeguard bourgeois interests from socialism. The bourgeois class consisted of two large factions, the big landed proprietors and the financial and industrial bourgeoisie; the internal divisions of this class, however, obstructed the development of an autonomous, united class-conscious ruling bourgeoisie. Marx attempts to show that the state was not a simple reflection of social forces but rather an example of the separation of the state from society: under the rule of the second Bonaparte, Marx wrote, the state seems 'to have made itself completely independent' so that all classes 'fall on their knees before the rifle butt'. Executive power embraced a broad strata, state officials numbering as many as half a million, and Marx depicts this bureaucratic state machine as an 'appalling parasitic body which enmeshes the body of French society like a net and chokes its pores'. State power soars 'high above society'. This mode of domination emerges historically 'when the proletariat is not ready (or able) and the bourgeoisie has lost the facility of ruling the nation' (Marx and Engels, 1962, Vol. 2, pp. 331–2). Marx is arguing that when no single class enjoys social and political dominance, the state emerges to act as mediator:

> The bourgeoisie confesses that its own interests dictate that it should be delivered from the consequences of its own rule; that, in order to restore tranquility in the country, its bourgeois parliament must, first of all be given its quietus; that, in order to preserve its own social power intact, its political power must be broken; that the individual bourgeois can continue to exploit the other classes and to enjoy undisturbed property, family, religion and order only on condition that their classes be condemned along with the other classes to like political nullity; that in order to save its purse it must forfeit its crown (Marx and Engels, 1962, Vol. 2, p. 288).

In sharp contrast, Marx analysed the events surrounding the Paris Commune to argue that the institutions thrown up spontaneously by the working class organising themselves against the bourgeoisie represented the only authentic alternative to the centralising trends of the modern state. The Paris Commune was essentially the political form of proletarian emancipation, direct democracy characterised by the recall of political representatives, a peoples' army and militia, 'the reabsorption of the State power by society as its own living forces instead of as forces controlling and subduing it, by the popular masses'. The Commune was the 'glorious harbinger' of a new type of society, 'the people acting for itself by itself'. And only the industrial working class could invent and put into practice the concept of Commune, of workers councils (Marx and Engels, 1971, p. 153).

Nevertheless, Marx was sharply critical of the policies pursued by the Commune describing its lack of socialist leadership and coherent socialist ideology: it was not socialist 'nor could it be'. Subsequent generations of Marxists drew the conclusion that a successful proletarian revolution required more than self-governing working-class institutions, but a disciplined revolutionary political party, Marxist theory and a centralised socialist administration. A close analysis of Marx's writings on the Commune, however, suggests that although he saw the events of 1871 as doomed to failure by muddled and incoherent leadership, he nevertheless regarded the Commune as embodying a struggle against the state and the centralising trends of modern society, a reassertion of the independence of civil society.

But Marx's work as a whole, from the philosophical critique of Hegel's authoritarian theory of the state to his hostile criticism of Bakunin's anarchist concept of the state as the source of all problems in capitalist society, is characterised by a sharp tension between a libertarian and democratic temper: the state is as an 'alienated social power' dominating civil society, an authoritarian, centralised structure constituting an essential element of society as a whole. The Commune's policy of democratisation – election to administrative posts, the power of recall and equality of pay – was defined by Marx as part of a process which sought to reverse the historical trend, set in motion by revolutions of the past, which invests the state and its apparatuses with control *over* civil society. But in works such as *The German Ideology, The Communist Manifesto* and the *Address to the Communist League* Marx emphasised that the state, founded historically on the division of labour, class interests and class conflict, was effectively the 'official form of social antagonisms in civil society': thus in the transition from capitalism to socialism greater rather than less centralisation would be necessary. A broadly similar standpoint emerges from his criticism of the Marxist programme of the German Social Democratic Party – the Gotha Programme of 1875 – in which he scornfully rejected the concept of 'free state', arguing that the issue was rather one of elaborating the social functions of the state in socialist society analogous to their functions in capitalism. In writings such as these the state is clearly defined as the instrument of class forces, as an integral structure of society: in socialism, therefore, the state, as the dictatorship of the proletariat will dominate civil society disappearing only with the advent of Communism. The state and its organs of repression remain firmly anchored within society. It was only after the experience of the Paris Commune that Marx began to shift his position and hesitantly advance the standpoint of state versus society and emphasise the necessity for civil society to absorb and abolish the distinct organs of political society and reverse the historical trend of increasing centralisation.

But this radical, libertarian strand remained muted: in their published writings both Marx and Engels tended to identify the domination and centralisation of *capital* as the critical issue, the 'despotism of capital' rather than the despotism of the state. This is particularly brought out in Engels's article, 'On Authority' (1872), written polemically against anarchist socialism, in which he explicitly rejected democratic, decentralising forms of authority. 'Wanting to abolish authority in large-scale industry', he wrote, 'is tantamount to wanting to abolish industry itself, to destroy the power loom in order to return to the spinning wheel'. Large-scale industry and social development are impossible without authority: Engels argued that authority was neither good nor bad but relative to the specific social situation. Socialism will effectively transform the political functions of the state 'into the simple administrative functions of watching over the true interests of society'. Engels's formulation asserts the centralising trend of industrialism: authority is imposed from above over civil society and not 'reabsorbed' into its institutional framework (Marx and Engels, 1962, Vol. 2, pp. 636–9).

The theory of class: Weber

Neither Marx nor Weber produced a complete theory of social stratification. Nevertheless, Weber's brief discussion of stratification as a 'multi-dimensional structure' embracing social class, status and party has become a fundamental source of modern social theory.

Weber's interpretation of Marx was based on the contemporary view of Marxism as a form of economic determinism. In general, Weber accepted this interpretation, widely propounded by Marxists such as Kautsky, in which the political was assimilated to the economic. In contrast Weber insisted that the political was not a secondary and derivative phenomenon but an active, autonomous element exercising a critical role in the formation of modern society. He rejected Marx's analysis of capitalism as a system structured in class struggle and internal contradictions, defining capitalism as a rational mode of organisation and thus clearly distinguished from previous social formations. This emphasis on the autonomy of the political and the pervasiveness of rationality within capitalism led Weber to reject the Marxist theory of the state as the instrument of class domination. Before examining Weber's theory of domination, however, it is essential to outline his general perspective on class and power.

Superficially, Weber seems to follow Marx: property, or the lack of it, constitutes 'the basic categories of all class situations' and the factor which produces class 'is unambiguously economic interest'. However, the 'class situation' is differentiated 'according to the kind of services that can be offered in the market'. Here Weber departs from Marx in stressing that skill may constitute a form of property productive of internal class differentiation: those offering services are differentiated 'just as much according to their kinds of services as according to the way in which they make use of these services'. It is 'chance' within the structure of the market which Weber identifies as 'the decisive moment which presents a common condition for the individual's fate'. In this sense class situation is ultimately 'market situation'. Writing of Marx's fragment on class, Weber noted that 'it was intended to deal with the issue of class unity in the face of skill differentials'. Thus Weber distinguished between 'ownership classes' (those who receive rents from the ownership of land, mines, factories) and 'acquisition classes' ('typical entrepreneurs' offering services on the market such as bankers and financiers, as well as members of the 'liberal professions' who enjoy a privileged position through their ability or training). Weber described these groups as 'positively privileged' comparing their market position with 'negatively privileged' groups such as wage-labourers who have neither disposable property nor specialised skills. For Weber, classes never constituted homogeneous wholes but were highly differentiated internally embracing a number of different interests. He argued that the basic tendency of capitalism was the expansion of the 'acquisition classes' with the result a more pluralistic social structure, one increasingly built around educational qualifications.

A pluralistic stratification system thus develops involving complex differentiation within dominant, middle and working classes. Weber described the stratification system within modern capitalism as consisting of working classes, petty bourgeoisie, 'intelligentsia' (a category lacking independent property but whose social position hinges on technical training, such as engineers, bureaucratic officials and other white-collar workers), and finally, a class which occupies a 'privileged position through property and education' (entrepreneurs, etc.). Given this complex stratification system there is clearly no simple relationship between class situation and class consciousness as conceived by Marx. Class constitutes a crucial objective factor in the formation of consciousness, affecting the 'life-chances' of individuals in a variety of ways, but there exists no automatic transposition of so-called economic and class interests into solidaristic class consciousness. Weber rejected the historical relation of class to social change, the concept of historically necessary objective laws of social development. Consciousness, therefore, is structured firmly within the present, within the empirical market situation, and quite clearly Weber's sociology has eliminated such notions as 'class-for-itself' (fully conscious of its historical interests).

Social stratification is further complicated by the existence of 'status groups'. Weber distinguished classes from status groups by arguing that class situation differs from status situation by virtue of 'a specific, positive or negative, social estimation of honour'. Class situation depends on the market; status situation hinges on the judgements which others pass on his, or her social position, thus attributing positive or negative esteem. Because a status group is characterised by a 'specific style of life', comprising social distance and exclusiveness, a repudiation of economic factors as the basis of membership and a commitment to patterns of non-utilitarian consumption, it approximates to a unified social class: 'With some oversimplification, one might thus say that "classes" are stratified according to their relations to the production and acquisition of goods; whereas "status groups" are stratified according to the principles of their *consumption* of goods as represented by special "styles of life".' There is, of course, a close relation between status groups and property and in this respect class and status are linked: an economically ascendent class will, through subsequent generations, achieve the position of a status group. Both propertied and propertyless individuals may belong to the same status group while economically declining groups exercise considerable social influence. Weber's point was that class and status constituted two distinct forms of group formation and organisation: thus although interrelated, class and status are competing structures of stratification relating specifically to the distribution of power. Power is not a separate dimension of stratification; classes, status groups and political parties are all phenomena 'of the distribution of power within a community' (Weber, 1964, pp. 424–9; Gerth and Mills, 1948, pp. 180–95).

Weber's pluralistic model of stratification is theoretically one which assumes the existence of a strong civil society. Power, for example, constitutes an expression of the distribution of interests within civil society; but at the same time power and class cannot be assimilated to economic elements, or political parties be considered solely as the expression of class interests. The principle of autonomy is important for defining the separation from the state and bureaucracy of institutions bound up with class, status and power. For Weber, civil society was a living force: thus theoretically parties can constitute class or status parties but because of the complex nature of industrial society they are more likely to be 'mixed types'. Weber's pluralistic approach to social stratification assumes conflict over interests and a fluid, mobile and open social formation. But, as with Marx, there are tensions between these formulations and Weber's awareness of the centralising trends of modern industrial society.

Capitalism, bureaucracy and democracy: Weber's theory of domination

Throughout his life Weber accepted the necessity for a strong, nation state, its primacy in all social and political spheres. His early studies into the agricultural conditions of Eastern Germany had pointed to the problems caused by an incursion of Polish workers into German territory and their potential threat to German culture. Germany at the end of the nineteenth century had developed into a strong, centralised nation state with its own distinctive national culture. Political unification was achieved during the first stirrings of industrial development and Weber emphasised that if Germany was to become a truly modern industrial nation then it could do so only under the guidance of new political leaders. The *Junker* landowning class still controlled large sections of German political life, yet in Weber's terms they constituted a declining class incapable of generating the necessary dynamic leadership. As for the industrial bourgeoisie Weber depicted this class as cautious and unpolitical, wholly dominated by the *Junkers*. The industrial working class was equally incapable of leadership being an immature class politically, its leaders in the Social Democratic Party contemptuously dismissed as mere journalistic dilettantes. Weber defined a politically mature class as one which repudiated sectional interests in favour of the political power interests of the German nation.

Weber's attitude to questions of power was uncompromising: all modern states, he argued, demanded a structure of domination through which some individuals ruled others.

Weber rejected what he regarded as utopian political concepts such as direct democracy (he discussed the example of Soviets in his essay, 'Parliament and Government in a Reconstructed Germany', written in 1918) on the grounds that in large, complex modern societies such institutions were technically impossible. He accepted the extension of democratic rights in modern societies but argued that the process of democratising society entailed an increasing bureaucratisation and centralisation of power structured in the rational norms of a bureaucratic state apparatus. In modern society the administrative function is determined by size: the administration of mass structures is radically different from the personalised relationships of administration in small associations; administration expands with the result that those with training and experience exercise technical superiority in the carrying out of complex tasks. The classic democratic doctrine, based on the sovereignty of the people, formed no part of Weber's theory of democracy. Writing to Robert Michels, whose book on *Political Parties* (1911) advanced similar arguments on the nature of organisation, Weber asked: 'How much resignation will you still have to put up with? Such concepts as "will of the people", genuine will of the people, have long since ceased to exist for me; they are fictitious. All ideas aiming at abolishing the dominance of men over men are "Utopian" ' (Mommsen, 1974, p. 87).

One of Weber's fundamental arguments was that the rise of modern political parties – itself a democratic development – entailed increasing bureaucratisation and the weakening of human initiative and action. His ideological support for a strong German state and his general distrust of 'mass' democracy was closely bound up with his sociological studies of bureaucracy, a legal–rational form of domination described as eliminating all personal, irrational and emotional elements from administration. Bureaucratic administration subordinated the individual to the rational, specialised division of labour and an increasing rationalisation of all spheres of social life. Pessimistically Weber described this process in terms of a 'new iron cage of serfdom' and a dehumanised, 'disenchanted world'.

For Weber, Parliamentary Democracy was largely passive in

its effects; the mass of the people were uneducated, politically ignorant and incapable of forming reasoned political judgements. The real objective of democracy was the creation of charismatic leaders who succeed in establishing leadership over the masses not through policies but by their personal qualities. In this way the inherent trends towards bureaucratisation might be checked by the emergence of a powerful personality with extra-mundane gifts who succeeds in integrating the propertyless masses into modern society. Modern mass political parties, however, are based on bureaucratic principles of organisation and the basic trend of modern society is for parties to select their leaders and offer them for election to Parliament: democracy becomes increasingly a mode of selection of leadership.

Weber insisted throughout his writings that the struggle for power was an inherent feature of all social life pervading every sphere of social action. Parties exist to achieve power. It is important to understand Weber's concept of power in this context: he did not accept the crude Marxist position which defined power in terms of economic interests and class structure. Power is defined in social action terms as 'the chance of a man, or of a number of men, to realise their own will in a communal action even against the resistance of others who are participating in their action' (Gerth and Mills, 1948, p. 180). Individuals do not necessarily strive for power merely because of possible economic rewards: power, including economic power, may be valued for itself, or for the social honour it confers. There is thus no single source of power and one of the consequences of Weber's argument is that changes in the economic organisation of society do not automatically result in changes in the distribution of power. Historically the major sociological challenge to this Marxist thesis had originally occurred in the work of the Italian political scientist, Gaetano Mosca (1859–1941). Many of Mosca's themes were developed by Robert Michels (1876–1936) and Max Weber. For Mosca and Michels power flowed from its source in political and bureaucratic organisations; Weber's theory of bureaucratic domination emerged as a more complex development of this theme.

In his *Elementi di Scienza Politica* (translated into English as

The Ruling Class), first published in 1896, Mosca appears superficially to follow Marx in his argument that 'in all societies . . . two classes of people appear – a class that rules and a class that is ruled'. Political power has always been exercised by organised minorities who impose their rule on the unorganised masses. His 'political', (or ruling) class, enjoys legal and factual authority and in democratic societies the selection of candidates by political parties is always the product of organised minorities. Mosca emphasised that the political class does not represent economic interests but constitutes an autonomous social stratum, a natural élite 'whose economic position is virtually independent of those who hold supreme power and who have sufficient means to be able to devote a portion of their time to perfecting their culture and acquiring their interest in the public weal'. For Mosca, this élite constituted the best elements of the ruling class. Thus he argued that the stability of nineteenth-century England had less to do with its Parliamentary institutions than with the continuity of its political class. The implication is that the state is not an expression of class interests but an institution resting on moral and material forces and seeking to achieve unity of all social groups within the nation (Mosca, 1939, pp. 144–5, 284–92).

Bureaucratic organisation is the key to understanding political power. Mosca's argument is often couched positivistically in terms of laws – the law of organised minorities – which have the force of natural laws: thus he departs radically from Marx's theory of socialism by postulating that 'no social organisation can be based exclusively on the sentiment of justice' for human nature is irrational and egoistic, a constant striving after wealth, power, worldly vanity. Mosca's critique of socialist collectivism was based partly on his theory of organisation and an ahistorical notion of human nature. Democracy thus becomes the rule of organised minorities which 'in spite of appearances to the contrary, and for all the legal principles on which government rests . . . still retain the actual and effective control of the state'. History teaches the lesson that social progress occurs only if those with power are controlled and balanced by others who enjoy positions of absolute independence and no common interest with those who wield power. It is this mediation of power, Mosca argues, which tends to disappear with the development of collectivism: a blind belief in the masses can lead only to the destruction of multiple centres of political power (Mosca, 1939, pp. 50–87).

Mosca's pessimistic sociology is thus a critique of so-called mass democracies and the threat posed to governing élites by the rise of bureaucratically organised political parties claiming to represent the interests of the 'irrational' masses. This is one of the themes also of Michels's *Political Parties* (1911) which adumbrates the sociological law of oligarchical inevitability: all organisations, however democratic their ideology, become necessarily oligarchic and bureaucratic. 'As a result of organisation, every party or professional union becomes divided into a minority of directors and a majority of directed'. Basing his arguments on the bureaucratic tendencies of the German Social Democratic Party (the major Marxist political party in Europe at the time of Michels's study, with a nationwide political organisation and deputies in Parliament) Michels sought to show, like Mosca, the inevitable trend to bureaucratic control of the state and the ways this process flowed directly from the organisational requirements of modern, 'mass' society. Michels's 'iron law of oligarchy', working through social institutions, means the rule of the bureaucratic official over democratically elected parliamentary representatives, the growth of authority based on position within a hierarchy of salaried officialdom. Bureaucratic organisation is a natural law which determines the structure of modern political parties and trade unions. Within capitalism administrators increasingly acquire an authority 'at least equal to that possessed by the private owner of capital', while under socialism the ideals of a classless society 'would perish in the moment of its adherents' triumph'. The necessity for bureaucracy gives 'birth to the domination of the elected over the electors, of the mandatories over the mandators, of the delegates over the delegators. *Who says organisation, says oligarchy*' (Michels, 1962, pp. 333–56).

As we have seen, Weber shared Mosca's and Michels's rejection of the 'utopian' ideals of socialism. He argued that the highly specialised division of labour, which forms the backbone of a modern economy, must inevitably lead to greater bureaucratisation: bureaucratic modes of organisation, technically superior to other modes, are essential for large-scale

189

planning and the mobilising of resources. Only through bureaucratic organisation has it been possible to develop the modern polity, economy and technology. The fully developed bureaucratic structure compares with other organisations as the modern machine compares with non-mechanical modes of production. Bureaucracy is characterised by the following characteristics: precision, speed, unambiguity, knowledge of the files, continuity, discretion, unity, strict subordination; the bureaucratic office has a clearly defined sphere of competence, its officials organised in a clearly defined hierarchy of positions, and appointed, not elected, on the basis of technical qualifications. Officials are personally free and subject only to authority in terms of their impersonal bureaucratic obligations. The development of modern society demands this mode of administration for the larger the association, the more complicated its tasks and the more it depends on rational organisation. In this sense the future belongs to bureaucratisation.

For Weber, the increasing bureaucratisation of social life formed the major structural form of modern capitalism: rationalised efficiency which results from bureaucratic organisation enables humanity to develop economically, technologically and politically, but this progress is achieved at some cost, 'a parcelling out of the human soul', a dehumanisation of the subject. As for socialism, rather than decentralising power, it will lead inevitably to a further centralising of institutions and the dictatorship of the bureaucratic official. Weber's pessimism is complete: modern society cannot escape from bureaucratic organisation.

Thus a contradiction is generated between the democratic trends of bourgeois society and the anti-democratic ethos of bureaucratic organisation. In Weber's analysis bureaucracy becomes the major source of authority in the modern world: 'Every domination expresses itself and functions through administration. Every administration, on the other hand, needs domination, because it is always necessary that some powers of command be in the hands of somebody' (Weber, 1954, p. 330). This is what Weber called 'imperative co-ordination', the probability that commands will be obeyed irrespective of their specific content or degree of supervision. Domination is distinguished from power in that domination carries the weight of legitimacy, that individuals obey not because of physical compliance, but through a belief in the validity of norms regulating the command. For Weber, domination was not the simply external fact of an order being obeyed, but involved a subjective component, as if those who are ruled had made the content of the command the basic maxim of their own activity. In this respect Weber differs sharply from Mosca in seeking a voluntaristic basis for power; 'It is an induction from experience', he writes, 'that no system of domination voluntarily limits itself to the appeal to material or affectual or ideal motives as a basis for guaranteeing its continuance. In addition every such system attempts to establish and to cultivate the belief in its "legitimacy" ' (Weber, 1964, p. 325).

Weber identified three ideal types of legitimacy: traditional, resting on a belief in the authority of 'immemorial traditions'; charismatic, based on the prophetic pronouncements of oracles and great leaders invested with 'magical' qualities; and finally, rational, based on a belief in the legality of enacted rules and the right of those in authority to issue commands that have their basis in law. Commands, then, always carry a minimum of voluntary compliance; they are obeyed because of a belief in the legitimacy of the authority. It is, therefore, not a question of an 'organised minority', or élite, imposing its rule on an unorganised mass, but rather of the process of institutionalising the 'inner support' of subjects for the different modes of authority. Weber's sociology of domination is ultimately less concerned with the sources of power in material forces, such as property ownership, than in the ideologies which legitimate different forms of rule.

Modern society is characterised by rational–legal domination centred in bureaucracy. Weber argued that capitalist production created 'an urgent need for stable, strict, intensive and calculable administration'; in the field of administration the choice lay simply 'between bureaucracy and dilettantism'. In his lecture on Socialism, given in 1918, he argued that modern democracy was increasingly a bureaucratised democracy, the administrative staff completely separated from the ownership of property; all bureaucratic enterprises, from factories to armies to schools, based on purely technical norms of efficiency and grounded in rational–legal authority, increasingly separate the individual from the means of work. Socialism would accelerate these trends and prepare the ground for 'a new bondage', a bureaucratic mode of domination stifling all freedom and independent human activity.

Weber's reflections are prescient in the light of later developments within capitalism and state socialist societies, all of which have witnessed an enormous growth in bureaucratic administration. There can be no doubt that Weber was right to emphasise the growing autonomy of the state and the legitimation needs of modern industrial societies: thus while Weber's typology of domination can be criticised for constituting a taxonomy, a formal structure of concepts, rather than a theory which investigates the actual functioning of different modes of domination, including the repressive apparatuses of the state – police, army, etc. – it nevertheless illuminated the necessary subjective element present in structures of authority. In his lecture, 'Politics as a Vocation' (1918), he quotes Trotsky's remark that 'every state is founded on force', but adds that the modern state is never simply a repressive apparatus but a community that successfully claims 'the monopoly of legitimate violence' (Gerth and Mills, 1948, pp. 78–83).

Yet while domination implies a subjective component and a consenting subject, Weber maintained a resolutely pessimistic view of modern democracy. The masses confer legitimacy purely passively: there is little sense of an active relationship between the various groups and classes of civil society and the state apparatus. Weber accepted Michels's theory of mass democracy and the inevitable rule of functionaries. The whole question of popular democratic control is eliminated on the basis that a modern industrial society necessitates bureaucratic administration *from above*. But, as was noted earlier in relation to Weber's theory of stratification, and indeed his theory of bureaucracy, the concept of domination is structured around the existence of an independent civil society. Only from within a strong civil society can the subject actively consent to domination, that is, confer legitimacy through political and social institutions. Weber depicts the technical necessity of rational–legal domination, and thus the emergence of functionaries within the state apparatus controlling modern society; and this, in itself, constitutes a democratic process facilitating mobility and promotion by merit. But this process of rationalisation that seems to lead inevitably to increasing centralisation and the rule of the few over the many, and thus the eclipse of civil society as an independent and living structure, is contradicted by Weber's insistence that social change and thus society itself is the product of human action. Weber failed to reconcile his pessimistic political sociology with his optimistic sociology of social action, for ultimately his sociology of bureaucracy and democracy lacks an adequate theory of civil society.

7
Marxism and Sociology

Marxism after Marx

When Marx died in 1883 Marxism as a distinctive body of knowledge, theory of society and scientific methodology had exercised little influence in the field of the social sciences. Discussion of Marxism was largely confined to the workers' movement and it was not until the 1890s that a wider debate was initiated involving scholars from different areas of the social sciences – economics, history and sociology. The main academic critics of Marxism – Weber, Durkheim, Pareto, Mosca, Croce, Stammler, Sorel – did not set out simply to refute historical materialism but were mainly concerned with the problems which Marx had identified within the social sciences and modern society. This growing interest in Marxism was partly the result of its increasing popularisation in the socialist movement, as well as the importance of socialism itself as an organised political trend based on the principles of class struggle, class consciousness and class solidarity.

Marxism was developed outside the academy by socialist intellectuals who defined it as a natural science of society emphasising the existence of specific laws of social development, the inevitability of class conflict, the polarisation of classes, growing economic crises and eventual collapse of capitalism. At Marx's graveside Engels had declared that as Darwin had discovered 'the law of development of organic nature, so Marx discovered the law of development of human history'. Engels's reference to Darwin and natural history is significant, for the Marxism which developed during the 1880s and 1890s made no distinction between the methods of the natural sciences and those of Marxism. The Marxism of the Second International was particularly positivistic in its early phases. During the 1890s the major political party advocating Marxist theory was the German Social Democratic Party whose leaders, Karl Kautsky (1854–1938) and Eduard Bernstein (1850–1932) enjoyed close ties with Engels; the Social Democrats were responsible for the publication of many of Marx's early and later writings such as the *Theories of Surplus Value*, part of *The German Ideology* and the final volumes of *Capital*. The party, having been legalised in 1890, polled one and a half million votes at the first General Election.

Kautsky, who wrote voluminously on the history of religion, socialism, ethics and economic and political theory – he was described as the 'Pope of Marxism' – represented the orthodox wing of Marxist theory; many of his ideas were shared by the Russian George Plekhanov (1856–1918). More than any other writers Kautsky and Plekhanov transformed Marxism into an integrated world view, defining its basic concepts in positivistic, evolutionary terms arguing that the task of intellectuals was merely to defend Marxist thought from bourgeois theory thus preserving its theoretical purity. Following the inspiration of Engels, in his *Anti-Duhring*, Marxism became codified into a set of rules and general materialist principles applicable to all social and historical phenomena.

During the 1890s the major Marxist works were largely polemical dogmatically defending Marx's method of analysis, his general theory of laws of development and the nature of capitalism as an exploitive system of production. In 1899 Bernstein published his *Evolutionary Socialism* in which he subjected these dogmatic concepts to the test of empirical reality. Contrary to Kautsky and Plekhanov, he argued that the historical development of capitalism did not support Marx's theory of crisis, the notion of inevitable polarisation of classes or the law of the centralisation of capital. The working class was not becoming impoverished, the middle classes were not disappearing, small businesses were developing and there was no evidence that capitalism as a system was doomed to historically inevitable collapse. Bernstein concluded that history demonstrated no 'iron laws', no 'historic necessity'; socialism must be validated, not by appeals to an historically inevitable future, but rather through the ethic of socialism, the *a priori* categories of Kantian moral philosophy in which individuals are regarded, not as means or instruments, but as ends in themselves. For Bernstein the movement was everything; there was no 'ultimate goal'. The political conclusions which Bernstein drew from his analysis came to be known as 'Revisionism', that as capitalism was gradually and peacefully evolving towards a more complex social structure than existed at the time Marx wrote *Capital*, so it was possible to extend democracy, citizenship and equality from within the system itself. The struggle for socialism was thus conceived as a piecemeal, evolutionary process and not as the violent conquest of state power by a disciplined party apparatus.

Bernstein's critique of Marxism was immediately rejected by Kautsky who merely repeated that Marx's analysis of capitalism was correct in virtually every detail: Bernstein had misinterpreted the statistics. The Revisionist controversy is important, however, because it highlighted the weaknesses of Marxism in the light of modern social science. In particular it focused attention on the changes within capitalism since the 1860s that could not be accommodated to the dogmatic prescriptions of orthodox Marxism. For all its claims as a science, Marxism had become ossified into a quasi-religious system which admitted the existence of no facts or historical evidence which might render it untenable. The Revisionist debate reflected many of the criticisms which academic scholars were increasingly levelling at Marxism.

The first significant discussion between Marxists and representatives of 'bourgeois' social science had taken place in 1894 at the first International Congress of Sociology; further debates took place in the 1890s and early years of the twentieth century. The Marxist theory of inevitable social change was particularly criticised, as was the concept of laws of natural necessity and the reduction of the human agent to a product of external conditions. Marxism, it was argued, postulated a rigid, mechanical notion of the relation between the economic 'base' of society and its ideological 'superstructure', a correspondence theory of knowledge which transformed ideas into a passive reflection of class interests. Kautsky developed this model to account for the necessary development of socialist theory itself as occurring outside the workers' movement, the product of intellectuals whose privileged position enabled them to escape from the socio-economic determinism which affected all other groups. The workers attained only a limited consciousness, broadly economic and oriented to trade union matters. As capitalism intensified the objective class struggle through heightened contradictions and tensions, the working class became increasingly receptive to Marxist theory. One important consequence of this élitist position was that the state was defined as an instrument of social transformation, the result of socialist leadership from above. This passive concept of consciousness is central to orthodox Marxism and was further developed by V. I. Lenin (1870–1923) in his theory of the 'vanguard' party discussed below.

Weber, Durkheim and Simmel rejected the Marxist concept of economic laws in favour of a voluntaristic sociology which also took account of the growing complexity, not homogeneity, of modern capitalist society. Criticism of the positivist elements in Marxism, however, did emerge from the Marxist movement itself and was not confined to those intellectuals outside the socialist movement. The Italian Marxist Antonio Labriola (1843–1904) and the French theorist of revolutionary syndicalism Georges Sorel (1847–1922) sought to combat the concept of Marxism as a self-contained system based on natural laws of development by invoking Vico's dictum that humanity knows only that which it has created. Sorel, who wrote extensively on Marxism during the 1890s and contributing an important essay on Vico, introduced Labriola's work into France especially the *Essays on the Materialist Conception of History* (1896). Sorel, however, was much more concerned with Marxism as a theory of action than Marxism as a theory of totality and it is interesting to see how these two elements were combined in Labriola's work.

Labriola accepted the concept of society as a whole, analysing social classes and individuals as parts developing in relation to the whole; he assimilated, too, the model of base and superstructure in which ideas correspond to specific social conditions. But he went beyond naturalistic Marxism by emphasising the uniqueness of historical formations and rejecting the simple triadic schema of social change –

thesis–antithesis–synthesis – in favour of a theory of change centred on human activity, consciousness and thus praxis. Like Sorel, Labriola attacked the whole notion of economic determinism and the theory that historical change can be explained entirely in terms of the economic factor. He defined the historical process as an historical totality in which intellectual and material culture are organically bound together. Unique historical events cannot be explained away by reference to simple, reciprocal economic causation. Labriola emphasised the economic *structure* of a society as the basis of its organic unity; it was not, therefore, a question of assimilating cultural forces to the economic and defining society in terms of one single *factor*. For Labriola, all elements of material life and intellectual culture were an expression of the historical epoch – an expressive totality – and could not be analysed in positivist terms, as external facts, because of their organic unity in an all-enveloping process of historical development. There was no 'dominant' element as such within this concept of totality: historical events and sociological processes existed in relation to economic forces but could never be reduced to them as mere passive expressions (Labriola, 1967).

Reality is not a given datum but created through human activity; the goal of socialism is not lying in wait in some distant future but result from *praxis*. There is no truth waiting to be discovered only a truth which must be *made*. Sorel praised Labriola's rejection of 'vulgar Marxism' and its crude theory of economic determinism. As the editor of two influential socialist journals, Sorel proposed to examine Marxism in depth and during the late 1890s contributed a number of critical essays on such topical issues as the Revisionist debate, Marxism as a science and the role of ethics in socialist theory. After 1903, however, he became increasingly disillusioned with orthodox Marxism and turned towards revolutionary syndicalism and his theory of the *myth* developed especially in his *Reflections on Violence* (1908).

Orthodox Marxism, Sorel argued, had degenerated into a species of historical fatalism built around the notion of periodic and catastrophic economic crises which supposedly culminate in a general crisis of the whole capitalist system and subsequent political transformation. The reductionist formulas of Kautsky *et al.* ignore the real 'authors' and 'actors' of history and the fact that social relationships are made by men as much as by the development of the productive forces. Sorel was a perceptive critic of vulgar Marxism: his work was influenced by what he called 'the treasures contained in the work of Vico', especially the notion of the social world as the work of humanity and that humanity understands only that which it has created. Thus for Sorel there was no natural history of society, no scientific socialism. In the debate on Revisionism he sided with Bernstein arguing that 'the problem for socialism is to develop in the working classes a superior culture, which would allow them to administer the productive forces . . . Today, the proletariat is far from possessing this culture' (Sorel, 1976, pp. 126, 157–64). Socialism is vindicated, not through appeals to the 'final end' of historical development but by the ethical superiority of proletarian institutions and culture.

Sorel's anti-scientism and his general distrust of theories of social change which minimised or eliminated the active human subject, led him to argue against the holistic approach of Marxist methodology and advocate an atomistic concept of society structured in the voluntaristic practice of actors. His fundamental point was that change occurs through will, collectively organised within the working class, but expressing the contradictions of the present system and a longing for an alternative society. The myth of the general strike functions precisely in this way as a system of images, which invokes through intuition the sentiments oriented towards socialism that form an integral part of working-class experience.

As we shall see below, Sorel's work influenced the Marxism of the Italian Gramsci, especially the critique of scientistic anti-humanist materialism, although in general Sorel's writings exerted little significance for the development of early twentieth-century Marxism.

Marxism as revolutionary consciousness: Lukács and the concept of totality

One of the most important Marxist theorists in the immediate post-1917 period was Georg Lukács (1885–1971). His work includes studies of aesthetics, literature, philosophy, politics and sociology. Lukács turned to Marxism during the First World War: his pre-war writings were informed by a strong anti-positivist outlook influenced by the work of Rickert, Simmel, Weber and Dilthey. In 1915 he belonged to a circle of Hungarian intellectuals which included Karl Mannheim, Arnold Hauser, Bela Bartok, Zoltan Kodaly and Michael Polanyi, all of whom were concerned with the problems of democracy and culture. Joining the Hungarian Communist Party shortly after its founding in 1918, Lukács began writing a series of essays dealing with the question of Marxism and modern bourgeois thought. In 1923 he published *History and Class Consciousness*, subtitled, 'Studies in Marxist Dialectics', a book which has the remarkable distinction of being banned by the Third International as non-Marxist and heretical, and yet a potent influence on the thought of such diverse thinkers as Martin Heidegger, Jean-Paul Sartre, Herbert Marcuse and Lucien Goldmann. *History and Class Consciousness* was directed against the evolutionary positivism that dominated the Marxism of the Second International and was particularly critical of the contribution of Engels to Marxism: Lukács argued that Engels had transformed Marxism from a dialectical into a mechanical social theory in which consciousness became the passive product of external forces, a reflection of objective conditions.

History and Class Consciousness is an attempt to relate Marx's social theory to its Hegelian origins in the concept of totality and dialectical method. Facts do not speak for themselves but have meaning only when integrated into a whole; the fundamental axiom of dialectical method is that the whole is prior to the parts and that the parts themselves must be interpreted in their relation with the whole. For Lukács, the whole has primacy over its parts; the meaning of facts lies in their mediation with the whole. Thus the 'ultimate goal' of the socialist movement is the *'relation to the totality* (to the whole of society seen as a process) through which every aspect of the struggle acquires its revolutionary significance'. The meaning of history, or truth, lies not in the study of the empirical, objective structure of capitalism but in grasping that the working-class movement constitutes the expression of a necessary historical progress. The proletariat simultaneously is both the subject and object of history, the knowing subject which approaches truth through 'knowledge of the real, objective nature of a phenomenon . . . of its historical character and the knowledge of its actual function in the totality of society'. The 'self-knowledge of the proletariat', its awareness of its position in the social structure as an exploited class, 'coincides with knowledge of the whole', its awareness that its class situation can be understood only from the standpoint of the whole society, its system of production and social relations. Thus knowledge of reality is inseparable from the class position of the proletariat (Lukács, 1971, pp. 12–23).

In these formulations Lukács defined Marxism as an ideology but an ideology more advanced theoretically than any other 'style of thought'. Marxism is, therefore, not a systematic body of knowledge based on historically objective laws and the application of natural scientific methodology, but a revolutionary *praxis* in which the individual becomes a subject not an object of the historical process. Marxism is wholly distinct from bourgeois thought, and while bourgeoisie and proletariat share the same social reality, capitalism, they comprehend it differently. Bourgeois thought is profoundly unhistorical accepting the given, empirically immediate forms, thus conceiving change as catastrophe rather than as mediated by the structural principles of the whole. In contrast, proletarian thought is self-knowledge of the real historical situation, comprising a rejection of the immediately given forms of society in favour of the 'immanent meanings' of the historical process as a whole. Lukács concludes that proletarian thought stands 'on a higher scientific plane objectively' than bourgeois thought since it refuses to consider objects in isolation from the total process.

Thus the proletariat comprehends society as a coherent whole and, unlike the bourgeoisie 'aspires towards the truth even in its false consciousness . . . and substantive errors'. Ontologically privileged, the worker is nevertheless transformed into a commodity, into an object by the nature of capitalist production so that his empirical condition corresponds to the capitalist transformation of social relations into relations between objects and things. The fact that labour-power is appropriated as a thing means only that the proletariat, as a class, can achieve a consciousness of its real position. In the act of knowing, subject and object coincide: the cognitive and practical components of knowledge are thus fused within proletarian thought. The proletariat's self-knowledge of society is identical with the revolutionary transformation of capitalism: the movement towards socialism and the consciousness of this movement are one and the same thing. Knowledge is no mere epiphenomena, no simple reflection of external objects but is bound up with the revolutionary practice of the proletariat (Lukács, 1971, Ch. 2).

Lukács's discussion of bourgeois and proletarian thought and his general critique of positivism is linked to his analysis of reification and alienation as critical elements in the formation of consciousness and social theory. Although Marx had discussed alienation in his early writings, the Marxism of the Second International had failed to notice its significance, partly as a result of the unavailability of the texts (many remained unpublished until the 1920s and 1930s), as well as the unreceptive nature of positivist Marxism to non-scientistic concepts as alienation and reification. With his Hegelian and hermeneutic philosophical background, Lukács was able to analyse *Capital* through the categories he discovered in the few texts of Marx's early years which had been published, notably *The Holy Family*. He argues that reification dominates capitalist culture stamping its 'imprint upon the whole consciousness of man', a process which is total:

> Reification is . . . the necessary, immediate reality of every person living in capitalist society. It can be overcome only by *constant and constantly renewed efforts to disrupt the reified structure of existence by concretely relating to the concretely manifested contradictions of the total development, by becoming conscious of these contradictions for the total development* [Lukács's emphasis] (Lukács, 1971, p. 197).

Yet how is it possible for the proletariat to aspire to truth given the total penetration of reification within the culture? Lukács argues that as a commodity, the proletariat embodies the whole process of reification, but because it is an object its class situation drives it towards consciousness, 'the self-consciousness of the object', which enables it to cut through the fetishised nature of capitalism.

In these formulations Lukács comes close to abandoning Marxist materialism altogether. Historically, the worker is not transformed into a *thing*, or mere object, for while the social world of commodities penetrates consciousness, disposing the worker to grasp society as a natural, objective datum, there is always within every situation forces which work against reification. If Lukács's theory was historically accurate, it would be impossible to understand the development of specific working-class institutions such as trade unions or the struggle of the English proletariat against the nineteenth-century Factory Acts: in the most advanced industrial society of the nineteenth century the English working class should have been wholly dominated by reification, yet they created the most powerful trade union movement in the industrialising world and struggled, successfully in many cases, to improve their economic, social and political status. Lukács's conception of reification as a total process flows from his theory of totality, that the whole is prior to its parts which are organically bound together and express the inner core of the whole itself. It should be clear that this conception of totality is neither empirical nor historical but an *historicist* category in which the whole is directly expressive of the historical process. The relation of parts and whole is thus symmetrical rather than uneven and contradictory.

Similarly, in his discussion of class and class consciousness Lukács postulates an abstract and non-historical conception of the relation between social structure and ideology. Class consciousness is equivalent to totality: 'For a class to be ripe for hegemony means that its interests and consciousness enable it to organise the whole of society in accordance with those interests' (Lukács, 1971, p. 52). For Lukács, bourgeois thought fails to grasp society 'from the centre, as a coherent whole', while proletarian thought strives towards a historical understanding of its historical mission as a universal class whose actions will transform the whole. Lukács thus distinguishes 'psychological' from 'imputed' class consciousness, the former consisting of the empirical, day-to-day consciousness of workers which is false and incapable of grasping the whole. 'True' class consciousness is the 'potential' consciousness of a class that corresponds with the Marxist theory of the historical process. Potential consciousness is the 'appropriate and rational reaction' of a class to its historical situation *if* it possessed the necessary knowledge of its relation to the social whole. Employing one of Weber's concepts, Lukács thus writes that 'the objective theory of class consciousness is the theory of its objective possibility' (Lukács, 1971, p. 79).

But what is 'imputed' or 'potential' consciousness? It is obviously more real than everyday consciousness and cannot be reduced to elements of the latter. Yet how is it to be constituted theoretically if not from the empirical forms of consciousness? The answer is the privileged position of intellectuals who genuinely understand the historical process and therefore impute to the proletariat its true consciousness. For Lukács, history is invested with a meaning outside its empirical, concrete determinations, its different phases expressing an essence which is the historical process conceived as a totality. Lukács's critique of positivism thus ends in idealism, the rejection of all principles of verification and empirical evidence as the basis of Marxist theory: totality cannot be reconstructed through its empirical parts, the facts cannot simply be accumulated before the whole emerges. If wholes cannot be structured in terms of the empirical but only in terms of the future, the maturation of the historical process, then all social science would seem superfluous.

Lukács's standpoint is Hegelian, for like Hegel's philosopher who could genuinely interpret the ruses of history, so Lukács's historicism allows scope for the socialist, revolutionary intellectuals to impute consciousness and grasp the meaning of the whole. But the whole must be known before facts can be integrated within it, and the only way that the whole is known is not by empirical method but by accepting the privileged historical standpoint of the proletariat. And, of course, this itself cannot be proved, only accepted as the truth of history.

Culture and domination: Gramsci and the concept of hegemony

Antonio Gramsci (1891–1937) has been described as the most original Marxist theorist of the first half of the twentieth century. Gramsci's work is characterised by a concern with problems of culture and the relation of cultural formations to political domination; the central concept of hegemony has become widely used in the social sciences, as popular a term as that of alienation. Like Lukács, Gramsci defined Marxism in opposition to positivism and all forms of economic determinism emphasising the role of consciousness and the human subject in the making of historical change.

One of the leaders of the Italian Communist Party, Gramsci spent the last years of his short life incarcerated in Mussolini's jails producing, often in elliptical form to avoid prison censorship, reflections and reviews of Marxist theory and the relation between Marxism and political science, sociology, philosophy and history. Arrested in 1926 Gramsci wrote 3000 pages of analysis as well as hundreds of letters: his activity firmly negated the intention of the prosecutor at his trial that 'this brain must be put out of action for twenty years'.

In the years following the Second World War, the Italian Communist Party published much of this material frequently in an abridged form to avoid embarrassing the party's rigid Stalinist standpoint. Not that Gramsci deviated widely from orthodox Leninism: he accepted the necessity for a revolutionary party and rejected his youthful advocacy of workers councils as constituting the basis for a total reorganisation of society. His writings during the great strike wave and factory occupations in Turin during 1919–21 parallel Lenin's reflections on the relation of state and soviets in *The State and Revolution*; influenced especially by the work of Sorel, Gramsci suggested that the working class, through its own independent institutions, can transform social relations from within civil society, and that social change will not be imposed from above through centralised authority. But as Lenin abandoned his concept of Commune state so Gramsci modified his views on working-class spontaneity. In 1924 he wrote that Bolshevism was the first movement to develop the conception of proletarian hegemony; in the *Prison Notebooks* he is more explicit noting that the concept of hegemony represented Lenin's 'greatest theoretical contribution to the philosophy of *praxis*' (Gramsci, 1971, p. 365). Yet there are significant differences between Lenin's notion of the dictatorship of the proletariat, with its assumption of a strong, coercive state apparatus (and which remained central to Lenin's Marxism apart from the single exception of *The State and Revolution*), and Gramsci's theory of hegemony. For Gramsci, hegemony is predicated on a resilient and independent civil society allowing autonomy to 'private institutions' such as education, church, political parties, trade unions, and so on, which form the source of *consent*. Equally, Gramsci's concept of Marxism differs sharply from Leninism being influenced less by Engels, Plekhanov and Kautsky than the anti-positivist elements in Labriola, Sorel and the Italian Hegelian, Benedetto Croce.

For Gramsci, Marxism constituted a form of 'absolute historicism'. All forms of thought and action express a global historical process. Thus philosophy and science are true in the sense that they express the 'real' development of history. Marxism is defined as a world view (a *Weltanschauung*) containing 'in itself all the fundamental elements needed to construct a total and integral conception of the world, a total philosophy and theory of natural science . . . everything that is needed to give life to an integral practical organisation of society, that is, to become a total integral civilization' (Gramsci, 1971, p. 462). Reality is thus always historical, made by active human subjects: science, philosophy, Marxism, are not objective modes of intellectual activity existing in an external relation with the subject but created through the sum of actions which constitutes *praxis*. All elements have meaning in relation to the whole and they are 'true' in that they express the immanent tendencies of the whole itself. Unlike Lukács, Gramsci rejects the dualism of nature and society arguing that the category nature is itself social and historical. Marxism, or as Gramsci phrases it in the *Prison Notebooks*, the philosophy of *praxis*, constitutes the expression of the collective will of the subordinate working class striving to educate and liberate themselves from exploitation and class domination. The historical process is characterised, not simply by economic forces, but by human will, organised into collective forms and becoming 'the driving force of the economy,' moulding 'objective reality' (Gramsci, 1977, p. 35).

Gramsci's emphasis on will, on voluntarism is brought out vividly in one of his first significant articles, his response to the 1917 revolution, called prophetically, 'The Revolution against *Das Kapital*'. Written shortly after the successful October revolution, Gramsci's article argued that the Bolshevik accession to power vindicated Marxism as a non-fatalistic, activist theory built around the concept of 'collective will' rather than objective, 'iron laws'. Throughout his early writings Gramsci continually emphasised the self-activity of the working class, arguing that fatalistic acceptance of the inevitability of socialism condemns the proletariat to passivity and defensive political action. For Gramsci, revolution was not the automatic product of external economic forces but the result of one class establishing a cultural domination over all other classes. A 'rising class', he wrote, will strive to establish its authority over other social strata both through economic, political and military power and 'intellectual and moral leadership'. All revolutions are preceded 'by an intense work of cultural penetration' as the rising class aims to subjugate allied and subordinate strata to its ideas. A dominant class is thus defined as one which saturates civil society with the spirit of its morality, customs, religious and political practices: 'The founding of a ruling class is equivalent to the creation of a *Weltanschauung*.' If the working class are to constitute a dominant class they must establish a culture that commands the support of other strata; its world view, Marxism, is thus not a class ideology as such, but the expression of the immanent structural trends of history. Cultural hegemony is prior to the act of revolution and must be created through collective action. Gramsci thus distinguishes hegemony – associated with consent and equilibrium between social classes – and domination, associated with coercion and the state. Hegemony is created within civil society and the private institutions which mediate the individual and the state; direct domination flows from the state apparatus, coercion through public institutions (Gramsci, 1971, pp. 77–84).

Gramsci first employed the term hegemony in his *Some*

Aspects of the Southern Question (1926), where he said that the proletariat 'can become the leading (*dirigente*) and the dominant class to the extent that it succeeds in creating a system of alliances that allow it to mobilise the majority of the working population against capitalism and the bourgeois state' (Gramsci, 1978, p. 443). Hegemony is effectively a synthesis of political, intellectual and moral leadership in which a class passes from defending its own 'corporate' interests to unifying and directing all other social groups. Two examples from Gramsci's work will illustrate his general argument. He suggests that only the bourgeoisie and proletariat strive to establish hegemony. Feudal society, in contrast to capitalism, is dominated by a closed caste, the dominant classes do not develop an organic passage from the other classes to their own but remain 'technically' and 'ideologically' separate. In contrast, the Jacobins, a specific social group, developed into a hegemonic class by representing all the popular forces ranged against the old regime and organising a national, popular collective will. Thus although possessing certain economic functions related to the developing bourgeois means of production, the Jacobins passed from a merely economic phase of development to an ethical–political stage with their own political party and *Weltanschauung*.

Gramsci, of course, was concerned with the possibility of revolution in the advanced capitalist countries. His analysis of hegemony suggests that the working class are not simply the passive victims of an overpowering structure of bourgeois ideology, but actively acquiesce in the persistence of bourgeois society. In Western Europe civil society is relatively strong thus enabling the bourgeoisie to rule through consent. Gramsci emphasises that hegemony is not wholly consensual but consists of a synthesis of consent and coercion, an equilibrium in which force does not prevail. The distinction between civil and political society is therefore not absolute since the capitalist social formation cannot be broken down into wholly separate and independent institutions. Thus he notes that education, while belonging, as an institution to civil society, is dependent on the state both economically and ideologically. In Hegelian terms, Gramsci argues for the ethical role of the state, that although defending the economic and political interests of the dominant class, the state is nevertheless instrumental in building up the institutions which contribute to the strength of civil society. This is Gramsci's way of expressing the problem of relative autonomy, that the state is not simply the organ one class uses to oppress another but the means whereby a modern complex society is created and legitimised, not through a class ideology, but a bourgeois *Weltanschauung*.

The whole tenor of Gramsci's Marxism was against reductionism of any kind: culture was not simply class culture, the state was not merely a class state, consent was not false consciousness. Hegemony implied a democratic relation between ruled and ruler, the existence of institutions which enable the subordinate groups to articulate their own interests and defend them, to build their own distinctive culture. Thus revolution is not simply the seizure of the state apparatus and the transference of economic forces to a new class: proletarian revolution is a process of mass participation, the exercise of collective will by a class whose culture enables it to become an active subject and hegemonic force thus enlarging civil society and its democratic structures.

Marxism and the sociology of intellectuals: Gramsci

One of Gramsci's most significant contributions to a sociology of modern society and the processes of hegemony was his theory of intellectuals. For Gramsci, intellectuals exercised a critical role in the formation both of ideologies and consent. Social cohesion was as much the function of intellectuals as of social structure. The failure of Marxism in the advanced capitalist societies posed questions both on the role of leadership as well as the function of intellectuals in society as a whole.

Gramsci defined intellectuals sociologically rejecting the conception of intellectual activity as intrinsic to a special social stratum. Such properties, he argued, were characteristic of everyone in society:

> What are the 'maximum' limits of acceptance of the term 'intellectuals'? Can one find a unitary criterion to characterise equally all the diverse and disparate activities of intellectuals and

to distinguish these at the same time and in an essential way from the activities of other social groupings? The most widespread error of method seems to me that of having looked for this criterion of distinction in the intrinsic nature of intellectual activities, rather than in the ensemble of the system of relations in which these activities . . . have their place within the general complex of social relations . . . All men are intellectuals . . . but not all men have in society the function of intellectuals (Gramsci, 1971, pp. 8–9).

Gramsci thus rejected the idealist notion of 'great intellectuals': intellectuals were defined in terms of knowledge production and work function. Discussing the Italian philosopher, Croce, Gramsci described him as a 'constructor' of ideologies in the interests of the governing class, although 'interests' and 'ideologies' cannot be assimilated mechanistically to class position. Intellectuals produce knowledge and ideologies which are always more than a simple reflection of class interests. As a social stratum intellectuals develop more slowly than other social groups and although giving expression to the interests of a dominant class they equally articulate the cultural traditions of a whole people. The development of capitalism, however, introduces a new type of intellectual, the technical organiser, the specialist who gradually replaces the older, traditional type organising society through the institutions of the state.

Gramsci defined intellectuals, therefore, as those who perform functions of organisation within the realm of production, culture, public administration, a concept wholly opposed to the élitist notion exemplified in Pareto's circulation of élites or Mosca's governing class which effectively divided society into a superior stratum of governors and inferior stratum of the governed. Underpinning Gramsci's theory of intellectuals was his awareness of the specific historical development of bourgeois society towards increasing centralisation – a national educational system, local and national civil service administration, the growth of the church and the professions and especially the rapid development of the state apparatus. In Gramsci's view certain economic 'corporate' classes – classes whose own narrow interests were wholly class conditioned – must necessarily pass into hegemonic classes if they are to become a dominant class. In this process intellectuals play a critical role linking the basic economic structure and basis of a class with the wider cultural institutions:

> Every social group, coming into existence on the original terrain of an essential function in the world of economic production, creates together with itself, organically, one or more strata of intellectuals which give it homogeneity and an awareness of its own function not only in the economic but also in the social and political fields (Gramsci, 1971, p. 5).

Gramsci argues that social classes do not develop their own intellectuals; a social class, striving for hegemony, must transform itself from its original amorphous structure into a homogeneous, ideologically unified group capable of generating, through its allied intellectuals, universal concepts. Intellectuals are defined both in terms of structure and function as well as consciousness.

Gramsci distinguished two types of intellectual: organic and traditional. Organic intellectuals belong to social groups aiming to direct the whole of society, 'experts in legitimation', who emerge as the result of changes in the mode of production; organic intellectuals express the aspirations of a class without themselves constituting a class. In contrast, traditional intellectuals evolve through a process of 'uninterrupted historical continuity' and unlike organic intellectuals are not so closely bound up with the mode of production. Traditional intellectuals are characterised by a caste-like structure; they define themselves independently of the dominant class. Traditional intellectuals are inter-class, existing within the intercises of society, linking the past with the present as an historically continuous process. Organic intellectuals produce ideas which mark a sharp break with the past. Traditional intellectuals include ecclesiastical intellectuals, lawyers, teachers, doctors, their function one of maintaining continuity between one social formation and another. Gramsci cited the eighteenth-century French clergy who, through their function in education and monopoly of religious ideology transformed themselves from traditional intellectuals into the organic intellectuals of the landed aristocracy. Gramsci's point is that any social group

211

striving to establish hegemony must conquer and assimilate the traditional intellectuals. In Italy, the bourgeoisie failed to create a 'hegemonic phase' remaining at the corporate level and thus used Piedmont, the northern monarchical state, as the means of domination. In Germany, the Junkers constituted the traditional intellectuals of the bourgeoisie retaining an independent economic and political base.

Gramsci's examples are hypotheses. He could not conduct empirical research into the complex relation of intellectuals and social structure. His purpose was largely theoretical to show that while all social groups necessarily forge links with different types of intellectuals, only the political party can carry out the task of welding together the organic intellectuals and the traditional intellectuals: 'The party carries out this function in strict dependence on its basic function, which is that of elaborating its own component parts – those elements of a social group which has been born and developed as an "economic" group – and of turning them into qualified political intellectuals, leaders and ·organisers of all the activities and functions inherent in the organic development of an integral society, both civil and political' (Gramsci, 1971, pp. 16–17). An economic social group – the landed interest, the industrialists, the proletariat – can only develop beyond the specific 'moment of their historical development' and become the agency of national and international activity through the fusion of the two types of intellectual within the structure of a political party.

As 'functionaries of the superstructure', intellectuals mediate the worlds of culture and production producing the ideas which the masses 'spontaneously' accept as legitimate because such ideas express more than the sum of the class interests of the dominant group. In this sense intellectuals are 'organisers' of social hegemony and Gramsci emphasises their critical role in the hegemonic structures of Western European civil societies in which direct forms of domination have been the exception. Gramsci's is not a pessimistic sociology of the intellectual: his concept of modern capitalism was not that of a mass society, although he noted the tendency towards bureaucratisation and centralisation, but a complex structure of independent, 'private' institutions (political parties, trade unions, church, professional associations, etc.) which formed the basis of consent and social hegemony. The vitality of civil society and the persistence of hegemony enabled intellectuals in the advanced capitalist countries to exercise their function as organisers of, and experts in, legitimation without forming a special élite dominating society from above. It thus follows that the proletariat, as a rising class striving for hegemony, must saturate civil society with its own distinct values and culture, not as simple working-class ideas or interests, but universalised as socialism – a world view – which compels the whole society and in particular the traditional intellectuals to accept *actively* the validity and historical necessity of its fundamental principles.

For Gramsci, then, intellectuals are structured in a hierarchy of functions relating to hegemony. At the apex are the creative intellectuals who produce the world views, ideologies and theoretical systems; at the base are administrative intellectuals whose function is one of diffusing the values and culture of the existing hegemony; and finally, in the middle ranges are the organisational intellectuals without which no dominant group could survive. The role of creative intellectuals is more significant in strong civil societies where they work to bring together a number of strata or groups into an 'historical bloc' (i.e. the English industrialists and the aristocracy, the German Junkers and industrialists). Gramsci emphasises that the withdrawal of their allegiance to hegemony will produce an 'organic' crisis, a crisis of authority and the possibility of social disintegration. Creative intellectuals are structurally and ideologically more crucial than the second order intellectuals, although these subaltern groups are functionally necessary if social hegemony is to work adequately and therefore they must be assimilated into the dominant intellectual bloc. In the transition to socialism it thus follows that intellectuals must articulate the consciousness of the working classes and allied groups: Gramsci formulated the concept of the political party as the 'collective intellectual', the institution which synthesises the creative vitality of the masses with the organisational, directing function of the organic intellectuals. Intellectuals are crucial for socialist transformation: it is not a question of the Party dominating the masses from above but rather of a dialectical and democratic relation of party to people. Yet although this formulation opposes authoritarianism and élitism it nevertheless leaves unanswered the question of how a socialist society, based on centralisation and collectivist ideology, can retain an independent civil society and thus autonomous intellectuals. In this sense the collective intellectual suggests an element of totalitarianism within Gramsci's general framework of a democratic socialism structured in the activity and culture of the masses.

Lukács and Gramsci on sociology

Both Lukács and Gramsci defined Marxism as a world view organically bound up with the 'rising' industrial working class. As a science of proletarian revolution Marxism expressed the active elements of human culture, *praxis*, through which human subjects created necessary historical change. Both writers were aware of developments in the field of sociology: Lukács knew the work of Simmel, Weber, Sombart; Gramsci was particularly interested in sociological studies of political parties and problems of methodology and was familiar with the writings of Mosca, Michels, Pareto, Weber, not to mention the nineteenth-century positivist tradition.

Both Gramsci and Lukács tended to identify sociology with positivism: sociology was thus criticised for the elimination of the active subject in favour of external, objective laws which dominate society and the individual. For Lukács, sociology defined the object as given, transforming historical processes into eternal and natural forces; the social world was thus reifed with consciousness reduced to a passive reflection of economic structure. The reification of the historical and social world within bourgeois thought makes it impossible to grasp the connections between the various elements that comprise society and the whole: society as a totality in a constant process of change is absent from bourgeois sociology. Indeed, bourgeois thought splits up social knowledge into separate spheres of inquiry – political economy, history, jurisprudence and sociology. Thus bourgeois thought cannot go beyond the surface of observable facts to determine their relation with the whole: the monographic method, Lukács concludes, the intensive, quantitative study of one element within the whole, constitutes the limit of sociology and confirms its status as ideology. All facts must be interpreted in terms of the historical process as a whole, its objective possibility.

Similarly, Gramsci criticised positivistic sociology for reducing social relations to the status of inviolable natural laws. He was particularly hostile to sociologists such as Michels, for postulating 'iron laws' of organisation that assumed incompetence and passivity on the part of the masses. Hegemony constitutes rather the triumph of consciousness, social action and *will* over external conditions: 'Structure ceases to be an external force', Gramsci wrote, 'which crushes man, assimilates him to itself and makes him passive [but] is transformed into a means of freedom, an instrument to create a new ethico-political form and a source of new initiatives' (Gramsci, 1971, p. 367). Gramsci followed Labriola in rejecting sociology on the basis of its inability to grasp the whole historical process: Labriola had coined the term, the philosophy of *praxis* as the 'essence' of historical materialism, defining it as the 'immanent philosophy' which pervades the entire historical and social individual. As a philosophy of *praxis*, Marxism cannot be reduced to sociology which for Gramsci was a science which sought to discover social facts, the causal relations between them and the general laws of social systems through the methods of the natural sciences. Marxism, as a world view, cannot be schematized into an external body of knowledge structured around the discovery of regular and objective laws since such a standpoint assumes the passivity of the historical subject. Gramsci admitted, however, that statistics were valuable, especially from the point of view of social planning, but his main thrust against sociology, as he conceived it, was that all statistical laws, and predictions based on these laws, defined as natural phenomena, ignored the essential component of all social situations, that of collective will. Reality is constantly changing through *praxis*; it is impossible to predict scientifically the effects of actions or the workings of elements on elements: one can foresee only in the sense that one acts and therefore contributes to the 'predicted' result.

As there were no sociological laws which facilitated prediction as in the natural sciences, so there was no 'Marxist sociology', since reality was always a created reality and the historical process an act of self-knowledge by the proletariat. For Lukács and Gramsci, sociology separated theory from practice: objective laws and objective facts exist only in a process of active mediation involving an historical subject. Ultimately both Lukács and Gramsci argue that historical knowledge is not possible merely as the product of empirical social science: empirical inquiry must be guided by historicism and humanism.

There were attempts from within Marxism to transform Marxism into a sociological system or theory, by the Austro-Marxist school (a term coined by the American socialist, Louis Boudin to describe a group of young Marxists active in the Austrian socialist movement prior to the First World War, the most prominent being Max Adler, Otto Bauer, Rudolf Hilferding and Karl Renner) and the leading Bolshevik theorist, Nikolai Bukharin whose textbook, *Hitorical Materialism*, subtitled *A System of Sociology*, originally published in Russia in 1921, exercised an influential role in the education of leading Marxists inside and outside the Soviet Union. Both Lukács and Gramsci polemicised against Bukharin (1888–1938) precisely because *Historical Materialism* had a greater intellectual impact among Marxists than the more academically oriented work of the Austro-Marxists who, in any case, did not belong to the Third International.

Both Lukács and Gramsci criticised *Historical Materialism* for dividing Marxism into a naturalist scientific sociology, combining history and politics, and a philosophical materialism embracing the theory of knowledge. One of the first Marxists to interpret historical materialism as a form of sociology, Bukharin sought to assimilate the burgeoning sociology of Weber, Simmel, Michels and others, to accommodate twentieth-century Marxism to twentieth-century sociology. He distinguished between 'proletarian science' and 'bourgeois science', the former assimilating the scientific insights of the latter. Yet as Lukács and Gramsci emphasised in their critiques, Bukharin's conception of Marxism is close to 'bourgeois natural scientific materialism' in its attempt to reduce the dialectic to general laws of motion working objectively and independent of human consciousness. In his criticism, Lukács argued that Bukharin's conception eliminated the category of totality from social science, the historical process was no longer grasped as a unifying whole; the relation of parts to whole is conceived mechanically and positivistically. In particular Bukharin's concept of society as a system with its law of equilibrium is close to the formulations of Comte and Pareto in assimilating human activity and human relationships to an underlying and dominating external structure. Lukács was especially critical of Bukharin's scientism, his uncritical acceptance of prediction in social science: only practice, not unmediated facts based on statistics, constitutes proof of empirical propositions, the transformation of reality by human activity and human consciousness. Bukharin's sociologised Marxism, concluded Lukács, was merely a form of 'passive' materialism' that divorces the active subject from the totality of the historical process (Lukács, 1972, pp. 135–42).

Gramsci, too, criticised Bukharin's scientism, for his failure to grasp that all objective economic and sociological phenomena derived from social relationships, human activity, values, culture and consciousness. Bukharin's concept of system, Gramsci argued, fetishised and hypostatised society. For Bukharin, society was defined as a system greater than the sum of its parts; it is not ideology (Lukács) or hegemony (Gramsci) which transforms the different parts into a whole, but a system of mutual interactions between the different members. In this way the subject plays a role but one severely circumscribed by external forces. For Bukharin 'each individual in his development . . . is filled with the influences of his environment, as the skin of a sausage is filled with sausage-meat . . . Like a sponge he constantly absorbs new impressions . . . Each individual at bottom is filled with a social content. The individual himself is a collection of concentrated social influences, united in a small unit' (Bukharin, 1969, p. 98). The parallel between nineteenth-century positivist sociology and Bukharin's Marxist sociology is brought out quite sharply in this formulation. Society is an organism consisting of different structures; the system dominates the individual who is linked to others through mechanical modes of interaction. An homologous relationship subsists between the material and economic 'base', and the culture of society; cultural institutions, ideologies and consciousness are epiphenomenal forces lacking all autonomy. The system normally exists in a state of equilibrium, a situation facilitated by morality and customs which co-ordinate human action to prevent social disintegration. But the existence of class interests and sources of conflict necessarily lead to adjustments and change and, in extreme situations, to revolution.

The important point about Bukharin's mechanistic and abstract concept of society is that it fails totally to develop a theory of civil society and the institutions through which social action occurs, values produced, culture transformed and with it the social individual, social groups and social classes. In Bukharin's formulation the human subject is passive, the product of external forces; social change is the result of a breakdown of equilibrium within the system, of necessary adjustments and thus the development of a new systemic equilibrium. Such ahistorical, excessively abstract and mechanical conceptions of society are strikingly similar to Pareto's *Treatise*, and its concern with developing a general theory of society to the exclusion of any detailed, empirical analysis of any one society and its constituent structures. Abstractly conceived, Bukharin's work fails to grasp, in Marx's and Engels's words, that 'civil society is the true source and theatre of all history' (Marx and Engels, 1964, p. 48).

In contrast, the explicit sociological Marxism of Austro-Marxism was mainly concerned with the specific development of capitalism, its class structure, and state institutions: they argued, rather like Weber, that civil society was changing, the class and occupational structure leading to the emergence of a broad middle class including what Renner called 'the service class' (managers and salaried employees), and a shift in authority relations from those based on private property to bureaucracy. Perhaps the most significant empirical study of the school was Hilferding's *Finance Capital*, which influenced Lenin's *Imperialism* in its depiction of modern capitalism as a fusion of banking and industrial capital within a structure dominated by cartels, trusts and monopolies. Hilferding emphasised the role of an increasingly interventionist state which prevented capitalist economic laws working out towards crisis and collapse: his concept of 'organised capitalism' emphasises the close relation between the nation state and private capital. The relation between state and civil society was thus close to the formulations of orthodox Marxism: thus the socialist programme advocated by the Austro-Marxists was broadly evolutionary, taking over the state apparatus and wielding it for the public good: there was no conception of the state being absorbed and abolished by the democratic institutions of civil society.

Thus although focusing empirically on changes within capitalism, the Austro-Marxists reached broadly similar conclusions to those of Bukharin and orthodox Marxism. The masses were largely passive; the human subject exercised no decisive role in change other than as determined by external forces. Thus their methodological orientation explicitly rejected the *verstehen* approach of Weber and Simmel arguing for the unity of the natural and cultural sciences: 'Nature and society . . . comprise the causal regularity of events as a whole . . . a social scientific standpoint . . . is logically on the same footing as natural science'. As a 'natural science of social beings and events' Marxism studied the law-governed interconnectedness of phenomena: the link between the Austro-Marxist methodology of scientific inquiry and their social reformism is brought out in Adler's concept of Marxism as 'a system of sociological knowledge' which grounds socialism 'upon causal knowledge of the events of social life'. Marxism and sociology 'are one and the same thing', the science 'of the laws of social life and its causal development', striving 'to deduce the development of socialism from capitalism as a matter of causal necessity' (Bottomore and Goode, 1978, pp. 60–4). As with Bukharin, the Austro-Marxists defined Marxism as a closed discourse based on positivistic scientism and evolutionism. The complex pluralism of modernity, the problematic autonomy of human agency, and the creative role of values and culture were assimilated to the primacy of economic forces.

Western Marxism and the problem of sociology

The many attempts to define Marxism as a sociology foundered over the specific nature of Marxism as a revolutionary, critical social science. Marxism was simplified, purified of its emphasis on contradictions and the role of ideas and collective agent in social change. Similarly, the complexity of sociology was assimilated to a unified, closed positivistic discourse. In this way the tensions and ambiguities within and between Marxism and sociology disappeared. By emphasising the centralising and collectivist nature of the emerging industrial, capitalist social order, Marxist theorists tended to assimilate the concept of civil society to historicism (Lukács, Gramsci) or the economic infrastructure and the causal laws of the social system (Bukharin). Gramsci's concept of civil society gives his work a sociological dimension but his historicism pulls it back both towards orthodox Marxism and what the French philosopher Merleau-Ponty termed Western Marxism (Merleau-Ponty, 1973).

Whereas orthodox Marxism was locked into a mechanical base/superstructure model of necessary economic causality, Western Marxists (notably Lukács, Ernst Bloch, T. W. Adorno, Max Horkheimer, Herbert Marcuse) redefined Marxism as a philosophical 'critique' structured in such humanist concepts as *praxis*, alienation, emancipation and utopia. Western Marxism was pre-eminently a philosophy of history concerned not with laws of development but rather with the fate of culture, with values, meaning, human purposes. Social consciousness and practice were no mere reflexes of economic laws.

A Marxism of the superstructure, Western Marxism owed more to Hegel's speculative philosophy than to Marx's materialist social theory, to Hegel's historicising of culture and society and the young Marx's reflections on alienation and dehumanisation. From Hegel came the concept of totality: social theory must address the problem of the whole culture of a society in its immanent development. Marx's materialist and historical category of totality, together with his analysis of social formations structured in objective, law-like processes, was dismissed as residues of nineteenth-century positivism. Bloch's *The Spirit of Utopia* is an exemplary work of Western Marxism with its totalising messianic view of culture, its utopian demand for a wholeness to heal the fragmented character of modern society. In Bloch and Lukács cultural critique is substituted for socio-economic analysis. Influenced by Simmel's pessimistic sociology of modernity and Weber's value pluralism, both theorists grounded historical truth in the historical process and the privileged ontology of a universal class. In his essay on reification Lukács identified the essential antinomies of bourgeois thought in its failure to grasp totality, splitting the whole into distinct specialist studies and fragments. Bourgeois thought, with its value relativism and immediacy, contrasted with the totalising *praxis* of the proletarian perspective. Socio-economic analysis of objective laws was not the route to critical knowledge (Lukács, 1971, pp 128–30).

But not every Western Marxist shared Lukács's and Bloch's revolutionary utopianism. In his analysis of social formations Gramsci develops the sociological principle of socio-historical specificity. The concept of hegemony focuses analytically on the genesis and structure of distinct socio-cultural-political levels of a social formation, while simultaneously identifying the collective agent as both making and being made by these forces. In the broad tradition of Western Marxism there exists a failure to analyse the mechanisms whereby moral and normative elements are constituted in social action. It is this sociological problem which Gramsci addressed in his theory of hegemony. How is social integration possible other than through coercion and fraud? By appealing to the supra-historical *praxis* of the revolutionary proletariat (Lukács) the whole question of the variability of class consciousness and class structure could be ignored. Bourgeois ideology deflects the proletariat from its true historical tasks. And for all his historicism Gramsci postulates a sociological account of the ways in which cultural elements structure social action, the various modes whereby values are institutionalised and the complex genesis and functioning of ideologies in relation to social consciousness.

Western Marxism culminates in the critical theory of the Frankfurt School (see Chapter 10). In the work of Adorno, Horkheimer and Marcuse, many of the critical problems raised by classical sociology in relation to modernity, the sources of social action, the role of values in social integration and political legitimacy, are theorised away, explanation

221

couched in ahistorical essentialist terms of a pervasive total ideology and a transhistorical striving for emancipation. Moreover, they failed to theorise the historically complex development of civil society, uncritically accepting the one-dimensional, finalising concept of culture advanced by Simmel and Weber. But Weber's rationality thesis embodied critical sociological implications which in the tradition of Western Marxism were buried under cultural determinism, historical pessimism and anti-capitalist romantic rhetoric.

PART III
MODERN SOCIOLOGY

8
Functionalism

Functionalism as a distinct methodology and theory of society originated first in the work of Comte, Spencer and Durkheim, and secondly, in late nineteenth-century and early twentieth-century anthropology especially the writings of A. R. Radcliffe-Brown (1881–1955) and Bronislaw Malinowski (1884–1942). Durkheim is often cited as the dominant influence on the development of sociological functionalism for his argument that social institutions exist solely to fulfil specific social needs. 'All moral systems', he argued, constitute 'a function of the social organisation', and apart from 'abnormal cases' every society develops a morality necessary for its adequate functioning (Durkheim, 1953, p. 56). In *The Rules of Sociological Method* he explicitly argued that the function of a social fact is social in that it necessarily produces socially useful effects. Thus:

> ... to explain a social phenomenon the efficient cause which produces it and the function it fulfills must be investigated separately (Durkheim, 1982, p. 123).

For Durkheim, cause and function related to specific ends, especially those concerned with social solidarity and the maintenance of society as an organic whole. Durkheim's holistic functionalism sought to explain social facts not solely by focusing on the cause on which they depended but by showing their function 'in the establishment of . . . general harmony' (Durkheim, 1982, p. 125). Thus in analysing the division of labour Durkheim established its efficient cause as increasing moral and material density, and its function as the social need it fulfilled, that is, to integrate the social struture of modern industrial society.

Durkheim was particularly concerned to show that the function of social facts was moral: social institutions 'normally' worked to promote the goals of social solidarity. Morality thus constituted a structure of social functions which embodied the collective conscience of society as a whole. Education and religion functioned in this way promoting moral values which integrated different individuals into the social collectivity. Similarly, crime, as a 'normal' and 'healthy' feature of all societies functions both to reinforce collective sentiments and to facilitate 'the normal evolution of morality and law'. Durkheim argued that the existence of criminal behaviour constituted an index of the flexibility of the *conscience collective*. A normal level of crime indicates that the collective conscience lacks the total authority to 'suppress' all 'divergencies' within society. Crime itself reflects the existence of social conditions which enables individuals to express themselves as individuals: 'If there were no crimes, this condition would not be fulfilled . . . collective sentiments would have attained a degree of intensity unparalleled in history . . . The authority which the moral conscience enjoys must not be excessive for otherwise no one would dare to attack it, and it would petrify too easily into an immutable form'. The existence of crime, therefore, shows that the collective sentiments are not too strong as to crush all sense of individuality and originality (Durkheim, 1982, p. 101).

Durkheim's functional approach to the study of institutions, while remaining tenuously within the framework of nineteenth-century evolutionism, tended to emphasise the synchronic, structural dimensions of society at the expense of the diachronic, the genetic and historical: the concept of society as a differentiated and integrated whole, in which the various elements exercise interdependent functions to sustain a complex unity, has the effect of separating 'function' from 'development' generating abstract, ahistorical social typologies such as mechanical and organic solidarity. In a broadly similar vein Malinowski and Radcliffe-Brown, in their studies of Pacific tribal communities (Trobriand and Andaman Islanders), rejected the evolutionary and diffusionist approach and argued for structural and systemic analysis. Rather than pose the question, how did this particular institution or custom originate, they asked how does it fit into the broader context, how does the part relate to the whole. In contrast to American cultural anthropology and German ethnology, early twentieth-century British anthropology developed a distinctive sociological approach to the analysis of social structure, defining society as an integrated system.

Radcliffe-Brown specifically abandoned the search for *origins*, the historical past of institutions and customs, arguing that each culture constitutes 'a functionally interrelated system' in which 'general laws or functions' operate (Radcliffe-Brown, 1952, p. 180). Anthropology, declared Malinowski, should deal with the totality of social, cultural and psychological elements of communal life 'for they are so interwoven that not one can be understood without taking into consideration all the others' (Malinowski, 1922, p. xvi). In this way magic was analysed as fulfilling 'an indispensable function' in primitive societies through satisfying a social need 'which cannot be satisfied by any other factors of primitive civilisation', while the function of the funeral ceremony 'is the part it plays in the social life as a whole and therefore the contribution it makes to the maintenance of the structural continuity'. For Radcliffe-Brown, a social system, that is, 'the total social structure of a society together with the totality of social usages', constituted 'a functional unity', a condition in which all parts 'work together with a sufficient degree of harmony or internal consistency, i.e. without producing persistent conflicts which can neither be resolved nor regulated'. Culture was thus an integrated whole: to explain any belief, rule, custom or institution demanded an analysis which linked the element functionally with the *structure* of the culture as a system (Radcliffe-Brown, 1952, ch. 9).

This model of society stresses the elements of harmony and consistency not those of conflict and contradiction. The functional unity of a system is defined in terms of social order. In defining society in holistic terms functionalism implies that as everything within the system is necessarily functional for the whole then change, based on conflict, must be conceived as a threat to the basis of the system itself. The tendency to regard functionalism as a conservative sociological theory largely stems from its central concern with integration and the analogy of society as a human organism in which social 'health' is identified with social order and 'disease' with social conflict. Thus the major problem in *The Division of Labour* lay in reconciling the increasing social differentiation of the advanced societies with the need for social integration, a means of regulating 'insatiable desires and appetites'. The function of the division of labour, Durkheim argued, as with elements of the human organism, was normally one of promoting unity, but its 'abnormal' form functioned to create dissension and conflict eventuating in a widespread state of anomie. Durkheim's holistic functionalism, concerned particularly with problems of social order, can be seen, however, as one attempt to develop an objective science of society which rejected the nominalist conception of society as constituted in individuals and explanation of social phenomena in psychological terms.

Given its early development in Durkheim's sociology functionalism was barely a significant presence in the mainstream of European sociology during the first years of the twentieth century. The early American sociologists – Albion Small, Robert Park, Charles Cooley and W. I. Thomas – were attracted to the individualistic, psychological approach of Tarde, and Simmel's theory of sociation, both, of course, criticised by Durkheim for a failure to grasp society as a collective phenomenon. American individualism, combined with empiricism and social psychology, effectively precluded the development of a *theory* of society in the manner of the European sociologists: a collectivist conception of society did, however, emerge in America during the 1930s in the form of a dogmatic Marxism although it failed to strike deep roots in American intellectual culture. Sociological functionalism developed as the major sociological paradigm after the Second World War, the first significant holistic conception of society developed by American sociology. In Kingsley Davis's *Human Society* (1949) society was defined in macrosociological terms with the main focus on integration and survival and the relation of parts to whole; and in the work of Talcott Parsons (1902–79) functionalism became codified into a form of systems analysis.

Talcott Parsons is the major figure in the transition from the predominantly individualistic social psychological theory of early American sociology to its post-war holistic, anti-psychological standpoint. Parsons was the first American sociologist to develop a coherent theory of society conceived as a whole in opposition to the dominant mode of anti-theoretical sociological empiricism. Yet Parsons's work during the 1930s, culminating in his *The Structure of Social Action* (1937), was not strictly speaking functionalist at all but a development of the anti-utilitarian, voluntaristic theory of action in which Weber and Durkheim were singled out for their insight that social integration is centred around a core of common norms and values accepted as legitimate by the members of society.

Parsons's theory of action, which explicitly relegated Marx to a minor position in the history of social theory, emphasised the need for central values at a time in American history – the Depression years of the 1930s – when American values appeared to be under strain. Parsons's voluntarism clearly opposed what he regarded as deterministic Marxist theories of inevitable class conflict, class ideologies and class struggle. For Parsons, the answer to social disorganisation lay in the furthering of moral values which would bind society together as a cohesive unity; and by emphasising the voluntaristic aspects of action, Parsons focused on the need for individuals to act and thus create the conditions necessary for social regeneration.

During the period following the end of the Second World War, however, beginning with his article, 'The Present Position and Prospects of Systematic Theory in Sociology' (1945), Parsons's action approach became a systems approach which diminished the voluntaristic element. Whereas in *The Structure of Social Action* Parsons's starting point was the 'unit' act, in books such as *The Social System* (1951), the starting point was that of 'the empirical system' and social structure focusing particularly on 'the integration of the motivation of actors with the normative cultural standards which integrate the action system'. In his later work Parsons attempted increasingly to link the actor with the social structure within the framework of system defined in anti-voluntaristic functionalist terms.

By the 1950s sociological functionalism was increasingly regarded not simply as one of many sociological approaches but *the* sociological method. In his 1959 paper, 'The Myth of Functional Analysis as a Special Method in Sociology and

Anthropology', Kingsley Davis proclaimed that functionalism was simply the method employed by all social scientists irrespective of whether they called themselves functionalists or not. Functionalism, he noted, was a method which related parts to whole and one part to another, a method characteristic of any science and if 'there is a functional method, it is simply the method of sociological analysis'. Critics of functionalism, however, have suggested that far from constituting an objectively neutral methodology for the social sciences, functionalism is simply an expression of conservative ideology. In seeking to explain the need for social stability and social order, sociological functionalism fails to provide an adequate analysis of social change and social conflict; the historical basis of society as a *process* and structure is assimilated to a static concept of social solidarity and social consensus. Functionalism, wrote Alvin Gouldner, in his extended critique of Parsons, 'resonates sentiments that favour the preservation of privilege . . . A social theory that takes as its central problem the maintenance of social order' and is thus 'more ideologically congenial to those who have more to lose' (Gouldner, 1971, pp. 253–4).

Gouldner's critique of functionalism, especially the work of Parsons, is broadly similar to C. Wright Mills's criticism during the 1950s which defined functionalism as an example of 'grand theory' reflecting the dominant values of American capitalism and which failed to account for the reality of power in society. In his analysis of Parsons in *The Sociological Imagination* (1959), for example, Mills argued that the 'normative order' which Parsons identified as the basis of every social system ultimately fails to explain the simple fact that in all societies some individuals make decisions while others obey them: Parsons's theory suggests that individuals virtually govern themselves through a social consensus which pre-empts any consideration that consent might be manipulated (Mills, 1959, ch. 2).

In general these criticisms miss the point: it is one thing to argue against the later Parsons that the human subject has disappeared within the framework of the social theory, and another to charge functionalism with a lack of substantive concern with power. Functionalism cannot be dismissed for ignoring power in society and the problems of social conflict and of 'vested interests'; Parsons's work includes many discussions of the sources of conflict and power, while his argument that in explaining social order he simultaneously focuses on those elements likely to produce social instability, a lack of cohesion and thus the possibilities of social change, is clearly persuasive in the sense that any sociological theory must incorporate analysis of both dynamics and statics. It is in this spirit that R. K. Merton has argued that far from embodying a conservative ideology, sociological functionalism can be radical and critical by pointing to the failures and weaknesses, the 'malfunctioning' of specific institutions for satisfying the collective needs of society. The introduction of concepts such as 'functional alternatives', 'dysfunctions' and 'moving equilibrium', and the identification, in some functionalist writings, of 'the postitive functions of social conflict', its creative role in systemic change, have tended to weaken the general criticism of functionalism as a theory of system maintenance and cohesion. Thus, for Merton, functionalism is methodologically neutral given an ideological colouring only by the politically motivated. Functional analysis, he writes, does not entail any specific ideological commitment which 'is not to say that such commitments are not often implicit in the works of functional analysts' but that they remain 'extraneous rather than intrinsic to functional theory' (Merton, 1957, pp. 38–43).

What, then, is sociological functionalism?

Sociological functionalism: general features

The basic characteristics of sociological functionalism can be briefly summarised:

1. Societies are wholes, systems of interrelated parts. Each part has meaning only in terms of its relation with the whole performing a specific function within the system; society is thus a system of interdependent elements all of which contribute to the integration and adaptation of the system as a whole. Social causation is thus multiple and reciprocal.

2. The concept of system, derived as a sociological concept from Pareto, is central to all forms of sociological functionalism.

It is the functional relation of parts to whole which distinguishes functionalism from other holistic approaches. Society is thus defined as a structure of elements possessing a patterned form; the point of departure is the system as a whole and those factors essential for its survival, evolution and adequate functioning. Systemic functionalism can be distinguished from general functionalism: systemic functionalism begins from the assumption that all elements contribute to maintaining the whole, while general functionalism is concerned only with the empirical functions of different items which may or may not contribute to maintaining the whole. Both types of functionalism, however, are concerned with what Merton describes as 'observable objective consequences', not 'subjective dispositions' (i.e. motives and purposes), which effectively constitute the basis of function.

3. All elements which make up the social system are indispensable to the extent that they perform special functions related to the 'needs' of the system as a system. Parsonian functionalism has developed the notion of functional prerequisites of social systems which 'refer broadly to the things that must get done in any society if it is to continue as a going concern, i.e. the generalised conditions necessary for the maintenance of the system concerned'. The functional prerequisites have included provision for an adequate relationship of the individual to the environment, role differentiation and role assignment, communication, shared cognitive orientations and articulated goals, normative regulation of means, the regulation of affective expression, socialisation and social control of deviant behaviour. Many of these functional prerequisites are implied in any concept of society and are therefore tautologous: all societies must have modes of socialisation and means of communication since without these society as a concept would be impossible, irrespective of whether the theoretical standpoint is functionalism, social action, sociological nominalism or Marxism. Parsons, however, has regrouped the prerequisites under four headings: Adaptation, Goal Attainment, Integration, and Latency (AGIL for short). Adaptation refers to activities by which the system adapts to its environment modifying, controlling it in terms of the needs of the system; Goal Attainment refers to the mobilising of resources to attain

specific goals and seeking such goals methodologically; Integration refers to the solidarity of the system, its survival as a cohesive whole; and finally, Latency, which refers to the accumulations and distribution of energy which takes the form of motivation (Parsons, 1967). In his later writings Parsons refers to the fourth variable as *pattern maintenance* or *tension management*. Although the emphasis is clearly on social cohesion and stability, change is present in the form of structural differentiation which enables a social system to respond to its needs; with increasing complexity societies evolve new modes of integration.

4. Nevertheless, integration of all parts of the system – the sub-systems – is never 'perfect'. Merton describes the postulate of universal functionalism as an ideal never found in reality: Durkheim's work, for example, stressed the instability, the extremely fragile nature of social solidarity within the advanced societies and the consequent problems of the integration of the individual into the social whole. The basic tendency of social systems is towards equilibrium and a harmonious balance between its various institutions. Elements of 'mal-integration' will, however, always be present hence the importance of social control mechanisms.

5. Deviance, tension and strains exist as 'dysfunctional' elements which tend to become institutionalised or resolved in the direction of social integration and equilibrium.

6. Social change is adaptive and evolutionary. If there is rapid social change it occurs within the cultural rather than within the economic institutions. Even rapid social change has a tendency to leave the basic institutional framework intact.

7. Social integration is achieved essentially through value consensus, 'shared cognitive orientations', that is, through a pervasive set of principles which legitimise the existing social, economic and political structure.

A distinction has sometimes been made between *general* and *normative* functionalism. The latter, associated especially with the work of Parsons, postulates 'shared value elements' as constituting the basis of social cohesion and consensus; society is defined as a system of interdependent parts. Normative functionalism emphasises the contribution of value consensus to the maintenance of an integrated, equilibrated social system. Normative functionalism attempts to synthesise Durkheim's concept of society as 'normally' integrated through shared values with Weber's action theory, the individual and the collectivity, emphasising the centrality to functionalist analysis of social roles, social processes, social norms and institutions all contributing to social control. Both types of functionalism are concerned with defining society as a system in which socialisation is the key element thus giving rise to the criticism that functionalism, in minimising individuality and 'eccentricity' (or defining the latter as deviant behaviour) works with an oversocialised conception of humanity. It is true that general functionalism minimises the functional integration of parts and postulates the dysfunctional consequences of differing and sometimes opposing values. But this distinction seems exaggerated: the work of so-called general functionalists – Davis and Merton for example – differs only in degree, not in kind, from normative functionalism. As will be argued below, both types of functionalism postulate the view that social integration is a consequence of both normative and structural forces and cannot be reduced to one or the other.

The concept of system

The concept of society as a system is most elaborately developed in Parsonian functionalism. Repudiating the atomistic, individualistic theorising of early American sociology, Parsons consistently argued that a theory of society cannot be built up from facts; the data of social science itself must begin from theory, derive from theory: a fact is always a statement of experience couched in terms of a conceptual scheme. Facts never reproduce an external objectivity; theory is essential and it is theory on a grand scale clearly different from Merton's more modest 'theories of the middle range'. Parsons's concept of system differentiates his functionalist approach from Merton's general functionalism. In *The Social System* the concept of system is linked with two analytically distinct systems, personality and culture. The social system consists of actors interacting in a socio-cultural situation, a process mediated by 'a system of culturally structured and shared symbols'. Parsons notes that every social system consists of four major sub-systems, kinship, social stratification, power and religion. The kinship system is the main socialising agency, stratification the means of distributing rewards within a differentiated social structure, and these two sub-systems effectively reinforce the pattern of inequality in society:

> The consequence of this is that the combination of an occupation-ally differentiated industrial system and a significantly solidary kinship system must be a system of stratification in which the children of the more highly placed come to have differential advantages, by virtue of their ascribed kinship status, not shared by those lower down (Parsons, 1951, p. 161).

These internal sub-systems, the economy, the polity, socialisa-tion and societal community (stratification, power, kinship, religion) are further sub-divided into the sub-systems of action (AGIL). Parsons, of course, is not defining society in terms of the interactions of individuals, or the totality of such interac-tions structurally patterned: society is defined in terms of the structure which links individuals with the whole, a systemic approach that emphasises the factor of motivation, that actors pursue goals within the framework of voluntaristic elements that is neither reducible to individuals or atomistic interaction.

For Parsons, system is an indispensable master concept, its meaning directly bound up with its relation to the concept 'environment'. The concept of sub-system enables Parsons to treat the individual in relation to this environment while still remaining part of a system of action. The system is thus highly centralised and organised around values as distinct from interests: there is little awareness of possible conflicting social worlds, with their own distinctive culture and values, within a social system, that a social system, while retaining its wholeness, may lack a coherent, unifying *centre*. The biological organism or system necessarily adapts to its environment. But the social system is made by humanity, social groups and social classes each seeking to establish their own identity within the social whole and striving to remain autonomous in terms of their institutions and values. In Parsonian functionalism there is no sense of society as a decentred, polyphonic structure built upon the basis of different interests *and* values. Rather, the system tends to total coherence possessing an inbuilt equilibrium which Parsons emphasises is constantly undergoing change – the 'moving equilibrium':

> The social system's own equilibrium is itself made up of many subequilibriums within and cutting across one another, with numerous personality systems more or less in internal equilibrium, making up different equilibrated systems such as kinship groups, social strata, churches, sects, economic enterprises, and government bodies. All enter into a huge moving equilibrium in which instabilities in one sub-system in the personality or social sphere are communicated simultaneously to both levels, either disequilibrating the larger system or part of it, until either a re-equilibrium takes place or the total equilibrium changes its form (Parsons and Shils, 1962, pp. 226–7).

Parsons's imagery does present problems when related to his concern with 'voluntarism' and social action. When he writes of the 'in-puts' and 'out-puts' of sub-systems and systems, for example, he seems to be rejecting normative functionalism in favour of what might be termed 'cybernetic functionalism' in which society has become a self-contained and self-equilibrating system. Parsons's work is dominated by a reified and dehumanised theory of society in which the process of equilibrium takes place outside human action and independently of consciousness, interests and struggle. Nevertheless, even here, Parsons is careful to qualify the usage of his concepts: equilibrium is not an empirical fact or reality for no society is equilibrated in the sense that its parts 'fit' together in complete harmony. Equilibrium is a heuristic device which is employed in conjunction with the concept of inertia: the absence of change within a system of action results in stasis, but in reality systems of action are constantly modified and changed by processes involving communication, decision-making and differentiation. This aspect is especially marked in Parsons's analysis of integration: since no system can be perfectly integrated it becomes essential to create institutions that mediate the possible conflict of interests, the 'internal conflict and other failures of co-ordination'; the integrative sub-system thus functions to adapt individuals to the 'goals of the social system' by generating legitimate values, 'the institutionalisation of value-patterns which define the main structural outline of society' bringing ' "into line" the behaviour of system units in accordance with the integrative needs of the system, to check or reverse disruptive tendencies to deviant behaviour and to promote the condition of harmonious co-operation' (Parsons and Smelser, 1959, pp. 16–23).

Equilibrium of *all parts of the social system* comprises the normal condition of human society, with conflict, although present, an essentially residual and abnormal element. Society is thus characterised by the existence of 'value orientations' held by certain 'solidary groupings' (professional occupations such as scientists) which, over time, pass into the 'value system' of the whole society. Parsons defines value system as 'the set of normative judgements held by the members of the society who define, . . . what to them is a good society' (Parsons, 1951, pp. 36–7). But not all members of a society would necessarily agree on what constitutes the 'good society'. In any case, Parsons's own approach seems to give individuals little choice in the matter: norms, values and collective goals govern and control individual behaviour and he follows Durkheim in emphasising the need to control the individual; collective and social, not personal goals motivate and orientate the individual to the social system. Internalising the collective goals the individual is thus socialised and social order augmented, a standpoint which suggests a passive not active relation of the individual actor to values, the internalisation of norms approaching simple habit formation and thus conformism to the status quo. Through explicit socialising agencies such as family, school and community the actor successfully internalises societal goals so that social order, far from being problematical is 'normal'. Like Durkheim, Parsons emphasises that constraint is not forced on the individual but develops organically from the collective conscience, that is, from society. 'In this way', he writes, 'the moral component of the *conscience collective* is social' comprising common, shared values internalised through the agencies of socialisation (Parsons, 1967, pp. 27–9).

Culture is a critical element in this process. Writing on

Marx, Parsons argues that an inadequate theory of personality led Marx to misunderstand that action 'is a function of the *organisation* of behaviour . . . in terms of generalised codes that permit the programming of widely varying particulars'; it is these 'cultural codes' which underlie the 'normative components of societies'. For, contrary to Marx's materialist theory, society is not dominated by social and class conflict; Durkheim's concept of organic solidarity is recommended as a more fruitful way of understanding modern society. For lacking adequate concepts of order and personality Marxist materialism must fail to explain what Parsons calls 'directionality of orientations to work and enterprise' – this being accomplished in Weber's study of Protestantism and capitalism. Thus remaining 'psychologically naïve' Marx's social theory failed to account for the significance of cultural factors in the maintenance of social order, social integration and equilibrium (Parsons, 1967, pp. 123–35).

Parsons's critique of Marx undoubtedly focuses on one of the major weaknesses of historical materialism as it developed in the analysis of modern capitalism (*Capital*) and became codified into a world view by later generations of Marxists. The voluntaristic element is assimilated to underlying laws and external structures: yet this is precisely Parsons's own theoretical position. For example, although dismissing Marxism for its notion of class conflict and structural contradiction, Parsons advances concepts such as 'strains', 'tensions' and notes that in modern society there is 'widespread' anomie all of which suggests the possibility of structural conflict. It is, nevertheless, the system which produces strains and tensions, the failure of its regulative, socialising institutions: within the closed field of the system there is virtually no scope for autonomous social action because there are no sources of legitimate opposition to the all-embracing central values, no institutional means for expressing the possibilities of social alternatives other than in the form of 'deviance'. Parsonian functionalism has successfully effaced the human subject from social theory other than as supports of the *system*.

Functionalism and the dialectic of social life: Merton

Writing on the functional necessity of religion for modern industrial society, Parsons accepted Durkheim's correlation of morality with the sacred noting his 'important insight' into the 'exceedingly close integration of the system of religious symbols of a society and the patterns sanctioned by the common moral sentiments of the members of the community' (Parsons, 1954, p. 206). In a similar vein two representatives of general functionalism write:

> The reason why religion is necessary is apparently to be found in the fact that human society achieves its unity primarily through the possession by its members of certain ultimate values and ends in common. Although these values and ends are subjective, they influence behaviour, and their integration enables this society to operate as a system . . . Even in a secularised society some system must exist for the integration of ultimate values, for their ritualistic expression, and for the emotional adjustments required by disappointment, death and disaster (Davis and Moore, 1969, p. 499).

Criticising this extreme functional interpretation of religion, R. K. Merton (1910–) has argued that although some kind of moral agency is functionally indispensable for society, religion can be both functionally unifying and dysfunctional. He points out that the Durkheimian orientation of functionalist analysis is one rooted in the function of religion in non-literate societies and thus the effective absence of several religions. In modern society the tendency is for a plurality of religions and an increasing secularisation of values and beliefs, processes which raise serious questions on the function of religion *as such* to promote or produce structural unity. 'In what sense does religion make for integration of the larger society, if the content of its doctrine and values is at odds with the content of other, non-religious values held by many people in the same society?' In non-literate societies there is usually a single religion which can thus be taken as a model of functional unity. Merton goes on to suggest that in modern societies the concept of 'functional alternative', or 'functional substitute', may be of more value in analysing the relation of values to social cohesion. Although

239

this still assumes the centrality of religious values for the concept of social unity it raises the question of the degree of unity found in the social and historical world.

Merton argues that the postulate of total functional unity is clearly contrary to social reality and an obstacle to social analysis, diverting attention from 'possible disparate consequences of a given social or cultural item' for the various social groups and individual members of groups. All human societies are integrated but few societies are characterised by that *'high degree of integration in which every culturally standardised activity or belief is functional for the society as a whole'.* Rejecting the whole notion of functional unity, or functional indispensability of elements, Merton advances the argument of a *net balance of functional consequences* which 'avoids the tendency of functional analysis to concentrate on positive functions' and focus on possible dysfunctional consequences. A major theorem of functional analysis, Merton concludes, is *'just as the same item may have multiple functions, so may the same function be diversely fulfilled by alternative items'.*

Merton defines function objectively as the 'observed consequences' which 'make for the adaptation or adjustment of a given system', while dysfunction is defined as the consequences which reduce the possibility of adjustment and adaptation. Further modifying the functional theory of coherence of systems, Merton distinguishes manifest from latent functions, the former consisting of the objective consequences facilitating adjustment and adaptation of the system and which are 'intended and recognised' by individuals, while latent functions are unintended or unrecognised. As an example he cites Thorstein Veblen's analysis of 'conspicuous consumption', human activity, which functions both to satisfy the needs of the individual consumers (manifest function) and to enhance social status since goods are bought not because of their utility but for their expensiveness (latent function). In this way what may appear to be irrational behaviour by members of different social groups to outsiders is actually functional for the group itself. For Merton latent functions constitute a significant development of sociological theory since they challenge all commonsense knowledge and focus on the 'hidden' components of processes (Merton, 1957, pp. 27–33, 51–8, 65–71).

Merton has sought to introduce a more flexible form of functionalist analysis, but in doing so has confused the distinction between actor and system: the concept of manifest function assumes some awareness on the part of the actor of the actual consequences of action. But does this imply that the actor is equally aware of the consequences for the system as a whole? Unanticipated consequences of action defined as latent functions are clearly systemic in nature linking the individual social actions collectively with society as a whole. Thus although he avoids employing the concept of system arguing that sociological analysis must begin from the 'units' or 'items' rather than from the system as a whole, Merton's notion of social structure, with its interdependence of parts, implies a systemic and deterministic approach. This is particularly brought out in his analysis of the latent functions of the phenomenon of 'Bossism' or 'political racketeering' in American society.

Superficially the illegitimate political machine violates all accepted legal and moral norms yet it succeeds in carrying out 'positive functions' inadequately fulfilled by other legitimate structures. Merton argues that the political machine functions first as a means of centralising the scattered bases of political power (officially devolved by the democratic ethos of the American Constitution), and secondly, to provide assistance for certain deprived sub-groups whose access to legitimate channels is restricted. The 'corrupt political machine' effectively 'fulfils the basic function of providing avenues of social mobility for the otherwise disadvantaged . . . in a society which places a high premium on economic affluence and social ascent for all its members'. 'Bossism' is therefore not merely the means 'of self-aggrandizement for profit-hungry and power-hungry individuals, but . . . an organised provision for subgroups otherwise excluded from or handicapped in the race for "getting ahead" '. Moral disapproval is irrelevant for an understanding of the structural and functional role of the political machine (Merton, 1957).

Bossism as a structure persists, therefore, not through fulfilling a vital need for the system as a whole, but for the reciprocal relationship it generates with smaller units. It is this 'norm of reciprocity' which enables the element to enjoy autonomy; the relation of part to whole is uneven rather than symmetrical. Nevertheless, the part, or sub-system, can be understood ultimately only in terms of the wider system. In this way unintended consequences are assimilated to an underlying structure similar to Smith's 'hidden hand' and Marx's dialectic of history. 'Bossism' is more than simple corruption but a process which functions at both the micro and macrolevel of the social system, its latent functions dependent on the failure of other institutions within the social whole. Merton's concept of latent function is therefore predicated on systemic analysis; it also minimises the role of the subject since it is the system itself which determines the functions, and thus the ends, unintended or not, of institutions at the microlevel.

The conservative implications of Merton's functionalism are thus clear: 'Bossism' is *explained away* by focusing on its effects on those individuals immediately involved in its workings: but the existence of widespread political corruption constitutes a threat to the legitimacy of the democratic political order and its persistence must ultimately weaken belief in democratic processes in society as a whole. Merton's functionalism fails to incorporate a genetic dimension so that social structures are never concretely related to interests and ideology. Historically, political 'Bossism' develops out of the weaknesses of civil society and a failure to thoroughly democratise society as a whole. Merton's analysis accepts *as given* what should be explained: that élitism, in whatever form, functions to promote specific interests against other opposed interests by organising society *from above*. The analysis assumes a passive population, subjects who can be manipulated by élites towards ends neither acknowledge.

Similar criticisms can be brought against one of Merton's most significant contributions to functionalism, the study of anomie and social structure. Here he presents a typology of individual adaptations to the disjunction 'between culturally induced high aspirations and socially structured obstacles to realisation of these aspirations', between the officially sanctioned cultural goal of monetary success (although Merton emphasises that American culture defines other success goals) and the legitimate institutional means of achieving such goals. Culture generates motivation; social structure constitutes the means of satisfying aspirations. But not everyone can be successful: anomie is likely to result when an acute disjunction exists between the cultural norms and goals and 'the socially structured capacities of members of the group to act in accord with them'. Merton thus considers five modes of adaptation:* (1) conformity to the goals and the institutional means, the most common form without which no society could survive; (2) innovation, in which the goals are accepted but non-institutional means employed for their realisation, such as white-collar crime, or the Robber Barons; (3) ritualistic adaptation in which the goals are 'scaled down' but the means accepted as legitimate thus allaying status anxiety – the ritualist is one who continues to follow compulsively institutional norms, e.g. the conformist bureaucrat; (4) retreatism is the rejection of both goals and means so while individuals may have assimilated both as norms, failure or frustration can lead to defeatism, quietism and resignation, the individual escaping into the private world of drug addiction, chronic alcoholism or vagabondage; and finally, (5) rebellion, a combination of accepting and rejecting the goals and the means, as with revolutionaries who seek to set up an entirely new society, or those who have become resentful and discontented with their failure to achieve the goals (Merton, 1957, ch. 4).

Merton argues that every society generates norms governing conduct but they differ 'in the degree to which the folkways, mores and institutional controls are effectively integrated with the goals which stand high in the hierarchy of cultural values'. Not everyone can be upwardly mobile or follow a middle-class life-style. Within Merton's model there are similar assumptions to those made by Durkheim on the nature of humanity –

* **A typology of modes of individual adaptation**
  + signifies acceptance, – signifies rejection

Modes of Adaptation	Cultural Goals	Institutionalised Means
Conformity	+	+
Innovation	+	–
Ritualism	–	+
Retreatism	–	–
Rebellion	±	±

striving competitively for success rather than co-operating with others – and the function of institutions to maintain social stability and thus the status quo. Merton's analysis is effectively couched at the level of system: it assumes the necessity for a systemic ideology which is accepted uncritically and passively as the norm by the population; institutions function not to mediate ideology but to serve as neutral means for the realisation of ideological goals. But individuals are not passively socialised into the dominant cultural norms: social class, family, trade unions, and other institutions function as mediators of 'official culture', generating co-operative values which may well include a rejection of the dominant goals and institutionalised means as defined by Merton. But this activity cannot be accommodated easily to Merton's typology which assumes that social stability, or equilibrium of the social system, to rest on an 'oversocialised' notion of humanity (Merton, 1957, pp. 77–8).

Functionalism, social conflict and social change

One of the most persistent criticisms of sociological functionalism, as it developed into the dominant paradigm of American sociology during the 1940s and 1950s, was its failure to explain social change and the persistence of social conflict within the advanced societies. Yet Parsons has not shirked from analysing the problem of social change, revolution and anomie. In his discussion of German fascism, written during the 1940s, he described Nazism as 'one of the most critical . . . social events of our times' (Parsons, 1954, ch. 6) while in *The Social System* a substantial part of the chapter on social change was devoted to analysing Russian communism and the 1917 revolution. In every social system, Parsons has argued, equilibrium is always precarious and its breakdown as 'scientifically important a phenomenon as its preservation' (Parsons, 1951, p. 338).

Parsons's analysis of German fascism is based on the assumption that in modern society the common value-system is always likely to break down and produce the 'strains' which result in disequilibrium and anomie. A revolutionary movement is one consequence of such strains, strains which gain ascendancy only if a number of specific conditions exist such as 'the presence in the population of sufficiently intense, widely spread and properly distributed alienative motivational elements'. Nazism succeeded because the rapid industrial and technological development of Germany created strains within the cultural sub-system leading to 'widespread insecurity' and 'a good deal of free floating aggression, a tendency to unstable emotionalism and susceptibility to emotionalised propaganda'. In short, a process of rationalisation, a 'secularisation of religious values', undermined 'traditional and conservative systems of symbols', producing 'imperfectly integrated institutional structures, ideological definitions of the situation and the psychological reaction patterns typical of anomie'. Parsons analyses fascism and communism as movements exemplifying a 'romantic' revolt against 'the whole tendency of rationalisation in the Western World'. Rapid social change produces a state of instability in which norms no longer regulate society; anomie results with fascism and communism emerging as mass movements able to canalise the 'free floating aggression' engendered by technology, urbanism and industry (Parsons, 1954, pp. 104–41).

Parsons is thus proposing a theory of cultural determinism. Although critical of Marx for failing to develop a theory of motivation, Parsons effectively proposes that a conjunction of certain cultural elements determined that Germany deviated from the 'normal' Western path of industrial evolution. His analysis of Bolshevism is couched similarly in terms of an equilibrium model leaving no room for human *praxis*: the events in Russia, as with those in Germany, were inescapable. Revolutionary movements are notably 'ambivalent in structure' fusing together utopian and realist elements, and although beginning from a perspective of total, uncompromising criticism of the existing social system, are increasingly forced to accommodate themselves to 'reality' after the revolution. No society, Parsons writes, can 'become stabilised on the basis that a fundamentally ambivalent motivational structure towards its central values and ideology became the norm'. The central values of the old society reassert themselves. Differential payments in industry and a rigid system of stratification emerge as 'the need for adaptive structures in the light of fundamental functional requirements ... and the re-emergence of conformity needs associated with the old society as such'. There is thus continuity in change and Parsons concludes his analysis with the hope that industrialisation will bring with it 'a universalistic-achievement pattern' of motivation to transform Soviet Russia into a broadly similar social system as America (Parsons, 1951, pp. 523–33).

Similarly, Parsons has never denied the factual existence of conflict in modern society: 'Class conflict certainly exists ... class conflict is endemic in our modern industrial type of society.' The point, however, is that class conflict for Parsons and other functionalists does not constitute the dominant structural element in a system of social stratification (Parsons, 1954, pp. 329–33). Conflict is not conceived as a source of change but rather as an indication of a breakdown of social control, a deviant response to inequalities of income, status and power. Parsons's equilibrium model minimises the importance of power and conflict; it does not deny the factual significance of these elements. Similarly, sociological conflict theory makes frequent reference to consensus and equilibrium. Both Parsons and Merton repudiate the argument that sociology can thus be divided into those theories which emphasise conflict and those which stress consensus. Using the analogy of biology Parsons notes that there are not two distinct theories referring to the health of the organism on the one hand, and its pathology on the other (Parsons, 1975). Nevertheless, a tradition has developed within sociology which accepts this dichotomy.

Sociological conflict theory developed originally during the late nineteenth century largely in response to Marxist class conflict theory: the major figures such as Gumplowicz, Ratzenhofer and Novicow were conservative theorists working within the organicist and Social Darwinist tradition. Early twentieth-century conflict theorists, such as the Americans, Veblen, Ross and Small, rejected the organicist model and emphasised the constitutive role played by social conflict for social life generally. In contrast, sociological functionalism has tended to categorise conflict as dysfunctional, or as a 'disease', thereby shifting attention away from its important constitutive role in the formation and maintenance of social structures.

Thus Lewis Coser in his *The Functions of Social Conflict* (1954), working within the formal sociological tradition of Georg Simmel for whom conflict constituted the 'essence' of social life, argued that social conflict functioned positively in terms of social structure. Criticising Parson's 'static' equilibrium model he suggests that 'conflict, rather than being disruptive and dissociating, may indeed be a means of balancing and hence maintaining a society as going concern'. Rather than tearing society apart, conflict performs 'group maintaining functions in so far as it regulates systems of relationships', functioning as 'safety valve' mechanism producing an 'equilibrating and stabilising impact'. Conflict creates new norms and values, re-establishes unity between different groups and the boundaries between them, and redresses potentially disruptive inequalities in power and authority. A society lacking conflict ossifies and stagnates; societies in which conflict has become institutionalised are correspondingly more stable and integrated than those with rigid structures:

> By permitting immediate and direct expression of rival claims, such social systems are able to readjust their structures by eliminating the sources of dissatisfaction. The multiple conflicts which they experience may serve to eliminate the causes for dissociation and to re-establish unity. These systems avail themselves, through the toleration and institutionalisation of conflict, of an important stabilising mechanism (Coser, 1956, pp. 153–5).

Coser's functional approach to conflict is primarily based on the assumption that institutionalised conflict will make a positive contribution to the adaptive capacity of the social system always providing that the social structure is sufficiently elastic. Social change occurs only when the conflict relations within a society co-operate with the unifying forces:

> What threatens the equilibrium of such a structure is not conflict as such, but the rigidity itself which permits hostilities to accumulate and to be channelled along one major line of cleavage once they break out in conflict (Coser, 1956, p. 157).

Pluralistic, democratic and open societies thus allow for underlying social change to develop through a process of institutionalising conflict: conflict establishes social unity and maintains a balance within the social structure. Coser's concern is not with systemic conflict, with basic contradictions within the system itself and thus the possibility of revolutionary change, but conflict as antagonisms between different parts of the system, such as social groups, communities, political parties. Nevertheless, Coser's general conclusion is of great significance: change *of* or *within* a system is closely bound up with the degree of cohesion that the system has attained. Capitalist democracies, with their strong institutional structures based in civil society, 'tolerate' and 'creatively utilise' group conflict; totalitarian societies are incapable of responding to conflict in this limited sense since the means of expressing diverging interests and values are virtually absent in a situation of an ideologically closed 'consensus'.

In its historical development sociological functionalism failed to confront the problem of social conflict, its social bases and relation with social change. This is not to suggest, however, that functionalism cannot account for social change: the difficulty is that functionalism defines change from within the closed field of the system, as the product of disjunctions between culture and social structure, or of strains and tensions which develop independently of groups or class interests, culture and ideology. Talcott Parsons's belated rediscovery of evolutionism in his 1964 paper, 'Evolutionary Universals in Society', does not advance much beyond the systemic formalism of his earlier work. The terms remain as before – 'adaptive capacity', 'system-needs' – but now combined with an evolutionary framework which emphasises the significance of cultural diffusion and two critical universal evolutionary universals, 'a well-marked system of social stratification' and a system of 'cultural legitimation'. Parsons's evolutionary schema, which culminates in the modern democratic polity, characteristically underemphasises the structural significance of conflict and power, ideology and culture of the lower social strata.

In general, functionalism assimilates conflict to an underlying process which effectively strips it of all active human components. In particular, functionalist theories of social change minimise the important reciprocal relationship between the institutions, or structures, and the human agents who comprise them; change is thus conceptualised as the disintegration of structural equilibrium and not as the result of a crisis in reciprocity and the corresponding changes in consciousness and values of the human subjects. At least on this level the frequent comparison between Marxism and functionalism is valid for both tend to reify society as an external system structured in equilibrium and hegemony, a whole superior to its parts; and both seek to eliminate the active human subject as the source of social relationships and social change.

Functionalism and stratification

In 1945 Kingsley Davis and Wilbert Moore published their paper, 'Some Principles of Stratification', in which they sought to elaborate a functionalist theory of social stratification. Their work proved to be one of the most widely discussed contributions to sociology; any debate on the nature of social stratification in modern industrial society would include some discussion of Davis and Moore.

Their starting point, unexceptionable in itself, was the proposition that no known society was classless. All human societies, they argued, were characterised by structures of inequality which comprised universal and variable features. All social systems must develop some means of allocating individuals to specific occupational positions some of which are more functionally important than others. If societies are to survive, then a functionally efficient means of fitting talented individuals to occupations must develop. Stratification is a system which determines that individuals are trained to the limit of their inherent ability to fill functionally essential positions which reward them with high remuneration and status. Stratification constitutes the mechanism 'by which societies ensure that the most important positions are conscientiously filled by the most qualified persons'. In this way individuals are motivated and placed in the social structure with the inevitable result of structured social inequality. Stratification effectively means inequality:

Social inequality is thus an unconsciously evolved device by which societies . . . differentiate persons in terms of both prestige and esteem (Davis and Moore, 1969, p. 497).

Although stratification and inequality are universal, their forms vary from one society to another depending on the level of social development, scarcity of resources and thus the need for special skills and talent (teachers are less functionally important in non-literate cultures than advanced industrial societies for example).

Davis and Moore's thesis hinges on two basic propositions: (1) the factual existence of functionally important occupations, and (2) the need for an adequate reward system which will motivate the most talented individuals to seek essential training. In his *Human Society* Davis modified the argument that stratification functions as the sole mechanism allocating talented individuals to social position by noting the important role played by birth and inheritance as elements in determining role position. But in general this is not seen as a great problem since the development of industrial society weakens the influence of inherited wealth and status. But it leaves open the problem of defining functionally important position. It could be argued, for example, that doctors are functionally more important than nurses in that their training and expertise enables them to fulfil the work tasks of nurses, but that nurses could not work as doctors. Comparable examples could be cited although in the long run the profession of doctors could not survive without the profession of nurses. They are both functionally necessary to each other because they involve a reciprocal relationship. To argue that doctors and other comparable higher professions require a high level of material rewards because of long, 'expensive' and 'burdensome' training ignores the equally 'burdensome' training undergone by nurses and others.

Historically, the higher professions have been associated with the upper strata of society: remuneration and status are less connected with *function* than with socio-cultural antecedents. The anti-historical, non-genetic nature of functionalism leads to explanations of social phenomenon which assume that their present form is their natural form. Can one really argue that plumbers are less functionally significant for industrial society than Professors of Divinity? Or electricians, or train drivers? How is talent to be measured? Many critics of functionalism have noted that social structures function to limit the inherent potential of individuals through various mechanisms associated with social class, education and the dominant culture. And what of motivation? Is this not also determined by the ways in which individuals define themselves in relation to others and to society as a whole? Motivation is not a neutral element but influenced by the class structure, culture and ideology.

The concept of functionally important position relates to the general functionalist argument that stratification works to integrate the social system around a core of values which legitimate existing inequality. This is the essence of the functionalist theory of stratification. Its undoubted truth, that a complex division of labour demands an efficient means of allocating individuals to necessary occupations which results in some degree of unequal reward, is common to all theories of class from Smith to Marx to Weber. Functionalism departs fundamentally from these writers by eliminating power and class interests as important and enduring structural principles in the formation of inequality. There is a great deal of evidence, much of it historical in character, which points to the divisive nature of stratification and the unequal distribution of power in modern industrial societies. Power is not a 'secondary phenomenon' but bound up with economic and class forces. Neither is the agent the passive product of the system, but an active presence involved in the production and reproduction of social life. It is over these issues that functionalism founders as a sociological explanation, attributing 'needs' and purposes to society as if society constituted an active subject rather than an historical system, a structure and a process which changes through the 'needs' and interests of actors or subjects.

Self, Society and the Sociology of Everyday Life

Action theory and the concept of self: the early and later Parsons

A major problem of classical sociology was the contradiction between its emphasis on the concept of society as a system or structure governed by objective laws, and the role of the subject, or actor, in the making of social structure and social change. A tension was generated within classical sociology between the concepts of subject and structure, voluntarism and determinism. Marxism, Functionalism and Sociological Positivism tended to assimilate the active role of the subject to an underlying economic, socio-cultural system. Social action theory, as it developed in the work of Simmel and Weber, sought to redefine the object of sociology as the study of human interaction. Talcott Parsons's *The Structure of Social Action* (1937) advanced the argument that a voluntaristic theory of action constituted the major preoccupation of Weber, Durkheim and Pareto, and although there were important differences between these sociologists, working apart from each other in their own distinctive national cultures, a real convergence of sociological theory was nevertheless taking place. For Parsons, the history of sociology was not a history of competing and opposing schools, 'that there are as many systems of sociological theory as there are sociologists, that there is no common basis, that all is arbitrary and subjective', but rather the development of 'a substantial common basis of theory' and 'sound theoretical foundations on which to build' (Parsons, 1961a, pp. 774–5). This convergence of sociological theory is towards a 'generalised theory of action'.

Parsons's broad argument was that a sociological theory of action could not develop on the basis of nineteenth-century positivism with its belief in the methods of the natural sciences. The stability of society, the existence of social order, cannot be explained solely in terms of natural laws. Social order has its basis both in the objective structure of society and in the subjective actions of individuals as they internalise the values of the culture. Thus utilitarian philosophy, with its conception of individuals seeking their own interests, embodied a strong action element. But utilitarian philosophy could not account for the persistence of social order through its central precepts of the randomness of ends, the rational orientation of individuals to such ends based on knowledge of the situation, and an atomistic conception of society. It was not sufficient for Bentham and the classical political economists to cite the 'hidden hand' which fused individual interests and ends with the interests of society as a whole and collective ends or, as with Spencer, to postulate a social contract existing between individuals as forming the basis of social order. Utilitarian rationality assumed that social order was possible through (1) the rational recognition of a natural identity of interests thus neatly solving the problem of a possible conflict of ends; and (2) the voluntarist postulate of a social contract which assumed that humanity consciously recognise the utility of government and social stability. Parsons argued that the whole utilitarian doctrine, built around an atomistic conception of society and rational norms which govern the means–ends relationship, was inherently unstable since it assumed that ends were both random and atomistic. All departures from the rational norms were regarded as irrational.

In contrast, Durkheim, Weber, Pareto and to a lesser extent Tönnies and Simmel, were concerned, not with 'interests' defined atomistically, but with the norms regulating human action which, internalised by the actor, were regarded as putatively desirable and therefore worthy to be realised. The voluntaristic theory of action thus refers to a process whereby the subject actively consents to the legitimacy of specific values. The norms regulating human action are therefore not external forces or constraints (as was the case with nineteenth-century positivism and Durkheim's early work) but elements organically bound up with the human actor. There is, in other words, an active not passive or adaptive relation between individuals and norms: the relation is both creative and voluntaristic.

For Parsons, however, human action is characterised by its systemic nature. The notion of human action as a system is central to Parsons's argument that late nineteenth-century sociological theory exhibited a movement towards convergence: thus although human action assumes motives, goals and wishes it can be studied scientifically only through objective, systemic analysis. The influence of Pareto on Parsons's thought is clearly in evidence here since neither Durkheim nor Weber developed a notion of system in this sense. Action constitutes a system: society is a system of action. And in the same way as the particle relates to classical physics so does the 'unit act' relate to the social system: as particles 'can be defined only in terms of their properties, mass, velocity, location in space, direction of motion, etc., so the units of action systems . . . have certain basic properties without which it is not possible to conceive of the unit as "existing" '. All action constitutes a structure of unit-acts involving actors. An act, therefore, involves an agent, an end to which the process of action is oriented and a situation (the 'conditions of action') involving elements some of which the actor may control and others over which he/she has no control. Within the situation there is always a choice of alternative means to ends, a 'normative orientation of action' (Parsons, 1961a, pp. 43–4).

A system of action can thus be broken down into parts or smaller 'sub-systems'. The unit-act is the smallest unit of an action system. A system of action constitutes an organisation of the interactions between actor and situation. Social action is built around rules, norms and patterns. It was Durkheim who particularly stressed the processes whereby collective representations become internalised by individuals to promote social order and a personality structure adequate to the social structure. Parsons argues that Durkheim's critique of positivism led him to define the social milieu in terms of an integrated system of norms which involve 'the existence of a common system of ultimate-value attitudes'. A common value system is one which is institutionalised. Action is thus objectively and subjectively institutionalised:

> The most fundamental theorem of the theory of action seems to me to be that the *structure* of systems of action *consists* in institutionalised (in social and cultural systems) and/or internalised (in personalities and organisms) patterns of cultural meaning (Parsons, 1961d, p. 342).

Thus ritual is a system of action involving sacred things performed without any utilitarian calculation of advantage and related to a symbolic means–ends relationship. Thus although the source of the sacred is the supernatural 'our symbolic representations of it are sacred things' and 'the attitude of respect to them is, along with respect for moral obligations, a manifestation of our ultimate-value attitudes which are social in so far as they are common' (Parsons, 1961a, pp. 709–13).

As an action theorist Parsons was concerned with the universality of action, the relation of the human agent or personality to the social system. *The Structure of Social Action* examined the possibilities of action in the social world by rejecting the extreme voluntarism of utilitarianism, with its focus on the freely choosing actor, and the determinism of positivism, with its emphasis on causes and effects. In short, Parsons attempted to analyse the subjective element of human society as an objective structure: ends, means and conditions were all theorised from the point of view of the actor and also as external datums. As I have already noted (pp. 228–9), in his later writings – *Toward a General Theory of Action* (1951) and *The Social System* (1951), for example, – action is redefined in systemic terms. The motivation of the actor in terms of goal attainment is determined by the 'needs' of the socio-cultural system. The voluntaristic component is thus diminished: the meaning of action is located within the system and not from the standpoint of the actor. Action is organised as a necessary function of the actor's relation to the situation. The social system is thus defined as

255

... a plurality of individual actors interacting with each other in a situation which has at least a physical or environmental aspect, actors who are motivated in terms of a tendency to the 'optimization of gratification' and whose relation to their situations, including each other, is defined and mediated in terms of culturally structured and shared symbols (Parsons, 1951, pp. 5–6).

In his explicitly functionalist writings Parsons describes action systems in terms of roles, stable patterns of behaviour bearing a specific status such as 'father', 'businessman', 'professional', etc. Although in his functionalist works, action and system are combined, as was noted in Chapter 8, Parsons tends to emphasise the predominant role of the system over the subject and propose a concept of closed rather than open system. Although the theory of action can be seen as a critique of nineteenth-century positivist reductionism, an attempt to bring back the human subject into sociological theory and define society in terms of everyday human actions saturated with meaning, it has led, in Parsons's work, to a reified notion of society and a conservative concept of personality. As a system of action the human personality is mediated and stabilised by a common culture involving language and socialisation: moral standards and '*all the components of the common culture* are internalised as part of the personality structure'. Thus moral standards constitute the core of 'the stabilising mechanisms of the system of social interaction' (Parsons, 1964, pp. 20–2). There is thus a 'fit' between the type of personality and the type of social structure, a standpoint difficult to reconcile with the voluntaristic and creative theory of social action outlined in Parsons's early work. *The Structure of Social Action* made no reference to Freud or Mead, but in his later writings Parsons has stressed both the importance of Mead's 'symbolic interactionist' sociology and, more significantly, the convergence of thought in Freud and Durkheim.

It is Freud, however, who has exercised the greatest influence on Parsons's concept of personality and its relation to the social system. Freud's great discovery 'of the internalisation of moral values as an essential part of the structure of the personality itself' converged with Durkheim's theory of the socially integrative role of moral norms. 'This convergence, from two quite distinct and independent starting points, deserves to be ranked as one of the truly fundamental landmarks of the development of modern social science' (Parsons, 1964, pp. 18–19). Nevertheless, Freud is criticised for an excessive emphasis on the individual and for failing to analyse personality as it interacts with others to form a system. The personality system is defined by Parsons as a system of action which functions in a relatively autonomous way in relation to its dynamic structure and needs. For Parsons, the personality does not internalise social objects individually, but rather assimilates systems of interaction between social objects. Many of Freud's basic psycho-analytical concepts – id, super-ego, ego, the Oedipus complex – are redefined sociologically by Parsons: the function of the super-ego, for example, is limited almost entirely to internalising patterns of social interaction and social roles, an integrative mechanism which exercises control over the personality. Similarly, the Oedipal phase of human development is linked specifically with industrial society and the nuclear family: in Freud's work the Oedipal phase was defined as a fixed, universal phenomenon of all human societies.

Freud's contribution to social theory will be discussed in the next section of this chapter. In relation to Parsons's attempt to sociologise psycho-analytic theory it is worth noting, however, that many of Freud's basic concepts are made to conform with a model of social integration that eliminates negative and contradictory elements. The concept of self, for example, is stripped of Freud's emphasis on the repression of instinctual drives; human sexuality is reduced to a matter of social role and social order. A fundamental harmony is assumed to subsist between the personality and the social system. Thus the development of personality, the stages through which it passes, is separated from Freud's notion of instincts or drives and from the repressive nature of culture. For Freud, socialisation was deeply problematical, but for Parsons it constituted an integrating and harmonious process of learning experiences and internalisation of dominant values.

257

Psycho-analysis and self: Freud

The science of psycho-analysis was officially inaugurated in 1908 with the formation of the Vienna Psycho-Analytical Society; in the same year the first international Psycho-Analytical Congress was held. Of those participating in the Vienna society the most important figure was Sigmund Freud (1856–1939). A contemporary of Durkheim, Weber and Pareto, Freud drew attention to the significant role played by non-rational elements in human action and culture. Like Weber and Pareto, Freud was deeply sceptical of such notions as the perfectability of humanity, nineteenth-century theories of progress and the claims of mass, popular democracy.

Freud's first interests had been in the general area of the physiology of the nervous system. He studied hysteria and its treatment through hypnosis. In the course of the 1890s he developed the technique of 'free association' in which patients were encouraged to say whatever came into their thoughts no matter how ludicrous or obscene. Many of Freud's patients mentioned sexual experiences and sexual problems and this led him to conclude that hysteria was not simply a biological malfunctioning of the organism but the result of sexual repression. Freud's emphasis on the role of sexuality in the aetiology of the neuroses differentiated his approach from orthodox psychology: through free association the patient recalled early childhood sexual experiences which had been subsequently censored by the mind. Freud thus advanced the argument that hysteria was the result of childhood sexual seduction carried out either by an adult or older child. But from 1900 onwards, especially with the publication of *The Interpretation of Dreams* (1900), *The Psychopathology of Everyday Life* (1901) and *Three Essays in the Theory of Sexuality* (1905), he argued that neuroses involved both the whole human personality and unconscious elements.

Freud rejected both the rationalist and mechanistic concepts of personality: no mental phenomenon was accidental or irrational but the effect of a complex process of causation. Symptoms were meaningful in relation to the patient's unconscious. Similarly, the apparently random actions of everyday life such as slips of the tongue, jokes, and forgetting of names together with dreams, equally involved unconscious elements in their causation: dreams and jokes became meaningful only when they were integrated into another structure which in Freud's theory was the structure of the unconscious mind. Freud also argued against a simple cause and effect model: mental phenomena were 'overdetermined', the combination of many elements and not the products of a straightforward process of reciprocal causation. Thus dreams may have several meanings and fulfil a number of different wishes; an element within a dream will combine a number of quite different features of many elements. And because a dream condenses a number of experiences into single composite figures and censors, those elements which might disturb sleep itself, the manifest content of the dream (what the individual remembers) is less significant than its latent content (the underlying structure which gives the dream its meaning or meanings). Freud regarded *The Interpretation of Dreams* as forming the basis of the psycho-analytical method and his most important work: the analysis of dreams, he argued, provided evidence of the deeper structure of the human mind:

> It was discovered one day that the pathological symptoms of certain neurotic patients have a sense. On this discovery the psycho-analytic method of treatment was founded. It happened in the course of this treatment that patients, instead of bringing forward their symptoms, brought forward dreams. A suspicion thus arose that the dreams too had sense (Freud, 1953, Vol. XV, p. 83).

Dream interpretation was thus 'the royal road to a knowledge of the unconscious activities of the mind'. The true meaning, or meanings, of a dream emerge only by analysing the complex ways whereby the dream wishes are distorted by 'dream-work'. Sleep relaxes control over the unconscious: dream-work functions to disguise the 'forbidden' and repressed elements of the unconscious as they surface within the dream. Thus dreams are censored by the processes of *condensation* and *displacement* (that is, by fusing a number of different traits into a composite figure, and by making emotionally significant elements insignificant).

Freud's theory of the self was built around the necessity for society to repress specific instinctual drives which then found their expression in dreams, symbols and fantasies. For Freud, the human organism was characterised by a tension between the 'pleasure principle' (the sexual instincts) and the 'reality principle' (the drive for self-preservation). The pleasure principle was related to sexual energy (or libido) which is constantly seeking release and gratification. Libido was diffused throughout the whole of human organism and sexuality embraced pleasurable bodily sensation as well as the 'sublimation' of feelings such as tenderness and friendship. The process of becoming social – the reality principle – involved the repression of instinctual sexuality. In *Civilisation and its Discontents* (1930) Freud drew attention to the inevitable conflict between civilised culture (industry, technology, education and art) and the irrational drives of Eros – sexuality – and Thanatos – the instincts of destruction and death. The nature of modern society demanded the renunciation of both instincts in the interests of social order. The result was widespread guilt and mental illness.

Freud's psychological theory of personality assumes a sociological dimension in terms of the mechanism whereby individuals internalise cultural values and norms, thus becoming social beings. In 1922 he published *The Ego and the Id* in which the human personality was described as a system comprising three autonomous and conflicting levels – id, ego and super-ego. The id is essentially amoral, instinctual and dominated by the pleasure principle. Reality is defined narcissistically as the extension of itself. In the process of adjusting to reality, however, the personality becomes differentiated into ego and super-ego. The ego, or self, develops first its primary function to protect and maintain the individual through adaption to the environment. But the ego as such cannot cope with the demands of a complex culture and thus the super-ego emerges as the moral conscience of the personality or the 'ego-ideal', remaining partly unconscious although controlling the actions of the individual *from within*.

Freud's main concern was with the super-ego and its relation with family structure. Initially the child takes both parents, but especially one, as the object of its erotic wishes. 'As a rule a father prefers his daughter and a mother her son; the child reacts to this by wishing, if he is a son, to take his father's place, and if she is a daughter, her mother's.' The resolution of these incestuous desires takes the form of the Oedipus complex in boys and the Electra complex in girls. But Freud was mostly concerned with the Oedipus complex, a term derived from Sophocles's play *Oedipus Rex* in which the king kills his father and marries his mother in ignorance of both identities. Sexual identity is not a given datum; human nature is basically bisexual. It is the object-choice and its resolution which for Freud determines the sexual character of individuals. Libido passes through a number of different stages in its maturation: the phallic phase for males, for example, begins roughly at the age of three years with awareness of, and interest in, the penis: this leads to an infantile desire for the mother and jealousy of the father. But the erotic feelings for the mother (pleasure principle) comes into conflict with the authority and fear of the father (reality principle, the fear being that of castration). The child abandons his desire for the mother by assimilating the father's male authority. In this way the super-ego develops out of the Oedipus complex: a strong parental influence and notion of self has been integrated into the structure of the personality. The female attachment to the father, which in Freud's interpretation is loosely based on the Greek myth of Electra who sought the death of her mother, Clytemnestra, is resolved by an acceptance of castration (in Freud's view girls develop penis envy) and a turning towards the father.

The development of the super-ego is thus closely bound up with the sense of guilt which the child experiences as the result of his or her erotic desire for the mother or father. The Oedipus complex exerts a more powerful influence on the process of assimilating parental values: thus Freud concludes that males develop a stronger super-ego than females. This is, perhaps, one of Freud's more speculative notions comparable to the 'primal horde' thesis of *Totem and Taboo* (1913) and his theory of religion as 'the universal obsessional neurosis of humanity' in *The Future of an Illusion* (1927). For Freud, the Oedipus complex is a universal phenomenon found in all human societies and social groups. Anthropologists, such as Malinowski in his study of the Trobriand Islanders in *Sex and Repression in Savage Society* (1937) concluded that family structure differed sharply from that implied in the theory of the Oedipus complex: social status and property is inherited not from the child's father but from the maternal uncle, and in general the father plays a far less significant role in the socialisation of the child than is the case with the middle-class European family.

Freud's significance for sociological theory, however, does not depend on the validity of his quasi-mystical notions of cultural development – the struggle between the life and death instincts, for example – and ahistorical categories such as the Oedipus complex, but in his attempt to develop an action concept of personality, with its emphasis on energy, and a notion of a creative self. The role of irrational, unconscious forces in the formation of self and society further suggests the potential absence of harmony between the individual and society. Ultimately, however, the relation of self to the social system and to everyday life, including ideological influences, remains absent from Freud's theory.

The social self: Mead and symbolic interactionism

Although the dominant trend of late nineteenth-century and early twentieth-century social theory was towards developing a concept of action, none of the major sociologists discussed by Parsons in *The Structure of Social Action* constructed an adequate notion of self. The self was defined anonymously as a disembodied actor assimilating norms and producing meanings in relation to the wider, macrosociological system. The self as a distinctive social being, as the source of action and energy, existed implicitly as the necessary voluntaristic component of an anti-positivist sociology. The self was defined in terms of institutions, ideologies, culture: but its rich complexity, its many-sided aspects, its forms of action and consciousness were largely absent. Only Simmel's sociology with its basis in sociation and interaction approached an adequate theory of the living, active social subject. And it was Simmel, not Durkheim, Weber or Pareto, who exerted the greatest influence on the theory of the self which developed in the social psychology, or social behaviourism, of G. H. Mead (1863–1931).

For much of his academic life Mead taught at the University

of Chicago. The first major school of American sociology developed at the University of Chicago in the work of Robert Park, who had studied with Simmel in Germany, W. I. Thomas, Florian Znaneicki and many others all of whom were largely concerned with micro rather than macrosociological issues especially the study of social interaction in the city, the process of urbanism and the ways in which individuals construct reality. Thus Thomas and Znaniecki argued that since the personal element is a constitutive factor of every social occurrence, 'social science cannot remain on the surface . . . but must reach the actual human experiences and attitudes which constitute the full, live and actual reality beneath the formal organisation of social institutions' (Thomas and Znaniecki, 1927, Vol. 2, p. 1834). The Chicago based *American Journal of Sociology* had published a number of Simmel's essays before 1914 while the first major textbook in American sociology, *Introduction to the Science of Sociology* (1921) written by Park together with E. W. Burgess, contained more references to Simmel than to any other European sociologist. Simmel's emphasis on the importance of subjectivity in social life and the deeply alienating nature of modern urban society found a ready response in the Chicago school's focus on the rootlessness of American culture, the increasing isolation of individuals from community and primary groups. 'It is plausible', writes Rock, 'that the greatly accelerated processes of capitalism in early twentieth-century America gave ontological primacy to the individual above all other categories. Theories which centred . . . on the European forms of class, could be discounted as irrelevant. The self became chiefly problematic' (Rock, 1979, pp. 95–6). But although problematic the self was not integrated within a sociological theory of society as a system: the Chicago school tended to define society atomistically. Indeed, the only available theory of the subject which conceived the self anti-atomistically, as a structure, derived from the social psychological approach of Mead.

Mead published very little during his lifetime; his influence on his contemporaries flowed from his lecture courses and scattered articles. After his death the lectures were published in book form, *Mind, Self and Society* (1934), *Movements of Thought in the Nineteenth Century* (1936), *The Philosophy of the Act* (1938) and his work reached a wider audience. Mead is important because he broke from the mechanical and passive notions of self and consciousness which had dominated early twentieth-century American psychology and sociology. Mead attempted to examine the genesis of the self both in terms of its practical social experience (its external aspects), as well as its experience as consciousness (its inner aspects). The intellectual influences on Mead's thought were numerous and varied: the philosophy of pragmatism (John Dewey, William James), Darwinian evolutionism, German idealism, nineteenth-century Romanticism and the sociology of Charles Cooley. Thus although the self was partly biological in that its development was dependent on the central nervous system it was only by adapting to its environment, and struggling continually to control it, that the human organism comes to identify itself as a subject. German idealism (Hegel, Fichte) and Romanticism had both emphasised the significance of a constituting subject in the formation and development of culture, but failed to ground it materialistically in the day-to-day experience of ordinary humanity. Mead criticised Cooley, for example, for a similar failure, a too-subjectivist notion of the self.

Charles Cooley (1864–1929) rejected the dualism of individual and society arguing that they both constituted 'collective' and 'distributive' aspects of the same phenomena. The self arises out of a process of communication with others and society as a whole: the 'I' is impossible without the 'you', the 'he', without the 'they'. In his most famous formulation Cooley described the genesis of a 'looking-glass self' which consisted of 'the imagination of our appearance to the other person, the imagination of his judgment of that appearance, and some sort of self-feeling, such as pride or mortification'. Society, however, and its 'solid facts' were ultimately constituted in 'the imaginations which people have of one another' (Cooley, 1902, pp. 184, 121). By defining the self almost entirely in terms of those ideas which others entertain of it, Cooley slipped into mentalism, society defined psychologically as a psychical whole. Mead, in his assessment of Cooley's contribution to American social theory wrote:

His method was that of an introspection which recognised the mind as the *locus* of the selves that act upon each other, but the methodological problem of the objectification of this mind he pushed aside as metaphysical . . . [But] in the process of communication there appears a social world of selves standing on the same level of immediate reality as that of the physical world that surround us. It is out of this social world that the inner experience arises which we term psychical . . . the *locus* of society is not in the mind . . . though what goes on in the inner forum of our experience is essential to meaningful communication (Mead, 1964, pp. 304–5).

For Mead, both mind and self were the social creations of everyday life: 'Human society as we know it could not exist without minds and selves, since all of its most characteristic features presuppose the possession of minds and selves by its individual members' (Mead, 1934, p. 227). Humanity, through mind and self, had the capacity to reason and to reflect. Two elements of the self which Mead analysed in great detail were its reflexive nature and ability to develop symbolic forms of communication. Moreover, the self exists only in relation to social groups 'because the individual himself belongs to a social structure, a social order' (Mead, 1934, pp. 1–7). Mind and self, consciousness and action, were thus collaborative not individual phenomena involving social roles, social relations and social institutions.

Mead was concerned with analysing the patterns of interaction, the social acts which constituted the basis of human society. Reality was not a fixed datum but constantly shifting as actors – selves – create new roles and new meanings, defining their situation in a variety of different ways all of which were 'real' to them. Communication is effected through 'significant gestures', self-conscious acts which distinguish human from non-human behaviour. The acts of dogs, about to fight each other, consist of what Mead called 'a conversation of gestures' but not of significant gestures: the animals instinctively react and adjust to the situation. Significant gestures are full of meaning because they involve ideas communicated through a system of universal symbols such as language. In this way human beings interpret the actions of others. Mead emphasised that the capacity of individuals to communicate through vocal gestures was closely linked to the evolution of society in which co-operative activity increasingly became the norm. Social acts were defined as acts involving the co-operation of more than one person within a framework of the group.

The self is thus individual only through its reciprocal relations with others and with the community. The self is both a subject and an object, the 'I' as the subject which thinks and acts, the 'Me' as the individual's awareness of self as an object in the world existing for others. Mead's notion of the 'I' is both biological and social, a synthesis of organic drives and social experience; it is not, therefore, easily separated from the 'Me'. Mead's emphasis on the role of language in the formation of the self, however, suggests that the 'Me' aspect of self arises out of dialogic speech acts, out of discourse, 'the inner flow of speech'. There is no 'I' or 'Me' in a conversation of gestures: it is only through dialogic communication that self-consciousness develops:

> The 'I' is the response of the organism to the attitudes of the others; the 'me' is the organised set of attitudes of others which one himself assumes. The attitudes of the others constitute the organised 'me', and then one reacts towards that as an 'I' (Mead, 1934).

A self exists, only then, when it interacts with itself and the other selves of the community: the self arises 'through its ability to take the attitude of the group to which he belongs' and assimilate the group's social habits, the common attitudes of the community (Mead, 1964, pp. 33–4). The individual takes not simply the attitudes of others towards him/her but seeks to integrate the 'whole social process' into individual experience. The self is finally organised into a unity by this 'generalised other'.

Thus the young girl who takes the role of mother, conversing with herself and acting towards herself as she believes mothers do, has succeeded in getting outside herself by adopting the role of a 'significant other'. For Mead, as for Freud, childhood constituted the first stage in the formation of the self: the second stage Mead described as the 'game' (as distinct from the 'play' of the first stage where individual roles are internalised) in which the child takes a collective role, the 'generalised other', the organised group. Mead illustrated this process in terms of a baseball team: the individual player must take account of the role of the whole team, its structure as a team, as a whole, which is always involved in his individual action. (Other examples were the family, education, political parties, trade unions, etc.)

Mead's theory of the self represented a marked advance on previous sociologies of the actor: the act and the self were structures bound up with social structure yet creative and reflexive. But as Mead's work became widely known during the 1940s and 1950s it was increasingly appropriated by social theorists who tended to stress the passive nature of roles and diminish the active properties of self. The 'Me' dominated the 'I' in the interests of the social system and social order. Yet there is a sense in which Mead's work inclines in this direction: through his emphasis on the collective community as a unity, a structure of commonly shared values, Mead's theory of self approaches a conservative standpoint. There is, for example, no awareness in his writings of the repressive character of culture – the generalised other – and the potential conflict between the creative, voluntaristic aspect of the self and the collective, conformist nature of modern industrial society. Mead's fundamental concepts assume a common core of values which arise spontaneously from within the common culture and community. It is the strong sense of community which effectively overrides the possibility of conflicting and alternative values.

Nevertheless, Mead's emphasis on the potential creativity of the subject constitutes a significant corrective to mechanistic and reified notions of self and society. In particular, the category of meaning is located within the common symbols of social groups and their modes of interaction. Other symbolic interactionists (the term was coined by Herbert Blumer in 1937) developed many of Mead's ideas concerning the role of gestures and speech in the formation and structure of human society. Mead's voluntarism and concern with the dialogic nature of everyday life stand opposed to the dominant assumptions of structural functionalism which one critic has conveniently summarised as 'the oversocialised conception of man' (Wrong, 1976). Thus for Herbert Blumer meaning is not a property intrinsic to an object but constructed through the interactions of group members. It is this notion of meaning as inter-subjective which links symbolic interactionism, in its Meadian and post-Meadian phases, with sociological phenomenology.

Sociological phenomenology: Schutz and the reality of everyday life

In the historical development of a voluntaristic sociological theory of action the work of Alfred Schutz (1899–1959) occupies as important a place as that of Freud and Mead. Like Mead, Schutz emphasised the creative and active role of the subject; social reality is a process constantly reconstructed through the everyday action of individuals. Schutz follows Weber in rejecting positivist methods for the exploration of social and cultural life, arguing that the object of sociology is the meaning-endowing actions of human agents.

Schutz's first significant work, *The Phenomenology of the Social World*, published in Germany in 1932 (and translated into English in 1967), set out to establish a distinctive phenomenological approach to the study of society. Schutz was influenced by the phenomenological philosophy of Edmund Husserl (1859–1938) whose work was primarily concerned with the structure of consciousness and the relation between subjectivity and scientific method. In his various writings Husserl advanced the argument that all the sciences had their basis in the pre-scientific world (*Lebenswelt*) of a common humanity. For Husserl, reality was 'intentional' in the sense that the human subject directed his/her consciousness to objects. Experience was always intentional and all modes of consciousness involved consciousness of objects: it was through the activity of consciousness that the objects acquired a structure and a meaning. Thus the meaning of an object was not inherent in the object itself but located in the inner life of the subject. But the subjective life-world, the consciousness, con-sisted of numerous accumulated experiences and pre-suppositions which hinder the process of understanding. Husserl thus advocated the method of 'phenomenological reduction' whereby consciousness abandons all ideas about the external world and its objects. Consciousness would become a pure consciousness. In this way society, culture, history are 'bracketed away', put on one side as it were, so that knowledge is the product of the 'intentionality' of the 'pure consciousness'.

Husserl called this procedure the *epoché*, a suspension of belief in the objects of experience: what is left afterwards is the 'transcendent ego', the pure consciousness free to discover its 'true' meaning, its essence. As Schutz described it: Husserl's 'transcendental phenomenological reduction . . . must deprive the world which formerly, within the natural attitude, was simply posited as being, of just this posited being . . . what is grasped in the epoché is the pure life of consciousness in which and through which the whole objective world exists for me . . . I abstain from belief in the being of this world, and I direct my view exclusively to my consciousness of the world' (Schutz, 1978, p. 124). Schutz's sociological version of this phenomenological reduction was to bracket away all scientific presuppositions about the socio-historical world: sociology must begin its task of analysis and understanding not from a conception of a world 'out there', but from the actions and consciousness of subjects who strive to construct and make sense of reality. Meaning is thus not waiting passively to be discovered but requires active construction.

Schutz defined the 'life-world' as a continuous flow of experience and action; the actor rarely reflects on this process. Now whereas Husserl had sought to purify consciousness of all empirical elements, Schutz starts from these experiences, from everyday life, common sense, the social actions of ordinary individuals. Social science begins from the 'taken-for-granted' self-evident nature of the social world that is the marked characteristic of those individuals who remain 'within the natural attitude'. The natural attitude is one which accepts the reality of the everyday world suspending all doubt that it can be other than it is. To understand this ordinary world the social scientist must account for the ways in which individuals define and reflect upon their situation and action (the actor's intentions and purposes), as well as examining its structure.

Schutz defines the everyday world as inter-subjective: the world is not private but shared with others, a plurality of interacting actors whose presence influences the development of ourselves. Social reality is thus the sum total of all the objects and occurrences within the social world. But this world has a structure – it is not an atomistic world – built around social relationships which involve various modes of communication. An actor has to make sense of the actions of others by learning to interpret what the action is about. To do this requires a stock of commonsense knowledge, commonsense understanding, which enables the individual to structure the social world in terms of 'meaningful configurations' such as ideal types or typifications. Schutz distinguishes between first order typifications (e.g. the act of posting a letter which assumes knowledge of specific types involved in the action, postmen, sorters, etc.) from second order typifications which the sociologist employs to analyse and reconstitute reality.

The stock of knowledge is based on individual experience which has, over time, become 'sedimented', congealed within the culture of the life-world and communicated through language since only a small fraction of the totality of such knowledge can exist in the consciousness of a single individual. The actor's stock of knowledge is simply taken for granted, practical, relating to how the world works. Thus the everyday world has its own distinctive structure which to a great extent coheres around the notions of 'cookery book' knowledge or recipe knowledge in which action becomes 'reduced to automatic habits of unquestioned platitudes' (Schutz, 1972, pp. 142–3). For Schutz, knowledge is defined by 'interests', usually practical in nature, which are bound up with an individual's 'project'. The life-world, is, therefore, further structured into domains or 'zones of relevance' which relate to certain group associations (marriage, business enterprises, clubs). The life-process is made up of these changing systems of relevance for individuals. In undertaking a project the actor is necessarily bound to a system of relevances intrinsic to the project. It is this process which enables the individual to select and interpret: 'All facts are from the outset, facts selected from a universal context by the activities of our mind. They are therefore always interpreted facts.' The individual thus structures the life-world through consciousness: the stock of knowledge, typifications and relevance constitute the categories through which the consciousness organises reality. Schutz's formulation is thus similar to Kant's analysis of causality, time and space as immanent categories of the mind which organise external matter rather than as elements intrinsic to the object.

Schutz's description of the life-world emphasises the importance of shared meanings, the notion of the world as 'ours' rather than 'mine', a linguistic community existing through mutual symbols:

> Our everyday world is, from the outset, an intersubjective world of culture. It is intersubjective because we live in it as men among other men, bound to them through common influence and work, understanding others and being an object of understanding for others. It is a world of culture because, from the outset, the life-world is a universe of significations to us, i.e. a framework of meaning which we have to interpret, and of interrelations of meaning which we institute only through our action in this life-world. It is a world of culture also because we are always conscious of its *historicity*, which we encounter in tradition and habituality . . . the men to whom I stand in relationships are my kind, my friends, or strangers. Language is not a substratum of philosophical or grammatical considerations for me, but a means for expressing my intentions or understanding the intentions of Others. Only in reference to me does that relation to Others obtain its specific meaning which I designate with the word 'We' (Schutz, 1978, pp. 134–5).

It is this 'We' relationship which constitutes the basic structure of everyday life; all other relationships depend on and relate to it. Schutz argues that the social world, centred around the individual, consists of a web of relationships ranging from the immediate, personal and unique (relations with *consociates* such as family and friends) to the indirect and more anonymous 'They' relations (with *contemporaries, predecessors* and *successors*). Knowledge of contemporaries is largely inferential and discursive based on typical not unique features. The pure 'We' relation, in contrast, 'involves our awareness of each other's presence and also the knowledge of each that the other is aware of him' (Schutz, 1972, pp. 142–3, 168).

For Schutz, then, society constitutes a structure of 'multiple realities' cohering around different 'zones of relevance', interests, consociates, etc. It is not strictly speaking a world of

271

objects but one constructed by the active subject. Schutz's social world lacks a fixed centre other than the vague notion of social order. It is a social world made meaningful through language, rules, roles, statuses. But it is a stable and conformist world:

> In order to find my bearings within the social group, I have to know the different ways of dressing and behaving, the manifold insignia, emblems, tools etc. which are considered by the group as indicating social status and are therefore socially approved as relevant (Schutz, 1962–6, Vol. 1, p. 350).

The social world is not therefore an objective system or structure; the social world flows from the shared stock of knowledge and common assumptions of different social groups and communities. Nevertheless, Schutz maintains that meaning forms an integral part of the interaction process and to this extent his sociology is objective: consciousness and action are meaningful in their relation with social structure and institutions.

Social action and interactionism: ethnomethodology

Parsons's action theory, symbolic interactionism and sociological phenomenology focus on the problem of social integration from the standpoint of subjectively mediated action. Mead's emphasis on social acts which fulfil specific needs through co-operative relations with others, deals with socialisation at the 'micro' level: as the child internalises the gestures of others by 'taking an attitude' so he/she begins to act. In Parsons's action theory the actor internalises both specific cultural values and the personality of the other in the process of interaction. Parsons rejected positivistic voluntarism for reducing action to the conditions of its context: cultural values, because they are linked with the integration of society as a whole, and enshrine universal not everyday, practical principles. The common culture of society defines what is desirable and valuable for the individual; these cultural values are simultaneously institutionalised in society and its sub-systems and internalised by personalities. These 'higher normative components of culture' enable individuals to transcend their particular concretisation in social institutions, their meaning realised through action which goes beyond empirical everyday experience (Parsons, 1989, pp 577–82).

Parsons, then, does not present the agent entirely as a passive, oversocialised product of social and cultural norms. There is an active relation between a rational agent and culture. Yet problems remain. Parsons's formulation suggests that the agent realises already existing values rather than actively producing them. The link between the actor and the system is clearly articulated, but it remains unproblematic, for in the very act of realising universal cultural values the bonds between the individual and normative culture is deepened. It is this aspect of Parsons's theory which has drawn criticism for an unreal distinction between the normative and the empirical order, between a higher and a lower reality. Parsons's agent, for all the emphasis on autonomy, is close to a 'judgmental' or 'cultural dope' whose actions comply with standardised expections and 'who produce(s) the stable features of the society by acting in compliance with preestablished and legitimate alternatives . . . that the common culture provides' (Garfinkel, 1967, pp 66–8).

It is ethnomethodology which sets itself the task of challenging the orthodox sociological concept of self. Developed initially by Harold Garfinkel during the 1960s, ethnomethodology (ethno – referring to the stock of commonsense knowledge available to individuals; method – referring to the strategies whereby the acting subject makes sense of the social world and seeks to communicate meaning) focused on 'practical actions as contigent accomplishments of organised artful practices of everyday life' (Garfinkel, 1967, p. 11). For Garfinkel, Parsons's action theory failed to explain how actors acquire knowledge and understanding, how 'persons discover, create and sustain' cultural norms. Actors are reflexive in relation to norms and action. In the choice of this or that goal, in assessing possible results of action, it is precisely the empirical mundane knowledge of 'members' (Garfinkel's term) which is crucial. It is the practical reasoning of members which is missing from Parsons's account. The agent makes sense of the world through 'accounting', by observing, reporting and commenting on different forms of action in which he/she is involved. A sociological theory of action must always include the actor's own account of that action.

The object of study for ethnomethodology is thus the commonsense activities of ordinary members of society. It is the emphasis on these activities as phenomena 'in their own right' which distinguishes ethnomethodology from traditional sociology which, with the exception of sociological phenomenology, had largely ignored the everyday world. In effect, ethnomethodology sought to reveal the implicit rules and planful nature of everyday life. It is a world consisting of reflexive social acts which embody a variety of meanings, and Garfinkel uses the term 'indexicality' to refer to the context-bound nature of meaning: there is no objective meaning as there is for Mead and Parsons. By constructing meaning, ordinary members are effectively 'doing sociology' and there is little to choose between the sociology of the professional and of the lay public. Social science itself is a practical accomplishment.

This is to abandon all hope for a sociology grounded in the complex relation of self to society, agent to structure. Ethnomethodology is the ultimate trivialisation of voluntarist sociology, the reduction of action to the freely constructed meanings of atomised individuals. Parsons's concept of cultural values (however problematic) succeeded in situating action in and beyond its immediate context. Ethnomethodology reverts to a positivistic model: all values are situational values, all meaning is situational meaning. Thus many of the examples cited by Garfinkel, students acting as lodgers in their own home, others making offers for already priced goods, action challenging pre-established conventions of interaction, eliminate the core element of interaction: that in one's own action account is taken of the other(s) by a process of internalisation and dialogue with their values, meanings, interpretations and action.

10
Critical Theory, Ideology and Modern Sociology

Two major themes dominated nineteenth-century sociology and Marxism. Through the critique of positivism the problem of social action and the relation of agency to structure was raised, the degree to which moral and normative elements played a critical role in the social integration of developing capitalist societies. And secondly, with the rapid growth of industrialisation and urbanism, specific cultural issues moved to the forefront of sociological theory. Western Marxism resolved the question of agency by appealing to the power of bourgeois ideology over nascent proletarian revolutionary consciousness. In the aftermath of the First World War, the abortive revolutions in Germany and Hungary and the 1917 Russian Revolution, the question of a consciously guided social transformation structured in ideology became a major issue within Marxism and sociology. The debate between Marxists and sociologists, which had characterised French and German sociology during the period 1890 to 1914, took on new urgency. Weber's concern with the sociology of culture, his theorisation of autonomous value spheres and eclipse of dominant world views, is echoed in the work of Karl Mannheim (1893–1947) and Max Scheler (1874–1928).

In a social world fragmented into competing ideologies and the relativism of values the question of knowledge became problematical. How was scientific knowledge possible? It was Scheler who coined the term, the sociology of knowledge, to describe the collective, social nature of knowledge, its distribution through cultural institutions and the reality of social

275

interests in its genesis. All mental acts, he wrote, were 'necessarily sociologically co-conditioned . . . by the structure of society' (Scheler, in Curtis and Petras, 1970, pp. 170–5). For Scheler, the sociological analysis of forms of knowledge served to illuminate what he, and other contemporary sociologists, defined as a crisis of values in a world dominated by such diverse philosophies, sociologies and psychologies as neo-Kantianism, phenomenology, Marxism, psycho-analysis, vitalism and formalism. In the realm of social theory, relativism in epistemology and agnosticism in methodology predominated; while a plurality of world views, socialism, Marxism, liberalism, fascism emerged, each with its particular claim to truth. The task of the sociology of knowledge was defined as the selection of the truthful, universal elements in each world view and their integration into a total conception (Scheler, 1970). Scheler's anti-positivism, Dilthey's conception of 'world view', Marx's theory of ideology were brought together in Mannheim's social theory of ideology.

Mannheim: the problem of ideology

Mannheim belonged to a generation of Hungarian intellectuals who were concerned above all with culture and human values: he was a member of a group consisting of Lukács, the art historian, Arnold Hauser, the composer, Bela Bartok and the philosopher, Michael Polyani. During the 1920s he sought to define an interpretative sociological approach in the analysis of different forms of knowledge. During the period 1921–9 he wrote a series of essays exploring the possibility of a sociology of knowledge. The most important of these works were 'On the Interpretation of *Weltanschauung*' (1921), 'Historicism' (1924), 'The Problem of a Sociology of Knowledge' (1925), 'Conservative Thought' (1926) and *Ideology and Utopia* (a book of three essays published in 1929). 'The sociology of knowledge', he wrote, 'is . . . the *systematisation* of the doubt which is to be found in social life as a vague insecurity and uncertainty.' The modern world is to blame for this situation with social life increasingly alienated, disorganised and anarchical. Mannheim wrote gloomily of 'the intellectual twilight which dominates our epoch', the 'appalling trend of modern thought' and the confusion into which social and intellectual life has fallen (Mannheim, 1960, p. 94).

These pessimistic comments are from one of Mannheim's most significant works, *Ideology and Utopia* (1929), in which he confronted the problems of objectivity and perspective that Weber and Lukács had raised in their sharply differing ways. If there is no objective reality but merely the sum of divergent perspectives then how is historical knowledge possible? In opposition to Weber's cultural relativism and sceptical sociology, Mannheim proposed an historicist solution, 'a dynamic conception of the truth', an absolute standard by which to judge the validity of different perspectives. Mannheim adopted the concept of totality arguing that although different types of knowledge are related to different social locations each new perspective which emerges in the course of historical development actually contains new and valuable insights into the nature of historical reality – Marxism emphasised the class struggle, Fascism the element of action in social life, Liberalism the importance of the autonomous individual. Each new perspective synthesises previous perspectives: different 'styles of thought' continually undergo uninterrupted fusion and interpenetration. Thus modern society, although characterised by intense fragmentation and polarisation, nevertheless lays the foundation for 'an ever-widening drive towards a total conception', in that each new perspective uncovers 'an approximate truth' that forms part of a 'larger body of meaning' within the structure of historical reality. All perspectives are necessarily partial 'because historical totality is always too comprehensive to be grasped by any one of the individual points of view which emerge out of it' (Mannheim, 1960, pp. 94–6, 134–5). This is the meaning of Mannheim's 'dynamic conception of truth'. In the essay on 'Historicism', for example, he argued that no single class, or group, could constitute itself as the bearer of the totalising movement of history. The whole can only be grasped by taking all perspectives into account, 'the whole contrapuntal pattern of all the voices'.

Mannheim thus adopts a version of Hegel's 'cunning of reason' in which the historical process immanently transforms ideological and interest-bound thought into objective truth. In

Ideology and Utopia Marx's theory of ideology is praised for identifying the link between class interests and forms of knowledge. But Marx failed to apply his theory to his own thought and conceived ideology as a 'privileged concept of socialists'. Although an advance on previous theories, the Marxist concept fused two distinct meanings of ideology: the simple (or particular) concept, referring to individual disguises and rationalisations of actions operating on a psychological level; and the total concept which refers to the thought of a social class, or epoch, to styles of thought. The latter meaning is sociological and therefore approximates to the truth. The total concept of ideology is non-evaluative seeking only to elucidate the relation of 'mental structures' to specific 'life-situations'; it enables the sociology of knowledge to explore the social determinants of thought and raise the question of truth and falsity (Mannheim, 1960, pp. 66–72).

All thought is socially determined. However, Mannheim exempts mathematics and the natural sciences from a dependence on social causation. In contrast to 'existentially determined thought' mathematics and the natural sciences are governed by immanent factors so that in the formulation $2 + 2 = 4$ 'there is no indication as to who did the thinking and where'. Many critics have pointed out the weakness of this distinction between formal and historical knowledge: if thought is socially determined then science, the product of human action and culture, is equally determined. In general, Mannheim failed to distinguish clearly between different types of knowledge assuming that political, ethical, historical and religious beliefs were the same as everyday values and ideas. For if knowledge is determined by extra-theoretic factors then logic and science, as well as political philosophy and epistemology, are relative in terms of the truth content.

In his early writings Mannheim had identified the problem of relativism as the basic problem of the sociology of knowledge since it clearly suggested the limits of the sociology of knowledge itself. His solution in *Ideology and Utopia* was to distinguish *relativism* (that all ideas are relative to a situation) from *relationism* (that knowledge, although related to specific contexts, is not thereby invalidated as truthful or not). But as we have seen, ultimately Mannheim adopted an Hegelian historicist standpoint so that although the sociologist of knowledge relates specific forms of thought to specific social locations, the truth content of different perspectives lies in their relation with 'supra-historical' reality.

In *History and Class Consciousness* Lukács had proposed the radical historicist solution to the problem of historical relativism: the optimum of truth lay with the ontologically privileged proletariat whose world view of Marxism embodied the principle of totality and thus of historical meaning. Like Lukács, Mannheim argued that some social locations enable a social group to understand historical reality at a deeper level than others; not all perspectives are equally valid. Mannheim rejected Lukács's assimilation of truth to class and advanced the view that the task of synthesising different perspectives lay with a privileged social stratum, the 'free-floating intelligentsia' (*freischwebende Intelligenz*), a group unattached to specific social interests and thus intellectually autonomous. Marx's theory of ideology could develop into the sociology of knowledge only through the actions of these independent intellectuals who occupied a social location outside the main institutions of capitalist society.

> It seems inherent in the historical process itself that the narrowness and the limitations which restrict one point of view tend to be corrected by clashing with the opposite points of view. The task of the study of ideology . . . is to understand the narrowness of each individual point of view and the interplay between these distinctive attitudes in the total social process (Mannheim, 1960, p. 72).

Only the intellectuals can achieve a total perspective and in *Ideology and Utopia* Mannheim adopted Alfred Weber's term describing the intelligentsia as a '*relatively* classless stratum' (Mannheim's emphasis), highly differentiated and unified by the bond of education. Mannheim distinguished between the 'socially unattached intelligentsia' (clergymen, engineers, writers, academics) and the 'socially attached intelligentsia' (the Church in the Middle Ages is mentioned as constituting a closed social stratum, highly unified internally) in an attempt to differentiate those intellectuals capable of autonomous cognitive activity from those whose function was directly interest bound and thus ideological.

279

The development of the modern intelligentsia is the result of a broad process of democratisation embracing the professions, education, communications and the cultural institutions of industrial society which effectively liberate the intellectual from patronage and total dependence on state institutions; the modern intelligentsia is thus an open stratum, lacking a unified world view, democratic and sceptical in outlook. Their marginal social position makes the modern intelligentsia highly sensitive to the political and cultural fragmentation of the modern world:

These unattached intellectuals are the typical advocate-philosophers, *ideologues* who can find arguments in favour of any political cause they may happen to serve. Their own social position does not bind them to any cause, but they have an extraordinarily refined sense for all the political and social currents (Mannheim, 1953, pp. 126–7).

As examples Mannheim cites both Enlightenment philosophy and Romanticism as currents of thought developed by intellectuals acting as the spokesmen for specific social groups. Intellectuals effectively give theoretical expression to the material interests of social groups and classes and in so doing become the allies of such groups and classes without belonging to them. Thus Mannheim describes Kant's critical philosophy as expressing the 'inner nature' of the French Revolution, not because Kant identified with its political aims, but 'because the form of his thought . . . (was) of the same brand as that which was the dynamic force behind the French revolutionaries' (Mannheim, 1953, p. 84).

Mannheim's sociological writings tended to emphasise the essentially passive role played by the intellectual in the formation of styles of thought: at times Mannheim's work approximates to vulgar Marxism especially the formulation of intellectuals as merely expressing the 'appropriate' thought of a specific social group or class. This is especially the case with one of his major studies, 'Conservative Thought' (1925). Here Mannheim distinguished 'Conservative' thought from 'Traditional' thought in terms of the former's reflective structure, arguing that in the wake of the French Revolution and the rise of more open, socially mobile societies, new secular philosophies and the disintegration of the static pre-industrial world view, 'Conservative' thought emerged as a self-conscious mode of opposition both to individualistic capitalism and the collective philosophy of nascent socialism. In particular 'Conservative' thought stressed the organic nature of society, the importance of family and corporations in opposition to the atomistic philosophy of Social Contract philosophy with its stress on the inalienable rights of the individual and values of popular sovereignty. Human life was fundamentally irrational and historical development conceived as an organic not mechanical process. In this way 'Conservative' thought legitimised opposition to industrial capitalism, individualism, liberalism and socialism.

The new industrial society of the early nineteenth century could no longer be legitimised through appeals to traditional values as such: thus the 'unattached intelligentsia', unable to articulate its own distinctive interests and secure an autonomous social position, identified with the conservative reaction against the values of Enlightenment (Mannheim's analysis focuses mainly on Germany with its weak industrial base and fragmented political system). It is precisely because intellectuals are relatively unattached to specific material interests that they lack their own ideology but remain highly sensitive to existing social and political currents: 'By themselves they know nothing. But let them take up and identify themselves with someone else's interests – they will know them better, really better, than those for whom these interests are laid down by the nature of things, by their social condition' (Mannheim, 1953, p. 127).

In Mannheim's later work, intellectuals constitute more than a passive instrument of a specific class. In *Ideology and Utopia* intellectuals have the task of elucidating the category of totality through synthesising different perspectives, a process not bound up with class interests (as with Lukács's proletarian and bourgeois thought concepts for example). Later, in the essay on the intelligentsia, written during the 1930s, although not published until after his death, this emphasis on totality is replaced by empathy. As an open stratum the relatively free intelligentsia participates in historical experience from a variety of different perspectives; reality is multiple and not single centred, the product of increasing social mobility and complexity of modern society. Thus intellectuals empathise with other standpoints and enter a critical dialogue developing an attitude of 'fruitful scepticism'. It is the structural and cognitive openness of the intelligentsia which Mannheim identified as the means of making sense of the many conflicting ideologies that characterise the modern age.

Ideology and Utopia

These arguments find their first formulation in *Ideology and Utopia*. In this work Mannheim distinguished ideology from Utopia by defining ideology as the process whereby the thought of a ruling group becomes so interest bound that it no longer comprehends the existence of facts which might undermine its claim to domination. Ideology implies 'that in certain situations the collective unconscious of certain groups obscures the real condition of society both to itself and to others and thereby stabilises it'. In contrast, Utopian thought reflects the struggles of oppressed groups to seek change thus seeing only 'those elements in the situation which tend to negate it'. Utopian thought is thus incapable of a valid analysis of an existing situation only of grasping the possible negative elements in situations: as examples of Utopian thought Mannheim cites the orgiastic chiliasm of the Anabaptists, Liberal humanitarianism, Communist socialism, all of which are structured around concepts 'incongruous' with the existing state of reality. Only intellectuals, from their privileged vantage point, can provide historically objective knowledge through their ability to synthesise the valid elements from different perspectives. Truth is historical and holistic: neither Utopian nor ideological thought can grasp the historical whole.

In *Ideology and Utopia* Mannheim sketched an evolutionary development of utopian thought beginning with chiliasm and ending with Socialist-Humanism. He noted the difficulties in distinguishing the utopian and ideological modes of action suggesting that the utopias 'of ascendent classes are often . . .

permeated with ideological elements'. Thus the world view of the ascendant bourgeoisie embraced the Utopian ideal of human freedom (in opposition to the static corporatist ideal of feudal society) which was ideological in that it was actually realised historically: Mannheim described bourgeois freedom as 'a relative utopia' (Mannheim, 1960, pp. 183–4). His basic argument remained resolutely historicist: 'our ideas and existence are components of a comprehensive evolutionary process (in which) conservative and progressive ideas appear as derivatives of this process' (Mannheim, 1952, p. 146). The result is that the distinction between Utopia and ideology is made *ex post facto* since it was clearly impossible at the time to know if bourgeois freedom could be realised in bourgeois society. Many of Mannheim's arguments have this *ex post facto* character and his sociological theorems on the relation of knowledge and society are couched in such terms as 'appropriate to the situation', 'in accord with the needs of the time', 'never by accident that' (Merton, 1957, pp. 498–9). In effect, the criterion of truth becomes the adequacy of thought to an existing reality, a functionalist rather than an historicist standpoint.

Mannheim's sociology of knowledge thus embraced two distinct theoretical positions: first, a correspondence theory of knowledge in which styles of thought were related to definite social groups and social locations, and secondly, an historicist conception of truth and validity in tension with the functionalist notion of 'appropriateness' and 'needs'.

The theory of mass society

Mannheim's historicism led him to develop a sociology of knowledge which lacked a distinctive sociological theory of society. Thus although he discussed the production of knowledge in its relation to social groups, social classes and social location, the links between these components of social structure and forms of thought are untheorised. In his later writings, following exile from Germany in the 1930s, Mannheim developed a theory of mass society which is close to that articulated by the Marxist Frankfurt School.

The school took its name from the Frankfurt Institute for Social Research established in Germany in 1923. Its leading members were Theodore Adorno (1903–70), Max Horkheimer (1895–1973), and Herbert Marcuse (1898–1978). Like Mannheim, they were deeply influenced by German idealism, the pessimistic cultural sociology of Simmel and Weber, and the philosophically oriented Marxism of Lukács and Karl Korsch (1886–1961). Unlike Mannheim, the Frankfurt theorists accepted the broad arguments of Marxism but followed Lukács and Korsch in criticising its tendency towards positivism, evolutionism and scientism. Marxism was predominantly a critique of capitalist society and its forms of knowledge; thus the emphasis was placed on consciousness, *praxis* and human values. But unlike Lukács and Korsch, the Frankfurt School remained aloof from politics believing that the proletariat had become integrated into what they called 'organised capitalism' and thereby lost its revolutionary historical role.

The Frankfurt School's theory of society is profoundly pessimistic. Mannheim, too, adopted a pessimistic standpoint. The rise of totalitarian governments – Communist and Fascist – led him to argue that the historical trend of modern society was one of increasing centralisation and atomism: the social and political institutions, essential for a democratic society, were increasingly losing their autonomy. An inevitable escalation of bureaucratisation, a burgeoning army of technical 'experts', a transformation of knowledge into a commodity to be manipulated in the interests of social order, all these effectively undermined the autonomous role of the intellectual. The relatively free intelligentsia becomes problematic as intellectuals are assimilated by centralised, bureaucratic state institutions. In 'The Problem of the Intelligentsia' Mannheim wrote:

> Free inquiry is . . . losing its social basis through the decline of the independent middle classes from which . . . an older type of the relatively unattached intelligentsia used to recruit itself. No other stratum or alternative plan has arisen to assure the continued existence of independent and uncommitted critics (Mannheim, 1956, p. 169).

Mannheim's thesis of the necessary rise of modern 'mass society' and the eclipse of a strong, independent civil society led him towards a concept of intellectuals as standing above all class interests and the dehumanising trends of modern society, an élite whose 'proper' function was as moral guardians of society as a whole.

The Frankfurt School, too, advanced a theory of mass society and mass culture: capitalism, they argued, had become increasingly centralised and its social structure progressively 'atomised'. In the nineteenth century the bourgeoisie had enlarged the 'public sphere', institutions separate from the state through which they conducted their business and organised their culture. But with the development of a centralised economy and polity, collectivist ideologies emerge which emphasise conformity to the social system. The public sphere shrivels: the social structure no longer contains strong, independent institutions that guarantee individual values. The autonomous individual disappears. In this process science played an important 'instrumentalist' role: the scientistic, anti-humanist principles of bourgeois science permeate society as a whole and lead inevitably to a new mode of domination centred in technology and bureaucracy. Consciousness and culture become alienated from the realm of human action, values and *praxis*. The relation between individuals increasingly becomes a relation between things.

The origins of critical theory

In his inaugural address as Director of the Institute in 1930, Horkheimer redefined historical materialism as 'critique' not science, and argued for the integration of philosophy with social science. Later, exiled in the United States of America as a refugee from German Fascism, Horkheimer coined the term 'critical theory'. Like Gramsci's notion of the philosophy of *praxis*, the term critical theory implied a Marxism which emphasised the active role of cognition and rejected the 'copy', or reflection theory of knowledge: theory was defined as an autonomous practice, a critical element in the transformation of society and culture. The leading figures of the Frankfurt School rejected Lukács's historicist identification of the proletariat with historical truth, but followed many of his other arguments such as the universality of reification within capitalism, and the methodological importance of categories such as totality, negativity, dialectics and mediation in the analysis of ideological and cultural forms.

Critical theory concerned itself with truth, with universality and emancipation. Mannheim's argument that knowledge was socially related to specific historical locations was rejected because it undermined the crucial distinction between 'true' and 'false' knowledge. The Frankfurt School were sceptical of the whole notion of the sociology of knowledge since they identified sociology with positivism, agnosticism and relativism. Marxism was not a sociology in this sense, concerned as it was with human *praxis*, meaning and emancipation. To suggest that the partial perspectives opened up by the historical process might be synthesised into truth by free-floating intellectuals was to advance a mechanical *Gestalt* theory of truth and a metaphysical notion of totality. Mannheim's sociology of knowledge assumed the existence of an objective historical reality which was reflected imperfectly in human consciousness: for the Frankfurt School, reality was created through *praxis* in which subject and object were dialectically unified. Underlying the Frankfurt School's epistemology was the Hegelian concept of totality and its expression in the laws of society and history. Critical theory did not relate different forms of thought to particular social groups, but rather sought to 'decipher the general social tendencies which are expressed in these phenomena' and thus bring to consciousness contradictions, negativity and the lack of harmony of individual to society (Adorno, 1967, p. 32).

In his essay, 'Critical and Traditional Theory' (1937), Horkheimer had argued that the goal of bourgeois, positivist science was 'pure' knowledge, not action. Whereas critical theory was based in *praxis*, traditional theory (that is, positivism) separated thought and action, establishing the authority of observation over imagination, and advocating the methods of the natural sciences, especially biology, in the analysis of socio-cultural phenomena. Knowledge was thus 'fetishised' as something standing apart from, and superior to, human action. But this kind of disinterested research was impossible within the framework of capitalist, mass society for it assumed an autonomous individual researcher. In reality, however, the researcher's perception was always mediated through social categories which in the context of modern society meant reification. Bourgeois science, including social science, was linked organically to technical control, technological domination and instrumental rationality. For Horkheimer, only in a non-reified, rational world was prediction – of of the principles of positivist science – possible. The basic distinction, therefore, between critical and traditional theory, was that the former rejected the bourgeois illusion of the autonomous scientist and the goal of a politically neutral objective knowledge. Critical theory postulated an inseparable relation between knowledge and interests. But knowledge was not produced automatically; it required the active intervention of intellectuals. Thus although rejecting Mannheim's sociology of knowledge, the Frankfurt School advanced a modified version of the concept of the free floating intellectual. For only intellectuals can consciously reveal the negative and contradictory forces at work within society through their commitment to critical thought and 'emancipatory interests'.

Methodologically, the Frankfurt School developed a notion of immanent criticism: they argued that the methods of social science should be 'adequate' to its objects. Since objects are neither static nor external but made through human action and mediated by human values and subjectivity, social scientific method must start from the concepts and principles of the object itself and not from its appearances and surface reality. The concepts, however, were not identical with the object because they sought to uncover both the object's immanent tendencies as well as its relation with the wider whole. The objects of social science become known only through practice, through the subject transforming reality. Thus truth constituted a 'moment' of 'correct' practice. But what was correct practice? For Horkheimer, correct action meant action linked with emancipatory interests which were distinguished from class or group interests by their universality and authenticity (Horkheimer, 1976).

287

ation, however, became increasingly problematic. *ilectic of Enlightenment* (1944), Adorno and Hork- plained the failure of proletarian revolution in the capitalist countries as the result of a conformist ture and control over social consciousness through the 'culture industry'. Following Weber, Adorno and Hork- heimer argued that Western culture was dominated by instru- mental (formal) rationality, its goal the control over human action and society through a dehumanised science and tech- nology. How, they asked, had the ideals of the Enlightenment, of freedom, justice, autonomy of self, led to a social world structured in conformism, the totalitarian systems of fascism and communism and the alienated administered world of modern capitalism? The answer lay in the inner tension of Enlightenment rationalism, between the universal ideals of science which freed individuals from the constraints of mytho- logy and unreason, and the positivist, quantitative and prag- matic goals of science empirically realised in the culture of utilitarianism. This tension is mirrored in the development of bourgeois society itself: the principles of calculation and systemisation have the effect of rationalising culture, trans- forming science and reason into modes of technological domi- nation which signal the eclipse of the autonomous individual.

Much of the analysis in *The Dialectic of Enlightenment* has only the most tenuous connection with Marxist social theory. In the post-war years Horkheimer abandoned Marxism alto- gether, while Adorno rejected the concept of totality, arguing that far from constituting the key to scientific knowledge 'the whole was untrue'. Critical theory effectively separated itself from the fundamental concepts of Marxism such as class struggle and the leading role of the working class in social change. Capitalist societies were analysed as closed systems in which all effective opposition had been assimilated and poli- tically neutralised. All modes of social communication were monologic; the system was as perfectly integrated as the models employed in structural functionalism. And while critical theorists such as Marcuse (in his *One Dimensional Man*, 1964) did identify potentially negative and oppositional for- ces, these were largely marginal to society as a whole (stu- dents and blacks, for example). In general the first generation of critical theorists failed to develop an adequate sociology of modern society, the relation between capitalism as a system and its structural differentiation with the emergence of civil society as an autonomous sphere separate from the State. Thus the critical sociological problem of social integration was resolved not in terms of a complex process of a subjectively mediated interaction but rather as a simple one-way process of cultural indoctrination. Society, wrote Adorno, has come to mean the domination of things over human action, so, although the product of human activity, its historical development obstructs subjects reaching consciousness of themselves as subjects: they identify their fate with the domination of market forces:

> In mockery of all hopes of philosophy, subject and object have attained ultimate reconciliation. The process is fed by the fact that men owe their life to what is being done to them . . . the mass appeal of sports, the fetishization of consumer goods, are all symptoms of this trend. The cement which once ideologies supplied is now furnished by these phenomena, which hold the massive social institutions together on the one hand, the psychological constitution of human beings on the other (Adorno, 1989, pp. 274–5).

Habermas: crisis theory

During the 1960s the work of the Frankfurt School became widely known and influential in the social sciences. The concepts of culture industry and one dimensional man, the theory of modern capitalism dominated by a dehumanised rationality, seemed to offer a more salient analysis of modern society than the dogmatic prescriptions of Leninist Marxism and the rigid formulations of structural functionalism. But as Jurgen Habermas (1929–   ), one of a new generation of critical theorists observed, the Frankfurt School programme set out by Horkheimer and Adorno had assumed an objective teleology in history underpinning the normative foundation of its critique of capitalist rationality. The historically complex, variable practices of the everyday world were thus ignored, reduced to ideological reflexes of the centralised culture industry. One of the major themes of Frankfurt School theory was that all capitalist societies were similiar in structure and ideology, dominated by a centralised state apparatus that formed an integral part of the capitalist mode of production. In general, both critical theory and more orthodox Marxism have tended to analyse the state structure in terms of concepts derived from the economic system, that is, the state reproduces the social conditions necessary for capital accumulation and functions in the long-run interests of the dominant class.

Such reductionism is challenged by Habermas, whose work owes a great deal to the Frankfurt School theory of state-regulated capitalism. His analysis of modern society incorporates many of the concepts of critical theory – knowledge is interest-bound; the goal of social theory as emancipation not technical control; science and technology have become increasingly enmeshed with production and administration; social consciousness has become technocratic and structured in instrumental reason. The emancipatory role of reason has become transformed into technical efficiency concerned with means not goals, the triumph of formal over substantive rationality. Instrumental rationality leads to impersonal modes of authority with decision making devolved to hierarchies of experts removed from open, public debate.

For Habermas, capitalist society has become a state–capitalist system, highly centralised and regulated. The public sphere, which functioned to mediate society and the state in nineteenth-century capitalism, has been eclipsed with the growth of technology and bureaucracy. Institutions which normally function to articulate and communicate public opinion have become commercialised and depoliticised. An atomised, mass society is the result.

Habermas focuses on the crises tendencies and the legitimation problems of state or 'late' capitalism. In his analysis Habermas employs categories derived from a variety of intellectual sources ranging from modern system theory to Marx, Freud, Mead, Piaget and Parsons. Sociological theory, he argues, must combine an emphasis on both action and system, subject and structure. The study of legitimation involves objective structures such as the state and economy, as well as motivation and patterns of communication. 'From Hegel through Freud to Piaget the idea has developed that subject and object are reciprocally constituted, that the subject can grasp hold of itself only in relation to and by way of the construction of an objective world.' Thus social systems are 'networks of communicative actions' involving socialised personalities and speaking subjects (Habermas, 1979, pp. 98–100). Crisis is defined at the level of the social system and the socialised actor:

> A social-scientifically appropriate crisis concept must grasp the connection between system integration and social integration. The two expressions 'social integration' and 'system integration' derive from different theoretical traditions. We speak of social integration in relation to the systems of institutions in which speaking and acting subjects are socially related. Social systems are seen here as *life-worlds* that are symbolically structured. We speak of system integration with a view to the specific steering performances of a self-regulated *system* . . . Both paradigms, life-world and system, are important. The problem is to demonstrate their interconnection (Habermas, 1976, p. 4).

Arguing that society must be conceived simultaneously as system and life-world, Habermas defines the life-world as the realm of culture, personality, meaning and symbols, all of which form the basis of communication: agents seek mutual understanding through the substantive reason embodied in speech and action. In contrast, action linked with instrumental reason works through the social system and its subsystems. For Habermas, modern society is characterised by the 'uncoupling' of life-world from system (in primitive society kinship structures were largely inseparable from the economic forces; in modern society the economic institutions are differentiated from those of kinship) and with it the 'uncoupling' of social from system integration. Working through market elements, integration becomes largely automatic. But as modern society evolves, the possibility of social integration through the life-world grows, on the basis of subjectively-mediated communication, not system imperatives. Nevertheless, system imperatives, based on bureaucratisation and monetarisation, constantly threaten to 'colonise' the life-world. The result is a permanent tension between life-world and system (Habermas, 1989, pp. 116–19).

Thus although working within the field of critical theory, Habermas rejects the Adorno–Horkheimer–Marcuse theorisation of a social system free of all significant structural contradictions and opposition. The life-world generates potential sources of conflict with system imperatives in the form of new social movements (notably the ecological and peace movements) bound to a free, open discourse rather than bureaucratically closed modes of communication. Moreover, he seeks to integrate a sociological concept of crisis within critical theory.

He identifies three sub-systems – economic, political–administrative, socio-cultural. Crisis tendencies within late capitalism can arise at different points within the social system and they are not simply economic in character. Habermas suggests a typology of four possible crisis tendencies (Habermas, 1976, p. 45):

Point of Origin	System Crisis	Identity Crisis
Economic System	Economic Crisis	—
Political System	Rationality Crisis	Legitimation Crisis
Socio-Cultural System	—	Motivation Crisis

Late capitalism has produced a shift in the pattern of motivation that characterised the historical development of capitalist society. A crisis of motivation occurs when the socio-cultural system (values oriented to labour, etc.) no longer functions to socialise individuals into roles, occupations and cultural institutions. A rationality crisis occurs when the administrative system can no longer reconcile and fulfil the 'imperatives received from the economic system', that is, the allocation of adequate rewards for labour (consumerism) and the necessity for capital accumulation. It is at this stage that a crisis of legitimacy may occur. The social system depends on a widespread acceptance of rules and laws, on patterns of normative integration and social identity thus enabling agents to recognise the 'worthiness' of the political order. But if culture becomes 'privatised' through consumerist ideology, an object of private enjoyment, it runs the danger of becoming separated from the socialisation process and therefore no longer functioning to integrate the personality system with the social system: 'The less the cultural system is capable of producing adequate motivations for politics, the educational system, and the occupational system, the more must scarce meaning be replaced by consumable values.' Legitimation becomes problematical with the development of 'inflexible normative structures that no longer provide the economic–political system with ideological resources, but instead confront it with exorbitant demands' (Habermas, 1976, pp. 91–3).

Habermas's crisis theorems are advanced as tentative hypotheses. Nevertheless, he seeks to describe the broad tendencies of advanced, late capitalist societies and his general theory rests on the Frankfurt School argument of a declining public sphere and a depoliticised public world. Historically bourgeois society was able to generate adequate motivational structures from its socio-cultural system. But with the development of a centralised state system institutions increasingly function to control and plan from the centre. If culture is privatised – or atomised – it leaves the administrative–political system with the task of producing motivational values; and this it cannot do. The state system produces ideological values which justify the existing structures. Thus the problem: the state apparatuses of late capitalism will inevitably encounter 'long-term insoluble problems', for if the state itself is identified as the producer of ideological values – as the source of social integration – a legitimation crisis develops: 'A legitimation crisis . . . must be based on a motivation crisis – that is, a discrepancy between the need for motives declared by the state, the educational system and the occupational system on the one hand, and the motivation supplied by the socio-cultural system on the other' (Habermas, 1976 pp. 74–5).

Thus system crises are both economic and rationality crises, while legitimation crises are those of social integration. If the system is perceived as failing then its whole legitmacy is questioned and a motivational crisis follows. Legitimation problems of late capitalism emerge through disjunctions between the various sub-systems and the failure of the socio-cultural sphere to supply adequate motivation for the 'needs' of the economic sphere.

Habermas's model is strikingly similiar to that of Parsonian functionalism: the system functions externally to agents and a crisis develops not through the collective actions of social classes and groups over the allocation of scarce resources but through the impersonal logic of system imperatives. In the real world, the life-world, for example, remains the site of struggle and conflict over economic imperatives: the system only works through collective action, through agents orga- nised in the pursuit of goals (economic, political, cultural) which necessarily involve them in both life-world and system. Rather than clarifying the relation of action theory to systems theory, 'the question of how these two conceptual strategies . . . can be related to and integrated with one another', Habermas has reinforced the division between them (Mouzelis, 1991).

Emancipation and communicative action

At the heart of Habermas's critical theory is a contradiction between a deterministic systems theory and a voluntaristic action theory. The life-world constitutes the sphere of human action and autonomy through language and communication with the 'project of Enlightenment', dismissed by Adorno and Horkheimer, remaining a possibility. Individuals possess the capacity for self-reflection, understanding and knowledge. A theory of emancipation is built on a model of communication not production, with Habermas positing as an ideal state of undistorted communication the 'conversation of free citizens', action oriented towards 'truth'. The life-world is the sphere of free and equal discourse, of rational understanding and a 'normative consensus' that flows 'from the cooperative in- terpretation processes of participants themselves'. The ration- alisation of the life-world signals 'a release of the rationality potential inherent in communicative action' (Habermas, 1989, p. 146) and opens the way for genuine emancipation. But as the life-world is constantly under threat from the system imperatives governing production and profitability, linguistically-mediated interaction may become distorted with language no longer embodying the rational and universal elements of truth. If the life-world is colonised the result is the centralisation of culture, increasing passivity and decline of authority.

Habermas's avowed 'reconstruction' of historical materialism with its emphasis on 'ideal speech communities', a communicative rationality which offers the possibility of 'negotiated' consensus effectively separates the collective agent from social and cultural production, transforming social action into disembodied ahistorical categories: the concept of the modern life-world as a forum for undistorted communication is sociologically naive and historically untenable. As Bakhtin has shown (see pp. 300–3), during the Middle Ages the communication structure of popular culture was one of debunking established authority (no fusion of life-world and system), while in the nineteenth century, language formed an integral part of economic and cultural domination (no separation of life world and system).

11
Structuralism

Since the 1950s a new social theory has emerged which shares many of the holistic assumptions of functionalism and Marxism. Originating in the study of languages, structuralism has exerted an enormous influence in the social sciences especially in the work of Lévi-Strauss (anthropology), Roland Barthes, Julia Kristeva (semiotics and literary theory), Althusser, Poulantzas (Marxism and sociology) Godelier (economics), Foucault (philosophy and the history of science), and Lacan (psycho-analysis). Although these theorists disagree about the exact nature of structuralism there is, nevertheless, a broad consensus that a structuralist approach to the study of human society and culture involves the notion of wholes (a structure is not a simple aggregate of elements), the idea of transformation (structures are dynamic, not static, governed by laws which determine the ways that new elements are introduced into the structure and changed) and the concept of self-regulation (the meaning of a structure is self-contained in relation to its internal laws and rules). Where structuralism differs from functionalism and positivist Marxism is in its rejection of objective social facts and a concept of society as an objective, non-problematic external datum. Social facts have to be reconstituted in a theoretical discourse if they are to have any meaning at all. In short, structuralism defines reality in terms of the relations between elements, not in terms of things and social facts. Its basic principle is that the observable is meaningful only in so far as it can be related to an underlying structure or order.

The development of structuralism: Saussure

The founder of modern structuralism was Ferdinand de Saussure (1857–1913), a Swiss linguist who taught in Paris between 1881 and 1891 and whose most significant work, *Course in General Linguistics* (based on lectures given at the University of Geneva between 1906 and 1911), was published after his death. An expert in Indo-European languages, Saussure worked on a general theory of languages during the 1890s and he followed Durkheim in regarding language as an example of a social fact. Durkheim, of course, did not regard social facts as simple, naturalistic datums but rather as elements related to morality and collective representations.

The contemporary French linguist, Antoine Meillet, who studied with Saussure and Durkheim, noted the significance of Durkheim's sociology for Saussure's theory of language. And Saussure himself followed the debate between Durkheim and Tarde (which we discussed in Chapter 4) on the nature of sociological method. Saussure accepted Durkheim's methodological collectivism not Tarde's methodological individualism: thus he distinguished between language (*langue*) and speech (*parole*) in terms of the collectivist character of *langue* and the individualistic speech – utterances of *parole*. For Saussure, language constituted a collective representation, an abstract system of linguistic rules which governed concrete language use, a formal and coherent structure, the product 'of the collective mind and linguistic groups' (Saussure, 1974, p. 5). Saussure rejected nineteenth-century reductionist accounts of language arguing against historical, psychological and causal explanations. Language was not reducible to the psychology of speakers or the historical evolution of society. As a social fact, exercising constraint on individuals, language constituted a definite system, or structure, which existed independently of individual speakers whose utterances were merely an imperfect reflection of the whole. No one could retain the whole of a language system just as no one could know the legal system as a whole: language, like law, exists in everyday life within the consciousness of individuals constraining their actions, its concrete forms meaningful only in relation to its structure as a whole, as a collective representation.

Saussure drew an important distinction between the study of language conceived synchronically (its existence at a specific moment in terms of its functioning as a system) and diachronically (its development through time, that is, historically). 'The opposition between the two viewpoints', he argued, 'is absolute and allows no compromise.' Synchronic linguistics 'will be concerned with the logical and psychological relations that bind together co-existing terms and form a system in the collective mind of speakers' while diachronic linguistics studies 'relations that bind together successive terms not perceived by the collective mind but substituted for each other without forming a system' (Saussure, 1974, pp. 99–100). By psychology Saussure meant collective, not individual psychology although he remained uncertain of the exact nature of a psychology of language. His main focus was on synchronic linguistics the study of which he frequently compared with the game of chess. Chess is meaningful only in terms of its internal rules, its grammar, its network of relationships in which the value of a single piece depends on its relation with the whole; and to move a single piece is to alter the relation of the other elements to the whole. To understand chess, in other words, it is necessary to account for it as a system: 'The respective value of the pieces depends on their position on the chessboard just as each linguistic term derives its value from its opposition to all the other terms.' The synchronic facts of a language, like the synchronic facts of chess, are characterised by their systemic nature. To adopt a diachronic perspective is not to observe language as a system but rather as 'a series of events that modify it' (Saussure, 1974, pp. 88–91). The facts of diachronic, historical linguistics lack a systematic character and are thus of secondary importance in the study of language. Language is a system where all parts can, and must, be considered in their synchronic solidity.

The units that comprise a system of language acquire their meaning from their formal position, location and function within the whole. Saussure's central argument, therefore, was that language was produced socially as a collective phenomenon, independent of human will and intentions, a system irreducible to individual utterances. Speech and communication were thus made possible because of an underlying linguistic code, a system of collective norms which give meaning to specific verbal acts. Although Saussure did not employ the concept of structure, his theory of language is structural: to explain and understand an individual utterance it must be related to the 'hidden' system of functions, norms and categories. Thus Saussure abandoned causal explanation in favour of synchronic analysis of the position and function of elements within a system. The rules of language thus explain how language itself is simultaneously unknown and present, hidden from consciousness yet structuring human action.

The concept of structure

Saussure's *Course in General Linguistics* was not published until 1916. His concept of language as a self-contained system and advocacy of synchronic over diachronic analysis influenced the development of language studies, literary analysis and cultural theory.

In the development of structuralism two distinct trends are apparent. The first follows Saussure's separation of synchronic from diachronic analysis; while the other seeks a more historically grounded approach. An example of the former is Vladimir Propp's study of fairy tales (*The Morphology of the Fairy Tale*, 1928) which later influenced the structural anthropology of Claude Lévi-Strauss. In his research, Propp advocated the primacy of the synchronic over the genetic arguing that in the analysis of fairy tales it was possible to identify a limited number of functions (thirty-one) which could then be organised into an underlying system or structure. In this way fairy stories, which originated in widely differing cultures, could be classified since the multiplicity of characters is in direct contrast to the limited number of functions which the characters exercise in the course of the action.

In contrast to Propp's synchronic analysis, the Russian sociologist Mikhail Bakhtin (1895–1975) developed an historical structuralism which defined language as social communication. For Bakhtin language was not an abstract linguistic system, as Saussure had argued, but essentially historical acquiring its living forms 'in concrete verbal communication'.

Saussure's separation of utterance (*parole*) from language (*langue*) postulated the view of language as a product passively assimilated by individuals and not 'a function of the speaker'. Saussure's dualism was rejected. Indeed, orthodox linguistics was criticised for a failure to examine dialogic relations, the linguistic interaction of different speakers. Saussure's binary opposition of a 'pure' language and an 'impure', historically specific, utterance was overcome through defining the word as dialogic. This is one of Bakhtin's most significant contributions to structuralist thought. He wrote: 'Language is alive only in the dialogic intercourse of those who make use of it. Dialogic intercourse is the genuine sphere of the life of language [which] is permeated by dialogic relationships' (Bakhtin/Volosinov, 1973, pp. 102–3). Language as discourse is active and productive, involving social evaluations of the present, the past and the possibilities inherent in the future. Semantic and logical relations of language lack the dialogic aspect until they become utterances and embody the positions of various speakers. Thus discourse links individuals in a chain of communication: 'Utterances are not indifferent to one another, and are not self-sufficient; they are aware of and mutually reflect one another. Each utterance is filled with echoes and reverberations of other utterances to which it is related by the communality of the sphere of speech communication . . . Each utterance refutes, affirms, supplements, and relies on the others . . . and somehow takes them into account' (Bakhtin, 1986, p. 91).

In Bakhtin's theory of language the dialogic character of the utterance involves an active, unfinalised relation of self to other in which the self, through its practical acquisition of languages of speech genres (highly flexible, diverse everyday modes of social conversation, for example), becomes the sum of its discursive actions. All discourse implies simultaneous understanding between the speaker who listens and the listener who speaks:

Any true understanding is dialogic in nature.
Understanding is to utterance as one line of dialogue is to the next . . . meaning belongs to a word in its position between speakers . . . realised only in the process of active, responsive

understanding . . . Meaning is the effect of interaction between speaker and listener produced via the material of a particular sound complex (Bakhtin, 1973, pp. 102–3).

Bakhtin's theory of dialogism is built around the notion of alterity, that the autonomy and individuality of the social self springs out of its necessary relation with the 'other', seeking an identity through dialogue with others, but maintaining individual differences. The social production of self involves action and performance, individuality as the product of open-ended practices. In Bakhtin's word, the self is the 'gift' of the other constituted in and through discourse as socially productive practice.

Bakhtin applied these concepts to the study of the novel which he defined as a literary genre that sought to represent the multiplicity of the languages of a specific era and thus all the social and ideological 'voices' claiming to be significant. He was particularly concerned with analysing the relation between cultural forms and the broader structure of popular culture. In one of his most significant sociological studies, *Rabelais and His World* (1940) he argued that writers such as Boccaccio, Cervantes, Shakespeare and Rabelais developed their artistic techniques and vision historically from the depths of a folk culture which 'shaped during many centuries . . . had defended the people's creativity in non-official forms, in verbal expression or spectacle'. Bakhtin shows in rich detail the organic relation of the 'popular–festive images' associated with the 'unofficial culture' of popular festivals and carnivals with Rabelais's 'grotesque realist' literary form:

> Thanks to this process, popular–festive images became a powerful means of grasping reality; they served as a basis for an authentic and deep realism. Popular imagery did not reflect the naturalistic, fleeting, meaningless, and scattered aspect of reality but the very process of becoming, its meaning and direction (Bakhtin, 1968, p. 72).

Bakhtin's extraordinary detailed analysis of Rabelais's novel, *Gargantua and Pantagruel*, its verbal imagery and the relation of its different parts to the whole is structured around the key element of carnival. As an archaic element in the process of cultural continuity with its origins in pre-industrial folk-culture, carnival cannot be assimilated to the economic system or defined as a reflection or reproduction of an historically given reality: carnivalesque literature does not signify ideology but the universal elements within popular, democratic culture. Carnival is an inherent element in human culture although its forms vary historically: it constitutes an alternative reality to official culture with its panoply of ecclesiastical and political cults and ceremonies:

> A boundless world of humorous forms and manifestations opposed the official and serious tone . . . of feudal culture. In spite of their variety, folk festivities of the carnival type, the comic rites and cults, the clowns and fools, giants, dwarfs and jugglers, the vast and manifold literature of parody – all . . . belong to one culture of folk carnival humour (Bakhtin, 1968, p. 4).

Carnival functioned to liberate humanity from the established order; it was 'the suspension of all hierarchical rank, privilege, norms and prohibitions . . . hostile to all that was immortalised and completed'. The unofficial popular culture emphasised equality of human relationships and defined humanity in dynamic, not fixed, secular terms. Folk laughter is identified as the laughter of the whole community, simultaneously mocking, triumphant, derisory, assertive, denying, burying, reviving. As part of the carnival crowd the individual 'is aware of being a member of a continually growing and renewed people' in which folk laughter represents an element of victory 'over super-natural laws . . . the sacred . . . death', over everything which is oppressive and restrictive.

In Bakhtin's analysis popular culture forms a living and open structure which liberates the individual from dogmatism and fanaticism. Perhaps the most striking feature of Bakhtin's analysis is the emphasis he places on the ambivalence of laughter and its role in culture. Laughter, he argues, refuses to allow seriousness to atrophy but seeks to maintain its unfinal-ised and open form. Thus the unity which characterises the human community is not imposed from above but flows organically from the depths of a popular and democratic culture. The development of capitalism, the growth of bureaucracy and the trend to rationalisation in culture tend to separate popular culture from the human community, although the implication of Bakhtin's work – the wider study of culture and languages – suggests the persistence of an open-ended, polyphonic culture within modern societies.

Bakhtin's theory of the dialogic, unfinalised nature of the human community and the complex ways in which this structure informs the work of specific writers represents one of the most important contributions to the development of a diachronically grounded structuralism.

The genetic structuralism of Lucien Goldmann (1913–70) follows Bakhtin's broad, humanist perspective. Goldmann was largely influenced by the early writings of Lukács, especially *History and Class Consciousness*, from which he derived the concepts of world vision, totality, consciousness, and the Swiss psychologist, Jean Piaget from whose work he adapted the notions of significant structure, function and structuration/destructuration. Basic to Goldmann's sociology was a conception of structure created and transformed by human activity. Structures were *made* through the *praxis* of the human subject. But the subject is not an individual but a collective category, a social group which constitutes the true source of cultural creation. This *collective subject* is, like cultural creation, a significant structure. All major cultural forms embody a significant structure, a world view which expresses the 'collective consciousness' of a significant social group. The world view unites the various elements and levels of a cultural form into unity and coherence. Thus Goldmann's sociology of literature begins by analysing the immanent structure of an art-work – the work as a whole – and then relates it to a social group. Since the art-work expresses the tendencies, actions and values of the collective subject it bears a functional relation with it. Thus to understand the totality of a literary work it is necessary to explain its historical genesis in the social life of the group. The cultural objects are analysed both synchronically (the work as a whole) and diachronically (the products of human action). Structures are meaningful only in relation to human action and communication. Purely diachronic study, Goldmann argues, 'which forgoes systems and structures, is scientifically impossible and inadequate', for reality is constantly undergoing a process of structuration and destructuration:

> History is the object of structuring processes and these cannot be studied if one has not first established models. Inversely, however, structures are only provisional, the result of men's behaviour in precise and concrete situations which they themselves transform within given structures. In this way they create new structures (Goldmann, 1980, p. 50).

Goldmann's emphasis on the creative, human dimension of structure distinguishes his approach from that of his contemporary, Roland Barthes (1915–80). Goldmann's genetic structuralism owed little to linguistic theory: defining structuralism in 1967, Barthes stressed its origin in the methods of linguistics and semiotics.

He defined semiology as the scientific study of human actions and objects in relation to an underlying system of rules and differences that enable a signifying process to take place. Culture consists of signifying phenomena and Barthes describes two such signifying systems, fashion and food. In his *Système de la mode* (1967) Barthes described fashion as a system which has the effect of naturalising the conventions on which the system itself rests. Underlying the *parole* of fashion and food is a distinctive code, or *langue*, defining which garment suits a particular event and the items of food that together constitute a 'course'. The cultural code is the system of distinctions and conventions which generate meaning for the members of different social groups.

One of Barthes early works in semiotic analysis was his study of mass culture, *Mythologies* (1957), in which he discussed the signifying systems of striptease, cars, margarine, detergents and toys. Describing these products of mass culture as 'collective representations', sign-systems, Barthes suggested that their function was to 'mystify' the true nature of modern capitalist society. On one level of signification soup was simply soup and French wine merely good wine; but as signs they communicate secondary meanings so that wine is not one drink among others but a sign of the superior French way of life, the drinking itself constituting a ritual, collective act producing a sense of social solidarity. Similarly, Barthes analysed the cover of the magazine *Paris-Match* in which a black soldier, in French uniform salutes the French flag: the first level of signification is a French soldier saluting the national flag, but the second level of meaning is the French Empire, lacking racial discrimination with its virtues exemplified by the zeal of the black soldier serving his alleged colonial oppressors: 'I am therefore . . . faced with a greater semiological system: there is a signifier, itself already formed with a previous system (*a black soldier is giving the French salute*); there is a signified (it is here a purposeful mixture of Frenchness and militariness); finally, there is a presence of the signified through the signifier' (Barthes, 1973, p. 116). It is at the second level of signification that the object or event becomes myth seeking to present its conventions (in photography, food, fashion, for example) as natural datums. As such, fashion signifies the cultural importance of the insignificant, the slight differences in dress; but as a signifying system fashion communicates secondary and ideological meanings.

For Barthes, bourgeois culture is built around these mythical, ideological meanings, generating norms which appear as facts of nature:

> The whole of France is steeped in this anonymous ideology: our press . . . films . . . theatre . . . the garments we wear, everything in everyday life, is dependent on the representation which the bourgeoisie *has and makes us have* of the relations between man and the world. These 'normalised' forms attract little attention, by the very fact of their extension, in which their origin is easily lost . . . bourgeois norms are experienced as the evident laws of a natural order (Barthes, 1973, p. 140).

As a means of communication myth is thus a language, which generates its own meanings. Meaning is enclosed and finalised within the code and stripped of its relation with the discursive practices of subjects. Barthes's semiotics, anti-historical, anti-genetic and anti-humanist, constitutes the triumph of the system over the subject.

Marxism and structuralism

During the course of the 1960s a distinctive form of Marxist structuralism, resolutely anti-humanist, developed in France. Its leading theoretician was the Communist Party philosopher, Louis Althusser. In a series of essays and analyses Althusser proposed a radically new, scientific 'reading' of Marx. Influenced by structural linguistics and the scientific rationalism of Gaston Bachelard, Althusser criticised all forms of positivist/ empiricist Marxism as well as the idealist, humanist-centred approach of Lukács, the Frankfurt School and those contemporary Marxists, such as Sartre, for whom Marxism was the philosophy of *praxis*.

For Althusser, Marxism was the science of social formations, the study of the inner logic, the relations between its various levels, or structures. The specific nature of a social formation – capitalism, socialism, etc. – is analysed from the standpoint of a complex totality consisting of economic, political–legal and ideological 'practices', the 'labour of transformation' which 'sets to work . . . men, means and technical method'. Althusser rejected the base-superstructure model of orthodox Marxism because it suggested an essentialist notion of society, that the social totality *expresses* a single dominant element, the labour–capital relation or the alienation of humanity. This 'expressive totality' is ultimately Hegelian since it conveys the notion of unity produced through a single essence. Althusser's concept of totality, in contrast, emphasises the multiplicity of economic, political and ideological structures, their relative autonomy and, employing a concept derived from Freud, *overdetermination*. Thus the most basic contradiction, the capital–labour contradiction, 'is never simple, but always specified by the historically concrete forms and circumstances in which it is exercised . . . specified by forms of the superstructure (the State, dominant ideology, religion . . .); specified by the internal and external historical situation'. Contradictions are not pure but are overdetermined, that is, determined and determining 'in one and the same movement'. There is no single contradiction which dominates, but many possible contradictions influencing each other. Hegelian philosophy and humanist Marxism tended to assimilate the complex diversity of 'a historically given society' to a single substance, or element, which functioned to determine all other elements of as well as the social whole itself (Althusser, 1969, pp. 106–13).

The concept of structure thus refers to the ways in which relatively autonomous levels combine into the 'structural complexity' of a social formation. Causality is structural not linear. Althusser illustrates this process by analysing the 1917 Russian Revolution. No single contradiction determined the development of the revolution but multiple contradictions such as those characterising 'a regime of feudal exploitation at the dawn of the twentieth century': contradictions between the advanced methods of capitalist production in the cities and the medieval condition of the countryside; contradictions between bourgeoisie and proletariat, the liberal bourgeoisie and the feudal landowners; contradictions between the Tsarist political system and nascent political democracy (Althusser, 1969, p. 96). There is thus uneven development between the various levels of a social formation; the structure and its effects determine each other with totality defined in terms of its effects. Social formations are asymmetrical in their structure. But what of the relation between the economy and the superstructure? Is the economic merely one structure among many or is it, as Marx, Engels and other Marxists have held, dominant? Althusser suggests that although the social formation comprises relatively autonomous levels, 'in the last instance' the economic determines which is dominant. This notion of a 'structure in dominance' allows Althusser to maintain the traditional Marxist emphasis on the primacy of the economic while at the same time advancing a pluralist conception of the social formation.

One result of Althusser's work has been an increasing emphasis in Marxist theory on the concept of mode of production and its relation with the superstructure, and the theory of ideology. For Althusser, the mode of production constitutes a number of different structures including the economic. It is the way in which these structures are combined which differentiates one mode of production from another. For example, the capitalist mode of production consists of a specific economic structure (the labourer, means of production, etc.) and a rational, legal system which forms part of the super-

307

structure. The economic structure determines the specificity of the various laws which relate to property and contract. A different combination of economy and law subsists within a socialist mode of production, the socialised economic relations determining a different set of legal principles and rights. Nevertheless, the legal system, as a structure of ideology, is relatively autonomous constituting a distinct level of the social formation. But as E. P. Thompson, in his extended critique of Althusser, has pointed out, such a formal, synchronic approach fails to grasp that law, as an historical phenomenon, was not part of a separate level but always 'imbricated within the mode of production and productive relations themselves . . . [intruding] . . . with religion . . . an arm of politics . . . [and] it was an academic discipline, subjected to the rigour of its own autonomous logic' (Thompson, 1978, p. 288). Because Althusser's structuralism has separated the human subject and human action from the structures themselves, one consequence is the reification of the social formation and its levels, the dominance of the system over the individual, and a tendency for the system itself to remain closed, emptied of all dialogic communicative relations. Structures, after all, do not make laws or change them.

The rigidity of Althusser's Marxism is particularly brought out in his analysis of ideology. The traditional Marxist definition of ideology as a 'false consciousness' (adumbrated in Marx's early work, especially *The German Ideology*), a distorted picture of the external world, illusory and unreal, is rejected by Althusser for its non-scientific humanism. Such a theory of ideology is centred on the notion of a 'constituting subject' and the assumption that knowledge, formed and reflected in human consciousness, develops only through the experiences of this subject. The true source of ideology is neither experience nor the subject, but objective, material reality; as an objective structure ideology cannot be reduced to the actions and consciousness of the subject. Ideology is thus defined as 'a system of representations', 'images and concepts' which 'impose' themselves as structures on social classes and individuals. Making a distinction between 'real objects' and 'objects of knowledge', Althusser located ideology as a real object forming an 'instance' of the social totality, a partly autonomous structure irreducible to the economic or political levels. Ideology is thus a system through which the individual exists as a social being, a 'lived' relation between the individual and the world, a relation which

> ... only appears as *'conscious'* on condition that it is *unconscious* .... not a simple relation but a relation between relations, a second degree relation. In ideology men do indeed express, not the relation between them and their conditions of existence, but *the way* they live the relation between them and their conditions of existence: this presupposes both a real relation and 'an imaginary, lived' relation (Althusser, 1969, p. 233).

Representing the 'imaginary' relations of individuals to the 'real' conditions of their existence, ideology forms an essential element of all social formations (including Socialism and Communism) since social cohesion is only possible through the 'practico-social' functions of ideology. Althusser here distinguishes science from ideology: science is 'theoretical knowledge', a system of concepts, a discourse which produces the objects of knowledge and which leads ultimately to the framing of scientific generalities. There is thus an important difference between theoretical knowledge and knowledge of the external world: the former does not depend on external proofs for its validity since it is purely theoretical; the latter is involved with ideology and thus the practico-social function dominates the theoretical function.

Ideology is produced, therefore, not by the intentions of subjects but by institutions, specific apparatuses which, in modern capitalism, are increasingly state organs. Ideology is anchored within institutions which themselves are the products of ideology. In his essay, 'Ideology and Ideological State Apparatuses' (1971), Althusser, responding to criticisms that his Marxist theory of ideology underemphasised the role of class struggle, argued that ideology constituted the 'site' of class conflict. Distinguishing between the Ideological State Apparatus (consisting of religious, educational, cultural institutions as well as political parties) and the Repressive State Apparatus (consisting of the institutions of coercion such as the army, police, judiciary) Althusser argued that the Ideological

State Apparatuses 'largely secure the reproduction specifically of the relations of production, behind a "shield" provided by the repressive State apparatus'. In pre-capitalist societies the Church functioned as the dominant ideological apparatus. In modern capitalism the educational institutions have become the dominant ideological apparatus:

> It takes children from every class at infant school age, and then for years, the years in which the child is most vulnerable; squeezed between the family State apparatus and the educational State apparatus, it drums into them, whether it uses new or old methods, a certain amount of 'know-how' wrapped in the ruling ideology (French, arithmetic, natural history, the sciences, literature) or simply the ruling ideology in its pure state (ethics, civic instruction, philosophy) (Althusser, 1971).

For Althusser, the ideological state apparatuses perpetuate submission to the established order reproducing the relations of production. But the model of society which Althusser proposes in this formulation comes close to a totalitarian system in which a process of complete ideological indoctrination into a dominant ideology is secured both by the passivity of an atomised population and the absence of alternative structures. Althusser's structuralist concept of ideology is historically and sociologically inadequate: the 'private' institutions which form part of the ideological state apparatus are centred in civil society and cannot be assimilated to state practices in the way that Althusser suggests. In capitalist society education is governed both by ideological assumptions and practices as well as by its own specific laws and values, that is, education is both dependent on the mode of production and class structure, and yet partly autonomous in terms of its immanent properties.

Althusser's emphasis on education as indispensable for the organisation and discipline of capitalist societies, together with his principle of structural causality, suggest a functionalist rather than a dialectical Marxist explanation. Although functionalist analysis has been defended as legitimate for Marxist theory (Cohen, 1978, pp. 283–5), it tends to assimilate the complex interaction between active, knowledgeable agents and the social structure to an underlying, ahistorical and deterministic process. Althusser's structuralism, like functionalism, eliminates the dialogic, humanist tradition of sociological thought: men and women become mere supports of structures. In his account of the Russian Revolution, for example, Althusser fails to include as a critical factor in its genesis the contradictions within the Russian socialist movement itself: contradictions within *theory* between those advocating an evolutionary road through a bourgeois republic (Plekhanov) and those who favoured a direct transformation to socialism skipping the bourgeois phase (Lenin, Trotsky). In the resolution of these theoretical differences both individual and collective agent played a crucial role to become a 'voluntarist' factor in the development of the revolution; similarly with the concept of Workers' Council or Soviet, a decentralising, plebeian form of democracy which arose out of working-class activity and culture, intellectually independent of its theoretical formulation in Marxist discourse. Both the concept and the institution can be grasped sociologically only by positing a collective agent within an historical framework which includes choices and possibilities.

The problem of agency and structure: structuration theory

The promise of structuralism lay in its proposals for a more rigorous method in the social sciences, one purged of humanism, essentialism, historicism. Its advocates made much of its anti-bourgeois, anti-individualistic stance. Meaning did not inhere in the actions of a creative subject but in a process which 'de-centred the subject'. But in focusing on structural transformations in discourse, language and history, structuralist analysis turned into the study of concepts which effectively became the object of research itself. Society and history became elusive and shadowy concepts. With the exceptions of Goldmann and Bakhtin structuralism failed to address the complex, historical nature of social structures, their contradictions, conflicts and transformation through the actions of collective agents. The de-centring of the subject eliminates the problem of choice, the possibility of alternative action, of

311

voluntarism, and the voluntaristic dimension of social structures and historical processes.

Anthony Giddens's work represents one attempt, from within sociology, to go beyond the sterility of much structuralist theory. Although acknowledging the importance of decentring the subject, Giddens seeks to restore the primacy of the agent, for while actors do not create social systems 'they reproduce or transform them, remaking what is already made in the continuity of *praxis*' (Giddens, 1984, p. 171). Actors are both 'knowledgeable' and 'skilful' although never fully aware of their action which is always bounded by historical contexts and situations not of their own choosing: routines, constraints, power.

Giddens defines structure as 'rules and resources' or 'sets of transformational relations' organised as properties of social systems. By system is meant the 'organisation and reproduction of social practices and relations' in which the structural properties are simultaneously 'medium' and 'outcome' of 'recursively organised practices'. This 'duality of structure' means that structure is not external to individuals but instantiated in practices that are grounded in practical, not discursive consciousness, in routines and encounters which 'happen' through the 'relexive monitoring of action' (Giddens, 1984).

Although these formulations seem to offer a dynamic alternative to structuralism and functionalism, structuration theory tends to a dubious subjectivity: the agent, through whose practices structures are transformed, remains vague and insubstantial, while structure is dissolved into action. This Weberian standpoint collapses society as a determinate external structure into agents' practices. But agents encounter society and its institutions as external elements seeking to understand, work with and possibly transform them. There is, in Giddens's analysis, a blandness, a lack of cutting edge, a failure to theorise the historically specific forms of action, collective and individual, in relation both to the latent openness and possibilities within social situations and to the prevailing modes of externality embodied in the coercive properties of institutions.

12
Modernity, Industrialisation and Sociological Theory

In this book I have argued that sociology originated in eighteenth-century philosophy, political economy and cultural history. Eighteenth-century social theory embraced both a voluntaristic pole – Vico for example – as well as a deterministic, systemic perspective – Montesquieu. The tension between these two approaches to the study of human society dominated the subsequent development of sociological positivism and Marxism. It needs emphasising that although Vico, Montesquieu, Ferguson and Millar laid the foundations for sociological theory their work was not sociology: the complex sociohistorical relation between action and structure remained untheorised. Ferguson's concept of the unintended consequences of human action was never integrated with the notion of society as a system: it was Hegelian philosophy which transposed Ferguson's voluntaristic element into an organic part of totality. Later Marx developed these negative and contradictory notions into the dichotomy of the capitalist system, structured in objective laws of change, and class agency, structured in collective consciousness and political organisation. Marx's contemporaries, Comte and Spencer, equally conceived society as an organic whole, its structure determined by specific laws of evolution, but the action element was ultimately subordinated to the system and the whole.

Comte, Marx and Spencer grasped the concept of society as a dynamic system evolving historically and inevitably towards

313

complex industrial structures. Although these writers differed sharply in their analysis of modern capitalist society they shared one common theme: that industrial society constituted a new form of social organisation built around the separation of state and civil society. Industrialism expanded the institutions of industrial society and thus produced the institutional framework that enabled individuals, as members of different social collectivities (associated with education, communications, political organisation, trade unions, etc.), to change society. Nevertheless, the early sociologists were deeply sceptical of bourgeois society: but it was classical sociology, with its themes of alienation, urbanism, anomie, rationalisation, bureaucratisation, reification, mechanisation which advanced a pessimistic theory of bourgeois culture. Durkheim, Tönnies, Weber and Simmel were as concerned with the collapse and disintegration of old, traditional social orders as they were with the rise of a fluid, dynamic industrial and egalitarian democratic society. Industrialisation seemed to lead to a culture hostile to human values. These tensions are nowhere more evident than in Weber's sociology which succeeds in analysing social change both in terms of objective structure and subjective human action, yet concludes pessimistically that the fate of humanity is necessarily one of increasing bureaucratisation and the domination, from above, of specialised élites.

Marxism, industrialism and modernity

The history of sociology and the history of Marxism are directly linked to these developments. At the turn of the century, European sociology engaged in a debate with Marxism which raised precisely the problems of democratic structures within the framework of advancing industrialism. The pessimism of classical sociology largely flowed from its failure to grasp the enormous democratic energies which capitalism in its historical development had, and would continue, to release. One might say that classical sociology lacked a dialectical sense of historical change. The structural complexity of the social formation was frequently assimilated to an abstractly conceived universal process, or universal history – the rationalisation of culture, total reification, functional consensus, mass society and mass culture.

As with sociology so with Marxism. In some of his writings Marx had emphasised the crucially significant and creative role played by the active human subject (*praxis*) in the formation of an open, decentralised, socialist society. Yet the basic trend of Marxist thought was away from such libertarian conceptions towards a deterministic, economic theory of historical change in which human action is meaningful only in ⁗ terms of the emergent social order lying within the womb of the old society: thus social institutions, social change, culture, could all be assimilated to the dominant underlying economic system. Human agents were effectively transformed into passive ⋇ objects. The inherent collectivism of Marxism, both its conceptual framework and political ideology, led to the evolutionary, undemocratic, élitist collectivism of German Social Democracy (so perceptively analysed by Michels), the centralised party of Leninist theory and the totalitarian ideology of Stalinism. The core of Marxist theory lay in its ideology of finalisation (history has a definite, single meaning) and collectivist political prescriptions (the rising class must organise society as a whole from the centre in terms of its specific interests). But the problem is that Marxist political and social finalisation contradicts the historical logic of capitalist industrialism. Modern industrial societies, far from being structured around a single dominant centre – contradiction or class force – increasingly developed open-ended, decentred social structures. Politically, Marxism leads to the annihilation of civil society as a living and active force built around democratic institutions. In general, the main trends of twentieth-century Marxism, the 'humanist' ✳ form that stems from a concern with alienation and dehumanisation of the subject, the so-called 'scientific' form associated with structuralism, have both denigrated the capacity of the human subject to democratise, humanise and understand the necessity for collectivist, democratic change *from below*. Implicit in both forms is a conception of Marxism as finalised ideology of both subject and structure.

Yet there is a crucial difference between Marxist finalisation and the pessimism of classical sociology. Tönnies, Weber and

Simmel described modern industrial society in negative terms but they also grasped the possibilities latent within industrial development. Classical sociology, unlike Marxism, stressed the complex ambiguity of modern society, its open structures – mobility, class relationships, democratisation, increasing dialogic modes of communication – as well as its tendency towards closure – rationalisation of culture, reification, lack of community. Both were present simultaneously.

The development of sociology is further bound up with modernity, a concept first theorised by Simmel and Weber. As with Enlightenment philosophy, classical sociology assumed that industrialisation and science generated the possibility of a more rational, humane and democratic society. In Weber's work modernity is grounded sociologically in the structural differentiation of society and culture – the value spheres – which lead to the autonomy of institutions and action. Weber's concept of subjectively mediated interaction further suggests an increasing role for the agent. Modernity thus implied voluntarism, choice and increasing purposiveness (Giddens, 1987, p. 223).

But under the influence of Nietzsche's philosophy, the early theorists of modernity rejected both totalising history and the autonomy of reason. For Nietzsche, modern society was structured in the pluralism of values, in relativism and fragmentation, a pessimism reflected in Weber's 'iron cage' of rationalisation and in the pathologies of modernity which classical sociology had identified – anomie, disenchantment, reification, mass society. In the development of modern sociological thought this dialectical notion of modernity tends to disappear, notably in structural functionalism, or become marginalised in the pessimistic sociology associated with one dimensional theories of mass culture. (Mills, 1956) New sociological theories of industrial society and culture have further challenged the pessimistic notion of modernity, notably the theory of post-industrialism.

The theory of post-industrial society

During the 1950s a number of eminent sociologists, such as Daniel Bell, S. M. Lipset, Raymond Aron and Ralf Dahren-

316

dorf, argued against what they saw as the static, ahistorical bias of Functionalism and the worn-out ideological historicism of Marxism by advancing a concept of post-industrialism (although the term varied from one sociologist to another – 'post-capitalist', 'post-bourgeois society', the 'technological society', the 'knowledge society' – in essentials it suggested the priority of technology, science and culture over private property and class divisions). Post-industrial society was contrasted with nineteenth-century capitalist society and twentieth-century industrial society in terms of the transformation of social structure: post-industrial society constituted a social formation in which private property, class interests and class conflict had lost their centrality as 'axial principles'. The social structure of capitalist and industrial society was largely organised around the axis of private property; post-industrial society is organised around the axis of 'theoretical knowledge'. In *The Coming of Post-Industrial Society* (1973) Bell argues that the 'energising principle' of modern societies will increasingly be centred within the educational, scientific and governmental institutions. The traditional business firm and the entrepreneur are in the process of being replaced by scientists, economists and engineers. The source of innovation and policy-making is no longer the business enterprise but the university.

Bell's general thesis rests on his argument that modern society is organised into three separate although related realms: the economy, the polity and the culture. The polity regulates the distribution of power and the different interests in society; the culture, as the realm of self-realisation, establishes meaning through the expressiveness of art and ritual: the economic realm relates to the social structure. Each is ruled by different axial principles: self-realisation in culture, equality in politics, efficiency in economics. Thus society as a whole is not organised around one dominant element or integrated into a single system. There is always a disjunction between the different realms so that culture, for example, may repudiate the axial principle of economic efficiency and rationality in favour of irrational, hedonistic modernism with its rejection of tradition and established institutions. Similarly, the axial problem of the polity 'is the relation between the desire for popular participation and bureaucracy' (Bell, 1976, p. 115). Each of these spheres has its own inner logic and contradictory nature. Prediction and forecasting generally in the cultural and political realms is thus hazardous and Bell's main emphasis is on the economic sphere. Thus:

> The concept of a post-industrial society is not a picture of a complete social order; it is an attempt to describe and explain an axial change in the social structure (defined as the economy, the technology and the stratification system) of the society. But such a change implies no specific determinism between a 'base' and a 'superstructure' . . . it is likely that the various societies that are entering a post-industrial phase will have different political and cultural configurations (Bell, 1976, p. 119).

As with other post-capitalist theses, Bell's concept of post-industrial society assumes the decline of manual labour and the rapid growth of white collar work, service industries, professional groups and greater expenditure on higher education, research and development. As society is transformed from one largely dominated by the production of goods to one dominated by the production of theoretical knowledge a new social structure will emerge. In modern societies, theory dominates empiricism in the areas of science, economics and computer studies. The scientist, the mathematicians, the computer-technologist and the economic theorist rise to prominence to form what Bell calls a distinct 'knowledge class'. At the heart of post-industrial society is a professional class embodying norms of social responsiveness derived from an ethics of service to the community. The profit motive has no place within the burgeoning research institutes and universities. This professional–scientific class will eventually saturate society with its professional values: Bell distinguishes his position from earlier writers such as Saint-Simon by defining the new class as those who apply their knowledge to the organisation of society as a whole. It is not a question of technocrats exercising power, but rather the production of new values and principles of organisation.

Bell's work describes many of the basic changes which are occurring within modern industrial societies, although he exaggerates the significance of the autonomy of theoretical knowledge. In many modern industrial societies, for example, the proportion of Gross National Product devoted to pure science is significantly smaller than that channelled into practical research and research in already established areas. Research and development is not yet dominated by theoretical knowledge. More pertinently, the argument that the new science-based professions generate their own immanent values (universal rather than particular, opposed to profit and for the community) is difficult to sustain in view of the frequent involvement of academic intellectuals in government defence projects and foreign policy objectives. The post-industrial thesis assumes, further, that market forces will eventually disappear as the axis of organisation and change: yet one of the most significant contributions to the development of pure economic theory in the last twenty years, monetarism, has focused both on the centrality of market forces in the formation of a democratic system and the irrelevance of government and centralised authority and bureaucracy to involve itself in economic management.

Many critics of the post-industrial thesis have emphasised the persistence of class inequalities, class conflict, the concentration of economic resources in a few hands, the unskilled nature of white collar work and the tendency towards the professionalisation of all occupations, thus diluting the norm of professionalism itself. But the most important aspect of Bell's theory is its advocacy, as historically inevitable, of a planned, centralised, rationalised and bureaucratised social system. The post-industrial theory thus maintains a continuity with classical sociology. But the logic of industrialism was not, as Bell and others have argued, to separate the economic from the political and cultural spheres and thus enable authority to be centralised and autonomous within the polity: the logic of industrialism was both to centralise society and produce the possibilities of democratic decentralisation. It is this dialectic which Bell assimilates to an élitist and finalised notion of post-industrialism. In Bell's theory the human agent plays no role in the shaping of the culture, the polity or the economy. The planners and the technocrats, basing their policy decisions on theoretical knowledge and a professional ethos, effectively neutralise popular democratic forms and active political institutions. A bureaucratic, administrative relation subsists between rulers and ruled: the logic of post-industrial society is thus to eliminate dialogic modes of communication and the ambiguity of human discourse and action.

Modernity and post-modernity

Since the collapse of sociological functionalism as the major paradigm of Western sociology only Marxism, in its various forms, and the mass society thesis have attempted to develop a total theory of industrial society. The theory of post-industrial society constitutes the single exception but it has yet to be developed as a general sociological theory comparable with Parsonian functionalism or Marxism. As I have suggested, Habermas's work advances a totalising conception of social science and is, in many ways, a return to 'grand theory'. Like Parsons, Habermas seeks to assimilate the systemic, holistic approach (drawing on Marxism and Parsonian systems theory) and a dynamic, voluntaristic theory of communicative human action (drawing on the work of Mead, Freud, Piaget and Goldmann). Thus like Parsons in the 1930s, Habermas is arguing for a convergence of sociological theory. But unlike Parsons, Habermas emphasises the 'emancipatory' role of social theory rejecting the scientistic objectivism and acceptance of the status quo characteristic of sociological functionalism and nineteenth-century grand theory. Stressing his continuity with the ideas of the Frankfurt School, Habermas attempts to synthesise systemic structural analysis with *praxis*.

Thus for Habermas modern sociological theory represents the renewal of the unfulfilled potential of 'the Enlightenment project'. The 'signature' of modernity lies in purposive activity and 'a concept of a communicative reason ingrained in the use of language oriented to reaching understanding . . .' Habermas's concept of modernity is based on the 'uncoupling' of a progressively rationalised life-world from the system domains of the economy and the state administration. The tension between life-world and system is both an index of potential crisis and emancipation (Habermas, 1989, pp. 303–6). But as was argued in Chapter 10, Habermas's concept of system is as closed as that proposed by Parsonian functionalism, action being subordinated to the dehumanising logic of system imperatives. Communicative rationality fails to deal adequately with real historical agents, with open, unfinalised modes of dialogic interaction.

Habermas's theory of modernity stresses its sociological character: post-modernity he rejects for its reactionary philosophical basis in subjectivism, relativism and unreason. The concept of post-modernity is linked historically with the post-industrial thesis with its emphasis on the decline of industrial production, class structure and interests, rise of consumerism, technological modes of communication and differentiated status structure. Whereas modernity separated the cultural from the social sphere and led to a fundamental division between mass culture and critical, 'high' culture, post-modernity unifies popular/mass 'commodity' culture with the forms of modernist aesthetics. The subversive, critical principle at work within modernity is assimilated to a bland, pluralist culture which has neither centre nor structure.

As the object of study for sociology, society is both structure and action: and if sociology is emancipatory it is so because it has adequately theorised a real historical development as society develops from pre-industrial, highly centralised systems to decentred, complex industrial systems, characterised by the growth of autonomous institutions that enable social groups and communities to define and articulate their specific interests in relation to others and enlarge society as a whole.

Sociology is both a humanism and a science conceiving society as an objective structure created through human action. It can never entirely escape the influence of the socio-historical context. But this should not imply subjectivism. Because it deals with the results of social action which, although structured, can never be predicted-accurately, sociological theory must remain provisional in its attempts to explain and comprehend the structure and development of human society. But its future as a human science lies with the fate of industrial society, whether Western societies become more centralised and civil society weaker, whether Soviet societies collapse and a revitalised civil society emerges. These are the issues of modernity which post-modernity ignores. The history of sociology is a history of the struggle of democracy and industrialism to assimilate the dialogic openness implicit in the notions of active subject and human structure.

Further Reading

1 Origins of Sociology

One of the most thorough works on the history of sociology (Szacki, 1979) traces the development of sociological thought from its intellectual origins in the philosophy of Plato and Aristotle, Renaissance thought and Vico, to modern social theorists such as Mead, Mannheim, Parsons. Mauss (1962), Nisbet (1967), Fletcher (1972, 1973), Hawthorn (1976) offer general histories and idiosyncratic interpretations, while Aron (1965, 1968) examines the major sociological figures from Montesquieu to Weber. Coser (1971) is especially valuable for relating sociological theory to social context and biography.

Shils (1980) offers a wide-ranging interpretation of the main traditions in sociology while a valuable collection of essays on the history of sociology is Bottomore and Nisbet (1979).

The most comprehensive study of Enlightenment philosophy and its relation with social thought and early sociologists such as Montesquieu and Ferguson is Gay (1967, 1970).

Vico's major work has been translated into English (Vico, 1948). A good discussion is Berlin (1976) while Cahnman (1981) examines the relation between Vico, Hobbes and Tönnies.

Montesquieu (1949) includes a penetrating introduction by F. Neumann.

A general overview of the Scottish Enlightenment is Chitnis (1977) while Swingewood (1970) and Therborn (1976) analyse the specifically sociological aspects. Ferguson's *Essay* has been republished (1966) while Millar's *Origin and Distinction of Ranks* is included in Lehmann (1960). For good discussion of Ferguson's contribution to sociology see Kettler (1965), MacRae (1969) while a useful collection of writings, including Ferguson, Kames, Robertson, Millar, is Schneider (1967).

2 Industrialisation and the Rise of Sociological Positivism

Useful histories of positivism include Simon (1963), Giddens (1977, Ch. 1), Halfpenny (1982). The relation of the French Revolution to the development of sociology is discussed by Nisbet (1967) and Gouldner (1971). A critique of Nisbet's thesis identifying sociology with conservative thought is advanced by Giddens (1977, Ch. 6).

Saint-Simon's writings relating to social theory have been translated in two collections (Ionescu, 1976; Taylor, 1975). Saint-Simon's importance to both nineteenth-century sociology and socialism is examined by Durkheim (1958) and his relation with the Enlightenment by Manuel (1962). Hayek (1955) has interpreted the works of Saint-Simon and Comte as laying the foundations for modern totalitarianism and methodological collectivism, while Bell (1976) explores the sources of the concept of industrial society in relation to Saint-Simon.

Comte's work was translated into English during the nineteenth century (Comte, 1896, 1877). His early essays have been recently republished (Fletcher, 1974). Two useful selections of Comte's sociological and philosophical writings are Andreski (1978) and Thompson (1976). Fletcher (1972) advances a sympathetic view while Marcuse (1954) develops a critical Marxist perspective of Comte's sociology. J. S. Mill's study is still worth reading (Mill, 1961). A short, lucid account of Comte's relation with nineteenth-century statistics and social surveys is Halfpenny (1982).

For J. S. Mill see Fletcher (1972), Feuer (1976). Mill's *System of Logic* is widely available: a good, recent edition is edited by Fletcher (Mill, 1976).

The most succinct introduction to Spencer's voluminous works is the popular *Study of Sociology* (Spencer, 1965). Spencer's opposition to collectivism, his advocacy of the organismic analogy in social science is best approached through the essays (Spencer, 1969a). Selections from Spencer's works include Carneiro (1967), Andreski (1971), Peel (1972). The most thorough discussion of Spencer's work which places it within the context of English nonconformity is Peel (1971). The wider debate on evolutionism is examined by Burrow (1966) and critically evaluated by Hirst (1976).

3 Marxism: A Positive Science of Capital Development

Marx and Engels's collected works are currently being published (Marx–Engels, 1975) but there is a useful two-volume edition which includes many of their most important writings including *The Communist Manifesto*, *The Civil War in France*, *The Eighteenth Brumaire of Louis Bonaparte* (Marx and Engels, 1962). The Penguin editions of *Capital* (Marx, 1976–80), *Grundrisse* (Marx, 1973) and the political writings (Marx, 1974–6) are highly recommended.

Selections from Marx's and Engels's writings include Bottomore (1964a) for the early works, Bottomore and Rubel (1961), McLellan (1980a).

The most exhaustive and stimulating study of Marxism is Kolakowski (1981) while a more sympathetic series of essays is McLellan (1983). One of the best defences of the Hegelian, humanist Marx is Avineri (1968). Cohen (1978) rejects the humanist core of Marxism arguing that concepts such as mode of production, rather than alienation, are more central to Marx's scientific project. He emphasises the role of technology in social development minimising the role of ideas and the subject. Other anti-humanist interpretations include Althusser (1969, 1971), Hindess and Hirst (1975). These works should be read in conjunction with Rosdolsky (1977) which contains a thorough analysis of the *Grundrisse* and its relation with the early and later works.

For Marx's relation with sociology see Gouldner (1980), Bottomore and Nisbet (1979), Therborn (1976) and Worsley (1982). Still worth reading is Schumpeter (1961).

4 Critique of Positivism: I Durkheim

The general social and intellectual background to the development of Durkheim's sociology is examined by Lukes (1973) and Clark (1973). Wolff (1964) includes a number of essays dealing with the social and political context that shaped Durkheim's sociology.

Durkheim's most important works have all been translated into English. There is a new edition of *The Rules of Sociological Method* (Durkheim, 1982) which includes some of Durkheim's articles relating to methodology and sociological theory. Other works include the study of suicide (Durkheim, 1952), studies in philosophy and social theory (Durkheim, 1953, 1964, 1965), the study of economic organisation (Durkheim, 1964, new translation 1984), professions (Durkheim, 1957), religion (Durkheim, 1961) precursors of sociology (Durkheim, 1958, 1965).

Selections from Durkheim's work include Giddens (1972b), Bellah (1973), Traugott (1978), and Thompson (1985).

The most thorough analysis of Durkheim's relation with nineteenth-century positivism remains Parsons (1961a). Other valuable discussions include Coser (1971), Giddens (1971), Aron (1968). The relation of Durkheim's theory of society to contemporary science has been discussed by Hirst (1975), to contemporary French Marxism by Llobera (1981) and his theory of politics analysed perceptively by Giddens (1977).

Douglas (1967) has advanced a phenomenological critique of Durkheim's use of official French suicide statistics. This argument should be read in conjunction with Pope (1978) and Taylor (1982).

5 Critique of Positivism: II Social Action

For a good, general survey of the *verstehen* tradition in social theory see Rickman (1967) and the stimulating historical and critical account of the reaction to positivism in late nineteenth-century and early twentieth-century social thought by Hughes (1959). Outhwaite (1975) is short, lucid and critical.

Dilthey (1976) is a useful selection and an important essay is included in Gardiner (1959). Rickert's major work is available (1962). For German sociology see Aron (1964). Baumann (1978) surveys the hermeneutic tradition from Dilthey to Parsons.

The development of formal sociology is discussed by Aron (1964), Szacki

Further Reading

(1979, Ch. 12). Tönnies's major work is available (Tönnies, 1963) and there are two good selections from his work (Tönnies, 1971, 1974).

Many of Simmel's works are now available in English translation: the early study of history (Simmel, 1977), studies in interpretative sociology (Simmel, 1980), conflict (Simmel, 1956), the role of money in the development of culture (Simmel, 1978), the theory of modern culture (Simmel, 1957) as well as selections from his essays (Wolff, 1950, 1965). The most recent study of Simmel is Frisby (1981). A negative view is argued by Sorokin (1928), pp. 501–5. Durkheim's assessment is reprinted in Coser (1965).

Weber's major works are all available in English translation: on interpretative sociology (Weber, 1968), the methodological essays (Weber, 1949, 1975, 1977), the specialised histories (Weber, 1923, 1976), the studies of religion (Weber, 1968, 1951, 1952, 1958a). Useful selections from his work include Runciman (1978), Gerth and Mills (1948). General discussions of his work include Bendix (1963), Giddens (1971), MacRae (1974), Stammler (1971), Wrong (1970), Parkin (1986), Albrow (1990).

The critical literature on the Protestant ethic is enormous but a good, recent survey is Marshall (1982). A negative argument is advanced by Samuelson (1961).

Pareto's major work has been translated into English in four volumes (Pareto, 1963). The classic account of his relation with Durkheim and Weber is Parsons (1961a), which strives to force Pareto's sociology into a convergence with action theory and voluntarism. Other sympathetic accounts include Sorokin (1928), Lopreato (1975, 1981).

6 The Sociology of Class and Domination

Marx's writings on domination are contained in Marx and Engels (1962, 1971). For Marx's early writing on the state and his critique of Hegel see Bottomore (1964). Marx's comments on Bakunin's *Statism and Anarchy* are included in the Penguin edition of his *Political Writings* (Marx, 1974–6).

There is a good, critical analysis of Marx's concept of centralisation in Kolakowski (1981), Volume I. Also of interest are Therborn (1976) and McLellan (1983).

Weber's writings on class and domination are widely available: Weber (1968) consists of three volumes which includes the important essay, 'Parliament and Government in a Reconstructed Germany'. The essays on 'Socialism' and 'Politics as a Vocation' are in Gerth and Mills (1948).

Weber's politics and concept of domination are ably discussed by Mommsen (1974), Beetham (1974), Giddens (1972). A Marxist critique is presented by Therborn (1976). Weber's relation with Marxism has been widely discussed but see especially Lowith (1982), Aron (1968), Giddens (1971, 1977).

On élites see Mosca (1939) and Michels (1962).

Further Reading

7 Marxism and Sociology

A lucid, critical account of the development of Marxism after Marx is offered by McLellan (1983). Kolakowski (1981) Volume 1 is indispensable. Anderson (1976) is a short, idiosyncratic account. Bernstein (1963) is the main text for the revisionist debate. Sorel's major theoretical writings are available in English translation (Sorel, 1950, 1969). The important essay on the disintegration of Marxism is included in Horowitz (1961). There is a good selection of his essays on Marxism and the revisionist debate (Sorel, 1976). Labriola's essays have been translated (1967, 1980) and there is a good discussion in Kolakowski (1981) Volume 2, Ch. VIII.

Many of Gramsci's writings have now been translated into English and published in three volumes (Gramsci, 1971, 1977, 1978). The important critique of Bukharin and sociology is in 1971, while the essay on the Southern Question, in which the first formulation of hegemony is advanced, is in 1978.

Lukács's early political writings, including the critique of Bukharin, are available (Lukács, 1972) as well as the difficult essays on dialectics and history (Lukács, 1971).

Gouldner (1973) has discussed the importance of Lukács's concepts for modern sociology although somewhat uncritically. Kilminster (1979) discusses the relation of Gramsci, Lukács and the Frankfurt School to Marx's social thought.

There is a useful selection of writings of the Austro-Marxists (Bottomore and Goode, 1978) and Hilferding's major work is now available in translation (Hilferding, 1980). There is a short, lucid account of the relation between Marxism and sociology, with reference to Lukács, Gramsci and the Austro-Marxists in Bottomore (1975).

8 Functionalism

Functionalist anthropological formulations are represented by Malinowski (1922) and Radcliffe-Brown (1952) while Merton (1957) advances a sociological approach. Gouldner (1973) includes the indispensable essay on reciprocity and autonomy in functionalist theory. Other useful discussions include Cohen (1968), Mulkay (1975), Rex (1961), Strasser (1976), Sztompka (1974), Craib (1984), Alexander (1985).

Parsons's writings are widely available: the difficult study of the social system (1951) is in sharp contrast to the more readable and stimulating essays (Parsons, 1954, 1961b, 1964, 1967). The key article on pattern variables, first published in 1960, is included in Parsons (1967) while a succinct theoretical view of the social system is in Parsons (1961b). Difficult texts which seek to reconcile action with systems theory include Parsons and Shils (1962) and Parsons and Smelser (1956). Parsons and Bales (1955) discusses the relation of the nuclear family to industrialism.

During the 1960s Parsons developed an evolutionary perspective: an early statement on 'evolutionary universals' is reprinted in Parsons (1967) and further argument is in Parsons (1966, 1971). One of his last statements sums up his attempt to develop a systematic and voluntarist social theory and brings out the importance both of Durkheim and Freud (the latter's concept of 'overdetermination') for his thought (Parsons, 1981).

Critical discussions of Parsons's work include Black (1961), Gouldner (1971), Part Two; Menzies (1977), Mills (1959), Rocher (1974), Bourricaud (1981).

A valuable collection of essays which discuss functionalism and conflict is Demerath and Peterson (1967). Coser (1956, 1967) attempts to synthesise conflict sociology with functionalism while Lockwood (1964) distinguishes system from social integration in a difficult but rewarding essay.

A classic statement by Aberle *et al.* on the functionalist theory of stratification is reprinted in Demerath and Peterson (1967). Davis's early statement is still available (Davis, 1949). The whole debate is critically discussed by Wrong (1976) and Tumin (1968).

9 Self, Society and the Sociology of Everyday Life

The major statement of action theory is Parsons (1961a): a shorter statement is Parsons (1961b). A more general view is Parsons (1978). For Parsons's attempt to integrate psychology into action theory see his essay on Freud (Parsons, 1971b) and the essays on psychological and social structure (Parsons, 1964). Useful discussions of Parsons's theory of personality includes Rocher (1974), Dawe (1979).

Freud's works are widely available both in the standard edition (1953–) and Penguin edition (1977–). The best introduction to Freud's theories is probably the introductory lectures (Freud, 1977, Vol. 1) and the three essays on sexuality (Freud, 1977, Vol. 7). A sociological discussion is Bocock (1983). A lucid introduction is Brown (1961) and other useful discussions include Wollheim (1971) and Rieff (1965). Marxist interpretation is provided by Marcuse (1962) and the relation between Freud's theories and the Frankfurt school is discussed by Jay (1973) and Held (1980).

Cooley's writings are an important source of social interactionism (Cooley, 1902, 1956) and are ably discussed by Coser (1971). The major study of the polish peasant contains much of value for sociological theory (Thomas and Znaneicki, 1927). Mead's works are widely available (Mead, 1934, 1936, 1938) and a useful selection from them is Mead (1964) which includes an essay on Cooley.

A valuable study which explores the complex relation between Simmel, German Idealism, American Pragmatism and the formation of symbolic interactionism is Rock (1979). Gouldner (1973) Ch. 11 argues that Chicago sociology was largely romantic, intuitive, anti-rationalist. A recent analysis of Mead in relation to Marx is Goff (1980). Blumer (1981) is a succinct summary.

Schutz's major work is available in English (Schutz, 1972). There are three volumes of essays (Schutz, 1962–6) and two studies of the life-world and meaning structures (Schutz, 1974, 1982). A wide-ranging collection of essays

Further Reading

include Outhwaite (1975), Heeran (1971). For ethnomethodology see Garfinkel (1967), Heritage (1984), Giddens (1976), Sharrock and Anderson (1986).

10 Critical Theory, Ideology and Modern Society

For Mannheim the most accessible of his works is the study of ideology (Mannheim, 1960) followed by his essay on conservative thought (Mannheim, 1953). His early essays are available (Mannheim, 1952) and there is a good selection from his work, including his review of Lukács's *Theory of the Novel* in Wolff (1971). The most readable account of his work is Merton (1957) which nevertheless tends to debunk Mannheim's approach as too philosophical and speculative. More subtle critics have emphasised the significance of Mannheim's critique of epistemology (Simmonds, 1978). A hostile view is advanced by Popper (1963) Vol. 2.

Some of Scheler's writings are available in English translation (Curtis and Petras, 1970). A general statement is Scheler (1980).

A good account of Mannheim's theory of intellectuals is Heeran (1971) and there are useful comments in Simmonds (1978) and Coser (1971). One of Mannheim's first statements on intellectuals (1960) should be read in conjunction with the later essay of 1933 (Mannheim, 1956).

For the Frankfurt School see the accounts in Jay (1973, 1988), Kellner (1988), Slater (1977), Held (1980). A good selection of essays is Connerton (1976) and Bonner and Kellner (1989). The critique of positivism is developed in Horkheimer (1972, 1976). Mannheim's study of democratisation is worth reading (1956) in conjunction with the mass society theory of the Frankfurt School. A hostile view of the Frankfurt School is advanced by Shils (1972).

Habermas's writings are widely available in English translation: they include philosophical and theoretical studies (Habermas, 1971), studies in the theory of the modern state and public sphere (Habermas, 1976, 1974, 1979a), studies in language, communication and historical materialism (Habermas, 1979b, 1984, 1989). An excellent introduction to Habermas's thought is Held (1980), while Wellmer (1974) discusses the philosophical and epistemological problems of Habermas's reworking of Frankfurt School critical theory. There is a volume of essays discussing all the aspects of Habermas's thought (Thompson and Held, 1982).

11 Structuralism

A short, lucid introduction to structuralism is Piaget (1971). Saussure's lectures are widely available (Saussure, 1974). A good account of Saussure's work and its importance for social theory is Culler (1976).

There are English translations of the most significant early structuralist works: Propp (1968), Bakhtin (1968, 1973).

Barthes's writings are widely available and include the early analysis of mass culture (Barthes, 1973) and semiology (1967). There is an informative study of Barthes's thought (Culler, 1983). Goldmann's approach to structuralism is best approached through his early study of methodology and theory (Goldmann, 1969) and his substantive study of Racine and Pascal (Goldmann, 1964).

For Althusser see especially his early essays on Marx (Althusser, 1969), the painstaking reading of *Capital* (Althusser, 1970) and the essays on ideology and state apparatuses (Althusser, 1971, 1972, 1976). The most extensive critique of Althusserianism is Thompson (1978) and other analyses include Kolakowski (1981) Vol. 3, Lorraine (1979). Other structuralist works which examine class structure include Poulantzas (1973, 1975), Hindess and Hirst (1975).

12 Modernity, Industrialisation and Sociological Theory

The theory of post-industrial society is developed by Bell (1976) in relation to economic and political structures, technology and science. Bell's book contains a valuable analysis of the concept of industrial society as it emerged in the work of Saint-Simon, Marx, Weber and Sombart. The discussion of culture in post-industrial and industrial society is developed in a later, stimulating volume (Bell, 1979). For criticism see Ross (1974) and Kumar (1978) which includes an excellent bibliography. Other studies of post-industrial society include Touraine (1971) and Dahrendorf (1959). For the debate on modernity and post-modernity see Habermas (1990) and Frisby (1985).

Bibliography

Adorno T.W. (1989) 'Society', in Bonner and Kellner.
Adorno T.W. and Horkheimer (1973) *Dialectic of Enlightenment* (London: Allen Lane).
Albrow M. (1990) *Max Weber and the Construction of Social Theory* (London: Macmillan).
Alexander J. (ed.) (1985) *Neo-Functionalism* (London: Sage).
Althusser L. (1969) *For Marx* (London: Allen Lane).
Althusser L. (1970) *Reading Capital* (with E. Balibar) (London: New Left Books).
Althusser L. (1971) *Lenin and Philosophy* (London: New Left Books).
Althusser L. (1972) *Politics and History* (London: New Left Books).
Althusser L. (1976) *Essays in Self-Criticism* (London: New Left Books).
Anderson P. (1976) *Considerations on Western Marxism* (London: New Left Books).
Andreski S. (ed) (1971) *Herbert Spencer: Structure, Function and Evolution* (London: Nelson).
Andreski S. (ed) (1978) *The Essential Comte* (London: Croom Helm).
Aron R. (1964) *German Sociology* (New York: Free Press).
Aron R. (1965, 1968) *Main Currents in Sociological Thought* 2 Vols. (London: Weidenfeld & Nicolson).
Avineri S. (1968) *The Social and Political Thought of Karl Marx* (Cambridge: Cambridge University Press).
Bakhtin M.M. (1968) *Rabelais and His World* (London: MIT Press).
Bakhtin M.M. (1973) *Marxism and the Philosophy of Language* (published under the name of V. Volosinov) (London: Academic Press).
Bakhtin M.M. (1986) *Speech Genres and Other Late Essays* (Austin: University of Texas Press).
Bales R.F. & Shils E. (eds) (1962) *Working Papers in the Theory of Action* (New York: Harper Torchbooks).
Barthes R. (1967) *Elements of Semiology* (London: Cape).
Barthes R. (1973) *Mythologies* (London: Paladin Books).
Baumann Z. (1978) *Hermeneutics and Social Science* (London: Hutchinson).
Beetham D. (1974) *Max Weber and the Theory of Modern Politics* (London: Allen & Unwin).

Bibliography

Bell D. (1976) *The Coming of Post-Industrial Society* (Harmondsworth: Penguin Books).

Bell D. (1979) *The Cultural Contradictions of Capitalism* (London: Heinemann).

Bellah R. (ed) (1973) *Emile Durkheim on Morality and Society* (Chicago: University of Chicago Press).

Bendix R. (1963) *Max Weber: An Intellectual Portrait* (London: Heinemann).

Bendix R. & Roth G. (eds) (1971) *Scholarship and Partisanship: Essays on Max Weber* (Los Angeles: University of California Press).

Benton T. (1977) *Philosophical Foundations of the Three Sociologies* (London: Routledge).

Berlin I. (1976) *Vico and Herder* (Oxford: Oxford University Press).

Bernstein E. (1963) *Evolutionary Socialism* (New York: Schoken Books).

Black M. (ed) (1961) *The Social Theories of Talcott Parsons* (New Jersey: Prentice-Hall).

Blumer H. (1969) *Symbolic Interactionism* (New Jersey: Prentice-Hall).

Blumer H. (1981) 'George Herbert Mead', in Rhea (1981).

Bocock R. (1976) *Freud and Modern Sociology* (London: Nelson).

Bocock R. (1983) *Sigmund Freud* (London: Methuen).

Bonner S.E. and Kellner D. (eds)(1989) *Critical Theory and Society* (London: Routledge).

Bottomore T.B. (ed) (1964) *Marx: Early Writings* (London: Watts).

Bottomore T.B. (1975) *Marxist Sociology* (London: Macmillan).

Bottomore T.B. & Goode P. (eds) (1978) *Austro-Marxism* (Oxford: Oxford University Press).

Bottomore T.B. & Nisbet R. (eds) (1979) *A History of Sociological Analysis* (London: Heinemann).

Bottomore T.B. & Rubel M. (eds) (1961) *Karl Marx: Selected Writings in Sociology and Social Philosophy* (Harmondsworth: Penguin Books).

Bottomore T.B. (1984) *The Frankfurt School* (London: Routledge).

Bourricaud, F. (1981) *The Sociology of Talcott Parsons* (London: University of Chicago Press).

Bramson L. (1961) *The Political Context of Sociology* (Princeton: Princeton University Press).

Brown J.A.C. (1961) *Freud and the Post-Freudians* (Harmondsworth: Penguin Books).

Buci-Glucksmann C. (1981) *Gramsci and the State* (London: Lawrence & Wishart).

Buckley W. (1967) *Sociology and Modern Systems Theory* (New Jersey: Prentice-Hall).

Bukharin N. (1969) *Historical Materialism* (Ann Arbor: University of Michigan Press).

Burrow J.W. (1966) *Evolution and Society* (Cambridge: Cambridge University Press).

Cahnman W. (1973) (ed) *Ferdinand Tönnies: A New Evaluation* (Leiden: Brill).

Cahnman W. (1981) 'Hobbes, Toennies, Vico: Starting Points in Sociology', in Rhea (1981).

Carneiro R.L. (ed) (1967) *Herbert Spencer: The Evolution of Society* (Chicago:

Bibliography

University of Chicago Press).

Cassirer E. (1951) *The Philosophy of the Enlightenment* (Boston: Beacon Press).

Chitnis A. (1977) *The Scottish Enlightenment* (London: Croom Helm).

Clarke T.N. (1973) *Prophets and Patrons: The French University and the Emergence of the Social Science* (Cambridge: Harvard University Press).

Cohen G.A. (1978) *Karl Marx's Theory of History: A Defence* (Oxford: Oxford University Press).

Cohen P. (1968) *Modern Social Theory* (London: Heinemann).

Comte A. (1877) *System of Positive Polity* (London: Longmans Green).

Comte A. (1896) *The Positive Philosophy* (London: Bell & Sons).

Connerton P. (ed) (1976) *Critical Sociology* (Harmondsworth: Penguin Books).

Connerton P. (1980) *The Tragedy of Enlightenment: An Essay on the Frankfurt School* (Cambridge: Cambridge University Press).

Cooley C.H. (1902) *Human Nature and the Social Order* (New York: Charles Scribners).

Cooley C.H. (1956) *Social Organisation* (New York: Schocken).

Coser L.A. (1956) *The Functions of Social Conflict* (London: Routledge).

Coser L.A. (ed) (1965) *George Simmel* (New Jersey: Prentice-Hall).

Coser L.A. (1967) *Continuities in the Study of Social Conflict* (New York: Free Press).

Coser L.A. (1971) *Masters of Sociological Thought* (New York: Harcourt Brace Jovanovich).

Craib I. (1984) *Modern Social Theory* (Brighton: Harvester Press).

Croce B. (1913) *Historical Materialism and the Economics of Karl Marx* (London: Howard Latimer).

Culler J. (1976) *Saussure* (London: Fontana).

Curtis J.E. & Petras J. (eds) (1970) *The Sociology of Knowledge: A Reader* (London: Duckworth).

Dahrendorf R. (1959) *Class and Class Conflict in Industrial Society* (London: Routledge).

Davis K. (1949) *Human Society* (London: Routledge & Kegan Paul).

Davis K. & Moore W. (1969) 'Some Principles of Stratification', in Heller, C. *Structured Social Inequality* (London: Collier-Macmillan).

Dawe A. (1970) 'The Two Sociologies', *British Journal of Sociology*, XXI, No. 2 (June).

Dawe A. (1979) 'Theories of Social Action', in Bottomore & Nisbet (1979).

Demerath N. & Peterson R. (eds) (1967) *System, Change and Conflict* (New York: Free Press).

Dilthey W. (1976) *Selected Writings* (Cambridge: Cambridge University Press).

Douglas J. (1967) *The Social Meanings of Suicide* (Princeton: Princeton Univeresity Press).

Douglas J. (ed) (1973) *Understanding Everyday Life* (London: Routledge).

Durkheim E. (1952) *Suicide* (London: Routledge & Kegan Paul).

Durkheim E. (1953) *Sociology and Philosophy* (London: Cohen & West).

Durkheim E. (1957) *Professional Ethics and Civic Morals* (London: Routledge).

Durkheim E. (1958) *Saint-Simon and Socialism* (London: Routledge).

Bibliography

Durkheim E. (1961) *The Elementary Forms of the Religious Life* (London: Allen & Unwin).

Durkheim E. (1964) *The Division of Labour* (New York: Free Press).

Durkheim E. (1965) *Montesquieu and Rousseau* (Ann Arbor: University of Michigan Press).

Durkheim E. (1982) *The Rules of Sociological Method* (London: Macmillan).

Durkheim E. & Mauss M. (1967) *Primitive Classification* (London: Routledge).

Easton L.D. and Guddatt K. (eds) (1967) *Writings of the Young Marx on Philosophy and Society* (New York: Anchor Books).

Engels F. (1942) *The Origin of the Family, Private Property and State* (New York: International Publishers).

Engels F. (1954) *Anti-Duhring* (London: Lawrence & Wishart).

Ferguson A. (1966) *An Essay on the History of Civil Society* (Edinburgh: Edinburgh University Press).

Feuer L.S. (1976) 'John Stuart Mill as a Sociologist', in Robson J. and Laine M. (eds) *James and John Stuart Mill* (Toronto: University of Toronto Press).

Feuerbach L. (1969) 'Preliminary Theses on the Reform of Philosophy', *Arena*, No. 19.

Finer S.E. (ed) (1966) *Vilfredo Pareto: Sociological Writings* (London: Pall Mall Press).

Fischer B.M. & Strauss A.L. (1979) 'Interactionism', in Bottomore and Nisbet (1979).

Fletcher R. (1972, 1973) *The Making of Sociology* (London: Nelson) 3 Vols.

Fletcher R. (ed) (1974) *The Crisis of Industrial Society: The Early Essays of Comte* (London: Heinemann).

Freud S. (1953–) *Complete Works*, ed Strachey J. (London: Hogarth Press).

Freud S. (1977–) *Selected Works* (Harmondsworth: Penguin Books).

Frisby D. (1981) *Sociological Impressionism: A Reassessment of George Simmel's Social Theory* (London: Heinemann).

Frisby D. (1985) *Fragments of Modernity* (Oxford: Polity Press).

Gane M. (1988) *On Durkheim's Rules of Sociological Method* (London: Routledge).

Gardiner P. (ed) (1959) *Theories of History* (New York: Free Press).

Garfinkel H. (1967) *Studies in Ethnomethodology* (New Jersey: Prentice-Hall).

Gay P. (1967, 1970) *The Enlightenment: An Interpretation* (London: Weidenfeld & Nicolson).

Gerth H.H. & Mills C.W. (eds) (1948) *From Max Weber* (London: Routledge).

Giddens A. (1971) *Capitalism and Modern Social Theory* (Cambridge: Cambridge University Press).

Giddens A. (1972a) *Politics and Sociology in the Thought of Max Weber* (London: Macmillan).

Giddens A. (1972b) *Emile Durkheim: Selected Writings* (Cambridge: Cambridge University Press).

Giddens A. (1976) *New Rules of Sociological Method* (London: Hutchinson).

Giddens A. (1977) *Studies in Social and Political Theory* (London: Hutchinson).

Giddens A. (1984) *The Constitution of Society* (Oxford: Polity Press).

Bibliography

Giddens A. and Turner J. (eds)(1987) *Social Theory Today* (Oxford: Polity Press).

Giddens A. (1987) *Social Theory and Modern Sociology* (Oxford: Polity Press).

Goff T.W. (1980) *Marx and Mead* (London: Routledge).

Goldman L. (1964) *The Hidden God* (London: Routledge).

Goldman L. (1969) *The Human Sciences and Philosophy* (London: Cape).

Gouldner A. (1971) *The Coming Crisis of Western Sociology* (London: Heinemann).

Gouldner A. (1973) *For Sociology* (London: Allen Lane).

Gouldner A. (1980) *The Two Marxisms* (London: Macmillan).

Gramsci A. (1971) *Selections from the Prison Notebooks* (London: Lawrence & Wishart).

Gramsci A. (1977, 1978) *Selections from the Political Writings* (London: Lawrence & Wishart).

Habermas J. (1971) *Knowledge and Human Interests* (London: Heinemann).

Habermas J. (1976) *Legitimation Crisis* (London: Heinemann).

Habermas J. (1979) *Communication and the Evolution of Society* (London: Heinemann).

Habermas J. (1984, 1989) *The Theory of Communicative Action*, 2 vols (Oxford: Polity Press).

Habermas J. (1990) *The Philosophical Discourse of Modernity* (Oxford: Polity Press).

Halbwachs M. (1970) *The Causes of Suicide* (London: Routledge).

Halfpenny P. (1982) *Positivism and Sociology* (London: Allen & Unwin).

Hawthorn G. (1976) *Enlightenment and Despair: A History of Sociology* (Cambridge: Cambridge University Press).

Hayek F. (1955) *The Counter-Revolution of Science* (New York: Free Press).

Heeran J. (1971) 'Karl Mannheim and the Intellectual Elite', *British Journal of Sociology* Vol. 22, No. 1 (March).

Heeran J. (1973) 'Alfred Schutz and the Sociology of Common-sense Knowledge', in Douglas (1973).

Held D. (1980) *Introduction to Critical Theory* (London: Hutchinson).

Heritage J. (1984) *Garfinkel and Ethnomethodology* (Oxford: Polity Press).

Hilferding R. (1980) *Finance Capital* (London: Routledge).

Hindess B. & Hirst P. (1975) *Pre-Capitalist Economic Formations* (London: Routledge).

Hirst P.Q. (1975) *Durkheim, Bernard and Epistemology* (London: Routledge).

Hirst P.Q. (1976) *Social Evolution and Sociological Categories* (London: Allen & Unwin).

Horkheimer M. (1972) *Critical Theory* (New York: Seabury Press).

Horkheimer M. (1976) 'Traditional and Critical Theory', in Connerton (1976).

Horowitz I.L. (1961) *Radicalism and the Revolt against Reason* (London: Routledge).

Horton J. (1964) 'The De-humanisation of Alienation and Anomie', *British Journal of Sociology* Vol. XV, No. 4 (Dec).

Hughes H.S. (1959) *Consciousness and Society* (London: MacGibbon & Kee).

Ionescu G. (ed) (1976) *The Political Thought of Saint-Simon* (Oxford: Oxford

Bibliography

University Press).

Jay M. (1973) *The Dialectical Imagination* (London: Heinemann).

Jay M. (1988) *Fin-De-Siècle Socialism* (London: Routledge).

Kahn J.S. & Llobera J. (eds) (1981) *The Anthropology of Pre-Capitalist Societies* (London: Macmillan).

Kautsky K. (1983) *Selected Political Writings* (London: Macmillan).

Kellner D. (1989) *Critical Theory, Marxism and Modernity* (Oxford: Polity Press).

Kettler D. (1965) *The Social and Political Thought of Adam Ferguson* (Columbus: University of Ohio Press).

Kilminster R. (1979) *Praxis and Method: A Sociological Dialogue with Lukács, Gramsci and the Early Frankfurt School* (London: Routledge & Kegan Paul).

Kolakowski L. (1981) *Main Currents in Marxism* 3 Vols. (Oxford: Oxford University Press).

Kolko G. (1960) 'Max Weber on America', *History and Theory* 1.

Krygier M. (1979) 'Saint-Simon, Marx and the Non-Governed Society', in Brown R. (ed) *Bureaucracy* (London: Arnold).

Kumar K. (1978) *Prophecy and Progress* (Harmondsworth: Penguin Books).

Labriola A. (1967) *Essays on the Materialist Conception of History* (New York: Monthly Review Press).

Labriola A. (1980) *Socialism and Philosophy* (Washington: Telos Press).

Lash S. (1990) *Sociology of Postmodernism* (London: Routledge).

Lehmann W. (ed) (1960) *John Millar of Glasgow* (Glasgow: Glasgow University Press).

Levine D. (ed) (1971) *Simmel: On Individuality and Social Forms* (Chicago: University of Chicago Press).

Levine D. (1981) 'Sociology's Quest for the Classics: The Case of Simmel', in Rhea (1981).

Lévi-Strauss C. (1968, 1977) *Structural Anthropology* (London: Allen Lane).

Lively J. (ed) *The Works of Joseph de Maistre* (London: Allen & Unwin).

Llobera J. (1981) 'Durkheim, the Durkheimians and their Collective Misrepresentation of Marx', in Kahn & Llobera (1981).

Lockwood D. 'Social Integration and System Integration', in Zollschan and Hirsch (1964).

Lopreato J. (1975) *The Sociology of Pareto* (Morristown: General Learning Press).

Lopreato J. (1981) 'Vilfredo Pareto: Socio-Biology, System and Revolution', in Rhea (1981).

Lorraine J. (1979) *The Concept of Ideology* (London: Hutchinson).

Lowith K. (1982) *Karl Marx and Max Weber* (London: Allen & Unwin).

Luckmann T. (ed) (1978) *Phenomenology and Sociology* (Harmondsworth: Penguin Books).

Lukács G. (1971) *History and Class Consciousness* (London: Merlin Press).

Lukács G. (1972) *Political Writings: 1919–1929* (London: New Left Books).

Lukes S. (1973) *Emile Durkheim: His Life and Work* (London: Allen Lane).

Lukes S. (1977) *Essays in Social Theory* (London: Macmillan).

MacRae D.G. (1969) 'Adam Ferguson', in Raison (1969).

MacRae D.G. (1974) *Weber* (London: Fontana).

Bibliography

Malinowski E. (1922) *Argonauts of the Western Pacific* (New York: Dutton).

Mannheim K. (1952) *Essays in the Sociology of Knowledge* (London: Routledge).

Mannheim K. (1953) *Essays in Sociology and Social Psychology* (London: Routledge).

Mannheim K. (1956) *Essays in the Sociology of Culture* (London: Routledge).

Mannheim K. (1960) *Ideology and Utopia* (London: Routledge).

Mannheim K. (1982) *Structures of Thinking* (London: Routledge).

Manuel F. (1962) *The Prophets of Paris* (New York: Harper).

Marcuse H. (1954) *Reason and Revolution* (New York: Humanities Press).

Marcuse H. (1962) *Eros and Civilisation* (New York: Vintage Books).

Marcuse H. (1964) *One Dimensional Man* (London: Routledge).

Marshall G. (1982) *In Search of the Spirit of Capitalism* (London: Hutchinson).

Martindale D. (1960) *The Nature and Types of Sociological Theory* (London: Routledge).

Marx K. (1957, 1958, 1962) *Capital* (London: Lawrence & Wishart).

Marx K. (1961) *The Poverty of Philosophy* (London: Lawrence & Wishart).

Marx K. (1963) *Economic and Philosophical Manuscripts* (London: Lawrence & Wishart).

Marx K. (1964–72) *Theories of Surplus Value* 3 Vols. (London: Lawrence & Wishart).

Marx K. (1971) *A Contribution to the Critique of Political Economy* (London: Lawrence & Wishart).

Marx K. (1973) *Grundrisse* (Harmondsworth: Penguin Books).

Marx K. (1974–6) *Marx: Political Writings* 3 Vols (Harmondsworth: Penguin Books).

Marx K. (1976–80) *Capital* 3 Vols. (Harmondsworth: Penguin Books).

Marx & Engels (1956) *The Holy Family* (London: Lawrence & Wishart).

Marx & Engels (1962) *Selected Works* (London: Lawrence & Wishart). This is a two volume edition.

Marx & Engels (1964) *The German Ideology* (London: Lawrence & Wishart).

Marx & Engels (1971) *On the Paris Commune* (London: Lawrence & Wishart).

Marx & Engels (1975–) *Collected Works* (London: Lawrence & Wishart). This, the first complete English edition of the complete works of Marx and Engels will include *Capital* and comprise 50 Volumes when complete.

Marx & Engels (n.d.) *Selected Correspondence* (London: Lawrence & Wishart).

Mauss H. (1962) *A Short History of Sociology* (London: Routledge).

McLellan D. (1969) *The Young Hegelians and Karl Marx* (London: Macmillan).

McLellan D. (1973) *Karl Marx: His Life and Thought* (London: Macmillan).

McLellan D. (ed) (1980a) *The Thought of Karl Marx* (London: Macmillan).

McLellan D. (1980b) *Marxism after Marx* (London: Macmillan).

McLellan D. (ed) (1983) *Marx: The First Hundred Years* (London: Fontana).

Mead G.H. (1934) *Mind, Self and Society* (Chicago: University of Chicago Press).

Mead G.H. (1936) *Movements of Thought in the Nineteenth Century* (Chicago: University of Chicago Press).

Mead G.H. (1938) *The Philosophy of the Act* (Chicago: University of Chicago Press).

Bibliography

Mead G.H. (1964) *On Social Psychology* (Chicago: University of Chicago Press).

Meisel J.H. (1962) *The Myth of the Ruling Class: Gaetano Mosca and the Elite* (Ann Arbor: University of Michigan Press).

Meisel J.H. (ed) (1965) *Pareto and Mosca* (New Jersey: Prentice-Hall).

Menzies K. (1977) *Talcott Parsons and the Social Image of Man* (London: Routledge & Kegan Paul).

Merleau-Ponty M. (1973) *The Adventures of the Dialectic* (London: Heinemann).

Merton R.K. (1957) *Social Theory and Social Structure* (New York: Free Press).

Michels R. (1962) *Political Parties* (New York: Collier-Macmillan).

Mill J.S. (1961) *Auguste Comte and Positivism* (Ann Arbor: University of Michigan Press).

Mill J.S. (1976) *A System of Logic* (ed Fletcher R.) (London: Nelson).

Mills C.W. (1956) *The Power Elite* (New York: Oxford University Press).

Mills C.W. (1959) *The Sociological Imagination* (New York: Oxford University Press).

Montesquieu (1949) *The Spirit of the Laws* (New York: Haffner).

Montesquieu (1965) *Considerations on the Greatness of the Romans and their Decline* (New York: Free Press).

Mommsen W. (1974) *The Age of Bureaucracy: Perspectives on the Political Sociology of Max Weber* (Oxford: Blackwell).

Mosca G. (1939) *The Ruling Class* (New York: McGraw Hill).

Mouffe C. (ed) (1978) *Gramsci and Marxist Theory* (London: Routledge).

Mouzelis N.P. (1991) *Back to Sociological Theory* (London: Macmillan).

Mulkay M. (1975) *Functionalism, Exchange and Theoretical Strategy* (London: Routledge & Kegan Paul).

Munch R. (1987) *Theory of Action* (London: Routledge).

Munch R. (1988) *Understanding Modernity* (London, Routledge).

Oberschall A. (ed) (1972) *Empirical Social Research in Germany 1848–1914* (New York: Harper & Row).

Ollman B. (1971) *Alienation: Marx's Theory of Man in Capitalist Society* (Cambridge: Cambridge University Press).

Outhwaite W. (1975) *Understanding Social Life: The Method called Vesthen* (London: Allen & Unwin).

Pareto V. (1963) *The Mind and Society: A Treatise on General Sociology* (New York: Dover).

Pareto V. (1965) *The Rise and Fall of Elites* (Towata: Bedminster Press) (First published in 1901).

Parkin F. (1982) *Max Weber* (London: Routledge).

Parsons T. (1951) *The Social System* (New York: Free Press).

Parsons T. (1954) *Essays in Sociological Theory* (New York: Free Press).

Parsons T. (1955) *Family, Socialisation and Interaction Process* (with Bales R.F.) (London: Routledge & Kegan Paul).

Parsons T. (1961a) *The Structure of Social Action* (New York: Free Press).

Parsons T. (1961b) *Structure and Process in Modern Societies* (New York: Free Press).

Parsons T. (ed) (1961c) *Theories of Society* (New York: Free Press).

338

Bibliography

Parsons T. (1961d) 'The Point of View of the Author', in Black (ed) (1961).

Parsons T. (1964) *Social Structure and Personality* (New York: Free Press).

Parsons T. (1966) *Societies: Evolutionary and Comparative Perspectives* (New Jersey: Prentice-Hall).

Parsons T. (1967) *Sociological Theory and Modern Society* (New York: Free Press).

Parsons T. (1971a) *The System of Modern Societies* (New Jersey: Prentice-Hall).

Parsons T. (1971b) *'The Interpretation of Dreams* by Sigmund Freud', *Daedalus* Vol. 103, pp. 91–6.

Parsons T. (1978) *Action Theory and the Human Condition* (New York: Free Press).

Parsons T. (1981) 'Revisiting the Classics', in Rhea (ed) (1981).

Parsons T. (1989) 'A Tentative Outline of American Values', *Theory, Culture and Society*, vol. 6, no. 4.

Parsons T. & Shils E. (1962) *Toward a General Theory of Action* (New York: Harper).

Parsons T. and Smelser N. (1956) *Economy and Society* (New York: Free Press).

Peel J.D.Y. (1971) *Herbert Spencer: The Evolution of a Sociologist* (London: Heinemann).

Peel J.D.Y. (ed) (1972) *Herbert Spencer on Social Evolution* (Chicago: University of Chicago Press).

Piaget J. (1971) *Structuralism* (London: Routledge).

Pope W. (1978) *Durkheim's Suicide* (Chicago: University of Chicago Press).

Popper K. (1963) *The Open Society and its Enemies* 2 Vols. (London: Routledge).

Poulantzas N. (1973) *Political Power and Social Classes* (London: New Left Books).

Poulantzas N. (1975) *Classes in Contemporary Capitalism* (London: New Left Books).

Propp V. (1968) *Morphology of the Fairy Tale* (Austin: University of Texas Press).

Radcliffe-Brown A.R. (1952) *Structure and Function in Primitive Society* (London: Routledge).

Raison T. (ed) (1969) *Founding Fathers of Social Science* (Harmondsworth: Penguin Books).

Rex J. (1961) *Key Problems of Sociological Theory* (London: Routledge).

Rhea B. (ed) (1981) *The Future of the Sociological Classics* (London: Allen & Unwin).

Rickert H. (1962) *Science and History* (New York: Van Nostrand).

Rickman H.R. (1967) *Understanding and the Human Sciences* (London: Heinemann).

Rieff P. (1965) *Freud: The Mind of a Moralist* (London: Methuen).

Ringer F. (1969) *The Decline of the German Mandarins: The German Academic Community 1890–1933* (Cambridge: Harvard University Press).

Rocher G. (1974) *Talcott Parsons and American Sociology* (London: Nelson).

Rock P. (1979) *The Making of Symbolic Interactionism* (London: Macmillan).

Rosdolsky R. (1977) *The Making of Marx's Capital* (London: Pluto Press).

Runciman W. (ed) (1978) *Weber: A selection* (Cambridge: Cambridge University Press).

Bibliography

Sahay A. (ed) (1971) *Max Weber and Modern Sociology* (London: Routledge).

Salamon L. (1981) *The Sociology of Political Praxis* (London: Routledge).

Samuelson K. (1961) *Religion and Economic Action* (London: Heinemann).

Saussure F. (1974) *Course in General Linguistics* (London: Fontana).

Sayer D. (1978) *Marx's Method* (Hassocks: Harvester Press).

Scheler M. (1980) *Problems of a Sociology of Knowledge* (London: Routledge).

Schneider L. (ed) (1967) *The Scottish Moralists on Human Nature and Society* (Chicago: University of Chicago Press).

Schumpeter J. (1961) *Capitalism, Socialism and Democracy* (London: Allen & Unwin).

Schutz A. (1962–6) *Collected Papers* 3 Vols. (The Hangue: Mouton).

Schutz A. (1972) *Phenomenology of the Social World* (London: Heinemann).

Schutz A. (1974) *The Structures of the Life World* (with T. Luckmann) (London: Heinemann).

Schutz A. (1978) 'Phenomenology and the Social Sciences', 'Some Structures of the Life World', in Luckmann (ed) (1978).

Schutz A. (1982) *Life Forms and Meaning Structures* (London: Routledge).

Schwendinger, H. & H. *The Sociologists of the Chair* (New York: Basic Books).

Sharrock W. and Anderson B. (1986) *The Ethnomethodologists* (London: Routledge).

Shils E. (1972) *The Intellectuals and the Powers* (Chicago: University of Chicago Press).

Shils E. (1975) *Centre and Periphery* (Chicago: University of Chicago Press).

Shils E. (1980) *The Calling of Sociology* (Chicago: University of Chicago Press).

Simmel G. (1956) *Conflict and the Web of Group Affiliations* (New York: Free Press).

Simmel G. (1957) *Philosophic Culture* (New York: Putnam).

Simmel G. (1968) *The Conflict in Modern Culture and other Essays* (New York: Columbia University Press).

SimmelG. (1977) *The Problems of a Philosophy of History* (New York: Free Press).

Simmel G. (1978) *The Philosophy of Money* (London: Routledge).

Simmel G. (1980) *Essays in Interpretation in the Social Sciences* (Manchester: Manchester University Press).

Simmonds A.P. (1978) *Karl Mannheim's Sociology of Knowledge* (Oxford: Oxford University Press).

Simon W.M. (1963) *European Positivism in the Nineteenth Century* (New York: Cornell University Press).

Slater P. (1977) *The Origin and Significance of the Frankfurt School* (London: Routledge).

Smith A. (1976) *Theory of Moral Sentiments* (Glasgow: Glasgow University Press).

Smith A. (1970) *Wealth of Nations* (Harmondsworth: Penguin Books).

Sombart W. (1967) *Luxury and Capitalism* (Ann Arbor: University of Michigan Press).

Sorel G. (1950) *Reflections on Violence* (New York: Free Press).

Sorel G. (1969) *The Illusions of Progress* (New York: Cornell University Press) (Berkeley: University of California Press).

Bibliography

Sorel G. (1976) *From George Sorel: Essays in Socialism and Philosophy* (New York: Oxford University Press).

Sorokin P. (1928) *Contemporary Sociological Theories* (New York: Harper & Row).

Spencer H. (1965) *The Study of Sociology* (New York: Free Press).

Spencer H. (1969a) *Man versus the State* (Harmondsworth: Penguin Books).

Spencer H. (1969b) *Principles of Sociology* (ed Andreski) (New York: Macmillan).

Stammler O. (ed) (1971) *Max Weber and Sociology Today* (Oxford: Blackwell).

Strasser H. (1976) *The Normative Structure of Sociology* (London: Routledge).

Swingewood A. (1970) 'The Origins of Sociology: The Case of the Scottish Enlightenment', *British Journal of Sociology* (June).

Szacki J. (1979) *History of Sociological Thought* (London: Aldwych).

Sztompka P. (1974) *System and Function* (New York: Academic Press).

Tagliocozzo G. (1983) *Vico and Marx* (London: Macmillan).

Tawney R.H. (1926) *Religion and the Rise of Capitalism* (London: Allen & Unwin).

Taylor K. (ed) (1975) *Saint-Simon: Selected Writings on Science, Industry and Social Organisation* (London: Croom Helm).

Taylor S. (1982) *Durkheim and the Study of Suicide* (London: Macmillan).

Therborn G. (1976) *Science, Class and Society* (London: New Left Books).

Thomas W. I. & Znaneicki F. (1927) *The Polish Peasant in Europe and America* 2 Vols. (Chicago: University of Chicago Press).

Thompson E. (1978) *The Poverty of Theory* (London: Merlin Press).

Thompson J.B. and Held D. (eds) (1982) *Habermas: Critical Debates* (London: Macmillan).

Thompson K. (ed) (1976) *Auguste Comte: The Foundations of Sociology* (London: Nelson).

Thompson K. (ed.) (1985) *Readings from Emile Durkheim* (London: Routledge).

Tiryakin A.E. (1979) 'Emile Durkheim', in Bottomore & Nisbet (1979).

Tönnies F. (1963) *Community and Association* (London: Routledge & Kegan Paul).

Tönnies F. (1971) *On Sociology: Pure, Applied and Empirical* ed Cahmann W.J. and Meberle R. (Chicago: University of Chicago Press).

Tönnies F. (1974) *On Social Ideas and Ideologies* (New York: Harper & Row).

Touraine A. (1971) *The Post-Industrial Society* (London: Wildwood House).

Traugott B. (1978) (ed) *Durkheim on Institutional Analysis* (Chicago: University of Chicago Press).

Tumin M. (1968) *Social Stratification: The Forms and Functions of Social Inequality* (New Jersey: Prentice-Hall).

Turner B. (1981) *For Weber* (London: Routledge).

Vico G. (1948) *The New Science* ed Bergin T. & Frisch M. (New York: Cornell University Press).

Weber M. (1923) *General Economic History* (London: Allen & Unwin).

Weber M. (1930) *The Protestant Ethic and the Spirit of Capitalism* (London: Allen & Unwin).

341

Bibliography

Weber M. (1949) *The Methodology of the Social Sciences* (New York: Free Press).

Weber M. (1951) *The Religion of India* (New York: Free Press).

Weber M. (1952) *Ancient Judaism* (New York: Free Press).

Weber M. (1954) *On Law in Economy and Society* (New York: Free Press).

Weber M. (1958a) *The Religion of India* (New York: Free Press).

Weber M. (1958b) *The City* (New York: Free Press).

Weber M. (1963) *The Sociology of Religion* (Boston: Beacon Press).

Weber M. (1964) *The Theory of Social and Economic Organisation* (New York: Free Press).

Weber M. (1968b) *Economy and Society* 3 Vols. (Towata: Bedminster Press).

Weber M. (1975) *Roscher and Knies: The Logical Problems of Historical Economics* (New York: Free Press).

Weber M. (1976) *The Agrarian Sociology of Ancient Civilisations* (London: New Left Books).

Weber M. (1977) *Critique of Stammler* (New York: Free Press).

Wellmer A. (1974) *Critical Theory of Society* (New York: Herder & Herder).

Wesolowski W. (1980) *Classes, Strata and Power* (London: Routledge).

Wolff K. (ed) (1950) *The Sociology of Georg Simmel* (New York: Free Press).

Wolff K. (ed) (1964) *Emile Durkheim: Essays on Sociology and Philosophy* (New York: Harper & Row).

Wolff K. (ed) (1965) *Simmel: Essays on Sociology, Philosophy and Aesthetics* (New York: Harper & Row).

Wolff K. (ed) (1971) *From Karl Mannheim* (New York: Oxford University Press).

Wollheim R. (1971) *Freud* (London: Fontana).

Worsley P. (1982) *Marx and Marxism* (London: Routledge).

Wright E.O. (1978) *Class, Crisis and the State* (London: New Left Books).

Wrong D. (ed) (1970) *Max Weber* (New Jersey: Prentice-Hall).

Wrong D. (1976) *Skeptical Sociology* (London: Heinemann).

Znaneicki F. (1965) *The Social Role of the Man of Knowledge* (New York: Harper & Row).

Zeitlin I. (1968) *Ideology and the Development of Sociological Theory* (New Jersey: Prentice-Hall).

Zollschan G.R. & Hirsch, W. (eds) (1964) *Explorations in Social Change* (London: Routledge).

Index

Index

Index

Index

Index

YORK NOTES

THE TAMING OF THE SHREW

WILLIAM SHAKESPEARE

NOTES BY REBECCA WARREN

 Longman

 York Press

Exterior picture of the Globe Theatre reproduced by permission of the
Raymond Mander and Joe Mitchenson Theatre Collection
Reconstruction of the Globe Theatre interior reprinted from Hodges:
The Globe Restored (1968) by permission of Oxford University Press

YORK PRESS
322 Old Brompton Road, London SW5 9JH

PEARSON EDUCATION LIMITED
Edinburgh Gate, Harlow,
Essex CM20 2JE, United Kingdom
Associated companies, branches and representatives throughout the world

First published 1999
This new and fully revised edition first published 2005
Second impression 2005

10 9 8 7 6 5 4 3 2

ISBN-10: 1-4058-0706-7
ISBN-13: 978-1-4058-0706-7

Typeset by Land & Unwin (Data Sciences), Bugbrooke, Northamptonshire
Produced by Pearson Education Asia Limited, Hong Kong

CONTENTS

PART ONE

INTRODUCTION

HOW TO STUDY A PLAY

Studying on your own requires self-discipline and a carefully
thought-out work plan in order to be effective.

- Drama is a special kind of writing (the technical term is 'genre')
  because it needs a performance in the theatre to arrive at a full
  interpretation of its meaning. Try to imagine that you are a
  member of the audience when reading the play. Think about
  how it could be presented on the stage, not just about the words
  on the page.

- Drama is always about conflict of some sort (which may be
  below the surface). Identify the conflicts in the play and you
  will be close to identifying the large ideas or themes which bind
  all the parts together.

- Make careful notes on themes, character, plot and any subplots
  of the play.

- Why do you like or dislike the characters in the play? How do
  your feelings towards them develop and change?

- Playwrights find non-realistic ways of allowing an audience to
  see into the minds and motives of their characters, for example
  soliloquy, **aside** or music. Consider how such dramatic devices
  are used in the play you are studying.

- Think of the playwright writing the play. Why were these
  particular arrangements of events, characters and speeches chosen?

- Cite exact sources for all quotations, whether from the text itself
  or from critical commentaries. Wherever possible find your own
  examples from the play to back up your opinions.

- Where appropriate, comment in detail on the language of the
  passage you have quoted.

- Always express your ideas in your own words.

These York Notes offer an introduction to *The Taming of the
Shrew* and cannot substitute for close reading of the text and the
study of secondary sources.

**CHECK
THE BOOK**

To read a selection
of traditional
sources on shrewish
wives and shrew-
taming, have a look
at Frances E. Dolan,
ed., *The Taming of
the Shrew: Texts
and Contexts* (1996).

READING *THE TAMING OF THE SHREW*

This play has attracted so much opprobrium during the past hundred years, including calls to have it removed from the theatrical repertoire, that it is difficult to know whether to begin these Notes with an apology for or defence of *The Taming of the Shrew*. Perhaps – since the ideas and actions it contains arouse such strong feelings – no apology is necessary for this **comedy**. While audiences, readers and critics find something to argue about, surely Shakespeare's version of a traditional wife-taming story is worth watching and discussing?

What has caused the controversy? The final sentence of the previous paragraph encapsulates the problem: this is a play in which a woman is starved into submission. Her husband, seen by some as a lively scamp and by others as a brutal scoundrel, employs a range of stratagems to curb his bride's headstrong humour: he deprives her of sleep, bombards her with lectures about wifely obedience, denies her clothes and kisses until she finally acts in a way that pleases him. Depending upon your point of view, the heroine is either taught how to behave in a manner befitting her sex and station in life, or forced to submit to a domestic tyrant. No wonder critics as illustrious as George Bernard Shaw have decided *The Shrew* is unfit for the stage. The events outlined above are doubtless objectionable to many modern readers and theatregoers. And yet *The Taming of the Shrew* continues to interest and absorb us.

CHECK THE FILM

The most recent reworking of the play is the 1999 Hollywood teen comedy *10 Things I Hate About You*, set in Padua High School.

Why does the play remain so stubbornly popular? Why have there been so many successful adaptations, including the Cole Porter musical *Kiss Me Kate*? The answer lies in the text's wit and exuberance. There are interludes of highly entertaining visual comedy. A modern audience often finds itself trapped in a curious position, rather like the heroine. While abhorring the sentiments of a drama that seems to advocate wife-taming as a prerequisite for a harmonious marriage, we find ourselves engaged by what is happening on stage. As well as being a rascal, Petruchio, the protagonist, is quick-witted, confident and funny: he is above all a wonderfully imaginative actor. His breathless wooing and wedding of the headstrong scold are theatrically compelling. And the minor characters are excellent comic foils, from Grumio, Petruchio's complaining manservant, to Tranio, the wily deceiver, who disguises himself in order to help his master Lucentio win the hand of fair Bianca. Added to the two fast-moving plots, which both focus on marriage, there is an entertaining and intriguing **Induction**, which frames the action of the play. This is the only induction in Shakespeare's drama, and it is a masterly example of the form, with another fine comic character in the shape of Christopher Sly, the Warwickshire tinker. The action in the Sly Induction foreshadows the events of both plot and subplot. The whole play is full of amusing intrigues and deceptions, and the wordplay is swift and hilarious. With the exception of Kate, the characters in *The Shrew* are having the time of their lives. And it is possible to argue that even Katherina learns that she will enjoy life more if she joins in with the game.

Shakespeare's tale of wife-taming was inspired by ballads, plays and folklore. It is part of a large body of literature dealing with the age-old war between the sexes, one of the stories most commonly reworked in every age. As such, it deserves attention. *The Taming of the Shrew* is also worth studying because it is an early comedy, and we see here some of the ideas that will preoccupy the dramatist in later works: the problematical relationships between parents and children and men and women, and the difficulty of negotiating appearances and reality. In *The Shrew* we see Shakespeare exploring the nature of romance and marriage, which he continued to do many times in subsequent plays. In particular, the playwright's evocation of the shrewish scold is intriguing, and troubling. This is his only drama in which a woman is severely punished for speaking her mind; later heroines are allowed to speak for and defend themselves. Kate is an interesting anomaly. By the time Shakespeare came to write *Much Ado About Nothing* (*c.*1598), the professed man-hater Beatrice is allowed to get away with a great many more jibes against the opposite sex, while still being presented as an attractive and desirable partner. The message of this play, that domestic harmony depends upon breaking a woman's spirit, or at least on marrying a quiet, obedient female, is not repeated elsewhere. Hero, the silent heroine in *Much Ado*, will suffer greatly;

> **CONTEXT**
>
> In his *Apology for Actors* (1612) the actor and playwright Thomas Heywood (c.1574–1641) defines comedy thus: 'In Comedies, *turbulenta prima, tranquilla ultima.*' Comedy, he says, begins with trouble, and ends in peace.

CHECK THE BOOK
To read about reactions to various twentieth-century productions of *The Shrew* and a discussion of how staging has changed, see Michael Mangan's *A Preface to Shakespeare's Comedies 1594–1603* (1996).

in this comedy, the seemingly submissive and modest Bianca reveals herself as a shrew. Perhaps, then, there are two messages to be taken from *The Shrew*: the second, that women will have their own way somehow, when it is least expected!

PART TWO

THE TEXT

NOTE ON THE TEXT

The history of the text we study and watch performed on stage today is complex, and its authorship has been the subject of dispute. Like Shakespeare's other plays, *The Taming of the Shrew* was not published during the playwright's lifetime. Another play, sometimes thought to be an imperfect reconstruction or early version of *The Shrew*, was published in 1594. *The Taming of a Shrew* shares the taming plot and romantic subplot with *The Shrew*, and Sly is present in both texts. The husbands' taming methods are similar, and occasionally there are verbal echoes of one text in the other play. Some have suggested that *A Shrew* should be regarded as a source for Shakespeare's drama. Other critics maintain Shakespeare's play came first. Shakespeare's sources are discussed in **Language and structure**.

The first version of *The Shrew* appeared in the First Folio, a collection of Shakespeare's plays published in 1623, seven years after the playwright's death. Modern editions of the text are based on this version, which is thought to have been taken from a manuscript, most likely a transcript or draft of Shakespeare's. It is difficult, however, to arrive at a date of composition or first performance for *The Shrew*. Some commentators argue that this early comedy is less sophisticated than *A Comedy of Errors* and must predate it (the date of this play is also contentious); others prefer to believe that *The Shrew* came later. The text's relationship to *A Shrew* adds to the difficulty. Brian Morris, editor of the Arden edition used in the preparation of these Notes – William Shakespeare, *The Taming of the Shrew*, ed., Brian Morris, The Arden Shakespeare, Methuen 1981 – argues that the play must have been written earlier than August 1592.

> **CONTEXT**
>
> Shakespeare does not seem to have taken any interest in editing or publishing his own plays. The playwright Ben Jonson (1572–1637) was the first writer to take responsibility for publishing his own plays, masques and poems: in 1616 his *Works* was published.

SYNOPSIS

CONTEXT

Critics have suggested that Shakespeare chose an Italian setting because of Italy's association with commercialism and the genre of classical romance.

Returning from hunting one day, a nobleman finds a drunkard, Christopher Sly, asleep outside a tavern in Warwickshire. He decides to play a trick on him, takes him into his house and has Sly dressed and treated as a lord. Sly is presented with a 'wife'. A group of actors arrive and the nobleman asks them to perform for the disguised tinker. The entertainment presented is a comedy about a rich Italian gentleman, Baptista Minola, and his daughters, Katherina and Bianca. Bianca, the younger daughter, has two suitors, Hortensio and Gremio, but Baptista refuses to allow her to marry until a husband has been found for her elder sister, Katherina, who is considered a bad-tempered shrew. Hortensio and Gremio agree that they will help to find a husband for Katherina and engage the services of tutors for Bianca to curry favour with her father. Meanwhile Lucentio, a well-born young man, arrives in Padua with his servant Tranio. He intends to pursue his education but falls in love with Bianca, disguising himself so that he can be engaged as her tutor, while Tranio takes on his identity. Petruchio, a friend of Hortensio, also arrives in Padua at this time. He is seeking a wealthy wife and agrees to court and marry Katherina. Hortensio assumes the disguise of a music teacher and is presented to Baptista in this role by Petruchio.

The courtship of Katherina is brief and rough, and Petruchio behaves very eccentrically at his wedding; the bride is carried off to her new home immediately after the ceremony. Here Petruchio sets about taming his wife. She is starved, kept awake and refused new clothes; essentially Katherina is tormented and deprived until she submits to her husband's will and acknowledges his right to rule her. Meanwhile, Baptista has promised Bianca to Tranio (whom he believes to be Lucentio). Tranio has persuaded a pedant to pretend to be his father so that a large dowry can be guaranteed; the aim is to outbid Gremio, who is still pursuing Bianca's hand in marriage. However, Lucentio's real father, Vincentio, arrives in Padua, and the real Lucentio has married Bianca secretly. Baptista and Vincentio are not amused, but are finally persuaded to accept their children's actions. Petruchio and Katherina have returned to Padua and at a wedding feast the success of the wife-taming is revealed publicly:

Katherina demonstrates that she is a more obedient and dutiful wife than either her sister or the wealthy widow whom Hortensio has married, neither of whom come when their husbands call for them.

DETAILED SUMMARIES

INDUCTION

SCENE 1

- Sly is thrown out of the inn.
- A nobleman decides to play an elaborate trick on him.

A tinker, Christopher Sly, is ejected from an alehouse by its Hostess and falls asleep in a drunken stupor on the ground, where he is found by a nobleman who has just returned from hunting. To amuse himself the Lord decides to play a trick on Sly, who will be carried off to his house, dressed magnificently and served delicious food. The intention is to see whether a 'monstrous beast' (line 32) can be persuaded to accept such a wild transformation in his circumstances as reality rather than a dream. The Lord adds further details to his plan; his huntsman is given elaborate instructions about the presentation of Sly's room and when he wakes up the tinker is to be told that he is a 'mighty lord' (line 63) who has been 'lunatic' (line 61) for fifteen years, to the chagrin of his wife and the rest of his household. When a troupe of strolling players arrive they are incorporated into the scheme. The actors are asked to perform for Sly (who, they are told, is an eccentric lord, given to odd behaviour). The Lord then sends a servant to his page, Bartholomew, who is to act out the role of Sly's wife. Bartholomew is to pretend to be overjoyed to see 'her' noble husband returned to health and sanity. The Lord intends that his own presence should serve to dampen any excessive merriment caused by what ensues.

COMMENTARY

This first scene of the **Induction** introduces a number of themes or issues that are mirrored in the taming plot. It is appropriate that the

CONTEXT

In 2003 the Globe Theatre, London, mounted an all-female version of *The Shrew*. At the end of the play Katherina and Petruchio could be seen arguing loudly after the final speech. It was clear that the shrew had not been tamed.

QUESTION

What is the dramatic importance of the Induction?

Lord has just returned from hunting; later we will learn that Petruchio, whom some critics see as a fortune-hunting rascal, comes 'to wive it wealthily in Padua; / If wealthily, then happily in Padua' (I.2.74–5). Having secured Kate he sets about taming her, as a lord might tame a falcon (see **Imagery**). Bianca's suitors might also be viewed as fortune-hunters, each seeking Baptista Minola's 'treasure' (II.1.32). The Lord's elaborate joke at Sly's expense foreshadows the taming plot too: can Petruchio bring about a radical change in his 'monstrous beast' (line 32), make her 'Conformable' (II.1.271)? We are introduced to ideas about role-playing; the Lord and his servants will adopt disguises in order to deceive Sly. Later, we watch as the male characters in both plot and subplot change their clothes and identities to pursue their aims. Layers of illusion become more complicated as the troupe of players arrive; the actors, who earn their living by deception, are themselves deceived by the Lord, who assures them that Sly is a nobleman. Here, the Induction is self-consciously theatrical, a point reinforced by the discussion of the role Bartholomew is to play: here we have a boy actor playing a male servant playing a lady. A **feminist** critic might assert that this self-conscious drawing of attention to the role of the boy actor suggests that women's roles and behaviour are constructed by the (male) playwright. Shakespeare deliberately uses his Induction to indicate that we are watching a topsy-turvy world. We might feel that it is implied that Katherina's shrewishness is part of the illusion; her 'unnatural' behaviour will be beaten out of her so that she becomes a more 'Conformable' woman and wife, just as Sly (and his 'wife') will be returned to their natural states when the Lord's whim is played out. It is also noticeable that Petruchio adopts outrageous clothes and eccentric behaviour in his 'taming-school' (IV.2.54) and uses them to impose his will on the Paduans, forcing them to accept his version of events. This is hinted at by Sly, who will be convinced that he is not dreaming when he wakes up. It is noticeable that the nobleman is to retain the upper hand, however; even when Sly is licensed to behave like a lord, the Lord will be on hand to 'abate the over-merry spleen / Which otherwise would grow into extremes' (lines 135–6). Do these lines hint at the control Petruchio is to exert?

The importance of social rank and identity is clearly highlighted in the Induction, and the role of language and its link to power is

---

CONTEXT

For several centuries, the Induction was cut from theatrical performances. It was only fully restored in a 1913 London production, in which Sly and his attendants remained on stage throughout as a surrogate audience.

---

suggested too. Sly's rank and identity are to be transformed and he is to be offered power: but only for a limited period and only as a joke. Note how Sly's language becomes transformed when he 'becomes' a lord; from the colloquial 'I'll feeze you, in faith' (line 1) to the more elevated and elegant courtly tone he adopts in the second scene of the Induction. This transformation will be mirrored in Katherina, who begins the play making what is characterised by the male Paduans as an infernal din, only to be silenced, before speaking with what many would argue is her husband's voice, in the final scene. Her famous final capitulation is perhaps an endorsement of male power and supremacy, just as the trick set up in the Induction is a lord's whim. The relationship between master and servant enacted in this scene hints at the resolution of the taming plot; for all the subversion that is implied by having Sly made lord for a day, we know he has no real power. The servants who wait on him are in fact serving their real lord, just as Petruchio's complaining servant Grumio serves his master, and Tranio acts the role of Lucentio to assist with his master's plans. (See also **Text 1** of **Extended commentaries**.)

www. CHECK THE NET
An easy starting point with comprehensive links and gateways is the web site of the Shakespeare Institute Library at **http://www.is. bham.ac.uk/ shakespeare/**

GLOSSARY	
1	feeze (dialect) beat, flog, drive off
4	Richard Conqueror in his ignorance, Sly mixes up William the Conqueror and Richard Lion Heart
5	*paucas pallabris* (Spanish) a mispronunciation of a Spanish phrase meaning 'few words'
	Sessa! be quiet!
7	denier small French coin
	Go by, Saint Jeronimy a misquotation from a popular revenge tragedy by Thomas Kyd (1558–94), *The Spanish Tragedy* (published in 1592). The hero of this play is Hieronimo (Jeronimo)
9	third-borough constable
14	tender look after
15	emboss'd foaming at the mouth through exhaustion
16	brach bitch
37	banquet dessert
38	brave dressed in fine clothes
	continued

55	diaper towel
99	the veriest antic a most eccentric person
100	buttery room where liquid refreshments were kept and served

SCENE 2

- Sly is duped into believing he is a lord.
- He settles down to watch the play that has been provided to entertain him.

When he wakes up Sly initially refuses to accept that he is a lord and calls for a pot of ale. He is gradually persuaded to accept that he is a nobleman when he is told of his wealth, possessions and beautiful wife. He is asked whether he wishes to hear some music, or would he prefer to go hunting or hawking? Bartholomew the page enters in disguise and announces that he is Sly's 'wife in all obedience' (line 108). Sly immediately suggests they go to bed, but his 'wife' informs him that doctors have decreed that this would 'incur your former malady' (line 123). A messenger says the same doctors have suggested that an entertainment would be a suitable way to drive away the melancholy that Sly's illness might have caused. Sly agrees to watch the play and calls on his 'wife' to sit by his side.

CHECK THE BOOK

Graham Holderness suggests Bartholomew is a 'wish-fulfilment fantasy of female subordination'. To read this critic's comments in full, see 'Text and Performance: *The Taming of the Shrew*' in *Shakespeare in Performance* (2000).

COMMENTARY

The action continues with the deception outlined in the previous scene. When Bartholomew declares that he is the drunkard's obedient wife we are offered a glimpse of what Katherina will become. Or are we? Is Shakespeare suggesting that the obedient wife is a fiction, just as Bartholomew the wife and Sly the Lord are impostors? We are reminded that we are watching an illusion when the actors take their places on the stage to entertain Sly.

The critic Stevie Davies makes some interesting comments about the classical references made in this scene, when Sly's 'possessions' are described to him, particularly the artworks. She notes that the pictures all depict scenes of transformation and sexual violence, and links these pictures to the relationship between hunting and 'the sexual chase' (see **Critical history**, on **Current approaches**). These ideas can clearly be linked to what is to happen in the play the troupe are to perform. It is noticeable that Sly is prevented from taking his 'wife' to bed: Petruchio will refuse to consummate his marriage until Katherina has conformed and capitulated.

CHECK THE BOOK

If you wish to see a range of images from film and TV productions of *The Shrew*, and discussions of these productions, have a look at *Shakespeare on Screen* (2000) by Daniel Rosenthal.

GLOSSARY		
1	small ale	cheapest weak beer
2	sack	white Spanish wine
3	conserves	candies or sweetened fruit
19	cardmaker	a person who made combs for spinning wool
20	bear-herd	the person who had charge of the performing bear
21–2	Hacket … Wincot	place names in Warwickshire
23	sheer ale	strong beer
36	Apollo	the Greek god of music
40	Semiramis	an Assyrian goddess, a legendary oriental beauty
42	trapp'd	decorated with ornaments
46	welkin	a poetical term for the sky
51–61	Adonis painted … tears are drawn	the tales behind the artworks described in this scene can be found in Ovid's poetry. Adonis was a young huntsman, who was loved by Venus. He preferred hunting to love. In the main plot, Petruchio will prove, perhaps, that it is possible to be a successful hunter and lover when Kate speaks with his voice in Act V
55	Io	a priestess loved by Jupiter, whom he changed into a heifer
58	Daphne	a nymph pursued by Apollo, who was turned into a laurel by the gods
88	present her at the leet	charge her at the assizes (manorial court)

continued

QUESTION

Many directors cut the **Induction** when the play is staged. What is lost if it is not included?

89	**stone jugs and no seal'd quarts** sealed quarts were stamped with an official seal; stone jugs were different sizes and held different amounts
106	**goodman** a peasant term for husband
137	**comonty** a mispronunciation of comedy
138	**gambol** dance
	tumbling-trick example of bawdy innuendo; Sly is eager to take his 'wife' to bed

ACT I

SCENE 1

- Baptista Minola refuses to allow his younger daughter, Bianca, to marry until a husband is found for her elder sister, Katherina.
- Lucentio falls in love with Bianca and changes clothes with his servant, Tranio.

CONTEXT

In Tudor society, clothes showed differences in rank, which people considered natural, and there were rules about the cloth or colours a person could wear. Critics have suggested that the theatre was subversive, since characters often changed clothes and adopted disguises associated with different ranks.

Lucentio, the son of Vincentio, a wealthy gentleman of Pisa, has come to Padua to continue his education. He is accompanied by his resourceful servant Tranio, who advises him not to take his studies too seriously: he should enjoy music and poetry as well as philosophy. While Lucentio is wondering what has happened to his other servant, Biondello, Baptista Minola appears with his two daughters, Katherina and Bianca, and Bianca's two suitors, Gremio and Hortensio. Lucentio and Tranio overhear their conversation. Baptista will not allow Gremio or Hortensio to court Bianca until a husband has been found for her elder sister, Katherina. Katherina has a reputation as a bad-tempered scold, who is 'too rough' (line 55) to attract a husband. Gremio and Hortensio clearly find her alarming, and suggest that she is unmarriageable, but Baptista is firm in his resolve. He announces that he is looking for tutors for Bianca. When he leaves the stage with his daughters, Gremio and Hortensio agree to put aside their rivalry while they attempt to find a suitor for Katherina.

After they have left, Lucentio declares that he has fallen in love with Bianca. Tranio reminds him that a husband must first be found for her 'curst and shrewd' sister (line 180). Master and servant arrive at a solution simultaneously: Lucentio should disguise himself as a schoolmaster so that he can gain admittance to Baptista's house. Meanwhile Tranio will pretend to be Lucentio. They exchange clothes. When Biondello arrives, he is perplexed by the role-reversal that has taken place, but is persuaded to accept that he should now treat Tranio as his master.

A servant asks Sly whether he finds the play entertaining; he replies that it pleases him but he hopes that it will soon be over (he wants to go to bed with his 'wife').

COMMENTARY

Katherina may have a reputation as a scold, but she says very little to merit the opprobrium she attracts; in this scene she speaks only twelve lines. Her detractors say far more, suggesting the male characters have the power to define the female, as the Lord had the power to give Sly a new identity in the **Induction**. However, Kate's few lines give a clear indication that she is not the Elizabethan ideal of the silent woman. Her opening speech and retort to Hortensio suggest that she is impatient and spirited. Is Katherina also contemptuous of men? Certainly, she dislikes her social position: she is the unwanted elder daughter, whose younger sister is desirable. This is degrading and Kate does not like to be publicly humiliated, as her querulous tone indicates. It seems clear that Baptista favours his quiet, apparently obedient child, who pleases him by 'humbly' subscribing to his 'pleasure', making no demands and taking herself off to study her 'books and instruments' (lines 81–2). Note the possessive pronoun 'my' Baptista adopts when addressing Bianca; he barely acknowledges Katherina, either speaking as if she were not there, or instructing her to stay outside when he leaves. By way of contrast to her sister, Kate asks questions and demands answers, which she does not get. When she leaves (line 104), it is already plain that her voice is ignored. Her father prefers to 'commune' with Bianca (line 101), suggesting that Kate is not a valued member of the family unit; quite the reverse: she is a troublesome outsider and a thorn in her father's flesh.

> **CONTEXT**
>
> The actress Fiona Shaw, who played Kate for the Royal Shakespeare Company in the 1980s, has commented: 'Along comes a man to tame the noisy one. And for almost five acts we never hear her speak.' To read Shaw's comments in full, see *Clamorous Voices: Shakespeare's Women Today* (1988), by Carol Rutter.

CHECK THE FILM

In the 1980 BBC production of the play, directed by Jonathan Miller, Katherina is genuinely upset when she describes leading apes into hell. She screams and cries and throws an apple at her father as she leaves the set.

QUESTION

Compare and contrast the Minola sisters.

CHECK THE FILM

In the 1999 Hollywood film *10 Things I Hate About You*, Kat (Katherina) is a teenage feminist who likes reading Sylvia Plath's poetry. She is scornful of boys. Pat (Petruchio) is the local bad boy, who is bribed by friends to take Kat to the prom so that her sister is allowed to date.

Gremio seems to sum up the masculine view of Kate when he says it would be a mercy to find someone who would 'thoroughly woo her, wed her, and bed her, and rid the house of her' (lines 144–5). The phrasing here ironically foreshadows Petruchio's brutal, breathless wooing and clearly indicates Kate is a nuisance the men need to be 'rid' of (Tranio's words at line 181 reinforce this idea). The language suggests that in Gremio's – and the other men's – eyes, Kate is barely human. The male characters view Katherina as a threat as well as a nuisance. They are scared of her. She is described as 'too rough' (line 55), 'stark mad or wonderful froward' (line 69), given to 'loud alarums' (line 127). More significantly, she is compared to the devil. This link between the shrewish scold and the devil was frequently made in Elizabethan folklore (see **Imagery**).

In contrast, the language used to describe Bianca suggests that she conforms to the Renaissance ideal of womanhood; she is silent, 'good', 'Sweet', 'this young modest girl' (lines 76, 139, 156). The lovestruck Lucentio compares her to classical beauties, and says that, like a courtly lover, he will 'burn ... pine ... perish' if he does not 'achieve' her (lines 155–6). No wonder her father is interested in *her* education; *this* daughter is indeed a prize, worth improving so that he can barter her successfully on the marriage market.

In spite of Lucentio's musings, marriage is firmly linked to money in this scene, most explicitly when Gremio ponders the likelihood of finding a mate for Katherina: 'Thinkest thou, Hortensio, though her father be very rich, any man is so very a fool to be married to hell?' (lines 123–5). These lines hint at events to come and set up a sense of anticipation. Having seen Katherina for ourselves, and heard her described as 'hell', we wonder what sort of specimen the man who takes her on will be. It is also abundantly clear that marriage is a financial game played by *men*, who jostle for position; at the moment the father holds all the cards because he has something Bianca's suitors want and a bargain must be struck before they will have a chance to court the 'treasure' (II.1.32). Baptista is wily; Gremio and Hortensio have not only agreed to try to find a husband for Katherina (saving her father the trouble); they will also be footing the bill for Bianca's education. We might see this as a fair financial exchange. It is recognised that Baptista is going to have to provide a large dowry to rid himself of Katherina, so it seems fair that the suitors should contribute to the adornment and improvement of the prize they seek. Lucentio's lovestruck musings are undermined by Tranio's pragmatism: 'I pray, awake, sir. If you love the maid, / Bend thoughts and wits to achieve her' (lines 178–9). Like Hortensio and Gremio, Tranio recognises that one has to *work* for a prize. It might be argued that this is exactly why Petruchio succeeds in his 'taming-school': he outwits Katherina (and the Paduans). At the end of the scene plot and subplot are interwoven and deception is the order of the day as Tranio and Lucentio exchange clothes. Key dramatic ideas – the importance of role-reversal and transformation, and the deceptiveness of appearances – are established here. All the male characters are focused on Bianca, but, ironically, they must consider the fate of her irksome sister first. This early comedy has started with unromantic subterfuge and bargaining, as it will proceed.

GLOSSARY

2	Padua an Italian university town; the university was established there in 1228
23	plash a puddle or pool
25	*Mi perdonato* (Italian) pardon me
31	stoics those who dislike and shun pleasure, taken from the Greek philosophers, the Stoics, who preached the endurance of suffering
33	Ovid the Roman poet of amorous poems used during the wooing of Bianca
34	Balk use in conversation
34–8	logic ... stomach serves you Tranio outlines the typical academic curriculum studied by the gentleman of the time: rhetoric (the art of argument), mathematics, poetry and metaphysics
38	stomach desire or inclination
41	Gramercies thanks
50	bestow find a husband for
56	cart her prostitutes were carried through the streets on a cart

continued

CONTEXT

The stage directions at line 47 reveal Shakespeare's *commedia dell'arte* sources. A '*pantaloon*' is a stock character, a silly old man who lusts after and seeks marriage with a younger woman.

CHECK THE NET

An excellent general web site about Shakespeare is 'Mr. William Shakespeare and the Internet' at **http://shakespeare. palomar.edu**

58	**stale** prostitute or laughing stock
64	**comb your noddle** hit your head
69	**froward** perverse (note how frequently you come across this word in the play); the implication is that froward women are unnatural
78	**peat** pet or favourite child (a term of contempt)
84	**Minerva** the Roman goddess of wisdom; an ironic allusion. Bianca is wise, but not in the way Lucentio expects her to be; she knows the value of silence
87	**mew her up** a hawking term meaning to cage
97	**Prefer** recommend
	cunning clever
108–9	**Our cake's dough on both sides** (proverbial) we will both fail
115	**parle** negotiate a truce
127	**alarums** trumpets, signalling the start of battle; the war **imagery** helps us understand how nervous Kate makes the men; ironically, her final speech of submission also includes imagery of war
154	**Anna** the sister and confidante of Dido, Queen of Carthage. She killed herself after suffering unrequited love for Aeneas. The story can be found in Virgil's *Aeneid*
162	*Redime ... minimo* (Latin) 'get yourself out of captivity as cheaply as possible', from the Roman comedy *The Eunuch* by Plautus
168	**the daughter of Agenor** Europa was the daughter of the King of Phoenicia. Jove, disguised as a bull, fell in love with her and carried her off to Crete. From Ovid
180	**shrewd** hard to rule or control; another word that is repeated many times
198	*Basta* (Italian) enough
207	**Uncase thee** take off your cloak
247	*The Presenters above* those introducing the play were standing above the stage
249	**Saint Anne** the mother of Saint Mary

SCENE 2

- Petruchio arrives in Padua.
- He agrees to court Katherina.

CHECK THE FILM

Pat in *10 Things I Hate About You* (1999) has the same sort of dangerous reputation Petruchio constructs for himself here. He flouts school rules, and is rumoured to have eaten a live duck and spent time in prison.

A second visitor, Petruchio, arrives in Padua with his servant Grumio. He has come to visit Hortensio, and is looking for a wealthy woman to marry. Hortensio tells him about Katherina, warning his friend that she is 'shrewd' and 'ill-favour'd' (line 59). Petruchio refuses to be put off by her reputation as 'an irksome brawling scold' (line 186) and wishes to be introduced to Katherina's father without delay. Hortensio explains that he is in love with Bianca. Like Lucentio, he decides to adopt a disguise in order to gain admittance to his beloved's house and asks Petruchio to present him to Baptista as a music tutor.

QUESTION

Examine the dramatic importance of Hortensio and Gremio.

Gremio arrives with the disguised Lucentio, whom he has engaged as a schoolmaster. He expects the young man – 'Cambio' – to plead his cause with Bianca. Hortensio lies to his rival, telling him that he too has found a tutor for 'our mistress' (line 172). Gremio is astonished when he hears that Petruchio is prepared to court and marry the 'wildcat' Katherina (line 195) but agrees to 'bear his charge of wooing' (line 214) with Hortensio. At this point the disguised Tranio appears, announcing that he is another suitor for Bianca's hand. He too says he will 'gratify' Petruchio (line 271), who, it seems, is to be handsomely rewarded for wooing the scold.

COMMENTARY

Themes and ideas established in the previous scene are further developed here. The introduction of Petruchio and the discussion of financial arrangements that accompanies the talk of wooing Katherina extend our understanding of the marriage market. Another disguise is planned, and Lucentio and Tranio continue with their deception. The opening altercation between Grumio and Petruchio hints at the latter's potential for violence. This quick-fire exchange also foreshadows the wooing of Katherina. We are immediately aware that Petruchio is interested in money; he has 'come abroad' (line 57) to seek his fortune and is breezily unconcerned about the character of his wife-to-be: so long as she is rich he will be satisfied. All his speeches in this scene are confident and direct and many include references to wealth. His brazen self-assurance is summed up by two lines: 'I know she is an irksome brawling scold. / If that be all, masters, I hear no harm' (lines 186–7). Petruchio appears to be a man of action; he restlessly says that he 'will not sleep' (line 102) until he sees Katherina, suggesting he wants to get on with the business of wooing the wildcat as swiftly as possible. Later he adds to the impression of masculine valour he is constructing when he outlines his previous life experiences in a wonderfully energetic speech (lines 197–209). It is clear that, unlike the Paduans, Petruchio is not scared of a woman's tongue. Grumio further enlightens us about his master's character, assuring Hortensio that 'scolding would do little good upon him' because 'he begin once, he'll rail in his rope-tricks' (lines 108–11). These lines are a clear indication that Petruchio will be more of a shrew than Katherina; she has met her match: a man as determined as she is, who has a reputation for powerful talking. And as in the previous scene, there is little romance (none at all in Petruchio's lines). When he speaks disparagingly of Katherina's shrewish tongue he belittles the female voice: later we will watch as Petruchio makes women's words meaningless. By the end of this scene the 'hero' is already speaking of Katherina as part of his goods and chattels, as he will on the wedding day. He warns Tranio off with these words: 'Sir, sir, the first's for me, let her go by' (line 254). Petruchio has made his decision and, with the force of will he displays in his first scene, he will carry all before him.

CONTEXT

Gremio's allusion to the twelve labours of 'great Hercules' at lines 255–6 suggests the taming of Kate will be an arduous business. Hercules carried a huge club and was renowned for his strength. Is this classical reference comic exaggeration, or a hint that Petruchio is a violent man?

GLOSSARY

7	**rebused** like Sly, Grumio mispronounces words. He means abused
17	**solfa** the notes on the scale
24	*Con tutto ... trovato* (Italian) with all my heart
25–6	*Alla nostra ... Petrucio* welcome to our house, most honoured Petruchio
27	*compound* settle
28	**in Latin** Grumio's Englishness is comic here; he can't tell Latin from Italian

32–3	**two and thirty, a pip out** the winning score in a card game like cribbage; here it means he is beyond himself
68	**foul** ugly
	Florentius' love Florentius appears in John Gower's *Confessio Amantis*. He was forced to marry a hag, but she was transformed into a beautiful woman; Chaucer uses this story in *The Wife of Bath's Tale*. This reference hints at the outcome of the play
69	**Sibyl** Greek prophetess
70	**Xanthippe** the wife of the Greek philosopher Socrates, a renowned scold
72–3	**as rough … seas** there are a number of sea **images** in Petruchio's speeches; appropriate since he is to behave rather like a pirate ('board her' later on in this scene, line 94, is a naval term for an attack on a sea vessel)
78	**aglet-baby** doll
	trot hag
104	**give you over** leave your company
111	**rope-tricks** meaning unclear: possibly rhetoric, the subject Lucentio has supposedly come to learn in Padua. Petruchio proves to be more interested in practice than theory
142	**A proper … amorous** an **ironic** comment from Grumio; like his master he is describing things as the opposite of what they are
159	**woodcock** a bird that was easy to catch, therefore a byword for stupidity
202	**ordnance** artillery
208	**a chestnut in a farmer's fire** chestnuts explode when roasted. Young lovers used chestnuts to find out how their love would turn out; if the nuts exploded in the fire it meant that there was quarrelling ahead
209	**bugs** bogeys or bugbears, hobgoblins used to frighten children
242	**Leda's daughter** Helen of Troy, who married Menelaus, King of Sparta. When she ran away with Paris, son of the King of Troy, she caused the Trojan Wars
247	**jade** an inferior, worn-out horse
255–6	**labour … Alcides' twelve** a reference to the twelve labours of Hercules (Alcides), who had extraordinary strength

continued

 CHECK THE FILM

In both the 1967 film version by Franco Zeffirelli and the 1980 BBC production by Jonathan Miller, Petruchio is very clearly a fortune-hunter. He only begins to pay close attention to Hortensio's early descriptions of Kate when he hears the word 'rich'.

CONTEXT

The pun on Kate's name at lines 113–14 ('no more eyes … cat') is one of many. This pun has undertones of violence, since the cat-o'-nine-tails was a whip used to tame shrewish wives.

271	gratify pay or reward
275	quaff carouses drink toasts
280	*ben venuto* (Italian) host, literally, 'welcome'

ACT II

SCENE 1

- Petruchio 'woos' and 'wins' Katherina.

The scene moves to Baptista's house, where Katherina is tormenting her sister. She has tied Bianca's hands and taunts her, demanding to know which of her suitors she likes best. Baptista releases his younger daughter and tells her to go inside. Katherina storms off, vowing revenge, and angry with her father because he appears to favour Bianca; she is also concerned about being humiliated if her younger sister is allowed to marry first. Bianca's suitors arrive, accompanied by Petruchio, who immediately requests permission to court the 'fair and virtuous' Katherina (line 43). The tutors are introduced: Hortensio is 'Litio'; Lucentio, 'Cambio'. Baptista sends them in to his daughters and continues his discussion with Petruchio, who makes enquiries about Katherina's dowry and assures his potential father-in-law that his future wife will be well provided for should he die. Baptista reminds Petruchio that he must win his daughter's love, and advises him that he should be 'arm'd for some unhappy words' (line 139) when he meets Kate. Petruchio refuses to be perturbed by yet another warning. With exquisite timing, Hortensio reappears, '*with his head broke*' (after line 141); Katherina has beaten him with his lute. Baptista goes in to fetch his elder daughter and Petruchio declares his intention to 'woo her with some spirit when she comes' (line 169).

The wooing is indeed rough; the pair of 'lovers' argue in (sexual) puns, with Petruchio insisting firmly that he is the man 'born to

CHECK THE FILM
In the 1980 BBC production Baptista is worn out by Kate. He appears depressed when Hortensio and Petruchio arrive, and does not seem overly hopeful about the new arrival's wooing prospects. He shakes hands with him to wish Petruchio luck.

tame' Kate (line 269). When Katherina strikes him, Petruchio restrains her physically; a visual **symbol** of his intentions. Baptista enters with Gremio and Tranio. Petruchio announces boldly that he has won Kate, while the latter castigates her father for permitting 'one half lunatic' to court her (line 280). Baptista allows himself to be convinced that Petruchio speaks the truth in spite of his daughter's obvious outrage and agrees that the wedding should take place the following Sunday. He then barters with Bianca's two suitors. Tranio outbids Gremio but is expected to provide a guarantee of the dowry he has offered. Alone on stage, Tranio – resourceful as ever – sees that he must set about finding 'a father, call'd suppos'd Vincentio' to back up the promises he has made (line 401).

COMMENTARY

The first part of the scene shows Katherina at her worst. Her violent behaviour is meant to be understood as a sign of her shrewish nature. Critics have made much of her abuse of Bianca, with some suggesting that the heroine's interest in her sister's suitors shows a subconscious desire to be married herself. Certainly Kate is concerned that she will be publicly humiliated, shown by her words to her father: 'she must have a husband, / I must dance barefoot on her wedding-day, / And for your love to her lead apes in hell' (lines 32–4). These lines are an allusion to the idea that unmarried women were said to lead apes into hell because they had no children. The opening exchanges in Act II Scene 1 suggest sibling rivalry, as well as parental favouritism, which was established earlier. Although we will not view Katherina favourably, it is hard not to feel some sympathy for her. Bianca's 'So well I know my duty to my elders' (line 7) can seem smug and sanctimonious, and her father's crude description of his eldest daughter, delivered to Kate's face – 'thou hilding of a devilish spirit' (line 26) – is unkind. We can understand Kate's desire to 'find occasion of revenge' (line 36). It is **ironic** that Kate draws attention to her sister's silence; it 'flouts' (line 29) Katherina here, but it is Bianca's speech and unexpected disobedience that will vex her husband in the final moments of the play.

Kate's sulky, stormy behaviour and physical abuse of Bianca prepare us for the encounter she is to have with Petruchio later in the scene, as does her abuse of Hortensio. Baptista's weary rhetorical question

QUESTION

Consider the Minola family. To what extent do her relationships with her father and sister explain Katherina's behaviour?

**CHECK
THE NET**
For a comprehensive
film database listing
Shakespeare
cinematic
adaptations, search
the Internet Movie
Database at **http://
www.imdb.com**

at line 37 also helps to prepare us for Petruchio's entrance. The new
arrival's appearance will prove to be an antidote to his grief. The
incongruity between what we have just seen of Katherina and
Petruchio's opening remark, 'Pray, have you not a daughter / Call'd
Katherina, fair and virtuous?' (lines 42–3) signals Shakespeare's
comic intentions for the wooing, as does Baptista's blunt response,
'I have a daughter, sir, call'd Katherina' (line 44). We see the first
glimpse of Petruchio's taming methods here. Throughout the
wooing and wedding, he will doggedly assert that Kate is mild
and meek, the opposite of what she appears to be. There are
different ways of interpreting Petruchio's absurd construction of
'Conformable' Katherina (line 271). Is he presenting the heroine
with a model of behaviour that she must follow in order to take her
place by his side in society? Is he seeking to liberate or dominate?
Or is this simply an example of a highly skilled actor taking on a
role? Perhaps we are to begin to see the fortune-hunter as a teacher
at this point; he brings the disguised Hortensio to assist in the
education of his bride-to-be. Note the difference between the polite
and formal way in which the men all greet one another, and the
boisterous and far from polite banter that Petruchio engages in with
Katherina.

Whatever disquiet a modern audience might feel about the idea of a
man taming and changing a woman, we are certainly supposed to
laugh at Petruchio's elaborate, polite descriptions of Katherina's
virtues, which are at odds with the businesslike tone the hero adopts
after 'Cambio' and 'Litio' have been sent indoors. From this point
onwards it is impossible to avoid the conclusion that female
education is intended to improve a woman's prospects on the
marriage market. In all the talk of dowries and estates, and
Petruchio's abrupt declaration that he cannot come to woo every
day, there is no hint of romance. Only Baptista's feeble insistence
that Petruchio must obtain his daughter's love suggests that
marriage is more than a business transaction, and we are unlikely to
be convinced by the father's late, brief concern for his daughter's
feelings. Quite the contrary: we will recognise that, as Petruchio
says, commenting on the likelihood of his engaging Kate's
affections, 'that is nothing' (line 130). Significantly, Petruchio then
launches into a description of his 'peremptory' qualities (line 131),

drawing attention to the fact that she *will* yield to him. The stage is set for the battle of the sexes, which is even more eagerly anticipated when Hortensio enters '*with his head broke*'.

Is Petruchio looking forward to meeting Katherina? It is possible to interpret his statements at line 160 as conveying genuine eagerness to meet a 'lusty wench'. But it is equally possible to feel that Shakespeare is simply aiming for laughs; perhaps this is yet another droll remark at Katherina's expense, intended to provoke mirth, and not a sign that the hero secretly wants a strong-minded female companion (the rest of the play suggests that this is exactly what Petruchio *doesn't* want). If we wish to see this line as part of Petruchio's character development, then I suggest we should read these words as an indication that the hero eagerly anticipates taming his bride-to-be; he knows he will enjoy asserting himself in a rough wooing. His **soliloquy** suggests a bright confidence about his prospects, as we are further informed about the methods Petruchio will use to 'woo her with some spirit' (line 169). The final line can be read as a definite indication of a strong will: Petruchio expects his words to prevail and when he speaks Katherina will listen and submit. He knows there will be a tussle, but he will emerge victorious. This soliloquy adds to the anticipation the audience will be feeling about observing the first meeting of the two protagonists. Note the repeated references to speaking in this soliloquy, hinting that Petruchio will 'out talk' Kate: 'say' appears five times, and there are eight other verbs describing speaking.

The wooing scene is undoubtedly intended to be comic, as the playful and witty repetition of Katherina's name suggests, although one critic, J. D. Huston, has described it as 'nothing less than psychological rape'. Petruchio's familiar and repeated use (and some would say abuse) of Katherina's name also confirms his authority: he has the power to define his chosen bride. By referring to her as 'my super-dainty Kate' (line 188) Petruchio demonstrates his right to possess her. The food **imagery** objectifies Katherina as a morsel to be eaten for his enjoyment. Throughout the rest of the scene there are many other lines that demonstrate the male's physical, mental and verbal authority and superiority. Immediately prior to her father's reappearance we see where the toying with Kate's name

CHECK THE FILM

Petruchio is eager to see Katherina in the 1980 BBC production. He moves restlessly to a doorway, hoping to get a glimpse of her when he hears her shouting off stage in Act II Scene 1. He repeats this movement later in the scene.

CHECK THE FILM

In Franco Zeffirelli's 1967 film the 'wooing' scene is a highly physical encounter. It includes a rooftop chase, several blows, and ends with the couple falling into bales of wool in a barn. Petruchio then locks Kate in a room so that he can report his 'triumph' unmolested.

will lead: she is to be brought 'from a wild Kate to a Kate /
Conformable as other household Kates' (lines 270–1). The
impersonality of these two lines suits Petruchio's project: he wants
a wealthy bride, and is confident that he can make the Kate he has
chosen conform with his standards for a wife. The fact that
Katherina has come off worse in the exchanges that precede this
firm declaration of what will be suggests that the shrew is going to
be tamed. Petruchio remains resolute and businesslike: 'setting all
this chat aside' he says as he moves on to 'plain terms': 'your father
hath consented / That you shall be my wife; your dowry 'greed on;
/ And will you, nill you, I will marry you' (lines 261–4). The force
and assurance of the modal verbs and the 'nill you' demonstrate the
bridegroom's determination to have things his way. It is interesting,
however, that Shakespeare then adds this line for Petruchio, 'I am
a husband for your turn' (line 265). Is there a suggestion that we
should see these two as a good match? This is perhaps the only hint
that Kate might have some needs. However, the phrase 'Thou must
be married to no man but me' (line 268) reinforces the male's power:
he marries; she is to be married. Kate is the passive victim. Her
passivity is demonstrated forcefully when her father returns and she
is rendered silent, no doubt outraged by the enormous presumption
of Petruchio.

Not that Katherina doesn't attempt to assert her own point of view:
she speaks with spirit and contempt, as we would expect. She is
almost as quick-witted as her combatant and **puns** with the same
alacrity that Petruchio demonstrates. But we know that she has lost
when she strikes him and he retorts, 'I swear I'll cuff you, if you
strike again' (line 218). As in her exchange with Bianca, Katherina's
physical violence is ultimately a sign of impotence. She may
defiantly declare, 'I care not' (line 233), but she is forced to stay
and listen when she would rather leave (see line 235). In spite of his
conventional praise of her virtues and beauty, Petruchio's behaviour
is aggressive and not lover-like (in a courtly sense) or gentlemanly.
Indeed, it is possible to read this 'praise' as ridicule. The
descriptions of Kate suggest she does not conform to Elizabethan
ideals of physical attractiveness; she is not fair-skinned or light
haired. Instead, she seems to resemble a country-bumpkin with her
brown-tanned skin. Petruchio's initiation of the sexual punning that

**CHECK
THE FILM**

In the 1980 BBC
production
Petruchio's voice
becomes more
intimate and
sensual when
he describes
Katherina's
appearance. He
means it when he
says he finds her
attractive.

occurs between lines 200–26 clearly demonstrates the male's sexual and physical superiority, and a very conventional view of women's roles. Women are 'made to bear'. The conclusion of this line – 'and so are you' – is a warning: Katherina will be forced to conform (line 200). Altogether, it is impossible to imagine a less romantic wooing than the meeting of Petruchio and Katherina. He threatens, mocks and talks down his 'lover' in bawdy and assertive language, refusing to admit her voice at all. We see that Petruchio has the power to assert his own view of reality, which he can persuade others to accept. In spite of the fact that there is no proof that his daughter looks favourably on her perverse suitor, Baptista agrees to the wooer's terms. Petruchio's reputation as a powerful talker is well deserved.

GLOSSARY

13	**Minion** spoilt favourite (from French 'mignon')
26	**hilding** baggage, jade
29	**flouts** challenges
54	**entrance to my entertainment** this is a theatrical **metaphor** Petruchio brings in the disguised Hortensio as his 'entrance fee'
73	**Baccare** (corrupt Latin) stand or get back
80	**Rheims** a university was founded here in the sixteenth century
126	**specialties** specific contracts
127	**covenants** promises
147	**break her to the lute** teach her to play the lute; to break an animal (e.g. a wild horse) is to tame it
156	**pillory** a punishment; stocks for the head and wrists
180	**banns** announcement of marriage, read in church
189	**dainties are all Kates** a **pun** on Kate's name: Kate/cake
197	**movable** a piece of furniture
200	**Women are made to bear** to bear children; women's roles are sharply defined in this play
204	**swain** a rustic fool
206	**Should ... buzz!** another example of wordplay; be/bee, buss/buzz – to kiss
	buzzard this word has two meanings: an idiot or a bird of prey

continued

CONTEXT
The name Cambio, appropriately, means exchange.

208	turtle a turtle dove (**symbol** of love); also easy prey for a buzzard
216	tongue in your tail Petruchio is being deliberately obscene with this reference to cunnilingus
223	coxcomb fool (a coxcomb was associated with the court jester)
225	craven a cock that refused to fight (a coward)
227	crab crab apple, sour tasting – sour person
252	Dian Diana was the Greek goddess of hunting and chastity
257	extempore impromptu or spontaneous
265	for your turn to suit you
271	Conformable passive and obedient
	household Kates still punning on Kate's name: domestic cats. Note the extensive use of animal **imagery** in this scene (see **Themes** and **Imagery**)
277	dumps low spirits
288	Grissel patient Griselda, a byword for female obedience (see Chaucer's *A Clerk's Tale*)
289	Lucrece Lucrece killed herself after the tyrannical king of Rome, Tarquin, raped her; see Shakespeare's *The Rape of Lucrece* (1594)
306	meacock timid or effeminate
332	Skipper a halfwit or a youngster
340	plate silver
341	lave wash
342	Tyrian costly purple cloth; the dye was made at Tyre
344	arras counterpoints counterpanes or bedspreads from Arras in northern France
346	boss'd decorated
350	milch-kine dairy cows
362	ducats common currency in Europe, first issued by the Duke of Apulia
363	jointure settlement
367	argosy merchant ship
371–2	galliasses … galleys types of ships
378	outvied appropriately this is a gambling term, meaning outbid

CHECK THE FILM

Throughout the wooing scene, Petruchio makes clucking noises to belittle Katherina in the 1980 BBC production. Initially they are made in response to her line 'no cock of mine' (line 225). At home in Act IV, Petruchio continues clucking like a chicken when he wants to warn Kate, or put her in her place.

383	cavil unimportant quibble or objection
398	fac'd it with a card of ten another gambling **metaphor**, from card-playing; the implication is that one of the players is bluffing
400	suppos'd Lucentio a direct reference to the source play *I Suppositi* (see **Structure**)

ACT III

SCENE 1

- 'Cambio' and 'Litio' woo Bianca.

Meanwhile, the disguised suitors have been attempting to woo Bianca, who refuses to be treated like a schoolchild by the two rivals; she decides which of her tutors should be allowed to give the first lesson. 'Litio' loses out to 'Cambio'. Ostensibly translating Ovid, Lucentio reveals his true identity and is offered some hope by Bianca, who rejects Hortensio when he offers her instruction in music. When Bianca is called away to help with the preparations for her sister's wedding, Hortensio declares that he is suspicious of 'Cambio' and adds that he will look elsewhere for a wife if his beloved is prepared to cast her 'wandering eyes on every stale' (line 88).

QUESTION

What is the dramatic significance of this scene in which 'Litio' and 'Cambio' woo Bianca?

COMMENTARY

The wooing of Bianca is in sharp contrast to the wooing of Katherina. Here the men do not really have the upper hand, although they work hard to exert themselves. In spite of the fact that she is idealised by her suitors as a perfect, modest maiden, there are clear signs that Bianca possesses a strong will. Her first two lines suggest that she will make her own decisions: 'Why, gentlemen, you do me double wrong / To strive for that which resteth in my choice' (lines 16–17). It can be argued that the command she shows in this scene – deciding whom to listen to and how much she will hear and 'learn' – mirrors the control Petruchio exerted over her sister. It is thus **ironic** that Lucentio and Hortensio should try to woo Bianca with typical courtly methods: music and poetry. We have begun to suspect that the goddess they see is not the real Bianca. This scene presents us with another example of the deceptiveness of appearances and it is ironic that the disguised wooers fail to look beyond Bianca's pleasing exterior. Their romantic approach is undermined by the suitors themselves, who squabble like schoolboys over who should 'teach' 'The patroness of heavenly harmony' (line 5).

A more prosaic reality breaks through in other ways. Bianca is shrewdly cautious about Lucentio's intentions, as indicated by line 49: 'In time I may believe, yet I mistrust.' And at the end of the scene Hortensio is decidedly unromantic when he announces peevishly that he will 'be quit with' Bianca if she casts her 'wandering eyes on every stale' (lines 88–90). Finally, it is highly ironic – and inappropriate – that the lovelorn Lucentio should attempt to woo Bianca with Ovid's poetry. Critics have pointed out that the work he quotes from can be read as a rather cynical manual for seduction and is certainly not a romantic tract. It seems that Shakespeare is intent on undermining traditional notions of romance in this play.

GLOSSARY

4	pedant schoolmaster
15	braves taunts
18	breeching scholar a schoolboy in breeches, who deserves a whipping
28–9	*Hic ibat ... celsa senis* (Latin) 'Here flowed the Simois, here is the Sigeian land, here stood the royal palace of old Priam [the King of Troy]', from *Heroides* by Ovid
30	Construe translate
36	beguile deceive
38	The treble jars the topmost string is out of tune
43	presume not ... despair not Bianca proves that she is as adept as Lucentio in acting out the role of courtly lover
48	Pedascule petty schoolmaster

50–1	**Aeacides … grandfather** Lucentio returns to Ovid. Aeacides is also called Ajax
58	**in three parts** for three voices
69	**past my gamut** beyond elementary teaching; in the Tudor period the gamut (order of notes in the scale) was six
75	**clef** musical key
76	**show pity or I die** more fitting courtly sentiments; earlier Lucentio said he would perish and die if Bianca did not love him; note how different Lucentio's approach is from Petruchio's: here there is a suggestion that the female has some power to choose
88	**stale** a decoy pigeon used in hawking
89	**list** want or wish
	ranging straying; note that the **metaphors** Hortensio employs here are similar to the hawking terms associated with Petruchio, hinting that he will settle for the wealthy widow

SCENE 2

- Katherina and Petruchio are married.
- Petruchio departs with his bride immediately after the ceremony.

Baptista, Katherina and the wedding guests await the arrival of the tardy bridegroom. Katherina is anxious and angry that she has been made a fool of by a man who 'never means to wed where he hath woo'd' (line 17). When Tranio attempts to comfort her, she leaves weeping, followed by Bianca. As Baptista is sympathising with his daughter, Biondello rushes in with the news that Petruchio is approaching, in fantastic garb, riding an old horse and attended by a servant, whose appearance is as inappropriate as his master's. Upon his arrival Petruchio behaves eccentrically. Refusing to change his clothes, he is impatient to greet, marry and kiss his bride as swiftly as possible. Baptista and the guests follow him off stage. Tranio and Lucentio discuss the latter's progress with Bianca and the possibility

CHECK THE NET
Use a search engine to find Peter Heaney's detailed discussion of the significance of Petruchio's horse.

of an elopement. Before long, Gremio reappears and describes the marriage ceremony. We learn that Petruchio behaved outrageously in church: swearing at and cuffing the priest, throwing wine at the sexton and kissing Katherina violently 'with such a clamorous smack / That at the parting all the church did echo' (lines 176–7). When the wedding party returns Petruchio announces that he must leave with his bride immediately, ignoring all pleas that he should stay for the wedding feast. Kate attempts to defy her husband and is determined to remain behind, but she is overruled. Declaring she is his property, Petruchio warns the party against trying to obstruct him as he 'defends' his wife and makes his leave. The remaining guests are bemused and puzzled; Bianca observes that 'being mad herself' Katherina has been 'madly mated' (line 242). Bianca and 'Lucentio' (Tranio, disguised) are to take Kate and Petruchio's places at the feast.

COMMENTARY

This scene is a comic tour de force, with many moments of high farce. Shakespeare sets up the visual comedy (Petruchio's appearance and dramatic exit with his bride) with elaborate descriptions from Biondello and Gremio, which make us eager to observe the interaction between the incongruous couple. The opening exchanges serve the same purpose: will Petruchio arrive? How will he behave? What will he say? After the rough wooing, we do not expect the wedding to pass off without incident. We are not disappointed.

Katherina's anxiety has been interpreted as a sign of her desire to conform: now that she has been presented with a man who will take her on, she sincerely wishes to be married. She certainly continues to dread social disgrace. **Ironically**, what is most striking about this scene is the way in which Petruchio refuses to conform to society's expectations of a bridegroom (just as, to the onlookers, Kate is an unconventional bride). The hero's tardiness suggests subversion immediately. He continues to ignore social conventions completely, as he did when he wooed Kate. Petruchio's dress, method of transport, behaviour in the church and refusal to stay for the feast are all subversive (and often hilarious on stage). Critics have suggested that Petruchio is attempting to demonstrate to Katherina that, really, *she* is at fault.

CHECK THE FILM

We know there is trouble to come for Katherina when a storm starts after the wedding ceremony in Franco Zeffirelli's 1967 film.

It is clear that Petruchio is playing a role throughout this scene: he is the 'mad-brain rudesby' (line 10), more bizarre and outlandish than his wife. His transformation into 'frantic fool' (line 12) demonstrates that Katherina too will be transformed and find another role to play. Petruchio's words and actions foreshadow his taming methods when he is at home in Act IV. We are intended to see that the bridegroom is deliberately killing his wife in her own humour.

However, as in Act I Scene 1, Katherina's shrewishness amounts to little more than voicing her feelings and we are likely to sympathise with her situation. She is forced to wait passively for her 'merry man' (line 14) to arrive and claim her, and then has to resort to pleading with him after the ceremony. It is only when he ignores her, addressing his servant as he makes preparations to leave ('Grumio, my horse', line 202) that Katherina tries to exert her own will to 'please myself' (line 210). By now we know her indignation is pointless: Petruchio has been allowed to marry her on his own terms, and will undoubtedly do as he pleases. Kate has been humbled in this scene, and will be further shamed until she becomes the wife her husband wants. Here we are presented again with the idea that the male is superior and possesses all the power. Petruchio's speech at line 220 makes this abundantly clear; Katherina is now told in no uncertain terms who her master is (lines 226–31).

These lines reiterate the idea that the male can define the female, as Kate is told how she should behave as a piece of Petruchio's property. She has been passed from one owner (her father) to another (her husband), and must accept that her old ways, which caused Baptista so much grief, are no longer acceptable. We will recall these lines when Katherina offers her public speech of submission at the end of the play.

The audience at the wedding have colluded with Petruchio. In spite of Baptista's disquiet when he sees Petruchio's garb ('But thus, I trust, you will not marry her', line 113) and Gremio's amazement at what occurs in the church ('Such a mad marriage never was before', line 180), Petruchio gets what he wants, says what he wants, leaves when he wants and continues to assert his own version of reality,

CHECK THE FILM
Directors have been keen to show the wedding scene on film. In the 1929 Hollywood film directed by Sam Taylor, Petruchio forces Katherina to say 'I do' by stomping on her foot. Franco Zeffirelli preferred a slightly less violent approach (1967). His Petruchio stops his bride's mouth with a kiss when she attempts to shout 'I will not [marry you]' during the marriage ceremony.

which includes furthering the illusion that he has 'a most patient, sweet, and virtuous wife' (line 193). The final absurd fiction he creates, when he 'rescues' Katherina from thieves, seals the supreme command of events he has shown throughout Act III Scene 2.

As in previous scenes, the other characters are forced to react to and accommodate the dominant male. They comment on Petruchio's behaviour and appearance, but do not really challenge him. They – and we, the audience – are forced to marvel at the protagonist's swaggering, boisterous display. As well as creating an obedient wife, Petruchio has also reconfirmed his masculine valour, amusingly setting himself up as a knight defending his lady-love. His exaggerated posturing further undermines the ideals of courtly love that Lucentio espoused in Act I Scene 1. As the newly-weds leave the stage, we are not likely to agree with Gremio's assertion that 'Petruchio is Kated' (line 243). On the contrary, we understand that the bridegroom's taming methods will be highly effective. At the end of the scene Baptista attempts to reassert the social conventions that have been overturned so dramatically when he replaces the bride and groom at the feast with 'stand-ins'. Perhaps these final lines are a sign that Kate is on the road to conformity. (See also **Text 2** of **Extended commentaries**.)

CHECK THE FILM

In Franco Zeffirelli's 1967 film Petruchio often manhandles Kate. In this scene he puts her over his shoulder and installs her on the horse so that he can leave.

GLOSSARY	
10	**rudesby** rude, rough fellow
42	**thrice turned** turned inside out three times (to conceal the wear)
45	**chapeless** without the metal plate on the scabbard to cover the point of the sword
46	**points** laces
	hipped with broken hips
47	**of no kindred** not from the same matching pair
48–53	**glanders ... shoulder-shotten** this horse has an impressive collection of ailments: swollen legs, jaundice, strained shoulders, tumours, loss of balance, worms
54	**near-legged before** knock-kneed
58	**crupper** the rear part of the saddle, used by passengers
68	**footboy** page

93	**wondrous monument** a bad omen
97	**unprovided** badly or inappropriately dressed
98	**doff this habit** take off these garments
138	**steal our marriage** elope
158	**by gogs-wouns** by God's wounds (Petruchio is cursing inappropriately here)
171	**sops** dregs
209	**You may be jogging … green** go as soon as you want to (a reference to boots being clean and ready for the journey)
211	**jolly** arrogant (or Kate could be offering an ironic comment about her husband)
222	**domineer** riot, lord it
226	**look not big** don't be proud
230	**my ox, my ass, my any thing** Petruchio is parodying the ten commandments here
237	**buckler thee** protect you with my sword
243	**Kated** a **pun** on mated/mad – the implication is that bride and groom both share the same bad temper
246	**junkets** delicacies

ACT IV

SCENE 1

- Arriving home, Petruchio sets about taming Katherina.

Complaining and cold, Grumio arrives home ahead of his master with orders for the other servants; they must light the fire and prepare the house and supper for the arrival of the bride and groom. We learn that the journey has been full of mishaps. When he enters, an enraged Petruchio shouts at the servants for failing to carry out his orders. This overbearing behaviour continues when the meal is served, with Petruchio striking the servants and throwing the

 QUESTION

How do you respond to the scenes set in Petruchio's house? Do you find them comic?

'overcooked' meat at them. Kate – who has wearily attempted to defend the men and calm her husband – is not allowed to eat. Instead she is hurried off to the bedchamber by her perverse bridegroom. When Grumio enquires where his master is, Curtis tells him that Petruchio has been 'Making a sermon of continency' to his dazed wife (line 170). Alone on stage, Petruchio outlines his plan to tame Katherina. He will deprive her of food and sleep and insist that 'all is done in reverend care of her' until she submits to his will (line 191).

COMMENTARY

As in the previous scene, we are prepared for Petruchio's entrance with informative and descriptive speeches. Grumio's physical abuse of Curtis foreshadows Petruchio's treatment of the servants. His loquacity mirrors his master's verbal dexterity. Grumio's words and actions also hint at his collusion with Petruchio (he will help starve Katherina into submission). His speech at line 64 alerts us to the fact that Kate is losing ground all the time. Not only is Petruchio (as we suspected) 'more shrew than she' (line 76), but Katherina has also suffered the indignity of falling off her horse in 'miry a place', becoming 'bemoiled' (line 67), while her husband 'left her with the horse upon her' (lines 67–8). Is this a mire of her own making? Some critics have argued that we are supposed to view Kate's ill-fortune on the journey as a sign that she will continue to find life difficult and unpleasant until she recognises the folly of her ways. Others argue that the treatment she receives at Petruchio's hands is out of all proportion to her supposed crimes as a scold.

When she does appear, it seems that Katherina's spirit has already been broken. She says very little, and when she speaks she pleads (see lines 143 and 155), making no personal demands. It is perhaps significant that she addresses her husband with the more formal 'you', rather than 'thou', which was a term of intimacy. Has she been cowed? Conversely, Petruchio continues to dominate the other characters on stage physically and verbally, and is a demanding, discontented master. We discover why he is behaving like a domestic tyrant when he is alone on stage at the end of the scene. He has 'politicly begun my reign' (line 175) and intends to maintain his supremacy in order to 'curb' Katherina's 'mad and headstrong humour' (line 196). The imagery of falconry he employs reflects his resolute taming methods. It also suggests that Katherina must become obedient so that she is an asset to her master, as a tame hawk reflects its owner's prowess. Some critics have suggested that the careful plan Petruchio outlines will make him suffer as much as his wife: he too must go without sleep in order to 'kill a wife with kindness' (line 195). However, the determined tone of the speech and the impersonality of the hawking metaphors and other references to Katherina (who is not once named in this soliloquy), would seem to indicate that Petruchio views the educational process he is engaged in, in a detached way. There is no mention of emotion. The protagonist could be speaking of any woman he had chosen to wed who 'will not be obedient' (line 183). The main topic of the speech is masculine control and the necessary methods for achieving it. The last two lines of the scene can be interpreted in different ways. Either Petruchio is asking for assistance (which he does not need: we know his methods are working) or he is boasting (his request is rhetorical). Either way, he is undeniably in charge in his own home.

CHECK THE FILM

In the 1980 BBC production the audience is encouraged to feel some sympathy for Petruchio during his soliloquy about wife-taming. It is delivered in a weary tone, as he sits quietly at the kitchen table. He yawns and rubs his eyes. He too is suffering, and is not simply a calculating sadist.

CHECK THE FILM

The hierarchy in Petruchio's home is conveyed when his servants line up to be inspected like army recruits in the 1980 BBC production, with one old servant blubbering with fear. Kate joins the end of the line.

GLOSSARY	
3	rayed dirtied or muddied
5	a little pot and soon hot a small man who is easily enraged
38	cony-catching deceiving simple people; there is a **pun** on 'catch'
44	Jacks ... Jills male and female servants
45	carpets coverings for tables and chairs
59	*Imprimis* (Latin) first
106	Cock's passion an oath: by God's passion
120	all unpink'd without proper decoration (ornamental holes pricked in the leather)
121	link black material, from torches, used to dye hats
144	beetle-headed thick-headed (a beetle was a mallet)
145	you have a stomach you are (a) hungry or (b) proud/hot-tempered
159	choler angry
180	haggard wild hawk

continued

183	bate and beat flutter and flap the wings
190	hurly chaos, disorder
195	to kill a wife with kindness (proverbial) this meant that the husband was too indulgent towards his wife, making her disobedient. Petruchio means the opposite of what he says here. There is a popular domestic tragedy by Thomas Heywood (c.1574–1641), *A Woman Killed with Kindness* (1603)

SCENE 2

- Hortensio rejects Bianca.
- Tranio persuades an old man, the Pedant, to play the role of Vincentio.

 QUESTION

Compare and contrast the couples presented in the play.

Hortensio and 'Lucentio' (Tranio) are spying on Bianca and 'Cambio' (Lucentio), who continues to woo his 'pupil'. Tranio professes outrage at the inconstancy of women (line 14). Hortensio reveals his identity and agrees that he too will forswear Bianca; he intends to marry a wealthy widow in three days' time. When he leaves, Tranio tells Bianca and his master what has happened. As they rejoice, Biondello appears with the news that he has found an old man who might be suitable to play the role of the supposed Vincentio. The Pedant is duped by Tranio, who persuades him that he is in danger in Padua. Fearful that he might be executed, the old man gratefully agrees to impersonate Vincentio and 'pass assurance of a dower in marriage' (line 118).

COMMENTARY

One disguise is cast off and another assumed as deceptions continue to proliferate in the subplot. Essentially, this scene furthers the action. It is clear that Bianca is in control of her own fate and her lover, as we see when Tranio says to Hortensio, 'See how beastly she doth court him' (line 34). This idea is reinforced by her remark about the prospect of Hortensio taming his widow at line 53. Hortensio remains deluded; he believes that he will now be satisfied by 'Kindness in women' (line 41) rather than beauty. His intention to be married to a wealthy widow suggests that he is as much a fortune-hunter as his friend Petruchio. Tranio dominates the final section of the scene, showing that he is as adept as Petruchio at controlling characters and events. We know that Lucentio would be lost without his guidance and cunning. The references to woman-taming and Petruchio in this scene reinforce the protagonist's dominance. It seems that his fame is spreading far and wide as others marvel at his success in transforming Katherina. Plot and subplot become more closely linked as two more couples move closer to matrimony. We will undoubtedly draw comparisons between these pairings.

CHECK THE NET

For a searchable online text of the play, search **http://www.online-literature.com**

GLOSSARY

3	**bears me fair in hand** encourages me
11	**proceeders** a proceeder was a scholar who had moved from a BA to an MA; therefore a quick learner
14	**despiteful** spiteful
20	**cullion** servant/wretch
24	**lightness** fickleness or disloyalty; there is also a **pun** on Bianca's name, which means 'white'
46	**napping** wooing (they are caught in the act of wooing)
57	**tricks eleven and twenty long** another reference to card-playing and gambling; this represents a high score. The implication is that there are lots of tricks being played
61	**An ancient angel** an old man
63	**mercatante** (Italian) merchant
83	**stay'd** kept in custody, under arrest. This is the second time this excuse has been used in the subplot; Lucentio told Biondello that he had been forced to change clothes with Tranio to save his life after killing a man
118	**pass assurance** give a guarantee

SCENE 3

- Petruchio continues the taming.
- He rejects a hat and gown that have been ordered for Katherina.

CHECK THE BOOK

There is an interesting discussion of the role and significance of clothing by Graham Holderness in 'Text and Performance: *The Taming of the Shrew*' in *Shakespeare in Performance* (2000), pp. 137–9.

Weary and starving, Katherina begs Grumio to bring her some food. He taunts and teases her with offers of wonderful delicacies, but does not give her anything to eat. Petruchio appears with Hortensio, bearing a dish of meat. When the trio sit down, Petruchio tells his friend to eat all the food in an **aside**. Before Kate has had a chance to assuage her hunger pangs, a tailor and haberdasher arrive. Petruchio rejects the hat and gown they have brought, ignoring Katherina's protests: she likes the garments and wishes to keep them. Petruchio abuses the tailor, who boldly defends the gown, saying that he followed the instructions delivered by Grumio. Grumio joins the fray, quibbling with the tailor and defending his own actions. The tailor is dismissed. In an aside Petruchio tells Hortensio to pay him later and sets about lecturing his wife: clothes and outward appearances are not important. Petruchio then announces that they will visit her father, leaving immediately. He deliberately mistakes the time and Kate tries to correct her husband. Petruchio warns her against contradicting him. The trip is cancelled.

COMMENTARY

There are further examples of **slapstick** and quick-witted verbal comedy in this scene, centring on the interlude with the tailor. Katherina makes a brave attempt to assert herself again, but is completely unsuccessful, because, as Hortensio says, Petruchio 'will command the sun' (line 193) if he chooses. He continues to dominate completely. We can see the efficacy of his taming methods at the beginning of the scene, when Kate outlines what has happened since we last saw her. From her descriptions of life in Petruchio's house it is clear that the plan outlined in Act IV Scene 1 has been followed to the letter and the young bride's words suggest bewilderment. We are reminded that Kate will be defeated when Grumio denies her food. This is the first of three attempts at breaking her will in this scene: the offer of food is followed by the visit from the tailor and Petruchio's plan to visit her father. On each occasion Kate attempts to assert her own point of view, but her voice continues to be ignored. Grumio has an important role to play in Petruchio's plans for thwarting his wife in this scene and his actions indicate that Kate is isolated. Her impotence grows with each successive scene, despite the fact that she has more to say for herself here.

The scene with the tailor is significant for a number of reasons. Some critics have suggested that Katherina's desire for a gown is further proof that she – secretly or subconsciously – desires to conform to society's codes; she wishes to be attired appropriately as a respectable man's wife. Others suggest that Petruchio withholds the gown because his wife is not yet fit to wear the garb of an obedient wife; she is still, in his word, 'crossing' him (line 190). The exchange with the tailor adds to our understanding of the theme of appearance and reality.

This scene includes clear proof that the male characters work together to exert control over Katherina throughout the play. By the close of Act V, Petruchio won't need any assistance.

CHECK THE FILM

Richard Burton's Petruchio in the 1967 Franco Zeffirelli film is a boorish, heavy drinker. During this scene he is physically violent, as he is in many other scenes. He regularly destroys furniture, fixtures and fittings, as well as the tailor's gown.

GLOSSARY	
11	spites me angers me
17	neat's foot ox or calf's foot
36	all amort melancholy or mortified
43	sorted to no proof come to nothing
56	farthingales hooped skirts
	bravery clothing
58	knavery nonsense
69	doth fit the time is fashionable
82	custard-coffin crust of a custard pie
87	masquing stuff clothing only fit to be worn as a costume at a masque; not proper clothing
91	censer incense burner
98	kennel street gutter

continued

102	**quaint** skilfully made
103	**puppet** a fool or a dressed up doll
128	**Ergo** (Latin) therefore
132	**loose-bodied gown** this might be an allusion to the kind of dress worn by prostitutes
145	**prove upon thee** a threat to fight in a duel
150	**mete-yard** a yardstick for measuring
167	**habiliments** clothes
177	**furniture** clothing or outfit

SCENE 4

- Deceived by Tranio and the supposed Vincentio, Baptista agrees to marry Bianca to 'Lucentio'.

Tranio ('Lucentio') and the Pedant, who is dressed to resemble Vincentio, arrive at Baptista's house. Biondello is part of the scheme to deceive Bianca's father; he has told Baptista that 'Vincentio' has recently arrived from Venice. When their prey comes out of his house 'Vincentio' confirms the dowry 'Lucentio' has offered. Baptista does not wish to draw up the wedding agreement in his own home because Gremio is 'hearkening still' (line 53) and agrees to go to 'Lucentio's' lodgings to complete the transaction. The real Lucentio (still disguised as 'Cambio') has been watching his servant Tranio manage the deception so efficiently; as Baptista's servant he is now ordered to inform Bianca 'how she's like to be Lucentio's wife' (line 66). When Tranio leaves with Baptista, Biondello explains what has happened to his rather dim-witted master, and urges him to move along swiftly with his secret marriage to Bianca.

QUESTION

How do you respond to the presentation of Bianca?

COMMENTARY

Role-playing through the use of disguises continues to draw our attention to the differences between appearance and reality in the subplot, as the interlude with the tailor in the previous scene highlighted this theme in the taming plot. Like Grumio, Tranio and Biondello assist their master in his matrimonial plans (the former is almost stage-manager in this scene, directing Lucentio's actions). There is **dramatic irony** in the fact that Baptista agrees to marry Bianca to 'Lucentio', commenting that the young people seem to be very much in love, 'Or both dissemble deeply their affections' (line 42). He unwittingly speaks the truth, having been completely taken in by the wily youngsters. The real Lucentio is as happily deluded as Baptista, believing that he has obtained an obedient and modest wife. His final speech contrasts vividly with the force of Petruchio's speeches before and after his wedding. Note the passivity of this line: 'I may and will, if she be so contented' (line 101). We might also feel that there is a hint of danger in the following line, particularly Lucentio's question: 'She will be pleas'd, then wherefore should I doubt?' The canny audience will be well aware that it is necessary to look beyond appearances, and realise that Lucentio's blissful lack of understanding cannot last much longer. There is further dramatic irony in the fact that the character who seeks to deceive is being deceived himself.

www. CHECK THE NET
The Shakespeare Resource Center at **http://www. bardweb.net** is a useful general site to visit.

GLOSSARY	
5	**Pegasus** the winged horse, a familiar name for English inns
7	**'longeth to** appropriate to
36	**curious** niggling
49	**affied** engaged
52	**Pitchers have ears** (proverbial) a reference to the possibility that the servants might overhear their plans; **ironic** here, since it is the servants who are plotting
59	**scrivener** a lawyer who drew up legal contracts
70	**One mess** one dish or course
89	**cum privilegio ... solum** (Latin) this phrase can often be found on the title page of books; it means 'with the right to be sole printer'
103	**roundly go about** approach frankly, or go straight in search of

SCENE 5

- Katherina capitulates to her husband.
- On the road to Padua they meet the real Vincentio.

Accompanied by Hortensio and their servants, Petruchio and Kate make their way to Baptista's house in Padua. As contrary as he was in Act IV Scene 3, Petruchio insists that it is night. When Kate says that it is day he declares that they will all turn round and return home. Katherina finally capitulates and says that she will see the world through her husband's eyes and contradict him no more. Petruchio immediately puts her to the test and greets an old man they meet on the road as if he were a young gentlewoman, urging Kate to do likewise. When she follows his instructions Petruchio scolds her. Katherina apologises for her 'mad mistaking' (line 48). The old man announces that he is Vincentio, on his way to see his son Lucentio in Padua. Petruchio informs him that Lucentio has married Bianca and the travellers continue their journey together. Spurred on by his friend's success, Hortensio is sure that he will be able to tame his widow 'if she be froward' (line 77).

? QUESTION

What is the dramatic importance of Act IV Scene 5?

COMMENTARY

Katherina finally capitulates. But how are we to view her submission? Some would argue that she has been worn down; as Hortensio points out, 'Say as he says, or we shall never go' (line 11). Others would argue that her liveliness and wit in this scene suggest that Kate has chosen to take on a new role herself, because she has recognised the 'game' that Petruchio is playing and decided to participate. Certainly it is possible to argue that the encounter with Vincentio is like a game, in which Kate shows off for the amusement of her husband. This meeting also provides Petruchio with an opportunity to test his wife's obedience, and we see that he has won the field completely when he succeeds in getting Katherina to change her mind with the same perverse, lightning speed that he has demonstrated. Some would argue that Kate begins to speak with a new voice in this scene, becoming more eloquent as she greets and then apologises to Vincentio in an exaggerated way, mirroring the style her husband has employed throughout the first four acts of the play. Is this voice Katherina's, or Petruchio's? Has the shrew been silenced, or transformed?

There is an inconsistency in the plot at this point. Petruchio informs Vincentio that his son has married his sister-in-law: he cannot know this, because the secret marriage has not yet occurred. Hortensio's final lines in this scene mirror Lucentio's words at the end of the previous scene: he too remains deluded about his own matrimonial prospects. He says that Petruchio has taught him how to be 'untoward' if his widow is 'froward' (lines 77–8); we know that he does not possess the same steely resolve as his friend and cannot hope to rule anyone. Some would suggest that Hortensio's and Vincentio's presence in this scene, which is public proof of Katherina's obedience, prepares us for her even more public submission in the final scene. It is perhaps appropriate that Katherina's submission is witnessed by other men; she has irked them, and we know that the Paduans feel that Petruchio has carried out a public duty in taking on and taming the shrew. If we are to accept this reading of the scene, then Hortensio's last lines, indeed the whole scene, can be read as proof of the successful outcome of a male wish-fulfilment fantasy. At the same time, we might argue that Shakespeare undermines Petruchio's triumph by closing the scene with his much more feeble friend. And Katherina does not sound humiliated when she speaks in this scene, even though she follows Petruchio's instructions and seems to make a fool of herself. Is it being suggested that a woman must follow even the most ridiculous commands her husband makes, or are Petruchio's absurd requests ironic? The answer depends upon whether we feel Katherina has gained or lost by her submission. Perhaps we cannot view this scene ironically; the reference to the sun and moon was a common analogy used during this period to describe the ideal relationship that should exist between husband and wife. The moon obviously 'follows' the sun and 'mirrors' its behaviour; just as a wife should behave in a way that reflects well on her husband as his subordinate.

 QUESTION

Janet McTeer, who played Petruchio in an all-female production of *The Shrew* in 2003, argues that this is a 'crucial scene' and that Katherina 'isn't defeated here; she merely wants peace. It is obviously a device and her spirit is not bowed.' Do you agree?

GLOSSARY

7	**what I list** what I please
14	**rush-candle** a flickering candle
23	**the field is won** the battle is won
24–5	**Thus the bowl … the bias** this is how things should be; a **metaphor** from the game of bowls
38–40	**Happy the parents … bedfellow** taken from Ovid
47	**reverend father** a respectable old gentleman or the head of the family
71	**pleasant** joking
75	**jealous** suspicious
77	**Have to** now for
78	**untoward** bad mannered or awkward

ACT V

SCENE 1

- 'Lucentio' and the supposed Vincentio are unmasked.
- Baptista and the real Vincentio learn that their children have married in secret.
- Kate kisses her husband in the middle of the street.

QUESTION

Consider the portrayal of the servants in the play. What are their dramatic functions?

Lucentio goes off to marry Bianca, Biondello having informed the couple that the priest is waiting. Petruchio shows Vincentio to his son's lodgings, where they discover the supposed Vincentio, who stoutly refuses to allow them to enter. The Pedant maintains that he is the real Vincentio. Gremio is standing in the street outside. When Biondello arrives he pretends that he does not know Vincentio, who questions the 'notorious villain' angrily (line 46). As he beats Biondello, the supposed Vincentio calls to Baptista. The real Vincentio is further astonished when Tranio appears, dressed in his son's clothes. He fears Lucentio has been killed by his servant.

Tranio calls for Vincentio to be arrested. Gremio tries to intercede; he swears that this new Vincentio is 'the right Vincentio' (lines 91–2) but Baptista has urged the officer to take the 'mad knave' away to prison. When Lucentio and Bianca arrive, Biondello, the supposed Vincentio and Tranio make off as fast as they can: they know they 'are all undone' (line 101). Lucentio begs his father to forgive him and explains to Baptista that he has married Bianca. The deceived fathers are not entirely satisfied, but go into the house together 'to sound the depth of this knavery' (line 126). Petruchio and Katherina have been watching 'this ado' (line 130) and she urges her husband to follow the others. Before they go Petruchio demands a kiss, which Kate reluctantly bestows on him.

COMMENTARY

The subterfuge of Lucentio and Tranio is uncovered in this scene: the masks come off. The timing of the revelations is significant. Katherina has been transformed, meaning that Petruchio can dispose of his disguise as 'mad-brain rudesby' (III.2.10); in the subplot the characters are forced to dispose of their disguises too. When Tranio and Biondello run away we know that when we next see them they will have returned to their 'proper' roles as servants, just as Kate has now become a 'proper' wife. Events move very swiftly here, but we know that the alarm the real Vincentio feels will not last long. Lucentio is penitent (he kneels to his father, signifying his respect and a return to the correct social order) and his partners in crime make themselves scarce. The threat of subversion is neatly disposed of. Both fathers regain the upper hand at the end of the scene when they go in to the house together. This is as it should be: control has been returned to the right hands. However, we know that Baptista's outwardly obedient daughter has succeeded in duping her father, as Lucentio has deceived his. And it is **ironic** that Lucentio, ever the romantic, claims that 'Love wrought these miracles' (line 113); we know that his success in wooing and wedding Bianca lies with the lady herself, and with Tranio and his clever plotting. The final scene is set up when Gremio retires from the field, content that he should get his 'share of the feast' (line 129). Like Hortensio, he is forced to satisfy himself – realistically – with what he can get. These two suitors' careers as wooers have not been auspicious or in any genuine sense romantic; but as we have already

CHECK THE BOOK

For a discussion of Shakespeare in the theatre, Stanley Wells's *Shakespeare in the Theatre: An Anthology of Criticism* (1997) brings together eyewitness accounts of performances from the eighteenth century to the present.

seen in the main plot, romantic ideas about matrimony are no preparation for the reality of wedded life. Interestingly, the scene ends with what some critics view as a moment of genuine affection as Petruchio asks Kate to kiss him. Others see his request as another example of the triumphant husband testing his wife. For those who wish to see this exchange as proof that this match has become a loving marriage, there are two pieces of evidence to point to. The first is that Petruchio and Kate are now in calm waters, observers of the 'ado' caused by Lucentio, his servants and Bianca. They watch the scene unfolding with mutual amusement, and, some might say, a feeling of superiority. The second is the more affectionate terms the married couple use when speaking to one another. Kate is now 'my sweet Kate' (line 137), while he is her 'love' (line 136). Their kiss prepares us for the consummation of the marriage which will be referred to at the end of the play.

CHECK THE BOOK

To read comic depictions of the shrew-taming story popular in the Renaissance, have a look at *A Merry Jest of a Shrewd and Curst Wife* (1550) and 'The Cruel Shrew', both reprinted in *The Taming of the Shrew: Texts and Contexts,* edited by Frances E. Dolan (1996).

GLOSSARY	
s.d.	*out before* at the front of the stage, or ahead of the rest
12	cheer refreshment, or there might be a suggestion that happy people can be heard ahead
34	cozen defraud or cheat
35	under my countenance masquerading
40	crack-hemp a rascal worthy of being hanged
59	copatain hat tall, conical hat
70	Bergamo traditionally the home town of servants in Italian comedy
107	counterfeit supposes false pretences; another direct reference to the source play (see **Structure**)
108	packing scheming

SCENE 2

- Petruchio wins his wager at the wedding feast.
- Katherina makes a speech in which she scolds the other women for daring to challenge their husbands' authority.

Lucentio welcomes the guests to the banquet, which is being held to celebrate his marriage to Bianca, as well as the marriages of Hortensio and his Widow and Petruchio and Katherina. There is much jesting about shrewish wives and the men engage in a wager. They bet on their wives' obedience. Biondello is sent out to call in the Widow and Bianca. Both refuse to come. Contrary to expectation, Kate obeys Petruchio's summons. She also fetches the other women when required to do so. Baptista is impressed and offers Petruchio a second dowry because his daughter is 'chang'd' (line 116). Petruchio charges Katherina to 'tell these headstrong women / What duty they do owe their lords and husbands' (lines 131–2). Kate lectures the Widow and Bianca, reminding them that they are weak women, who should serve and submit to their menfolk. She offers to place her hand beneath her husband's foot as a token of her duty. Petruchio is delighted with his wife and takes her off to bed.

COMMENTARY

The final scene begins with Lucentio in complacent mood, and his tone is cheerful and celebratory as he welcomes everyone to the feast. As the characters sit down to 'chat as well as eat' (line 11), it seems that all is resolved and social harmony has been restored, with each person in their rightful place. But we quickly realise that this is not so. Petruchio crows that 'Hortensio fears his widow' (line 16), and a new battle begins. The Widow's challenge to Katherina begins the tussle and introduces the wager: marriage is still linked to money. Now the men bet on the obedience of their wives, reviving the competition that occurred early in the play as suitors fought to be allowed to court Bianca. We are further prepared for the wager by Hortensio and Petruchio urging their wives to put each other down. There are hints that the Widow and Bianca will not be ruled: both assert their own points of view before they leave at line 48. When they have left, the betting begins in earnest. Petruchio employs **images** of hawking, reconfirming the idea that an obedient wife does credit to her master (and in this case, in a financial as well as **metaphorical** sense). Shakespeare builds up the dramatic tension which leads to Katherina's long speech of submission with the refusal of the Widow and Bianca to return. Does the audience expect Katherina to refuse to come too? Probably not; in spite of

CONTEXT

Katherina's descriptions of women as physically weak echo the words of the *Second Book of Homilies*, in which it was claimed 'the woman is a weake creature, not induced with like strength and constancy of minde'.

CHECK THE FILM

Katherina's power is conveyed physically and verbally in Franco Zeffirelli's 1967 film when she drags the other women back to the feast in an armlock. She then paces around the hall as she delivers her final speech, hands on hips in a very confident attitude.

her spirited retorts to the Widow earlier in the scene, we know she has been tamed. The drama of the scene comes from the fact that all the male characters, with the exception of Petruchio, are flabbergasted by Katherina's lecture.

What are we to make of this speech? There are a number of contradictory readings of it. Some critics have argued that it should be delivered in an **ironic** tone; that Katherina is not serious. Others suggest she is playing her husband's game through choice, because it has liberated her (she has found love and a place in society). Others suggest that she does not speak with her own voice here; that a masculine voice has replaced the voice of the scold. Has Shakespeare killed off his original Katherina and replaced her with a female Petruchio impersonator? Certainly the arguments Katherina expounds are 'masculine' and she speaks on cue when requested; she suggests that women should be ruled by men because they are biologically and culturally inferior to the male sex. She also seems to be reconfirming the rights of the patriarchal hierarchy, which decreed that the husband should be the 'head' and 'sovereign' (line 148) of the household, just as the monarch was head and sovereign of the kingdom. Kate's reference to the duty 'the subject owes the prince' (line 156) reinforces this idea. She employs imagery of war too, supporting the idea that Petruchio has won the battle of the sexes. And it is ironic that Kate's longest and most eloquent speech, and the only one that is really heard, is a speech in which she declares her own – and other women's – weaknesses.

But should we believe her? The play does not prove that women are weak, merely that a man has to work hard to subdue a scold. It is ironic that Kate's speech rounding off the play virtually silences the stunned men. Is Shakespeare confirming Petruchio's superiority and triumph, but undermining the other male characters, who remain dupes? Are we to understand that Katherina's speech is a joke against the men? (In spite of Kate's words, and the fact that she seems to be taking on Petruchio's role of tamer when she lectures her 'froward' sisters, the other wives are clearly not malleable.)

Those who wish to see Katherina as a subversive figure may like to consider the irony implied by the fact that she delivers what is in effect a sermon. The content of her final speech would have been familiar to the sixteenth-century audience, but it would have been highly unusual to hear this message about marriage eloquently delivered by a woman, and in a public setting. Elizabethans were used to hearing such sentiments – from male ministers in church. Is Kate mocking and subverting a traditional masculine role?

This reading is plausible if we remember one of Petruchio's first actions on arriving home with his bride. Grumio tells us that he makes 'a sermon of continency' (IV.1.170) to Katherina, which leaves her dumbfounded ('she, poor soul, / Knows not which way to stand, to look, to speak', IV.1.171–2). Now, in Act V, it seems that the heroine has turned the tables on her husband, and the other males who scorned her. The Paduans are as astonished when they hear Kate's sermon as she was on her wedding night when Petruchio railed at her. The shrew is every inch the impressive public speaker; as effective and eloquent as a minister or an overbearing bridegroom. She has usurped their roles: it is she who speaks longest, loudest – and uninterrupted – in the final moments of *The Taming of the Shrew*.

Those who would argue that Katherina's final speech is not ironic point to the fact that she goes further than saying she is an obedient wife; she offers to place her hand beneath her husband's foot in a gesture that suggests excessive humility. But could we read this as a test of Petruchio? Is she attempting to see how far he will push her? This seems doubtful. As soon as she has finished speaking she gets her reward (a kiss and consummation), just as Petruchio has had his reward for taming her (a second dowry from Baptista). Evidence suggests that Katherina is acting out the role that her husband has cast her in, and that the final lines of the play are not ironic: they all point to the men's admiration for Petruchio's taming methods. Hortensio says unequivocally that he has 'tam'd a curst shrew' (line 189). Or are we to read Lucentio's subsequent line as undermining this? It is indeed 'a wonder' (line 190) that Katherina has delivered this speech: perhaps we are intended to reserve doubts about her future conduct. This is a plausible reading if we consider that one shrew may be vanquished, but another two have revealed their true natures. However hard we try, it is not entirely possible to feel a

CHECK THE FILM
In the 1929 Hollywood film, the final speech is made ironic when Kate winks at Bianca, suggesting that she still has a mind of her own.

QUESTION

One actress who played Kate has argued that Katherina's final submission makes her powerful, and that 'the play lands back in her hands. It's her play at the end.' Do you agree?

CHECK THE BOOK

Carol Rutter's book *Clamorous Voices: Shakespeare's Women Today* (1989) includes comments from actresses who have played Katherina.

sense of closure at the end of this play. (For further comments on this scene see **Text 3** of **Extended commentaries**.)

GLOSSARY	
33	To her! go for her!
40	hasty-witted quick-witted
46	bird prey or game
52	slipp'd me let me off my leash (a hunting metaphor)
56	at a bay defending itself against the hounds in the hunt
58	gird taunt, a stroke of wit
61	glance away rebound
63	in good sadness in all seriousness
105	Swinge beat
140	bite the meads attack the meadows
170	unable physically weak
177	vail your stomachs throw off your pride and anger
	no boot in vain
186	sped defeated or finished
	hit the white archaic term and **pun** on Bianca's name

EXTENDED COMMENTARIES

TEXT 1 – INDUCTION 1.1–42

Sly is found lying outside the inn by the Lord.

SLY: I'll feeze you, in faith.

HOSTESS: A pair of stocks, you rogue.

SLY: Y'are a baggage, the Slys are no rogues. Look in the
Chronicles, we came in with Richard Conqueror.
Therefore *paucas pallabris*, let the world slide. Sessa!   5

HOSTESS: You will not pay for the glasses you have burst?

SLY: No, not a denier. Go by, Saint Jeronimy, go to thy
cold bed and warm thee.

HOSTESS: I know my remedy, I must go fetch the third-
borough.   [*Exit.*] 10

SLY: Third, or fourth, or fifth borough, I'll answer him
by law. I'll not budge an inch, boy. Let him come,
and kindly.   *Falls asleep.*

Wind horns. Enter a LORD *from hunting, with his* TRAIN.

LORD: Huntsman, I charge thee, tender well my hounds.
Breathe Merriman, the poor cur is emboss'd,   15
And couple Clowder with the deep-mouth'd brach.
Saw'st thou not, boy, how Silver made it good
At the hedge corner, in the coldest fault?
I would not lose the dog for twenty pound.

FIRST HUNTSMAN: Why, Belman is as good as he, my lord.   20
He cried upon it at the merest loss,
And twice today pick'd out the dullest scent.
Trust me, I take him for the better dog.

LORD: Thou art a fool. If Echo were as fleet,
I would esteem him worth a dozen such.   25
But sup them well, and look unto them all.
Tomorrow I intend to hunt again.

FIRST HUNTSMAN: I will, my lord.

LORD: What's here? One dead, or drunk? See, doth he
breathe?

SECOND HUNTSMAN: He breathes, my lord. Were he not
warm'd with ale,   30
This were a bed but cold to sleep so soundly.

LORD: O monstrous beast, how like a swine he lies!
Grim death, how foul and loathsome is thine image!
Sirs, I will practise on this drunken man.
What think you, if he were convey'd to bed,   35
Wrapp'd in sweet clothes, rings put upon his fingers,
A most delicious banquet by his bed,
And brave attendants near him when he wakes,
Would not the beggar then forget himself?

> **CONTEXT**
>
> Throughout the
> **Induction**,
> Shakespeare
> plays on words
> associated with
> illusion: 'practice',
> 'flatt'ring dream',
> 'worthless fancy',
> 'play', 'usurp'. All
> these words are
> designed to draw
> our attention to
> the artifice of the
> scene.

FIRST HUNTSMAN: Believe me, lord, I think he cannot choose. 40

SECOND HUNTSMAN: It would seem strange unto him when he wak'd.

LORD: Even as a flatt'ring dream or worthless fancy.

CHECK THE BOOK

If you wish to learn more about the social and economical background of Shakespeare's times, have a look at D. M. Palliser's *The Age of Elizabeth: England Under the Later Tudors, 1547–1603* (1983).

The opening of the Induction serves as an ironic commentary on the action of the play that follows it and foreshadows events and themes that will become important in both plot and subplot. The exchange between Sly and the Hostess, which concerns the drunkard's refusal to accept responsibility for his behaviour and pay for the glasses he has broken, anticipates the verbal sparring of Katherina and Petruchio, and hints at the heroine's waywardness. Sly's defiance and determination to stand up for himself mirror Kate's, but she is as powerless socially as her counterpart in the Induction. Sly is the lowest of the low, a 'beggar', just as Kate, as a woman, is considered worthless when she is a scold. The 'foul and loathsome … image' the tinker presents reflects the fact that sharp-tongued Katherina is abhorred as a 'fiend of hell' (I.1.88): both project repugnant images. It is clear that Sly – like Katherina – will be acted upon by more powerful men: either the law ('the third-borough') or the Lord's tricks will ensnare him. We might compare the public humiliation of the stocks that the Hostess threatens Sly with, with the public punishment that is dealt out to Katherina during her taming. Sly and Katherina are not allowed to exercise their own wills; as the huntsman points out, Sly 'cannot choose': neither can Kate. She is married off and tamed against her liking.

Sly will be made to believe that he is a lord. The language used to describe the process – 'flatt'ring dream … worthless fancy' (line 42) – suggests the magical transformation that will take place. This is exactly what occurs in the main plot, in which the other characters see the heroine's metamorphosis into an obedient wife as a 'wonder' (V.2.190). Kate is bewildered as if in a dream during her taming. Some would argue that because the Lord's trick on Sly is described as a 'fancy' we can view Petruchio's taming of Kate as a male wish-fulfilment fantasy: it is just as unexpected and preposterous. In the Induction it seems that Sly's transformation is to be a source of entertainment; but in the main plot Petruchio is in deadly earnest. Disturbing as it may seem, it is possible to view the reactions of the other characters to Katherina's humiliation at the wedding ceremony as proof that the pugilistic hero is providing his Paduan audience with a comic interlude: Gremio says, 'Went they not quickly, I should die with laughing' (III.2.239). This amusement is foreshadowed later in this scene of the Induction when the Lord says that he will remain on hand to ensure that the hilarity caused by his tricks does not become too great. The Lord's delineation of Sly as barely human – he is a 'monstrous beast' (line 32) – reflects the fact that the male characters all view Katherina as an inhuman devil when she exercises her tongue. Is the playwright suggesting it is legitimate to treat these inferior creatures as objects of ridicule to be used in sport? It is intriguing, and perhaps ironic, that Sly will be subjected to an onslaught of elegance and riches in his 'dream'; this is the opposite of the treatment that Kate will endure. The rogue tinker is to be made to accept his transformation through the demonstration of excessive kindness, Kate the scold through deprivation.

Sly's confused concern for his social status (his family arrived with 'Richard Conqueror') reflects the social concerns of the play. Kate is worried that she will be publicly humiliated by her family and her husband, shown by her angry words in Acts I–III, and then by her dismay when the tailor is dismissed in Act IV. Petruchio will subvert society's codes in order to force his wife to conform, and he uses his masculine power to achieve his ends. The Lord is involving himself in a reversal of the social order for the same reason. We are introduced to ideas about male linguistic power in this extract. The difference between Sly's colloquial speech ('I'll feeze you') and the Lord's and huntsmen's more elegant style is amusing, and we immediately see who will dominate. Petruchio's forceful verbal style will similarly overrule Kate's shrewish persona; like Sly asleep, Katherina is largely silent as she is tamed.

The references to hunting and the treatment that the dogs, described in this extract, are to receive are ironic. More care is lavished on these beasts than is meted out to tinkers and women like Kate; we might argue that this is because the dogs perform a valuable service

CHECK THE BOOK

To read the additional passages of the Sly frame from *The Taming of a Shrew*, see p. 53 of Stanley Wells and Gary Taylor's edition of Shakespeare's plays, *William Shakespeare: The Complete Works* (1988).

to their owner and heighten his reputation. When she submits to her husband's authority Kate is given the praise that Echo, Merriman and the rest have deserved for their efforts during the hunt. The hunting **motif** runs through *The Shrew*, clearly linking Petruchio with the Lord; both are the superior and controlling males in the scenes in which they appear. Petruchio takes on the shrew, which makes 'a little din' (I.2.198), and turns her from a 'haggard' (IV.1.180) into a tame falcon, who will perform so as to add to his prestige. The coupling of Clowder with the 'deep-mouth'd brach' (line 16) perhaps hints at the couplings we will see later in the play. Pairing him off is to be an important part of the Lord's scheme for deceiving Sly: in the next scene he will be presented with a 'wife'. The exhaustion of the 'emboss'd' dog mentioned at line 15 foreshadows the weary state Katherina will find herself in during her taming. Sly is linked to the animal world when he is compared to a 'swine' (line 32); animal imagery will continue to suggest the natural order of things in this play, in which unattractive animals are brought into line. The competitive discussion of the dogs' different merits foreshadows the tussle for Bianca's hand in marriage, and the comparison that will be made between the three wives who grace the table in the final scene. There is a clear indication that there is a natural order in this scene. We will not be able to escape the conclusion that women are meant to be like tame dogs and falcons, part of their husband's goods and chattels, for men to train and enjoy as and when they please. 'Tomorrow' the Lord intends to go hunting again; Petruchio will expect his Kate to speak and perform on cue too.

We might feel that the **slapstick** and verbal comedy that are notable features of *The Shrew* are established here. The joke that the Lord sets up will involve visual comedy, and Sly's drunken slumber is comic. The incongruity of the elegant language used to describe the dogs and the more direct and pithy exclamations of and about Sly prepare us for the wit and linguistic ingenuity that we will come to associate with Petruchio and Tranio in particular. The theme of deception, the importance of appearances and the power of transformation are also established here. Complex layers of theatrical illusion are hinted at: we suspect that Sly will be given new clothes as well as a feast when he wakes up, anticipating the

CHECK THE BOOK

To read a **feminist** discussion of the play in relation to stage and film versions, see Diana E. Henderson's essay 'A Shrew For the Times' in the New Casebook *Much Ado About Nothing and The Taming of the Shrew,* edited by Marion Wynne-Davies (2001).

use of disguises in the subplot. Are we to understand that the roles people play are a construction? Sly is to be given a false identity by the Lord, just as the women in *The Shrew* are defined by men. The important role clothes are to play in the taming plot is hinted at when we learn that Sly is to be attended by 'brave' servants (in fine array). When she fits in with the plans that have been made for her Kate will be rewarded with a new dress. Like the Lord, Petruchio will be able to choose the clothes that he and his wife wear, proving where the power lies. Finally, just as Petruchio will give Kate no time to think about what is happening to her, the Lord makes a lightning decision to play a trick on Sly. When the drunkard wakes up in the next scene he is immediately bombarded with new sensations.

TEXT 2 – III.2.189–231

Petruchio prepares to return home with his bride after the wedding ceremony.

> PETRUCHIO: … If you knew my business,
> You would entreat me rather go than stay.   190
> And honest company, I thank you all
> That have beheld me give away myself
> To this most patient, sweet, and virtuous wife.
> Dine with my father, drink a health to me,
> For I must hence, and farewell to you all.   195
>
> TRANIO: Let us entreat you stay till after dinner.
>
> PETRUCHIO: It may not be.
>
> GREMIO: Let me entreat you.
>
> PETRUCHIO: It cannot be.
>
> KATHERINA: Let me entreat you.
>
> PETRUCHIO: I am content.
>
> KATHERINA: Are you content to stay?
>
> PETRUCHIO: I am content you shall entreat me stay;   200
> But yet not stay, entreat me how you can.

? QUESTION

Explore the dramatic importance of the wedding scene.

KATHERINA: Now if you love me, stay.

PETRUCHIO: Grumio, my horse.

GRUMIO: Ay, sir, they be ready; the oats have eaten the
  horses.

KATHERINA: Nay then,   205
  Do what thou canst, I will not go today,
  No, nor tomorrow, not till I please myself.
  The door is open, sir, there lies your way,
  You may be jogging whiles your boots are green.
  For me, I'll not be gone till I please myself.   210
  'Tis like you'll prove a jolly surly groom,
  That take it on you at the first so roundly.

PETRUCHIO: O Kate, content thee, prithee be not angry.

KATHERINA: I will be angry; what hast thou to do?
  Father, be quiet; he shall stay my leisure.   215

GREMIO: Ay, marry, sir, now it begins to work.

KATHERINA: Gentlemen, forward to the bridal dinner.
  I see a woman may be made a fool
  If she had not a spirit to resist.

PETRUCHIO: They shall go forward, Kate, at thy command. 220
  Obey the bride, you that attend on her.
  Go to the feast, revel and domineer,
  Carouse full measure to her maidenhead,
  Be mad and merry, or go hang yourselves.
  But for my bonny Kate, she must with me.   225
  Nay, look not big, nor stamp, nor stare, nor fret;
  I will be master of what is mine own.
  She is my goods, my chattels, she is my house,
  My household stuff, my field, my barn,
  My horse, my ox, my ass, my any thing,   230
  And here she stands. Touch her whoever dare!

CHECK THE BOOK

In *Shakespeare and the Nature of Women* (1975) Juliet Dusinberre claims 'For avaricious fathers love is for women and cash is for men. When the dramatists uphold the love match against the mercenary marriage … they uphold women's values against men's' (p. 123). Whose values are upheld in this scene?

From the courtship onwards Petruchio has been in control of events, and this extract confirms his authority. He refuses to stay for the wedding feast, in spite of entreaties from Tranio and Gremio.

His repeated denial becomes more forceful (from 'It may not be' to 'It cannot be'), and then when his wife makes the same request, his answer is indirect. He forces Katherina to question him so that he can put her in her place. We might feel he is reminding her that she must get used to the idea of asking for his consent and approval ('I am content you shall entreat me stay'). The repetition of the word 'entreat' suggests that Katherina will become accustomed to verbal submission. This does not come as a surprise. The opening of this extract hints that the wife-taming has begun in earnest now; perhaps this is the 'business' Petruchio refers to at line 189. It is rather chilling that Petruchio believes that the Paduans would 'entreat me rather go than stay' if they knew what his intentions were (line 190). Are his methods to be too shocking or unpleasant to witness? It is significant that Petruchio's reference to his 'business' is immediately followed by a description of his 'most patient, sweet, and virtuous wife' (line 193). We might feel that these lines are a reproach to Kate, who clearly possesses none of these qualities in this scene. This description is also a declaration of intent: she will be forced to assume these qualities. The final lines of the extract suggest that Petruchio has the power to make this happen, since he is now Katherina's owner, she part of his 'household stuff'. Throughout this scene, Petruchio speaks with complete authority, indicated by his use of commands in the final speech ('Obey the bride ... Go to the feast ... Carouse full measure ... go hang yourselves') culminating in a forceful statement: 'she must with me'. The modal verbs Shakespeare puts in the protagonist's mouth have become increasingly purposeful: 'must' allows no contradiction. This is entirely in keeping with the way in which Petruchio has been portrayed so far. He remains determined, single-minded and assured.

Petruchio's behaviour retains some of the boisterous high spirits and playfulness we have come to associate with him too. He is verbally dexterous, quibbling with the Paduans and his wife, and asserting his own seemingly fantastic reality. His audience are more or less silenced by his lively final speech, and can only watch as the groom carries away his reluctant and outraged bride, pretending that she has been beset by thieves ('Touch her whoever dare!'). Petruchio continues to play the role of 'mad-brain rudesby' (III.2.10), although he is perhaps more serious here than his garb

CHECK THE FILM

Franco Zeffirelli's 1967 film gives a strong sense of marriage as a public act. Huge crowds witness the wedding, and the discomfort caused by being shamed publicly by your partner is made very clear when Kate is laughed at loudly by the citizens of Padua while she stands waiting for Petruchio to arrive.

and behaviour in the church, as reported by Gremio, suggested earlier in the scene. Why is he acting out the role of subversive? Why won't he stay for the feast? Essentially, Petruchio has made a farce of his wedding because he wishes to show his wife that she must conform, or continue to suffer humiliations like those she experiences in this scene. He is attempting to alert Kate to the social chaos her shrewish behaviour leads to, and he is trying to shame her into submission by being even more perverse than she is. By being more shrew than she, Petruchio clearly shows his wife that it is useless to resist the authority of the dominant male. He can and will shout louder and longer. His refusal to stay for the feast is an example of his taming techniques: a punishment because Kate won't conform. Until she behaves in the way society expects an obedient female to behave, she will not be allowed to participate in its rituals. When she does conform Katherina will be allowed to celebrate and eat. As yet, Petruchio does not feel there is anything to be jubilant about; his wife still insists she will 'please myself' (line 207). Petruchio continues to deny her food in Act IV, when he has her at home. The reference to her 'maidenhead' hints at what will occur. Petruchio will not consummate his marriage until his wife has submitted to him publicly in Act V. By making a mockery of the celebrations that have been set up Petruchio undermines Katherina, but not himself. He gets precisely what he wants in this extract.

We might feel that Petruchio ridicules the Paduans too; the idea that they will leave to 'revel and domineer' without the bride and groom suggests that he has, in a strange way, got the better of them. In spite of Gremio's belief that 'now it begins to work', Petruchio will have the last laugh and dispel all doubts that he will not be able to master his wife. The Paduans may feel the joke is on him (he has a shrew for a wife and Gremio's line suggests that they have a voyeuristic pleasure in seeing how the Punch and Judy show will turn out), but the audience suspects they misjudge the situation. Those who laugh at Katherina now for being 'madly mated' (III.2.242) will be made uncomfortable by the revelation that the supposedly docile Widow and Bianca are in fact shrews. Petruchio, who makes use of illusions and role-play, proves that he is the only character on stage with true understanding, or rather, he is the only character in this play forceful enough to create his own reality.

 CHECK THE FILM

In the 1999 film *10 Things I Hate About You* it is the hero Pat who has to change his ways in order to impress Kat. He gives up smoking and looks after her when she gets drunk at a party. Later he sings her a love song, 'Can't Take My Eyes Off You'.

But what of the shrew herself? In this extract she delivers her last truly energetic and indignant speech about wishing to please herself, although she will try to assert her point of view when the tailor visits in Act IV. We know that there is a good deal of work to be done to bring Katherina into line when she says, 'Do what thou canst, I will not go today' (line 206). Kate also pours scorn on her 'jolly surly groom', echoing her words in the earlier courting scene. But we know that she will not prevail, in spite of the fact that she can still silence some men (her father). Kate uses the same forceful modal verbs as her husband 'I *will* be angry … he *shall* stay my leisure [my italics]' – but the fact that she is ignored at line 202 suggests that the female voice has little power. There is a hint that the heroine is already being worn down and perhaps already accepts that she wants to conform. Her uncertain question 'Are you content to stay?' suggests this, as does her next line: 'Now if you love me, stay' (lines 199 and 202). This request might be a challenge, but because Kate was so worried about being jilted at the altar at the beginning of the scene, and because she is also clearly concerned about not being allowed to participate in the public triumph of her own bridal feast, we might sense that she will submit. The only – preposterous – power she is allowed in this scene is to tell the guests to go forward to the wedding feast, a command which is hijacked by her husband and revealed as an absurdity. Petruchio's pretended gallantry at this point ('They shall go forward, Kate, at thy command') further undermines her, as the description of her supposed virtues did earlier. Her stamping, staring and fretting make her seem ridiculous too. Kate may 'look … big', but she doesn't have the verbal power to achieve anything.

The reference to Petruchio's horse is important, part of the pattern of animal **imagery** that informs our understanding of the play. This reference hints at what will occur on the journey home, when Kate comes off her horse in the mire; a visual **symbol** of her ultimate submission. Earlier in the play Katherina referred to her wooer as a 'jade' (a worn-out, useless horse, II.1.201), and he invited her to 'sit on' him (II.1.198); when she falls under her horse we know Petruchio will win. This extract suggests that it is Kate and not Petruchio who is the real 'jade': she is no use to her master because she remains stormy and defiant. Petruchio's reference to his horse

> **CONTEXT**
>
> In *The Woman's Prize, or The Tamer Tamed* (c.1611), a **comedy** sequel to *The Shrew* by John Fletcher, Petruchio finds it impossible to assert himself against his new wife Maria. In Act V he has to resort to pretending to be dead and having himself carried on stage in a coffin in order to gain her sympathy and a truce.

 QUESTION

Theatre director Michael Bogdanov argues that the play is about 'a male wish-fulfilment dream of revenge on women'. Do you agree?

also reminds us of his arrival at the wedding on a broken-down horse suffering from every possible ailment (III.2.46–61). This entertaining description of the decrepit beast is a **metaphor** for Kate the useless wife, and Petruchio's arrival on it an insult to her dignity. We will see many more examples of the protagonist's perverse eccentricity in the next act.

TEXT 3 – V.2.117–48

The men bet on the obedience of their wives, and Katherina scolds her sister and the Widow for their 'froward' behaviour.

QUESTION

How fitting do you find the final scene as an ending to the play?

PETRUCHIO: Nay, I will win my wager better yet,
    And show more sign of her obedience,
    Her new-built virtue and obedience.

      Enter KATHERINA, BIANCA, *and* WIDOW.

See where she comes, and brings your froward wives   120
As prisoners to her womanly persuasion.
Katherine, that cap of yours becomes you not.
Off with that bauble, throw it under foot.   *[She obeys.]*

WIDOW: Lord, let me never have a cause to sigh
    Till I be brought to such a silly pass.   125

BIANCA: Fie, what a foolish duty call you this?

LUCENTIO: I would your duty were as foolish too.
    The wisdom of your duty, fair Bianca,
    Hath cost me a hundred crowns since supper-time.

BIANCA: The more fool you for laying on my duty.   130

PETRUCHIO: Katherine, I charge thee, tell these headstrong
    women
    What duty they do owe their lords and husbands.

WIDOW: Come, come, you're mocking. We will have no telling.

PETRUCHIO: Come on, I say, and first begin with her.

WIDOW: She shall not.   135

PETRUCHIO: I say she shall. And first begin with her.

KATHERINA: Fie, fie! Unknit that threatening unkind brow,
And dart not scornful glances from those eyes,
To wound thy lord, thy king, thy governor.
It blots thy beauty as frosts do bite the meads,   140
Confounds thy fame as whirlwinds shake fair buds,
And in no sense is meet or amiable.
A woman mov'd is like a fountain troubled,
Muddy, ill-seeming, thick, bereft of beauty,
And while it is so, none so dry or thirsty   145
Will deign to sip or touch one drop of it.
Thy husband is thy lord, thy life, thy keeper,
Thy head, thy sovereign ...

These lines provide **closure** of a kind, but also raise questions. On the surface it seems that Petruchio has won 'peace ... and love, and quiet life, / An awful rule, and right supremacy' (V.2.109–10), and, significantly, his wager. Love, marriage and women are linked once again to money and Petruchio's supremacy over the others in all these fields is demonstrated visually and orally. Firstly, having come when she was called for, Kate throws her cap under her foot as a token of obedience. She then obeys Petruchio's command to lecture the other women on the 'duty they do owe their lords and husbands' (line 132), speaking in a style and tone that reflect many of Petruchio's earlier speeches, both in content and construction. The comparison that Katherina makes between an unruly woman and a muddy fountain, which no one will 'deign to sip', can be linked to the way food was withheld during the taming scenes. Kate can eat now because she is a good wife; she is her husband's 'super-dainty Kate' (II.1.188). Her listing of 'thy lord, thy life ...' recalls earlier speeches made by Petruchio too, most notably his defiant description of Katherina as part of his 'household stuff' in Act III. Has she been so cowed that she now takes on her husband's voice? Or are we to assume that this couple are well matched because she has learned to speak his language? Kate's rhetorical skill reflects Petruchio's verbal mastery of events, suggesting that he has prevailed completely. It is significant that Katherina does not speak until she is requested to. Her scolding of Bianca and the Widow – 'Fie, fie! Unknit that threatening unkind brow' (line 137) – recalls

CHECK THE BOOK
Stevie Davies argues that 'Kate's life is finished, because she concedes her voice.' To read her discussion of the final scene in full, have a look at her Penguin Critical Studies guide *The Taming of the Shrew* (1995).

his commands to her, which she has now learned to obey. And Petruchio does not simply get his wife to show her obedience and use her 'womanly persuasion' to put down the other women; he shows that he is still in control verbally. He silences the Widow with these forceful words: 'I say she shall.' It seems that Petruchio maintains his taming ability, even when his own wife is tamed; now he has so much power he can even get his wife to 'tame' the others: she carries on the war against shrews for him. A number of critics suggest that Kate's speech silences the other women in this scene. Because Petruchio has won an enormous amount of money during the play for taming Kate, we have to see him as the real winner here. And his confidence and continued domineering behaviour suggest he is well pleased with his work: he is keen for his wife to speak and show off *his* skill.

However, many critics have claimed that Katherina's speech and behaviour must be read as an **ironic** deconstruction of the patriarchy she seems to be endorsing. As Bianca says, it is ridiculous to throw off a cap and put it under a husband's foot: does this 'foolish duty' undermine Petruchio's triumph? Equally, Katherina's speech can seem exaggerated and rather ridiculous; the war **imagery** she utilises ('dart not … those eyes … wound') which is carried on through the rest of the speech might be seen as a deliberate absurdity. The same might be said for her rhetorical listing: is she parodying Petruchio in order to suggest that *she* has in fact triumphed? When she speaks with his voice, perhaps she defeats the Paduans, who have not had a good word to say for her. And how can we be sure that the 'brawling scold' of the early scenes has gone for ever, particularly when two other shrews unmask themselves? The scorn and defiance that the Widow and Bianca display here mirror Kate's early defiance, suggesting that a woman may 'break out' at any time. Really, perhaps there is no choice: all women are shrews. Hortensio's silence and Lucentio's peevish and impotent comments suggest that there is a perceptible loss of male power in this scene.

Nevertheless, it remains possible to argue that this extract proves that a happy marriage depends upon female submission. We know that two out of three couples are in for a rough ride, and the fact

CONTEXT

Critics have argued that Katherina's final speech shows that she has a growing awareness of her body as a source of erotic pleasure when she speaks of the female form being 'soft' and 'smooth' (V.2.166).

QUESTION

Does Petruchio transform Katherina, or does she transform herself?

that Petruchio seems well pleased with what occurs ('Why, there's a wench!') endorses the view of those who would argue that this final scene cannot be read ironically, for all the questions it raises. Here, women are reduced to sport when the men bet on their obedience; marriage remains a game for *men* to win or lose. The fact that money is linked to love and marriage again here suggests that the patriarchal hierarchy remains in place. Men control the money, and the most successful man gets the largest share, because he has been most successful in the terms of the world of the play, in which matrimonial bargaining has been repeatedly linked to mercantile bartering. Petruchio's goods and chattels are worth most. And the masculine competition and sporting of the wager suggests that it has all been a game, undermining the seriousness of the whole business of marriage.

CHECK THE FILM
The 1980 BBC production ends harmoniously. Katherina and Petruchio enjoy a lengthy kiss and then the assembled guests all sing happily together.

PART THREE

CRITICAL APPROACHES

CHARACTERISATION

This play contains many elements of **farce**. Great depth cannot be expected from characters who are required by the kind of **comedy** Shakespeare was writing to move at high speed, without much introspection. The subtlety of characterisation noted in the dramatist's later works is perhaps missing in this early play, and we are not intended to be troubled by the transformations of personality that occur: Kate is required by the genre to change. Having said this, a modern audience is likely to want to analyse the presentation of the characters in detail and seek out and account for any inconsistencies or incongruities that present themselves. It is, of course, legitimate to question Shakespeare's portrayal of his cast in the search for meaning. And it is true that Shakespeare does individualise and transform the stereotypes and stock characters he uses.

PETRUCHIO

For an audience watching and reading the play today, the problem with Petruchio is this: he is outrageous, his behaviour deeply repugnant to modern sensibility, but it is also possible to be enormously entertained by him. The theatrical qualities of the role make him engaging. Petruchio is at times deliberately farcical (the wedding ceremony, his behaviour at his home in Act IV) and he seems to be at the centre of some of the cruder **slapstick** comedy. He is also verbally energetic and linguistically imaginative. His early speeches in Act I Scene 2 are full of machismo, but they are witty. At times Petruchio is also – perhaps surprisingly – poetic (see his descriptions of Kate's appearance in Act II Scene 1). The verbal dexterity the protagonist displays can make him, if not endearing, then certainly appealing as a theatrical creation. Our reception of Petruchio depends partly upon the shrewishness of Kate and whether or not he is portrayed as sinister and violent, as well as direct, lively and playful. There are elements of all these qualities in his characterisation.

CHECK THE FILM

A stage tradition of Petruchio brandishing a whip began in the eighteenth century. In the 1929 film version of the play, it was Mary Pickford, playing Kate, who carried a whip, which Petruchio ultimately flung in the fire.

Petruchio is undoubtedly a fortune-hunter, associated with money
and animal-taming from the beginning of the play. Within moments
of his arrival on stage he has announced that he is seeking a wealthy
wife. The action of the play suggests that he is rewarded financially
for taming the shrew. His wooing costs are met by the men who
wish to get Kate out of the way so that they can court Bianca,
and he wins the wager in the final scene. Impressed by the
transformation of his daughter, Baptista offers his triumphant son-
in-law a second dowry. We might be tempted to feel that Petruchio
has been paid for performing a public service, rather than for
embarking on a mercantile and risky personal business venture.
The protagonist's piratical behaviour continues when he woos
Katherina. He sweeps in, overpowers her verbally, threatens to do
the same physically, and then sweeps out, nonchalantly announcing
when he is prepared to come and claim his bride. We are forced
to marvel at the presumption of the man, as eventually the
dumbfounded Katherina does.

As the play progresses Petruchio moves on to new feats of eccentric
swaggering, before setting about the taming in earnest in Act IV.
The wedding ceremony may look like a game (Gremio's
descriptions of the scene in the church and Petruchio's 'mad attire'
suggest we should laugh at the incongruity before us), but really, the
protagonist is preparing us for his resolute rule, as his speech at the
end of Act III Scene 2 shows (see lines 220–37). The confidence and
sense of superiority established in earlier speeches are reconfirmed
here. We can never be in any doubt that Petruchio intends to be
master of what he owns, and he is prepared to take on a role and
work hard to achieve his aims. He is extremely single-minded, and
does not waver from his purpose. Not once does he admit that
Katherina has her own point of view.

But what does he want? His ambitions are actually quite small, and,
ironically, at odds with the swashbuckling persona he assumes for
much of the play: he declares that he values domestic peace and
harmony. All the noise and chaos he causes are intended to secure
a quiet life at home. So how does he ensure that he achieves this?
Partly by being a fine actor and doggedly and consistently asserting
that everything is the opposite of what it seems, but mainly because

**CHECK
THE FILM**

Petruchio's power
at the end of the
wooing scene is
clear in the 1980
BBC production –
he has Kate in an
armlock.

PETRUCHIO continued

he possesses a will stronger than anyone else's. The other (male) characters also collude with and assist Petruchio, who is undoubtedly the most masculine and dominant male: he is cock of the walk. There are lines that suggest the master is teacher and educator, but there are also lines that suggest brute force and an uncompromising desire to dominate ruthlessly. Undoubtedly, his educational methods are harsh. His violent tendencies are all directed at his subordinates, and his abuse of those who serve him is intended to remind his wife that she may be next on the list. And if Petruchio does not actually resort to beating his wife, she certainly suffers physically while in his care. The neglect and disinterest of her father's house are replaced by deprivation: no food, no sleep, left in the mire under her horse, and no new clothes or kisses. Petruchio forces his wife to give up her voice by asserting his own right to speak and define the world as he sees it. It becomes clear that his unnatural and eccentric behaviour is licensed while Katherina's is not. We are encouraged to believe that Petruchio is using his role as 'mad-brain rudesby' (III.2.10) to re-educate his wife. At the end of the play we know that Hortensio and Lucentio will need to join Petruchio's 'taming-school' (IV.2.54) if they are to enjoy peaceful marriages with their wives.

> **CONTEXT**
>
> Petruchio's strategies to gain control of his wife, as outlined in his soliloquies, are reflected in the advice moralists and ministers offered Renaissance husbands in texts and sermons. They urged men to use 'policy' rather than beatings to achieve a happy marriage.

Is Petruchio a playful suitor or misogynist bully? It depends upon whether or not we feel that Katherina has gained or lost by meeting and marrying him. Petruchio's **soliloquies** do not hint at much affection, although at the end of the play we can see that he is satisfied with the wife he has moulded and subdued. The line 'Why, there's a wench! Come on, and kiss me, Kate' (V.2.181) suggests approval. We might feel that the kisses in the play chart the hero's increasing pleasure in his creation. At the wedding ceremony Petruchio kisses Katherina in order to humiliate her; then at the end of Act V Scene 1 he uses a public kiss in the street to test her obedience. Finally in Act V Scene 2 he rewards Kate – and himself – for her obedience by kissing her prior to the consummation of the marriage. Some see this kiss, and the line quoted above, as proof that Petruchio has really been seeking a companionate marriage (although we must not forget that a happy marriage depends upon female submission in this play). *The Taming of the Shrew* clearly demonstrates the importance of female behaviour for a man's reputation: the hawking **imagery** underlines this point. In the closing moments we will certainly view Lucentio and Hortensio as lesser men because they cannot rule their wives. Unlike Petruchio, they do not possess the energy and wit to tame their shrews. Their reputations have suffered, while his has prospered.

KATHERINA

Kate can be seen as a prototype for Shakespeare's energetic, licensed female talkers, Beatrice (*Much Ado About Nothing*) and Paulina (*The Winter's Tale*). However, many feel that the heroine's voice is never given the credit it deserves in this early play. It is possible to argue that Katherina is both defined and destroyed by the male tongue. Her early utterances reflect her reputation as a scold, but the male characters exaggerate her shrewishness. She says less than half as much as Petruchio and her longest and most compelling speech is made – **ironically** – after she has been tamed and given up her distinctive female voice. Prior to this speech, the men have dealt with Katherina by ignoring or contradicting her. Petruchio silences her by being more shrew than she. At the end of the play it is hard to resist the conclusion that Kate is only allowed to deliver her lecture because it has been endorsed by and will please a man. Essentially, Kate has a stereotypical role to play out, one which would have been familiar to the Elizabethan audience from folklore and **ballads**: she is the scold who must be punished for her waywardness. The treatment she receives bears some resemblance to the traditional methods used to shame shrewish females: the scold's bridle and the ducking stool, both of which were intended to humiliate the scold physically and publicly. Although Petruchio does not resort to the crude physical violence of these methods, he certainly threatens to cuff and restrain Kate.

If Kate is a stereotype, does her character develop? In more positive readings of the play, some critics suggest that she is liberated by Petruchio, who frees her to grow into a contented wife, with a useful role to play outside her father's house. Thus it can be argued that she benefits from the rather brutal education she is forced to endure. Some critics note Katherina's insistence on erotic and emotional pleasure in her final speech, in which she declares that women should submit to their husbands because they work hard to

CHECK THE FILM

In Franco Zeffirelli's 1967 film Katherina is shown to desire a 'happy family' when she smiles fondly at some children and then glances wistfully at her husband during the final feast.

keep their wives 'secure and safe' at home (V.2.152). Are we to assume that she has finally understood the point of being ruled by men? Her lines towards
the end of her lecture suggest she has 'seen the light' and accepted patriarchy's rules (see V.2.170–6).

These lines hint at a change of mind. It is possible to argue that Katherina's style and tone indicate that she has 'grown' and changed. In Act V Scene 2 she speaks eloquently, forcefully and gracefully, with a measured tone that contrasts sharply with her outbursts in Acts I and II. During Act IV, her combative wit becomes more playful, as we see from her exchanges with Petruchio about the sun and moon in Act IV Scene 5. Perhaps her quick-wittedness, once employed to snarl and sneer at her unwanted suitor, is now utilised to entertain a husband she has accepted gratefully.

CHECK THE BOOK

To read comments by actresses who played Kate in the 1970s, have a look at Judith Cook's *Women in Shakespeare* (1980). The actress Janet Suzman argues that Katherina and Petruchio find allies in each other.

It is possible that these comments are too generous, and do not allow for the outrage that might be felt when watching the heroine being humiliated. Modern audiences are likely to feel that Kate has some cause for her early discontent and shrewishness: the Paduan males are puny, her sister is sanctimonious, and her father mercantile and cold. No one listens to her. Later she has every right to be outraged by Petruchio's treatment of her, from the wooing scene onwards. A modern audience might also feel that Kate is diminished by the events of the play. Rather than grow, perhaps she is obliterated. The Katherina who speaks at the end of the play seems to possess a masculine view of the world, as if a new persona has been unconvincingly grafted on to the female stereotype by the playwright, who is not really concerned with the consistency of his heroine's characterisation. Katherina becomes the ideal Kate outlined by Petruchio in Act II Scene 1. Are we then to view her as a figure intended to satisfy a male wish-fulfilment fantasy? As Katherina goes from making demands to following instructions, many would argue that she becomes an increasingly powerless figure: her transformation negates rather than confirms the value of the female. As the title of the play suggests, the taming is more important than the shrew.

It is briefly worth considering Kate's looks, which are not so important to the drama as her scolding tongue, but significant nonetheless. Is the shrew ugly or fair, like her sister? Outward appearances are consistently deceptive in this play, in which men judge women according to their physical attributes and silence. Critics are divided about whether or not Kate's looks are as abhorrent as her voice. There are conflicting descriptions in Act I Scene 2; the heroine is 'ill-favour'd' (I.2.59) early in the scene, becoming 'young and beauteous' (I.2.85) as Hortensio realises that Petruchio will take her on. Petruchio then complicates matters by seeming to praise Katherina's appearance in Act II Scene 1:

> Why does the world report that Kate doth limp?
> O slanderous world! Kate like the hazel-twig
> Is straight and slender, and as brown in hue
> As hazel-nuts and sweeter than the kernels. (II.1.246–9)

He adds that her 'beauty ... doth make me like thee well' (II.1.267). However, all these words are uttered in a scene in which Petruchio often asserts the opposite of what he knows to be true. Is this another example of the hero taunting the heroine? If his praise is **ironic**, then Katherina looks even more like a victim.

Katherina's relationship with the other female characters in the play is important. Unlike Shakespeare's other heroines of comedy, Kate has no female friend or confidante: her isolation perhaps shows us how at odds she is with society. Both before and after her taming, she seems to remain antagonistic towards other women. Some critics have suggested that she redirects the venom she displayed towards Bianca in Act II at the Widow in the final scene. Neither her sister nor the Widow respond to her final speech; the male characters are alone when they celebrate the taming of the shrew. Has Kate turned on her 'sisters' in a different way? Can we view her as an enemy of her own sex, having been misled into believing that she was an enemy to men?

BIANCA

Bianca's characterisation is sketchy but intriguing. To begin with she seems to be as much a female stereotype as her sister: she is the

CONTEXT

In the sequel to *The Taming of the Shrew* by John Fletcher, *The Woman's Prize, or The Tamer Tamed* (c.1611), Petruchio's second wife Maria declares: 'that childish woman / That lives a prisoner to her husband's pleasure, / Has lost her making, and becomes a beast, / Created for his use, not fellowship.' In view of these lines, how do you interpret Katherina and Petruchio's relationship?

CHECK THE BOOK

Stevie Davies suggests Bianca proves 'that a man has two alternatives: a shrew ... and a shrew'. To read her comments in full, see her Penguin Critical Studies guide *The Taming of the Shrew* (1995).

silent, obedient maiden whom suitors flock to worship. But if Shakespeare seems to insist that the scold can be brought into line in the taming plot, the opposite is true in the subplot. From early on the playwright hints that Bianca will please herself, although she initially appears to be a victim. Like Katherina, she is mewed up and thwarted at home; but this female rebels by seeming to conform. By cultivating a silent and demure exterior, Bianca dupes others. It is noticeable that she says more, and speaks more assertively, as the play progresses, providing a point of contrast with her sister, who is becoming less vocal. Bianca's submissive outward appearance gives her some power: she is able to choose a husband by deceiving her father. There is a good deal of **irony** in her characterisation. Is she the real shrew in this play, far more dangerous than her railing, brawling sister? Because Bianca is unmasked as a shrew, there is no real **closure** at the end of Act V. One scold is silenced, but the other has gained what she wanted, and her reign has just begun.

BAPTISTA

Baptista Minola is a conventional Elizabethan patriarch. He is attached to at least one of his daughters, but views both as objects to be bartered on the marriage market. The clever father keeps Bianca in reserve while he follows the custom of marrying off his eldest daughter first; this is canny: it will raise her price, suggested by the fact that Bianca gains suitors as the play progresses. Baptista uses Bianca's suitors to find a husband for his difficult daughter, thus saving him the troublesome task of locating a man to take Katherina on. Many critics comment on his lack of concern for Kate, and consider the Minolas dysfunctional. Generally, Baptista disregards his eldest daughter's feelings, although he shows some sympathy for her on her wedding day when Petruchio is late. However, this remark and his rather lame insistence that Petruchio must win his daughter's love (see II.1.128–9) are unconvincing. Essentially, Baptista allows the pirate to make off with Kate because, as Gremio and Hortensio recognise, he wants to be rid of her. It seems just and appropriate, then, that his conniving younger daughter gets the better of him. This is **ironic**, because Baptista puts more energy, effort and guile into disposing of his 'treasure' (II.1.32). He plays the suitors off against one another, looking for the most advantageous match, simultaneously proving himself to be as careless of his younger daughter's feelings as he was of the elder's. His lines in Act IV Scene 4 show this. Here he speaks brazenly of knowing Bianca's heart and mind: we know he does not. Ultimately, however, the father is not punished for his mercantile approach to matrimony. He is humiliated by Lucentio, Tranio and Bianca, but the former is an eminently suitable match, socially and financially: he is the kind of son-in-law Baptista would have chosen. Because this is a **comedy**, the deception and self-delusion of the father do not lead to tragedy, as they will in *King Lear* (1605) and *The Winter's Tale* (1611).

THE SUITORS

Lucentio

Lucentio is presented as the young Elizabethan gallant, idealistic but rather ridiculous in his romantic aspirations. He is the opposite of Petruchio and, unlike the more vigorous wooer, requires some education himself if he is to achieve a happy marriage, his goal from the first scene in which he appears. Unlike the self-sufficient protagonist, Lucentio has to rely on others to organise his wooing and wedding, hinting at the fact that he will be duped by Bianca. In the end, like Hortensio, he is no match for the duplicitous female he is united with, in spite of the fact that he too has acted the role of deceiver. Lucentio is a benign, comic figure, whose courtly approach and classical allusions are undermined and ridiculed by the robust action and outcome of the play.

Hortensio

Hortensio provides another point of comparison with Petruchio, the successful woman-tamer; and Lucentio, the courtly lover. He lacks the masculine vigour of the former and the romantic conviction of the latter, although he professes to be very much in love with Bianca in Act I (see I.2.173–4). Hortensio's lack of success with women makes him a source of comedy; rejected by Bianca, he is physically abused by Katherina and bested by his Widow. He is an impotent figure, no match for the other men or women in the play. Like Lucentio, he has a lot to learn. Hortensio's attitude to marriage highlights the social and financial concerns of the

> **CONTEXT**
>
> Lucentio is similar to the 'Inamorato' from the Italian *commedia dell'arte*, whose role was that of the romantic young lover.

Elizabethan male. He declares he will no longer court Bianca when he discovers she has looked at another man, and settles for a wealthy widow instead. Hortensio's admiring responses to Petruchio's taming methods, and his assistance in the subjection of Kate in Act IV Scene 3, demonstrate the superior attitude of men towards women in this play. But this male is not assertive enough to capitalise on the lesson he is presented with.

Gremio

Gremio's characterisation is inspired by the 'Pantaloon' from Italian *commedia dell'arte*, in which wealthy old buffoons unsuccessfully and foolishly court young women. Gremio adds to our understanding of the masculine values that dominate this play, showing a traditional male abhorrence of the scold. He frequently makes derogatory comments about Kate, and serves as another comic foil in the subplot, as a rival to Hortensio and Lucentio. After the wedding of Katherina and Petruchio his role is not significant, although he continues to comment on the action, adding to our understanding of characters and events (particularly the Kate–Petruchio match) and to the confusion in the scene of unmasking that occurs in Act IV. His forced resignation from the battlefield of love is accepted with good grace, and he is content to obtain a hearty meal instead. Thus we might feel that his unsuccessful wooing, like Hortensio's, undermines the romantic Lucentio's approach.

THE SERVANTS

As is often the case in Elizabethan and Jacobean drama, the servants in *The Taming of the Shrew* are lively, resourceful figures, as quick-witted as their masters (often more so). They assist with the matrimonial plans and intrigues, taking on roles in order to participate in the action. However, in each case, the servant's subversive or anarchic potential is contained.

Tranio

Tranio is the most important servant in the play. Without his clever plotting, Lucentio would not 'achieve' (I.1.156) fair Bianca. He has a persuasive tongue and is able to transform himself at will. Tranio

QUESTION

Identity is a key theme in the play. How does Shakespeare use Tranio to explore this theme?

seems to be well educated, as his classical allusions in Act I Scene 1 show: he easily takes on his master's role and language. He is accepted and adept in his disguise, becoming increasingly active as he pursues his plots. At times he seems to be stage-managing the action of the subplot, most notably when he sets up his master's wedding and involves the Pedant in their affairs. However, we have to remember that Tranio is at all times serving Lucentio's ends; he is not punished for assuming the role of a wealthy gentleman because, essentially, he has always maintained his role as servant. As in *Twelfth Night*, the role-reversal is licensed and temporary. Tranio is put back in his place firmly in Act V after the high jinks are over, and has never really been a threat to the hierarchy, although he has caused the older male characters some disquiet. He speaks – as Katherina learns to – when called upon to do so.

Biondello

Shakespeare has fun with Biondello, who plays the role of cheeky page, just as he does with Tranio. This character is a helpful messenger. His lively descriptions of the wedding and quick-witted improvisations add to the comedy of the play. Like Tranio, he resembles his comic ancestors from *commedia dell'arte* and the servants in the sources Shakespeare used (see **Structure**).

Grumio

Grumio is most important as a foil for Petruchio, although he makes astute remarks about other characters too (most notably Gremio). He is a clownish figure, rather like a licensed court jester, who tells the truth about and to his master, affording us another view of the protagonist's character. Grumio alerts us to Petruchio's shrewish tendencies and potential for violence, thereby helping to set up the verbal combat that occurs during the 'courtship' of Katherina. This servant shares his master's verbal dexterity, sharp wits, and ability to argue his listener into submission. His 'backchat' in Act I Scene 2 might be seen as subversive, but, like Tranio, Grumio faithfully assists in his master's schemes. Following Petruchio's example and instructions he taunts Katherina with food in Act IV, playing his part in the taming. This is not unexpected; at the wedding he was 'caparisoned like the horse', 'a very monster in

> **CONTEXT**
>
> During the Renaissance the household was considered a microcosm of the state. Thus male dominance was seen as 'correct' because 'the goodly order of God' was being preserved.

apparel' (III.2.63–8). Like Biondello, Grumio is a source of verbal comedy. In Act IV Scene 1 he describes off-stage events in a colourful way. This narrative of the journey home is vivid and amusing. His treatment of Curtis mirrors and anticipates Petruchio's approach to his goods and chattels, demonstrating that Katherina will be brought into line. The 'pecking order' is made clear in Act IV Scene 1. Interestingly, Grumio gets away with far more than Katherina is ever allowed to: his cheek is tolerated.

CHRISTOPHER SLY

CONTEXT

Some theatre directors who have kept Sly on stage give him lines to say during the main action. In the 1939 Stratford production he was given Tranio's line from Act I Scene 1: 'That wench is stark mad or wonderful froward' (line 69). Sly also made several attempts to join in. What effects do you think the director intended?

Sly's situation parallels Katherina's: he is transformed. However, his is a temporary metamorphosis, like Tranio's. Like Lucentio's clever servant, he enjoys being allowed to take on a new social identity and lording it in a different class, although he has more difficulty adapting to his changed role. Perhaps his struggle foreshadows Katherina's. Certainly his initial bewilderment in Scene 2 of the **Induction** mirrors her dazed reactions to Petruchio in Act IV. Sly's energetic speeches anticipate Katherina's shrewish voice of Acts I and II and he is a source of verbal and visual comedy, ridiculous but entertaining as he calls for a pot of ale in his luxurious and elegant surroundings.

Sly is perhaps the only truly realistic character in *The Taming of the Shrew*. Critics have commented on the fact that Shakespeare deliberately casts him as a Warwickshire man, and his down-to-earth style is the opposite of the romantic and more artificial, courtly tones of Lucentio and the Lord. Sly is a man of the street and the tavern. Perhaps his vigour foreshadows Petruchio, whom some critics also characterise as true to life (see comments in **Critical history**). Sly's urgent desire to bed his 'wife' is human and unromantic, and leads the way for the unromantic and **farcical** comedy that is presented for his entertainment. His boredom with the play seems proof of his earthy vitality. Like Petruchio, he 'would fain be doing' (II.1.74).

THEMES

ROMANCE AND MARRIAGE

Some critics suggest that we must view *The Taming of the Shrew* as a romantic **comedy**; others believe there is little romance in this knockabout **farce** concerning the war between the sexes. The play ends with the traditional gathering of married couples, but their progress towards the altar has been characterised by tricks, ruses and brute force. It can be argued that the action of the taming plot systematically undermines the romantic impulses and gestures that we see enacted in the Bianca subplot. Through his portrayal of Kate and Petruchio, Shakespeare perhaps rejects the notions of courtly love the naive Lucentio espouses.

Matrimony is clearly the chief concern of all the characters in this play, but, with the exception of Lucentio, none of the characters appears to adopt a genuinely romantic approach to wooing and wedding a suitable partner. Baptista plays 'a merchant's part' throughout (II.1.319). Hortensio and Gremio, ostensibly romantic wooers drawn by Bianca's beauty, are actually engaged in a masculine competition, which involves providing a 'good deal' for her father and hiring suitable schoolmasters. When Tranio enters the field in disguise, they are concerned because he appears to be a very wealthy young gentleman, and is therefore a better prospect. Hortensio reveals his true colours when he settles for a wealthy 'lusty widow' (IV.2.50). Lucentio's romantic musings would lead nowhere without Tranio's practical scheming. Worshipping from afar simply will not do; he won't 'achieve' the maid this way (I.1.156). When he does 'achieve' her, Lucentio finds that Bianca is not the goddess of maidenly modesty and sobriety he took her for. Lucentio's values are foolish: he has a faulty approach to love and marriage. The careers of Hortensio and Lucentio suggest that matrimony is as hazardous as business. This idea is summed up by Baptista when he refers to the way in which he has to 'venture madly on a desperate mart' in his quest to marry Bianca off to the highest bidder (II.1.320).

The anti-romantic Petruchio is presented as a 'winner' (V.2.188), confirming that wooing is a competition. Pursuing the female is not

CHECK THE BOOK

Lawrence Stone's *The Family, Sex and Marriage in England 1500–1800* (1977) is an excellent source of information about family relationships in the sixteenth century.

the only challenge; establishing the way in which a happy marriage will work is also a contest. This is the focus of the main plot. Petruchio's mercantile approach, which fits in with the 'merchant's part' his father-in-law plays, is established within minutes of his arrival on stage. During the course of the play his wealth increases dramatically as he takes on and tames his bride. Is this a brutal or realistic view of the way marriages operated during the Renaissance? In later plays Shakespeare seems to insist that mutual affection is a vital part of a good match, although he also suggests that a down-to-earth approach is necessary; his heroes who do not look beyond appearances often find themselves in trouble. In *The Shrew* the message seems to be that a happy marriage depends first and foremost on female subordination, a model that we find unpalatable today. But critics have argued that Kate's final speech does not just show the importance of female submission. Some argue that she outlines the idea that men and women have duties to one another. While the woman lies 'warm at home, secure and safe', her mate goes out into the world, 'To painful labour by both sea and land'. Because he works for her 'maintenance' the woman owes her husband 'love, fair looks, and true obedience; / Too little payment for so great a debt' (V.2.149–55). It seems that both sexes have distinct roles in marriage. However, Kate uses language that makes some commentators uneasy; she speaks of 'payment', suggesting that the traffic is perhaps still one way, as it was when Baptista played Bianca's suitors off against one another earlier in the play. The dismay Lucentio displays when he realises his wife is not a dove shows that he has made a bad bargain. We cannot avoid the conclusion that the best kind of woman to marry is silent, or one whose tongue is used to serve and support men. Bianca is so attractive initially because she is quiet; when she voices her opinions in Act V she becomes troublesome. Conversely, Kate is licensed to talk at the end of the play because she speaks on cue, when she is asked to do so. She is no longer assertive and does not use her tongue to make demands any more.

Some critics have argued that this play represents an anachronistic view of marriage, that was already out of date at the time the play was first performed; others remain convinced that the message the play offers of the desirability of wife-taming was to be taken seriously. Katherina's offer to place her hand beneath her husband's foot was a gesture inspired by a part of the wedding ceremony that had been prohibited forty years before Shakespeare wrote *The Shrew*. And it is true that marriage was an institution being redefined at the end of the sixteenth century. A number of Elizabethan commentators suggested that wives should be seen as joint governors in the household, who should not be beaten. At the same time domestic violence was not illegal, and many writers of books and homilies which offered advice on how to conduct oneself in marriage held that it was legitimate to use force if it was necessary for maintaining right supremacy. Historians have proved that domestic violence was widespread. And it was often a source of comedy in **ballads** and puppet shows during this period, as well as a suitable subject for humour on the stage. Because this play is a comedy, and the beatings that occur are intended to make us laugh, it seems that the play might be seen as subscribing to 'old' rather than new views about matrimony. However, the fact that Petruchio, as one critic puts it, 'creates chaos in the central locations of marriage [the dining table and the bed]' and then resolves this disorder without resorting to his fists (although he does of course beat his servants) suggests that the protagonist is not entirely unenlightened. But he has a long way to go before he becomes the Elizabethan equivalent of a 'new man'.

Money and society

Money is a prerequisite for marriage – wise fathers and wooers think of little else. Petruchio is attracted to Kate solely because of her dowry; if he does, as some critics feel, find that he loves her, then this is a bonus. He states clearly that money alone would be enough: 'I come to wive it wealthily in Padua; / If wealthily, then happily in Padua' (I.2.74–5). Petruchio is rewarded for taming his wife with a second dowry, also gaining financially as a result of the wager in Act V. Lucentio is an acceptable son-in-law in spite of his subterfuge: he is the son of a wealthy gentleman. Significantly, the women have no part in the financial dealings that concern their futures. This play suggests patriarchy is alive and well.

We see an acquisitive middle class and very masculine society in *The Taming of the Shrew*. It is run along hierarchical lines, from

CONTEXT

Traditionally, prior to *The Taming of the Shrew*, shrewish wives were portrayed as reluctant to take up their domestic responsibilities, such as baking, brewing or washing. Why do you think Shakespeare decides not to focus on Katherina as housewife?

CHECK THE NET
Another general site about Shakespeare is **http://ise.uvic.ca**, where you can see a text of *The Taming of the Shrew* in its original spelling.

the Induction onwards. The Lord toys with his social inferior Sly for amusement, and his pursuits (hunting) are those of a gentleman. His servants obey him absolutely. Those who are allowed to usurp the positions of their betters in the subplot (Tranio, Biondello) are eventually returned to their roles, just as Bartholomew the page and Sly will probably return to a more mundane reality when the dream is over (although there is no **epilogue** to show that this is what the dramatist intended). Similarly, Kate will learn what role she should play and take her place in the hierarchy accordingly. Social status and middle-class life are evoked by references to possessions and leisure pursuits; boots, clothes, books, instruments, dogs, horses and hawks are all signs of social standing. Women are **symbols** of men's power, or lack of it. Baptista has one marriageable daughter and a shrew, who is presented as worthless until she is tamed. Hortensio and Gremio are laughable figures because they fail to 'achieve' the woman of their dreams. Petruchio's obedient Kate increases his prestige. Altogether, this is a play about masculine assertiveness, masculine negotiations and game-playing (see the repeated references to betting and card games), and masculine ideals. These ideas are reinforced by Shakespeare's use of competitive and supportive male 'double acts' throughout the play. For example, Petruchio and Grumio's verbal bantering, Petruchio and Hortensio baiting Kate in Act IV, 'Litio' and 'Cambio' vying for Bianca's attention. There is a constant masculine jostling for control and position.

DECEPTION

The theme of deception can be linked to illusion and transformation; these ideas are woven seamlessly together in *The Shrew*. There is much deceit in the play, creating numerous examples of **dramatic irony**. Disguises are used to achieve transformations in character and circumstances. In the Induction the Lord uses both illusion and reality to convince Sly that he is a nobleman, his fortunes transformed. Concrete details – pictures, music, food, clothes and a 'wife' – all persuade the tinker that he is a lord. But we know that he will come down to earth with a bump when the real Lord becomes bored with acting out his fantasy. Some would argue that the presence of the fake lord (Sly) on stage during the main play means that we should understand that Petruchio's taming of his wife is simply a temporary 'wonder' (V.2.190), like the beggar's changed circumstances. Others argue that this reading of Act V Scene 2 is hard to sustain because there is no final framing scene or epilogue involving Sly after the taming story is finished. By this point we will – probably – have forgotten the artful theatrical induction that introduced the action; so, as a number of critics observe, a strong illusion of reality surrounds Kate's final speech. It is difficult *not* to believe in her transformation. We will remain more convinced by her 'act' (if act it is) as an obedient wife than Sly's performance as a lord.

The differences between appearances and reality established in the Induction are highlighted by the use of disguises in the plot and subplot. Tranio and Lucentio set up a hoax as elaborate as the Lord's, and Biondello is brought in, like Bartholomew, to help carry out the scheme. This subterfuge is intended to provide Lucentio with a new role: that of husband to the divine Bianca. We realise that Lucentio is intent on presenting himself as a bold adventurer (rather like Petruchio) when he deceives Biondello with a story of his having to assume a disguise because he has 'kill'd a man' (I.1.231). His fantasies don't stop there, and he is punished for not looking beyond Bianca's appearance. As is frequently the case in *The Shrew*, it is **ironic** that the deceiver is deceived. Hortensio's disguise leads to failure of another kind. He congratulates himself for discovering that Bianca is courting 'Cambio', but does not look closely enough at his Widow. Petruchio, meanwhile, has been busy acting out the role of eccentric wife-tamer in order to create a new reality for himself as a married man. He uses his disguise to effect what he hopes will be a lasting transformation in his wife. As in the Induction, the dominant male is attempting to change another character's understanding of and response to the circumstances she finds herself in. But is Petruchio really in disguise? The protagonist is consistently upfront about his motives and does not deceive anybody, least of all Kate, about his intentions. Until the last act of the play, many doubt that he will be able to carry his project off. It is ironic that the one character whose behaviour is considered odd is proved to have been telling the truth all along. Petruchio does, however, use his storytelling and acting powers to transform his wife. Bianca is just as successful at acting as he, and she too gets what she wants. These two wily creatures prove that power can be

QUESTION

The Taming of a Shrew, which may be a version of *The Taming of the Shrew*, includes an epilogue, in which Sly comments that the shrew-taming he has witnessed was 'the best dream' he ever had. If Shakespeare had included such a line in *The Shrew*, would it undermine or reinforce Petruchio's actions?

QUESTION

On Shakespeare's
stage, Katherina
would have been
played by a boy
actor. Do you
agree with critics
who have
suggested that
this 'transvestism'
exposes the fact
that gender roles
are constructed
and artificial,
and that the
play is therefore
subversive, rather
than an
endorsement of
patriarchy?

gained by playing a role with your eyes open, if you have enough
determination, and a clear understanding of those you seek to
influence.

IMAGERY

Although patterns of **imagery** are not used so extensively and
densely in *The Taming of the Shrew* as they are in Shakespeare's
later works, an analysis of the **figurative language** helps to inform
our understanding of characters, events and themes.

THE DEVIL

On several occasions Kate's shrewish disposition is commented
on, particularly in the early scenes of the play. Images of hell are
invoked to demonstrate the men's abhorrence of her wayward
tongue and behaviour; and they help to establish the idea that many
of the male characters are rather frightened of the heroine. This
comes across clearly in Hortensio's and Gremio's utterances in
Act I, particularly Hortensio's line, 'From all such devils, good
Lord deliver us!' (I.1.66). Kate is 'this fiend of hell' (I.1.88), fit only
to 'go to the devil's dam' (I.1.105). Gremio wonders whether he and
Hortensio will be able to light on 'any man [who] is so very a fool
to be married to hell' (I.1.124–5). Even her father refers to Kate as a
'hilding of a devilish spirit' (II.1.26). All these references establish
the scold's unnatural and inhuman persona. Kate lives up to her
diabolical reputation when she breaks the lute over Hortensio's
head, showing, as he suggests, a 'most impatient devilish spirit'
(II.1.151). Her actions and the men's words seem to fit together.
Or do they? Some critics suggest that the exaggeration of these
invocations of devilry are absurd; surely the worst we can accuse
Kate of is possessing a bad temper? It is significant that Petruchio
disregards all the warnings he receives about uniting himself in
matrimony with 'hell'. After the episode with the lute he announces
boldly that he loves her 'ten times more than e'er I did' (II.1.161),
effectively undermining the legitimacy of the imagery the other
male characters use. To be sure, he is exaggerating as much as they
are, but Petruchio shows his superior masculinity when he proves
that he is willing and ready to do battle with the forces of evil. The

Paduans are the fools, not Petruchio. The linking of shrews and hell was traditional during the period in which the play was written; the creatures were commonly associated with dark, sinister forces. The 'little din' (I.2.198) that the shrew Kate makes is intended to add to her characterisation (and some would say vilification) as a scold; shrews were thought to be noisy, aggressive and voracious little beasts.

MADNESS

The Taming of the Shrew contains several references to madness. There are different ways of reading them. In the first scene in which she appears, disobedient Katherina is labelled 'stark mad' by Tranio (I.1.69). We may expect her to be described in this way, given the genre, title and subject matter of the play, and most readers will assume 'stark mad' suggests disapproval. On stage, however, Kate's 'madness' may make her a figure of pathos, since she is ignored, scorned and isolated by all the other characters. It is even possible to take pleasure in Katherina's 'madness'. Surely Gremio and Hortensio deserve to be treated with the same contempt that they mete out?

Interestingly, the protagonist is described in similar terms to the scold, and it quickly becomes clear that the adjective 'mad' is applied to acts of verbal or physical abuse. Petruchio's 'madness' is established early on when he wrings his servant by the ear, and the suffering Grumio boldly exclaims, 'My master is mad' (I.2.18). This complaint – like Tranio's observation about Kate quoted above – draws attention to antisocial behaviour. The wringing of Grumio's ear is the first example of Petruchio's propensity for violence, which is demonstrated many times, even before he carries his bride off home to his 'taming-school' (IV.2.54). As Katherina becomes more subdued, the same cannot be said of Petruchio, who develops from 'madcap ruffian' (II.1.281) in the wooing scene to 'mad-brain rudesby' at his wedding (III.2.10).

It is necessary to consider whether we view the antisocial actions of the hero through the same eyes that we use to judge the heroine. Some critics have suggested that Petruchio's 'madness' is licensed and acceptable because he is a male, while Kate's is not. To a certain extent, this is true. However, while Petruchio's eccentricities are

 CHECK THE NET
Questions and answers on *The Taming of the Shrew* can be found at the TES web site **http://www. talkingto.co.uk**. This useful site covers material on a wide range of Shakespeare's plays.

tolerated, they do cause alarm to characters on stage (and, arguably, to members of a twenty-first-century audience). This is demonstrated in Act III Scene 2, when Petruchio rolls tardily into town on his horribly diseased horse, wearing 'mad attire' (III.2.122). Looking at him in horror, Baptista cries, 'Fie, doff this habit, shame to your estate, / An eyesore to our solemn festival!' (III.2.98–9). Baptista's words betray what we might today call 'status anxiety'. He doesn't want to be humiliated in public by a son-in-law who looks like a vagabond and behaves like a lunatic.

While we sympathise with Baptista, we are also likely to be laughing at the foolish patriarch, and his absurd notion that his wildcat daughter and a 'madcap ruffian' (II.1.281) could be expected to behave with the decorum called for by a 'solemn festival'. Indeed, many in the audience, including those who sympathise with Kate's plight as unwilling bride, would be disappointed if Katherina and Petruchio suddenly became models of sobriety. Petruchio does not let us down. The most outrageous acts of antisocial behaviour in the play occur off stage during the wedding ceremony. The account of events is truly shocking. We are told that the bridegroom 'stamp'd and swore' at the vicar (III.2.165), guzzled the communion wine and then 'threw the sops all in the sexton's face' (III.2.171). Small wonder that Gremio says, 'Such a mad marriage never was before' (III.2.180). However, while being amused by this violence, we might also admit that the hero has gone too far, and much further than his bride is ever allowed to go. Petruchio's 'madness' – whether it is temporary, and assumed specifically to 'cure' his wife, or a permanent feature of his characterisation – can look increasingly gratuitous and self-indulgent as the play progresses.

CHECK THE FILM

In the 1967 film by Franco Zeffirelli, we see all Petruchio's outrageous acts in church, which the congregation laugh at. Petruchio is also clearly drunk throughout the scene.

Why are Kate and Petruchio both presented as 'mad'? Perhaps their shouts, threats and swaggering encourage us to believe that the warring couple are well matched, that each has found the partner who will fulfil their needs, as some critics have suggested. Petruchio's 'madness' becomes the driving force in the play, and eventually it appears to lead to harmony. In Act IV Scene 5 Katherina accepts and emulates her husband's wilful craziness when she embraces Vincentio on the road to Padua and calls him a 'Young budding virgin, fair, and fresh, and sweet' (IV.5.36). Petruchio seems to chide her: 'Why, how now, Kate, I hope thou art not mad. / This is a man, old, wrinkled, faded, wither'd' (IV.5.41–2). We are now witnessing a different kind of madness. It seems that antisocial madness has been replaced by linguistic game-playing. Because Vincentio is not offended and calls Kate 'my merry mistress' (IV.5.52), we know that the combative couple are now ready to take their place in society. At this moment, it is possible to view 'mad' Petruchio as one of Shakespeare's licensed jesters, a witty figure who has helped to establish an atmosphere of carnival and misrule.

The shared humour of Act IV becomes problematic when the events and speeches in Act V are considered. It seems that Petruchio remains as overbearing at the end of the play as he was at the beginning. Hints of the antisocial 'madcap ruffian' remain when he urges his wife to abuse the Widow with the command 'To her, Kate!' (V.2.33). Throughout this scene he enjoys causing dissent among the Paduans, as he did on his wedding day. He leaves the stage boasting, ''Twas I won the wager … / And being a winner, God give you good night!' (V.2.187–8). This is the same smug egotism Petruchio began his marriage quest with. In the tragedy *King Lear*, madness leads to enlightenment. In this **comedy**, it seems that it is only the female who needs to learn, not her mad master. We are forced to conclude that a man can behave as crazily as he pleases and still be allowed to control his own – and his wife's – destiny.

ANIMALS, HUNTING AND HAWKING

There are many **images** of animals, hunting and hawking throughout the play. All these references are intended to evoke the natural order, the hierarchy that decreed that women were inferior to men. Animal imagery informs our understanding of Petruchio's wife-taming methods too. At the time the play was written falconry was an expensive and laborious pursuit, not exclusively the preserve of the aristocracy, but certainly associated with it: thus Petruchio is presented as the most 'worthy' character in the main play. He has the skill to tame his wife, just as the aristocrat developed the skill to tame his hawk.

In the first scene of the **Induction**, set in a natural environment, the Lord returns from hunting, discussing the merits of his hounds.

CONTEXT

In the early seventeenth century, Puritans began to suggest that companionate marriages were the ideal. In *A Godly Forme of Household Government* (1598), John Dod and Robert Cleaver wrote: 'the wife ought … to labour to bee in favour and grace with her husband: So likewise the husband ought to feare to be in disgrace and disliking with his wife.' Are there any companionate marriages in *The Shrew*?

It seems that everything is in order here: the hierarchy of the two huntsmen and their polite obedience, the dogs' fine efforts out in the field, the Lord in command. This is the harmony that Petruchio will work hard to achieve in his own household. Like the Lord, the protagonist might be considered a willing and determined huntsman (the Lord intends hunting again the following day). Petruchio comes to Padua to 'wive it wealthily' (I.2.74). At the end of the play Tranio will refer explicitly to Petruchio's achievements as a hunter (V.2.52–6) who has succeeded in turning his 'wildcat' wife (I.2.195) into a 'slow-wing'd turtle [dove]' (II.1.207). The hawking **motif** that runs through the play is established early when Petruchio and Katherina meet for the first time. Kate is asked whether 'a buzzard' should 'take thee?' (II.1.207). Outlining his scheme to achieve domestic dominion Petruchio is quite clear about his intentions:

> My falcon now is sharp and passing empty,
> And till she stoop she must not be full-gorg'd,
> For then she never looks upon her lure.
> Another way I have to man my haggard,
> To make her come and know her keeper's call,
> That is, to watch her ...
> She ate no meat today, nor none shall eat;
> Last night she slept not, nor tonight she shall not. (IV.1.177–85)

CONTEXT

The hawking term 'haggard' was often used to describe assertive or wayward women during the Renaissance. The term refers to a wild bird which needs to be tamed by the falconer.

In this way he hopes to 'curb' his wife's 'mad and headstrong humour' (IV.1.196). His methods exactly match those used by a gentleman training his hawk. We might feel that a hawk is most natural when it is a 'haggard' (wild), but the imagery forces us to understand that a husband's successful 'reign' (IV.1.175) depends upon showing his wife that she must 'know her keeper's call'. The hawk must not be in control of its master. The final scene demonstrates this most clearly.

Petruchio's use of his horses adds to our impression of him as successful hunter and shrew-tamer. The ailing beast he rides to his wedding humiliates Kate as much as his clothes (the long description of it by Biondello suggests its importance). On the way home Katherina's horse stumbles, 'and she under her horse ... in how miry a place' (IV.1.65–7). Grumio adds the telling detail 'how

she was bemoiled'. It could be argued that the horse has punished
the shrew for her attempted defiance at the end of Act III, when she
stamped her feet and declared she would not leave until after the
feast. When Kate comes off in the mire, and Petruchio leaves her
there, we know she is floundering: the animal-tamer will have his
way. Some critics feel that it is significant that Kate finally submits
to her husband in the open air, on the journey back to Padua: has
she finally demonstrated that she is 'at one' with nature and the
hierarchy? In the closing scene there are images that suggest that the
natural order has been achieved in one marriage, but subverted in
two others, causing grief. Bianca reproves Petruchio when she says,
'Am I your bird? I mean to shift my bush, / And then pursue me as
you draw your bow' (V.2.46–7). The implication of these lines is
that Petruchio may have tamed *his* 'bird', but Bianca remains at
liberty and may 'shift' her 'bush' and act as she pleases. However,
harmony has been restored elsewhere. Tranio has returned to his
proper station in life, signalled by his rueful statement 'O sir,
Lucentio slipp'd me like his greyhound, / Which runs himself,
and catches for his master' (V.2.52–3). His acting out the role of
gentleman has never really been a threat to the natural order.
The banter continues with further animal imagery. **Ironically**, the
Paduans still believe that Petruchio's wife is unruly: ''Tis thought
your deer does hold you at a bay' (V.2.56) says Tranio. But the
suspense is soon over and Petruchio shows that he does not have
'the veriest shrew of all' (V.2.64). The wager is very much like a
modern bet on horses or dogs. Petruchio says that he'll venture
'twenty times so much upon my wife' as he would on 'my hawk
or hound' (V.2.72–3). It comes as no surprise when the most daring
gamester wins and Katherina performs, as P. J. Gabriner suggests,
rather like a 'trained bear' (see **Critical history**).

EDUCATION

References to teaching and learning add to our understanding of
Petruchio's wife-taming methods, and perhaps indicate that we
should see the protagonist in a slightly more favourable light than
some commentators suggest. But it is not just Katherina who is
educated; other characters learn lessons in the course of the play.
When he first arrives in Padua we are told that Lucentio has come
to 'institute / A course of learning and ingenious studies' (I.1.8–9).

**CHECK
THE BOOK**

To read P. J.
Gabriner's
comments in full,
see his essay
'Hierarchy, Harmony
and Happiness:
Another Look at
the Hunting Dogs
in the "Induction"
to *The Taming of
the Shrew*' in
*Reclamations of
Shakespeare*, edited
by A. J. Hoenlaars
(1994).

**CHECK
THE FILM**

In the 1999 film *10
Things I Hate About
You* Bianca's suitor
learns French in
order that he can
teach her, and thus
have an excuse to
get to know her.

This is appropriate for a young gentleman of his status. However, he swiftly throws off all thoughts of 'sweet philosophy' (I.1.28) when he sees Bianca. Lucentio then uses education to pursue his amorous aims, taking on the role of schoolmaster as he attempts to woo Bianca. We swiftly realise that he is the one in need of teaching. Shakespeare perhaps undermines traditional ideas about the value of book-learning in his portrayal of this young lover. For all his reading, Lucentio not only needs the assistance of the more practical Tranio to win his fair lady, but he also fails to look beyond her beautiful, mute exterior. Lucentio's use of Ovid's *The Art of Loving* further undermines him. Brian Morris, editor of the Arden edition of *The Taming of the Shrew* used in these Notes, says that this book is 'a witty, cynical textbook for seducers', 'anything but a manual for romantic lovers'. That Lucentio fails to notice this suggests his naïveté. **Ironically**, the other naive male suitor, Hortensio, also takes on the role of schoolmaster. The fact that Baptista places such a high value on his favourite daughter's education hints at the delight and admiration he will feel at the end of the play when he learns that his son-in-law Petruchio has succeeded in 'educating' his other daughter Katherina.

> **CONTEXT**
>
> Domestic violence was legal in Shakespeare's day, and many saw it as a husband's duty to keep his wife in line by whatever means necessary. Popular songs reflect this, for example 'Dub a dub, kill her with a club, / Be thy wife's master'.

Petruchio's approach is altogether more down to earth. His experience of the world, not the university, will help him in his 'taming-school' (IV.2.54). The hero has 'heard lions roar', 'heard the sea, puff'd up with winds', 'heard great ordnance in the field, / And heaven's artillery thunder in the skies' (I.2.199–203). Thus he is well prepared to take on and silence 'a woman's tongue' (I.2.206). When Gremio says that he comes from the wedding ceremony 'As willingly as e'er I came from school' (III.2.148), we get a hint that Petruchio's educational methods, while rather perplexing, are already efficacious. By the end of the play the male characters have realised this. Hortensio says that Petruchio has 'taught' him to be 'untoward' if his Widow 'be froward' (IV.5.77–8). Petruchio has proved the truth of a moral lesson: that peace and harmony in marriage depend upon wifely submission.

FOOD AND CLOTHING

Allusions to food and clothing suggest that this is a play very much concerned with the material world. This fits in with the portrayal of marriage as a business venture (see **Themes**).

References to clothes also help the dramatist explore ideas about appearance and reality. In the **Induction**, Sly is fooled by his own and others' outward appearances. When he is put in 'a costly suit' (Ind.1.57) and presented with a 'wife' (a page in disguise) he gradually becomes convinced that he is a lord. This suggests just how powerful attractive outward appearances can be. In the subplot disguises abound. Ironically, no one looks beyond Bianca's pleasing exterior; the 'sweet beauty in her face' (I.1.167) conceals a strong will. For a long time Tranio fools everyone too, causing Gremio and Hortensio, as well as the real Vincentio and Baptista, a good deal of worry before he is unmasked as an impostor. While his unmasking is comic, and leads to the restoration of order, Bianca's unmasking is more problematic for those she has deceived.

Petruchio's use of a 'disguise' is as calculated as the other characters'. It is both comic and serious. He takes on the role of 'mad-brain rudesby' (III.2.10). When he arrives at the wedding 'mean-apparell'd' (III.2.71) he presents an extraordinary picture, which never fails to raise a laugh on stage. He defends his peculiar attire thus: 'To me she's married, not unto my clothes' (III.2.115). This line suggests that he, unlike Lucentio and Hortensio, has the wit to look beyond appearances. But his costume serves another purpose too; he is mocking his bride by going against accepted customs of dress, demonstrating to her the importance of complying with conventions. For the same reason he rejects the tailor's gown in Act IV Scene 3. Katherina has not yet submitted to him, so she doesn't deserve new clothes. When she has a new persona, she gets her cap and gown, **symbols** of her status as obedient married woman. At the end of the play Kate shows that she has conformed by throwing her cap on the ground when her husband asks her to.

The numerous references to food serve a number of purposes. The delights of a good feast are established in the Induction when Sly is plied with all manner of delicacies. He betrays his class origins by calling for 'a pot o' th' smallest ale' (Ind.2.76), but we see the importance of appetite. We also learn in the Induction that Sly is presented with a play because it is thought that this will drive away

CHECK THE BOOK

Books by coaches aimed at actors often have great insights into the energy of Shakespeare's verse. See Cicely Berry's *The Actor and His Text* (1987) or Patsy Rodenburg's *Speaking Shakespeare* (2002).

the 'melancholy' (Ind.2.133). Food and good mental health are linked in the main action of the play. Katherina is deprived of food and not allowed to participate in a wedding feast until she has emerged from her diseased state as shrew. Petruchio tells her that he will not let her touch the meat that has been prepared because 'it engenders choler, planteth anger' (IV.1.159). Her submission is the source of celebration in the final scene, when the delayed festivities take place. A cheerful mood is established when Lucentio calls on the guests to 'chat as well as eat' (V.2.11). It is intended that the banquet will 'close our stomachs up / After our great good cheer' (V.2.9–10). These lines indicate that the quarrelling is over. This is because Kate, whose name was a source of **puns** (Kate/cake), is now palatable. Women are further linked to food when Gremio says 'My cake is dough' (V.1.128), recognising that his chances of marrying Bianca have been swept away. Wisely, he settles for his share of the feast instead. However, we know the man who got the cake will not find her as delicious in the eating as he expected.

LANGUAGE AND STYLE

The Taming of the Shrew is written in prose and **blank verse** (unrhymed iambic pentameter), which Shakespeare uses flexibly. Prose was traditionally used by low or comic characters and the dramatist follows this convention to an extent; Sly, Grumio, Biondello and Curtis habitually converse in prose, often to great comic effect (see Biondello's description of Petruchio's arrival in Act III and Grumio's account of the journey to Petruchio's house in Act IV for good examples of entertaining, swift-moving prose). Prose is employed to draw social distinctions. However, the servants occasionally speak in verse, depending upon the effect that Shakespeare wishes to achieve; for example, Grumio delivers a rather clumsy rhyming couplet in I.2.128–9, neatly encapsulating the problem Petruchio faces when he agrees to woo Kate ('Katherine the curst, / A title for a maid of all titles the worst'). The servants make effective use of puns, as befits their roles as comic foils (see Grumio's exchange with Petruchio at the opening of Act I Scene 2). Sly shifts sharply from prose to verse while under the Lord's influence in the second scene of the **Induction**,

CONTEXT

Blank verse is the commonest metre in English verse, and the usual medium of Elizabethan and Jacobean drama. It is also the form used in most of the greatest narrative works in English literature, such as John Milton's *Paradise Lost* (1667), William Wordsworth's *Prelude* (1850) and Alfred Tennyson's *Idylls of the King* (1842–85).

suggesting the power of transformation. The effect is again comic; the idea of a drunken tinker adopting the polite and formal mode of his social superiors makes us laugh. It is noticeable, however, that Sly finds it hard to speak this language consistently; at line 126 in the same scene he returns to his humbler prose. In the subplot Tranio presents an interesting case. Although he is a servant, and of a superior kind to Biondello, he speaks in verse. His understanding and use of classical and literary allusions, typical of the lovelorn Lucentio, mark him out as a bright and witty fellow. We are not surprised that he has none of Sly's difficulty in adopting a new voice; in fact, the measured style he uses when he appears as 'Lucentio' in Act II Scene 1 is as assured as his earlier speeches in Act I Scene 1. He certainly convinces Bianca's other suitors that they have cause to worry. Part of Tranio's success must be attributed to his quick-witted ability to use his tongue persuasively: he is able to convince the Pedant that he is in danger and almost gets away with his disguise because the Paduans find him so convincing in the role of gentleman.

Lucentio speaks in a style appropriate to a courtly lover with romantic aspirations, for example his speech with classical allusions in I.1.167–70. The grandiose, mock-heroic and rather stilted style is appropriate to the naive young man. We know that we should regard his poetic approach as comic when Tranio immediately tries to bring his master down to earth in the lines that follow this speech. Lucentio's style contrasts neatly with the language that we come to associate with Petruchio. As befits the man who wins the day because he is able to 'rail in his rope-tricks' (I.2.110–11), the protagonist's speech is lively and varied, and he has a great deal to say for himself. Petruchio is capable of the heroic (see his description of his adventures in Act I Scene 2), and of rhetoric (see his speech about his 'household stuff' in Act III Scene 2). But much of what he says is direct and pithy, devoid of the romantic **imagery** so beloved by Lucentio. He does make classical allusions in Act I Scene 2 but their effect is comic rather than proof of a romantic disposition (see glossary for Act I Scene 2).

Petruchio is associated with oaths, threats and abuse, with imagery of hawking and hunting, and with swift and successful wordplay.

His wooing of Katherina is a devastating example of the latter. In this combat, which proceeds in **stichomythia** (a dialogue carried out in single alternating lines), he makes a number of bawdy **puns** which show his ability to talk his audience down. We have been prepared for this dialogue by his argument with Grumio in Act I Scene 2. Petruchio is an effective storyteller, as we see when Baptista returns to the stage after this contest. He constructs a tall story of what has just occurred: 'She hung about my neck, and kiss on kiss / She vied so fast, protesting oath on oath, / That in a twink she won me to her love' (II.1.301–3). This comic and ludicrous exaggeration is typical of Petruchio and his methods of persuasion: he describes things as he would have them and ultimately gets his own way because he is prepared to stick to his version of reality. The breathless energy of Petruchio's wooing style exactly foreshadows his actions later in the play.

QUESTION

The actress Jane Lapotaire, who has played Kate, argues that 'both meet their match and therefore fight as equals'. Is this how you view Kate and Petruchio?

The text is full of linguistic competitiveness, appropriate since the play focuses on the war between the sexes. Kate interrogates her sister. Hortensio and Lucentio vie for Bianca's ear and heart. Gremio and Tranio/'Lucentio' try to outdo each other with descriptions of what they have to offer as suitors. At the wedding there is an altercation when Kate tries to persuade her husband to stay in Padua for the feast. In Act IV she finds arguing is pointless, because Petruchio either contradicts her or delivers a sermon. The couple continue to scrap about food, clothes and whether the sun is the moon. The increasing absurdity of these 'discussions' is comic, culminating in the scene in which Kate submits (perhaps the most absurd scene of all?). On the road to Padua Katherina meets Vincentio, and at her husband's request greets him as 'Young budding virgin, fair, and fresh' (IV.5.36). It seems that she has learned a few verbal tricks from her master; her inappropriate descriptions show that she has given up quarrelling. From now on she will describe and see the world in the way that Petruchio wants her to.

In the final scene Kate demonstrates an even more impressive ability to speak her husband's language when she delivers her speech about the duties wives owe their husbands. This is important. Early in the play we learn that Kate's language and style make her objectionable;

now she is allowed to speak at length because she speaks on cue. Her early talk was characterised by forceful, direct, short speeches, full of indignant questions, which nobody wanted to hear. Her final speech is utterly different: formal, measured, full of imagery of war, it hints that her husband has won the battle. It is rhetoric, reminiscent of Petruchio's longer speeches. His triumph is displayed through her rhetorical skill. Kate speaks half as many lines as Petruchio: her linguistic power has never been as great as his, indicating what the outcome of the play will be. We might feel that the lack of soliloquies for Kate reveals the masculine bias of the text: the taming is more important than the shrew. Petruchio delivers only two soliloquies, but they are not used to reveal a complex inner life; they are a means by which the audience finds out how he will woo and tame his wife: they are proof of power. His aside to Hortensio at IV.3.50 serves the same purpose; it shows us that the hero is in control. Elsewhere asides are used to reveal thoughts and feelings and make subversive jokes. The style and construction of the play, which includes few very long speeches and a lot of fast-moving, witty dialogue, reflect Petruchio's methods and complement the visual comedy. In Petruchio's case, language is power. The exuberance of his verse is a large part of what makes the play so entertaining on stage, and Petruchio the most compelling talker. Silence is important too. The fact that the women are often bystanders suggests that they are less important than the men, and Katherina's dumbfounded silence can certainly indicate powerlessness. But Bianca's silence means something different, hinting that we might consider her sister's silence more closely too. Bianca uses silence to get what she wants: a voice that her husband will be forced to listen to unless he can tame her. What else does her silence mean? Subversion? Wilful wiliness? Duplicity? Does her unmasking as a shrew hint that Katherina may again break out and speak her own language once more?

A final comment on the language of this play. In spite of the Italian names and phrases and Latin quotations that appear, this is a very English play, as the colloquial descriptions of Grumio and Biondello demonstrate. The Italian phrasing adds colour, but the really inspired passages are most definitely English. Comically, Grumio cannot even tell the difference between Latin and Italian,

CONTEXT

In the eighteenth century, David Garrick's *Catharine and Petruchio* (1754) was highly popular. In this version of *The Shrew*, it was Petruchio who delivered the final lines of Kate's sermon about shameful women refusing to 'kneel for peace'. Garrick also omitted Katherina's offer to place her hand beneath her husband's foot. What effects do you think Garrick was aiming at?

 CHECK THE BOOK

David and Ben Crystal's *Shakespeare's Words: A Glossary and Language Companion* (2002) is a good source of information about Shakespeare's language.

betraying his English roots immediately. The use of Italian and Latin hint at the sources Shakespeare used (see **Structure** below).

STRUCTURE

A discussion of the sources that Shakespeare used when writing *The Taming of the Shrew* will show just how skilfully his play is constructed. The Bianca subplot is taken from George Gascoigne's **comedy** *Supposes* (1566), which was essentially a translation of *I Suppositi* (1509), an Italian comedy by Ludovico Ariosto (1474–1533). A 'Suppose', according to Gascoigne's prologue 'is nothing other else but a mystaking or imagination of one thing for another': hence the disguises that we find in *The Shrew*. Italy was often used as a setting for plays of intrigue during this period. Although the subplot follows Gascoigne and Ariosto quite closely, there are differences that suggest that Shakespeare wished to make his comedy of mistaken identifies and subterfuge more romantic than the original. In *I Suppositi* the Bianca character has already been seduced; and her seducer is seeking a wife with a handsome fortune: he does not fall in love at first sight. These are typical features of classical comedy, which was more **farcical** than the comedy Shakespeare wrote. Shakespeare complicates the plot by introducing more suitors and disguises than feature in the source play, adding to the theatrical appeal of *The Shrew*.

CONTEXT

The Taming of a Shrew has a complete Sly framework, perhaps suggesting that Shakespeare's play had a similar structure, and that scenes may be missing from the text we read today.

In *I Suppositi* the heroine has no sister. The character of the shrew Katherina is introduced to provide a point of contrast; her wooing and wedding are to be very different from Bianca's. Shrew-taming stories were part of folklore; there were **ballads** and folk tales dealing with the subject, and a number of literary antecedents too, in the form of early Tudor plays and poems. It is possible that Shakespeare's play was inspired by an English comedy, *The Taming of a Shrew*, which resembles *The Shrew* in a number of ways (see **Critical history** for references to books you can refer to if you wish to read discussions about *The Taming of a Shrew*). But Petruchio's wife-taming methods are unique in the literature of this period; he does not beat or trick his wife. What is most remarkable is the fact that Shakespeare manages to marry his two plots, from very different literary traditions, and interweave them into a cohesive whole. He manages this by focusing on the same themes in both plots (money, marriage, men and women), encouraging us to compare the characters' experiences. As *The Shrew* progresses, plot and subplot become more and more closely linked, culminating in a scene where all the characters are on stage together (as they are at the wedding ceremony, although Act III Scene 2 is solely concerned with Kate and Petruchio). Leading up to Act V Scene 2, Shakespeare moves between his two wooing plots, focusing on one sister and then the other. Hortensio provides a neat link between the two strands of the story: he begins as a suitor in the subplot, but is then a witness to Petruchio's taming methods in Act IV. Hortensio is also suitor to a third female, the Widow. Shakespeare introduces this 'plot' to provide another point of contrast with the other couples on stage.

The differences in mood and sentiment in the alternating scenes are effective. In the taming plot there are more examples of verbal and physical violence, although the subplot includes moments of visual comedy too, centring on the use of disguises. The subplot is driven by intrigue and improvisation, while the taming plot proceeds in a more direct way: we know what Petruchio intends from Act I Scene 2 onwards because he is open about his plans. It is possible to argue that the main plot has more theatrical power because it focuses on the conflict between two individuals, while there are a number of characters jostling for position in the subplot. Both plots, however, involve a degree of suspense. Will Lucentio and Tranio get away with their disguises? Will Petruchio tame his wife? The two plots are driven by conflict and competition. In both the servants play supporting roles, helping their masters with their plans. It is **ironic** that plot and subplot, for all the mirroring that occurs, ultimately lead in different directions. The taming plot culminates in the revelation of marital peace and harmony, while the subplot, which seems more romantic, ends in discord. Realism is pitted against romanticism, and wins.

Although the play centres on the wooing of Bianca to begin with, Petruchio becomes the dramatic focus when he appears in the second scene. It can be argued that the whole play is driven by Petruchio, structured around his progress and the ways in which the

? QUESTION

In the eighteenth century David Garrick omitted the subplot from his version of *The Taming of the Shrew*, which was called *Catharine and Petruchio* (1754). Do you agree that the subplot is inferior to the main plot?

other characters respond to him. Petruchio is the only character who is given **soliloquies** and he dominates both verbally and physically, mirroring the role the Lord played in the **Induction**. Repetition is a key feature of the taming plot. In each phase a pattern is repeated; Petruchio makes a decision about what he wants and then sets about achieving his aims in a very single-minded way. He wants to woo Katherina; he woos her. He decides when he will marry her; he marries her. He decides to tame her at home; he carries her off and breaks her will. Finally, Petruchio returns to Padua to prove he has tamed his wife and she demonstrates his success. As Brian Morris suggests in his introduction to the Arden edition of the play, this is a pattern of taming, teaching and testing, and suggests forward movement. In each phase, until the final one, there is an argument between hero and heroine; Kate comes off worse each time, so we know how the plot will be resolved. Other characters are used to demonstrate Petruchio's ability to dominate; he conquers Grumio, Baptista, his servants, the tailor and finally the whole gathering at the wedding feast in Act V when he wins his wager. Descriptions of events off stage add to his power and make us eager to see Petruchio in action. Throughout the play, characters in the subplot comment on the action of the main plot, further adding to its impact. There is one other feature of the structuring of the play that adds to Petruchio's power as a theatrical creation. Three key scenes, always 'highlights' on stage, focus on the fortune-hunter: the first meeting of Kate and Petruchio, the wedding ceremony and the final feast. The scene with the tailor might be added to this list. It is clear from this list that social ceremonies and rituals are an important part of the structure of *The Shrew*.

How does the Induction fit into the structure? The two main plots run parallel to one another, along lines set up by the frame. Here we see a plan outlined in one scene and carried out in the second, foreshadowing both plot and subplot. Themes are established in the Induction: illusion and transformation can be added to the list offered above. There is a tension between romance and reality; the tinker Sly is contrasted with the well-educated Lord. Most importantly, we have an introduction to the use of deception and disguises. The Induction is an ironic foreshadowing of the main action; most significantly in the transformation of Sly into a lord.

This introduces us to the idea of Kate being tamed. This Induction is the only frame of its kind in Shakespeare's work, and it too has literary antecedents: for example the tale of a beggar who is transformed into a prince in *The Arabian Nights*. The Warwickshire drunkard is a unique theatrical creation, however. Some critics have argued that the self-conscious theatricality of the Induction (the drawing of attention to the boy actor playing Bartholomew and the players who provide the entertainment, as well as the brief comments by Sly at the end of Act I Scene 1) indicates that Shakespeare wishes to undermine the validity of the wife-taming that occurs: is *everything* we see an illusion? Are *all* the characters impostors? Critics continue to discuss whether or not there was an **epilogue** (a final framing scene) that has been lost. Some directors feel that the Induction does not serve a useful purpose. Often it is dispensed with when the play is performed. But without the Induction we have a less sophisticated play, and a good deal of **dramatic irony** is lost. The frame is an important part of the whole, and Sly is an entertaining and vigorous character in his own right.

CHECK THE BOOK

Graham Holderness argues that the play would be very different without the Induction. To read his comments in full, see the New Casebook 'Text and Performance: *The Taming of the Shrew*' in *Shakespeare in Performance*, edited by Robert Shaughnessy (2000).

PART FOUR

CRITICAL HISTORY

CONTEXT

The Woman's Prize, or The Tamer Tamed (c.1611), John Fletcher's sequel, was written approximately twenty years after *The Shrew*. In this sequel Kate has died and Petruchio remarries. His new wife Maria refuses to sleep with him until she has tamed him.

CONTEXT

It is possible that *The Taming of the Shrew* and *The Woman's Prize, or The Tamer Tamed* were played as a popular double bill in the seventeenth century. There is evidence for a joint production in 1633. More recently, the Royal Shakespeare Company revived the two plays in 2003.

THE PLAY IN PERFORMANCE

The Taming of the Shrew has been a popular play in performance, inspiring a number of adaptations and even a comedy sequel (John Fletcher's *The Woman's Prize, or The Tamer Tamed*, c.1611). Because of the difficulty of knowing whether Shakespeare's play or the anonymous *The Taming of a Shrew* (see **Note on the text**) is being referred to, it is difficult to say when Shakespeare's play was first played and commented on. It seems possible that *The Shrew* was performed at St James's for the King and Queen in 1633 and was well received. Thereafter its fortunes languished until the nineteenth century. After the Restoration Grumio was elevated to the central role (Sander) in a rather brutal reworking of the play by John Lacy of 1667 (*Sauny the Scot*), and the actor David Garrick cut the text to arrive at his own extremely popular *Catharine and Petruchio*, first performed in 1754. This version of the shrew-taming story dominated the stage for almost thirty years. Brian Morris, editor of the current Arden edition of the play, argues that this adaptation and its predecessors succeeded in keeping Shakespeare's play off the stage until the middle of the nineteenth century. Garrick's adaptation was used by Frederick Reynolds for his opera of 1828, and then in 1948 another musical version of the story appeared, the enormously popular *Kiss Me Kate* by Cole Porter. It was not until 1844 that Shakespeare's text was revived on the stage, but by the end of the century it was being performed regularly. There have been a number of productions since, and the play is now a firm favourite with audiences, in spite of the fact that a number of modern critics find its philosophy objectionable.

EARLY VIEWS

As mentioned above, it is difficult to be sure whether the early comments that survive are remarks about Shakespeare's text, or *A Shrew*. However, it is clear that Samuel Pepys (1633–1703) found the version of the play he saw in 1667 unsatisfactory and 'silly'. Dr Johnson (1709–84) was more positive. He felt that 'the two plots are so well united, that they can hardly be called two, without injury to the art with which they are interwoven. The attention is entertained with all the variety of a double plot, yet is not distracted by unconnected incidents.' He found 'the part between Catharine and Petruchio … eminently sprightly' and declared the play 'very popular and diverting'. The critic William Hazlitt (1778–1830) shared similar views, although he rejected Johnson's readings of Shakespeare elsewhere. He saw a 'downright moral' in *The Shrew* and noted the 'bustle, animation, and rapidity of action'. For him the play 'shows admirably how self-will is only to be got the better of by stronger will, and how one degree of ridiculous perversity is only to be driven out by another still greater'. At this point in history it is clear that it has not yet occurred to critics to question whether a man has a right to get the better of a woman with his 'stronger will': this idea was taken up by twentieth-century critics.

It is noticeable that earlier critics responded favourably to Petruchio and his antics. Hazlitt continues: 'Petruchio is … a very honest fellow … He acts his assumed character to the life, with the most fantastical extravagance, with complete presence of mind, with untired animal spirits, and without particle of ill humour from beginning to end …' By the end of the nineteenth century, commentators began to question how we should respond to Petruchio and his wife-taming tricks. The playwright George Bernard Shaw (1856–1950) was contemptuous of the adaptation that he saw on the stage in 1888, commenting in *The Pall Mall Gazette* on 8 June that 'In spite of [Petruchio's] winks and smirks when Katherine is not looking, he cannot make the spectacle of a man cracking a whip at a starving woman otherwise than disgusting and unmanly.' Elsewhere, Shaw's comments on *The Taming of the Shrew* were contradictory. He felt that Shakespeare's comedy was 'realistic', Petruchio 'an honest and masterly picture of a real man, whose like we have all met' and the play as a whole 'quite bearable', 'because the selfishness of the man is healthily good-humoured and untainted by wanton cruelty', adding, 'it is good for the shrew to encounter a force like that and be brought to her senses'. It is hard to reconcile these remarks with his verdict on the final scene, which

CHECK THE BOOK
Russ McDonald's *Shakespeare and the Arts of Language* (2001) discusses Shakespeare's use of prose and verse, drawing on examples from across the plays.

CHECK THE BOOK

Michael Billington's comments can be found, with a selection of others, in The Cambridge School Shakespeare, *The Taming of the Shrew*, edited by Michael Fynes-Clinton and Perry Mills (1992).

CONTEXT

A Turkish production of *The Taming of the Shrew* was played as tragedy. Katherina's final speech was delivered by the actress with a shawl over her arms. At the end of the speech she revealed that she had slashed her wrists, and the play closed with her death.

was, he declared, 'altogether disgusting to a modern sensibility. No man can sit it out in the company of a woman without being extremely ashamed of the lord-of-creation moral implied in the wager and the speech put into the woman's own mouth.' Shaw concluded that a producer would need 'some apology' for presenting the play. In recent years, the theatre critic Michael Billington has expressed the same view, calling the play 'totally offensive' and suggesting that it should be left on the shelf. Shaw was among the first to note that there is an incongruity between Katherina's speech in the early acts and the final scene. This idea preoccupied a number of twentieth-century critics, undecided about whether or not the play is repugnant or legitimately entertaining and lively.

TWENTIETH-CENTURY VIEWS

As we have seen, Katherina has not yet attracted much critical attention, although Petruchio's character was dwelt on. The balance has been redressed, particularly since the development of **feminist** criticism in the second half of the twentieth century. But before we consider more current observations on the play, it is worth considering what earlier twentieth-century commentators said about *The Taming of the Shrew*.

Critics remained divided about the dramatic interest of the subplot, depending upon whether they believed Shakespeare was responsible for writing all three parts of the drama (**Induction**, plot and subplot). Gradually, as the authorship of the text has become less contentious, the views expounded by Dr Johnson and Hazlitt have come to dominate. Most critics agree that Shakespeare has interwoven his plots and themes effectively. The network of intrigues and deceptions that we are presented with continues to delight and impress audiences and readers. Attention has been paid to the sources Shakespeare used, and the influence of Roman and Italian comedy on the construction and content of *The Shrew*. H. B. Charlton (1938) sees a 'germ of romanticism' in the play because the lovers Bianca and Lucentio mean to marry (in the source play they have enjoyed an illicit love affair that results in pregnancy). Yet he casts doubt on Petruchio as a lover, characterising the central couple as 'dwellers in a menagerie'. Charlton feels that there is 'a brutal insistence on the animal in man' in the main plot. We are slowly moving away from the untroubled early readings of the presentation of the relationship between the sexes. Unlike Shaw, however, Charlton does not feel that Shakespeare intended us to take the message or moral of the play seriously. He argues that no Elizabethan or modern man or woman 'could really hold to the underlying assumption that marriage is mainly an economic arrangement'. Charlton's views raise questions that have continued to perplex readers and critics.

Overall, the predominant view before the 1950s was that Shakespeare's comedies were 'happy' plays. Gary Waller characterises this approach as one which saw the comedies as 'escapist crowd pleasers, golden effusions of romantic celebration and sentimentality'. Commentators concentrated on what they saw as universal themes and values: 'appearance and reality, courtship and marriage, idealism and cynicism, innocence and experience, order and disorder' (see Waller, 1991, p. 4). Critics also began to moralise about and psychologise the characters, following in the steps of A. C. Bradley, whose critical approach and methods had been influential since the beginning of the 20th century. Critics explored the ways in which society's most important and meaningful rituals and myths were explored in Shakespeare's plays. The comedies were linked to pre-modern community festivals and rituals, or, as Leo Salingar suggests, 'the ideas of holiday pastime and courtly revels'. In *The Shrew* this critic sees 'knockabout, practical jokes and disguises, of a kind appropriate to the Tudor Christmas holidays, the season of Misrule'. Salingar feels that Shakespeare is deliberately attempting to compare 'romantic love and acquired culture', noting the transformative powers of the former. But he also notes that Shakespeare treats Lucentio's romantic assumptions with **irony**: a view that has been more or less universally accepted today. Another critic writing in the 1970s, Alexander Leggatt, suggests that there is a sense of dislocation produced by the way in which Petruchio and the Lord work on their victims' minds. This critic comments on the self-consciously theatrical nature of the text, making much of the dreamlike and

CHECK THE BOOK

The Literary Language of Shakespeare by S. S. Hussey (1982) discusses Shakespeare's language in the contexts of history, poetry and rhetoric.

CONTEXT

In Shakespeare's plays, those who scorn love are usually portrayed as too proud, and heading for a fall: for example the male characters in *Love's Labour's Lost* and Beatrice and Benedick in *Much Ado About Nothing*. These characters deserve tricks to be played on them, because they are designed to do them good. Is this how you see *The Taming of the Shrew*?

illusory qualities it contains. The self-consciousness of the text is a central theme in current critics' discussions of *The Shrew*.

CURRENT APPROACHES

QUESTION

Why do you think some modern critics argue that *The Shrew* should be classed as a 'problem play' rather than a **comedy**?

CHECK THE BOOK

Natasha Korda's essay 'Household Kates: Domesticating Commodities in *The Taming of the Shrew*' offers a Marxist feminist reading of the text. It can be found in the New Casebook *Much Ado About Nothing and The Taming of the Shrew*, edited by Marion Wynne-Davies (2001).

More recently critics have redirected their approaches to Shakespeare's comedies. Now commentators are more inclined to relate them to the era in which the plays were written; they are no longer seen as possessing and expressing universal, enduring values: they are a product of a specific time, place and culture. Modern critics concentrate on gender and class issues, becoming increasingly interested in the subversive and self-consciously theatrical elements of the text. **Feminist, new historicist** and **psychoanalytic critics** have had a good deal to say about *The Shrew* and how its meanings are constructed. Contradictory readings continue to proliferate.

Feminist critics are divided about whether or not we can view the action of this play as supporting or subverting the patriarchal hierarchy that is described in Katherina's last speech. After discussing Kate's shrewish literary antecedents, Lisa Jardine (1983) argues that there is an 'entire absence of any locating tone' in the final lecture, which allows for 'conflicting and contradictory readings'. However, she feels that it is only the critic who 'imputes a celebratory tone to Kate's utterance at all'. To support her case Jardine considers the way in which the female tongue seems to signify impudence and immodesty in this play: 'the woman with the sharp tongue breaks the social order: she is distinctly disorderly … she threatens to sabotage the domestic harmony which depends upon her general submissiveness'. So, in order for harmony to be restored, Kate's chattering and scolding must cease. By way of contrast, Leah Marcus feels that it 'is by no means clear' that Katherina is 'converted' at the end of the play, in spite of the fact that there is 'a strong illusion of reality' surrounding this final speech. Marcus argues that Katherina learns to speak the 'pedagogue's language of social and familial order' thereby showing that she is a fine student of '**humanist** doctrine'. Other feminist critics have argued that we must view Kate's final speech as an **ironic** construct. These critics would suggest, as Germaine Greer has, that the heroine is lucky to meet a man who suits her so well. Many would dispute this. Jardine, in terms familiar from much feminist criticism of *The Shrew*, calls Petruchio a 'fortune-hunting rascal', marking a radical departure from the early positive descriptions of the hero by male commentators. Some feminists argue that the play is a satire on male chauvinism. Others would reject this, defining *The Shrew* as a product intended to affirm traditional views of men and women's roles. The debate about whether or not the play is sexist and/or misogynistic will doubtless continue to rage.

New historicist readings of *The Shrew* are often linked to feminist critiques, as commentators examine Elizabethan and Jacobean texts as 'articulations of the society's dominant cultural forces'. Karen Newman considers family politics in their historical context and produces a persuasive reading of the play, which concludes that the representation of gender is both 'patriarchally suspect and sexually ambivalent'. She suggests that the play clings to 'patriarchal ideology' while also 'tearing it away by foregrounding its constructed character'. She points to the use of the framing device and the presence of boy actors on the Elizabethan stage to support her views. Leah Marcus also draws attention to the Sly **Induction** in her arguments about the way patriarchy is presented in the play; she suggests that the drunkard's presence highlights and casts doubt on the hierarchy that is seeking to tame Kate. Joel Fineman adds to these ideas by suggesting that we become conscious of the constructed nature of speech in the play; Petruchio takes on a woman's shrewish tongue in order to beat his wife into submission; but whereas her tongue is powerless, he is 'never more patriarchal' than when he is acting the shrew. In her Penguin Critical Study of *The Shrew*, Stevie Davies is interested in class issues too. She says that the play 'reflects the blurring of class distinctions in the exchangeability of Tranio and his man'. She argues that both plots 'raise the ghost of possible revolt on the part of the servant class' (p. 79), although she does not believe the text ultimately endorses rebellion. She does, however, suggest that Petruchio's 'pathologically violent verbal and physical behaviour exposes the basis of force upon which the patriarchal system of marriage, the subordination of women and the ownership of property are

 QUESTION

Janet McTeer, the actress who played Petruchio in an all-female production of the play at the Globe Theatre in 2003, argues that it is not just Katherina who goes through a learning process. The hero has to learn 'responsibility, kindness, tolerance, self-control'. Do you agree that Petruchio has learned these things?

founded' (p. 6). More positively, Frances E. Dolan suggests that the play explores the ways in which husband and wife have to 'negotiate' their relationship. In her view the text also shows us the 'disparity between public and private conduct' and 'the clash of ideals' in Renaissance marriage.

CHECK THE BOOK

For a new historicist reading of the text, see Lynda E. Boose's essay 'Scolding Brides and Bridling Scolds: Taming the Woman's Unruly Member' in the New Casebook *Much Ado About Nothing and The Taming of the Shrew*, edited by Marion Wynne-Davies (2001). Boose looks at the punishments that were dealt out to real-life shrews.

Psychoanalytic critics consider the 'struggle for differentiation between child and parent' that occurs in the comedies. For these commentators, the family becomes a 'site of instability ... a place where often one parent is missing and where its harmonies are tentative, patched and together, founded on a utopian wish rather than reassuring coherence' (see Waller, p. 16). It is certainly possible to argue that *The Shrew* highlights these dilemmas. The Minolas are a dysfunctional family, who some might feel are 'cured' by Petruchio: he is astute enough to work out a suitable treatment for the reluctant bride. There have been attempts to account for Katherina's shrewishness using modern psychology: she is a neglected, hysterical child with an unpleasant family she needs to escape from in order to 'heal'. The ending of the play does not suggest that there is a 'reassuring coherence' to the events that we have seen. Hortensio and Lucentio are going to have to negotiate for domestic harmony with their partners; they cannot take it for granted.

PART FIVE

BACKGROUND

WILLIAM SHAKESPEARE'S LIFE

There are no personal records of Shakespeare's life. Official documents and occasional references to him by contemporary dramatists enable us to draw the main outline of his public life, but his private life remains hidden. Although not at all unusual for a writer of his time, this lack of first-hand evidence has tempted many to read his plays as personal records and to look in them for clues to his character and convictions. The results are unconvincing, partly because Renaissance art was not subjective or designed primarily to express its creator's personality, and partly because the drama of any period is very difficult to read biographically. Except when plays are written by committed dramatists to promote social or political causes (as by George Bernard Shaw or Bertolt Brecht), it is all but impossible to decide who among the variety of fictional characters in a drama represents the dramatist, or which of the various and often conflicting points of view expressed is authorial.

What we do know can be quickly summarised. Shakespeare was born into a well-to-do family in the market town of Stratford-upon-Avon in Warwickshire, where he was baptised, in Holy Trinity Church, on 26 April 1564. His father, John Shakespeare, was a prosperous glover and leather merchant who became a person of some importance in the town: in 1565 he was elected an alderman of the town, and in 1568 he became high bailiff (or mayor) of Stratford. In 1557 he had married Mary Arden. Their third child (of eight) and eldest son, William, learned to read and write at the primary (or 'petty') school in Stratford and then, it seems probable, attended the local grammar school, where he would have studied Latin, history, logic and rhetoric. In November 1582 William, then aged eighteen, married Anne Hathaway, who was twenty-six years old. They had a daughter, Susanna, in May 1583, and twins, Hamnet and Judith, in 1585.

 CHECK THE BOOK

There are a number of biographies of Shakespeare – many of them very speculative – but the most authoritative is still Samuel Schoenbaum's *Shakespeare: A Documentary Life* (1975).

CHECK THE NET
There is some very useful information on Shakespeare's London at **http:// www.britannia. com/hiddenlondon**

Shakespeare next appears in the historical record in 1592 when he was mentioned as a London actor and playwright in a pamphlet by the dramatist Robert Greene. These 'lost years' 1585–92 have been the subject of much speculation, but how they were occupied remains as much a mystery as when Shakespeare left Stratford, and why. In his pamphlet, *Greene's Groatsworth of Wit*, Greene expresses to his fellow dramatists his outrage that the 'upstart crow' Shakespeare has the impudence to believe he 'is as well able to bombast out a blank verse as the best of you'. To have aroused this hostility from a rival, Shakespeare must, by 1592, have been long enough in London to have made a name for himself as a playwright. We may conjecture that he had left Stratford in 1586 or 1587.

During the next twenty years, Shakespeare continued to live in London, regularly visiting his wife and family in Stratford. He continued to act, but his chief fame was as a dramatist. From 1594 he wrote exclusively for the Lord Chamberlain's Men, which rapidly became the leading dramatic company and from 1603 enjoyed the patronage of James I as the King's Men. His plays were extremely popular and he became a shareholder in his theatre company. He was able to buy lands around Stratford and a large house in the town, to which he retired in about 1611. He died there on 23 April 1616 and was buried in Holy Trinity Church on 25 April.

SHAKESPEARE'S DRAMATIC CAREER

Between the late 1580s and 1613 Shakespeare wrote thirty-seven plays, and contributed to some by other dramatists. This was by no means an exceptional number for a professional playwright of the times. The exact date of composition for individual plays is a matter of debate – for only a few plays is the date of their first performance known – but the broad outlines of Shakespeare's dramatic career have been established. He began in the late 1580s and early 1590s by rewriting earlier plays and working with plotlines inspired by the classics. He concentrated on comedies (such as *The Comedy of Errors* and *The Taming of the Shrew*) and plays dealing with English history (such as the three parts of *Henry VI*, 1589–92), though he also tried his hand at bloodthirsty revenge tragedy (*Titus Andronicus*, 1592–3, indebted to both Ovid and Seneca). During the 1590s Shakespeare developed his expertise

in these kinds of play to write comic masterpieces such as
A Midsummer Night's Dream (1594–5) and *As You Like It*
(1599–1600) and history plays such as *Henry IV* (1596–8) and
Henry V (1598–9).

As the new century begins a new note is detectable. Plays such as
Troilus and Cressida (1601–2) and *Measure for Measure* (1603–4),
poised between **comedy** and tragedy, evoke complex responses.
Because of their generic uncertainty and ambivalent tone such
works are sometimes referred to as 'problem plays', but it is tragedy
which comes to dominate the extraordinary sequence of
masterpieces: *Hamlet* (1600–1), *Othello* (1602–4), *King Lear*
(1605–6), *Macbeth* (1605–6) and *Antony and Cleopatra* (1606).

In the last years of his dramatic career, Shakespeare wrote a group
of plays of a quite different kind. These 'romances', as they are often
called, are in many ways the most remarkable of all his plays. The
group comprises *Pericles* (1608), *Cymbeline* (1609–11), *The Winter's
Tale* (1610–11) and *The Tempest* (1610–11). These plays
(particularly *Cymbeline*) reprise many of the situations and themes
of the earlier dramas but in fantastical and exotic dramatic designs
which, set in distant lands, covering large tracts of time and
involving music, mime, dance and tableaux, have something of the
qualities of masques and pageants. The situations which in the
tragedies had led to disaster are here resolved: the great theme is
restoration and reconciliation. Where in the tragedies Ophelia,
Desdemona and Cordelia died, the daughters of these plays –
Marina, Imogen, Perdita, Miranda – survive and are reunited with
their parents and lovers.

THE TEXTS OF SHAKESPEARE'S PLAYS

Nineteen of Shakespeare's plays were printed during his lifetime
in what are called 'quartos' (books, each containing one play, and
made up of sheets of paper each folded twice to make four leaves).
Shakespeare, however, did not supervise their publication. When a
playwright had sold a play to a dramatic company he sold his rights
in it: copyright belonged to whoever had possession of an actual
copy of the text, and so consequently authors had no control over
what happened to their work. Anyone who could get hold of the

CHECK THE FILM

There are lots of anachronisms and inaccuracies in *Shakespeare in Love* (1998) – that's half the fun of it – but its depiction of the hand-to-mouth world of the commercial theatre has something of the energy and edginess from which Shakespeare drew his artistic power.

CONTEXT

A quarto is a small format book, roughly equivalent to a modern paperback. Play texts in quarto form typically cost sixpence, as opposed to the cost of going to the theatre at a penny.

CONTEXT

Plays were not considered as serious literature in this period: when, in 1612, Sir Thomas Bodley was setting up his library in Oxford he instructed his staff not to buy any drama for the collection: 'haply [perhaps] some plays may be worthy the keeping, but hardly one in forty'.

text of a play might publish it if they wished. Hence, what found its way into print might be the author's copy, but it might be an actor's copy or prompt copy, perhaps cut or altered for performance; sometimes actors (or even members of the audience) might publish what they could remember of the text. Printers, working without the benefit of the author's oversight, introduced their own errors, through misreading the manuscript, for example, and by 'correcting' what seemed to them not to make sense.

In 1623 John Heminges and Henry Condell, two actors in Shakespeare's company, collected together texts of thirty-six of Shakespeare's plays (*Pericles* was omitted) and published them in a large folio (a book in which each sheet of paper is folded once in half, to give two leaves). This, the First Folio, was followed by later editions in 1632, 1663 and 1685. Despite its appearance of authority, however, the texts in the First Folio still present many difficulties, for there are printing errors and confused passages in the plays, and its texts often differ significantly from those of the earlier quartos, when these exist.

Shakespeare's texts have, then, been through a number of intermediaries. We do not have his authority for any one of his plays, and hence we cannot know exactly what it was that he wrote. Bibliographers, textual critics and editors have spent a great deal of effort on endeavouring to get behind the errors, uncertainties and contradictions in the available texts to recover the plays as Shakespeare originally wrote them. What we read is the result of these efforts. Modern texts are what editors have constructed from the available evidence: they correspond to no sixteenth- or seventeenth-century editions, and to no early performance of a Shakespeare play. Furthermore, these composite texts differ from each other, for different editors read the early texts differently and come to different conclusions. A Shakespeare text is an unstable and a contrived thing.

Often, of course, its judgements embody, if not the personal prejudices of the editor, then the cultural preferences of the time in which he or she was working. Growing awareness of this has led recent scholars to distrust the whole editorial enterprise and to repudiate the attempt to construct a 'perfect' text. Stanley Wells and Gary Taylor, the editors of the Oxford edition of *William Shakespeare: The Complete Works* (1988), point out that almost certainly the texts of Shakespeare's plays were altered in performance, and from one performance to another, so that there may never have been a single version. They note, too, that Shakespeare probably revised and rewrote some plays. They do not claim to print a definitive text of any play, but prefer what seems to them the 'more theatrical' version, and when there is a great difference between available versions, as with *King Lear*, they print two texts.

SHAKESPEARE AND THE ENGLISH RENAISSANCE

Shakespeare arrived in London at the very time that the Elizabethan period was poised to become the 'golden age' of English literature. Although Elizabeth reigned as queen from 1558 to 1603, the term 'Elizabethan' is used very loosely in a literary sense to refer to the period 1580 to 1625, when the great works of the age were produced. (Sometimes the later part of this period is distinguished as 'Jacobean', from the Latin form of the name of the king who succeeded Elizabeth, James I of England and VI of Scotland, who reigned from 1603 to 1625.) The poet Edmund Spenser heralded this new age with his pastoral poem *The Shepheardes Calender* (1579), and in his essay *An Apologie for Poetrie* (written about 1580, although not published until 1595) his friend Sir Philip Sidney championed the imaginative power of the 'speaking picture of poesy', famously declaring that 'Nature never set forth the earth in so rich a tapestry as divers poets have done ... Her world is brazen, the poet's only deliver a golden'.

Spenser and Sidney were part of that rejuvenating movement in European culture which since the nineteenth century has been known by the term 'Renaissance'. Meaning literally 'rebirth' it denotes a revival and redirection of artistic and intellectual endeavour which began in Italy in the fourteenth century in the poetry of Petrarch. It spread gradually northwards across Europe, and is first detectable in England in the early sixteenth century in

 CHECK THE NET
You can consult texts by Spenser and Sidney, and other contemporaries of Shakespeare, at Renascence Editions **http://www. uoregon.edu/ ~rbear/ren.htm**

the writings of the scholar and statesman Sir Thomas More and in the poetry of Sir Thomas Wyatt and Henry Howard, Earl of Surrey. Its keynote was a curiosity in thought which challenged old assumptions and traditions. To the innovative spirit of the Renaissance, the preceding ages appeared dully unoriginal and conformist.

That spirit was fuelled by the rediscovery of many classical texts and the culture of Greece and Rome. This fostered a confidence in human reason and in human potential which, in every sphere, challenged old convictions. The discovery of America and its peoples (Christopher Columbus had sailed in 1492) demonstrated that the world was a larger and stranger place than had been thought. The cosmological speculation of Copernicus (later confirmed by Galileo) that the sun, not the earth, was the centre of our planetary system challenged the centuries-old belief that the earth and human beings were at the centre of the cosmos. The pragmatic political philosophy of Machiavelli seemed to cut politics free from its traditional link with morality by permitting to statesmen any means which secured the desired end. And the religious movements we know collectively as the Reformation broke with the Church of Rome and set the individual conscience, not ecclesiastical authority, at the centre of the religious life. Nothing, it seemed, was beyond questioning, nothing impossible.

Shakespeare's drama is innovative and challenging in exactly the way of the Renaissance. It questions the beliefs, assumptions and politics upon which Elizabethan society was founded. And although the plays always conclude in a restoration of order and stability, many critics are inclined to argue that their imaginative energy goes into subverting, rather than reinforcing, traditional values. They would point out, for example, that Katherina's speech on wifely submission to patriarchal authority in *The Taming of the Shrew* (V.2.137–80) appears to be rendered **ironic** by the action of the play in which it occurs. Convention, audience expectation and censorship all required the status quo to be endorsed by the plots' conclusions, but the dramas find ways to allow alternative sentiments to be expressed. Frequently, figures of authority are undercut by some comic or parodic figure: against the Duke in *Measure for Measure* is set Lucio; against Prospero in *The Tempest*, Caliban; against Henry IV, Falstaff.

CHECK THE NET
The Luminarium site has links to a wide range of historical information on sixteenth-century topics including astronomy, medicine, economics and technology: **http:// www.luminarium. org**

Despairing, critical, dissident, disillusioned, unbalanced, rebellious, mocking voices are repeatedly to be heard in the plays, rejecting, resenting, defying the established order. They belong always to marginal, socially unacceptable figures, 'licensed', as it were, by their situations to say what would be unacceptable from socially privileged or responsible citizens. The question is: are such characters given these views to discredit them, or were they the only ones through whom a voice could be given to radical and dissident ideas? Is Shakespeare a conservative or a revolutionary?

Renaissance culture was intensely nationalistic. With the break-up of the internationalism of the Middle Ages the evolving nation states which still mark the map of Europe began for the first time to acquire distinctive cultural identities. There was intense rivalry among them as they sought to achieve in their own vernacular languages a culture which could equal that of Greece and Rome. Spenser's great allegorical epic poem *The Faerie Queene*, which began to appear from 1590, celebrated Elizabeth and was intended to outdo the poetic achievements of France and Italy and to stand beside works of Virgil and Homer. Shakespeare is equally preoccupied with national identity. His history plays tell an epic story which examines how modern England came into being through the conflicts of the fifteenth-century Wars of the Roses which brought the Tudors to the throne. He is fascinated, too, by the related subject of politics and the exercise of power. With the collapse of medieval feudalism and the authority of local barons, the royal court in the Renaissance came to assume a new status as the centre of power and patronage. It was here that the destiny of a country was shaped. Courts, and how to succeed in them, consequently fascinated the Renaissance; and they fascinated Shakespeare and his audience.

But the dramatic gaze is not merely admiring; through a variety of devices, a critical perspective is brought to bear. The court may be paralleled by a very different world, revealing uncomfortable similarities (for example, Henry's court and the Boar's Head tavern, ruled over by Falstaff in *Henry IV*). Its hypocrisy may be bitterly denounced (for example, in the diatribes of the mad Lear) and its self-seeking ambition represented disturbingly in the figure of a Machiavellian villain (such as Edmund in *Lear*) or a malcontent

 CHECK THE BOOK
Benedict Anderson's book on the rise of the nation and nationalism, *Imagined Communities* (revised edition, 1991), has been influential for its definition of the nation as 'an imagined political community' – imagined in part through cultural productions such as Shakespeare's history plays.

CHECK THE FILM
We can get a modern equivalent of the effect of this displacement from Christine Edzard's film of *As You Like It* (1992). Here, the court scenes are set in the luxurious headquarters of a bank or company; the woodland scenes amid a sort of 'cardboard city' of social outcasts and the vulnerable.

(such as Iago in *Othello*). Shakespeare is fond of displacing the court to another context, the better to examine its assumptions and pretensions and to offer alternatives to the courtly life (for example, in the pastoral setting of the forest of Arden in *As You Like It* or Prospero's island in *The Tempest*). Courtiers are frequently figures of fun whose unmanly sophistication ('neat and trimly dressed, / Fresh as a bridegroom … perfumed like a milliner', says Hotspur of such a man in *1 Henry IV*, I.3.33–6) is contrasted with plain-speaking integrity: Oswald is set against Kent in *King Lear*.

When thinking of these matters, we should remember that stage plays were subject to censorship, and any criticism had therefore to be muted or oblique: direct criticism of the monarch or contemporary English court would not be tolerated. This has something to do with why Shakespeare's plays are always set either in the past, or abroad.

The nationalism of the English Renaissance was reinforced by Protestantism. Henry VIII had broken with Rome in the 1530s and in Shakespeare's time there was an independent Protestant state Church. Because the Pope in Rome had excommunicated Queen Elizabeth as a heretic and relieved the English of their allegiance to the crown, there was deep suspicion of Roman Catholics as potential traitors. This was enforced by the attempted invasion of the Spanish Armada in 1588. This was a religiously inspired crusade to overthrow Elizabeth and restore England to Roman Catholic allegiance. Roman Catholicism was hence easily identified with hostility to England. Its association with disloyalty and treachery was heightened by the Gunpowder Plot of 1605, a Roman Catholic attempt to destroy the government of England.

Shakespeare's plays are remarkably free from direct religious sentiment, but their emphases are Protestant. Young women, for example, are destined for marriage, not for convents (precisely what Isabella appears to escape at the end of *Measure for Measure*); friars are ambiguous characters, even if with benign intentions, as in *Much Ado About Nothing* or *Romeo and Juliet*. (We should add, though, that Puritans, extreme Protestants, are even less kindly treated: for example, Malvolio in *Twelfth Night*.)

The central figures of the plays are frequently individuals beset by temptation, by the lure of evil – Angelo in *Measure for Measure*, Othello, Lear, Macbeth – and not only in tragedies: Falstaff is described as 'that old white-bearded Satan' (*1 Henry IV*, II.4.454). We follow their inner struggles. Shakespeare's heroes often have the preoccupation with self and the introspective tendencies associated with Protestantism: his tragic heroes are haunted by their consciences, seeking their true selves, agonising over what course of action to take as they follow what can often be understood as a kind of spiritual progress towards heaven or hell.

SHAKESPEARE'S THEATRE

 CHECK THE NET

Find out more about Shakespeare's new Globe Theatre at **http://www. shakespeares-globe.org**

The theatre for which the plays were written was one of the most remarkable innovations of the Renaissance. There had been no theatres or acting companies during the medieval period. Performed on carts and in open spaces at Christian festivals, plays had been almost exclusively religious. Such professional actors as there were wandered the country putting on a variety of entertainments in the yards of inns, on makeshift stages in market squares, or anywhere else suitable. They did not perform full-length plays, but mimes, juggling and comedy acts. Such actors were regarded by officialdom and polite society as little better than vagabonds and layabouts.

Just before Shakespeare went to London all this began to change. A number of young men who had been to the universities of Oxford and Cambridge came to London in the 1580s and began to write plays which made use of what they had learned about the classical drama of ancient Greece and Rome. Plays such as John Lyly's *Alexander and Campaspe* (1584), Christopher Marlowe's *Tamburlaine the Great* (*c.*1587) and Thomas Kyd's *The Spanish Tragedy* (1588–9) were unlike anything that had been written in English before. They were full-length plays on secular subjects, taking their plots from history and legend, adopting many of the devices of classical drama, and offering a range of characterisation and situation hitherto unattempted in English drama. With the exception of Lyly's prose dramas, they were in the unrhymed iambic pentameters (**blank verse**), which the Earl of Surrey had

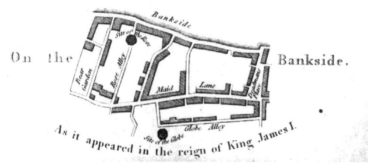

THE GLOBE THEATRE,

On the Bankside.

As it appeared in the reign of King James I.

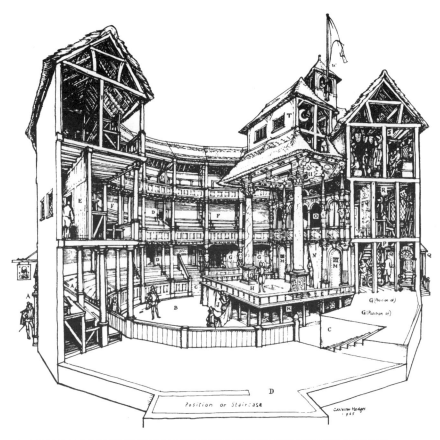

A CONJECTURAL RECONSTRUCTION OF THE INTERIOR OF THE GLOBE PLAYHOUSE

AA	Main entrance	N	Curtained 'place behind the stage'
B	The Yard	O	Gallery above the stage, used as required
CC	Entrances to lowest galleries		sometimes by musicians, sometimes by
D	Entrance to staircase and upper galleries		spectators, and often as part of the play
E	Corridor serving the different sections of the	P	Back-stage area (the tiring-house)
	middle gallery	Q	Tiring-house door
F	Middle gallery ('Twopenny Rooms')	R	Dressing-rooms
G	'Gentlemen's Rooms or Lords Rooms'	S	Wardrobe and storage
H	The stage	T	The hut housing the machine for lowering
J	The hanging being put up round the stage		enthroned gods, etc., to the stage
K	The 'Hell' under the stage	U	The 'Heavens'
L	The stage trap, leading down to the Hell	W	Hoisting the playhouse flag
MM	Stage doors		

CHECK THE BOOK
The most authoritative book on what we know about the theatre of Shakespeare's time is Andrew Gurr's *The Shakespearean Stage* (1992).

introduced into English earlier in the sixteenth century. This was a freer and more expressive medium than the rhymed verse of medieval drama. It was the drama of these 'university wits' that Shakespeare challenged when he came to London. Greene was one of them, and we have heard how little he liked Shakespeare setting himself up as a dramatist.

The most significant change of all, however, was that these dramatists wrote for the professional theatre. In 1576 James Burbage built the first permanent theatre in England, in Shoreditch, just beyond London's northern boundary. It was called simply 'The Theatre'. Others soon followed. Thus, when Shakespeare came to London, there was a flourishing drama, theatres and companies of actors waiting for him, such as there had never been before in England. His company performed at James Burbage's Theatre until 1596, and used the Swan and Curtain until they moved into their own new theatre, the Globe, in 1599. It was burned down in 1613 when a cannon was fired during a performance of Shakespeare's *Henry VIII*.

CONTEXT
Whereas now we would conceptualise a visit to the theatre as going to *see* a play, the most common Elizabethan phrase was 'to go *hear* a play' (Christopher Sly is told that 'they thought it good to hear a play' Ind.2.134) – thus registering the different sensory priorities of the early modern theatre.

With the completion in 1996 of Sam Wanamaker's project to construct in London a replica of the Globe, and with productions now running there, a version of Shakespeare's theatre can be experienced at first hand. It is very different to the usual modern experience of drama. The form of the Elizabethan theatre derived from the inn yards and animal baiting rings in which actors had been accustomed to perform in the past. They were circular wooden buildings with a paved courtyard in the middle open to the sky. A rectangular stage jutted out into the middle of this yard. Some of the audience stood in the yard (or 'pit') to watch the play. They were thus on three sides of the stage, close up to it and on a level with it. These 'groundlings' paid only a penny to get in, but for wealthier spectators there were seats in three covered tiers or galleries between the inner and outer walls of the building, extending round most of the auditorium and overlooking the pit and the stage. Such a theatre could hold about three thousand spectators. The yards were about 80ft in diameter and the rectangular stage approximately 40ft by 30ft and 5ft 6in high. Shakespeare aptly called such a theatre a 'wooden O' in the Prologue to *Henry V* (line 13).

The stage itself was partially covered by a roof or canopy which projected from the wall at the rear of the stage and was supported by two posts at the front. This protected the stage and performers from inclement weather, and to it were secured winches and other machinery for stage effects. On either side at the back of the stage was a door. These led into the dressing room (or 'tiring-house') and it was by means of these doors that actors entered and left the stage. Between these doors was a small recess or alcove which was curtained off. Such a 'discovery place' served, for example, for Juliet's bedroom when in Act IV Scene 4 of *Romeo and Juliet* the Nurse went to the back of the stage and drew the curtain to find Juliet apparently dead on her bed. Above the discovery place was a balcony, used for the famous balcony scenes of *Romeo and Juliet* (Act II Scene 2 and Act III Scene 5), or for the battlements of Richard's castle when he is confronted by Bolingbroke in *Richard II* (Act III Scene 3). Actors (all parts in the Elizabethan theatre were taken by boys or men) had access to the area beneath the stage; from here, in the 'cellarage', would have come the voice of the ghost of Hamlet's father (*Hamlet*, II.1.150–82).

On these stages there was very little in the way of scenery or props – there was nowhere to store them (there were no wings in this theatre) nor any way to set them up (no tabs across the stage), and, anyway, productions had to be transportable for performance at court or at noble houses. The stage was bare, which is why characters often tell us where they are: there was nothing on the stage to indicate location. It is also why location is so rarely topographical, and much more often **symbolic**. It suggests a dramatic mood or situation, rather than a place: Lear's barren heath reflects his destitute state, as the storm his emotional turmoil.

None of the plays printed in Shakespeare's lifetime marks act or scene divisions. These have been introduced by later editors, but they should not mislead us into supposing that there was any break in Elizabethan performances such as might happen today while the curtains are closed and the set is changed. The staging of Elizabethan plays was continuous, with the many short 'scenes' of which Shakespeare's plays are often constructed following one after another in quick succession. We have to think of a more fluid and

> **CONTEXT**
>
> We do not know much about the props list for a theatre company in Shakespeare's time, although the evidence we do have suggests that there were some quite ambitious examples: one list dating from 1598 includes decorated cloths depicting cities or the night sky, items of armour, horses' heads and 'one hell mouth', probably for performances of Christopher Marlowe's famous play *Doctor Faustus*.

much faster production than we are generally used to: in the prologues to *Romeo and Juliet* (line 12) and *Henry VIII* (line 13) Shakespeare speaks of only two hours as the playing time. It is because plays were staged continuously that exits and entrances are written in as part of the script: characters speak as they enter or leave the stage because otherwise there would be a silence while, in full view, they took up their positions. (This is also why dead bodies have to be carried off: they cannot get up and walk off.)

In 1608 Shakespeare's company, the King's Men, acquired the Blackfriars Theatre, a smaller, rectangular indoor theatre, holding about seven hundred people, with seats for all the members of the audience, facilities for elaborate stage effects and, because it was enclosed, artificial lighting. It has been suggested that the plays written for this 'private' theatre differed from those written for the Globe, since, as it cost more to go to a private theatre, the audience came from a higher social stratum and demanded the more elaborate and courtly entertainment which Shakespeare's romances provide. However, the King's Men continued to play in the Globe in the summer, using Blackfriars in the winter, and it is not certain that Shakespeare's last plays were written specifically for the Blackfriars Theatre, or first performed there.

READING SHAKESPEARE

Shakespeare's plays were written for this stage, but there is also a sense in which they were written *by* this stage. The material and physical circumstances of their production in such theatres had a profound effect upon them. Unless we bear this in mind, we are likely to find them very strange, for we will read with expectations shaped by our own familiarity with modern, largely realistic, fiction and drama. If we try to read them like this, we shall find ourselves irritated by the improbabilities of Shakespeare's plot, confused by his chronology, puzzled by locations, frustrated by unanswered questions and dissatisfied by the motivation of the action. The absurd ease with which disguised persons pass through Shakespeare's plays is a case in point: why does no one recognise people they know so well? There is a great deal of psychological accuracy in Shakespeare's plays, but we are far from any attempt at realism.

CHECK THE BOOK

Deborah Cartmell's *Interpreting Shakespeare on Screen* (2000) is recommended for its clear and interesting sense of the possibilities and the requirements of approaching Shakespeare through the cinema.

The reason is that in Shakespeare's theatre it was impossible to pretend that the audience was not watching a contrived performance. In a modern theatre, the audience is encouraged to forget itself as it becomes absorbed by the action on stage. The worlds of the spectators and of the actors are sharply distinguished by the lighting: in the dark auditorium the audience is passive, silent, anonymous, receptive and attentive; on the lighted stage the actors are active, vocal, demonstrative and dramatic. (The distinction is, of course, still more marked in the cinema.) There is no communication between the two worlds: for the audience to speak would be interruptive; for the actors to address the audience would be to break the illusion of the play. In the Elizabethan theatre, this distinction did not exist, and for two reasons: first, performances took place in the open air and in daylight which illuminated everyone equally; secondly, the spectators were all around the stage (and wealthier spectators actually on it), and were dressed no differently to the actors, who wore contemporary dress. In such a theatre, spectators would be as aware of each other as of the actors; they could not lose their identity in a corporate group, nor could they ever forget that they were spectators at a performance. There was no chance that they could believe 'this is really happening'.

This, then, was communal theatre, not only in the sense that it was going on in the middle of a crowd but in the sense that the crowd joined in. Elizabethan audiences had none of our deference: they did not keep quiet, or arrive on time, or remain for the whole performance. They joined in, interrupted, even getting on the stage. And plays were preceded and followed by jigs and clowning. It was all much more like our experience of a pantomime, and at a pantomime we are fully aware, and are meant to be aware, that we are watching games being played with reality. The conventions of pantomime revel in their own artificiality: the fishnet tights are to signal that the handsome prince is a woman, the Dame's monstrous false breasts signal that 'she' is a man.

Something very similar is the case with Elizabethan theatre: it utilised its very theatricality. Instead of trying to persuade spectators that they are not in a theatre watching a performance,

---

CONTEXT

The Romantic critic Samuel Taylor Coleridge argued that literature requires our 'willing suspension of disbelief': but it is not clear that the theatre of the Shakespearean period did require its audience to forget that they were in a theatre. Certainly, remarks calling attention to the theatrical setting are commonplace – in comedies such as *Twelfth Night* (III.4.125) and *As You Like It* (II.7.139–43), and in tragedies including *Macbeth* (V.5.23–5) – making it more difficult to forget the theatricality of the stories depicted.

Elizabethan plays acknowledge the presence of the audience. It is addressed not only by prologues, **epilogues** and choruses, but in **soliloquies**. There is no realistic reason why characters should suddenly explain themselves to empty rooms, but, of course, it is not an empty room. The actor is surrounded by people. Soliloquies are not addressed to the world of the play: they are for the audience's benefit. And that audience's complicity is assumed: when a character like Prospero declares himself to be invisible, it is accepted that he is. Disguises are taken to be impenetrable, however improbable, and we are to accept impossibly contrived situations, such as barely hidden characters remaining undetected (indeed, on the Elizabethan stage there was nowhere at all they could hide).

 CHECK THE NET
The 'Designing Shakespeare' database at PADS (**http://www.pads. ahds.ac.uk**) has an extensive collection of photographs from different productions available online.

These, then, are plays which are aware of themselves as dramas; in critical terminology, they are self-reflexive, commenting upon themselves as dramatic pieces and prompting the audience to think about the theatrical experience. They do this not only through their direct address to the audience but through their fondness for the play-within-a-play (which reminds the audience that the encompassing play is also a play) and their constant use of **images** from, and allusions to, the theatre. They are fascinated by role-playing, by acting, appearance and reality. Things are rarely what they seem, either in **comedy** (for example, in *A Midsummer Night's Dream*) or tragedy (*Romeo and Juliet*). This offers one way to think about those disguises: they are thematic rather than realistic. Kent's disguise in *Lear* reveals his true, loyal self, while Edmund, who is not disguised, hides his true self. In *As You Like It*, Rosalind is more truly herself disguised as a man than when dressed as a woman.

The effect of all this is to confuse the distinction we would make between 'real life' and 'acting'. The case of Rosalind, for example, raises searching questions about gender roles, about how far it is 'natural' to be womanly or manly: how does the stage, on which a man can play a woman playing a man (and have a man fall in love with him/her), differ from life, in which we assume the roles we think appropriate to masculine and feminine behaviour? The same is true of political roles: when a Richard II or Lear is so aware of the regal part he is performing, of the trappings and rituals of kingship, their plays raise the uncomfortable possibility that the answer to the question of what constitutes a successful king is simply: a good actor. Indeed, human life generally is repeatedly rendered through the imagery of the stage, from Macbeth's 'Life's but a walking shadow, a poor player / That struts and frets his hour upon the stage / And then is heard no more' (V.5.23–5) to Prospero's paralleling of human life to a performance which, like the globe (both world and theatre), will end (IV.I.146–58). When life is a fiction, like this play, or this play is a fiction like life, what is the difference? 'All the world's a stage ...' (*As You Like It*, II.7.139).

CONTEXT

The poet Walter Raleigh wrote a poem on this image of life as theatre, which begins 'What is our life? A play of passion', in which 'Our mothers' wombs the tiring houses be, / Where we are dressed for this short comedy'. There's a twist at the end of the short verse: 'Only we die in earnest, that's no jest.'

World events	Shakespeare's life (dates for plays are approximate)	Literature/Drama
1492 Christopher Columbus sets sail for America		
		1509 Ludovico Ariosto, *I Suppositi* (source)
		1513 Niccolò Machiavelli, *The Prince*
		1528 Castiglione's *Book of the Courtier*
1534 Henry VIII breaks with Rome and declares himself head of the Church of England		
		1554 Matteo Bandelli, *Novelle*
1556 Archbishop Thomas Cranmer burned at the stake		
1558 Elizabeth I accedes to throne		
		1562 Lope de Vega, great Spanish dramatist, born
	1564 (26 April) William Shakespeare baptised in Stratford-upon-Avon	
		1566 George Gascoigne, *Supposes* (source)
1570 Elizabeth I excommunicated by Pope Pius V		
		1576 Erection of first specially built public theatres in London – the Theatre and the Curtain
1577 Francis Drake sets out on voyage round the world		
		c.1580 Sir Philip Sidney, *An Apologie for Poetrie*
	1582 Marries Anne Hathaway	
	1583 Daughter Susanna born	
1584 Walter Raleigh's sailors land in Virginia		**1584** John Lyly, *Alexander and Campaspe*
	1585 Twins, Hamnet and Judith, born	
	LATE 1580s – EARLY 1590s *1–3 Henry VI* and *Richard III*	

World events	Shakespeare's life (dates for plays are approximate)	Literature/Drama
1587 Execution of Mary Queen of Scots after implicated in plot to murder Elizabeth I **1588** The Spanish Armada defeated		**1590** Sir Philip Sidney, *Arcadia*; Edmund Spenser, *The Faerie Queene* (Books I–III)
1592 Plague in London closes theatres	**1592** Recorded as being a London actor and an 'upstart crow' **1592–4** *The Comedy of Errors*, **The Taming of the Shrew** and *Titus Andronicus* **1594 ONWARDS** Writes exclusively for the Lord Chamberlain's Men **1594–5** *Two Gentlemen of Verona*, *Love's Labour's Lost* and *Richard II* **c.1595** *Romeo and Juliet* and *A Midsummer Night's Dream*	**1592** Christopher Marlowe, *Doctor Faustus*; Thomas Kyd's *The Spanish Tragedy* published **1594** *A Pleasant Conceited Historie called The Taming of a Shrew* (authorship unknown) entered in the Stationers' Register **1595** Death of William Painter, whose *Palace of Pleasure* provided sources of plots for many Elizabethan dramas
1596 English raid on Cadiz; Drake dies	**1596–8** First performance of *The Merchant of Venice* **1597** *1–2 Henry VI* **1598–9** Globe Theatre built at Southwark; *Much Ado About Nothing*, *Julius Caesar*, *As You Like It* and *Henry V* **1600** *A Midsummer Night's Dream*, *Much Ado About Nothing* and *The Merchant of Venice* printed in quartos **1600–1** *Hamlet* and *The Merry Wives of Windsor* **1600–2** *Twelfth Night* **1601** *Troilus and Cressida*	

World events	Shakespeare's life (dates for plays are approximate)	Literature/Drama
	1602 *All's Well That Ends Well*	
1603 Death of Queen Elizabeth Tudor; accession of James Stuart	**1603** ONWARDS His company enjoys patronage of James I as the King's Men	**1603** Thomas Heywood, *A Woman Killed with Kindness*
	1604 *Othello* performed; *Measure for Measure*	
1605 Discovery of Guy Fawkes's plot to blow up the Houses of Parliament	**1605** First version of *King Lear*	**1605** Cervantes, *Don Quixote de la Mancha*
	1606 *Macbeth*	**1606** Ben Jonson, *Volpone*
	1606–7 *Antony and Cleopatra*	
	1607 *Coriolanus* and *Timon of Athens*	
	1608 *Pericles*; the King's Men acquire Blackfriars Theatre for winter performances	
1609 Galileo constructs first astronomical telescope		
1610 William Harvey discovers circulation of blood		
	1611 *Cymbeline, The Winter's Tale* and *The Tempest* performed	**1611** John Fletcher, *The Woman's Prize, or The Tamer Tamed*; King James's translation of the Bible
1612 Last burning of heretics in England		**1612** Thomas Heywood, *An Apology for Actors*
	1613 *Henry VIII*; the Globe Theatre burns down	
		1614 John Webster, *The Duchess of Malfi*
	1616 Dies	
1618 Raleigh executed for treason; Thirty Years War begins in Europe		
		1622 Birth of French dramatist Molière
	1623 First Folio is published, which includes *The Taming of the Shrew*	

TEXTS OF THE PLAY

Brian Morris, ed., *The Taming of the Shrew* (The Arden Shakespeare), Methuen 1981
 This is the edition of the text used in preparation of these Notes

Michael Fynes-Clinton and Perry Mills, eds., *The Taming of the Shrew* (The Cambridge School Shakespeare), Cambridge University Press, 1992

Stanley Wells and Gary Taylor, eds., *William Shakespeare: The Complete Works*, Clarendon Press, 1988

CRITICISM

Jonathan Bate, ed., *The Romantics on Shakespeare*, Penguin, 1992

John C. Bean, 'Comic Structure and the Humanising of Kate in *The Taming of the Shrew*', in *The Woman's Part: Feminist Criticism of Shakespeare*, eds. Carolyn Ruth Swift Lenz, Gayle Greene, Carol Thomas Neely, University of Illinois Press, 1980 (1985)
 Bean takes on the revisionists and antirevisionists, arguing for a **humanist** reading of the play, in which Kate 'discovers her own identity'

H. B. Charlton, *Shakespearean Comedy*, Methuen, 1938 (1967)
 Charlton looks closely at the traditions of comedy in Europe and at the models Shakespeare used while working on *The Shrew*

Judith Cook, *Women in Shakespeare*, Harrap, 1980

Stevie Davies, *The Taming of the Shrew* (Penguin Critical Studies), Penguin, 1995
 A thorough **feminist** examination of all aspects of the text, including its historical context

Frances E. Dolan, ed., *The Taming of the Shrew: Texts and Contexts*, Bedford Books of St. Martin's Press, 1996
 Includes the text of the play, comments on the historical context of the play, and extracts from a number of Renaissance texts on marriage, the household, shrew-taming. Extremely useful for any student wishing to view the play in relation to social, literary and historical contexts

Juliet Dusinberre, *Shakespeare and the Nature of Women*, Palgrave Macmillan, 1975

Joel Fineman, 'The turn of the shrew', in *Shakespeare and the Question of Theory*, eds. Patricia Parker and Geoffrey Hartman, Methuen, 1985
 Fineman looks at the use of male and female discourse in the play

P. J. Gabriner, 'Hierarchy, Harmony and Happiness: Another Look at the Hunting Dogs in the "Induction" to *The Taming of the Shrew*', in *Reclamations of Shakespeare*, ed. A. J. Hoenlaars, DQR Studies in Literature 15, Rodopi, Amsterdam, GA, 1994
 Gabriner argues that Kate is 'liberated into her true nature'

F. E. Halliday, *Shakespeare and His Critics*, Gerald Duckworth and Co. Ltd, 1949

Graham Holderness, 'Text and Performance: *The Taming of the Shrew*', *Shakespeare in Performance* (New Casebooks Series), ed. Robert Shaughnessy, Palgrave Macmillan, 2000
Offers a history of the play in production, with some interesting comments on *The Shrew* in comparison with *A Shrew*

J. D. Huston, *Shakespeare's Comedies of Play*, Columbia University Press, 1981

Lisa Jardine, *Still Harping on Daughters: Women and Drama in the Age of Shakespeare*, Harvester Press, 1983
Chapter 4 focuses specifically on *The Shrew* ('Shrewd or shrewish? When the disorderly woman has her head'). Jardine looks at the historical and literary contexts closely and writes persuasively about the text

Alexander Leggatt, *Shakespeare's Comedy of Love*, Methuen, 1974
Leggatt looks at the clashes and contrasts of style in the play (romance versus realism), and at the use of dreams

Alexander Leggatt, ed., *The Cambridge Companion to Shakespearean Comedy*, Cambridge University Press, 2001
Includes an introduction to the play, and information on the context

Laurence Lerner, ed., *Shakespeare's Comedies: An Anthology of Modern Criticism*, Penguin, 1967

Michael Mangan, *A Preface to Shakespeare's Comedies 1594–1603*, Longman, 1996

Leah Marcus, 'The Shakespearean Editor as Shrew-Tamer', in *Shakespeare and Gender: A History*, eds. Deborah Barker and Ivo Kamps, Verso Books, 1995
Marcus focuses on the **Induction**, arguing that it reinforces the idea that Kate is tamed, and looks closely at *The Taming of a Shrew*, discussing the merits of this play

Karen Newman, 'Renaissance Family Politics and Shakespeare's *The Taming of the Shrew*', in *English Literary Renaissance*, Vol. 16, 1968, pp. 86–100
Newman's essay can also be found in the Waller collection mentioned below

Walter Raleigh, ed., *Johnson on Shakespeare*, Oxford University Press, 1908 (1968)

Carol Rutter, *Clamorous Voices: Shakespeare's Women Today*, Routledge, 1989

Leo Salingar, *Shakespeare and the Traditions of Comedy*, Cambridge University Press, 1974

Emma Smith, *Shakespeare's Comedies* (Blackwell Guides to Criticism), Blackwell, 2003
Smith covers key critical debates under five headings: genre; history and politics; gender and sexuality; language; and performance. She also includes a chapter on pre-twentieth-century criticism with excerpts from Johnson, Hazlitt and Coleridge

E. M. W. Tillyard, *Shakespeare's Early Comedies*, Athlone Press, 1965 (1983)
> There is a useful introduction on the dramatic, narrative and anthropological range of Shakespeare's comedy; there is a sympathetic reading of Petruchio's character too

Gary Waller, ed., *Shakespeare's Comedies*, Longman, 1991
> The introduction is extremely thorough, charting the history of approaches to Shakespeare's comedies in the twentieth century

Marion Wynne-Davies, ed., *Much Ado About Nothing and The Taming of the Shrew* (New Casebooks Series), Palgrave, 2001
> Includes essays by Joel Fineman, Karen Newman, Lynda E. Boose, Natasha Korda and Diana E. Henderson

GENERAL READING

Benedict Anderson, *Imagined Communities*, Verso Books, revised edition, 1991

Deborah Cartmell, *Interpreting Shakespeare on Screen*, Palgrave, 2000

Andrew Gurr, *The Shakespearean Stage*, Cambridge University Press, 1992

D. M. Palliser, *The Age of Elizabeth: England Under the Later Tudors, 1547–1603*, Longman, 1983

C. T. Onions, *A Shakespeare Glossary*, Oxford University Press, 1911 (frequently reprinted)

Daniel Rosenthal, *Shakespeare on Screen*, Hamlyn, 2000

Samuel Schoenbaum, *Shakespeare: A Documentary Life*, Oxford University Press, 1975

Lawrence Stone, *The Family, Sex and Marriage in England 1500–1800*, Weidenfeld & Nicholson, 1977

Stanley Wells, ed., *Shakespeare in the Theatre: An Anthology of Criticism*, Clarendon Press, 1997

LANGUAGE

Cicely Berry, *The Actor and His Text*, Virgin Books, 1987

David Crystal and Ben Crystal, *Shakespeare's Words: A Glossary and Language Companion*, Penguin Books, 2002

S. S. Hussey, *The Literary Language of Shakespeare*, Longman, 1982

Russ McDonald, *Shakespeare and the Arts of Language*, Oxford University Press, 2001

Patsy Rodenburg, *Speaking Shakespeare*, Palgrave Macmillan, 2002

aside common dramatic convention, in which a character speaks in such a way that some of the characters on stage do not hear what is said, while others do. It may also be a direct address to the audience, revealing the character's inner thoughts, views, motives or intentions

ballad (French 'dancing song') poem or song which tells a story in simple, colloquial language. There are traditional oral ballads, folk and literary ballads. The subject matter of ballads is usually tragic, and often violent. During the Elizabethan period ballads were accessible to a wide section of the populace; they were sung in the streets by their sellers, and mass produced. There were a number of comic ballads about shrewish wives

blank verse unrhymed iambic pentameter: a line of five iambs. One of the commonest English metres. It was introduced into England by Henry Howard, Earl of Surrey, who used it in his translation of Virgil's *Aeneid* (1557). Thereafter it became the normal medium for Elizabethan and Jacobean drama. The popularity of blank verse is due to its flexibility and relative closeness to spoken English

closure the impression of completeness and finality achieved by the ending of some works of literature

comedy (Greek 'merry-making, comic poet') a broad genre which encompasses a large variety of different kinds of literature; however, 'comedy' is used most often with reference to a kind of drama which is intended to entertain the audience, and which ends happily for the characters. In this meaning of the word, comedy, like tragedy, is an ancient form dating at least as far back as the fifth century

commedia dell'arte (Italian 'comedy of the professional actors') a form of drama that evolved in sixteenth-century Italy in which travelling companies of actors improvised comic plays around standard plots, using stock characters. A typical play might involve a young lover, the 'Inamorato', tricking Pantaleone ('Pantaloon'), a rich old father, into giving up his daughter. Arlecchino ('Harlequin'), the cunning servant, and Pulcinella ('Punch'), the hunchback clown, were other stock types. The play was enlivened by dancing, singing and **slapstick** buffoonery. Many elements of the form are visible in comic plays by Shakespeare, especially *The Taming of the Shrew* and *The Comedy of Errors*

dramatic irony feature of many plays: it occurs when the development of the plot allows the audience to possess more information about what is happening than some of the characters on stage. Characters may also speak or act in an ironic way, saying something that points to events to come without understanding the significance of what they say

epilogue (Greek 'speech on') concluding speech or passage in a work of literature, often summing up and commenting on what has gone before; the epilogue may help to achieve closure

farce (Latin 'to stuff') drama intended primarily to provoke laughter, using exaggerated characters and complicated plots, full of absurd episodes, ludicrous situations and knockabout action. Farcical episodes date back to Aristophanes and occur alongside serious drama in all ages

feminist, feminism broadly speaking, a political movement claiming political and economic equality of women with men. Feminist criticism and scholarship seek to explore the masculine 'bias' in texts and challenge traditional ideas about them, constructing and then offering a feminine perspective on works of art. Since the late 1960s feminist theories about literature and language, and feminist interpretations of texts have multiplied enormously. Feminism has its roots in previous centuries; early texts championing women's rights include Mary Wollstonecraft's *A Vindication of the Rights of Women* (1792) and J. S. Mill's *The Subjection of Women* (1869)

figurative language (Latin 'to shape, form or conceive') any form of expression or grammar which deviates from the plainest expression of meaning is designated 'figurative language'. Departures into more decorative language are further defined by a large number of terms. **Metaphor** is probably the figure of speech which most clearly characterises literary language: hence 'figurative language' can specifically refer to metaphorical language as well as to language abounding in other figures of speech

humanist originally refers to a scholar of the humanities, especially classical literature. At the time of the Renaissance European intellectuals devoted themselves to the rediscovery and intense study of first Roman and then Greek literature and culture, in particular the works of Cicero, Aristotle and Plato. Out of this period of intellectual ferment there emerged a view of man and a philosophy quite different from medieval scholasticism: in the nineteenth century this trend in Renaissance thought was labelled 'humanism'. Reason, balance and a proper dignity for man were the central ideals of humanist thought. The humanists' attitude to the world is anthropocentric: instead of regarding man as a fallen, corrupt and sinful creature, their idea of truth and excellence is based on human values and human experience. They strive for moderate, achievable, even worldly aims, rather than revering asceticism

imagery, image (Latin 'copy', 'representation') in its narrowest sense an image is a word-picture, a description of some visible scene or object. More commonly, imagery refers to the **figurative language** in a piece of literature (**metaphors** and similes); or all the words which refer to objects and qualities which appeal to the senses and feelings. Thematic imagery is imagery (in the general sense) which recurs through a work of art: for example, images of card-playing, hunting and hawking are all invoked in *The Taming of the Shrew* to suggest the way in which the male characters relate to their womenfolk (see **Imagery**)

induction (Latin 'leading in') an archaic word for the prologue introducing a work

irony (Greek 'dissembling') saying one thing while you mean another. However, not all ironical statements in literature are as easily understood; the patterns of irony – of situation, character, structure and vocabulary – may need careful unravelling. Sometimes the writer will have to rely on the audience sharing values and knowledge in order for his or her meaning to be understood. Ironic literature characteristically presents a variety of possible points of view about its subject matter

metaphor (Greek 'a carrying over') goes further than a comparison between two different things or ideas by fusing them together: one thing is described as being another thing, thus 'carrying over' all its associations

motif (Old French, from Latin 'moving') some aspect of literature (a type of character, theme or **image**) which recurs frequently. An individual work may have its own recurring motifs, or leitmotifs, repeated phrases, images, descriptions or incidents. In *The Shrew* there are a number of repeated words, phrases and images, most frequently to do with hunting/wife-taming

new historicist, historicism the work of a loose affiliation of critics who discuss literary works in terms of their historical contexts. In particular, they seek to study literature as part of a wider cultural history, exploring the relationship of literature to society

psychoanalytic criticism Freud developed the theory of psychoanalysis as a means of curing neuroses in his patients, but its concepts were expanded by him and his followers as a means of understanding human behaviour and culture generally. Literature and creative processes always figured largely in his accounts of the human mind, as both example and inspiration: he asserted that many of his ideas had been anticipated in great literary works, and the terms he devised for his concepts (such as the Oedipus complex), illustrate his reliance on literary models. Critics who adopt a psychoanalytical approach explore the psychological conflicts in texts, seeking to uncover the latent content and psychological realities that underlie the work of art; they look at **symbolism** and hidden meanings

pun (possibly from Italian 'fine point') a 'play on words': two widely different meanings are drawn out of a single word, usually for comic, witty or playful purposes

slapstick broad comedy with knockabout action, fighting, clowning, people falling over each other. So called after the stick carried by the Harlequin in *commedia dell'arte* which was constructed of two pieces of wood which slapped together to produce a loud crack when used in mock fights

soliloquy (Latin 'speak alone') curious but fascinating dramatic convention, which allows a character in a play to speak directly to the audience, as if thinking aloud about motives, feelings and decisions. The psychological depth which the soliloquy gives to Shakespeare's tragedies in particular is inestimable. Part of the convention is that the soliloquy provides accurate access to the character's innermost thoughts

stichomythia a dialogue carried out in single alternating lines

symbol something that represents something else (often an idea or quality) by analogy or association

Rebecca Warren is the author of York Advanced Notes on *King Lear, Othello, Richard III, The Mayor of Casterbridge, The Glass Menagerie* and Sylvia Plath's *Selected Poems.*

General editor

Martin Gray, former Head of the Department of English Studies at the University of Stirling, and of Literary Studies at the University of Luton

Maya Angelou
I Know Why the Caged Bird Sings

Jane Austen
Pride and Prejudice

Alan Ayckbourn
Absent Friends

Elizabeth Barrett Browning
Selected Poems

Robert Bolt
A Man for All Seasons

Harold Brighouse
Hobson's Choice

Charlotte Brontë
Jane Eyre

Emily Brontë
Wuthering Heights

Shelagh Delaney
A Taste of Honey

Charles Dickens
David Copperfield
Great Expectations
Hard Times
Oliver Twist

Roddy Doyle
Paddy Clarke Ha Ha Ha

George Eliot
Silas Marner
The Mill on the Floss

Anne Frank
The Diary of a Young Girl

William Golding
Lord of the Flies

Oliver Goldsmith
She Stoops to Conquer

Willis Hall
The Long and the Short and the Tall

Thomas Hardy
Far from the Madding Crowd
The Mayor of Casterbridge
Tess of the d'Urbervilles
The Withered Arm and other Wessex Tales

L.P. Hartley
The Go-Between

Seamus Heaney
Selected Poems

Susan Hill
I'm the King of the Castle

Barry Hines
A Kestrel for a Knave

Louise Lawrence
Children of the Dust

Harper Lee
To Kill a Mockingbird

Laurie Lee
Cider with Rosie

Arthur Miller
The Crucible
A View from the Bridge

Robert O'Brien
Z for Zachariah

Frank O'Connor
My Oedipus Complex and Other Stories

George Orwell
Animal Farm

J.B. Priestley
An Inspector Calls
When We Are Married

Willy Russell
Educating Rita
Our Day Out

J.D. Salinger
The Catcher in the Rye

William Shakespeare
Henry IV Part I
Henry V
Julius Caesar
Macbeth
The Merchant of Venice
A Midsummer Night's Dream
Much Ado About Nothing

Romeo and Juliet
The Tempest
Twelfth Night

George Bernard Shaw
Pygmalion

Mary Shelley
Frankenstein

R.C. Sherriff
Journey's End

Rukshana Smith
Salt on the snow

John Steinbeck
Of Mice and Men

Robert Louis Stevenson
Dr Jekyll and Mr Hyde

Jonathan Swift
Gulliver's Travels

Robert Swindells
Daz 4 Zoe

Mildred D. Taylor
Roll of Thunder, Hear My Cry

Mark Twain
Huckleberry Finn

James Watson
Talking in Whispers

Edith Wharton
Ethan Frome

William Wordsworth
Selected Poems

A Choice of Poets

Mystery Stories of the Nineteenth Century including The Signalman

Nineteenth Century Short Stories

Poetry of the First World War

Six Women Poets

For the AQA Anthology:

Duffy and Armitage & Pre-1914 Poetry

Heaney and Clarke & Pre-1914 Poetry

Poems from Different Cultures

Margaret Atwood
Cat's Eye
The Handmaid's Tale

Jane Austen
Emma
Mansfield Park
Persuasion
Pride and Prejudice
Sense and Sensibility

Alan Bennett
Talking Heads

William Blake
*Songs of Innocence and of
Experience*

Charlotte Brontë
Jane Eyre
Villette

Emily Brontë
Wuthering Heights

Angela Carter
Nights at the Circus

Geoffrey Chaucer
The Franklin's Prologue and Tale
*The Merchant's Prologue and
Tale*
The Miller's Prologue and Tale
*The Prologue to the Canterbury
Tales*
*The Wife of Bath's Prologue and
Tale*

Samuel Coleridge
Selected Poems

Joseph Conrad
Heart of Darkness

Daniel Defoe
Moll Flanders

Charles Dickens
Bleak House
Great Expectations
Hard Times

Emily Dickinson
Selected Poems

John Donne
Selected Poems

Carol Ann Duffy
Selected Poems

George Eliot
Middlemarch
The Mill on the Floss

T.S. Eliot
Selected Poems
The Waste Land

F. Scott Fitzgerald
The Great Gatsby

E.M. Forster
A Passage to India

Brian Friel
Translations

Thomas Hardy
Jude the Obscure
The Mayor of Casterbridge
The Return of the Native
Selected Poems
Tess of the d'Urbervilles

Seamus Heaney
*Selected Poems from 'Opened
Ground'*

Nathaniel Hawthorne
The Scarlet Letter

Homer
The Iliad
The Odyssey

Aldous Huxley
Brave New World

Kazuo Ishiguro
The Remains of the Day

Ben Jonson
The Alchemist

James Joyce
Dubliners

John Keats
Selected Poems

Philip Larkin
*The Whitsun Weddings and
Selected Poems*

Christopher Marlowe
Doctor Faustus
Edward II

Arthur Miller
Death of a Salesman

John Milton
Paradise Lost Books I & II

Toni Morrison
Beloved

George Orwell
Nineteen Eighty-Four

Sylvia Plath
Selected Poems

Alexander Pope
*Rape of the Lock & Selected
Poems*

William Shakespeare
Antony and Cleopatra
As You Like It
Hamlet
Henry IV Part I
King Lear
Macbeth
Measure for Measure
The Merchant of Venice
A Midsummer Night's Dream
Much Ado About Nothing
Othello
Richard II
Richard III
Romeo and Juliet
The Taming of the Shrew
The Tempest
Twelfth Night
The Winter's Tale

George Bernard Shaw
Saint Joan

Mary Shelley
Frankenstein

Jonathan Swift
*Gulliver's Travels and A Modest
Proposal*

Alfred Tennyson
Selected Poems

Virgil
The Aeneid

Alice Walker
The Color Purple

Oscar Wilde
*The Importance of Being
Earnest*

Tennessee Williams
A Streetcar Named Desire
The Glass Menagerie

Jeanette Winterson
*Oranges Are Not the Only
Fruit*

John Webster
The Duchess of Malfi

Virginia Woolf
To the Lighthouse

William Wordsworth
*The Prelude and Selected
Poems*

W.B. Yeats
Selected Poems

Metaphysical Poets

P

UNTIL THE BRIGHTER TOMORROW

"A modern-day rags-to-riches story, this book inspires, strengthens, and gives you the determination to strive for all things possible and succeed."

—Michelle Taylor-Jones, CEO, The Taylor Group

"I'm a picky reader, but there is nothing I didn't love about this brutally honest book—the story, the cover, the title, even the typeface. When you devour this masterfully written memoir, you will fall in love with the author as I have. Though I suggested to Valerie long ago that she write her crushing story so the world could learn her lessons, I had no idea how adroit she was with pen and paper. The narrative, insights, and prescriptive dialogue will educate, inspire, and empower you. *Until the Brighter Tomorrow* is simply a book to love and a must-read for those who are serious about navigating life's tragedies to lead a fulfilling life. My heartfelt thanks goes out to Valerie for providing us all a clear way to manifest our destiny. Don't miss this important gem."

—George C. Fraser
Author, *Success Runs in Our Race* and *Click*

"What an incredible story! Women everywhere suffer through many of these same life challenges but often carry the burdens of shame and guilt, sometimes losing their sense of self altogether. *Until the Brighter Tomorrow* is an inspiring must-read—a raw, authentic account that reminds us of the power of courage, strength, and perseverance."

—Carol Evans
President, Working Mother Media

"All I can say is WOW!—this memoir reads like a novel. Although I have heard many parts of Valerie's story before, I continue to be captivated and inspired."

—Marsha Haygood, Co-author, *The Little Black Book of Success: Laws of Leadership for Black Women*

"Our environment shapes us but doesn't define us. Valerie took her adversity and through hard work and vision, became an outstanding servant leader who made and continues to make a significant difference in the lives of others."

—Audra Bohannon
Senior Partner, Korn-Ferry International

"Stories of personal tragedy are often too painful to speak about openly, and even more painful to publish for the world to read. But Valerie's courage in sharing her story gives hope to readers of any age or background who have suffered loss, extreme adversity, or emotional heartbreak, illustrating for them that tenacity and faith are the antidote for despair, even when brighter days seem impossible. An incredible story definitely worth devouring."

—Sheila Robinson
Publisher & CEO, Diversity Woman magazine

"Valerie has an incredibly giving spirit, and this book is a testament to who she is and her commitment to helping people push past life's adversities, even in the midst of their seemingly darkest moments. She is a remarkable business coach, and this book is an amazing personal tool and gift."

—Cheryl B. Walker-Robertson
President & CEO, Protocol International

"*Until the Brighter Tomorrow* is an absolute must-read. This inspirational true story has transformed my interpretation of difficult events endured at any age and outside of one's control, and is a testament to the power, love, and thought in each of Valerie's words, captivating and motivating her readers to believe that ANYTHING is possible."

—Vera S.
Recent college grad and survivor of family suicide

UNTIL

the

BRIGHTER

TOMORROW

ISBN: 978-0-9905193-1-7

Published by Elloree Press, New York.

Cover photo: Dunbar Apartments, New York City. Courtesy Wikimedia Commons; author, Beyond My Ken.

Editing and book design by Stacey Aaronson

Printed in the United States of America

UNTIL

the

BRIGHTER

TOMORROW

———◆———

ONE WOMAN'S
COURAGEOUS CLIMB *from*
the PROJECTS *to the* PODIUM

VALERIE IRICK RAINFORD

ELLOREE PRESS

NEW YORK, USA

In memory of my mom,
a woman of incredible strength.

Dedicated to my daughters,
Avaree and Alyssa.

Let my story be full of lessons and inspiration for you
of the importance of never giving up.

And THANK YOU to my husband
and lifelong partner Tony
for standing by me through this journey.

I love you all.

Mommy

ACKNOWLEDGMENTS

There are so many people to thank for helping me not only see the value of telling my story out loud, but also of penning it in the form of a book to help those who are struggling to find their strength and purpose amidst a life of adversity.

I am who I am because of many people to whom I owe my success and tremendous gratitude. To my beloved mother, for instilling in me the value of hard work and for teaching me that I could be anything I put my mind to—despite her inability to see a way of achieving more for herself.

To my grandmother, who taught me the power of faith and resilience, and my dad and brother, Ankie, who exemplified how to enjoy life despite your circumstances. I am grateful that they each passed on these gifts to me before leaving this earth. I am each of them.

I am equally blessed to have a wonderful cheerleading squad surrounding me who encourage my every dream ...

To my big brother Jay, who is my longest running champion. I understand that my telling our story is hard for you but appreciate your supporting me in doing so anyway. To my biggest supporters, my daughters Avaree and Alyssa, the pride you show in this work I am determined to do fuels me even more. And then there's the anchor to my cheering squad—the person who has stood at the center bringing support and gentle encouragement for thirty years—my wonderful husband, Tony. I am so grateful for you.

The idea for telling my story is credited to George Fraser, the author of *Success Runs in Our Race* and *Click*. While my motivation for finally completing it is the result of a chance meeting with another great author and transformation genius, Lisa Nichols—contributor to the book and movie *The Secret*—both of these giants were instrumental in encouraging me to share my story with the world.

Lisa Nichols and her colleague Nicole Roberts Jones are credited with connecting me with my first book editor, the "Words Lady," Marlene Oulton, who helped me draw out the raw emotion in the story so readers would experience the journey with me. God then blessed me to discover Stacey Aaronson, also known as "The Book Doctor," the genius who put the finishing touches on my story, title, and cover design. If it weren't for Stacey, it would have been another five years before getting this precious gift into your hands.

There are many more family, friends, mentors, and mentees who encouraged me along the long journey of birthing this baby—too many to name here. But I would like to offer a special thank you to the following few who committed their time to reading and contributing to various drafts along the way: Marsha Haygood, Michelle Taylor-Jones, Milca Esdaille, Donna Cuomo, and Nancy Andre.

I am grateful for you all.

CONTENTS

THE PAIN

GRIEVING AND HEALING

THE NEXT CHAPTER

THE PAIN

1

IS THAT YOUR MOTHER?

I T STARTED AS A pleasant Sunday morning in September of 1984. We were newlyweds in our new, tiny apartment overlooking the Hudson River in Yonkers. My husband, Tony, and I had both grown up in the Bronx, and now here we were, barely adults, breaking out on our own to start living as a couple. Life was good, although the months preceding had been tough. I had finished my sophomore year at Fordham University in the Bronx and worked part-time as a bank teller while I planned our wedding; Tony had worked the night shift as a coupon clerk in New York City. Consequently, we didn't see each other much before our wedding day.

Our blessed event was attended by 250 family members, friends, and work colleagues from both sides. My brother Jay came from South Carolina with his family, and both of his children were in the wedding party. My parents helped me buy the beautiful white wedding gown I wore as I walked down the aisle at St. Luke's Episcopal Church in the Bronx; the reception followed in the church hall down in the basement. Tony's dad, who worked as a mechanic at the Rolls Royce Carriage House in New York City, arranged for us to wrap up the day in style by driving away in a vintage Rolls Royce.

It was a grand wedding by anyone's standards, and we were exceedingly happy. What made it even more special was that with the exception of my dress and that fancy car, almost every dime of the wedding had been paid for with the money Tony and I had saved over the prior year.

Now settled in our beautiful one-bedroom, made even lovelier with the bedroom and living room sets our parents had given us as wedding gifts and a spectacular river view, we knew we would struggle financially. I still worked only part-time as a bank teller with student loans funding my education, but we were in love and that's all that mattered.

We had mapped out our future living expenses before the wedding—a bit burdened with unexpected credit card debt and no savings to fall back on in case of emergencies —hoping that the monetary gifts we would receive would help us get back on track. When we tore through the envelopes on our wedding night to see how much money our guests had gifted us, however, we discovered that we hadn't found the proverbial pot of gold. In fact, we received just enough to take a little spending money on our honeymoon to the Bahamas. We shared a humble laugh over our dashed expectations and felt grateful nonetheless.

Nassau was lovely. It was my first time traveling outside of the United States. Tony was born in England and had spent a good part of his childhood in Jamaica with his maternal grandmother so he knew island life well; I, on the other hand, was thoroughly fascinated. We walked the beach, visited straw markets, took island boat tours, and spent equal time in our hotel room as madly-in-love honeymooners often do. Then, after five days and four nights, it was back to New York—to our little apartment, to school, to work. By mid-September we were settling into the groove of life together—happy to have the hectic wedding-planning days behind us—and I had started my junior year of college.

Then, everything changed.

WE HAD PLANNED TO have a quiet day that September 23rd. We would sometimes travel on weekends from Yonkers down to the Bronx to visit our families, but on that particular Sunday, we decided to stay home. I hadn't seen my mother since the prior week, and because we had only made it a quick trip, I didn't even make it up to her apartment. We talked a bit while standing on the sidewalk outside of her building, and then we rushed over to Tony's family's house for a short visit there. Everyone understood that as newlyweds we were eager to spend time together on weekends since we didn't see each other much during the week, so despite the fact that our previous family visit was only a brief one (and we felt a bit guilty about it), we longed for a day to ourselves.

I woke up feeling great, poised to make my first-ever pot roast for my new husband. When I called my mother to ask her for the recipe, she seemed distant but calmly told me what to do. We finished the call with my telling her that I would phone her later that day to tell her how my meal turned out.

After preparing my roast and being pleased with how it looked simmering in the oven, I tried calling Mom to tell her about my cooking success, but there was no answer. *Maybe she stepped out*, I thought. Oh well, I would try again in a bit.

I was still in the kitchen when the phone rang a short time later. A woman claiming to be a friend of my mother's told me that Mom had been in an accident and was in Jacobi Hospital in the Bronx. I never stopped to ask her name; I just knew I had to get to the hospital right away. We didn't own a car, so Tony called our good friend Michael to come give us a ride.

Driving down to Jacobi, I could only hope that Mom was okay. They hadn't said what happened, so I assumed she had been in a car accident. I had this terrible feeling in the pit of my stomach, but Michael and Tony kept reassuring me that she would be fine. I kept telling myself the same.

We arrived at the hospital, jumped out of Michael's car, and ran through the front doors. The hospital—one of the busiest in New York City—felt empty ... or so it seemed. As we slowed from a run to brisk walking, I don't remember seeing a soul in the hallway. The place felt creepy, lonely, and eerily hollow with a strange odor in the air.

As we proceeded down the empty hall, a woman dressed in a white lab coat approached us and asked if I was Valerie. *How did she know who I was?* I wondered, as I nodded in the affirmative. I recognized her voice as that of the woman who had called me on the phone and followed her as she escorted us down the quiet hall to the room where I thought my mom would be.

My cousin Lewis was already in the room and he hugged me. His presence should have alerted me that something was seriously wrong, but everything was happening so fast. They sat me down in a cold metal chair.

"Lewis, what happened?" I asked. "Where's Mom? What's happened to her?"

Lewis looked me straight in the eye. "There was an accident."

"Valerie," the lady in the white lab coat said gently, "I have your brother Jay on the line and he would like to speak with you."

I took the phone. "Jay, what happened?" I practically yelled into the receiver.

I'm sure he must have said more in our brief conversation, but I only recall four distinct words.

"Val, Mommy is dead."

I shook my head in disbelief. "No, no, no ..." I said. "That can't be. I just spoke with her. She told me how to make roast beef."

Tony wrapped his arms around me as I realized what my brother said had to be true. I wanted to scream but only tears came instead. Oh my God, how I cried. I have no idea how long it took for that first wave of tears to subside; all I remember is that as the news started to sink in, I brought the phone back up to my ear where my brother was still waiting.

"What happened?" I asked through my tightened throat.

Silence.

I asked again.

"Baby girl," my brother said calmly. "Mommy killed herself."

I stared ahead in shock, afraid to breathe. It made no sense, but I knew my brother wouldn't lie to me so I didn't question him. The only thing I remember with total clarity was sitting in that room, being held by Tony and Lewis, crying until my reservoir of tears ran dry.

When I finally settled down, my brother's voice came through the telephone line again.

"Val, there's something I need for you to do."

I heard my brother take a deep breath.

"One of us needs to identify Mommy's body, and since I can't get there today, we need you to do it."

I don't remember my reaction to his words, nor do I recall any more tears. It was as if my brain had shut down and there was no space for any additional information.

The next thing I recall is standing at a door with a covered window, Tony on one side of me and the lady in the white lab coat on the other. Lewis, I am sure, was somewhere nearby, but I can't remember. I heard the woman say to me that when she pulled back the curtain to the window, I would see my mom, but only from her eyes down to her chin. She explained that the rest of her would be covered.

As she slid the window covering back, I saw Mom's closed eyes. There were no signs of worry on her face. She looked like she was simply sleeping.

"Is that your mom?" the woman asked.

The tears once again began flowing down my cheeks. "Yes," I whispered.

I LATER LEARNED WHY I was not allowed to see her entire face. My mom had placed a gun to her head and pulled the trigger, one month after my wedding day and ten days after my 20th birthday.

2

CAN YOU HEAR ME?

Val, baby, stop crying. Please stop crying. Oh my God, what have I done?!

"Oh my God, she can't hear me. What did I do? What was I thinking? I didn't mean to hurt you. Please don't hate me. I can see you and I can hear you, but you can't hear me. I can hear you sobbing. How could I not have realized how much this would hurt you? I wasn't thinking clearly.

"It's okay, baby girl. Stop screaming so you can hear me. I know this is hard. I didn't mean to cause you this much pain. I need you to stop crying so you can hear me. Val, please baby, listen to me. I need to explain ...

"I just couldn't take it anymore. I was so tired of everything, of working three jobs and never getting ahead. Life has just been so hard, one battle after another. I know I've told you that 'trouble don't last always,' but it seems that didn't apply to me lately. I tried to fight through it, but I just didn't have anything left.

"But you're going to be okay. You're in college. That was my dream for you and you did it. You've married a good man. I know he'll take good care of you. Lean on him as you're doing right this moment. He'll help you get through this. Please understand everything I ever did was for you. My life revolved around you. THIS, however, is not about YOU. It was about me, about me being tired of fighting.

"You need to fight for YOU now. Fight through this. You can do this, I know you can. I wish I could change things, but I can't. Don't let this ruin things for you ...

"Oh, how I wish you could hear me ..."

3

FOREVER ETCHED ON MY SOUL

I COULDN'T LOOK ANYMORE through that glass square in the door. The only thing I could do was sob. My sole memory of that moment standing at the morgue window was my screaming and sobbing ... and seeing Mom's closed eyes draped in those white sheets. I didn't need to see the rest of her face. Her eyes in that moment are forever etched on my soul.

The sobs were so intense they felt like they came from deep within. They seemed to never stop, blurring my actions for days afterward. I don't remember when my brother Jay arrived in New York from South Carolina for the funeral, but I know he was there. I don't remember making any funeral arrangements either, but I know I must have been involved in the planning.

The wake was held at McCall's Funeral Hall in the Bronx where hoards of people came to pay their respects. I don't know who or how many; I only remember the line of people waiting to hug me—an ongoing stream of obscure faces that seemed like it would never end.

A week later, Mom was memorialized at Brown Chapel church in South Carolina—the church that she and my dad were raised and schooled in—then buried next to my brother Ankie in the Brown Chapel cemetery. She was in an open casket wearing the beautiful pink gown she had worn to my wedding. She looked beautiful in the dress, but I couldn't look at her long without remembering her eyes draped in those white sheets—the ones that covered the damage caused by the single bullet wound to her head.

⁂

MY HOME IS FILLED with pictures of my mother, images of her before that dreadful day surrounded me. My wedding album sits on the coffee table in the living room; photos of her are on the wall in the family room. A picture of her in her youth sits on the nightstand in the guest room that would have been hers had she lived. I didn't put that picture there consciously, but I realize now in my writing and reflecting that this room is set up for her as she would have liked it had she ever visited us.

On the wall of the private bathroom is a portrait of an

old woman's hands as she quilts. I found it in a book on black history, clipped it, framed it, and hung it on that wall years ago because it reminded me of my own grandmother who was a talented quilter. That photo soothes me as I know it would have also soothed my mother. But I still can't look at her eyes without remembering how she looked through that single window in the morgue.

4

THE NOTE

THE WEEKS, MONTHS, AND even years after Mom's suicide are still a fog to me. In hindsight, likely due to the effects of mental shock, my memories are vague. What I'll never forget, however, is how lost, confused, scared, and terribly guilty I felt.

How could she do this? I thought. *What the hell was she thinking? What could have been so bad? What did I do to contribute to her actions? What could I have done to keep it from happening?*

The first time I went to Mom's apartment after the day she committed suicide, I found the note, perched just inside the front door of her apartment. It was attached to an envelope with my name handwritten on the front.

Val, I'm sorry. I couldn't take it anymore.
Take care of yourself.
I love you.

Inside the envelope was a small life insurance policy, just enough to pay for her funeral. She had left it there specifically for me to find.

Having locked it away in my home safe, I hadn't looked at the note until I was writing this book for fear of reliving the moment I found it. When I finally got up the courage to bring it out, I cried as if that day was happening all over again.

IT ISN'T SURPRISING THAT in addition to all of the other emotions that plagued me during that time, I was also very angry. Ironically, I didn't spend too much time being angry with my mother; perhaps the pain and guilt were too deep. I knew how difficult life had been for her, and I also knew how hard she had always tried. Although I had moments of being angry with her for deserting me, they would be short lived, pushed aside by sadness and guilt. My anger would instead be directed first at me and then at Tony. I believed I had abandoned my mother when she needed me most, that I should have been there for her, that I should have never left home to get married.

It made for a terrible way to start Tony's and my life together. Outward, I was sad and frequently reserved, plagued by my thoughts; inside I was heartbroken and scared, often taking my frustrations out on the man I had just wed. He comforted me during the emotional roller coaster I was on, never realizing that I was sometimes resentful of him for taking me away from her.

My mind was a shambles, making me wonder if I was destined for the same end as my mother. My brother Jay and I actually made a promise after my mother killed herself that we would reach out to each other if we ever felt like killing ourselves too, often wondering if suicide was hereditary. Not only had our mom chosen to end her life this way, but our brother Ankie had taken his life only a few years earlier.

I walked around for a long time pondering if I could ever become so overwhelmed that I would put a gun to my head and pull the trigger. Would death be instantaneous? Would I even be able to make the call to my brother Jay—before I did anything drastic—as I had promised him?

And then I received a call that added a whole new layer to my guilt and emotional pain.

Soon after Mom died, one of her "friends" reached out to me. Miss Ann was supposedly a God-fearing, churchgoing woman, and she and Mom had been friends for years, having worked together as nurse's aides at Misericordia Hospital in the Bronx.

Miss Ann called to check on me and see how I was doing. We chatted for a bit about how much she missed Mom and what a good friend she had been over the years. Then, toward the end of the call, she said, "Val, did your mother happen to mention that she owed me some money?"

I felt a stab in my already broken heart. I was too

stunned at first to speak, but after a few moments I responded, "No."

"Oh," she went on, "I thought she may have mentioned it to you. Well, as things settle down, please keep me in mind. I could really use it."

I was stunned, not knowing what to say.

Miss Ann broke the silence. "Well, you take care of yourself and that baby."

"Excuse me?"

"You have to be careful in your condition" she said. "You *are* pregnant, aren't you?"

"No, I'm not."

"Oh, we all thought you were pregnant. Isn't that why you got married so early?"

Who the hell was "we all"? I thought, but out of respect didn't ask.

"Miss Ann, I got married because I was in love."

"Oh," was all she could say.

After another awkward pause, she closed the conversation by saying, "Well, okay then. You still take care of yourself and let me know if you come up with any money for me, okay?"

That was the last time I ever heard from Miss Ann, my mother's so-called friend. I never asked the amount my mother owed her, but I knew her well enough to know that it was not a huge sum, plus Miss Ann likely didn't have much excess money to loan anyone in the first place. I also knew that whatever the amount was, it had to trouble Mom to ask for it. I knew that at times she would borrow money from family and friends to make ends meet, but she didn't like to do it and it was always an amount she knew she could pay back.

"If you find yourself having to borrow money from someone," Mom would say, "make sure you always pay them back. You never know when you might need them again."

Miss Ann never called again "to check up on me" or to ask me for the money. Perhaps she realized the absurdity of her call. If the situation was reversed, I am certain that my mother, no matter how bad things were, would never have made such a call to Miss Ann's family.

Despite her apparent lack of common decency, Miss Ann's call laid bare the idea that the lifetime of money struggles Mom experienced had finally overwhelmed her. I often wondered if I should have stayed at home and continued to work and help her pay the bills, or if my moving out caused her breakdown. And though it crossed my mind, I didn't dwell on the question about my being pregnant as that was plain stupid. My mom would have confronted me if she suspected that were the case.

No matter how I tried to reconcile the cause, however, her suicide still didn't make any sense to me. I continued to question whether it was my fault, plagued by persistent guilt. I had an aversion for years to cooking roast beef—or even looking at it in the supermarket—as if it were a bad omen, a glaring symbol of sadness and fear. I even blamed myself for letting her buy that pink dress for my wedding. *How could I have been so thoughtless, so selfish?* I thought. *She couldn't afford that dress!* She had bought it because she wanted me to be happy with how wonderful she looked on my wedding day ... and then we had buried her in it—the most expensive dress she had ever owned.

I carried the guilt for years of all the "what-ifs" I couldn't answer, of how she had sacrificed so much for me and I had let her down, even deserted her. Was the amount she had borrowed from Miss Ann larger than I thought? I wished I would have asked how much it was when Miss Ann called. Now, I would never know.

Ultimately, the guilt overpowered the anger, and to his credit, Tony was wonderfully patient with me. He was always there and incredibly supportive even through my emotional shifts, which was all the more heroic when I realized I wasn't the only one grieving.

Tony and Mom were very close. She would cook for him when he came over to see me, and since they both worked nights, on Saturday mornings after work they would both arrive at the apartment at around the same time for us all to have breakfast together. When we wanted to go out on a date to the movies, she would generously loan him her car. I would often complain that he could borrow the car with nary a question or complaint, but I couldn't take it around the corner. Mom would simply brush off my comments. The truth was, she trusted him with her car—and also with me.

I only remember one occasion when Mom got angry with Tony. We had borrowed her peach-colored Chevy Monte Carlo to go to a track meet, Mom saying that we could take her car as long as we were back by 10:30 p.m. so that she could go to work that night. We left the stadium a little early—and with enough time to get home by our assigned curfew—but soon realized we had rushed into the stadium without taking note of where we parked.

We walked around and around the still-full stadium parking lot to no avail, stunned that we couldn't find a peach-colored car. We then panicked, knowing Mom was going to be upset and would probably never loan us her car again. We thought of calling to let her know we would be late, but that would have meant going back into the stadium to find a pay phone. Besides, how would we explain that we had lost her car?

It wasn't until after midnight when the event was over and the parking lot was nearly empty that we spotted Mom's car. We jumped in and raced home. When we reached the apartment, Mom quickly grabbed the keys as we tried to explain, rushing out of the apartment saying she "couldn't afford to lose her job over our foolishness."

We learned a valuable lesson that night. To this day, we share a chuckle and take a mental note of where we park our car in large parking lots, remembering how panicked we were the night we lost Mom's car for a few hours.

After the incident blew over, Mom continued to loan us—or rather loan *Tony*—her car when we wanted to go out, remaining very supportive of our relationship. I suspect that she was also relieved that night when we arrived home safe and sound.

BELIEVE IT OR NOT, Tony and I have never talked about the details of Mom's suicide. He held me when I needed to be held and let me be quiet when he knew I needed to simply think. My silent anger toward him dissipated over time as I thought about their relationship and how much Mom loved him and supported our being together.

While I'll never know specifically why Mom killed herself, I have come to believe that she would never have done so if it weren't for Tony's presence in my life. She held on and kept fighting until she knew someone else was there to take care of me. I believe she knew that Tony would see me through that terrible time, and he did. She had fought the good fight for years until she had no more fight left, knowing that in leaving me, I would be in good hands.

GRIEVING
AND
HEALING

5

HER CHALLENGING BEGINNING

OM'S CHILDHOOD WAS ONE based on hard manual labor in the cotton fields of Elloree, South Carolina. My maternal grandparents, Otis and Corinne, had six children: three girls and three boys, including my mother Betty. Otis died in 1935 when the youngest of those children, Aunt Flossie, was only one year old and my mother was six. The eldest of the children was my Uncle Junior (Otis Junior) who was fourteen.

Prior to my grandfather's death, my grandparents worked the fields for years on Mr. Houck's land, one of the local white landowners. They earned a living by harvesting his cotton in exchange for pennies a pound, while living in a three-room shack on Mr. Houck's property. Each day, from sunup to sundown, my grandfather and the older children would work the fields harvesting crops on the surrounding land. Only days after the accident in which my grandfather and his horse and buggy were run off the road by a car and he was left to die in a ditch, my grandmother was put out of her home and left homeless with six children.

Mr. Houck's land was intended for sharecropping. Without my grandfather, it would be hard for Grandma to tend the land—and hard for old man Houck to make an income as a result—so he put a lock on the barn where all her tools and equipment were located, leaving my grandmother to fend for herself.

Grandma's parents were long deceased—with her own mother, Winnie, dying years before during the Bubonic Plague of the 1920s—so with nowhere else to turn, my grandmother was forced to live with her mother's sister, Aunt Florence.

Five of the six children picked cotton during harvest season alongside Aunt Florence instead of attending school. Off-season they went to school at the family church, Brown Chapel African-Methodist Episcopal, where three grades were taught basic reading, writing, and arithmetic in a single classroom. Mom went to school during harvest season, and after that worked in the fields full-time for the rest of the year. She never had the opportunity to return to school after the sixth grade.

My grandmother worked hard at various jobs to provide for her children, doing everything she could to earn money—from working the fields to cooking and cleaning houses. She even planted trees for the government's Work Projects Administration (WPA), President Roosevelt's New Deal program of the 1930s. Her children were left to sharecrop with Aunt Florence during the day while she would walk miles each morning to her job to plant trees along South Carolina highways. Whenever I'm back in South Carolina, I can't help but wonder which of the beautiful trees that line the roads were planted there with my grandmother's bare hands almost 100 years ago.

Grandma was a stern matriarch, no doubt concerned about raising her children without a man in the house. My Uncle Junior carried the greatest burden to help his mother raise and feed his siblings, telling tales of picking a little extra cotton that he kept on the side to sell for himself rather than turn it in with his other sharecropping. He would also keep an egg or two when gathering a dozen, or keep a couple of peaches when collecting a full crate. He was even known to steal a chicken or two to make sure all the children had enough to eat. While not an honest living, it was certainly a necessary one under the circumstances. And the girls worked nonstop too. In addition to sharecropping and chopping wood, they were also required to clean house, and wash and iron the family clothes.

This grueling daily scene was my mother's life until she was seventeen. She would often tell me how much she hated that period of her life, and that as she got older, she would look out across the fields at the boys "cropping," searching for the man of her dreams who would take her out of the fields and save her blistered hands.

One day, she got sweet on a "red-skinned" young man by the name of Ed. Edward Irick was four years older, and he had just returned home from a tour in the Navy where he served as a cook on a ship toward the end of World War II. He and his family sharecropped nearby land and also attended the same church and school at Brown Chapel. Soon, he and my mother began courting, and not long after got married on Valentine's Day in 1947, just one month before my mother turned eighteen. Nine months later, Betty and Ed were blessed with a baby boy they named Edward Irick, Jr., who they would nickname "Jay."

Mom's middle sister, Wilhelmina (who they called Bill), gave birth to a son named Lewis one month later. Jay and Lewis grew up as close as brothers, learning how to sharecrop alongside their mothers. They would also learn a bit from our Uncle Junior about survival, cultivating their own stories about skimming peaches off the pickings for the day.

In 1953, six years after my brother Jay was born, my parents were blessed with another son they named Anthony, affectionately referred to as "Ankie."

My mother and father worked tirelessly and eventually fulfilled their wish of moving their family out of the country to nearby Columbia, South Carolina. There, my father—who was also limited by a sixth grade education—was only able to find work as a truck driver and auto mechanic. Always handy, he would often pick up odd jobs working on local homes doing everything from fixing doors to making cabinets. My mother supplemented their income by performing domestic work.

When I entered the world in September of 1964, I joined my family in the first home my parents were able to buy—at 118 Paul Street in the Greenview section of Columbia. My brothers would tell me stories of how much they loved having a new little sister, but how much they hated that Mom made them take me with them whenever they wanted to go out. My brother Jay now jokes about how he eventually got used to taking me with him and even liked it once he realized that I was a "chick magnet." All the girls wanted to be with the cute guy who took such good care of his baby sister.

Because my parents were always working two and three jobs to make ends meet, my brothers provided a lot of my care, including combing and braiding my "mess of hair," according to them. But when Jay left for Vietnam in 1965, Ankie was left to take care of me a lot on his own while our parents worked.

By the time I turned four, my parents divorced. I didn't know the circumstances of their breakup as my parents never talked about it, but my aunt later told me that it was over money. I suspect that it was more than that, but it probably didn't help that they never had enough to make ends meet, making it understandably stressful on their relationship.

When my parents divorced, our family essentially split apart. Jay was still off at war and Dad moved to Connecticut where some of his siblings now lived. Around this time, Ankie's teenaged girlfriend became pregnant and they started living together, so it was mostly Mom and I from then on.

Life became even tougher for Mom after the divorce. She had few options and very little money, but she worked diligently to provide for us. Dad sent what he could, when he could, and wrote letters to keep in touch.

Mom couldn't afford child care, so I started going to work with her when I was five. At the time, she was working as a cook in a drive-in burger joint in Greenview, which wasn't really a "drive-in" or a "drive-thru" as we refer to them today, but rather a walk-up restaurant, very similar to a small, local neighborhood ice cream parlor. It had one small window, and typically one person took the orders, cooked the food, and served the customers. Friday and Saturday nights were the busiest, so those were the times I would help out. I had my own box to stand on to help take the food orders through the window, and after a while, the customers were all familiar faces who knew Mom and me well. They didn't mind that the line chugged along; the cute little girl behind the window always drew their attention.

Mom taught me how to take orders, write them down on a little pad, and even help collect and count money. My fondest memories to this day are the smiling faces that always seemed to be admiring me as I worked, and I liked showing them that I knew how to work hard. What's more, I looked forward to the extra nickel or dime that I was sometimes given for doing a good job.

Though we maintained that routine for a while, things continued to be tough on my mother. Struggling to make ends meet, she eventually migrated up north to New York where her sisters and one brother lived, while I stayed behind in South Carolina with a close friend of my mother's named Aunt Babe (pronounced "Baby") and her family.

Aunt Babe and her husband, Uncle Ed, had four daughters, and they raised me as their fifth child. I did everything with them as if they were my own family, and they never treated me like an outsider. For about a year, it was as if I had four older sisters and no worries. I ate well, had a nice warm bed to sleep in, and a family who loved me. I had everything in the material sense of the word ... but I didn't have my mother.

I would eventually move to New York at the age of six, just in time for first grade. With the help of Aunt Flossie, Mom landed a nurse's aide position working at the same hospital, Misericordia in the Bronx. It was a steady job with meager pay, but Mom was grateful for the opportunity. For a woman with little education, she knew how to get and keep a decent job. She mostly worked as a nurse's aide at night and as a home care attendant for the elderly during the day. Sometimes she cooked and cleaned on the side as well, following in her mother's footsteps, doing what was needed to care for her family.

Once I moved to New York, I was able to see my dad more often. Even though we had to change residences quite a bit—for one reason or another, things just never worked out as planned—he would drive down to the Bronx to pick me up to spend alternate weekends with him in Connecticut. I enjoyed visiting him and getting to know my relatives there. Dad and I would go to the beach or go fishing, and he even took me to the rifle range once when I was about ten years old. I remember everybody scattering when the backfire from the gun scared me and I threw the rifle down on the ground. Needless to say, we never did that again.

I can count at least six different apartments we lived in when I was between the ages of six and twelve before things somewhat settled down. Either the landlord was abusive, there was no heat during the winter, or the place was rodent infested. There was always something wrong. We just couldn't catch a break.

Because we lived in so many places, I also changed schools a lot. Nearly every year I was in a different school —a total of six by the time I got to seventh grade. It was hard to make friends or feel secure with so much instability in my home life, but the one constant was that my mom and I always had each other.

Living paycheck to paycheck, my working and helping out was never an option for me; it was simply expected and never questioned. In fact, when I turned twelve, I got my own job to help Mom with the bills. In the evenings after school, I would sometimes cook our dinner, and every night I would put curlers in Mom's hair as her arms were often too tired for her to put them in herself. She would lie down and fall asleep while I did this—never a night went by that I didn't perform the ritual for her. My grandmother had a similar routine of brushing, braiding, and wrapping her hair each night as well. It's funny what habits we inherit—to this day I can't go to bed without making sure my hair is prepared for the next day.

In caring for my mother's hair each night, I'd nudge her when one side was done so she could turn over in her sleep. I'd then put curlers in the other side of her hair until the job was finished. Sometimes, I would even rub her tired feet with warm rubbing alcohol to help take away the pain. After that, I had a few hours to do my homework while Mom slept before rising at 10 p.m. to get ready for her 11:00 p.m. shift at the hospital.

I'd stay up until Mom left each night in order to secure the locks on the apartment door after she left. There were three deadbolts, and after Mom stepped outside, she wouldn't leave until she heard the click of the locks for each one. She would call me to check in when she arrived at work and then the following morning to wake me up for school.

Mom and I were a team. I knew how tirelessly she worked so I in turn did the same. I never wanted to disappoint her or let her down. When I moved out at nineteen to get married, however, I wasn't thinking about the team my mother and I had become over the years, or how my leaving would affect her. I was madly in love and she seemed happy for me. I selfishly only thought of the new bond I was creating with Tony, but in the aftermath of her suicide, I could only think that I had deserted her. After years of caring for each other, I had walked out on her, and the guilt of having done so weighed me down.

But I knew my mother was a survivor. She had taught me the same work ethic she learned from her own mother, and although I watched her struggle, she wasn't one to get tired of hard work or give in to weakness.

So what did that note she left for me mean? I wondered. *What was she tired of? What couldn't she take anymore?* Maybe she thought she was helping me understand by leaving the note, but it simply left me with more unanswered questions.

6

MOSES

I CONTINUED TO DWELL on memories of our time together for answers to my mother's suicide, and one I couldn't let go was the memory of Moses.

I was around seven years old and had moved to New York the prior year. My mother was working at the hospital and had recently gotten remarried. I was in the second grade and attending P.S. 23 down the street from their apartment near 169th Street and Tinton Avenue in the South Bronx.

Moses didn't pay me any attention and I was grateful. He never talked to me, never even acknowledged me. I wondered if he even knew my name. He wasn't a very nice man, and since he never seemed to want me around, I suspected I was the reason he would always argue with my mother.

My one vivid memory of living in that place was a night when Mom and Moses had another of their many spats. He had been drinking, which he did often, and when he drank, he became argumentative and verbally abusive to my mother. Since Mom was not the kind of person to back down from a fight, she would always stand up to him. The arguments were loud, but they mostly occurred when I was in another room where I could only hear and not see them.

That night, I was in my room when the harsh words began to fly. I stayed in my bed, trying to block out the noise, but when the arguing escalated and my mom screamed, I jumped out of bed to see what was happening. I saw Moses chasing after her, trying to grab her but stumbling in his drunkenness, so I ran out of my room yelling, "Leave my mommy alone! Leave my mommy alone!"

Ignoring my pleas, he kept after her, grabbing at her with one hand while pushing me away with the other. Next thing I knew, he snatched a half-empty beer bottle from a nearby table and hit her over her head with it, smashing the bottle and splattering glass all over the room. Mom stopped screaming and fell to the floor. Moses dropped the broken bottle and ran from the apartment, leaving me crying over my mother's lifeless body, begging her to wake up. I had no idea what to do. I thought he had killed her.

Mom opened her eyes a few moments later and I

hugged her with relief. She told me not to worry and said everything would be okay as she stumbled toward the telephone. She called her brother Paul who came right over.

After Uncle Paul took my mother to the hospital, he took me home with him to spend the rest of the night with his wife and daughter. Throughout that night I lay awake, crying and wondering whether everything was really going to be okay as Mom had promised.

JUST BEFORE DAWN, my uncle returned home with my mother. The doctors had removed the glass from her head, and there was a shaved spot where stitches now resided.

I don't remember if we went back to that apartment, but I do remember Mom sending me back to South Carolina to live with Aunt Babe again, where I finished the last half of second grade.

Moving around so much, I often have to pause and think of which school I attended for which grade. Most kids can look happily back on their school years and friends during that time, but for me, there was simply too much going on to remember every detail.

I do know that by the fourth grade, we were living back up in the northeast Bronx and I was attending P.S. 78. Moses was no longer around, though he would occasionally call my mom to ask to get back together—or so I would overhear her telling her sister, my Aunt Bill. Mom didn't take him back and I believe that was because of me. She was resolute to not ever have me see her in that situation again.

The disastrous marriage to Moses was another in a long line of setbacks for my mother. She had male friends after that, but she never remarried. She would always drill into my head, however, the importance of finding a good man and of never letting a man raise his hand to me. She told me to never stay in a relationship that was unhealthy, and to always make sure I had the means to get out of any bad situation if I needed to. She was constantly prescribing the need to be independent, telling me to always be able to take care of myself.

In reflecting back on the Moses period in our lives, the image is reinforced of Mom as a woman of great strength. Being weak was not in her nature or vocabulary. If she was in a bad situation, she would fight through it and eventually get out of it, determined not to repeat the same mistake—and even more determined that *I* not repeat her mistakes either, leaving me with yet another reason why the words she left in her note to me made no sense at all.

7

———◆•◆———

CAN'T CATCH A BREAK

———◆•◆———

WHEN I WAS IN fifth grade, we moved into a house on Boller Avenue, a dead-end street right beside the Hutchinson River Parkway in the Bronx. My Aunt Bill helped Mom find the two-bedroom basement unit in the dual-family home (where she and her family lived in the main apartment upstairs), and while we lived there, I attended P.S. 111 on Baychester Avenue. The backyard was part of the infamous swamp that Co-op City is reportedly built on, and my bedroom was at the front of the apartment, while Mom's was toward the back behind the kitchen.

One night while I was asleep, I felt something strange and heavy on my chest. At first, I moved a little and it went away. A short time later when I felt it again, I realized that something was on top of me. I jumped up on my bed and screamed, sending Mom running into my room.

When she turned on the light, a swamp rat nearly the size of a cat was crouched in the corner of my room staring at us. I was petrified and couldn't help but scream while Mom chased the rat out of the room, throwing her bedroom slipper at it as it scampered away.

I don't remember where we slept that night; I only recall being scared and trembling as my mom comforted me and held me tight. We were grateful the rat hadn't bitten me, but it did scare the daylights out of me. Even today, there are nights I startle awake with sweat pouring down my face, trembling at the memory of little feet scampering across my chest.

The next day, Mom had it out with our landlord, Mr. Anderson, which resulted in us packing again. This would be our sixth move in six years.

IN OUR VOLATILE CIRCUMSTANCES, Mom always tried to have a little extra cash on hand for emergencies. Though it never amounted to much, she always stressed the importance of being prepared for unexpected difficulties. Mom would let me know her hiding places "just in case anything ever happened to her," as she drilled into me the importance of saving a little for a rainy day. Frankly, there were a lot of rainy days in my childhood years and there never seemed to be enough money to see us through them, but she held strong to her advice nonetheless.

Mom didn't believe in keeping her money in the bank —her philosophy was to always have a small sum she could get to quickly—so she stashed her savings in creative places where no one would ever be able to find it. In this particular case, her hiding place was in the living room. Back in those days, window curtains had hems at the bottom that were three to four inches tall. Mom had let the seam out at the bottom of one of the curtains and tucked her cash just inside for safety. She was sure that no burglar would ever think to look in a curtain hem, and to her it was safer there than in any bank. To make it even more burglar proof, Mom pushed the sofa up against the window so that her makeshift safe was behind it. In hindsight, it was pretty creative hiding on her part.

As we packed and prepared to move yet again, Mom pulled the sofa away from the window to retrieve her rainy-day stash.

"Oh my God, NO!" she screamed.

I ran into the room to see what had happened. The money was there, or at least pieces of it were. The rats had eaten holes in the bills that Mom had worked so hard to save. With their sharp teeth, they had chewed through the curtain hem, shredding the money beyond repair. Mommy was crushed as I stood there and watched her cry. All she kept saying was "Dear Lord, why can't I catch a break?!"

But Mom was determined to get her baby out of

harm's way, and within a week or so, we moved out of that apartment. I didn't know where she got the money for us to move until recently, when my cousin Lewis told me that Mom "hit the number" and borrowed the rest. Back in those days, an illegal numbers game was run out of the local fish and chip restaurant owned by one of Mom's friends. Apparently her favorite number was drawn soon after the rat incident and she won enough money to help us move.

Mom repeated her oft-quoted phrase as we drove away from that rat-infested apartment: "Don't worry baby, things will get better. Where there's a will, there's a way."

What she didn't know was that I wasn't worried. I trusted Mom to always find a way.

8

THE UNFORGETTABLE LESSON

LIFE FINALLY STARTED TO settle down for us when I entered junior high school in the seventh grade. It was the first time since coming to New York that we would live in one place for any length of time, and that I would attend a single school for longer than one year. It was also the first time I started to make friends and hang out like other teenagers in the neighborhood on a regular basis.

We lived in a two-bedroom apartment in a four-story walk-up building on the third floor. Hillside Homes on Fish Avenue in the Bronx was an apartment complex with better living conditions than we had ever had. The kitchen and my bedroom window overlooked the street below, facing a row of buildings on the other side identical to ours.

Once again, my Aunt Bill helped us find a new place to live. It was a rent-controlled complex for low-income families. I remember the three of us—Mommy, Aunt Bill, and I—going into the rental office for our initial visit and being turned away. Mom wanted a two-bedroom apartment so that I could have my own room, but she was told that she made too much money to qualify for a one-bedroom and not enough to qualify for a two-bedroom. In addition, she was told that since I was a female child under the age of thirteen, they expected us to sleep together in a one-bedroom apartment—the one she oddly she didn't qualify for.

None of it made any sense. We left the rental office that day disappointed, but Mom was determined not to take no for answer.

The following week, we returned to the rental office and submitted a new application. This time we had two additions that would help us qualify for the larger apartment. The first was a letter written by my dad stating that he provided my mother with $250 per month in child support, which helped us meet the income requirement for the two-bedroom. The second was a letter written by my Aunt Bill declaring that my mother was the legal guardian for her son—my cousin—Kenny, who would now be living with us. With a boy child listed on the application, we now qualified for the two-bedroom apartment.

We moved, and as the two sisters expected, we never had heat, rat, or landlord problems again. In fact, we never moved again. What's more, Kenny never lived with us a single day, and I was able to have my own bedroom just like Mom wanted.

While we lived there, I got a steady job working most days after school and all day on Saturdays in the neighborhood restaurant called Brown's Fish & Chips—the one run by a friend of Mom's—located in the heart of the nearby Edenwald housing projects. I started working there when I was thirteen, before being of legal age to get my working papers, so I was paid in cash. I cooked, cleaned—you name it, I did it, including cleaning the fish and chicken that was deep fried and loved by everyone in the neighborhood.

Fridays and Saturdays were the days I worked the hardest. It seemed to be the same crowd every week that came to the restaurant—even my school friends were regular customers. The fish and chips were delicious, mind you, but that's not all they came out for. Truth be told, the restaurant was a front for an illegal bookie operation—where my mom had "hit the number"—in the days long before Lotto, Mega-Millions, and Powerball were instituted by the state.

As I think back on the setup of the place, the cash register to make your illegal bet was located in plain sight at the front of the store, less than five feet away from the second cash register where you paid for your meal. I took orders and collected payment for food but was never allowed near that other cash register. Somehow I didn't find it strange at the time; I was well aware what that register was for, but it never bothered me, nor did it worry me that I was associated with something illegal. In fact, I doubt anyone who worked or bought food there was bothered by it. I was making money to help Mom out and funding my own pocket money so she didn't have to give me cash out of her own meager wages.

No doubt our comfort level with being part of an illegal operation was helped by the fact that some of our most frequent customers were New York City police officers from the 47th precinct, located a mere three blocks down the street from the restaurant. The beat cops loved Brown's Fish & Chips, and my boss, Mr. Brown, was very friendly with the officers. Out of respect for them, he would never take a bet when they were in the restaurant. Most times, he would even give them their food without charging them. Needless to say, we never had a problem with those officers.

Mom worked during the day cooking and cleaning for elderly white folks when I was in school, and she slept in the evenings after I got home from school before she would get up and leave for her night shift at the hospital. Mom always wanted me home before she went to sleep in the evenings so she knew I was safe. On the days I didn't come home straight from school because I was working at the restaurant, she was able to sleep comfortably knowing that Mr. Brown would see me home.

Sometimes, when Mom was off from work and I didn't have to be at the restaurant, I would hang out with the neighborhood kids, but I had to stay where she could see me when she looked out the kitchen window at the street below. I always had to be in the house by the time the street lights came on, and if I was hanging with friends away from the block, I would always let my mother know before I ventured away from our street. Mom was adamant about knowing where I was at all times.

In junior high, my mother stopped dropping me off and picking me up from school, as the walk from our apartment to school was only about fifteen minutes through Edenwald. By this time, my Aunt Bill and her family had moved from the rat-infested house on Boller Avenue and now lived in the Edenwald Projects in an apartment along the route that I walked home from school.

Many of my friends in junior high school also lived in Edenwald, including my best girlfriend Stephanie, whose single mother had ten kids. Her dad only visited occasionally—just long enough to father a baby before leaving again for months on end.

Stephanie and her one older sister and eight younger brothers lived in an apartment that the city had retrofitted for them. It was actually two apartments where the walls between the two had been removed. Stephanie's apartment was just around the corner from where my aunt lived, and since we visited Auntie a lot, I sometimes got to see her when we were there.

One day after school, my friends were talking about hanging out a little before heading home. Stephanie was going with the group so I decided to tag along. They were going up to the rooftop of one of the apartment buildings to "smoke some weed and get high." I looked at my watch and thought that I had enough time to hang out a little and still get home before my mother would be expecting me.

Up on the rooftop, I took two puffs off the joint, thinking that two puffs would be all I needed to look cool. I had never smoked pot before, but I had watched my friends do it, so I knew what to do to look cool like the others.

Before I knew it, I had lost track of time and was now running late. I knew Mom would be worried so I said my goodbyes and ran like a madwoman down the stairs of the building, determined to get home before my mother started looking for me.

As I reached the ground floor and wrenched open the door, guess who was standing at the front of the building waiting for me? You got it—my mother.

SHIT! I thought. *How did she know where I was?*

When I didn't arrive home on schedule as expected, my mother had walked the entire school route looking for me, asking if anyone had seen me. Someone told her they had seen me enter that particular building, so she stood out front and waited. She was waiting there with a "switch" in her hand and was ready to use it when I came out.

A switch is what we called a flimsy tree branch used to whip bad kid's asses. Usually your parents made you go pick your own tree branch or "switch" that they then whipped you with as punishment for something you'd done wrong. My mother was standing there packing her own handpicked switch.

When I saw her, she had fury in her eyes and I knew that I was in a world of trouble. She looked at me and immediately knew I had done something I had no business doing.

My mother whipped my ass with that switch all the way back home. It seemed that we would never get to our apartment. As my friends came out behind me from the building, they immediately scattered like dust. They must have seen the wrath in my mother's eyes. All she kept saying as she practically dragged me down the street was, "Is this what you want to do with your life? Is this what I work so hard for? What the hell were you thinking? I can't believe you would do this. I thought you had more sense than this!"

Mom was so disappointed. I should have been mad at her for whippin' my ass in front of all my friends and the entire neighborhood, but I wasn't. I was sore from the lashes, but more embarrassed that my friends and neighbors saw me get a whooping and ashamed that I had let my mother down. Today, she would probably be arrested for how she whipped me in the street that day. Surely someone watching would have called Child Protective Services or the police, but it was a different time, and folks looked out for each other's kids in a different way. My guess is that they instinctively knew that my mother meant well and that I was getting what I deserved.

When we finally reached home, Mom fell exhausted into a kitchen chair. I was bruised and crying. She looked at me and asked again, "What on earth were you thinking?"

"Momma, I didn't do that much, I swear! I was just trying to be cool like my new friends."

"Your cool, new friends ain't going nowhere!" she said. "You, on the other hand, can be anything you set your mind to if you stop following them dumbass kids! You need to pick better friends, and by the way, if I ever catch you doing that shit again, you will never be able to sit down in a chair ever again! Now go and take a bath. I need to get some sleep so I can go to work tonight!"

That was it. She went into her room and I went to take that bath I sorely needed. I doubt either of us slept much that night. I remember barely being able to sit the next day, swearing to myself never to do anything to get another whippin' like that one. I knew she would live up to her promise that it would be worse the next time.

I still hung out a little after school with that crowd, but never again did I join them on the rooftop. I refused to follow someone doing anything that I knew my mother wouldn't approve of. I never wanted to disappoint her again, and my friends never questioned me when I would make excuses to leave. I think they knew my mother was a badass who would whip them too, if necessary. Her message was loud and clear that day: No child of hers would do drugs.

When my girlfriend Stephanie got pregnant later that school year, all my mother kept saying was, "See what I told you?! Is that what you want for your life?"

AS JUNIOR HIGH SCHOOL wrapped up, my friends were all looking forward to entering Evander Childs High School in the Bronx, which was rumored among the neighborhood kids as a place where weed was plentiful.

I'd usually just sit back and listen when the other kids talked about what we had to look forward to in high school. They were eager to go to Evander, but I was scared shitless. Stephanie was pregnant and would be going to a school in the city for pregnant girls. Others in my circle of friends were pregnant too, and Derrick, the boy I liked, was now a regular pothead. I wasn't having sex or doing drugs, but I was hanging out with kids who did both regularly. If I ever felt pressure to do either, my excuse was that I had to leave to get to work.

During a trip to my dad's house one weekend, I kept thinking about how much I didn't want to go to Evander. I was afraid I would eventually cave in to all the pressures to do the things that were happening all around me. When my dad took me home that Sunday, I went to my room, but I could hear him and Mom whispering in the kitchen. After a few minutes, Mom called me.

"Daddy says that you were extra quiet this weekend. Is everything okay?"

I was normally a quiet kid, but with everything going on in my head, I had been more silent than usual that weekend.

I looked at Mom and Dad and with no warning burst out in tears. "Please don't make me go there!" I said. "I don't want to go! I don't want to be like them!"

My poor parents had no idea what I was talking about and simply stared at me. My dad probably thought I was saying I didn't want to go back to Connecticut with him ever again.

Daddy then said, "Baby girl, what are you talking about? Where don't you want to go?"

"I don't want to go to that high school. I hear there's nothing but drugs there. I'm afraid to go. Please don't make me go. I don't want to be like them!"

I threw myself into my mother's arms. "Mommy, please don't make me go there. I can't. I'll do anything. Please!"

Together my parents settled me down. I think they were lost on what to do about the situation, being caught off guard as they were. In hindsight, I'd caught myself off guard too.

"But that's the school the kids in this area are assigned to attend," my mother said. "Where else could you go?"

"What about one of those private schools?" I asked. "Could I go to one of those?"

"But Val, we can't afford those schools," my mother said.

"I'll pay," I said. "I'll work and pay as much as I can. Please, Mommy? Please, Daddy?"

My eyes pleaded to both of them as they looked at each other and stared back at me. They clearly saw my fear —and determination.

"Let's look into it and see what we can do," my dad said.

That night I started looking up schools in the phone book. I already knew of one Catholic school in the area, Cardinal Spellman High School, because I walked past it every day walking to and from junior high. But I found another all-girls Catholic high school across town I hadn't heard of before named Saint Catharine's Academy. It didn't matter to me that it was foreign and not close to home. I was determined to do something different and avoid being like the friends I was hanging out with.

Both schools required an application and $250 in monthly tuition. When I presented the options to my mom and dad during his next visit, they looked at me as if I had lost my mind.

Mom said, "Val, but we aren't Catholic!"

"Please Mommy," I pleaded, "just let me apply and see if they'll take me. If I get in, I've figured out how many hours I have to work to help pay at least $100 of the tuition each month if you guys can cover the rest."

My parents agreed to let me apply. I suspect they didn't anticipate a non-Catholic to be allowed into either school, but they went along with it, no doubt without any idea of how they would cover the monthly payment. They must have thought that once I wasn't accepted, the issue would simply go away.

A few weeks later, I received acceptance letters to both schools. Cardinal Spellman, however, offered me a conditional acceptance, requiring that I attend summer school and take prerequisite courses. I couldn't do that because I had to work to start saving money for my tuition, so by process of elimination, I accepted the offer to attend Saint Catharine's.

AS PLANNED, I LEFT my junior high school friends who were headed to Evander, with no idea where the thought of leaving my friends and going to a different school came from. It hadn't even crossed my mind before the words came pouring out of my mouth that day in the kitchen with my parents.

I didn't know what I wanted to do with my life, but I sure as heck knew I didn't want to be like most of the kids I'd been hanging around with. I wanted to make my mother proud; I would pay the entire tuition if I had to. While it was a huge sacrifice for me, I was confident that I could work hard and help pay my way through high school; I was less confident that I would survive the high school pressures that would follow my friends as they entered Evander Childs High School.

"Is that what you want?" continued to echo in my mind. My mother had said those words after catching me trying pot, then again when my best girlfriend got pregnant, and they had stuck with me—so much so that I made a conscious decision not to follow the crowd, to make my own way. Their kind of life would not be mine.

9

THE OTHER SIDE OF THE TRACKS

ENTERING HIGH SCHOOL, I felt like a fish out of water. The Hillside apartments where we lived were mostly filled with low-income minority families, and the restaurant where I worked served mainly minorities who were poor and barely making ends meet. Saint Catharine's Academy couldn't have been more different. I had run away from an environment full of drugs and the pressures of urban teens, only to run right smack into a world I knew nothing about.

At home, I rarely saw white people, yet at school, there were very few blacks. The student body was ninety percent white Italians who all lived in two-parent homes their family owned. Not only was it my first time in a predominantly white environment, it was also more difficult academically than what I was used to. When I was in junior high, I got away with doing my homework between school and work. Now, I needed to stay up late to get through it.

While it was initially awkward adjusting to a new school, more demanding schoolwork, and new friends, I eventually settled in and became more comfortable in my new environment. My lifelong experience with change over the years had prepared me for adjustment once again.

Shortly after I entered high school and got my working papers, I changed jobs. Because I needed to work every day after school and as much as I could on weekends to help pay my tuition, I was thrilled to land a job as a cashier at a Key Food supermarket not far from school. I didn't have enough time to get there by bus, so Mom would pick me up from school and drop me off at work. Then she would go home, sleep some, wake up at 10:00 p.m., and drive back across town to pick me up from work, drop me off at home, and then head to work herself in time for her midnight shift at the hospital. That was when I would complete my homework for the day.

Working at the supermarket was very different from the restaurant. I didn't know anyone, nor did I recognize any of the customers, but it was a legitimate job with a real paycheck, which was all I cared about. I was really good at that job too. I had taken a typing class in junior high, so in addition to being good with money, I was also a fast typist on the register. In fact, I was the fastest, most accurate cashier on the front end during the time I worked there, for which I was very proud.

Supermarkets in those days didn't have the fancy scanner machines of today. You had to know how to add, use a real cash register, and most importantly, handle money and count change without the machine doing it for you. Having worked in the restaurant business, I was grateful for my extensive experience with money.

The area where the Key Food supermarket was located was a predominately Jewish community, which was another first experience for me. Although it's a stereotype, the customers who shopped there always seemed eager to find a bargain. The little old people loved coming through my line, loaded down with the coupons they had clipped out of the Sunday paper. In those days, we didn't have the little discount cards everyone carries around today on their keychains. If you wanted the sale, you had to work for it by going through the paper and cutting out the five- and ten-cent coupons for the items you wanted. When "double coupon days" would come around, we were even busier because the little old Jewish ladies would save up their coupons for those days to get the extra savings. I had never seen anything like it. No one used coupons at the Fish & Chips restaurant, or in any of the local bodegas in my neighborhood for that matter. But these people were determined not to waste a cent they didn't have to.

Heeding my mother's words, "Whatever you do, be the *best*," it didn't take long for me to get promoted to front-end supervisor and then eventually night book-keeper. Here I was, only in high school, and I was now closing the books for the supermarket. It goes without saying that I learned a lot from that job. I even started clipping coupons for when Mom and I would go to the grocery store. Because I'd noticed that the prices there were always cheaper than in our neighborhood, we now shopped at the supermarket where I worked. Just like the little old Jewish people who didn't seem to have much, we were now saving a little bit too.

I worked in the supermarket for two of the three years I was in high school, but by senior year, I had switched to being a part-time teller in Dollar Dry Dock Savings Bank in Co-op City in the Bronx, another heavily populated Jewish community during that time.

Again, I was in a job that suited my skills. I was always a good performer who was well liked by my regular customers—they enjoyed coming to my teller window to carry out their banking transactions. Many of the customers who became my regulars had similar charac-teristics to those who had become my regulars in the supermarket. Like those who clipped the five- and ten-cent coupons every Sunday to save every penny they could, these people also dressed very simply, often wearing the same clothes each time they came in. They didn't look like they had any money to speak of ... or so I thought.

While working at the supermarket, I learned that saving every little bit helps; and while employed at the bank, I learned that looks can be deceiving. Imagine my surprise when I discovered that the same kind of people who pinched pennies in the supermarket were doing so to stash the bulk of it in their bank accounts!

Rarely did my customers come into the bank to withdraw money from their accounts. Instead, they would come in once a month to cash their checks and then deposit most of it. They would then give me their savings account passbook and ask to update their balances. They never touched their savings; they simply watched the money grow.

The same type of people—white people with worn clothes, eager for double-coupon savings—would make a regular trip once a month to bring their passbook to the window just to have their interest posted to their account. Hundreds of thousands of dollars sat idle collecting interest. I had never seen that much money in my life and definitely didn't know anyone else in my neighborhood who had that kind of cash tucked away.

I would go home and tell my mother about the hoards of money these people had stashed away and she would listen attentively and tell me, "These are good lessons you're learning that one day you'll put into practice."

Saint Catharine's turned out to be the blessing I needed to see a new world of possibilities for myself. The change in environment in school and work were eye-opening experiences for me as I got to see a different way of life: one that was unlike what my friends and I were learning in Hillside and Edenwald.

It wasn't that Saint Catharine's didn't have some of the same pressures of Evander; it certainly did. When school let out at the end of each day, for example, there was a line of boys waiting outside to pick up their girlfriends in their fancy cars. What we did on rooftops back in my neighborhood, these kids did in parked cars that their families could afford to buy for them.

The experience of seeing how these other people lived —and saved—made me curious. *How did they do it?* I often wondered. *How could they live in such nice houses?* The people back in my neighborhood knew nothing about this life—and neither would I had I not made the dramatic shift across town to Saint Catharine's Academy.

Mommy and me, circa 1965.

*Aunt Babe,
my "sisters"
and me,
circa 1969.*

*Jay and Ankie, circa 1958
(cousin Lewis, who was like a brother to
us, is sitting on the porch).*

Mommy and Ankie, circa 1978.

Daddy and me, circa 1988.

Tony's and my wedding day,
18 August 1984.

10

ANKIE

I WAS DOING WELL AND **Mom** was too. Things were looking up for us, and I was starting to think about going on to college.

One day, Mom and I were relaxing at home—I was in my bedroom and Mom was in hers—when the doorbell rang. I ran out to find my cousin Lewis on the doorstep. I let him in and gave him a big hug.

"Hi, kiddo," he said a bit solemnly. "Where's your Mom?"

"Mom, Lewis is here," I called out as I went back to my room.

Minutes later, I heard my mother crying, so I dashed

back out front to see what was happening. Lewis had come to break terrible news: my brother Ankie had died.

I immediately broke into tears and ran back to my room. My brother hadn't lived with us in years, but he was very special to me. No matter how busy he was or how far apart we lived, Ankie often called to check on me and ask how I was doing in school. When we visited him, he always treated me in the most special way. As a matter of fact, both my brothers doted on me when we were together. They were fiercely protective of their little sister.

When my mother came into my room a short time later, she found me crouched in the corner of my closet, shaking and crying silently. I had seen from her initial reaction to the news that she, too, was devastated, so I had crawled into the closet, not wanting her to see me cry or to upset her any more than she already was.

When she discovered me, she simply held her arms out for me to come to her. She had no words this time. We just held each other and cried.

MY BROTHER WAS TRULY a wonderful man. He was a friendly, kind, considerate person who loved to laugh and have fun, and we all loved being around him. But although he was a hard worker, he—like my mother—always seemed to struggle financially.

Both my brothers learned to be handy like my father, going on to have careers in the construction industry after the military. My brother Ankie attended technical school to become a tradesman, specializing in hanging sheetrock. My brother Jay still says that he has yet to meet anyone who hung and plastered sheetrock as perfectly as our brother Ankie did. He worked doggedly and was good at what he did, but he constantly struggled to keep money in his pocket.

Ankie and Mommy had a strong, unbreakable bond. He would call to talk to her often, and when she didn't hear from him, she would call to check on him. If he needed money, she would send what she could. So when the news of my brother's death reached her, I believe my mother's heart was permanently broken. It was as if the minute his heart stopped beating, hers was forever shattered. Like her, he was incredibly industrious and always strived to do the right thing, but he had more going on in his life than any of us realized.

My mother's instinct was to protect and save each of her children like she had done for me throughout my life. She was determined that we not fall prey to drugs. But on that day, we learned my brother had a drug problem. He hadn't died of an overdose, though. He had put a gun to his head and pulled the trigger.

Knowing my mother, I imagined she was silently blaming herself for not knowing the full extent of his struggles, for not doing more to save him. Mom stood tall amidst her heartbreak, but I don't believe she ever recovered from Ankie's suicide. Sometimes I would catch her with tears in her eyes, but she would brush them away and focus on me. Mom became even more protective of me after Ankie's death, and even more determined that I work hard and be successful. Months later, when she was still in pain over his death, she nonetheless showed no outward signs that she had lost hope. I thought she was okay because she always was.

WHEN I GRADUATED FROM high school, my mother was overcome with pride. My parents, my brother Jay, and my cousin Lewis were all at my graduation to cheer me on, going out of their way to make the day happy for me. My brother Jay kept putting his arm around my shoulder and saying, "I'm proud of you, baby girl." Lewis, who was like a brother to us, was right there smiling and hugging me too.

I cried at the memory of our brother Ankie who should have been there to cheer me on too as I crossed the stage to accept my diploma. But I knew that even though he wasn't there physically, he was with me in spirit, proud that I had successfully completed that stage of my education and was headed to Fordham University at Rose Hill in the fall. I had always wanted to return to South Carolina for college, but I decided to stay in New York and attend nearby Fordham in the Bronx to stay close to Mom, who I knew still needed me.

I I

TONY

I ENTERED FORDHAM UNIVERSITY in the Fall of 1982 and almost immediately met a guy I was smitten with at a school basketball game. He was skinny, crazy tall, and incredibly handsome, and his name was Tony Rainford. His best friend Michael Cooper was a senior and star player on the Fordham basketball team. Tony was visiting Michael to see him play, but he spent more of his time staring and smiling up at me from the stands below as I cheered on the team. Fordham won that day, and we both went to the celebration on campus that followed. Once again Tony kept smiling and staring. I pretended not to notice, but I was definitely attracted to him as well.

A few days later, the phone rang. It was Tony. He and Michael had looked me up in the Fordham freshman directory and found my name and number. I was flattered that he went to all that trouble to track me down, and we talked on the phone for four hours that night. The following day, he met me after class and escorted me home from school. We were instantly inseparable.

My mother adored Tony, and my dad and brother Jay liked him as well, so we had their "approval" to date. We attended Fordham basketball games together and went dancing and to the movies. We also loved to play arcade games—especially Ms. Pacman—at the neighborhood bowling alley on Gun Hill Road in the Bronx.

But the date that will go down in history as my favorite was when Tony stopped the car in the middle of Times Square and got out to dance in the middle of the street, telling me that he loved me. He didn't care that people were honking their horns at him. Crazy in love, that's what we were. If only my mother knew that he had stopped traffic in Times Square, he would have never been able to borrow her car again.

I was only nineteen and he twenty-three when Tony asked me to marry him, but I didn't hesitate to say yes. And although our families were initially resistant, they eventually gave us their blessing. I was actually surprised Tony didn't back out of the proposal from the scrutiny he received from Jay and my father—they both made a point of making sure Tony knew that he needed to take good care of me, but it was my father who tried to make Tony run like mad in the opposite direction.

Tony and I had borrowed Mom's car to drive up to Connecticut to visit Dad, who was an avid hunter and gun collector. He stored his guns in the basement of his home and was known for making his own bullets to use when hunting deer. During that visit, Daddy invited Tony down to the basement to see a new gun he had recently purchased. After showing off his new gun, Daddy said, "Tony, have I ever showed you how to make your own bullet?"

"No, sir," Tony replied.

"Oh, well then let me show you how it's done."

Daddy instructed Tony how to load the shell with gunpowder. He had never made a bullet before, so Tony was beaming when he finished.

"Good for you son," Daddy said. "You've just made your own bullet!"

"Thanks, sir."

"Now let me explain something to you, son, about this particular bullet," Daddy went on. "This bullet that you just made, it's the bullet I plan to shoot you with if you don't take good care of my daughter. Do I make myself clear?"

Tony laughs when he tells that story today, but he wasn't laughing that day. In fact, he almost peed his pants. I knew without a doubt he loved me if he still wanted to marry me after the stunt my father pulled.

We were young but we had everyone's blessing. We got married during the summer break between my sophomore and junior year at Fordham, not wanting to wait because we couldn't bear to be apart. We had such dreams and delighted in planning every detail of our life together, but never could we have planned for the tragedy that would occur just one month after our wedding day.

12

A MOTHER'S PAIN

AFTER MY MOTHER DIED, I was lost and confused. I quit working and dropped out of college as I couldn't concentrate on anything. School didn't matter anymore. Nothing did. My head was filled with conflicting thoughts and my heart was too heavy with grief to make room for schoolwork.

Perhaps my heaviest burden was that nothing made sense. It seemed as if the one major belief I held while growing up—that hard work was all that mattered—was a lie. My mother was the most hardworking person I knew, yet she ripped herself out of my life with no warning or explanation.

I floated through my days in a fog but was increasingly grateful to have Tony by my side, who was there for me at every turn. My brother Jay was there for me too, but he was miles away in South Carolina, dealing with his own pain over our mother's death.

But the relationship from which I drew the greatest solace during this time was with my maternal grandmother, Corinne. Always an incredible force in our family, she continually inspired me with her resilience because her life, like my mother's, was also fraught with great sadness and struggle.

Descendants of emancipated slaves, Grandma had no formal education. She had her first child when she was sixteen and was a widow at the age of thirty. She didn't learn to read or write until she was in her sixties, in 1965, after the passage of the Voting Rights Act when blacks were required to read in order to exercise their right to vote. She would practice by reading the Bible, her favorite book.

My grandmother was a faithful servant to the Lord first and to her family second. She was a quiet woman, rarely speaking unnecessarily, but when she did, you knew to pay attention because what she had to say was important.

As a child I loved to visit her down in the countryside of Elloree, South Carolina, but by the time I moved to New York at age six, Grandma was living there as well with my Aunt Flossie, the youngest of Grandma's children. The rest of the siblings had also left home and migrated north in search of better job opportunities.

My Aunt Flossie was the only one of Grandma's children to finish high school. She went on to complete nursing school and land a position at Misericordia Hospital in the Bronx, where, as I mentioned earlier, she helped my mother get a job as a nurse's aide.

Grandma would take care of my cousin Darryl and me at night while our mothers worked the midnight shift at the hospital. It was during this time with Grandma that both Darryl and I built an incredible bond with her. Grandma was by now seventy years old and could no longer work the fields, but she was still physically strong. She loved to cook and care for us, and Darryl and I would sit and talk with her while she combed my hair at night. We would then take turns combing her long white hair and braiding it into a single plait before she went to bed. Grandma encouraged us to do well in school, saying, "I'm counting on you two to take care of me when I can no longer take care of myself."

Grandma's watching over us lasted for a little over a year before she announced to the family that she was moving back to South Carolina. After living alone as a widow for thirty-eight years, she had found love again. She and Mr. Willie Dash—a man she had known all her life—had exchanged love letters during the time she was in New York caring for us, and they planned to get married.

I recall the day that our entire family—uncles, aunts, cousins, and grandchildren—traveled down to the Port Authority in New York City to see Grandma board the Greyhound bus back to South Carolina. She was glowing with happiness. Mr. Dash had sent her the bus ticket so she could return home to become his bride. As she hugged Darryl and me together to her bosom, she reminded us that she was counting on us to finish school and be successful so we could take care of her like she took care of us. We cried all the way home, melancholy to see her go.

My grandmother and Mr. Dash were a wonderful couple, and he was the only grandfather I ever knew; my other grandparents had all passed away before I was born. Mr. Dash, like Grandma, had been widowed many years prior to their marriage to each other, and after a lifetime of being a sharecropper, he lived in a home on old Mr. George Allen's land. The Allens had built the home especially for Mr. Dash and his first wife to live in while sharecropping the surrounding fields. The first Mrs. Dash had died leaving her husband with no children of his own, and he had lived alone in that little house for years. Now, with my grandmother as his wife, he would finally have a companion to share his life with.

Grandma and Mr. Dash were faithful members of Brown Chapel African Methodist Church, the same one where my parents attended school as children. The church was founded by freed slaves and has been our spiritual home for generations. All of my known ancestors are buried in the Brown Chapel cemetery, starting with my great-grandparents—my grandmother's parents—Winnie and Sole Snider.

Mr. Dash was a senior trustee and church treasurer, and Grandma was once again one of the church matriarchs. Back home and happy, she was—perhaps for the first time in her life—married to a man who loved her unconditionally.

Having given up sharecropping, Mr. Dash worked on

the assembly line at the local peanut factory. Though well into his seventies, he would leave for work every day with the lunch box my grandmother packed for him, and when he returned each evening, he'd call out to her, "Shug, I'm home."

It warmed our hearts to see our grandma with a true gentleman. He pampered her, opened doors for her, drove her around town to do her shopping on the weekends, and held her hand walking into church. "What else do you need me to do, Shug?" he'd often ask. He cared for her like she had never been cared for before, making these, no doubt, the best years of her life.

In return, my grandmother was a consummate homemaker. She tended to the chickens while he was at work, and she picked and canned the figs and peaches from the trees he had planted around the house. Grandma was also a phenomenal cook. He'd sit on his favorite stool in their tiny kitchen where she prepared his favorite meals and say things like, "Shug, can I have a little more of that sweet tea? You sure do make the best sweet tea."

After dinner, they would head out to the front porch and sit together holding hands in their dual rocker as they watched the sun go down each evening. When my grandmother wasn't cooking, cleaning, or tending to their home, she would quilt. Every bed in her house—and in the houses of her children—has a quilt made by our grandmother. They are some of our most prized possessions.

Grandma and Mr. Dash were married for almost eighteen years when he died—within a year after my mother. Grandma was once again a widow, but at eighty-eight years of age, Mr. Dash had made sure that she lived at least eighteen of those years happy and loved.

After Mr. Dash died, the Allens gifted my grandmother the right to live in that house indefinitely—that is, until she died. We have no doubt that Mr. Dash had prearranged that gift with Mr. Allen before his death, ensuring that his "Shug" would always have a place to live. Never again would she be put out of her home, as she had when my grandfather died, with nowhere to go.

The small two-bedroom home with the wood stove in the living room would always be my grandmother's home. The elder George Allen vowed that it was built for the Dashes and would only ever be occupied by a Dash, and his descendants have kept his word for generations. No one has lived in that house since my grandmother died. It sits there now, vacant and overgrown with the pecan and fig trees surrounding it that Mr. Dash planted so many years ago. Even the chicken coop and original outhouse are still standing in the backyard.

On a recent trip to South Carolina, I visited that old house. I peered through the overgrown trees at the porch they had loved to sit on together after dinner—the same porch I would sit on when I visited Grandma after Mom died.

I LOVED TO VISIT GRANDMA. Being with her was always a reminder of what it took to survive anything life threw at you. She had come through many struggles, never complaining, preaching hard work and faith as the answer to overcoming any obstacle life sent your way. She would often say, "You can get through anything if you work hard enough AND pray hard enough."

In the years after Mom died, I'd go back to South Carolina as much as I could, often alone, to visit Grandma and stop by the church cemetery to pay my respects to Ankie and Mom, who are buried side by side. Without my mother to guide me, I desperately needed time with my grandmother to keep moving forward with my life.

During one such trip, shortly after Mom's death, we were sitting on the front porch in silence, just Grandma and me, swaying back and forth in the rocker. I adored being in her silence, staring out over the cotton fields. I was always at peace whenever I was with her; we didn't need words to communicate.

On this particular day, she said out of nowhere, "Do you really believe she did it? Maybe there's something we don't know. I don't believe it, do you?"

I just looked at her, stunned, realizing at that moment for the first time that Grandma—the rock and strength and wisdom of our family—was also hurting. I also grasped that our roles in that moment had instantly changed, that she wouldn't be the one to explain Mom's death to me. Silence passed between us for a few minutes before I gave her the only response I could without breaking down myself.

"She did it, Grandma," I said.

Upon hearing my words, tears came to her eyes and began streaming down her cheeks. It didn't make sense to either of us, and it was the first time I had ever seen my always-strong grandmother cry. I imagined that was how she cried when she was left betrayed, widowed, and evicted from her home, all those years before.

I turned to her and put my arms around her shoulders, not allowing myself to cry though I desperately wanted to. It was her time to grieve and my turn to be there for her. In that moment, I remembered all of the times Grandma said, "I'm counting on you two to take care of me when I can no longer take care of myself." She had spent her entire life tending to everyone else and being strong. Now she needed someone else to lean on, and that someone needed to be me.

Grandma was still healthy and physically strong, but her heart was broken beyond repair. Watching my grandmother cry, I began to understand what my mother must have felt three years before when my brother Ankie had committed suicide. Mom was so focused on me, I wondered if she ever took time to grieve Ankie's death. In her sorrow, she had to pretend to be strong for me and others in our family, but did she have any shoulders to lean on? Did anyone see her sorrow? I know I didn't.

I knew at that moment that I needed to clear my head, to be there for my grandmother, and not have her worry about me as my mother did.

Later that evening, Grandma and I knelt at the side of her bed as she did every night. We bent our heads and recited our prayers together before climbing into her bed.

Now I lay me down to sleep,
I pray, Dear Lord, my soul to keep.
If I should die before I wake,
I pray, Dear Lord, my soul to take.

Before Mr. Dash died, I would sleep in the front bedroom, usually with one of my cousins accompanying me. But I was too afraid to sleep in that bedroom alone now, preferring instead to sleep in Grandma's bed and feel her warmth next to me throughout the night.

Sometime during the night I felt cold. It was pitch black in the room and I couldn't see anything. I reached over for Grandma, but she wasn't there. I bolted up and called out for her but there was no answer. I grabbed the flashlight on the nightstand and clicked it on, sweeping the small light over the room. I saw nothing, so I went to search for her.

I had never walked through Grandma's house at night by myself. Once you were in bed, that's where you stayed. Even if you had to use the bathroom during the night, you never went to the one at the back of the house; instead, you used the "slop jar." As you might imagine from the sound of it, I preferred to hold off going until morning.

The bathroom in my grandmother's house was chilly that night. Indoor plumbing was a recent addition to the home and the warmth of the wood stove didn't reach that section of the house. I didn't think she would be back there since no one ever ventured there at night, especially if it was cold, but I also knew she wouldn't have left me in the house alone. My worry increased thinking about how sad she had been on the porch earlier that day, so I kept roaming through the house until I finally found her in the back of the house, slumped over the toilet bowl. It looked as if she had fallen down and was holding her head in her hands.

"Grandma, what happened?" I whispered. "Are you okay?"

She didn't answer.

I tried again, louder this time. "Grandma, please answer me."

This time I saw her move. Relieved, I knelt down beside her. Then she turned and looked at me.

"Gurl, don't ever interrupt Grandma when I'm prayin'!"

I remained quiet as she bent her head back down for a few more seconds, then she grabbed my hand so I could help her get on her feet. We walked back to her room in silence, hand in hand, then crawled into bed in our quiet ritual, me hugging her tightly. I had a hard time falling asleep this time around, but the next thing I knew, the rooster was crowing in the daylight.

Blinking awake, I saw that Grandma wasn't next to me. Though I was still a little concerned about her well-being, I knew she typically got up with the chickens, so I wasn't worried about her absence. I padded into the kitchen to find her making breakfast and humming one of her favorite gospel hymns, "What a Friend We Have in Jesus."

What a Friend we have in Jesus,
all our sins and griefs to bear!
What a privilege to carry everything to God in prayer!
O what peace we often forfeit,
O what needless pain we bear,
All because we do not carry,
everything to God in prayer.

When she saw me, she smiled. "Good morning, my girl. Are you ready for breakfast?"

"Yes, ma'am."

"Well, go brush your teeth and come sit down then. Everything's ready."

As I passed through the kitchen toward the bathroom, I kept looking for yesterday's sadness in her face, but none of it showed.

I LEARNED A LOT about my grandmother—and my mother—in that 24-hour period. As a child, Grandma was always the first one up in the house. When the rest of us would finally stumble out of bed, she was busy doing some sort of chore: feeding the chickens, collecting their eggs, or cooking so that there would be plenty of food to eat in the house. And whatever she was doing, she was always humming either a gospel tune or a Negro spiritual song.

I realized that morning with Grandma that my mother often did the same. She, too, could be found singing a hymn—some church song with words of her faith in God —while working around the house. I wondered if my mother's singing was also an antidote for her pain and suffering. How often had my mother called on God in song to ease her tired hands and broken bank account?

It came to me that both of these strong and seemingly impenetrable women had their own personal moments of weakness, and that in the darkness of night, when no one could see their pain and worry, they had likely relied on their faith in God to help them get past the pain and struggle.

LATER THAT DAY, sitting again on the front porch, rocking and staring out over the fields in silence, my grandmother simply said, "She forgot."

I knew that she was talking about my mother.

"What, Grandma? What did Mom forget?"

"She forgot what I taught her," she said, turning to me. "She forgot that the good Lord don't put no more on you than you can bear." Then, pointing and staring at me dead in the eyes, she added, "You. You must never forget." Then she rose up from the rocker and went inside.

I realized in an instant that my grandmother had probably prayed the night before for an answer to why my mother killed herself, an answer that would ease her grief and align with her unwavering faith in God. It was the only explanation that made sense to my grandmother, and as she said it, it was the only explanation that made any sense to me. My mother had gotten tired of fighting. She knew how to fight to keep going when things were rough, but for some reason she had lost her will, her hope, and her faith that tragic day. She forgot to call out to God for strength through prayer. Maybe she did but found that God had not answered in that moment. She failed to do what she had done on so many occasions before: keep going, keep pushing, and keep praying until her prayers were answered.

My grandmother's words were a reminder to me that survival takes more than hard work. When we work hard, it's because we're reaching for something. We continue to fight because we understand that there is something better coming—a light at the end of the tunnel, the hope for a brighter day. But none of it matters if you lose your faith. When the hard work doesn't seem to be making a difference, faith can keep you putting one foot in front of the other, day after day, until that brighter tomorrow shows up.

When I went back into the house, I found my grandmother humming another of her favorite gospel tunes in the kitchen.

Amazing Grace, how sweet the sound,
That saved a wretch like me
I once was lost but now am found,
Was blind, but now I see.

Grandma and I never talked about Mom's death again after that day. We had both said all that needed to be said, and from there we would move on. On that day we both accepted the fact that my mom had taken her own life and we had no idea why, so we latched on to the only explanation that made any sense: that she had lost her faith.

Like so many families, we didn't talk about the tragedies. Though the pain was always present, we tucked the sad times away in a safe place, not wanting to air our dirty laundry. Yes, we talked about her, but it was about the good and the funny times. Grandma's outward strength and positive memories of Mom helped me to think of her in the same way, and watching how Grandma dealt with the pain helped me learn how to deal with it as well. It was clear that Grandma didn't understand what happened or why and that she was heartbroken over it, but she moved on. She helped me move on as well.

Grandma would say, "Everything in life happens for a reason. You may not understand and may not be able to explain it when it happens, but keep your faith in God and He will eventually help you understand."

After that particular visit, I went back to New York and re-enrolled at Fordham. I was determined to finish my degree and make my grandmother and mother proud. It was what my mom had worked so hard for. I couldn't give up on that dream now.

13

LETTING GO OF WHY

M Y FATHER RETIRED BACK to South Carolina in 1988, and I would see him when I visited my grandmother. Despite the fact that I mostly only saw him on weekends growing up, we had a nice relationship. He was a simple, pleasant man who rarely lost his temper—I can actually count on one hand the times I saw him lose his cool, and it was never with my mother or me. What's more, he never seemed sad. In fact, I can recall seeing my father cry only twice, when a single tear rolled down his cheek at the funerals of my brother and my mother.

My father loved to tell jokes and fun-loving stories of my brothers growing up and getting into mischief—how

Ankie was the one to get them *into* trouble and Jay was the one to get them *out*. "Ankie would pick the fight and Jay would finish it," Daddy would say, "always stepping in to defend his little brother."

After my mom died, my father made sure to stay in touch with me, and my relationship with him became stronger. He always called at 6:00 a.m. sharp on Saturday or Sunday mornings, and Jay and I would laugh and compare notes about who he'd call first each week and what funny thing he had to say to us. He would quip, "What are you doing in bed, girl? If the chickens are up, you need to be up." Or, "You can't get nothing done laying in the bed all day! What's a young girl like you doing in the bed so late? Don't you have things to do?"

"But, Daddy, it's 6:00 in the morning!" I'd say. "Some people don't wake up with the chickens."

"Well, if I'm up, you need to be up. Don't you have to go to work today?"

"No, Daddy. It's Saturday. I don't work on Saturdays. Remember?"

He clearly didn't remember because those 6:00 a.m. calls kept coming. To this day I still pop out of bed by six after so many years of receiving Daddy's early-morning phone calls. I also call or text Jay at that same hour, knowing that, like me, he developed the habit of rising early.

Our parents both dated other people while I was growing up, but to my knowledge never reconnected with each other. My mother remarried Moses, but "Thank God she had the good sense to leave him," as my grandmother would say. But my father never remarried, and if you heard the loving way in which he talked about my mother, you would think they hadn't been divorced for almost twenty years when she died. After all that time, he still referred to her as "my wife."

My father lived for seventeen years after my mother passed. During those years—first with him and my grandmother, and then with only Daddy after Grandma passed—none of us ever talked about Mom taking her own life. It was as if it was too painful to say out loud. I eventually came to understand what my grandmother and father no doubt understood: that sometimes things happen in life that we just can't explain.

SOMETIME DURING THE TEN years after my mother killed herself, I finally stopped questioning why. I no longer needed to know. I eventually accepted the reality that the explanation of "why" died with her. I came to realize that it wasn't healthy for any of my relationships for me to keep dwelling on a question that I would never know the answer to.

I also ceased blaming myself and instead began to focus on the fullness of her life—and of my brother's too—balancing the sadness with the goodness inherent in each of them. I convinced myself that that one day would not define her forever in my mind. Had I not learned to do that, I probably would have gone crazy a long time ago.

I can only imagine the countless number of people who've experienced a tragedy and spent the rest of their days on earth questioning why, blaming themselves when there was likely nothing they could do. My grandmother's simple explanation, that Mom simply forgot that "the good Lord don't put no more on you than you can bear," eventually became enough for me. I now understand, however, that that simple explanation is not actually simple at all.

AFTER MY GRANDMOTHER DIED, she continued to guide and coach me from afar. I could hear her words, sense her speaking to me regularly as if she were still here on earth with me. "Pray on it," she'd often say. And when she would come to me in a dream, it was always with warm words of encouragement.

Ironically, as I started to let go of the guilt and accept my mother's death, she too would come to me. I couldn't hear her when my mind was swirling with what-ifs and guilt, but later—once I began to let go of those emotions—I could hear her saying, "I'm sorry. I wasn't thinking. I made a mistake. Please don't hate me. I was just so tired. I should have hung in there."

But her words of encouragement came to me too. When I was doing well at work, she'd say, "Baby girl, I am so proud of you!" When I felt down or was losing confidence, she'd say, "You can do this. You can be everything I couldn't be." After a rough day at work, I'd hear, "You get up, dust yourself off, and go back in there tomorrow with your head held high. You're gonna run that damn place one day."

Even in death, my mother was a badass and still my biggest cheerleader.

THE
NEXT
CHAPTER

14

SHARING MY STORY

HEN I RETURNED TO Fordham University in the Spring of 1985, six months after my mother died, I was determined to finish on time because that was what she would have wanted me to do. I doubled up on classes, took summer courses, and made up for the lost time, and Fordham allowed me to walk through graduation in June 1986 with my original classmates despite being three credits short of my degree requirement. I sat in the audience with tears rolling endlessly down my face, crestfallen that my mother wasn't there to see me achieve her dream for me. I finished the one remaining course in the fall and officially received my degree the following January.

With the help of Fordham's Career Planning and Placement office, I secured an interview on campus that resulted in a job offer and subsequent placement at the Federal Reserve Bank of New York. I entered the working world and rose quickly through the ranks, building a reputation as a hard worker with an excellent performance record. Early on, I was tapped for the Fed's elite Management Training Program, after which I moved up and around the organization, breaking records and achieving firsts. When I was thrown difficult assignments —ones that required me to pull all-nighters, sweat bullets, and cry—I remembered that my mother and grandmother often worked three jobs with little sleep and zero complaints, so who was I to complain? I was doing what my mother taught me to do and what my grandmother would remind me to do for ten years after my mother died.

What I discovered about myself as I progressed in my career was that I excelled in problem solving and crisis management—no surprise given that much of my life was one crisis after another. As a result, I built a reputation for being able to enter any challenging situation, quickly assess the issues, and devise a plan of action to resolve the problem.

Whether I was in the role of Team Leader, Project Manager, or Operations Executive, when things were in upheaval mode and many of my colleagues went into what we referred to as the "spin-cycle" (also known as blaming and explaining), I remained calm and quiet. While others spent their time dwelling on the past when faced with problems—How did we get here? What went wrong?

Who is at fault?—I typically re-directed focus to What are we trying to achieve? How do we get there? and Who can help us get there?

I essentially took a lifetime of dealing with personal challenges and new situations and turned it into a valuable skill that made me incredibly successful—without anyone's realizing where my knack for managing change and solving complex problems emanated from. No one at work ever knew my story, not because I couldn't deal with it or was ashamed, but because I simply didn't want pity. I thought that if I shared my mother's and brother's tragic end, people would feel sorry for me. Handouts and pity were not what I wanted.

When I think back on my rise in two high-profile, well-regarded organizations, I was merely doing what I was taught: work hard, push through difficult issues, and always perform with excellence. Without consciously knowing it, I was emulating my mother. The only difference between her and me was that I was fortunate to have a formal education—which I was determined to make good use of—along with the words, wisdom, work ethic, and faith taught to me by my two angels.

AS MY CAREER PROGRESSED, I became known for being a strong mentor to individuals who were trying to climb the corporate ladder or who were working through difficult circumstances, both personal and professional.

After seeing so many women who needed coaching and mentoring, Renoka—a colleague at the Federal Reserve—and I created a support group for them called

MOSAIC. Although it wasn't initially sanctioned by the company, we'd meet with the women as a group once a month over lunch and guide them in the various challenges they were facing at work and in their personal lives. We had previously experienced much of what the women were going through—the challenges of balancing personal challenges with professional growth, feeling inadequate and ill-prepared for the corporate scene, or standing out as "the only one" in the work environment. We coached them and helped them role-play difficult conversations with their bosses while boosting their confidence that they belonged there and could be successful no matter where they started or what they were currently going through. In those sessions, I would share with them some of my struggles and offer advice on how to overcome their own challenges. In exchanging these real life experiences, the women thrived knowing that if I could do it, so could they.

It was with the success of this group that I first realized the power of my story. After one year of meeting with these women, every single one of them said that the group had changed their lives and career, giving them the strength to keep pushing forward. Some of these women had changed roles from one that was not working for them to another where they felt confident and empowered; others had been promoted. All attested to having benefitted from the support, coaching, and counseling we gave them.

Through this group, I became more comfortable telling snippets of my story. I was hesitant in sharing every detail, as much of it was still too painful to say out loud, but I found a way to share enough of it to give others hope that success—despite what they were presently going through—was possible.

At that point, I began to consider giving full voice to my story. If I could make that kind of difference with corporate women, I wondered what I could do for those in the communities like the ones my mom and I had lived in. Once this spark was ignited, I was spurred on to do more. I accepted volunteer assignments working with single women and girls, and I was invited to give talks called "The Secrets of My Success" to various groups. In those settings, I began to test the waters by sharing more details of my life's tragedy and subsequent successes. When I'd say that first my brother committed suicide and then my mother did the same three years later, the reaction would be a deep collective sigh from the crowd. The pity I was so determined not to incite seemed to envelop me, yet it also felt as if the audience could feel my pain.

As I would continue speaking, I witnessed people in the audience scrunching their brows and cocking their heads to one side while looking at me, seemingly asking themselves, *How is it possible that she made it through all of that?"* I then began to give more details—of Moses, the constant moving, the different schools, experimenting with smoking pot, and the decisions I made to change my own circumstances. When I shared these parts of my past, I noticed that their eyes would open wide, not in judgment of me, but rather as if something in my story felt familiar to their own. I sensed that they felt hope that if I could do it, maybe they could too.

Over time, the crowds at my talks became bigger, and more requests came in to tell my story. The more I shared, the more I was asked to speak to groups to inspire them with how I used the struggle of my past to achieve success in my present. Lines would form at the end of my talk with participants who wanted to speak to me. Some would hug me and say how much my story inspired them to think about their lives differently. Others whispered to me that someone in their family had taken their own life as well, and they had struggled with it for years until they heard me speak about how to get past it. After receiving this feedback, I couldn't help but believe in the impact my story might have on the lives of others.

But that was only part of my healing.

Even though I was speaking publicly about my past, I still wasn't talking about my brother's or mother's deaths at home or with family. My daughters, now teenagers, were completely unaware of my family tragedies. My closest adult friends didn't know; most of my work colleagues didn't either. But my mentees and complete strangers were now finding out, and this disparity was something I was going to need to reconcile ... I just didn't know quite how or when.

15

———◆•◆———

AN UNEXPECTED GIFT

———◆•◆———

A S I GAINED COURAGE to tell my story in public, numerous people asked me if I ever thought about writing my story down on paper. While I was flattered, writing a book was the furthest thought from my mind; I was perfectly happy telling my story to small-to-medium crowds where I knew it was helping change lives.

One day over lunch, a young mentee named Ken—who also worked at the Fed—and I were sharing stories of growing up in tough circumstances. His mother had lived a hard life and ultimately died of a drug overdose after years of addiction. She had imparted a great deal of wisdom to him on her good days as he fought his own demons throughout his life, and she had made it a priority to show him that other possibilities besides a life filled with drugs existed. She didn't want him to be like her.

Ken was in the process of writing a book and he encouraged me to do the same. Though many others had encouraged me to write, Ken's words struck a different chord.

"Valerie, you've got to tell your story," he said." You're already impacting so many lives. Imagine how many people you can inspire if you tell your story more broadly. You need to make it your business to tell it while you can before someone is standing over you telling it for you! Your story will be more impactful and long-lasting if *you* tell it."

Ken's words hit me like a brick. No one else had made that point so clearly for me before. He kept talking, trying to convince me, but I didn't hear anything he said after that pointed comment. Instead, I heard my grandmother's words: "Baby girl, people come into your life for a reason. Sometimes it's not always clear when you're dealing with them, but always know there's a reason, lesson, or message that they come bearing."

I left that lunch determined to start writing, intent on changing more lives. I didn't know the first thing about writing a book, but now I was curious about doing so.

A short time later, Renoka and I were invited to participate in a conference at Spelman College in Atlanta, Georgia, to share the story of how we started and built our successful women's group, the first of its kind at the bank.

At that conference, I had the pleasure of meeting George Fraser, who was also a featured speaker and the author of the book, *Success Runs in Our Race*. I had never heard of him before that trip, but I was captivated by his message of networking and strengthening minority communities. I felt an immediate connection to his story of growing up as a poor orphan.

After George's delivery, the crowd flocked to him to get his autograph on their copy of his book. I asked for his business card but didn't join the crowd that surrounded him; I merely stood back and watched. There was something about this man and his story—and his ability to call people to action—that had my attention.

Back in my hotel room that evening, I kicked myself. *Why didn't I go up to him?* I thought. I wanted to know how one went about writing a book, and I could have asked him whether he thought my story was worth putting down on paper for a broader audience.

That night, I couldn't fall asleep. *What a missed opportunity* played over and over in my mind. But then I heard, *You have his card. Send him a note.*

I can't do that, I thought. *He probably wouldn't remember me.*

It plagued me all night until finally, near dawn, I sat at the hotel desk, drafted an email, and sent it to the address on his business card. I asked if he would have any time to meet with me as I was thinking about writing a book.

When I checked my email later that morning, I was excited to see a response. George was from Ohio but was planning an upcoming trip to New York. He agreed to meet with me for coffee when he was in town, which left me flattered yet nervous for the day of our meeting to arrive.

⁂

GEORGE AND I MET a few weeks later, and as I still wasn't clear on what I wanted to say, I simply jumped right into the conversation, giving him the highlights of my story, how I had started to tell it in small groups, and the reactions I was getting from people—namely how it was changing their lives.

I further explained that I was struggling with how to begin. I wanted to write about my mom, about navigating the corporate environment, about money management, about empowering women—the list was long, and I had no idea where to start.

George then said: "Valerie, did it ever occur to you that *this* is your life's purpose? That what happened to you occurred so that you could overcome it the way you did, and that now you can teach others to do the same? You've got a story to tell and lives to change, and you need to get to it. My gut tells me that you need to unleash the story of your mother to the world first. That will free you and provide the foundation to teach all the other things you have learned along your journey. We all need your story— to be inspired by your story. Do you know how many people out there are suffering through the same struggles as you and your mother did? They need your lessons of survival. They need your life as an example of what is achievable. Our women *especially* need to know all that is possible."

As I absorbed the impact of his words, he generously laid out tips for collecting my thoughts—guidance that became the basis for the writing of my story. After I left that lunch with George, I felt I had a roadmap, and I was filled with eagerness at the prospect of creating a book.

But despite the fact that I became more comfortable sharing my story wherever I went, that I possessed a newfound enthusiasm and confidence, and even that I believed my two heavenly angels would be proud of me for doing so, I knew I couldn't fully put my heart out into the world without first putting it out to my earthly angels ... my daughters.

16

STANDING TALL

IT WAS A SATURDAY, and I was at my youngest daughter Alyssa's soccer game, chatting on the field with a few other moms as we waited on the sidelines for the game to get started. The local news that day had reported a story of a man from our area who had committed suicide after losing his job, leaving his wife and two kids behind to mourn his loss.

As we discussed the story, I was consumed with the feeling that the man had lost hope. I imagined he hadn't discovered an alternative to the bad situation he was in and simply gave in to the pressure. As I reflected on what he must have been thinking—as I had done hundreds of times before when thinking about my mom—one of the women said, "He must have been deranged or mentally unstable." I froze. She said it with such authority, as if that was the only possible answer for his actions, and then the other women began to chime in, agreeing and diagnosing his mental state in great detail. They talked about his "poor" wife and kids. They remarked that they had never seen signs of him being deranged, but yet in a split second, they determined he must have been. Last week he had been a good husband, a hardworking family man, and a great dad; this week, however, as his wife and kids suffered through planning life after his suicide, he was now a closet manic-depressive.

I couldn't sit on the sidelines of the conversation any longer, so I volunteered a different perspective: "Well … maybe he just lost hope."

They all turned and looked at me as if I had two heads. "Hope?! He had everything going for him!" one woman said angrily. Another chimed in. "Yeah, a beautiful home, caring wife, and good kids." The other woman simply said, "He was a selfish bastard!"

How ironic, I thought. In their eyes, the ʿamily members were the victims and he was the deranged criminal. Yet what resonated most with *me* was the incredible pressure he must have been under. I wondered: *Were there signs of his struggle? Had he ever been in such a scenario before? Did he have anyone to confide in? Was he just tired? Maybe he was depressed and losing his job pushed him over the edge.* But whatever his circumstances, who were they to judge?

When I think about my brother who put a bullet in his head when I was sixteen, or my mom who did the same, I think about their state of mind at the moment of their actions. Both were sane people. What they had in common with each other—and probably with the man who had just taken his own life—was being overcome by the pressure and struggle with which they walked through life at times in silence. Perhaps no one was aware of the stress they felt, or that they fought hard to meet the expectations of caring for their families no matter the weight of their burden. They were good people who, in a moment that appeared to have no options for them, gave into their feeling of hopelessness.

But these women, all they could do was demoralize this dead man they barely knew. I considered walking away from their ignorant chatter, but instead I blurted out, "My brother committed suicide and he wasn't crazy!"

They all turned abruptly toward me in silence, their mouths wide open.

"And by the way," I went on, "my mother committed suicide too, and she wasn't crazy either! Did it ever occur to you that this man lived with incredible pressures to provide for his family? Perhaps he lost hope when he ran out of options to continue to do so!"

I realized that I had actually screamed those words at them, so I turned and walked to the other side of the stands. Throughout the game, I caught them occasionally glancing over at me, probably thinking I was the deranged one, but it angered me how they demonized that poor man. *Maybe his wife should have found a damn job to help him instead of hanging out with her soccer mom friends all day*, I thought. Good thing I had walked away before I said that out loud. I had somehow managed to keep that one to myself.

As I sat in the bleachers, feeling good about standing up for the man while furious with the women for their condemnation, I began to feel unsettled about what I had just done. I had never told my children of the circumstances of my mother's death, yet I had just blurted it out to a bunch of local moms.

I hadn't consciously kept it a secret; it just didn't seem appropriate to talk about, especially when my girls were small. When I spoke of her to them, I would simply say, "After my mom died ..." or "When my mom died ...." I was never questioned, so I never explained. As they got older, I knew I needed to share the details with them, but finding the right time and way to tell them was important—particularly because one of my daughters is quite sensitive and I knew it would hit her the hardest.

Knowing how small-town news would travel through the entire neighborhood by late morning, I went home after the game and devised a plan to tell my daughters. I had no idea how they would handle it, but I didn't have a choice. I couldn't let them find out from someone else.

⁓❧⁓

THE NEXT DAY WAS Mother's Day. I decided that sharing the story would be my gift to my girls, and I imagined my angels cheering me on. "It's about time," my grandmother said. "You have nothing to be ashamed of," my mother added.

I decided the best way to share the story was to read from the draft manuscript of the book I was in the process of writing, which not even my husband had read. Tony was supportive of my plan, but I realized I couldn't read it to my daughters without crying—and I wanted to be clear-minded to answer their questions—so I decided to print a copy for everyone, allowing the four of us to each read it together and talk about what happened as a family.

When the following morning arrived, I called everyone together and explained the gift I wanted to give them for Mother's Day. This was no longer about the soccer moms' dialogue the day before; in the hours that had passed, I now *wanted* to tell my daughters, wanted them to know the truth. I believed the incident the day before had happened to make me realize it was time.

The only guidance I gave them before passing them the book was that they had to read each chapter together and not move forward until the others had finished reading. I promised to answer any of their questions in between each chapter, and the girls were both excited. They knew that I was writing a book about my life; they just didn't know all the details.

They began by reading Chapter 1: Is That Your Mother? Alyssa kept glancing at me and frowning as she read, then when she was finished, she simply stared at me while waiting for her sister. Avaree, on the other hand, seemed captured by the story and never looked up. When they were both finished, Alyssa asked, "Mommy, is this a true story?"

"Yes," I said.

"Can we keep reading?" Alyssa asked.

"Yes, sweetheart."

By the middle of Chapter 2, Avaree needed a tissue. She said nothing, only cried. But Alyssa wanted answers. "*Why*, Mommy? Why did she do it?"

"I don't know, baby girl," was my only response.

As they proceeded to read, Avaree continued to cry. By Chapter 4, Alyssa was determined to know why while Avaree remained silent in her tears.

After a few more chapters, I asked them to stop reading so we could discuss what happened. I explained to them that for a long time I questioned everything surrounding my mother's death, but that eventually I realized I would never truly know the answer to why my mother killed herself. I shared with them that my mother had had a hard life and simply gave up one day, that I believed she felt she had run out of options and didn't know where to turn. I wanted them to understand that she didn't have a clear head that day and had made a mistake by taking her own life.

Alyssa, the analytical child, needed to understand every action, while Avaree, the sensitive child, could only cry and hug me as if she felt my pain. In many respects, my own reaction to my mother's death was a combination of the two.

A few hours later, the girls finished reading the partial manuscript. I felt a mix of emotion having fulfilled my Mother's Day gift to my children, but when each one told me she understood me even better after reading the manuscript, it was an incredible gift to me. They saw me in both my mother and my grandmother, and they now had a different viewpoint of why I always encouraged them to push through any challenge facing them.

IT TOOK ME MANY years to share my story with my daughters, but I have no regrets about not telling them sooner; I actually suspect the timing of sharing the story with my children—in their pivotal high school years when teen pressures are at their highest—may have been perfect.

While I don't tell my daughters who to be friends with, they acknowledge from my own experience why it's crucial to pick their friends wisely. They likewise understand why I constantly tell them that no one is perfect, that everyone makes mistakes, and that the key is to learn from them and to ask for help when you can't work through an issue by yourself. They also now grasp why I'm compulsive about our family finances, why I get riled when others joke about or demonize suicide, and why I can't sit through a movie that has a suicide scene. Most importantly, they understand the unquenchable passion I have to use my life to inspire others.

It also helped that I could hear my angels in the background saying, "Now, that wasn't so bad, was it?"

17

THE LITTLE BLACK GIRL
THAT COULD

NOT EVERY PARENT FEELS comfortable bringing their past out into the open with their children, and not every child will embrace a parent's—or any adult's—cautionary tale and walk a different, better path because of it. I've been fortunate thus far with my own children, but I also know from experience that hearing the story of a stranger can often have more impact than one any relative can tell. I don't exactly know why that is, but I've seen it happen numerous times when I've been asked to speak. I also know that *how* the story is delivered—especially when talking to teens—can make all the difference.

A few years ago, my good friend Arlene invited me to speak at a teen summit after hearing me tell snippets of my story during talks at corporate and non-profit professional programs. She was impressed and believed that my story should be told to teenagers, to help them realize their full potential as they deal with many of the same teen pressures I did.

The event was structured as a half-day of training around resume writing, leadership, peer pressure, and even a discussion on sexual abstinence. I was asked to kick off the program and spark their interest in the workshops to follow.

Time passed and the date of the summit approached. I hadn't given a lot of thought to how I would present my story or meet Arlene's objective of inspiring these young people beyond their current circumstances, and since I had never spoken in front of a teen crowd, I began to worry about how I would grab their attention, knowing how difficult it was to keep my own two teenage daughters focused on any one thing for long.

On the eve of the event as I was preparing my speech, I glanced over at Avaree, who was about the same age as the teens I would be addressing, and wondered if she could help me with my concerns of how to capture the teens' attention. As she sat near me watching television, I explained my dilemma of having to give a talk the following day, and of not being sure how to make it impactful for that age group.

"Mom," she said, her eyes fixed on the television, "kids in my school hate when grown-ups come in and preach to us about what we should be doing with our lives." Then she turned to me. "We get these visitors all the time who come into our school auditorium and stand up there and just *talk*. Kids don't want to hear that stuff; they want people who will encourage us. So give them examples that will make sense to them, and then they'll listen."

It was as simple as that. She resumed watching her show, and I just stared at her, pondering the wisdom of her words. I then worked the rest of the evening to craft my talk in a way that would grab the attention of the young people with whom I would be speaking, exactly like my daughter suggested.

I decided to write a story of a little girl who had suffered through incredible difficulties in her life. This story would include many examples of the struggles that the little girl faced in a way that the teens could connect with. There was so much material to write about that I didn't finish the story that night, but I wasn't worried because I had an idea for how to wrap it up, make my point, and also meet Arlene's objective of inspiring my young audience.

I formatted the manuscript into book form, and the finished product actually looked like a real book that I had borrowed for the occasion from the library. I titled it "The Little Black Girl That Could," paraphrasing the title from the well-known children's story, *The Little Engine That Could.*

I arrived early the next day while the kids were having lunch. They were your typical group of teenagers: some had come from community groups and after-school programs, and almost all were black with a few Hispanics and

Caucasians mixed in. Group counselors and a few parents accompanied them, and the kids were hanging out and having fun, much like they would in the school cafeteria.

I floated through the crowd to hear what they were talking about with each other. They had no idea—nor did they seem to care—who I was. I imagined that to them I was probably just another counselor or chaperone in the crowd checking up on them. The girls were being cute, flirting with the boys. The boys were being cool, checking out the girls. It was a Saturday morning, but somehow it felt like another typical school day for them before they rushed off to another required class.

When lunch ended, the adults shepherded the teens into the connecting auditorium-style room, and I hung back while they got organized. At this point there were still only a few adults in the room who knew who I was and why I was there. Arlene called the program to order, then walked the audience through the day's itinerary and introduced me as the keynote speaker. I meandered toward the front of the room as Arlene read my professional biography in detail, which sounded pretty impressive, even to me!

The teens gave their undivided attention as she went on to introduce me as a senior banking executive, then numerous pairs of eyes flicked my way as she continued to read. I wondered whether they were staring because they suddenly realized I was the individual who had been checking them out at lunch, or because they were surprised that such a senior person would be there to share the day with them.

Arlene shared my career accomplishments, including the fact that I had risen to be the most senior African-American woman working in the Federal Reserve Bank of New York. At that point, everyone's gaze was locked on me. As I walked to the podium, I prayed that I could keep them as engaged as they seemed in that moment.

The crowd welcomed me with applause as I stepped to the microphone and thanked Arlene. I looked into the eyes of the teens in the front rows.

"I want to start off by reading you a story that I came across, a story that will help you understand why you're here today. The title of the story is 'The Little Black Girl That Could.'" Then I looked down at my notes and began to read.

⁓⁂⁓

"THIS IS THE STORY of a little girl who was born to a family living in the South. She was the youngest of three children with two older brothers. The eldest brother left home to serve in the Vietnam War shortly after the little girl was born. The second brother was twelve years old when his little sister arrived. By the time he was sixteen, he and his girlfriend were having a baby of their own. They got married with the consent of their parents and gave birth to a baby boy. That brother continued to attend school, but he now had to work after school to support his new family. When he turned eighteen, he too joined the military as a way to support his family.

"In many respects, the youngest child, the little girl, lived as an only child. She doesn't remember ever living with her brothers. She did, however, become close to both of them later in life when she was a teenager.

"The parents of these three kids were sharecroppers. If you've never heard that term before, sharecroppers were typically black farmers who worked the farms of white landowners after slavery and were paid for the crops they grew. The little girl's family picked cotton and grew peanuts for the local white landowner. For their work they were paid two cents for a pound of cotton, or about two dollars a day.

"As soon as the sharecropper's children were ten years old or so, they dropped out of school to work on the farms full-time, with their parents picking cotton all day for pennies a sack to help support their families. As was common in these circumstances, the little girl's parents only went to school through the sixth grade."

I paused, looked up at my audience, and said: "Think about that. They never got to go to high school like you guys do." I had their attention so I looked down at my notes and continued reading.

"The girl's parents could read and write, but beyond that their education was limited. With little education, raising their family was hard. The parents both worked multiple jobs to keep things going. When the little girl was nearly four years old, her parents divorced, which was about the same time the girl's middle brother became a father.

"The divorce of her parents broke up the family. The father moved away and the little girl lived with her mother. It was just the two of them but not for long because the mother had difficulty finding work. She was now a single mom with a young child to support. After a period of struggle and little help from others, the mother decided to move up north to New York—where other members of her family had moved—and find work. She wanted a better life for her daughter, but that meant leaving her behind until she could get settled and send for her."

I looked up at the crowd and their eyes were locked on me, so I continued.

"The little girl stayed behind in the South, living with friends of the family. The mother of the family she was left to live with was a close friend of the little girl's mother. They were a big family, and she was well cared for, but they were not *her* family, whom she missed very much. Despite that, she lived a happy, stable life with them. Her mother sent for her in time to attend first grade, so the girl started school up north, but that didn't go too well. By that time her mother had remarried, and the little girl's stepfather was abusive. He was a nice man until he got drunk. When he drank, they would fight, and he would beat the little girl's mom."

When I looked up again at the audience, I could see they were visibly upset.

"He never hurt the little girl," I reassured them, "but the mom must not have wanted the little girl to see her be beaten anymore, so she sent her back down south."

The crowd muttered "Awww ..." at the thought of the little girl being separated from her mother again.

"For third grade, the little girl was back down south in a new school. Her mom had separated from the abusive husband and sent for her again in time for her to begin fourth grade in New York. They had their own apartment in a private house, but they realized after moving in that it was rat-infested. The little girl's mother wouldn't tolerate that, but she didn't want to send her daughter away again. So they up and moved yet again. Another apartment, another school … but at least they were together. The mother was determined not be separated from her daughter again.

"They moved a few more times until they found a place that was warm, free of rats, and that they could afford. The only problem was that the little girl would end up attending six different schools between kindergarten and sixth grade. She never had a chance to make any real friends."

I deliberately paused but didn't look up. I wanted them to think about how many friends they had sitting right there in the room with them, but how the little girl in the story had none.

"Her mom worked during the day while the girl was in school, and she worked a second job as a nurse's aide at night. The girl would take care of herself every night, all night, while her mom was at work. This started around the time she was ten years old, creating a lot of responsibility for her at such a young age.

"When she started junior high school, she finally made some friends, which made her *so* happy. Her best friend lived in a nearby building and sometimes they would go there after school and hang out. She had never had a best friend before; she had never been in one school long enough to develop true friendships and she wanted to be liked. She loved having a best friend she could confide in, but her new friends came with a lot of pressures too.

"One day, she and her best friend went to a nearby building rooftop to hang out with a few of the boys. Thank God she didn't follow all of her buddy's activities during that time because not long after she started hanging out with them, her buddy became pregnant. They were still in junior high school, and her friend was only fourteen years old.

"As high school loomed in the near future and more and more teen pressures were mounting, fear caused the girl to ask her mother if she could go to a different high school than the rest of her friends. Everyone around her seemed to be falling prey to the same pressures, and they were all slated to go to the local district high school that was well known as 'drug city.' The little girl, now a young lady, had many friends who were getting high or getting pregnant. She didn't want to be like them.

"All of the other schools in the area were private ones that neither of her parents could afford to send her to because of the tuition costs. But the girl asked if she could apply to those schools and promised that if she was accepted, she would work to help pay the monthly tuition. Her parents reluctantly agreed, not expecting her to get in. But she did. She was accepted into an all-girls Catholic school across town, and shortly after, she found a job and started working just as she promised.

"Her high school was a very different place. Uniforms, nuns, and religion class—and she wasn't even Catholic. It was scary at first, but she just kept reminding herself that staying with her friends would have been much, much scarier. She traveled across town every day to attend school. Her friends didn't understand why she had made this choice, and most of the neighborhood kids stopped speaking to her, calling her names like 'stuck up' and 'miss goodie two shoes.' They didn't want to be around her anymore. It was hard, but luckily she had school and work to fill her days.

"Her job was near her school and she worked every day until night to help pay her tuition. Her mom would pick her up from school and drop her off at work to make sure she arrived on time. She typically worked until 10:00 p.m. during the week and also on Saturdays. Then her mom would pick her up at night after work, drop her off at home, and then head to her own job at the hospital to work the night shift. The girl never had time for homework, yet despite that, her grades in school were good. She did the best she could because anything was better than what her old friends were experiencing back at the neighborhood high school.

"As time moved on, she got used to the new school and the difficult schedule while managing her schoolwork. Things were feeling stable until one day the news came that her brother, the middle one—the one who got married at sixteen to be an honorable father and joined the military to provide for his family—had committed suicide. The little girl's heart was broken. She had looked up to her brother and knew how hard he had tried to do the right thing. Her mother was distraught."

I paused and looked into the crowd. They were sitting on the edge of their seats fully engaged with the story, seeming to feel the little girl's pain.

"Things were never ... ever ... the same," I continued. "Time passed and a few years later, the young girl's mother committed suicide too."

At that point, gasps of "Oh my God" floated toward me. I then looked into their eyes, and after an extended pause said, "Rather than me read any more, why don't you guys tell me what *you* think happened to the little girl after her mother committed suicide."

They erupted in chatter with each other, visibly upset for the girl, debating her fate. I heard them trying to figure out whether she killed herself or whether she gave into drugs. They couldn't decide. I merely observed from behind the podium, fascinated with how deeply they connected with the story.

I had purposely left out some of the details of the little girl's story to keep their attention, but while I was preparing it, I had no idea what their reaction would be. Now, however, I admit I wasn't surprised by how they were questioning the girl's fate.

After a few minutes, I raised the big question.

"Okay, by a show of hands, how many of you think the little girl killed herself?"

Almost every hand in the room went up. Those who disagreed began to speak up. "No, she didn't," they said, igniting more discussion amongst themselves as they contemplated what happened.

"Okay," I said. "How many of you think the girl is alive, but turned to drugs or is an unwed mom with a houseful of babies?"

Many hands went up and more chatter began. They

were upset because they knew that something terrible must have happened to the girl, but they were in disagreement about what it was. The discussion continued as I stood there watching them. Their reaction, of course, was typical—the media had taught them that only bad things follow a life of struggle. Negative outcomes were all they could imagine since, more than likely, that was all they had experienced. Their expectations mirrored what they had seen and been taught. They weren't even considering that anything good could have happened to the girl.

Finally, I took back control of my audience.

"Okay guys. Let me have your attention. Let's talk about it together. The girl has had a terrible life, right?"

Comments of agreement came from the group.

As I reopened the book, I purposely looked down, pretending that there were more words written on the page. "Okay," I said. "Let me ask you just one more question before I continue reading so that we can find out what happened to the girl."

They were all silent, their eyes fixed on me.

"Tell me, why do you guys think I'm here?"

I looked into their eyes, but all I received were blank stares. They were clearly confused, having no idea why I had been invited to speak to them. I glanced at the adults lining the back wall of the room, some of whom began to smile.

I looked back into the questioning eyes of my teen audience and said, "I'm here because I am the little girl."

Gasps and stares followed my declaration. I then

stepped away from the podium, leaving the book behind, and walked out into the crowd. I wanted them to know that I was real, that I knew what they were going through. I wanted them to know that no matter the difficult circumstances life dealt them, they could overcome them with a determination to be different, that their lives didn't have to follow a negative path, that they didn't need to believe or model everything they saw on TV ... that they didn't have to be another statistic within our urban communities.

⚶

I RECEIVED VERY FEW questions from my audience that day. After the program ended, many of them simply stared at me as they left the room and headed to their workshop classes. They were clearly shocked by the twist in the story, like a surprise in a movie where you think you know what's going to happen, but something sidelines you. After the lives they'd led up to that point, they simply couldn't fathom a positive end to the little girl's story.

As I prepared to leave, the adults thanked me for sharing my story. I was pleased to hear they thought the presentation was impactful, but I was more interested in what the kids thought. I could tell they had been engaged, but I couldn't help but wonder if they would merely go home and resume their pressure-filled lives.

As I watched them walk out of the auditorium that day, I knew I had left them thinking about a lot of things, but I didn't know if any of them would do anything differently in their lives or seek new opportunities for themselves as a result. It left me wishing I had made a way to keep in touch with them to know how many were impacted in a positive way. Instead, I had to resign myself to the fact that I would likely never know.

EPILOGUE

ONE YEAR AFTER THAT teen summit, I was invited to speak at the Harlem YMCA's 40th anniversary awards dinner. As a long-time supporter of the organization, the president and CEO of our company was asked to address the audience but was not available to attend. They had honored me the prior year at the same event as a Black Achiever, so I was invited in his stead to speak to the more than 1,000 people who would attend.

I addressed the crowd just before dinner with an intermission following my speech. As I left the stage, a woman came rushing over to me holding the hand of a young man dressed in a suit and tie.

"I just had to meet you," she beamed, putting her arm around the boy. "My son hasn't stopped talking about you since he attended a workshop last year where you presented to his teen group. He came home saying, 'Mom, if that woman can get past all that happened to her, what can I do?' Your story made quite an impression on my son. He's more focused on his schoolwork now, and I just wanted to say thank you."

I was shocked, yet excited. Never did I expect to learn about the fate of one of my teen protégés at this completely unrelated event. Beyond congratulating the young man and thanking his mother for seeking me out, I was otherwise speechless. We chatted for a bit and then went our separate ways. Only after the event did the impact of what happened hit me. Again, as on the day of that teen summit, I wished I had gotten his contact information to stay in touch.

Although I may never know how that young man's life has played out since, that one encounter was enough for me to become more deliberate about sharing my story. I already knew it was an inspiration to folks in the community and to my mentees at work, but now I had validation in the power of my story to change the lives of young people, to show them the world of possibilities that existed for them with hard work, focus, a determination to be different—and, of course, faith.

～⁂～

SOME TIME LATER, I received an email from another mother. She explained that she was one of the parent chaperones at the teen summit with her son on that day when I gave the "The Little Black Girl That Could" talk.

She had kept the business card I gave her and had just found it in an old pocketbook. I called her after receiving her email, touched that she had reached out to me.

She wanted me to know that her son had just graduated from Morehouse College, class of 2012, where President Barack Obama gave the commencement address. It was important to her that I know that not only did I make a difference in her son's life, but that she, too, had finished nursing school and was thriving, in large part because she had been touched by my story that day.

Once again, I was thrilled to know that my story was one of hope and inspiration to others. I told her about the book I was writing and she encouraged me to continue, convinced that many more needed to hear it. This time, I made sure we could keep in touch and have ever since.

With the passing of time, I understood it was no accident that these individuals were finding me to validate the power of my story. They were placed in my path, as my grandmother would say, to bring me a message, and I felt that message was to finally finish the book so I could inspire the world to believe that brighter tomorrows lie ahead.

⁂

MY HEART SWELLS WHEN I think of these two boys out of that group of 150 teens, knowing at least two lives were changed after hearing my story that day. And while I often wonder how many more of those young people left more focused on their future and determined to be different, what I do know is that we each have the opportunity to change a life every day, to share wisdom from experiences that can help one another, even if we don't get to hear the triumphant follow-up story. What counts is what we give to lift others up around us, no matter how big or small our gift may be. Whether you're a teacher who gives your heart to your classroom every day, or a coach who guides and inspires ... a leader who brings out the best in those around you to help them develop and grow, or a blue-collar worker who sets an example of hard work and ethics to your coworkers ... an entrepreneur who uses your gifts of innovation and creativity to help others fulfill a goal or dream, or a parent who's raising loving, compassionate children ... a professional who helps others heal, or a regular ol' honest employee who's doing your best on the job and for your family ... you have the opportunity to make a difference, even if a smile is all you have to give in the moment.

Not only was George right—that I do have a story to tell—but I've been blessed to meet many more people whose lives were changed because of my story. I may not have been able to save my mother, but I have since saved others who needed a dose of hope ... and that's what I plan to keep doing.

Being honored by the Harlem YMCA.

(left)
Lewis, me,
and Jay.

(below)
Aunt
Flossie,
me, and
Aunt Bill.

Tony and me today.

*My earthly angels, my daughters,
Avaree and Alyssa.*

My heavenly angels,
my grandmother, Corinne,
and my mother, Betty,
cheering us all on.

AUTHOR'S NOTE

Nothing fulfills me more than knowing I had a part in changing a life, in improving someone's outlook.

If my story touched you in some way, please send me a note at:

info@valerierainford.com

I would sincerely love to hear from you.

Here's hoping you achieve your brighter tomorrow …

QUESTIONS & TOPICS
FOR DISCUSSION

1. How did Valerie's story affect you? Could you feel her journey as she wanted her readers to?

2. What was the most impactful chapter for you personally?

3. In what ways did you relate to Valerie and her story? Have you had similar adversity to overcome?

4. Do you know anyone who grew up in similar circumstances to Valerie's? Did he/she succumb to those circumstances or supersede them as Valerie did?

5. What was your reaction to Betty's marriage to Moses? Were you surprised she left him? How do you think that decision affected young Valerie's opinion of her mother?

6. Do you know anyone who committed suicide? What was the impact on his/her loved ones? What are your thoughts on the topic of "loss of hope"?

7. Do you know anyone who is blaming themselves for the loss of a loved one to suicide? What would you say to them after reading Valerie's book?

8. Why do you think Valerie's mindset was so different from that of her friends, despite living in the same impoverished environment?

9. Valerie shielded her family heartache for many years. Do you believe in forming the support groups with women, she unwittingly formed a support group for herself?

10. What was your opinion of how Valerie delivered her talk at the teen summit? Do you think her choice to tell a third-person story had greater impact than a first-person version?

11. Did you find Valerie's story to be universal? Do you think it transcends race, gender, and environment to speak to a broad audience?

12. Although Valerie is a strong, driven person, do you think she would have had the courage to write her story had she not received encouragement from others to do so? Why or why not?

13. What do you think parents and educators can do to inspire more young people in similar circumstances to strive for a better life?

14. Did Valerie's story shift your thinking about how to deal with challenge and adversity?

15. Why do you think Valerie's inspiring story of hope, tenacity, and faith will change some lives for the better and not others?

ABOUT THE AUTHOR

VALERIE RAINFORD is the youngest child of southern sharecroppers who believes that everything that occurred in her life was intended to test her will and resilience and to prove that success can be achieved no matter where you start or what you may currently be going through. After enduring a series of trying circumstances in her young life, including the suicides of her brother and mother, Valerie stayed true to the strong ethics passed down to her from her parents and grandparents, determined to beat the odds.

After graduating from Fordham University with a Bachelor of Arts degree in Economics, she was appointed as an officer at the Federal Reserve Bank of New York at the age of 29—the youngest ever at that time in the Fed's history. By the age of 35, she was promoted to Senior Vice President, becoming the most senior African-American woman in the company's history; at 42, she was recruited by JPMorgan Chase to bring her well-regarded problem-solving skills to the private sector.

Valerie is currently a senior executive with one of the world's largest financial services firms, as well as a freelance writer, speaker, coach, and mentor who uses her work to inspire others to see past their current circumstances, whether in the workplace or in their personal lives, to reach their full potential and live their brighter tomorrow.

Valerie was honored in 2007 by *Network Journal* magazine as one of "25 Influential Black Women in Business" and in 2009 by the Harlem YMCA as a "Black Achiever in Industry." She has appeared on TV shows such as *Black Enterprise Business Report* and *Brooklyn Savvy*, and has been featured in multiple publications including *Black Enterprise* magazine and the Adecco Group's "Leadership Tribute to Women." She resides in New York with her beloved husband and two daughters.

Connect with Valerie at:
www.valerierainford.com
info@valerierainford.com

CPSIA information can be obtained at www.ICGtesting.com
Printed in the USA
BVOW05s1346241014

372240BV00002B/4/P

Topps® LEAGUE Story

STEAL THAT BASE!

· BOOK TWO ·

By **Kurtis Scaletta**

Illustrated by **Eric Wight**

Amulet Books
New York

For Byron, who stole our hearts.

Special thanks to Sean, T.J., and
Dylan of the Saint Paul Saints.
—K.S.

To Ethan & Abbie.
—E.W.

Cataloging-in-Publication data has been applied for and
may be obtained from the Library of Congress.

ISBN: 978-1-4197-0287-7 (hardcover)
ISBN: 978-1-4197-0262-4 (paperback)

Copyright © 2012 The Topps Company, Inc.
All Rights Reserved. Topps and Topps League are
trademarks of The Topps Company, Inc.

Book design by Chad W. Beckerman

ABRAMS
THE ART OF BOOKS SINCE 1949

115 West 18th Street
New York, NY 10011
www.abramsbooks.com

CHECKLIST

☐ **#1 JINXED!**

☐ **#2 STEAL THAT BASE!**

☐ **#3 ZIP IT!**

☐ **#4 THE 823RD HIT**

It was five minutes before midnight and the bottom of the ninth inning, and I was about to break a promise.

I was a batboy for the Pine City Porcupines. When I took the job, I promised my parents I would try to be home by ten o'clock and would *never* work past midnight. "That's just too late for a boy your age," Dad had said.

But there had been a rain delay and the game started late. The Porcupines were tied with the Attica Finches, 3–3. If the Porcupines didn't score here, the game would go into extra innings.

I'd also made a life-long promise to my uncle Rick that I would never leave a baseball game before it was over. Uncle Rick took me to a game when I was six. The Porcupines fell behind by ten runs, and I wanted to go home. "If you leave early, you might miss a thrilling comeback," he'd told me. "You might miss a walk-off home run. Never leave before the last out, Chad."

"I won't," I told him, and I meant it. The Porcupines ended up losing that game, but they did get a grand slam in the eighth inning. We would have missed it if we hadn't stuck around.

Tonight there was no way to keep both promises unless the Pines scored really soon.

Victor Snapp's deep voice boomed over the speakers. "Now batting: the designated hitter, Sssssammy Sssssolarisss!" Victor Snapp had been the announcer for the Pine City Porcupines since before I was born. He was my idol. I wanted to be a baseball announcer when I grew up.

"Come on, Sammy!" I shouted. Sammy was the best hitter on the team.

He swung at the first pitch. The ball sailed into the outfield. The Finches' center fielder ran after it.

"It's a gapper!" said Victor Snapp. He said that whenever a ball got between two outfielders. My heart nearly leaped out of my chest.

The ball hit the fence and rolled back toward the outfielder. Sammy took a big turn at first base, then stopped.

I went to fetch the bat.

"Solaris stretched that double into a single!" I heard someone shout. It had to be Ernie Hecker. Ernie had the biggest mouth in Pine City, and he always shouted stuff at the players and umpires. This time he was right. Most baseball players would have reached second base easily on a hit like that.

Sammy took his lead off first. The pitcher didn't even look at him. There was no way Sammy would try to steal a base.

"Now batting: the first baseman, Teddddddddy Larrrrrabeeeee!" Victor Snapp announced.

Teddy hit the ball hard, and it sailed to the right field corner. The outfielder caught it. Sammy took a couple of steps toward second, then changed his mind and stayed at first.

The crowd groaned again. Most runners would have tagged up and advanced a base.

"Now batting: the right fielder, Danny O'Brien!" Victor announced.

Sammy must have heard the crowd boo, because he did something crazy. The pitcher threw an off-speed pitch to Danny, and Sammy took off. He kicked up a cloud of dust and started toward second.

Danny didn't swing. The catcher threw the ball to second. The second baseman took two steps off the base to catch it. He ran back to the base and tagged Sammy.

Sammy was out by a mile.

"I could have stolen that base from up here!" Ernie Hecker shouted.

"Sammy Solaris is caught stealing!" said Victor Snapp. "And so we head to the tenth inning."

Sammy returned to the dugout and slumped onto the bench.

"Good try, Sammy," I told him.

"Nice of you to say that," he said.

"I didn't signal for you to steal a base," said the Pines' manager. His name was Harry Humboldt, but everybody called him Grumps.

"You'll know when I do, because it'll be never. That's when it'll happen. *Never*."

"Ah, come on. I just thought I'd get into scoring position," Sammy replied.

I missed the rest of their talk because Wally tugged on my sleeve. "You got a phone call."

Wally was the clubhouse manager. He was my boss.

"Thanks. It's probably my dad. I'll have to go home."

"That's all right," Wally said. "You should go home. We want you kids fresh for tomorrow."

I went back to the locker room to take the call. The phone was the old-fashioned kind, with the receiver wired to the base and the base stuck to the wall.

"I'm waiting out in front," said Dad. "Are you ready?"

"I just have to change."

"Hey, ask Dylan if he wants a ride too," said Dad.

"Sure."

Dylan was the other batboy for the Porcupines. He was working in the Finches' dugout for tonight's game. We took turns helping the opposing team.

"See you in a sec," I told Dad.

I changed clothes, grabbed my baseball card binder, and went to the Finches' dugout.

Even though he's a batboy, Dylan isn't a big baseball fan. I showed him my baseball card collection sometimes—well, *part* of it: I had more than 5,000 cards! I told him about my favorite players. I explained plays during the game. Dylan didn't know it, but he was my secret mission: By the end of the season, I was going to make him the greatest fan of the world's greatest game!

I found Dylan sitting on the edge of the bench in the visitors' dugout.

"Hey." I nudged his elbow.

"Shh." Dylan pointed at something.

I scanned the infield and didn't see anything unusual.

"What?"

"It's right there!" He pointed again, and I realized he was pointing at the fence that protected the dugout from foul balls. I set my baseball card binder down and knelt by the fence to get a better look.

There was a little creepy-crawly thing sitting on the chain link.

"It's just a bug," I said.

"It's not a bug. It's a spider," said Dylan.

"Spiders are bugs."

"Not exactly. They're arachnids. Bugs are insects. Hey, look. It's spinning a web."

"Great," I said. "Wally said we should go home. My dad will give you a ride."

"Thanks," Dylan replied. "I want to stay and watch. I can call my parents later."

"I thought baseball bored you."

Dylan had admitted that when we first started working for the Porcupines.

"I mean watch *that*," he said. He nodded at the spider.

"Of course."

I knew Dylan liked animals, but did a spider count as an animal?

ust after I got home I had one of the worst moments of my whole life. I'd forgotten my card binder! I'd left it in the Finches' dugout when I was talking with Dylan about that stupid spider. It felt like I'd left my right arm somewhere.

I called the Finches' locker room. Dylan answered.

"It's me. Is the game still going on?"

"Yeah. And Sparky is done with his web!"

"Sparky?"

"Sparky the Spider."

"You named that thing?"

"No, I just call him Sparky."

"That's naming him!"

"Maybe. By the way, you left your binder here."

"I know—that's why I called. I wanted to make sure it was OK."

"It's fine. Do you want me to put it in your locker?"

"Keep it overnight," I said. "Take good care of it. But feel free to look through it. There're some cool cards in there."

"Sure," Dylan promised. "Gotta go. I want to see if Sparky's caught any bugs yet."

• • •

I overslept the next morning. We batboys had to be at the ballpark two hours before the game started. I would have to hurry to get there on time.

It was my own fault. I'd listened to the rest of

the game on the radio before I went to sleep. The Porcupines finally won in the thirteenth inning. Tommy Harris hit a triple, and Mike Stammer brought him in with a sacrifice fly. It would have been so great to be there. I knew what Uncle Rick meant about never leaving a game early. Too bad Mom and Dad didn't understand.

I got dressed, bounded down the stairs, and ate a bowl of cereal.

Mom saw me put the bowl in the dishwasher.

"Do you need lunch?" she asked.

"I can get a hot dog at the ballpark."

"You've been eating a lot of hot dogs lately," she said. "Why don't I pack you a lunch while you walk the dog?"

"Oh, yeah." It was my job to walk our dog in the morning. Penny was near her food bowl. She looked up at me with great big eyes and made a whimpering noise.

"Hi, girl." I reached for the food bin.

"She's already had breakfast," said Mom.

"Aw, Mom. She wants more," I said. Penny was still staring at me. "It would make her happy."

"She's happy when she's eating a second breakfast," said Mom. "She's not happy when she's all out of breath on a short walk."

"She just has little legs." I took a handful of kibble and put it in my pocket.

Mom didn't notice. "Walk the dog while I make your lunch," she said.

I could still be on time if I hurried. I put the leash on Penny and took her out for a quick trot around the block.

Mom was right—Penny was panting before we got to the corner. She was getting kind of roly-poly these days. She was still cute, though.

"Hi, Chad!"

I turned and saw Abby. She waved at me

from across the street. Abby worked for the Pines too, and was in my grade at school. She ran across the street to meet us.

"I'm going to the ballpark early," she explained. She reached out and let Penny lick her hand. "It's a big day. They're giving out bobbleheads. Hey, aren't you supposed to be there by now?"

"I'm leaving as soon as I'm done walking the dog." I took the dog food from my pocket and fed it to Penny.

"I'll walk to the ballpark with you," said Abby.

"We're going to have to walk fast," I told her. Usually I rode my bike.

"No problem. I can walk superfast."

We took Penny home, and Mom gave me my lunch. I peeked at it. It was pasta salad and baby carrots.

"There's not even a cookie," I said.

"Just eat your lunch first," said Mom. "If you're still hungry, you can see if they have something at the ballpark that's halfway good for you."

"All right."

"Have fun and work hard," Mom said. She planted a smooch on top of my head. I was glad Abby had waited outside.

• • •

Abby and I walked six blocks, crossed a field, waited for one traffic light, crossed the street, and turned the corner.

We stopped.

"Holy cow!" said Abby.

There were about a billion people crowded around Pine City Park.

"There are always lines on bobblehead day," I told her.

"But the game doesn't even start for two hours!"

"They're *Spike* bobbleheads," I reminded her. Spike was the Porcupines' new junior mascot. He was the biggest star of the season. Everybody loved that quill-covered porcupine kid. "Not everyone will get one," I added. "They're 'only available while supplies last.'"

"They must really want those bobbleheads," said Abby. We both knew something most people didn't: Abby was Spike. She put on a porcupine costume and played the part. She was great at it.

We started across the parking lot.

"Dad!" a little girl tugged on her father's shirttail. "Those kids are cutting!"

"Hey, what's the big idea?" the man asked.

"We're with the Pines," I said. "I'm a batboy."

"And I work in fan services," said Abby.

"Oh, I see," the man said. "Sorry for bothering you." He let us go past.

"No fair!" said the little girl.

"It's all right, Petunia," her dad said. "They work for the team."

"But it's not fair!" she said again. "They'll get the last two Spike bobbleheads. I just know it."

"No, they won't, Petunia," her father said.

"Show me your ticket, so I can see your seat number," Abby said to the girl. "I'll make sure you get a Spike bobblehead."

"Promise?" Petunia asked.

"Promise," said Abby.

"You can believe it," I added. "Abby and Spike are good friends."

3

It's you!" said Wally when I got to the locker room. Several of the players were getting suited up for the game.

"Yeah. Sorry I'm late," I said. I put my lunch in the team fridge. "Mom wanted to make me lunch, I had to take the dog for a walk, and the line outside was really long."

"I'm just glad you're here," said Wally. "I wasn't sure either of you boys would make it after that marathon last night."

"You mean Dylan isn't here yet?"

Dylan had never been late before.

"His mother called and said he wasn't feeling well. Maybe he's just tired. I know I am."

Maybe he got bit by that spider, I thought. Maybe he wasn't "sick." Maybe I'd be working with Spider-*Boy* . . . That could be cool! Still, I hoped Dylan didn't feel too bad.

"I'll hold down the fort here," said Wally. "You go help the Finches. I know you'd rather help the Pines, but we're in a jam."

"No problem."

"And here, take this. I was only able to get one," said Wally. "You're here, so it's yours. At least now there won't be a fight over it." Wally pulled a white box out of the traveling case and handed it to me.

"All right!" I guessed what it was right away. I slid out a Spike bobblehead and unrolled it from the Bubble Wrap. I gave the

little porcupine head a tap and set it nodding. Awesome!

"Hey! Hey, Chad," said Sammy Solaris. "Don't forget about my corn dogs before you go, buddy."

I rewrapped the bobblehead and stowed it in my locker. "No problem," I said. I fetched Sammy two corn dogs before every game.

"Do you ever think about having something besides corn dogs?" asked Teddy Larrabee, the first baseman. "Like a regular hot dog, or a chili dog, or a Chicago-style hot dog, or a Carolina-style dog, or a bratwurst . . ."

"Or a frankfurter?" said Wayne Zane, the catcher.

"A frankfurter *is* a hot dog," said Teddy.

"I'm just sayin'," Wayne replied.

"I like corn dogs," said Sammy. "That's my thing. I eat two corn dogs before every game."

"You don't want to mess with tradition," said Wayne. "Especially when you're hitting like Sammy."

"Listen to him," said Sammy. "He's wise."

"By 'wise,' he means 'old,'" said Wayne.

"I agree about traditions," said Lance Pantaño. "Every time I pitch, I drink four cups of coffee before the game. And only from this." He took a big gulp from a Porcupines mug. The mug had an old piece of tape on it that said "Property of Lance."

"If I drank that much coffee, there'd be a seventh inning stretch in every inning, and I'd be spending it in the bathroom," said Mike Stammer.

"That's why I drink only four cups when I pitch," said Lance. "When I'm not pitching, I'm a nine-mug man. Nine innings, nine coffees."

"What about last night's extra innings?"

asked Wayne. "Wouldn't thirteen coffees keep you up all night?"

"Decaf," Lance replied.

"I don't know how you can have *anything* before a game," said Tommy Harris, the third baseman. He was the newest and youngest Porcupine player. He'd just come up from rookie league. "I'm too nervous to eat."

"I'm too hungry to be nervous," said Sammy. He looked at me and patted his stomach.

"On it, Sammy," I said. "I'll go get your corn dogs."

I ran out of the locker room and out to the plaza. The gates were now open, and the fans were swarming in. A lot of people were carrying Spike bobbleheads. Kids shook the toys and made the porcupine's oversized head rock back and forth.

The woman at the food stand saw me and

waved me up to the counter. I didn't have to wait in line. That was one of the perks of working for the team.

"Corn dogs, coming right up!" she said even before I ordered. She knew that Sammy Solaris had corn dogs before every game.

The smell of hot food made my stomach rumble, but I'd promised Mom I'd eat healthier today.

I forgot to tell the woman at the counter that. She set down three corn dogs and winked. Two were for Sammy, but the extra corn dog was always for me.

I hurried back to the Pines' locker room and gave Sammy all three dogs.

"You get an extra today," I said. "My mom made me lunch."

"But that's not the tradition," said Sammy. "I eat two corn dogs before every game. Not one corn dog. Not three corn dogs. *Two* corn dogs." He held up two fingers.

"Well, just imagine what you can do if you eat three," said Teddy.

"Don't mess with tradition," said Wayne.

"Traditions have to start somewhere," said Teddy. "Maybe you'll hit for the cycle. Maybe you'll steal a base."

Sammy's eyes got wide. "You think so?" He dipped one of the dogs in mustard and took a bite.

"You never know until you try," said Teddy.

"I tried stealing yesterday," said Sammy. "It didn't go so hot."

"But you only had two corn dogs."

"Don't mess with Sammy's system," said Wayne. "He eats two corn dogs, and he gets a lot of doubles and homers. It works for him."

"I do need to steal a base, though," said Sammy.

"You don't *need* to," said Wayne.

"Yes, I do," said Sammy. "On the last off day, I visited my niece's softball team. I was giving them a pep talk, and I told them they could do anything if they set their mind to it. Later on my niece asked me, 'Uncle Sammy, did you ever steal a base?' I said no. She asked me why not, and I said I wasn't that kind of player. So she said, 'If you put your mind to it, you can do it, right?' What could I say? I said, 'Yeah, of course I can.'

"So she said, 'Do it this weekend, Uncle Sammy,' and I said I would. That's why I tried it last night."

"Sweet story," said Wayne. "But a corn dog isn't going to help you run faster, unless you're chasing a corn dog truck."

"You're hilarious," said Sammy.

"Just sayin'," said Wayne.

"You've never stolen a base?" Tommy asked in surprise. "I've only been with the team a month, and I've stolen five!"

"Yeah, yeah. I know," said Sammy. "You're a jackrabbit out there. I just need to steal one base this weekend so I don't let down Wendy. That's my niece."

"Tell her you hit a lot of homers," said Myung Young. "Those are better than stolen bases."

"He's right," said Danny O'Brien. Or maybe it was Brian Daniels. I always got those two guys confused. Their names were similar, and they looked the same: unruly red hair and big freckled noses. "Tell Wendy you just set your mind to hitting home runs," said Danny or Brian.

"It's not just Wendy," said Sammy. "I want to prove to *myself* that I can steal a base."

"So take one from the equipment room," said Wayne.

Sammy glared at the catcher.

Zane shrugged. "I'm just sayin' . . ."

"You're no help," said Sammy. "But I know who will be. I'll get Chad the batboy to help me."

I popped my head up. "Who, me?" What was I supposed to do?

"Yeah. You gave a magic baseball card to Mike Stammer. That card helped him turn an unassisted triple play."

"Sure did," said Mike. "I haven't had a single error charged against me since I got it." He patted his hip pocket to show he still had the card I'd given him.

"The baseball card isn't *magic*," I said. "It's just a reminder that . . ."

"Listen, batboy." Wayne leaned in and

whispered in my ear. "If Mike thinks it's a magic card, then it's a magic card."

"I don't need a card as powerful as Mike's," said Sammy. "It just has to be a little bit magic. Stealing a base is a lot easier than turning a triple play all by yourself."

"It doesn't hurt to try," said Mike. "Who else do you have in that binder?"

"Rickey Henderson," said Brian or Danny. "That's who you want. Henderson stole more bases than anyone else in the history of baseball."

"Or Ty Cobb," said Myung Young. "He was famous for stealing bases."

"I don't have a Ty Cobb card," I said. "Ty Cobb played a hundred years ago. His cards are worth a fortune."

"How about Ichiro Suzuki?" asked Tommy. "Or maybe Juan Pierre? Those guys steal a lot of bases and they're still playing. It can't be that hard to find their cards."

"Good choices," said Myung.

"I do have an Ichiro card, but I don't have it with me," I said.

"Hey, look," said Sammy. "I'll take Kenny Lofton or Carlos Beltran. Anyone who ever stole a base."

"I don't have *any* baseball cards with me," I said. "I can go to the gift store and buy a pack. Maybe you'll get lucky and get one of those guys."

"Nah, I think the card has to be from that red binder of yours," said Sammy. "That's what makes it magic."

I started to say, "They're not magic," but then I remembered what Wayne had whispered to me.

"Let me settle this!" Grumps's voice rattled

the lockers. The Porcupines' manager stomped over to the group. He wagged a finger in Sammy's face. "If I don't give you the sign, you better not try to steal a base."

"But you never give me the sign," said Sammy.

"Exactly," said Grumps. "You're a slugger That's your role." Grumps patted Sammy's shoulder. "Just go out there and slug, all right?"

"Oh, all right," said Sammy. He didn't look happy about it.

I grabbed my lunch and set off for the other dugout.

"Good luck, Sammy," I whispered on my way out.

The Attica Finches were warming up, so I had to walk the long way around the diamond.

"Chad . . . Chad . . . Hey, Chad!"

I turned. There was a porcupine right behind me. Spike came close enough to whisper. "Remember the little girl outside?" Abby said. "I promised her a bobblehead?"

"Yeah. Her name is Petunia."

"Petunia!" Abby snapped her fingers. "I couldn't remember her name."

"How can you forget a name like Petunia?"

"I just remembered it was a flower. I was thinking Rose, Lily, or Violet."

"Those are normal names," I said. "I've never heard of anyone named Petunia that wasn't a cartoon character. And a pig."

"I think it's a pretty name," said Abby. "But I don't have a bobblehead to give her."

"*You* didn't get one? But you're Spike!"

"I know! But the bobbleheads are all gone. Every last one."

"Well, maybe Petunia got into the ballpark before they ran out."

"No way," Abby said. "She and her dad were way at the back of the line, remember?"

"Oh, yeah." I thought about the bobblehead back in my locker. I really wanted to keep it. I wanted to collect things from my time with the Porcupines. I already had a signed baseball that Mike Stammer gave me.

"I shouldn't have said I'd get her a bobblehead," said Abby. "She'll say Spike broke a promise. It'll be in the newspaper. 'Junior Mascot Lies to Little Girl.'"

"It won't be in the newspaper," I said.

"Well, what if she goes home sad? What if she never wants to come to another game?" Abby's voice rose higher. "What if she ends up hating the Porcupines?"

"You're right. This is serious . . . Hmm. I have a bobblehead you can give Petunia. I mean, if you can't find one any other way. I have to go work the Finches' dugout, but I can get it during the seventh inning stretch."

"Promise?" Abby asked.

I gulped. "Sure."

"Thanks, Chad! You're

36

a hero!" Abby remembered she was in costume, and shouldn't shout. "Thanks," she whispered.

• • •

There was a note taped to the fence in front of the Finches' dugout.

Please don't do anything to this spiderweb. The spider worked really hard on it.

Thanks, Dylan

P. S. It is not the kind of spider that bites people.

The web was still there, and so was the spider. I saw it hiding under one of the links in the fence. Dylan would be happy.

The Finches finished practicing and came back into the dugout.

One of the players sat down and pulled the brim of his cap over his eyes. "Last night's game went way too late."

"Tell me about it," said another player.

"Yawn."

"Zzzz."

Two seconds later, everybody had to jump up for "The Star-Spangled Banner," and then it was time to play ball.

Lance Pantaño was pitching for the Pines. He struck out the first batter.

"Nice breeze blowing back here!" Ernie Hecker hollered from the stands.

The next batter for the Finches took an awkward swing at the first pitch and bounced the ball to the shortstop. Mike Stammer fielded the ball and threw to first for the out. He'd been great on defense lately. There were rumors that he would get called back up to the big leagues any day now.

Lance got ready to throw his next pitch, but nobody was in the batter's box.

"Wake up Jonny!" a Finch shouted.

"Yo, Jonny!" A player reached out and tugged on his teammate's foot. "You're batting."

"What? Oh." Jonny got up, pushed his cap back, rubbed his eyes, and headed for the plate.

"You'll need this." I handed him his bat.

"Oh, yeah. Thanks."

"Hey, pitcher!" Ernie Heckler hollered. "Take it easy on this guy. He looks like he just woke up."

Jonny yawned and tapped his bat on the plate. The pitch sailed past him. Jonny didn't even lift his bat off his shoulder.

"Umpire, make sure that guy is still alive!" shouted Ernie.

Jonny stepped back and watched another pitch zoom by.

"Strike two!" the umpire shouted. Jonny had forgotten to ask for a timeout. He swung at the third pitch but missed it by a mile. He headed for the dugout and started to sit down.

"That's three outs, Jonny," said the Finches' manager. "Time to play defense."

"Oh, right." Jonny put on his catcher's gear and headed toward the plate.

"Stay awake out there," shouted the manager. "Don't let them catch you napping."

Usually that's just a saying, but with this guy it could happen! It might be a good day to steal a base—even for Sammy Solaris.

I ate my lunch while the Porcupines batted. The pasta salad was OK, but it was no corn dog. The baby carrots would have been better with nacho cheese.

Sammy batted fourth in the inning. Tommy Harris was on third and there were two outs. The pitcher walked Sammy on four pitches. It was baseball strategy. If Sammy got a hit, Tommy would score. But since the bases were not loaded, Tommy couldn't score on a walk.

Now would be a good time to steal second. If

the catcher's throw to second base wasn't perfect, the runner on third could come home. They call that a double steal. I looked over at Grumps standing in the Porcupines' dugout. Sometimes he'd slap his legs and his shoulders and tug on the brim of his hat. It was a sign to the base runner. It might mean "steal a base" or "run on contact."

There was no sign this time. Grumps just stood there and stared at Sammy Solaris. I knew that look from Mom and Dad. It meant: Don't even think about it.

Sammy didn't budge.

Wayne Zane flied out on the first pitch. Then Mike Stammer struck out, and the inning was over. Sammy Solaris didn't get one foot closer to stealing a base.

Victor Snapp's deep voice bellowed over the speaker system. "Please welcome the Porcupines' senior and junior mascots . . . Pokey and Spike!"

The crowd cheered. The two porcupines rolled out in a golf cart and stopped in the infield.

Spike jumped out of the cart and set down a giant boom box. The little porcupine pushed a button and rap music blared. Spike danced and the crowd clapped.

Pokey covered his ears and shook his head. He climbed out of the cart and punched a button on the boom box. The music died.

The crowd played along. They booed Pokey.

Pokey covered his ears but finally gave in and turned the music back on. Spike started dancing again. Everyone cheered.

"I'm with the big porcupine," Ernie Hecker shouted. "This song is terrible!"

Spike looked up to where Ernie was sitting and thumbed his porcupine nose. The crowd loved it.

ustavo Perez, the Finches' first baseman, poked at the dugout fence. The spider dropped to the turf and scurried away.

"What are you doing?" I asked.

"Trying to smoosh that spider," Gustavo said. "Did you see where it went?"

"No—don't!"

"Look, kid, spiders get smooshed sometimes. And I don't like spiders."

"I know, but Dylan likes that spider."

"Who's Dylan?"

"He's the other batboy. He's the one who

wrote that note." I pointed at the paper taped to the fence.

"'It is not the kind of spider that bites people,'" Gustavus read aloud. "How does your friend know?"

"Because he's really good at science," I said.

"Spiders eat insects," the Finches' pitcher said from the bench. His name was Todd Farnsworth. "I'll bet this one gobbles up gnats and mites. Would you rather have gnats and mites in your face, Gus?"

"No," Gustavo admitted.

"Then leave the kid's pet spider alone."

The Finches' catcher was sitting next to him. He yawned and rubbed his eyes. "Maybe that thing can play in the outfield," he said.

We all looked at him.

"It can catch flies. Get it?"

"Go back to sleep, Jonny," said the pitcher.

Not much happened for the next two innings. In the bottom of the fourth inning, a couple of the Finches' bench players asked me to fetch some sunflower seeds.

"Three bags of sunflower seeds," I told the woman at the food stand.

"That's all the Finches want?"

"Yep."

"They're named for birds and they eat like birds," she said. "Anything for you?"

"Sure." I remembered what Mom had told me. "I need something halfway good for me."

"We have tropical fruit kebabs."

"Tropical fruit ke-whats?"

"Tropical fruit kebabs. They're new." She took a skewer from the cooler and handed it to me. It had pineapple chunks and bananas and jumbo marshmallows and some orange-colored fruit that wasn't oranges.

"What's that?" I pointed at one of the orangey chunks.

"Mango."

I nibbled at a piece of mango. "It's good."

"Take some kebabs back to the players," she said. "Nobody's ordering them, and the fruit won't keep." She loaded a cardboard tray with fruit kebabs.

I took it all back to the dugout and set the tray down on the bench. I nibbled on my own tropical fruit kebab and watched the game.

There was nobody out, and Sammy was on first base after a clean single to left field. He took a step off the base and looked at the Porcupines' dugout for the sign. Grumps gave him his stone-faced look again. Sammy stepped back on the bag.

It was for the best, because Wayne got a hit and Sammy got to second anyway.

Later in the inning either Danny O'Brien or Brian Daniels hit a double.

"He's faster than a skyscraper!" shouted Ernie Hecker as Sammy lumbered home. It was a run for the Porcupines! The crowd cheered.

When the inning ended, I crossed the field to pick up a bat. Sammy stopped me. "Hey, Chad, never mind about that magic baseball card. I can't use it. Coach won't let me steal a base."

"Maybe he would if the situation was right?"

"No way. He won't ever give me the sign. I'll just have to tell my niece that you can do anything if you put your mind to it *and* Grumps lets you do it."

"I'll find you a card anyway," I promised.

"Thanks, Chad." Sammy headed back to the Porcupines' dugout.

Either Brian Daniels or Danny O'Brien

grounded into a double play, and the Finches came back to the dugout to bat. It was the top of the fifth inning.

Todd Farnsworth, the Finches' pitcher, picked up one of the fruit kebabs.

"Where did these come from?"

"The kid brought them," a player said. "Try one. They're good."

"I never liked marshmallows, but I could go for some fruit," said Todd. He slid off a marshmallow and started to toss it toward the trash.

"Hey, what are you doing?" said Gustavo. "That's the best part." He took the marshmallow and popped it in his mouth, then grabbed a skewer and took off more marshmallows. He popped them all into his mouth at once.

Todd ate a couple of pieces of fruit off the skewer. "These are great! You guys should try them." He pushed the tray down the bench.

Several of the players took one.

Gustavo mumbled something.

"We can't hear you, Gus," said the shortstop. "Your mouth is full of marshmallows."

Gustavo pointed at the shortstop's fruit kebab, then at himself.

"Gus wants all of your marshmallows," Todd explained. The players started handing him their marshmallows. Gustavo couldn't keep up.

"Perez, you're supposed to be on deck!" the manager shouted. Gus stuffed the marshmallows into his pocket and headed out of the dugout.

"Hope he doesn't have to slide," said Todd. "Could get messy."

Gustavo hit a home run to tie the game.

"Pass me a marshmallow," said the second baseman.

ylan showed up during the seventh inning stretch. The game was still tied, 1–1. The fans were singing "Take Me Out to the Ball Game," with Ernie Hecker's voice rising above the rest of the crowd.

"I thought you were sick," I told Dylan. I was putting some bats away. "Is getting well quick one of your new spider powers?"

"Nah, Mom just wanted me to get more sleep," he said. "After I got up, I decided to web-sling my way over here. How's Sparky?"

"Er . . . OK, I guess." I put the last bat

away and went back to the Finches' dugout.
Dylan was right behind me.

"You can go back to the Pines' dugout if you
want," he said. "I'll help the Finches."

"Sure," I said.

Then I realized that Dylan had frozen in
place, his mouth wide open.

"He's gone!" Dylan pointed at the empty
web. "Sparky is gone!"

"He might come back."

"Nobody smooshed him, did they?"

"Nobody smooshed him," I said. "That
spider just dropped and ran away. I saw him
do it."

"I hope he's all
right," said Dylan. He
crouched and peered
through the fence at the
infield.

"I gotta go," I said. I had to hurry to the Porcupines' dugout, because the Pines were going to bat. "I'll let you know if I see Sparky."

I watched for spiders on my way around the diamond, but didn't see any. I did bump right into Spike.

"Hey!" said Abby.

"Sorry."

"Never mind. So, um . . . I can't find another bobblehead for Petunia." Abby said. "Can I still have yours? You did promise."

"I know." When I'd made that promise, I was sure Spike could find a Spike bobblehead. No such luck. "Let's go get it."

Abby followed me into the Porcupines' dugout.

"Hey, Spike is here!" Wayne Zane gave Spike a high five.

"You're great, Spike," said Tommy. "You crack me up every time."

Spike toed the ground and looked bashful.

"Be right back." I ran and fetched the porcupine bobblehead from my locker. I opened the box to make sure the toy was still in there. That bobblehead would have looked great on my bookshelf, right next to my baseball cards. I was sad to lose it.

"Make sure Petunia takes good care of this," I said when I handed the box to Spike.

The mascot did a huge exaggerated bow, then gave me a Porcupine hug, which is like a bear hug, only you've got to watch the quills. Spike didn't leave the dugout, though.

"What's wrong?"

The little porcupine tugged on my arm and pulled me off to the side where nobody could hear us.

"I forgot Petunia's seat number," Abby whispered.

"Oh, no!"

"Do you remember it?"

"No, I didn't even look at the tickets." I bit my lower lip and thought about it. "Maybe you can go into the stands and find her. It's not that big a ballpark."

"There isn't much time left in the seventh inning stretch," Abby replied. "What if I don't find her?"

"I have an idea. Can you be batboy for a few seconds?"

"I don't know how."

"Just make sure that the bat for the next batter is ready, and return the bat to the rack when he's done. The players' names are on the bats, and you can match up their names to the numbers on the lineup card . . . "

"Whoa, slow down," said Abby.

"No time. Do the best you can," I said. I ran through the locker room and out onto the concourse. I had to talk to my idol.

• • •

Victor Snapp sat in a booth in between the upper and lower decks, directly behind home plate. The door was propped open. He was hunched over a scorecard, making flecks with his pencil for every pitch. "Remember," he said into the microphone, "Teddy 'the Bear' Larrabee is today's Papa's Pizza Pick to Click. If Larrabee gets a hit in today's game, fans will receive a five-dollar coupon good on any large pizza."

Victor's voice was deep and booming and smooth all at the same time. I practiced talking like that all the time but never came close.

I'd only met him once, when I crashed into him and spilled nacho cheese all over his shoes. What if he remembered me? What if he was still mad?

I'd have to try. He could make an announcement: "Petunia, please pick up your bobblehead from Spike at the Fan Services booth after the game." I didn't know her last name, but how many Petunias could there be at one ball game?

Teddy knocked a fastball over the head of the third baseman.

"There it is!" said Victor. "A base hit for the Bear! The Porcupines have a base runner, and you have a five-dollar coupon good for any large pizza at Papa's Pizza. And it looks like Spike the Porcupine is fetching the bat! Now I've seen everything."

He saw me by the door, hit a button on the microphone stand, and waved me in.

"You're that batboy," he said.

I gulped. He did remember me. "I am. I'm sorry I spilled food on you. It was my fault."

"It takes two to bump into each other," Victor said. He offered me a handshake. His hand was huge, and it buried my hand whole. "Pleased to finally meet you," he said.

"Me too!" I said. "I'm a big fan. I want to be a baseball announcer when I grow up."

"You don't say? Do you want to announce the next batter?" he asked.

"What?"

"Just say his name. It's written down right there." He pointed at his scorecard.

"I know who's batting!" I said. "I set up the bat rack enough times."

"So go for it," Victor said. He pushed the microphone at me and undid the mute button.

I remembered all the times I practiced at home. I could do this. I made my voice deep and booming. "Now batting for the Porcupines: the left fielder, BRRRRIAN DANNNIELS!" I heard my own voice echoing over the speakers. It was amazing.

Victor grabbed the microphone. "Of course he means the *right* fielder, *Danny O'Brien*!" He hit the mute button.

"Ulp. Sorry," I whispered. I always got those two confused.

"Easy mistake," Victor told me. "Anyone could make it." He picked up his pencil.

"Thanks," I said. I hung my head and went back down to the Porcupines' dugout. I was so mad at myself, I forgot to ask Victor to make the announcement.

I hoped that nobody noticed my mess-up. That hope didn't last long.

"I heard your voice on the speakers," Abby whispered as soon as I got back to the dugout.

"Huh? It must have been some other kid."

"It sure sounded like you. What did you do? Did you find Petunia?"

"No, I kind of blew it," I admitted. "But we still have two more innings."

"I'll go greet fans and try to spot her," said Abby. She tucked the box with the bobblehead under her arm. "I'm off to find Petunia."

"Good luck."

"Never say that to an actor. It's bad luck. You're supposed to say 'Break a leg.'"

"How about 'Break a quill'?"

"Perfect!"

Spike went out onto the field and waved at fans, then went up the stairs to shake hands with people.

I watched the game. The Porcupines were still batting. It sure was a long inning, but the Porcupines hadn't scored. Everything was just taking forever. I saw Gustavo reach into his pocket, then pop something in his mouth. He was still eating marshmallows, even while he was playing!

Sammy Solaris sat down next to me.

"Hey, was that you on the PA system?"

"Nope," I lied. "It was some other kid."

"Nah, it was you," said Sammy.

"OK, yeah. It was me. I messed up the name. I got Brian confused with Danny."

"Ah, don't worry about it," said Wayne. "Even they can't tell each other apart—can you, Danny?" He looked at a player returning to the dugout.

"I'm Brian."

"See what I mean?" said Wayne.

The seventh inning was finally over. Most of the players grabbed their gloves and headed back to the field. Sammy stayed behind because he was the DH, or designated hitter. The DH hits instead of the pitcher.

"Now pitching for the Porcupines . . . Nate Link!" said Victor Snapp.

Nate is what they call a sidewinder. Instead of pitching overhand, he pitches from the side.

He threw a few warm-up pitches to Wayne Zane behind the plate. Wayne had to reach way out to catch one. He didn't look too happy.

"Uh-oh. Looks like Nate doesn't have his best stuff today," said Sammy.

Pokey and Spike came out and played catch with an oversize baseball. Spike kept throwing the ball far away from Pokey. When Pokey ran to get the ball, Spike turned to the audience and grinned. The fans laughed.

"I can give you a baseball card now," I told Sammy. "Dylan brought me my binder."

"It doesn't matter," he said. "I'll have to tell Wendy that her uncle can't steal a base no matter how hard he puts his mind to it. Even if I get to bat again, and even if I reach base, Grumps will never give me the sign."

"He might," I said. "In the right situation."

I got the binder and flipped through the

pages. I looked at the stat for SB, or stolen bases.

"If you do give me one, it doesn't have to be a world-class base stealer," said Sammy. "Just someone who steals a base once in a while."

"How about this guy?" I gave him my 2010 Bengie Molina card.

"Ha. Good one," Sammy said, but he handed the card back to me.

"What's wrong?"

"Molina's a good hitter and a great catcher. But he's a slow runner. If me and him and a snail and a turtle were in a race . . ." Sammy thought it over. "Well, the turtle would win, but I'd beat the snail and Bengie Molina."

"That's the point! He's still stolen a few bases." I showed Sammy the back of the card. "See? Three stolen bases. And this doesn't show the one he stole in the playoffs."

"He must have gotten lucky."

"Maybe. Or maybe the situation was just right. Anyone can steal a base in the right situation."

"I don't know." Sammy looked at the card. "You know, I do like Bengie. He's a great player. I like all three of the Molinas." Bengie had two brothers who also played Major League Baseball. All three Molinas were catchers. "So if Bengie can steal a base, I can too?" he asked.

"In the right situation," I told him.

"How do I know when that is?"

"You'll get the sign."

"The sign from the manager?" Sammy asked.

"Yeah."

"I heard that," said Grumps from the other end of the bench. "Don't hold your breath."

"Just wait for the right situation," I whispered.

"All right," Sammy whispered back. "Me

and Bengie are going to steal a base for Wendy." He tucked the card in his pocket.

Grumps didn't say anything, so I guess he didn't hear *that*.

• • •

The first batter for the Finches in the top of the eighth inning was Gustavo. He popped a marshmallow in his mouth, went to the plate, and hit his second home run of the game.

"Now we're losing," said Sammy. "I don't like that."

"Him and his marshmallows," I said.

"What?"

"Nothing. It's just a fluke." I didn't want to give Sammy any ideas. He couldn't steal a base if he filled up on marshmallows.

Spike came back to the dugout before the next batter got to the plate.

"Your porcupine friend is here again," said Sammy.

"Yeah." I stood up so Abby could whisper to me.

"I can't find Petunia anywhere," she said. "It's just a sea of people. And she's so small. What am I going to do?"

Did I dare go back to Victor Snapp? I gulped. Did I have a choice? Hmm . . . I did.

There was one other person at the ballpark practically everyone could hear.

"I'll be right back," I told Abby.

I went to the seating area above the visitors' dugout. I was looking for the man with the loudest mouth in all of Pine City: Ernie Hecker.

I knew his voice, but I didn't know what he looked like. I had never met him. I only knew his name because everybody knew it. "There goes Ernie Hecker again," people would say every time he hollered.

I needed something to happen. Something Ernie would *have* to comment on.

Sammy was right. The Pines' pitcher, Nate

Link, did not have his best stuff going on. He'd given up that home run to Gustavo, and then he had walked a batter. Nate was one pitch away from walking the next batter.

He threw ball four. The batter took first, and the runner on first moved to second.

I waited for Ernie to yell something snarky. He didn't. Everyone in the section was just watching the game.

Maybe Ernie had left early?

The next batter stepped into the box. It was Jonny, the sleepy catcher. Nate sped a fastball by him. The umpire called it a ball. The next pitch got by the catcher (*both* catchers) and rolled to the backstop. Wayne went to get it.

"That's a wild pitch," said Victor Snapp, "and Wayne Zane seems to have tripped over somebody crawling around in foul territory."

I leaned over the dugout fence and craned

my neck to see what was going on. Dylan was crawling around in the dirt between the dugout and the backstop. The umpire tapped him on the shoulder. Dylan stood up, and the umpire spoke to him.

"It's a batboy," said Victor Snapp. "A batboy was crawling around in foul territory. What was he doing?"

"HELPING NATE LINK FIND THE PLATE!" Ernie Hecker answered.

Every single person in the ballpark must have heard him. A lot of them laughed.

And I had found my man. Ernie was in the third row. He wore glasses and a red polo shirt and was mostly bald.

"Excuse me." I edged past some fans and got to Ernie. The seat next to him was open.

"Hi," I said. "Can I please sit here a minute?"

"Help yourself," said Ernie. "It's my brother's seat, but he's not here today."

I sat down. Dylan was walking back to the visitors' dugout with his shoulders slumped.

"So, who are *you*?" asked Ernie.

"I'm your second biggest fan," I told him.

"I'm an accountant. Accountants do not have fans."

"I'm a fan of the stuff you say during the game. You know, like that joke you just made."

"It's called *ballpark patter*," he said. "I do take pride in my patter. I admit it."

"Your ballpark patter is great," I said.

The woman on the other side of me looked at me and shook her head.

"Anyway, I'm your second biggest fan," I told Ernie. "Your *first* biggest fan is my friend Petunia. Will you please wave to her? It would make her day."

"Who's Petunia?" Ernie asked.

"She's right over there." I started to point

and stopped. "I don't know where she is," I said. "But if you just say 'Hi, Petunia!' She'll hear you."

"'Hi, Petunia'?"

"Yeah."

"You want me to say 'Hi, Petunia.' What's the joke?"

I shook my head. "No joke."

"There must be," said Ernie. "It's like when I ask you for a henway."

"What's a henway?"

"Three or four pounds." He laughed and slapped his knee.

I thought about it. "No, it's not like that."

"Or like when I say, can you lend me a hammerfor."

"What's a hammerfor?"

"Pounding!" He laughed even harder at that one.

"It really isn't a joke," I told him. "Please say 'Hi, Petunia.' She'll hear you and wave, and then you wave back."

"No way am I doing it," Ernie said. "I am not saying 'Hi, Petunia.'"

"Please?"

"Hi, Petunia. Hi, Petunia. Hi, Petunia." He repeated it several more times. He was loud even when he wasn't trying. "Is that supposed to sound like something else? I don't get it."

"Look." The woman next to me pointed. A little girl was standing on the steps, three sections over. She was looking our way. She waved.

I waved back.

The little girl waved again.

I saw a big *G* on the stair. I counted: ten rows back.

Petunia!

Ernie didn't wave.

"She's my biggest fan?" said Ernie. "She's only four years old, tops."

"Yeah. Thanks!" I said. I rushed through the row—"Excuse me, excuse me"—and back to the aisle.

"I still don't get it!" Ernie shouted after me.

By the time I got back to the Porcupine's dugout, the score was 4–1, *not* in the Pines' favor. And the Finches were still batting.

Abby was fielding a foul ball, which wasn't easy to do in a porcupine costume. The fans laughed and clapped for her.

"Section G, ten rows back," I told her.

"Great," she said. She grabbed the box with the bobblehead, bolted from the dugout, and ran across the field. She forgot the inning was still going.

The second base umpire tried to stop her, but she ran right past him. The fans cheered.

"Spike is storming the field," said Victor Snapp. "The game is in a brief delay while an umpire chases a porcupine across the field. And now I really have seen everything."

Spike reached the seating area steps and ran up. The second base umpire went back to his spot on the field.

The mascot bounded up the steps and gave Petunia the bobblehead. The little girl jumped up and down and then gave Spike a big hug.

Nate Link pitched, and the batter bounced into a double play. The inning was finally over.

"The Finches get three runs on four hits," said Victor Snapp. "The inning also had two walks, a wild pitch, a distracted batboy, and a disruptive mascot. Figure out how to put that on your scorecards! We go to the bottom of the eighth inning."

It was mostly a happy ending, except for the fact that the Porcupines were losing—and I didn't have a bobblehead.

• • •

George "President" Lincoln batted first for the Porcupines. He was the second baseman. He hit a single. Tommy was next, and he hit a single, too. Myung came to the plate and grounded out. The runners were able to advance, so at least the Porcupines had two runners in scoring position.

Mike Stammer hit a double, and the crowd went wild as both runners scored. Now the Porcupines only needed one more run to tie the game, and there was a runner at second base.

Sammy Solaris came to the plate. The crowd stood up and clapped.

He took a ball, then swung at the next pitch and missed, then hit a foul ball.

I felt my stomach tie up in knots. Sammy had been on base every at-bat this game. What were the odds he could do it again?

He swung and smacked the ball. It soared toward the fence. The crowd gasped.

The ball hit the fence and bounced back. That was enough to score Mike Stammer. Sammy turned at first base.

"Go! Go! Go!" people shouted at Sammy, but he didn't go.

The center fielder fielded the ball and threw to the second baseman. He had an arm like a cannon. Maybe Sammy made the right choice by staying put. If he'd tried to go to second, he might have been out.

Grumps turned back to look at the bench. He nodded at Luis Quezada, a utility infielder and pinch runner. Luis leaped up. Grumps was taking Sammy out of the game. He went to signal to the umpires that he was putting in a replacement. He stopped and brushed at his leg. He slapped his left thigh three times. He drummed his fingers on his right shoulder. He took off his cap and swiped at his shoe while hopping on one foot.

I didn't know the signs, but Sammy's eyes lit up.

Todd was still pitching. He glanced at Sammy, saw he was still on base, and turned back to face Wayne Zane at the plate. He pitched.

Sammy took off.

The crowd roared. Grumps turned purple.

Wayne didn't swing. The catcher fumbled with the ball.

Sammy kept on running. He was halfway to second base.

Jonny finally got a grip on the ball and flung it to second. The second baseman caught it and braced himself to tag Sammy.

Sammy put on the brakes and started back to first.

Grumps covered his eyes.

Gustavo, the Finches' first baseman, caught the ball and got ready to tag Sammy as he bolted back to first. Sammy stopped, turned, and headed back to second.

"They have Sammy picked off," said Victor Snapp.

It was the slowest rundown I ever saw. Sammy strode to second. The second baseman toed the bag and waited for Gustavo to throw back the ball.

Gustavo took a few steps, and pumped. But he didn't throw the ball. He took another few steps and made like he was going to throw, but

the ball didn't leave his hand. He gave up and started running after Sammy.

Sammy slid. The second baseman got out of the way. Sammy's heel reached the bag a split second before Gustavo caught up and tagged him. The second base umpire signaled . . .

SAFE!

"He's safe!" Victor Snapp shouted. "Sammy Solaris just stole second base! That's the first stolen base in his career. What a game!"

The crowd stomped and cheered.

The Finches' pitcher shook his head in disbelief. Gustavo tried to throw him the ball, but still couldn't get it out of his hand.

Todd had to go take it by force. He glared at the ball and tossed it to the umpire for another.

Gustavo wiped his hand on his pants, and suddenly I knew what had happened. He couldn't make the throw because he had a hand full of marshmallow goo!

Grumps called a time-out and sent Luis to pinch-run for Sammy. Sammy got a standing ovation as he came in from the field. He was beaming. His smile could have lit up a night game.

"I stole second base," he said. "I can't wait to call Wendy!"

"I didn't give you the sign to steal," Grumps barked.

"It sure looked like you did. You touched your leg and took off your cap. That's the sign, coach. All that other stuff was funny to watch, but it didn't change the sign."

"I had a spider on me! I was shaking it off," Grumps said. "Can't you tell the difference?"

"I can't see a spider all the way from first base," said Sammy.

"Bah."

"Coach, it's OK," said Sammy. "I was safe. All's well that ends well."

"You got lucky."

"I'll take lucky," said Sammy. "Or magic." He patted his hip pocket and gave me a thumbs-up sign, then went to the locker room to call his niece.

I started to ask Grumps what happened to the spider, but decided it was not a good idea. He was called Grumps for a reason.

Wayne Zane hit a long single, and Luis Quezada sped home. The Porcupines took a one-run lead. Ryan Kimball, the Porcupines' closer, started warming up in the bull pen. Teddy Larrabee struck out, and then either

Danny O'Brien or Brian Daniels flied out to right field.

"The Porcupines get four runs on five hits, and the strangest stolen base I've ever seen," said Victor Snapp. "So we go to the top of the ninth!"

I went to the dugout door and searched the ground. I didn't see Sparky. I didn't see a dead spider, either, so that was good news.

10

ylan and I searched the field for an hour after the game. We found plenty of bugs but no spiders.

"You know," I said, "a spider is pretty small, and a ballpark is really big."

"I know," Dylan replied. "What's one little spider, anyway? There are billions of spiders in the world."

But he kept searching the grass.

"I'm going home," I said. "I have to get back in time for supper." I stood up and jogged toward the locker room. Just in the nick of time, I spotted a tiny black splotch against the white line around the on-deck circle. I almost smooshed it but stopped short. I hopped a couple of times before I got my balance. I knelt and took a closer look. Something wiggled. It could have been Dylan's spider, but it was hard to be sure.

"*Psst.* Dylan." I waved him over and pointed.

"Is that Sparky?"

"I think so." He put his hand out and let the spider crawl into his palm.

"And you're sure it's not the biting kind?"

"Yep. Unless you're an insect," said Dylan. "I'm going to move him outside the ballpark. Too many people stamping around in here."

"That's all baseball is to you?" I asked. "People stamping around?"

"I guess it is fun sometimes," Dylan admitted. The spider tried to crawl out of his hand. He swapped it into his other hand. "When the two guys were chasing Sammy back and forth. And when the mascot tore across the field. That was awesome."

"Yeah. Those sure were highlights. And you know, when Sparky makes a web. That's pretty awesome, too."

"Well, it's not exactly a high-speed chase," he said.

"Neither was that rundown!"

He laughed. "Thanks for helping me find Sparky," he said. "I just like animals. No matter how small. Some people don't get it."

"It's not much different being a big fan of Single-A baseball," I told him.

• • •

There was a green car parked in our driveway. I saw it from the corner and took off running. I would know that car anywhere, even before I saw the ballpark bumper stickers plastered all over it.

"Uncle Rick!" I shouted, banging through the front door.

"Hey, it's the all-star batboy!" Uncle Rick jumped up to give me a hug. He looks like Dad, but with more hair and less stomach. It turned out he'd just arrived, and Mom and Dad hadn't even known he was coming. Uncle Rick lives in the city. He explained that he'd been driving back from a trade show and took a detour to surprise us.

Uncle Rick is the biggest baseball fan I

know. He's the one who explained the rules of the game to me when I was little, and taught me all the ballpark slang, and showed me how to keep score. He even gave me all his baseball cards. That was huge. I knew Uncle Rick loved those cards. "They just sit around at my place," he'd said. "I don't have much time to enjoy them, but you do."

When Uncle Rick goes on vacation, he figures out a route where he can see as many baseball games in as many different ballparks as he can. Some years he goes to spring training in Florida or Arizona. I hope one day he'll take me with him. Uncle Rick has a great life for a grown-up, even if he spends most of his days selling dental supplies.

Over dinner I told Uncle Rick all about being a batboy. I told him about Grumps's nickname and Wally's mustache and Wayne

Zane's bad jokes. I told him about Mike Stammer's unassisted triple play and Sammy Solaris's stolen base.

"You never know what's going to happen," Uncle Rick said. "That's why I never leave until the game is over."

"I did leave a game before it was over," I admitted. "It was just last night. I missed a great walk-off hit."

"I made him do it," Dad explained. "It was way past his bedtime."

"Well, do what your parents say, even when they're wrong." Uncle Rick winked and got himself some more spaghetti. "I left a game early once," he admitted. "I found out later the pitcher finished a no-hitter. I could have been there for a historic moment, but I left after only four innings."

"*Why?*" I couldn't believe that Uncle Rick

of all people would leave in the middle of a no-hitter.

"I found out my nephew was coming, and I wanted to be there to meet him," he said.

"What?" I was his only nephew, and I didn't remember that. Then I realized what he meant—the day I was born.

"I can't believe you missed a no-hitter for *that*," I told him.

"Well, it was only the fourth inning," he said. "I didn't *know* it was going to be a no-hitter . . ."

Mom and Dad laughed, but I think Uncle Rick was being serious.

ncle Rick spent the night. We have a small house, but the couch in the office pulls out into a bed.

"Are you driving home after breakfast?" I asked him.

"Well, I was hoping to see a ball game," he said. "I want to root for my favorite batboy. I just hope there is a game." He pointed out the window at dark, gloomy clouds. "It looks like a big storm is coming."

Sure enough, it started drizzling when I was out walking Penny. I tried to jog home, but she started panting and I had to slow down.

"Sorry, girl. I forget how short your legs are." She used to keep up with me, but my legs used to be shorter. Besides that, she was getting plump. Mom was right.

We were both damp when we got home.

"Did Wally call?" I asked. I was afraid they'd canceled the game already.

"Nope," said Dad. He was in his favorite chair, reading a thick book about farming in the Middle Ages. He's always reading thick books about weird things.

"Are you coming with us?" Uncle Rick asked him.

Dad shook his head. "Sorry. I'll be at the next game. I really want to finish this book. There's another one I want to get to."

"Is it about the history of the rutabaga?" Uncle Rick guessed. "Or how worms worm?"

"Fungi," said Dad. "It looks really interesting."

"Well, at least a book has never been called on account of rain," said Uncle Rick. "Let's go, Chad!"

• • •

The ticket office wasn't open yet, but the guard let both of us in.

"Morning, Chad!" he told me. I felt pretty cool leading a grown-up past the gate and into the "Employees Only" entrance.

"I've never been behind the scenes like this," Uncle Rick said.

"Really?"

"I've been to a lot of ballparks, but I've never seen the guts of one," he admitted.

"Wow." I couldn't believe it. I could actually teach Uncle Rick something about baseball!

Wally had just made coffee, and the

machine was whistling and blowing steam.

"Wally, this is my uncle Rick. Is it OK if I give him a tour?"

"It's all right with me, as long as you get everything done," Wally said. "There probably won't be a game, anyway. They just never call it until the last minute."

Some of the players were sitting on the benches in the locker room.

"Hey, guys, this is my uncle Rick."

"Teddy Larrabee." Teddy shook his hand. "You got a good batboy for a nephew."

"He's not only good, he's great," Mike Stammer said. "I'm Mike Stammer."

"You're the one with the unassisted triple play!" Uncle Rick said.

"Yep," said Mike.

"Chad's more than great," said Wayne. "He's outstanding in the field. Especially during batting practice. Ha! Get it?" Nobody laughed. "Just sayin'," he added.

"And you must be Wayne Zane," said Uncle Rick.

• • •

There was a bolt of lightning and a crash of thunder during batting practice. It started to pour. We ran off the field so the crew could roll out the tarp. Uncle Rick had gone to buy his ticket, but he'd probably have to take a rain check.

Sammy was in the dugout studying the Bengie Molina card.

"Can I keep this a while longer?" he asked.

"I guess." I didn't like breaking up my page of Molina brothers in the binder. "If you think it'll help you steal another base."

"I don't need to steal another base," said Sammy. "I just wanted to steal one in my career, and now I have. But I see here that Bengie's got five triples." He pointed at the stats on the card. "I think he hit another one since then, too. I want to hit a triple before I'm done."

"Did your niece put you up to it?"

"No, I wanna do this one for me." Sammy tucked the card into his pocket. "By the way, I think I'll skip the corn dogs today. I need to put my mind to dropping a few pounds."

I started setting up the bat rack, knowing it was probably for nothing.

"The game is now postponed," Vincent Snapp announced over the PA system. "You can exchange your ticket stub for any remaining Porcupines' game this season. Thanks for coming, and try to stay dry!"

I hoped that Uncle Rick had made it to the ticket office. If he had bought a ticket, then he'd have to come back this summer and see a game.

Dylan came running from the other dugout.

"Guess we get a day off," he said. "But I hope Sparky's all right out there."

"Spiders can take a little rain," I said. "If they couldn't, there wouldn't be any spiders left."

• • •

Abby caught me and Dylan on our way out of the ballpark. She was dressed like Abby, not like Spike.

"Oh, good. You're still here." She flipped the hood of her rain poncho. We stood under the overhang by the gate, where it was dry. I could see Uncle Rick's green car in the distance. He flashed his lights to show he'd seen us, and started cruising across the lot to get us.

"This is for you." Abby handed me something damp. It was covered in plain white paper with baseballs drawn on it.

"Wow. Thanks. What is it?"

"Yeah, what's that?" Dylan asked.

"Chad gave me his Spike bobblehead so I could give it to a little girl. She loved it, by the way! I wanted to make it up to you . . ."

I tore open the paper. There was a white box. The same box the bobblehead had come in!

"You found another one?" I asked Abby. I opened the box. There was something inside, bundled in Bubble Wrap. I unrolled it. "Where did you get another bobblehead? Oh!"

I was holding a misshapen, handmade Spike bobblehead made of modeling clay. It was the kind of clay you dry out in the oven.

Abby hadn't found another bobblehead. She'd *made* one.

"I did the head separate, so it bobbles," said Abby. "See?" She gave it a tap. "My dad helped me put the pieces together."

The head wiggled—not really a nod, more like the clay porcupine was trying to shake water out of its ear.

"It's awesome!" I said.

I had something rarer and cooler than a Spike bobblehead. I had the only Spike bobblehead in the world that was made by Spike!

About the Author

Kurtis Scaletta's previous books include *Mudville*, which *Booklist* called "a gift from the baseball gods" and named one of their 2009 Top 10 Sports Books for Youth. Kurtis lives in Minneapolis with his wife and son and some cats. He roots for the Minnesota Twins and the Saint Paul Saints. Find out more about him at www.kurtisscaletta.com.

About the Artist

Eric Wight was an animator for Disney, Warner Bros., and Cartoon Network before creating the critically acclaimed *Frankie Pickle* graphic novel series. He lives in Doylestown, Pennsylvania, and is a diehard fan of the Philadelphia Phillies and the Lehigh Valley Iron Pigs. You can check out all the fun he is having at www.ericwight.com.

Come On into the Topps® Reading Clubhouse!

It's Chad's first summer as batboy, and the Pine City Porcupines are up against the league-leading Heron Lake Humdingers. Suddenly, Chad's got a whole lot lineup of problems: his favorite player, shortstop Mike Stammer, thinks he's jinxed; Dylan, the other batboy, doesn't even like baseball; and there's a goofy new porcupine mascot running around the field. To make matters worse, Chad has to serve as batboy for the Herons. Good thing there's something in the cards—his baseball cards, that is—that can help him sort it all out.